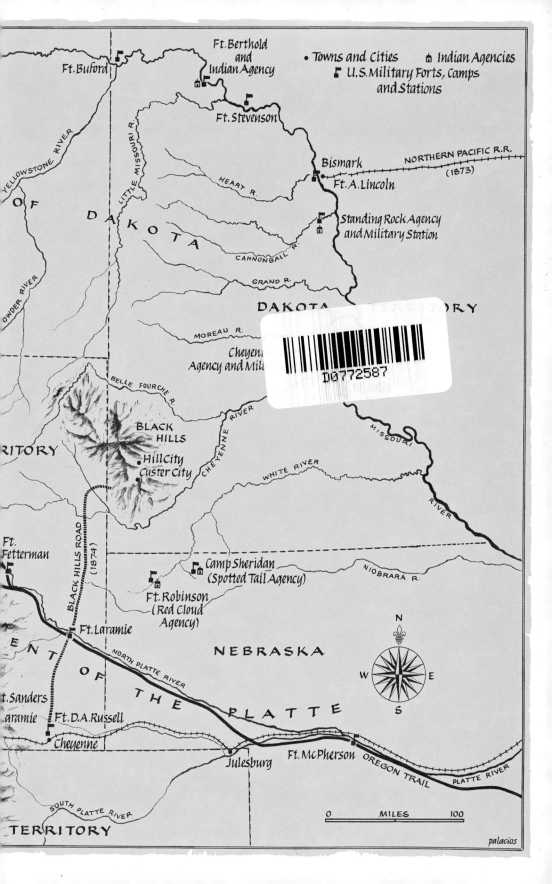

The Snowblind Moon

A NOVEL OF THE WEST

BY

John Byrne Cooke

Simon and Schuster *New York*

1 2 3 4 5 6 7 8 9 10

Library of Congress Cataloging in Publication Data
Cooke, John Byrne.
  The snowblind moon.
  1. Indians of North America—Fiction.   I. Title.
PS3553.0556S64   1984   813'.54   84-14009
ISBN: 0-671-45089-1

FOR MY FATHER, WHO HELPED TO INSTILL IN
ME A LOVE OF BOOKS, WHICH WAS EASY, AND
OF HISTORY, WHICH TOOK SOMEWHAT LONGER.

When I was a boy the Sioux owned the world; the sun rose and set in their lands; they sent ten thousand horsemen to battle. Where are the warriors today? Who slew them? Where are our lands? Who owns them?

—SITTING BULL

Department of Interior
Washington, December 3, 1875

Hon. E. P. Smith
Commissioner Indian Affairs
Washington, D.C.

Sir,

Referring to our communication of the 27th ultimo, relative to the status of certain Sioux Indians residing without the bounds of their reservation and their continued hostile attitude toward the whites, I have to request that you direct the Indian Agents at all Sioux Agencies in Dakota and at Fort Peck, Montana, to notify said Indians that unless they shall remove within the bounds of their reservation (and remain there) before the thirty-first of January next, they shall be deemed hostile and treated accordingly by the military force.

Very respectfully,
    your obedient servant,

    Z. Chandler
    Secretary

Prologue

For the moment, he was content. The wind gusted snow in Hardeman's face and he could hear the hard flakes striking the skeleton branches of the willows that stood around him in the valley bottom. On either side of the narrowing valley, snowy hillsides wooded with lodgepole pine and naked aspens rose into the soft layer of cloud that obscured the ridgetops. Saddle leather creaked as the horse shifted its weight to one hind leg and crooked the other hoof up on its toe. The sounds were clean and sharp in the cold air. Hardeman could make out the noise of two branches rubbing together twenty yards away and the rush of water over a rock in the small open patch of river nearby. For the most part the river was still snowbound, but the water flowed with a swollen urgency that spoke of spring. Even the river had been fooled by the chinook wind that had warmed the plains for two weeks, luring young boys in the settlements out of doors to play in the mud.

The horse rubbed its head against Hardeman's back, trying to slip the bit from its mouth.

"Go on, now." Hardeman pushed the animal's head away. The roan was tough and compact, born wild on the plains, obtained in trade for Hardeman's big chestnut before he and Johnny Smoker had left Kansas. He hoped he would never again have use for a horse that needed grain to survive. This one would make it through the winter on cottonwood bark if need be. He tethered the horse to a stout willow branch and stood looking about him at the falling snow. He felt as if a layer of deadening callus, carelessly acquired during years of neglect, had suddenly slipped away from him, allowing him to see and hear properly for the first time in a long while.

He was alone in the river bottom, a man in his forties, strong and compact, standing near middle height. The eyes set deep beneath his brow were a color for which there was no proper name, verging from brown toward green, or perhaps blue, depending on the light. They seemed to look on the world from a secret redoubt. A small scar stood out over his left cheekbone, pale against the skin. The hair of his close-trimmed beard was flecked with gray, as were the curls that covered his neck and ears between his hat and the upturned collar of his slicker. The hat showed none of the wide-brimmed Texas influence that was moving steadily northward with the southern cowhands. It was made of silver-gray beaver, now gone brownish from years of dust and sun. Except for its age and the ringed sweat stain above the simple horsehair band, it would not have been out of place on the streets of Philadelphia or New York.

9

Stock-still in the wind and snow, Hardeman was comfortably warm. His winter longjohns and high wool socks, kersey-wool pants and wool shirt and buckskin jacket and St. Paul canvas slicker with its heavy blanket lining guarded him well. In the bottoms of his high army field boots were carefully cut pieces of mountain sheepskin with the wool still on. Today the oilskin was unbuttoned and the cardigan he sometimes wore beneath the jacket was stowed away in a saddlebag. When he and Johnny left Kansas even the St. Paul coat had been rolled up and tied behind his saddle, but the thaw had ended when they reached Cheyenne. The chinook had died away and a new wind had come from the northwest, returning an honest winter chill to the plains and blowing straight in the faces of the two riders as they made their way from Cheyenne to Fort Fetterman and beyond.

He had been gone from these regions for eighteen years.

During that time the Union had been tested by rebellion and held together by the will of a brooding country lawyer from Illinois, dead these ten years and more. Now the nation was strengthened by a band of iron rails spanning the continent. Since the war, Wyoming and Montana territories had been hewn from Dakota and Idaho and Utah; Kansas and Nebraska had become states; Colorado was to enter the Union this year, on the nation's one hundredth birthday. The frontier, that invisible line said by those who lived behind it to separate civilization from what they called "wilderness," had moved west across the plains from the Missouri settlements and now threaded its way among the peaks of the Rockies. Everywhere new towns were growing and the buffalo grass was turned under by plowshares; but the land north of the old Oregon road, from Fort Laramie and the Black Hills west to the Big Horns, in whose southern flanks Hardeman now stood, had changed not at all. It still belonged to the Sioux.

His contentment vanished abruptly at the thought. He turned to contemplate the two rifles, a model 1873 Winchester and a Sharps buffalo gun, that hung in scabbards on either side of his saddle. From the agencies in Dakota there was word that the Indians there were slipping away to the west in small groups, to the Powder River country, to join the wild bands. Two days before, Hardeman and Johnny had passed through Fort Fetterman, but since then they had seen no sign of man nor a single pony track. The hostile Sioux were keeping well away from the old emigrant trails.

Hardeman took the Winchester, leaving the thunderous Sharps behind. There was no sense waking the dead just to get a little meat. He set off through the willows on foot, glancing from time to time at the wooded slope on his right, calculating where a deer might come down to drink. If he found an elk he would have to get close with the Winchester, but he thought it unlikely that he would see an elk. There was precious little sign in these hills and not even a rabbit track so far this morning in the new snow that was still falling.

As he moved silently along the riverbank his eyes sought every swirl in the wind-packed snow, each blade of dead grass left over from summer, every broken twig. These were the signposts of the mountains, telling the man who could read them that one animal or another, four-footed or two-footed, had passed this way, or that no creature had passed here at all. Knowing the signs could mean the difference between eating and going hungry, between living and dying. The mountains were not generous with information, but they provided enough for those willing to learn how to find it. Hardeman had learned. Remembrance flooded through him and he felt once again in touch with this world.

He had been seventeen when he first came to what was now the Wyoming Territory, a Philadelphia youth determined not to waste precious time behind the desks of a boys' academy or a university while other men opened up a continent. His father's urgings had kept him in the academy until his studies there were done, but within a week of receiving his diploma he had left Philadelphia to make his way across Pennsylvania on foot, and when he tossed his bedroll to the Negro deckhand and jumped aboard the riverboat at Pittsburgh, he knew only that he was going west. That summer of 1851 the Oregon Trail was crowded with wagons hurrying to the gold fields of California, but when young Chris Hardeman made his way across what was then known as the Great American Desert, already an apprentice scout on his first passage west, he had gazed in awe at the Big Horn Mountains looming to the north and the Wind Rivers standing sharp against the western horizon, and even before he carved his name deep into the weathered sandstone of Independence Rock he knew that no faint promise of gold flakes in the bottom of a pan could keep him long from these sights.

He had been as green a youth as ever set foot in new country, but he had learned quickly. Seven years a wagon scout on the Oregon road and by the end of that time one of the best; just twenty-five years old when he left off guiding wagons to explore other parts of the West, first for government survey parties and later for the army. Fortune had delivered him into the enterprise for which he was perfectly suited, from which he derived the most satisfaction. He had left home to take part in a great adventure, to make his mark on the frontier, and from the first it seemed that other men welcomed him and made room for him to set his shoulder next to theirs, where they pushed along the great wheel of progress. Wagonmasters and generals and common people cut from every cloth had depended on him and he had taken constant pleasure in leading the way, a man at home in what most thought of as wilderness. He had been happy at the thought of living out his days as a scout, certain with the sureness of youth that the need for such men would continue through his lifetime.

If he had followed the path his father had staked out for him, he might have become a lawyer, like his father, like the Illinois rail-splitter, but he had jumped that fence. And before he had found time to go home for a visit, to tell his parents of the life he had found, the typhoid had taken them. The news reached him six months after the fact, convincing him, in the midst of his grief, that the law was not proof against the twists of fate that inevitably changed the lives of men in ways that could not be foreseen. In the western mountains a different kind of law held sway, one not made by men and not subject to their lapses in enforcement. It was just, and truly blind, and Hardeman was comfortable under its rule.

He paused and looked around at the wooded slopes. He felt deep within himself a calm he had not known for a long time, and he realized as if it were a new notion how much he loved this high country of the Rocky Mountains. He wondered whatever could have kept him away for so long.

Pain stirred in an old wound. He shifted the rifle to his left hand and rolled his right shoulder slowly, giving an invisible nod to a God he rarely addressed. It was fitting that the shoulder should trouble him now, to remind him of how much had changed seven winters before, on the Washita River down in the Indian Territory. On a cold November morning two bullets had brought a sudden end to his scouting and had created in a moment a relationship of wounds between him and the boy called Johnny Smoker, a bond in blood as strong in most ways as any between father and son, he guessed, although he had no children of his own. He and the boy were seven years older now, Johnny nearing twenty, most likely, although neither one knew just when Johnny had been born. Johnny was downstream in the night camp, waiting for Hardeman to return with fresh meat.

He started off again along the riverbank, picking his way silently among the clumps of willow. He felt the emptiness in his stomach and wished he had stopped to have a bite of jerky or a cup of coffee before leaving the camp. He had come awake an hour ago, leaving sleep behind in a moment, as a man should in the mountains. Looking about in the dull blue light of predawn he had discovered Johnny building a sweat lodge. It was not large but was perfectly made in the plains style, four slender willow poles on a side, all bent down and tied together and covered with the blankets from the boy's bedroll. And there was Johnny in his longjohns and boots, hunkered in the snow, warming rocks on a small fire in front of the lodge as patiently . . . as an Indian. Hardeman had grown suddenly and irrationally angry and had saddled up and ridden off without a word to get fresh meat if he could find it. In those first wakeful moments, seeing something so unexpected, he had suddenly doubted for the first time his reasons for coming here.

How could he doubt leaving the settlements, where he had never wished to be? How could he doubt returning to these mountains, standing so real and comforting around him? The doubts seemed unfamiliar now, dreamlike, a memory from before waking, not after.

His roving eyes found the signs they were seeking—a depression in the new snow betrayed a pathway worn in the old snow beneath; tufts of hair were caught in the brush along the narrow trail through the willows. Close at hand the water tumbled over a fall of rocks, moving fast enough to keep the drinking place open in all but the deepest winter cold. He shut the other thoughts from his mind and concentrated on the hunt. They were half a day's ride from Putnam's Park and he wanted to arrive there with a full belly and meat tied behind his saddle. It didn't pay to be beholden to anyone when you were bringing bad news.

He turned his head, feeling the wind on his cheek, and backed away to a thicket of willows downwind where he would be hidden from all sides and still have a clear view of the pathway to the water. He hunkered slowly in the brush, cocking

12

the Winchester and testing once the single motion that would bring it from his knees to his shoulder. He grunted softly at the pain that sprang from the old wound. It bothered him more these days, especially in the cold.

I'm getting old, he thought, and laughed aloud, surprising himself. He looked quickly around, but the nearest game was still somewhere else. "You want to see meat today, you best keep shut," he told the willows and the snow, and fell silent. Not too long before, he had seen a Kansas judge sentence a mule thief to ten years in prison. As the man was taken away he had called out to the judge, begging for a reduction in sentence on account of his advanced age. The thief was forty years old. It had struck Hardeman that a man could give up and grow old any time he pleased, but he didn't figure to let that happen to him. He had his mind half made up to see the new century come in before he died—if a horse didn't fall on him or if he didn't get taken by some sickness that lurked wherever there were too many people. If he didn't let the wrong man provoke him to anger. If he lived out the month, which was perhaps least likely of all.

He drew the collar of the oilskin close about his neck and settled himself for a long wait, glad for the moment to be alone with the stream and the mountains. He passed his mind back over the half mile he had covered since leaving his horse, and found that although part of his attention had been occupied with other things, he could remember every fallen log, each clump of willow, every turn of the creek. He could find this place at night if he had to. He was pleased by the thoroughness of his recollection and was glad he had not fallen on careless ways. This was not safe country for fools. A man could not predict what weather a wind or a cloud might bring in any month of the year, nor what else might befall him unexpectedly in the mountains. All he could do was to be ready for whatever came. There was no certainty here, and Hardeman grinned at the awareness, a familiar feeling he had once known daily and had left behind like a worn-out shirt.

A breath of wind twisted through the willows, whisking the snow off the branches and depositing it in a cloud over the squat form of the man. Hardeman did not move. He willed himself to be a part of the mountains, like a rock or a stump. A measure of his earlier contentment returned and he recognized now the feeling that had comforted him so. He felt at home. Perhaps the settlements had not dulled him as much as he had feared. He would need all his old cunning, for he had returned to scouting after seven long years, determined once more to lead the way. At his own request, and in violation of a silent oath he had sworn that bloody morning at the Washita, he was scouting for the army again, and the army was going to war.

Book One

In a sheltered upland valley, circled by ridges and accessible in winter only through a cut in the hills where the river flowed between a low cliff on one side and a wagon track cut into a steep hillside on the other, the smell of woodsmoke hung in the air. Up against the wooded foothills at the north end of the valley the wagon road ended among the buildings of a small settlement dominated by a two-story log building that for more than twenty years had been the largest private dwelling and public house between the Black Hills to the east and South Pass far to the west, at the foot of the Wind River Mountains. Behind the building stood a large barn, a chicken coop and a pigpen, and a scattering of sheds and out-buildings. Closer to the creek, standing against the woods, was a tipi of northern plains design, painted in the style of the Sioux. From the peak of the tipi and from two rear chimneys of the main building, smoke drifted away to disperse in the winds that occasionally gusted a plume of snow from the long front porch of the big house.

In the snow-covered meadow below the settlement a tall black man and a teenaged boy tossed hay from a large sled drawn by two draft horses. Strung out behind the sled were fifty or sixty mixed-breed cattle browsing on the hay, a few horses and mules among them. The two men pitched the hay in even lines on either side of the sled, careful to spread it out so the less aggressive feeders in the bunch would have room to get enough.

"That's about the last of it," said Julius Ingram. Hutch nodded. Julius said the same thing every morning. Every morning they loaded the big sled with hay and hauled it to the bawling cattle in the meadow and every morning when the hay was almost gone Julius would say "That's about the last of it," and Hutch would nod, saying nothing.

At first he hadn't said much because he'd never worked for a nigger boss before. Not for a lady boss either, for that matter, although he was used to both of them now, to his own surprise.

"Whoa." Julius spoke no louder than if he were talking to Hutch, and the two Belgians stopped in the traces. The short hair that curled beneath the flat brim of the Negro's hat was gray. His mahogany skin lay smooth over every bone and muscle in his face; the effortless movements of his broad shoulders as he cleaned the last of the hay off the sled suggested reserves of strength untapped by the morning's work. He wore a new corduroy coat and wool pants that had once been light blue but were now so faded and stained and patched that they could not be said to have any distinct color.

At seventeen, Hutch had attained nearly his full height and still he was a good

17

head shorter than Julius. Unlike the tall black man, who appeared lean despite his strength, Hutch's form was stocky and heavily muscled, his movements short and economical. He took off his wool knit cap and stuffed it in a pocket of his old blanket-lined canvas jacket, enjoying the feeling as his scalp cooled in the wind. The thaw that had lasted for nearly two weeks was over and done with but the day was tolerable even so, nothing like the bitter cold days of midwinter. The snow that had been falling since before dawn was thinning now, and for the first time that morning he could see across the creek and the broad expanse of willow marsh to the far side of the valley. He breathed in deeply and noticed, not for the first time, how the smell of smoke from the stoves in the main house stayed in the air on a day like this when the clouds were low.

"When the chimney smoke's on the rise, you'll see clear skies," his mother had told him. "When the smoke hangs low, it's bound to snow." But the rhyme hadn't explained how low-hanging smoke in the hot Kansas summertime back home had foretold the coming of black thunderheads and sudden violent wind squalls and crackling lightning that you could see walking all around you on the endless plains. Hutch wondered if it was the same here in the mountains in the summer.

He had come upon the little mountain park with the first snow in autumn, getting plenty anxious about where he was going to spend his first winter away from home, looking for some cattle spread that didn't already have all the winter hands it needed. All the outfits along the Front Range in Colorado said they couldn't use another hand and if they could they'd hire on some man who had worked for them before, or a man anyway, not some runaway kid from Kansas so green he wouldn't catch light in the midst of a prairie fire. So Hutch kept heading north and west, toward the new ranges opening up in the Wyoming Territory, hoping he wouldn't have to go all the way to Montana to find work. But in Wyoming the story was the same—Sorry, boy, you best try farther on, up Virginia City way, mebbe, but stay west of the Big Horns if'n you reckon to hang on to your hair. He never would have come on the Putnam place at all if he hadn't gone wrong at the fork, mistaking the Putnam Cutoff for the old Oregon road. Not long before he rode into the valley and saw the big house he had realized he was lost, and heading deeper into Sioux country. The farther west he had come on his travels the more talk he had heard about new trouble with the Sioux, and he had been considerably relieved to see a white man's outfit and a welcoming face at the door, even if that face had been the dark visage of Julius Ingram. Hutch hadn't felt too particular about a man's color just then, so long as it wasn't red and decorated with war paint.

Miss Putnam had taken him on, wanting to know only if he was willing to work hard. "Yes, ma'am," he had said. "Everyone calls me Lisa," she said, but it went against Hutch's upbringing to call a white woman twice his age by her first name, so he settled for Miss Lisa and after a while she had settled for that too.

She had asked him another question that first day. It had seemed a strange one to Hutch and for a moment he had wondered if it were a condition of his employment—she asked if he could play the guitar or banjo. When he said he played the banjo a little she had fetched an old banjo from the attic. It was in good repair, only in need of tuning. He began to play a little tune his uncle had taught him and he didn't even notice when the tall darky named Julius reached up and took a fiddle off the wall. Before he knew it the fiddle had joined in as pretty as you please and for the first time Hutch suspected he had found not just a place to spend the winter, but a place where he might be happy into the bargain. It seemed a considerable deal, and more than he had hoped for.

The music appeared to mean a lot to Miss Lisa and the others. Hutch found that Julius knew a few hundred tunes of his own, white man's songs from the southern mountains as well as Negro dance tunes. Hutch and Julius traded songs, and with their music they had warmed the kitchen in the Big House on many an evening while winter got down to business outside. It was only later that Hutch was told the banjo he played had belonged to Lisa's father, who had died back in the fall.

That there was a painful gap in the ranks here had been as obvious to Hutch from the start as the empty chair at the head of the table and the fresh grave on the knoll behind the main house. It was too early for the people here to talk much of Jedediah Putnam, but Hutch gathered that a man was gone whose kind passed this way all too rarely. In bits and pieces Hutch had learned more about the former mountain man from the almost mythical company of Jim Bridger and Kit Carson, Joe Meek and Jedediah Smith, until Jed Putnam had assumed in Hutch's imagination the stature of a giant, almost a living presence, or perhaps more a sort of benevolent ghost, still protecting and presiding over Putnam's Park.

"Zeke!" Julius' voice was sharp. The lead horse had been slacking in his harness, letting his partner, Zeus, do the work. Now Zeke leaned into the collar and the sled jerked forward. The two Belgians were half of a team of four. The two pairs served alternate duty, and the full team was used every few days, for breaking new trails. The feed lines were moved regularly so the manure the cattle produced in winter would be spread across the hay meadows by spring and just need a pass with a tooth harrow to break it up so the grass would grow under the dried-up pies. During the recent thaw, all four horses had been used often, and even so there had been days when feeding took all morning, what with getting the sled unstuck three or four times.

Hutch liked the daily ride back up the valley to the barn after the hard, sustained work of loading the rack from one hay crib or another and feeding the cattle. On the cutting cold days, of which there had been many, he and Julius sat on the sled with their backs against the plank front, sheltered from the wind. On warmer days like today, Hutch stood in the middle of the rack and looked at the hills and the valley bottom and the settlement so perfectly situated at the head of the park. Keeping his balance against the uncertain motion of the sled was a game he played with himself, adding to his enjoyment. Today he had timed his reaction to Zeke's lunge perfectly, and he smiled. The work here was hard, as Miss Lisa had said it would be, but Hutch didn't mind hard work. He had quickly learned that Julius was a fair man, and worked half again as hard as Hutch could on his best day. At home, Hutch had been the strongest in the family, his father included, but he couldn't stay ahead of Julius. Before long, Hutch had stopped thinking of Julius as a nigger.

He was beginning to feel at home here, even if it wasn't much of an outfit. The beef herd was small, and the cattle were some kind of Longhorn-Shorthorn cross that Jed Putnam had been experimenting with, not the familiar Texas Longhorns Hutch had known in Kansas. The Texas cattle didn't require any such coddling as winter feeding. Just turn 'em loose and they'd fend for themselves all right. A Longhorn thrived on neglect. He would grow fat on range a lizard would shun for lack of cover. He would walk all day without water and gain weight on the trail. Or so the Texas drovers claimed. But he took four years to grow to market weight.

The notion that this was a fault had come as a surprise to Hutch when Julius first pointed it out. Hutch had seen the first huge herds of Longhorns driven past his pa's place when he was just eight, and as he stood there goggle-eyed and drop-jawed he had decided in that moment that as soon as he was old enough he would become one of the youths folks were already calling "cow-boys." Without giving it much thought, he had accepted the commonly held idea that the Longhorn was the very paragon of bovine development. But it was strange how a new notion could make an old one seem to fade, where once it had shone so brightly. When he thought about it, it made good sense that a steer that gained weight faster than a Longhorn was a better deal from a stockman's point of view, and Hutch had begun to look with new interest at Jed Putnam's mixed-breed cattle and to ask questions about them. He had been surprised to learn that steers he had taken for three-year-olds were not yet two.

Old man Putnam had only been running cattle for a handful of years, Julius said. After the fur trade gave out he had been a wagon guide for a time, leading emigrants to Oregon and California, and then in the fifties he had turned to road ranching, which was to say he ran a kind of a cross between a trading post and a hotel, the way Hutch understood it. He had pioneered the Putnam Cutoff and built his outfit here in what came to be called Putnam's Park, providing a place where the westbound emigrants could restock with supplies and rest their weary draft animals. Hutch thought it odd that Putnam had picked a place so out of the way up here in the Big Horns. He had seen other road ranches on his travels, pretty tumbledown affairs, most of them, and most were abandoned now, but at least they were right there on the road where a person didn't have to take a detour just to find them. Of course, there weren't so many wagons on the old trials now anyway, what with the railroad. By the look of things, old Jed had turned to raising cattle in the nick of time.

To Hutch, the days of road ranching and prairie schooners on the western trails and the even more remote years of the mountain men and the beaver trade were only slightly more real than the fairy tales his mother had read to him. By the time he saddled his mule and lit out on his own, the settlement of the western territories was no longer in question, and the struggles and deeds that had achieved that certainty were known to Hutch only in the broadest outlines as part of the folklore of the times. Like any sensible youngster, his eyes were firmly fixed on what lay ahead, not on the past. What had drawn him west in his own turn were the new tales of the growing boom in beef cattle that now reached beyond the Kansas trailheads up into the northern plains, where there were opportunities born every minute for a young man who wasn't afraid of hard work. When the snow melted he would move on to the kind of big spread he dreamed of, where he could become top hand by the time he was twenty-five and raise as much hell as he liked in town on Saturday night, once they built a town close enough so he could get to it. Miss Lisa and Julius talked of building up the herd in Putnam's Park, but this would never be the kind of place Hutch saw in his mind's eye. He'd have his pick of any ranch on the north plains when his reputation was made, and someday maybe even marry the boss's daughter. It unsettled him somewhat that on this place here the boss's daughter was the boss, and she was as old as his own mother, who was thirty-four and already had five children of which he was the eldest. Lisa Putnam had none, and no husband either, if it came to that, which Hutch thought was strange considering that she wasn't half bad-looking for an older woman, but that was her business. It was enough that her place was a good place to winter, a place where Hutch could learn the rudiments of cow-boying without making a fool of himself in front of a lot of other boys his own age. Come spring he'd move on, but for now he was content. He still didn't say much, but it was no longer because he felt like a stranger. A lot of talk just wasn't in his nature.

Once they reached the yard the horses knew the way without guidance and they picked up the pace, anticipating their daily ration of oats. The sled skimmed along, the rack creaking and the pitchforks wagging back and forth like drunken lookouts, held upright by the iron ring Harry Wo had bolted to the frame of the rack, their butts resting in an old bucket nailed in place below the ring.

"Whoa." Julius stopped the team beside the corral fence. As he moved around the Belgians, unbuckling the harness from their steaming flanks, he enjoyed the practiced ease in Hutch's movements and his familiarity with the complicated tack. Even that morning back in December when they had gone off to feed the cattle for the first time, it had been obvious that the boy knew horses. He could get milk from a cow too; right from the start he had taken to helping Harry with the milking before breakfast. But it was plain when Lisa signed him on that young Hutch didn't know straight up about beef cattle. He was learning, though. Julius guessed that the boy was from a farm back in Kansas. He spoke of Kansas now and again, but he hadn't offered the story of his short life and a man didn't ask that kind of question without some kind of invitation. Julius appreciated that aspect of frontier custom more than most, although he had nothing in his past to hide. It was just that he was used to his freedom now and guarded the right to keep his past to himself. What and where he had been was his own concern.

He felt the defensive anger rising in him without cause and he caught himself.

There was no need to get his back up. Nobody here had ever pried into his past. Lisa knew his story because what old Jed hadn't told her Julius had told her himself. She enjoyed hearing him talk about the Southwest and his years on the Texas cattle trails, although to Julius his own stories had always seemed pale in comparison with the fables old Jed had liked to spin around the glory days of the fur trade back in the twenties and thirties, when he and Bridger and Meek and the rest had roamed the Rocky Mountains as free trappers. The barest hint that you would like to hear one of those tales could set old Jed or his brother Bat going for hours. It was a wonder to Julius that the mountain men had found any time to catch beaver, judging by the way they liked to sit and jaw. He smiled at the memory of Jed Putnam.

"Something funny?" Hutch asked. They had turned the horses into the corral and poured a measure of grain onto the packed snow and put away the harness, all without a word said between them. There was no need for constant talk when two men had worked together for three months doing the same job each morning, just the way there was no need for too much conversation when they all sat down together at mealtimes. Some days they would go through three meals without much more than "Please pass the salt" or "I'll have that last piece of pie if nobody wants it," and some days they would sit around the kitchen table after the noon meal, drinking coffee and laughing and talking until finally Julius stood up and said they'd better get to work before it was too dark to do anything but mend harness. People in close quarters either fit together or they didn't. Julius's father had taught him that, before he was sold upriver to Macon. Folks had to fit together and make life bearable, either that or somebody had to go. Hutch was good company. He'd make a good hand if he stayed on.

"I was thinking about old Jed."

"He was something more than just an ordinary man, I guess."

Julius shrugged, unwilling to deny the common humanity that Jed Putnam had possessed in such uncommon measure. "You look close at his brother Bat. He's cut from the same cloth."

As they left the barn they heard a woman's scolding voice issue from the buffalo-hide tipi that stood alone near the woods. Julius put out a hand to stop Hutch and together they watched the tipi, grinning in anticipation. The dependable frequency with which this scene repeated itself was a comfort to them.

A mongrel dog leaped through the entrance flap, followed by a white man, gray bearded and gaunt, dressed in the buckskins of a mountain man. He wore a skunk-fur cap and a hooded blanket capote that hung from his shoulders and flapped about his leggings. The hood of the capote was thrown back despite the falling snow; the plaits of hair that hung on either side of the man's head were greased with animal fat and wrapped in otter skin. In one hand he held a long percussion rifle. Without looking back he set off for the main house, his thin legs making long strides on the narrow path beaten in the snow. Behind him a short Indian woman stepped out of the tipi, still scolding in her native tongue. She was Hunkpapa Sioux. The women of her people

22

were not afraid to tell a husband his responsibilities when he shirked them, or to make clear what he should do to put things right, but they would never scold a man to his face, least of all in front of others. The woman bent to pick up a few sticks of firewood from a small pile near the tipi's entrance, as if that were her only purpose in coming outside, but she continued to speak to the world at large, to the sky and the trees and the snow, glancing at the man just once and raising her voice when she saw that he was making for the house. Perhaps her husband thought that the deer and elk walked right up to the lodge and lay down to be butchered, she suggested. Perhaps he only left his lodge now because it was so full of meat that there was no room in it for him.

The old man marched ahead, never pausing or looking back. The woman made more observations, equally as pointed, but at last she fell silent. Once a man was set on a course of action, a good woman held her tongue.

Julius had understood some of what the woman had said, enough to grasp the nature of her complaint, and he was shaking with silent laughter. Hutch knew none of her words, but he knew perfectly well what was going on, and he too was laughing.

"Good huntin' lately, Bat?" Julius inquired innocently.

The mountaineer stopped in his tracks and glared at Julius and Hutch, whom he had not noticed until now. They were still laughing as they entered the door to the kitchen of the main house.

"Wagh!" Bat Putnam let out a grizzly bear's snort, the fur trapper's all-purpose interjection of surprise, pleasure, disgust or general exclamation. It was poor doings for a man to be forced out of his own lodge without so much as a bite of *wasná* by a wife who says if he's grown too old or lazy to hunt, he'd best get used to going hungry; it was worse yet to be mocked in front of his wife by a good-for-nothing darky and a bantam rooster too young to crow for real. The two of them put together didn't amount to a heap of goat shit. Well, they'd get no more satisfaction out of John Batson Putnam, not this day. With a cup of Lisa's coffee to warm him, he'd show those two that this coon could still raise sign in whatever weather God in his considerable humor decided to ply the mountains with.

He resumed his march toward the house.

It seemed to Lieutenant Whitcomb that he was entering a land where the Creation was incomplete. He had imagined the western country as gently rolling and covered with grass, perhaps looking from afar somewhat like the rolling swells of the Atlantic on a peaceful day, as he had often seen it from the beaches of Cape Henry. Around Cheyenne the pleasant grasslands had met his expectations, but here the countryside was broken, unfinished, as if God had deemed it unworthy of any further effort. To the south and west a range of mountains cloaked blue-black in evergreens rose into the gray clouds that stretched flat and featureless in all directions, but near at hand the land was unclothed. What few stalks of grass there were had clustered together for comfort, and the landscape was devoid of trees except for a few stunted specimens on the low buttes and a ribbon of tall cottonwoods hidden down in the bottomland of the North Platte, which hereabouts flowed in a shallow canyon a half mile off to Whitcomb's right. Even the brownish-yellow soil that served as the earth's poor flesh in these regions was insufficient, for on every slope and low summit the rocks—the bones of the planet—showed through.

The alien surroundings heightened Whitcomb's sense of loneliness. Overhead the twin strands of telegraph wire picked up the hum of the wind and he wondered if they were also carrying other messages, more comforting and friendly. He had only to follow the wires to reach Fort Fetterman, for they ended there, but as he topped each rise he saw only the telegraph poles marching onward and no glimpse of the fort. For a day and a half he had seen no living soul and had no company save for his horse, and so when he spied another rider approaching the wagon road from his left flank he greeted the sight with a surge of profound gratitude.

A glance was enough to identify the man as white. By his appearance Whitcomb took him for a wandering mountaineer or perhaps a scout for Crook's command returning to the fort from a reconnaissance of the surrounding country. The man was cloaked from neck to stirrup in a long fur coat and he kept his seat with perfect ease as the horse covered the rough ground at a steady trot. A rifle rested across the rider's lap and the body of an animal—Whitcomb guessed it was an antelope—was tied behind the saddle. A black-and-white border collie trotted behind the horse, content to let the larger animal break a path through a shallow drift of old snow. When horse and rider reached an expanse of bare ground, the dog trotted ahead.

24

Earlier that morning Whitcomb had led his own horse on foot for more than an hour, trying to walk off the cold that had chilled him to the bone ever since the clouds had covered the sun scarcely an hour after it rose, but he had remounted some time ago, anxious to keep up his pace. Now he touched his spurs to the tired animal, urging him into a faster walk in order to intercept the other rider as he reached the road. The man would know how much farther it was to the fort and some talk would be welcome—anything to forget the cold and wind. He pulled the collar of his dark blue greatcoat higher about his neck.

Second Lieutenant Hamilton Whitcomb was twenty-two and knew that he looked younger. His sandy hair and hazel eyes and open, unlined face contributed to an impression of untried youth. But he was wiry and he had endurance. "You have the build of a cavalryman," his father had said, certain that the family tradition of military service had been doomed to extinction by the surrender of the South. Whitcomb was conscious of the heavy gold West Point ring on his left hand. He was the only one of the Virginia Whitcombs presently in uniform and his father could not forget that the uniform he wore was that of the South's conquerors.

He had traveled alone from Fort Laramie, eighty barren miles to the southeast along the old Oregon Trail. From Cheyenne to Laramie he had ridden with a dozen replacement troopers whom he had escorted west on the train from department headquarters in Omaha. The road was choked with gold seekers hurrying north toward the Black Hills of Dakota, and everywhere along the way the small contingent of troops had been greeted alternately with shouts of encouragement in their task of quelling the Indians and jeers for having failed to do so thus far. The numbers of the argonauts had astonished Whitcomb and he had hurried his little troop along, all the more anxious to join General Crook.

Six months had passed since the latest peace commission had failed to negotiate a successful purchase of the hills from the Sioux. Smarting from the many promises that had been made and quickly broken by the whites during the course of their successive encroachments into Indian lands, the Sioux had demanded staggering sums for the Black Hills, which they revered as the "sacred center" of their nation. The amounts named by the various chiefs had ranged upward from thirty million dollars. The peace commissioners had offered six million, which the Sioux promptly refused, but the country needed new capital to speed its recovery from the financial panic of '73, and from Washington City the rights of the Sioux appeared small compared with the hunger for gold that pervaded the halls of the Capitol. Two years before, General George Custer had conducted a military reconnaissance of the hills and had reported the presence of gold "from the grass roots down," in the words of his exuberant dispatch. Since then, troops had struggled halfheartedly to root out white miners who slipped into the hills past the army roadblocks. With the failure of the peace commission the troops had been withdrawn and thousands of prospectors flooded into the hills. Throughout the winter they had scrabbled for gold with one hand while fighting off the angry warriors of Crazy Horse with the other. As spring drew near, the matter was still unresolved and new hordes poured daily into the diggings. The presence of the miners served as a goad to remind the Sioux that the advance of the white race could not be denied, while the planned military campaign, which Whitcomb was to join, would round up the last of the hostile bands in the Powder River country west of the Black Hills and complete the containment of the nomadic warriors on the Dakota reservation. With the spirit of resistance broken, a final settlement of the Black Hills dispute would quickly follow.

Whitcomb felt his pulse quicken at the thought of the coming campaign. He had feared during his years at West Point that the Indian wars would end before he could take part, denying him what might be his only chance to win recognition on the battlefield, and until a week ago he had despaired of obtaining field duty on the frontier. But then his orders had arrived, unexpected and electrifying: a three-pronged assault was about to be launched against the hostile Sioux, with General Custer leading the Seventh Cavalry from Fort Abraham Lincoln in Dakota Territory, Colonel John Gibbon moving southeast from Fort Shaw in Montana, and General George Crook, commander of the Department of the Platte, advancing northward from Fort Fetterman; if Whitcomb could reach Fetterman in time he could join Crook's force and take part in the campaign. The fact that Crook, whose command comprised Utah and Wyoming Territories and the state of Nebraska as well, had chosen to lead the expedition himself attested to its importance, and within an hour of receiving the message, Whitcomb was packed and on his way. In a handful of days he had crossed two-thirds of the continent, but when he reached Fort Laramie it seemed that his haste might have been in vain. The company to which he was assigned, E Troop, Third Cavalry, had already gone on to Fetterman, and the post adjutant at Laramie, to whom Whitcomb delivered the replacement troopers, informed him that Crook was reportedly impatient to be off and would certainly set out as soon as the last elements of his command reached him.

"But I have to get there before he leaves!" Whitcomb had protested desperately. "What arrangements have been made for my travel to Fetterman?"

"Arrangements?" The post adjutant had looked perplexed. "Why none, I'm afraid. Departmental orders state that no one shall travel alone west of Laramie, and I can't spare an escort. We've got the Black Hills road to police, you know, and you've seen what a job that is." He saw the disappointment on Whitcomb's face and he looked the young lieutenant up and down thoughtfully. "Of course I'm a pretty busy fellow," he said. "I can't be expected to bring every new shavetail up to date on all the standing orders." And with that he had returned to the papers on his desk, ignoring Whitcomb completely.

It had taken Whitcomb only a moment to see the opportunity the post adjutant had offered him. Somewhat taken aback by his own audacity, he had tiptoed silently from the adjutant's office and left Fort Laramie alone. He had made ten miles before seeking shelter at dusk in one of the countless ravines that cut the desolate red-clay countryside; there he had built a small fire of scrub cedar, hoping that the warming glow would not be seen by unfriendly eyes, and he had managed to get some sleep in the buffalo robe he had bought from the post trader at Laramie. That had been the night before last. Yesterday he had covered fifty miles under a brilliant sun, following the wagon tracks that paralleled the North Platte. Bunchgrass grew in the ruts now where twenty years before the emigrant wagons had often traveled ten abreast.

The other rider was drawing near and Whitcomb was about to call out a greeting when he crested a low ridge and saw Fort Fetterman before him, less than two miles away, its buildings grouped along the edge of a plateau overlooking a section of the Platte where the bottomland stretched out broad and wide. He could easily make out a beef herd foraging under guard near the fort and a much larger horse herd farther away. Plainly, a large force was in the garrison. The dozens of wagons grouped by the road would belong to the expedition's supply train.

Whitcomb felt his heart pounding in his chest. Crook was still at Fetterman and his lonely journey had been worth all the risks.

"Good morning, Lieutenant," the rider said as he gained the road. He's a scout, Whitcomb thought, or he wouldn't be able to read my rank so easily. As the fur-coated rider slowed his horse to a walk, Whitcomb drew himself up in the saddle, eager to make a good impression no matter who the man might be, although it was with some difficulty that he contained his excitement. He was proud of himself and his new field uniform, and glad that he presented a neat and relatively clean appearance despite the rigors of his journey.

"Good morning. It's a splendid day."

The man nodded politely. He was in his late forties, Whitcomb judged. He wore brown corduroy trousers beneath his bearskin greatcoat, and scuffed army boots. The bottoms of the corduroys were burned, as was the brim of the man's felt Kossuth hat, which was faded from black to a sun-bleached brown. There was a dark patch on the crown where an insignia had been torn away. It was a cast-off hat, no doubt given him by a generous officer, and had probably been used to beat out many a campfire. The man's blondish beard was unkempt, but his blue-gray eyes were calm and level and something about him conveyed an innate dignity.

"It could be that a change in the weather is coming," the rider observed, seemingly unaware of Whitcomb's scrutiny. His speech was that of an educated man, but that was not so surprising. Men of every sort came west, Whitcomb knew, and educated men could be found in any occupation. He regarded the low clouds for several moments, feeling the northeast wind on his cheek, trying to decide how to respond. A few flakes of snow were in the air now and it did seem warmer than the day before, in spite of the wind and clouds, but he decided to be cautious; if there was one thing the scout would know, it was the weather.

"I'm not familiar with the plains," he offered. "Until a week ago I had never been west of the Alleghenies."

"You are from the South, I believe. Virginia?"

Whitcomb stiffened involuntarily. The number of Southerners at West Point had increased steadily in recent years, and by the time Whitcomb graduated, there were almost as many Southern cadets at the academy as there had been before the war. The Northerners had grown accustomed to hearing Southern accents and Whitcomb had almost forgotten that there were men who might form certain opinions of him on the basis of his speech alone. But he had nothing to hide.

"Petersburg," he said, confirming the man's guess and leaving unsaid everything that name meant to anyone who had lived through the last year of the war. While Grant had kept Lee and his army bottled up at Petersburg, Sherman had made his devastating sweep through Georgia, and after nine agonizing months of siege, Lee had been forced to withdraw from Petersburg in defeat. A week later he had stepped into the McLean farmhouse at Appomattox Court House to surrender his army, and the last hope of the Confederacy.

"You are too young to have fought in the Rebellion," the scout said. It was not a question.

Whitcomb felt the blood rise to his face. The man was offering him a chance to disassociate himself from the Rebel cause. "My father fought with Jeb Stuart until the general's death," he said firmly. "Both of my uncles served with the Army of Northern Virginia." The scout was a Yankee, that was certain. No Southerner spoke of the Rebellion. Ham Whitcomb's father and uncles called it the War Between the States, or the War for the Southern Confederacy, or the War for States' Rights, but only a Yankee would call it the Rebellion. A rebellion implied a revolt against a legitimate government and the South had denied the legitimacy of an unbreakable Union. But Ham's father and uncles had fought their war and they had lost. He had no wish to revive the struggle, but neither would he allow a stranger to cast doubt on his family's honor.

The scout merely nodded in a way that implied no judgment and they rode for a time in silence while Whitcomb's anger cooled.

"I imagine you have come from Fort Laramie."

It was Whitcomb's turn to nod calmly, as if riding alone across eighty miles of frozen plains was something he did without a second thought. Too late he realized that he would have preferred to invent a different route by which he had arrived at Fetterman. If the scout should mention a young lieutenant riding alone from Laramie, things could go hard for Ham Whitcomb.

"They sent you on without an escort?"

"My regiment has been ordered into the field," Whitcomb replied, deliberately avoiding the question. It was an army tradition that an officer whose regiment was ordered into the field in his absence would cut short his leave and go to any lengths to join his men.

"I imagine we must all cast a blind eye at regulations now and then," the scout said.

So he knew of the standing orders. Well, there could be no going back now. "'Pity the warrior who is content to crawl about in the beggardom of rules,'" Whitcomb said. "That's from Clausewitz. I don't imagine you have read him.

28

But don't misunderstand me. I only disobeyed a rule that was keeping me from my duty."

The scout nodded, seeming to accept this. "Was there any sign of Indians along the way?" he asked.

"I saw no one, red or white." Whitcomb was glad of the change in topic and some of his former excitement returned. "Frankly, I've heard that the danger may be overrated. At Laramie they say there are only five hundred hostiles outside the reservation."

The scout smiled fleetingly. "Oh, there may be a few more than that. Still, with a little luck we may have them on the run before long."

"You're going on the expedition?"

The scout nodded.

"I think you're right, about having them on the run, I mean. With Crook and Terry and Gibbon all in the field, we should bring the hostiles to bay."

Whitcomb was surprised to see no reaction from the scout, only another nod of acknowledgment, but then he remembered the telegraph. Fort Fetterman must have been notified that General Alfred Terry instead of Custer would lead the column from Fort Abraham Lincoln. The news had reached Fort Laramie only hours before Whitcomb and his troopers arrived at the post, and it had been the topic on every lip. After a winter's leave, during which he had been lionized by Washington and New York society matrons, Custer had returned to his regiment a week ago only to be summoned back to Washington at once by a House committee that was investigating corruption in the handling of Indian affairs. Custer had requested that he be allowed to testify by deposition, but the House was controlled by Democrats who wanted to miss no opportunity to embarrass President Grant, and they had insisted that Custer should appear in person. The "Boy General"—a nickname that had stuck with Custer since the war, when he had been promoted brevet major general at the age of twenty-six—was widely known, and he would bring much attention to the hearings. In Custer's absence, General Terry, the commander of the Department of Dakota, had assumed direct command of Custer's regiment.

That Custer had been summoned to appear had come as no surprise to Whitcomb. For four years at West Point he had prepared himself for duty on the frontier by learning all he could both about the native peoples there and the officers that now sought to quell their warlike ways, and he knew that despite their very different temperaments, both Generals Crook and Custer abhorred any underhanded dealings on the part of Indian agents, not only for the practical reason that such thievery aroused justified resentment on the part of the savages, but also because it offended each man's sense of honor and fair play. Crook's success in taming the fierce Apaches with his scrupulous fairness was well known, and Custer had spoken loudly on the subject of Indian Bureau corruption more than once, frequently offering his written opinions to the newspapers. Such attention on Indian affairs only served to emphasize the failure of Grant's Indian policy, which had been intended to end the corruption and assure the Indians a secure future in American society.

As the white race pushed steadily westward both before and after the Civil War, successive tribes had been persuaded to accept small reservations in place of their formerly limitless homelands in exchange for payments of money and the long-term delivery of annuity goods, so called because they were usually delivered on an annual basis. The budget of the Indian Bureau expanded rapidly to provide for the goods, and the opportunities for corruption increased in direct proportion. The position of Indian agent paid just fifteen hundred dollars a year, but it was widely charged that an agent could retire comfortably in three years on the graft that would virtually be thrust upon him. Contracts were bought with bribes, the agents pocketed first-class payments while obtaining tenth-rate goods, and some supplies were privately sold to white citizens instead of being disbursed on the reservations. Even as these practices became widespread, some government officials, both military men and civilians, urged a policy of outright extermination of the Indians, saying that they were subhuman brutes who could never have a place among civilized people. In his first inaugural address, Grant had attempted to lay such talk to rest. He spoke of the Indians as "the original occupants of this land," and expressed his sincere hope that they could indeed be civilized and in time become citizens who were equal in all respects to their white brothers. His first Commissioner of Indian Affairs was Ely S. Parker, a full-blooded Seneca Indian. Together they attempted to institute policies that would treat the Indians fairly and begin the process of educating them in civilized ways. To stop the rampant corruption, Grant passed control of the reservations to the various religious denominations, in the hope that men of God would have as their first concern the welfare of the Indians' souls rather than filling their own pockets with the government's gold. But now, as Grant's second term drew to a close, it was apparent that human frailty had proved more than a match for the President's dreams. Most of the schools promised for the reservations had never been built; annuity goods were often late or insufficient, or they simply did not appear at all while greedy men grew fat on Indian hunger.

As Whitcomb had learned these painful facts, he had found himself agreeing with those who proposed that the Indian Bureau be returned to the War Department from the Department of the Interior, whose minions sat in their offices in Washington City and remained almost wholly ignorant about the distant lands they administered. His learning was as yet untried, but now, seeing this foreign landscape for the first time, it seemed to Whitcomb that the politics of Washington City and the conflicting proposals of groups both in and out of government were forces so remote from these vast regions that they could have no relevance here, a hundred miles from the nearest railroad and centuries in time from the marble columns of the nation's capital. Surely, trying to administer the Indians and their lands from Washington City was an enterprise with no greater chance of success than attempting to warm the chill winds by the application of Greek philosophy.

He looked around him and wondered what sort of men the Indians were, to choose this place for their home.

Custer's appearance before the House committee might bring matters to a head, and if Crook's campaign succeeded, perhaps that would convince the Congress that the officers of the frontier army were the men best suited to deal with the Indian problem.

The scout had made no reply to Whitcomb's expression of hope about bringing the hostiles to bay and Whitcomb decided to elaborate on it a bit. He was confident that he could hold his own on matters of tactics and strategy, no matter how much experience the scout might have on the plains.

"Even if there are a thousand or more on the loose, the capture of a single village should break their spirit. That's Sheridan's plan."

The border scout's collie spotted a jack rabbit in the brush and bolted suddenly across the road in hot pursuit. Whitcomb's horse shied, but he controlled the animal in an instant without moving his hands on the reins, using only a slight tightening of his knees. Horsemanship was something else he wouldn't concede to the scout.

"You agree with General Sheridan?" The scout regarded him calmly.

"Yes, I do." General Philip H. Sheridan was commander of the army's Division of the Missouri, within which General Crook's Department of the Platte was situated. It was Sheridan who had instigated winter campaigns against the hostiles in late 1868 on the southern plains. In that winter George Custer had obtained a signal victory over some Cheyenne camped on the Washita River in Indian Territory. Despite a lingering controversy over whether or not the Cheyenne had actually been hostile, Custer's success had proved the virtue of Sheridan's tactics.

"In summer the Indians have a tactical advantage over us, one of mobility," Whitcomb explained. "They can live off the country and move about quickly, while we're tied down by our supply trains. Even with several columns converging from different points we can't make them fight unless they want to. If they don't like the odds they just slip away. But in winter the advantage is ours. The Indian horses are too weak for prolonged reconnaissance and the warriors stay close to the villages. If we surprise one camp and take the savages under guard to Dakota, it may convince the rest that resistance is useless." He realized that much of what he had said would be known to the scout as a matter of common sense, if not as strategy, and he added, "At least that's the way I understand it. I'm sure you know more about this than I do."

"I'm always glad to hear some fresh thinking on the subject."

Whitcomb didn't feel that he had added any thoughts that were remotely fresh, and he realized that he would do well to keep his opinions to himself from now on. There was a cold reception awaiting young lieutenants fresh out of West Point who sought to educate their superior officers. It occurred to him belatedly that anything he told the scout might be reported to those same officers, and he wished he had been more guarded in his speech.

"I see you have been hunting," he said, hoping to shift the conversation to safer ground. He would let the other man do the talking for a while. Scouts were notorious storytellers, and it wouldn't hurt him to hear some tales of these wild lands that were so new to him.

"The officers enjoy some wild game now and again," the scout said. "Have you had antelope?"

"I'm afraid not."

"You will have it tonight." The scout lapsed into silence.

Disappointed to find the man so taciturn, Whitcomb was nonetheless cheered by the thought of hot food. Since leaving Fort Laramie he had eaten nothing but hardtack and jerky. He had been in the saddle before dawn that morning in the hope of reaching Fetterman in time for the noon meal.

They were nearing the first of the fort's outbuildings now, passing by a large corral where a stable sergeant was supervising the installation of a new water trough. Whitcomb returned the sergeant's salute as the scout waved a greeting. Not far away two companies of cavalry were firing at makeshift targets. Whitcomb took this as evidence of the thoroughness with which the troops were being prepared for the campaign. Target practice was not a regular feature of the soldiers' training, and on the frontier, where ammunition was scarce, it was virtually unknown.

Like many another frontier post, Fetterman had been a fortified bastion during the constant Indian troubles of the middle sixties, but the high plank fence that had once enclosed the headquarters building, barracks and parade ground had mostly been taken down since then, leaving only a tall log gateway, where three guards stood at ease, and a few sections of fencing behind the barracks. The stables were half a mile to the east of the main buildings, together with shops where blacksmiths, wheelwrights and saddlers practiced their crafts. Between the stables and the rest of the fort a ravine descended to the river plain, some hundred feet below the level of the plateau, and as the two riders rode past the ravine Whitcomb saw parallel lines of army tents on the bottomland. There were twelve companies in Crook's command, ten of cavalry and two of infantry, and by the look of it the entire force was encamped on the river plain. Beyond the neat rows of canvas tents stood a cluster of what appeared to be Indian tipis.

"Are our men using captured Indian tents?" Whitcomb inquired of the scout.

"Those are real Indians, Lieutenant. Thirty-six lodges of Arapaho. The Indians know we're up to something and the Arapaho are going in to the agencies. If there's to be trouble, they want to be well out of it. The chief of this group is named Black Crow. He is one of the reasons we expect to find a good many hostiles up north. He calls all Sioux 'Minneconjous,' and he says there are plenty of them up toward the Yellowstone. 'Heap plenty Minneconjous,' he told me. 'Makeum tired countum.'"

"I see." Whitcomb absorbed this sobering information with interest, but much of his attention was on the fort and its surroundings. Here and there among the buildings he spied a figure in dress and sunbonnet—an officer's wife or laundress—but the women were all but lost in a sea of men; everywhere about the plateau, squads were drilling on foot and horseback; packers moved among the wagons and worked over the rows of mule packs spread on the ground near the supply train; there were no idlers and nothing out of place. The scene confirmed everything Whitcomb knew about General George Crook, who was reported to concern himself with the workings of his command down to the smallest detail, and to have no patience for carelessness or neglect. He was also said to take a great interest in the welfare of his men, and Whitcomb hoped he might have a chance to meet the general during the course of the campaign, but he was careful to keep his expectations within reason. Even General Crook would have little time to chat with junior lieutenants.

The bugle notes of recall-from-drill sounded from the parade ground, and the squads began to disperse and make for the mess halls and kitchens on the far side of the large quadrangle. Whitcomb smiled. He had made dinner with fifteen minutes to spare.

"Just in time," the scout echoed Whitcomb's thoughts. He quickened the pace of his mount slightly. The collie ran ahead through the gate and paused to look over his shoulder, waiting for his master.

Whitcomb liked the scout. He found himself inventing a history for the man. Perhaps he was a gentleman of good family, one who had failed in life through some misfortune and come west in middle age. Men of every description had done so, some taking new names to give themselves a fresh start or to avoid the law, which might reach even into the territories if the crime was serious enough, but Whitcomb felt sure the man was not a criminal.

"It's been a pleasure riding with you," he said as they approached the gateposts. "I'm Lieutenant Whitcomb. I would be pleased to know your name."

The guards came to attention. Whitcomb returned the salutes, surprised to notice that the scout did so as well.

"Velcome back, Herr General." The German corporal of the guard pronounced "general," with a hard *g*.

"Thank you, Corporal," said Whitcomb's companion.

Ham Whitcomb felt a soft pounding begin in his ears as the blood rose to his face and banished the last trace of chill from his ears.

"General! I see you had good hunting, sir." A lieutenant a few years older than Whitcomb strode rapidly toward them. He was solidly built and round-faced, of medium height. His mustache had been allowed to grow long until it nearly covered his mouth.

"Only fair, Mr. Bourke," said the "scout" as he reined his horse to a halt and returned the lieutenant's salute. "There were two of them. I missed the other. Lieutenant Whitcomb, this is Lieutenant Bourke. Lieutenant Whitcomb is joining our little expedition, Mr. Bourke."

Whitcomb thought the pounding in his ears would deafen him. He knew his normally ruddy cheeks were flushing crimson with embarrassment, but he could do nothing except sit rigidly in his saddle, wishing the ground would open beneath him and swallow horse and rider whole. How could he have failed to recognize Crook? He had seen photographs! But in the photographs Crook's beard, which had a tendency to fork naturally in the middle, was neatly combed into two precise points, while he would certainly not bother to comb his beard before setting out to hunt by himself, as he was well known to do!

"Pleased to have you along, Lieutenant," Bourke said, smiling at Whitcomb. "To what troop are you assigned?"

"Company E, Third Cavalry," Whitcomb managed to say in something resembling his normal tone of voice. He chose to use the formal designation "Company" in the general's presence, although the practice of referring to cavalry companies as "troops" was common usage throughout the army. "Naturally, I will report to the post adjutant as soon as possible," he added quickly.

"I can save you the trouble," Bourke offered. "I'll be seeing him right after dinner and I'll tell him you've arrived. Your troop commander is Major Corwin. You can report directly to him."

"As you wish, Mr. Bourke. Thank you."

"Colonel Stanton informs me his scouts believe a change in the weather is coming," Bourke said to Crook. "They say it will snow tonight."

"What does Grouard say?"

"The same thing, sir."

"And Pourier? Garnier?"

Bourke smiled. "I believe for once the scouts are unanimous in their opinions."

Crook gave a short grunt that might have been a laugh. "It could only happen on the twenty-ninth of February. Please tell Colonel Stanton I agree with his scouts and ask him to report to me this evening after supper. Convey my respects to General Reynolds and ask him to see me at his convenience this afternoon."

Bourke saluted and withdrew, leaving Whitcomb alone with the general.

"The worse it gets, the better," Crook said. "I prefer to hunt Indians in bad weather. It's the only way you can surprise them." He dismounted stiffly. The dog flopped down at his feet, looking perfectly at home. "I hope you will forgive me for not introducing myself, Mr. Whitcomb. I like to know my officers and to hear them speak frankly. Unfortunately, frank talk is not all that common when general officers are on hand. I meant no deception."

"Yes, sir. I understand, sir." Whitcomb sat at attention in the saddle, looking straight ahead.

"Your father is Colonel Cleland Whitcomb, I believe."

34

Whitcomb looked at Crook now and saw that the general was regarding him kindly. "Yes, sir," he replied.

"He is a gallant officer. He was at the Point when I was there. A year or two ahead of me, as I recall. I hope he is well."

The officers and men passing by on their way to dinner glanced at the pair, alone on the parade ground, but the general spoke in a conversational tone that did not carry.

"He has been in failing health, I'm afraid, sir," said Whitcomb, feeling the hurt again. Cleland Whitcomb had returned from the war a broken man, bitter and unforgiving, and his health had declined rapidly until he was little more than an invalid. He had not spoken a word to his only son since Ham's appointment to West Point had arrived in the mail. Ham's mother and his uncle Reuben came to his graduation ceremony, but there had been no word from his father. Feeling unwelcome at home and having nowhere else to go, Ham had refused the leave that was customary for newly graduated cadets, and he had been assigned to staff duty at the headquarters of the Department of the Platte in Omaha until a field post could be found. But then before Ham could entrain for the West, his father had taken a turn for the worse and Ham had gone on leave after all, at first spending the quiet autumn days in a deathwatch over the comatose elder Whitcomb, and then, when his father regained consciousness and Ham was banished from the sickroom, wandering the wooded hills with his dog and his shotgun as he had done in his boyhood. In time he had accepted garrison duty at one of the posts near Petersburg, and when it seemed likely that his father would live for months or years rather than just days, he had once again requested transfer to the frontier. Providentially, some of the companies being assembled for General Crook's campaign against the hostiles were short of officers and Ham was offered one of the vacancies. He had taken the next westbound train after a final visit to his father during which he had received only a cold stare in reply to his expressions of farewell.

"I am very sorry to hear that he is not well," Crook said, and Whitcomb heard the sincerity in his voice. "Well, I enjoyed our ride, Mr. Whitcomb. I am glad to have you in my command."

"Yes, sir. That is, thank you, sir." Whitcomb came even more stiffly to attention in the saddle and gave the general a perfect salute, his eyes fixed straight ahead on an icicle dripping from the eaves of the telegraph office fifty yards distant.

Crook returned the salute and led his horse away, the tattered bearskin coat flapping about his ankles, the dog following behind.

Whitcomb dismounted slowly, his limbs weak from the cold. He held on to the saddle for a moment to steady himself, conscious of the many glances directed his way.

"Oh, Mr. Whitcomb." The general had paused and turned to call out to him.

"Sir?"

"You had better find some proper clothing."

Lisa Putnam's Journal

Tuesday, February 29th. 10:30 a.m.

It is mild this morning, twenty-five degrees when I went in to put on the kettle and rising nearly to freezing as it began to snow just before first light.

Six months ago today, on the day after my father's stroke, I began to keep this journal. I have grown used to the daily ritual of writing. It helps me to order my thoughts and to view my own life with some dispassion. I am glad that I decided to continue this family tradition. At least one Putnam in each of the last seven generations has kept a journal that has been placed, after the author's death, in the family library in Boston. I believe I am the first of my sex to take on the task.

I have put off my writing until mid-morning today in order that I may have a bit more time to myself. This seems to be a day for looking back, a habit my father did not encourage unless it enabled one to go forward with renewed determination. It is in that spirit that I have looked back on his life to see what lessons it may provide.

The pain I felt upon his death has diminished with time, and in looking back now, the first thing I feel is anger—anger at myself for not seeing while he was alive just how remarkable a man he really was. I loved him very much, but I took him for granted. To me he was just a father, which is to say a great deal: disciplinarian, taskmaster, comforter and friend. But it has only been during the months just past, when I tried to diminish my loss by getting to know more about him through his journals and letters, that I have come to see his full height.

He summed himself up quite well, without realizing that he did so, in a letter he wrote my mother in the summer of 1851. It was written in the Sink of the Humboldt River, in what is now Nevada Territory, and posted some weeks later in Sacramento. It came to us around the Horn. "I have a good deal of time to think, ranging out in front of my train," he wrote. "I am beginning to get the makings of an idea. I believe a fellow could make a living by helping the emigrants; not by guiding them but by helping them along their way from the trailside. Old Gabe—you recall how often I spoke of him—is situated on Black's Fork of the Green and is doing well for himself. He ferries folks across the river and sells them whatever they need. It's a life I think we could take to, if I find the right place. I was a pretty fair trapper and I intend to be pretty fair at what I do next, and this road-ranching business, as they call it, tickles my fancy. Of course, the migration won't last forever, but it may offer a way to live

36

in the mountains and a way to pass the time until we see what is coming along next. The fly in the ointment is that there's not a spot right handy to the Oregon road where I would ask you to live, but I have a notion about that too. Do you suppose these good people would do us the kindness of going a little out of their way? I don't mean to tease you, but I won't say what I'm thinking until I'm sure of myself."

As this reveals, he dedicated himself to changing successfully with the times, and I believe that to be his greatest achievement. It was no mean accomplishment for a man born in the year of the Louisiana Purchase. Like the majority of men, my father never by his own hand guided the course of the nation at some turning point in history, but unlike the majority he had an inclination of mind that allowed him to see those turning points as they passed by and to adapt himself accordingly, and in the end I believe he survived the changing fortunes of the frontier better than most of his contemporaries.

As a young man he left the home his ancestors had established in Boston and came west to lands that were then marked on the best French maps as terre inconnue. He helped to make them known and he had a hand in the great expansion and prosperity of the fur trade. He came for three years and stayed for fifteen, and when the trade declined he viewed that decline with regret but moved on willingly to other things, first back in New England and on voyages abroad; before long he returned to the West to assist the great migration that has now largely accomplished its purpose: to extend the Union across the continent. And yet even as he took part in events that had significance far beyond his own life, even as he saw and understood the historical forces at work around him, he lived a life of true independence, seeking a freedom few men are willing to shoulder. He chose to place his home far beyond the reaches of what we call "civilization," and here he found his greatest happiness. And then, near the end of his life, he undertook what he believed to be the enterprise of the future, establishing beef cattle in the northern territories. He charted this new course with as much confidence as any of his sea-merchant forebears when they set sail on the trackless oceans.

And yet this recounting of my father's life omits the one accomplishment he would like other men to notice. He wanted it known that by his presence here and his good relations with Sun Horse's band over so many trying years, together they have shown that it is possible for the red men and white to live side by side in peace, without either one being compelled to give up his way of life. He hoped they might serve as an example to others, and to some extent his hope has been justified, as long as peace prevails over the region. But he wished no praise for this success, nor for the others. "A man's got a duty to live right, like his Maker intended," he used to say. "He does that, he don't need no pats on the back from them that ain't up to it."

And so he leaves a twofold lesson: first, one must choose a way of life that has some part in the larger scheme of things; and second, no matter what enterprise *one chooses, one must live "right," as he put it so simply. I will try to follow his example. The immediate challenge at hand is to build up the herd with the new stock and make a go of raising beef. That seems like more than enough to keep me (and Julius, and the small crew we have assembled here) busy for the foreseeable future.*

Julius and Hutch will be in soon. I must help Ling with dinner. She was in the kitchen before me again today and had the fire going, even though I have begged her to rest in her bed in the morning. She is in her eighth month now, perhaps her ninth. We are not certain. I worry for her, but she tells me not to. Chinese women, like Indian women, are accustomed to work right to the beginning of labor, and I believe this habit would benefit Caucasian "ladies" as well. Surely none of us is more frail than little Ling. Harry says nothing about his wife's condition, but I think he would be glad to have a doctor in attendance at the delivery. (There is no chance of that, I am afraid.) In this wish as in so many other things, Harry has adopted the thinking of his new land.

There have been no white travelers through the park for more than three months now. The last were the two Mormons who shared our Thanksgiving dinner on their way to the Salt Lake. I have welcomed the solitude, but now I look forward to spring.

CHAPTER
THREE

Lisa heard the men open the outer door to the small entryway off the kitchen, laughing and stamping the snow from their boots. She touched the huge enameled coffeepot on the back of the stove and jerked her hand away with a sharp intake of breath, more startled than hurt. The pot was unexpectedly hot.

Ling Wo turned, anxious. She was a short and delicate Chinese, beautiful by the standards of the Orient and pleasing to Western eyes as well.

"You hurt?" The small woman took Lisa's hand and examined it closely before letting go. "Okay. You be careful." She turned away, her huge pregnant belly preceding her as she returned to the bread dough she was kneading on the broad wooden counter.

Lisa touched a finger to the chunk of butter on the sideboard and rubbed a little on the burned finger. She had inherited her mother's fine-boned patrician beauty along with her father's more rugged constitution, yet she dressed in a way that accentuated neither. Her hair, which shone from patient brushing, was piled loosely on top of her head and held in place with a simple whalebone comb, the single ornament she permitted herself for daily wear. Her long dress of indigo-dyed wool was bought from a catalogue, with nothing to distinguish it from countless other simple woolen dresses to be found in countless outposts of the West. But she had her father's cool blue eyes, and like him she had something in her look and manner that commanded attention. Those who shared her life in Putnam's Park were rarely unaware of her presence, and none was more solicitous of her welfare than Ling Wo.

The Chinese woman's predominance in the Big House had increased following Jed Putnam's death, as Lisa's attentions were drawn more urgently to the larger concerns of the ranch, and it was from the kitchen that Ling administered her bailiwick. The big room had pots and pans, and stovetop and counter space sufficient to prepare meals for a hundred, and the pump by the galvanized sink was a time-saving convenience, making it unnecessary to go outside for water. Years had passed since the facilities had been put fully to the test, but for Ling, disuse was no cause for neglect. The spare cookware and china was kept spotless, neatly stacked in cupboards and on shelves, as if she expected a train of wagons to appear on the river road at any time. The second cookstove was seasoned and blackened, free of rust, even though it had not felt the warmth of a fire in many years. The long plank counters were scrubbed clean between meals and the gingham curtains on the windows were kept washed and pressed. The heavy kitchen table that could seat a dozen hands at haying time always bore a vase of fresh flowers in the center, so long as flowers bloomed in the park or in the beds that Lisa's mother had planted around the Big House. In winter the same vase contained delicate arrangements of dried grasses and leaves that Ling picked in the fall and carefully preserved for the winter months. Yet in spite of Ling's loving efforts to make the kitchen and the rest of the house welcoming and cheerful, Lisa couldn't escape a feeling that some essential element of life had gone from the house years before and would never return, leaving the quiet hallways and empty bedrooms somehow incomplete and superfluous. She was glad when mealtimes brought some gaiety at least to this one room. She wrapped her hand in her apron and lifted the coffeepot, marveling at the way Ling treated her sometimes like a child with no sense of her own.

It's because I'm not married, Lisa thought. She thinks there is something deficient about a woman thirty-three years old and not married. Perhaps there is. If I had lived somewhere else, where I could have met some men other than emigrants and drummers and miners. . . . But that wasn't the reason she hadn't married, and she knew it.

Lisa had been just ten when Jed Putnam sent for his wife and child to join him in the house he was building beyond the Missouri in the Big Horn Mountains. Eleanor Putnam had groaned inwardly when she first saw the huge structure of logs, but Jed was sensitive to his wife's civilized background and he had already begun furnishing the house with certain comforts he had had shipped and hauled all the way from Massachusetts—carpets and paintings and some small items of furniture—and more he had bought at exorbitant prices in St. Louis and St. Joe. Eleanor had taken a deep breath and then she pitched in to help, and she had made the house a true home. In later years she wouldn't have traded Putnam

House, which they simply called "the Big House" within the family, for the finest mansions of the Cabots or the Lowells.

From the outset, Lisa had taken to life in the park the way a beaver took to water. She was the first to spy incoming wagons on the river trail and she rode out to meet them in every kind of weather as she grew from a flaxen-haired girl to a willowy sapling no longer a girl, to the striking young woman she had become when she returned in the war years from the fancy school back in Massachusetts where she had been sent at her mother's insistence. Her hair darkened as she grew until it was the color of a fine bay horse. The sunlight seemed to shine along each individual hair and linger there, flashing with a light of its own in the lampglow or firelight of evening. More than one bachelor emigrant had forsaken the conventions of courtship and had asked her, after knowing her for less than a day, to go with him and become his wife in the promised land of California, but she had sent these impulsive supplicants on their way without regret. Often she had accompanied departing wagons to the crest of the West Pass just for the pleasure she took in riding back alone into the comforting embrace of the small valley.

She had cast her lot with Putnam's Park.

Unbidden, an image arose from her memory of a summer day in the park and a troop of soldiers riding up the wagon road. She had been twenty-four that year. At the head of the column rode a young officer whose eyes belonged to an older man. He was a veteran of the war and when he met Lisa something in him had become suddenly open and vulnerable. . . .

"What's the matter with you today? You feel okay?" Ling asked, concerned anew.

"I'm all right." Lisa set aside her dangerous thoughts of the past and put out two cups as Julius and Hutch entered the kitchen, leaving their overboots and coats behind them in the entryway.

Beneath the stove there was a small movement as a large orange cat shifted position in his blanket-lined sleeping basket. He looked at the newcomers blearily and closed his eyes again. His name was Rufus, and he had been picked from a litter of barn kittens by Ling six years before, shortly after she and Harry came to Putnam's Park. He was the only animal permitted in the house. He was long-haired and massive, and Lisa liked to imagine that he belonged to some small, rare species of bear, because he adopted a state of virtual hibernation throughout the winter months, usually venturing from his basket only to eat and answer the other requirements of nature.

"That bad-eye cow's gonna calve first," Julius said. "Another week or two."

"How is her eye?" Lisa poured the coffee, knowing the answer to her question. The cow's cancer could not be cured. She was a good mother who raised fat and healthy calves. This one would be her last.

"Getting worse." Julius moved to the washbasin to clean his hands.

"The brindle cow might win out."

"Two bits on Bad Eye." Julius brightened, taking the bait.

40

"Done," said Lisa. Lord, if my mother knew I gambled, she would turn over in her grave. But Julius was smiling. Lisa knew the moods of her crew as well as she knew the weather in Putnam's Park. A moment of discouragement at the wrong time could sour a whole day and today she didn't want that to happen. Whether she and the others could fulfill her father's vision of a cattle ranch in Putnam's Park was very much in doubt, but this was no time to linger over uncertainties. She planned a lively noontime to raise the spirits of her crew and turn their thoughts to the future. Every job on the ranch had but one purpose— to assure the survival and good health of the calves, and the start of calving was the first sign of spring, the renewal of the annual cycle. Each season had its jobs and the shifting from one to the next marked the passage of time more certainly than the changing pages of the Currier and Ives calendar that hung on the wall by the entryway door. Even now there were fences to mend, work that should already have been done before the demands of calving grew too great. As soon as calving was over, the calves would be branded and then driven with their mothers out of the park onto the surrounding mountainsides, where they would wander higher as the green grass advanced up the slopes. In the park the meadows would be dragged with harrows to disperse the manure left during the winter, the irrigation ditches would be inspected for badger or gopher holes that could cause sudden washouts, and the irrigation system would be extended a little, claiming more land from the sage and bunchgrass as the feeder ditches were lengthened by Harry and his plow. As the days grew longer Lisa and Julius and Hutch would walk the ditches, raising the water level with planks and stones and lumps of sod, forcing the water over the banks to trickle everywhere among the green shoots. Irrigation was a job that continued through the summer, and Lisa enjoyed the peaceful quiet of days spent walking in rubber boots with a shovel over her shoulder. Then, when she and Julius agreed that the grass was mature, the water was cut off and haying began, and when the cribs were full and the meadows reduced to golden stubble, the cattle were gathered and driven back to the park, where the herd was culled of old cows and poor mothers. These, together with the mature steers, were driven to the railroad in Rawlins, and if the first snow had not fallen before Lisa and the drovers returned, it would fall soon, heralding the arrival of yet another winter, to be followed by another spring and another crop of calves. It was a stately progression of events, a continuity from which Lisa derived much pleasure, but this year she looked forward to the arrival of the first calf with a special anticipation. She needed the living proof of rebirth and new life as a sign that this particular winter and her time of mourning were done.

She was about to say something more to keep up the talk of calving and its attendant chores when the entryway door opened again and her uncle Bat stepped into the kitchen.

The mountain man nodded to the room at large, leaving his long rifle in the corner of the little entrance hall so the heat of the kitchen wouldn't sweat out moisture inside the barrel where it might foul the charge of powder just when he finally had meat in his sights. He shut the door behind him and glanced at the cup warming Hutch's hands. "Lisa, you got a cup of java for a poor feller's been pitched out'n his own home?"

Lisa smiled. "There's plenty of coffee, Uncle Bat. What have you done now?" She handed him the steaming cup she had poured for herself.

"Penelope says don't come back without I fetch some meat. Didn't put it in so many words, but she made herself plain. Meat, she says, to the feller that's kept her fed since Cain was a pup. This child knows sign, and that's the truth, but I ain't made a raise since afore Christmas. Ain't no man set eyes on more'n a scrawny doe or two since then, and them scarce as horns on a duck."

"You can have some beef, I imagine," Julius said, expressionless.

"Beef! She won't have none of it! *Pte gleshka*, she says. White man's buffalo! No good, she says. Got no heart." He smote his chest with a fist. "No sir, this child's got some cold trackin' to do 'fore he gets fed."

For more than thirty years Bat Putnam had lived with a small band of Sioux now led by Sun Horse, the aging Hunkpapa peace man. Bat and his wife, Otter Skin, whom he called Penelope for reasons he had never explained, had arrived in Putnam's Park in October, a month after his brother Jed's death, having been notified by an Oglala hunting party that someone had died here. The Oglalas had chanced to pass by the park on the day of the burial and they had observed it unseen from the shelter of a wooden ridge. When they encountered Sun Horse and his band near the Yellowstone on their fall hunt, they had passed on the troubling news, for they knew that the band wintered near the white settlement. Bat and Penelope had arrived as soon as they could, and not long after that the Sun Band, as Sun Horse's people were called, had gone into winter camp in their own valley seven miles to the north. Bat and Penelope had stayed in the settlement through the winter months and Lisa had been comforted by their presence.

Bat turned to Hutch now, his eye carefully noting the steaming pots on the stove behind the boy. "How you gettin' by, Hutch? This old nigger workin' you to death?"

"Not too bad." Hutch grinned. He was used to the trading of insults between these two. At first he had expected one or the other of them to be dead within days, if not hours, judging by the reckless claims each made about the other's character and ancestry, but before long Hutch had perceived that the gibes old Bat and Julius hurled so freely were just their way of letting the other one know that while he was clearly worth no more than a long-dead horse, he had a friend in this world.

Lisa moved to set the table, smiling inwardly. Winter doldrums were quickly banished at the hands of her uncle's often merciless good humor. No one else could have referred to Julius in such a manner and received a smile in return, but Julius knew very well that in the trappers' *patois*, "coon" and "nigger," "critter" and "child" were applied to oneself or a companion without rancor and with no regard for color. Lisa's father had clung to the mountain man's way of talking until his death, although he, like Bat, could drop its mannerisms if he wished. For the Putnam brothers it was not just a style of speech but a way of thinking, a way of living, as well. Its usage kept alive memories of grand adventures and "shining times" long past.

Lisa opened a drawer and began to gather silverware. "You better eat something before you go out into that," she said to her uncle, nodding toward the window. Outside, it had begun to snow again.

Bat sipped his coffee, trying to count the forks in Lisa's hand to see if she had already got one for him or if she was waiting for the stalking game to go a few steps further. She kept the silver hidden from him. "I dunno." He shrugged. "A man don't cut trail too good on a full belly. Takes the keen eye of hunger to make a good tracker."

"Good thing," Julius said, grinning as he dried his hands on a ragged muslin towel. "I don't set to table with white trash, 'specially not with no squaw man too feeble to lift a gun."

Bat snorted, ignoring Julius as if such a comment from that quarter was worth no notice at all. He watched attentively as Ling lifted the lid of an iron cauldron that had already filled the kitchen with smells of slow and careful cooking.

"Good dinner today," said the small Chinese, stirring the pot. She too had her part to play in this ritual. "Beef stew, beans, biscuits, dry-apple pie."

Bat thought of the way Ling laced her dried-apple pie with molasses and a touch of salt, and he felt the juices start to run inside his mouth. He winked at Hutch. "Oh, well, long's you ain't makin' that heathen Chinee food."

"You like Chinese food!" Ling stamped her foot. "I make *Kung Pao* beef, you eat it all! Don't leave none for Julius!"

Bat grinned. Here was a child whose goat could be got every time, rain or shine. Pass a remark about her cooking and Hannah, bar the door. "Was that Chinee food?" He feigned surprise. "I figgered it for Mexican. So hot it like to tore me a new throat."

"You know it is Chinese food!" Ling shook her large wooden spoon at him. "Mexicans don't know nothing about hot food. Chinese people make hot food two thousand years before Mexicans! Mexicans probably send some old fool like you to learn how to cook. Marco Polo come to China, he bring your grandfather. Old fool die on the way home, nobody remember how to cook right so Mexicans throw everything in pot, hope it come out okay." Ling turned back to the stove, muttering in Cantonese.

Bat was struck momentarily speechless by the chronology and geography of this pronouncement, and before he could frame a reply the kitchen door opened again and Harry Wo entered, bowing slightly to Lisa, who bowed in return. Harry was only a few inches taller than his wife but he was nearly three times as wide, even in Ling's pregnancy, and so solid that when he was standing still he seemed to be rooted where he stood as firmly as a tree trunk. His years as a railroad worker and blacksmith since coming to America had merely reinforced an already formidable strength, and in all the time he and Ling had been in Putnam's Park, no man had bested Harry Wo in arm wrestling, that most frequent physical contest of the western territories, which was conducted with every emotion from good-natured horseplay to mortal determination. He glanced around the kitchen now, noticing the smiles on every face except that of his wife, who was still muttering as she ladled stew into a heavy earthenware serving dish. Harry addressed her briefly in Cantonese.

Ling replied with a few short words and gestured with the ladle in Bat's direction. Bat grinned and Harry suppressed a smile as he took his place at the table, his stout body moving with an unnatural grace. His shirt and trousers were western, but his hair was braided in the traditional queue of his homeland. What had once been a mark of servitude to the Manchu overlords in China had become in America a badge of stubborn pride for Harry; it had pleased him to discover that the horse-riding Indians so feared by most Americans also wore their hair long and sometimes tied at the back.

Lisa carried the first serving dish to the table and in clearing a place for it she almost accidentally rearranged a few things she had concealed behind the breadbasket. When she moved away, Hutch saw that an extra place setting had suddenly appeared. Try as he might, he couldn't keep a grin off his face. The whole thing puzzled him almost as much as it pleased him. Whenever Miss Lisa's uncle had a fight with his Sioux wife or just got tired of eating jerky and pemmican and dog stew, he'd walk down to the house and pretend he didn't want to stay to the meal he'd come just in time for. There would be a little talk that didn't lead anywhere and never got around to old Bat accepting the invitation outright, and pretty soon they would all sit down and Bat would sit right along with them. How it made them all feel so good, Hutch didn't know, but it made him feel good too. It was kind of like watching a pickaninny do a perfect little dance step to somebody playing the mouth harp; a simple thing, but it made a person glad to see it.

As if it were no more than his birthright, Bat Putnam sat down at the table. Ling was at the sink now, washing a few carrots in a pan of clear water, and it struck Hutch that sticks of raw carrot were one of Bat's favorite additions to a meal. Ling was doing her best to look serious and annoyed, but there seemed to be the beginnings of a smile playing around her mouth. Julius saw that he couldn't throw his wash water into the sink and so he turned to the door, preparing to pitch it out into the snow instead, and he too was smiling, glancing back over his shoulder. He opened the door and turned to step into the entryway, and he found himself face to face with a gray-haired, blanket-wrapped Indian, who grinned and gave a loud whoop, shaking his feathered lance in Julius's face. Julius took an involuntary step backward, spilling some of the wash water on his boots and wool trousers.

"*Hau, kola,*" the Indian said solemnly.

Hutch found it necessary to sit in a convenient chair. If the whole episode between Bat and Ling Wo had been planned, it couldn't have been better preparation for the Indian's arrival. Hutch too had been startled at first, and a little afraid, but when he recognized Hears Twice he gave himself up to laughter at Julius's expense along with the others in the kitchen, who made no effort to conceal their delight at his surprise and discomfort. There was something about spending long winter months cooped up with a handful of people that led to outbreaks of practical joking. More than once, Hutch had suffered a similar fate at Julius's hand. He laughed until he choked and then he laughed some more as Bat pounded him on the back to stop the choking.

Julius looked the Indian up and down. "Some friend," he snorted. "You creep around like that, some day I'm gonna shoot first and see who it is later. You do better to walk right up and knock like a white man." He brushed past the old Indian and opened the outer door. A gust of cold air and snow swirled into the entryway and kitchen as he tossed the panful of water into the snow. A horse was tethered at the hitching rail close outside the back door. Julius slammed the door against the wind and stepped back into the kitchen. It serves me right, he thought, letting someone get that close to the house without being seen or heard.

"Well, just don't stand there," he said. "Come in and get warm if you've a mind to." Hears Twice was a frequent visitor to the settlement. He had initiated his own participation in the winter games on a day years before, when he had shaken hands with Julius and left the astonished black man holding the hand and forearm of a recently deceased Crow warrior, which Hears Twice had concealed under his robe. An invisible score sheet was kept, on which the old Sioux had just drawn even, making up for the time Julius had put salt in the sugar bowl before offering him a cup of coffee.

The Indian set his lance aside and stepped into the kitchen.

"What you got there?" Julius demanded. Ever since he had opened the door, Hears Twice had kept one hand behind his back.

The old man brought out two dead rabbits and laid them on the countertop. "*Le mashtínchala lila washtepi, Julius. Lila chépapi. Aghúyap'na tehmugha tunkché wachín.*" These rabbits are very good, Julius, very fat. I want bread and molasses for them.

Like Bat's wife, Hears Twice spoke Lakota, the tongue of the western Sioux, using simple words and phrases but always testing the black man's rudimentary grasp of the language by using a few words he might not know. As he spoke, the old Indian moved his hands gracefully as an aid to understanding, indicating the rabbits, pointing at the bread now rising in covered pans, crossing his forefingers to indicate the exchange of goods.

"I'll trade you bread for 'em," Julius said, choosing to conduct the bargaining in English today. "I cain't trade no molasses, not till we get more. We're about out."

"*Tehmugha tunkché,*" the Indian insisted. "Mola-say."

"No molasses." Julius was indifferent, in control now. He knew how much Hears Twice loved fresh bread. "The bread'll be ready after dinner. Think of it all hot and crusty. Fresh bread. *Aghúyapi lila washté.*"

Julius picked up one of the rabbits and felt the frozen corpse to judge how much meat lay beneath the thick winter coat. He was careful to conduct his dealings with Hears Twice with the imperturbable dignity that was expected, always observing each formality in turn. If the Indian ever took it into his head that he could get the better of Julius in trade, there would be no end of trouble.

Finally he nodded his satisfaction and set the rabbits on the counter. "You want some coffee? It's hot. *Pezhuta sapa, washté?*"

The Indian's face broke into a broad, gap-toothed grin. "*Hau,* Julius! *Pezhuta sapa na mitákola sapa, lila washtéyelo!*" Yes, Julius! The black medicine and my black friend are both very good! *Wakályapi* was the proper word for brewed coffee, whereas *pezhuta sapa* referred to the beans or dry ground coffee, but Hears Twice did not correct the black man, preferring to make the play on words. He laughed softly, well satisfied with the trade. He would ride home later with fresh bread wrapped in his blanket and he would take home the other three rabbits that he had found in his trapline this morning. He was an old man, but still he brought home food when he could. His daughter Mist would be pleased. Her husband had urged her once, in the quiet of the night, to put the old man out in the cold. He is useless, said Little Hand, but Mist had said that as long as there was food in her lodge she would share it with her father. He was a man of power, a man whom Little Hand would do well to respect, as Sun Horse respected him. Neither one knew that Hears Twice had overheard.

Hears Twice moved around the kitchen now, smiling and shaking hands with everyone in turn. Shaking hands was one of the whiteman's few good customs. Show that you hold no weapon; clasp the stranger's hand with your own, each feeling the other's strength. The practice had caught on quickly among the people of the plains and mountains. A whiteman welcomed to a large village could find himself shaking hands with everyone in camp until his own was sore from the effort.

When he reached Bat Putnam, Hears Twice made a few quick motions with his hands.

"Pretty good, Hears Twice," Bat responded. "How's yourself?"

Hears Twice answered with more signs, his hands weaving rapid patterns in the air, each gesture of one or both hands conveying a word or phrase graphically and with surprising speed: the edge of a hand passed across the belly to show the cutting pain of real hunger; a slight fluttering of the hand to signify uncertainty or a question; both hands raised beside the head with index fingers curving upward to evoke the horns of a buffalo.

Bat grew more serious, switching entirely to the sign language now, his own hands moving quickly.

Julius tried to follow what was said. He had first encountered the silent language of the hands when he was with the cavalry in Texas and Arizona. It was known throughout most of the continent, enabling tribes whose spoken languages were more different than English and Chinese to conduct trade or arrange a treaty, or just to exchange insults or declare war. Good sign talkers could carry on a conversation more rapidly than two people could speak any tongue, white or Indian, losing no subtlety or nuance in the process. Hears Twice used the gestures often, for he spoke very little, and Bat was his equal in fluency. Julius missed half of the signs, but he could gather the meaning. Sun Horse's people were experiencing poor hunting, and hunger had entered the village.

Hutch didn't see how anyone could make out the individual signs, but he knew it was possible. Maybe he would ask Julius or old Bat to teach him the sign talk. It might not be a bad thing to know how to parley with Indians. He had seen the signs used by the Kickapoos and the Sac and Fox Indians in eastern Kansas and he already knew a few of the most basic gestures.

"How come he won't talk out loud to nobody but Julius?" The question had been bothering Hutch all winter and he realized that there was no longer a reason not to ask it. He felt enough at home now to ask something that was really none of his business.

"Talkin's bad for his medicine," Bat said. "He's called Hears Twice on account of he hears everything twice, once afore it happens and again when it happens. He claims he hears better if he don't talk much."

"But he talks to Julius." Hutch was watching the old Indian warily, half suspecting that Bat was pulling his leg and half fearing that what the mountain man said was true.

"Julius speak good Lakota," said Hears Twice. He gave Hutch a wink and chuckled as if this were some kind of private joke.

CHAPTER ————————————————————————
FOUR

"Wagh!" Bat leaned forward, his eyes ablaze. "Them Injuns come out'n that gully like ants stirred up by a stick, and only four of us, so we put out for tall timber, but old Meek's mule, she wouldn't budge." His hooded capote was put aside now and his buckskins gave off an odor of smoke and old grease that was discernible among the other kitchen smells.

In a pause between the stew and the pie, they were all caught up in his tale. The meal was one at which everyone had had something to say as the stew and beans and biscuits were consumed in prodigious amounts, but as the comfort of a satisfying meal began to sink in and the conversation lagged, Lisa had prompted her uncle to recall the adventures of his youth, and he had needed little urging. Bat catalogued his past with stories, remembering battles and discoveries and deaths and high times in the words by which a friend had later told the tale, or

47

as he liked to tell it himself. This was one of his own, and he told it with broad gestures, often half rising from his seat to imitate an action he was describing, sometimes slapping a hand for emphasis on the heavy pine planks of the table, which were aged a rich and mottled brown by years of hot dishes and spills and wiping with linseed oil. As usual, Hutch was spellbound.

"He's a-poundin' on that critter's head 'n' kickin' her ribs, but there she stands, just as ca'm as ca'm. Meek, he sees the Blackfeet comin' for him and he reckons he'd like some company to help fend 'em off, so he hollers 'Hold on, boys! Thar ain't but a few of 'em! Let's stop and fight!' Well sir, I was coverin' ground pretty good about then. Passed a herd of antelopes and made such a wind it tore the hides plumb off their backs." He paused and looked closely at Hutch to see how much the boy would swallow. Hutch was grinning hugely. "Well, maybe it just ruffled their hair a mite, but I was goin' *some*, and that's truth. But I says to myself, 'Hoss,' I says, 'Meek's in trouble and Meek's your friend,' so I yanks my cayuse 'round and starts back and the other boys they come too, but just about then that mule of his caught her first whiff of Bug's Boys, and if there was one thing like to give that mule a fit, it were to catch the scent o' Blackfoot. She took out for the Yellowstone, and afore you could say 'I'm a nigger,' Meek was leadin' the pack of us and I'm bringin' up the rear, Blackfeet close enough to hit with a stick, and they was a passel of 'em and that's truth. The boys, they holler at Meek, 'Hold on, Meek! Let's stop and fight!' But Meek warn't lonesome no more, ner hankerin' to fight a hunnert Blackfeet neither, so he hollers back, 'Run for yer lives, boys! There's a thousand of 'em! They'll kill us all!' Fact was, that mule had the bit in her teeth and he never did turn her till he got clear 'cross the Yellowstone. We didn't set eyes on him for a week."

Bat sat back in his chair, looking anywhere but at Hutch.

"But how'd you get away from the Blackfeet?" Hutch wanted to know.

Julius had heard the same story a few dozen times over the years and it was a marvel to him the way the one greenhorn in a room would always walk into such a simple trap with his eyes wide open.

"Never did," said Bat, as solemn as a judge. "My horse went down and they was all over me like wolves on a lame buffler."

"But you—" Hutch saw his error too late, and now the laugh was on him. That was the trouble with Julius and Bat, you couldn't stay ahead of them for a minute. But he had to admit that the rules of the winter jokes were fair: each was made the butt in his turn, and there was no malice.

As the conversation resumed, Hutch plunged back into it, the others drawing him along and being so attentive until he felt proud enough to bust that he had been allowed to give them a good laugh at his expense.

Only Bat stayed withdrawn from the renewed gaiety, once he'd had his laugh, choosing instead to remain for a while in a backwash of memories, reliving in his mind the happy times of fifty years before, when an impulse of his father's curiosity had launched him and his brother Jed into the short-lived society of the mountain men, the freest and most exhilarating life Bat had ever known.

Jed had been the eldest of Joseph Putnam's three sons, and he had come west first, in the spring of '22. It was only by a blink in the eye of Fate that he, and Bat after him, had avoided being sent to sea instead. The Putnams were a Boston family of seafaring merchants, and it was a family tradition that those who were later to run the business should learn firsthand how its lifeblood was sustained; upon reaching eighteen years of age, the male offspring were berthed for three years on a Putnam ship, there to be tested and toughened, and, it was hoped, to grow into the kind of men the family or one of its ships might be glad to have at the helm. But Joseph Putnam was a man of some foresight and not inextricably wed to blind tradition. There were stirrings on the American frontier a dozen years after the epic explorations of Lewis and Clark; the elder Putnam suspected that new opportunities would arise in the vast domain beyond the Mississippi and he wanted to miss none that might profit J. Putnam & Sons. In 1821, the year his son Jed turned eighteen, Joseph Putnam was interested in rumors that American investors were about to enter the fur trade again after some tentative failures in recent years. The manufacture of gentlemen's hats and gloves guaranteed a never-ending market for beaver plews, as the hides were called; beaver had been the fur of choice used in making fine felt for hundreds of years, and showed no signs of falling from grace. It was said that the lands near the headwaters of the Missouri River were a fur kingdom of unparalleled wealth, but many wild tales were told of those unknown regions; Joseph Putnam was a prudent man and he wanted reports from someone he trusted. And so Jedediah had received on his eighteenth birthday, when his brother John Batson was just ten years old, an unexpected choice: spend the traditional three years at sea or three years instead on the western reaches of American territory, beyond the broad waters of the Mississippi. Young Jed had already felt within him the stirrings of a wanderlust that he suspected would not be satisfied by coursing over salt swells that stretched from one horizon to the other; he chose the frontier, and in April of 1822 he made his way up the Missouri with a brigade of trappers launched by William Ashley and Andrew Henry, the first Americans to enter the fur trade for keeps. Their one hundred and fifty men were to employ the river highways of the Missouri and its tributaries, traveling by keelboat and wintering in forts they built on the rivers, as the French and English had trapped the northern waterways of the continent for more than a century. But the enterprise was thwarted in its infancy by the implacable hatred of the Blackfoot Confederacy, which sat astride the Missouri's upper reaches.

The Blackfeet showed uncommon tenacity in bearing a grudge. Two of their number had been killed by the Lewis and Clark expedition in a half-baked mêlée set off by some petty thievery on the part of the redskins. The Blackfeet viewed the deaths as an inexcusable overreaction. In retaliation, they declared perpetual open season on whites, who thereafter found themselves treated as fit subjects for stealing from, shooting at, or inflicting slow death upon whenever the slightest opportunity permitted. The trappers came to regard the Blackfeet as the Devil's children; "Bug's Boys" they called them, with a mixture of respect and defiance.

Denied the upper Missouri, the Ashley-Henry men turned inland, moving

49

westward across the Great Divide into the valley of the Green River and beyond. There they found the promised fur kingdom and something else besides, something that in the end was more cherished by the trappers than the pelts they sought, for it was here that the trapping profession grew to full size. Freed from dependence on the Missouri for transportation and resupply, the trappers soon abandoned the habit of wintering back in a company fort. They stayed in the mountains year-round, learning the streams and backwaters and all the ways of the country until they belonged no longer to the rivers and forts and keelboats, but only to the mountains.

They were supplied at an annual *rendezvous* held in the trapping country, where Jed Putnam and the others gathered by the hundreds to trade the season's take for Galena lead and Du Pont powder and sharp Green River knives made in Massachusetts and transported in gross lots as far as St. Louis by J. Putnam & Sons, along with blankets and trinkets and all manner of foofaraw to trade with the Indians who flocked to the Rendezvous in the thousands. The elder Putnam was waiting for the moment when he could take a hand in the fur trade itself with some degree of safety. Three years came and went, but the uncertainties in the trade remained constant, and Jed gladly obeyed a suggestion that he stay on in the mountains he had come to love. He kept his father apprised of developments by means of discerning, enthusiastic letters that often took six months or more to reach Boston, where they were read to the assembled family in the drawing room after dinner; Jed's news was absorbed by young John Batson like water in sandy soil.

At the Rendezvous of '27, held at Bear Lake, Jed was astonished to see Bat among those arriving with the supply train. The younger Putnam was grinning from ear to ear, unfazed by the thunderous mock attack the trappers and Indians launched in waves on the pack train. Bat had jumped the gun a bit, coming west at age sixteen and without benefit of parental consent, but Jed's letters had fired his imagination until he could stand the waiting no longer. The middle brother, Jacob, had duly gone to sea upon reaching eighteen two years after Jed. He was back now and had taken his place in the business, proving himself as sober and industrious as his father. The truth was that although Jed and Bat were separated by eight years of age they had always been of much the same spirit and neither one particularly liked Jacob, who was cast from a different mold. The present arrangement suited them perfectly.

Jed took Bat under his wing when the Bear Lake Rendezvous broke up and they traveled together. They were among the first to turn free trapper, owing allegiance to no company, taking orders from no *bourgeois*, or booshway, as the Americans called the men who led the brigades. They lived as unfettered as the hawks, traveling the length of the mountain chain and out to the Columbia bar, wintering in Taos with the *señoritas* or in the Bitterroots with the bighorn sheep, returning in summer to the Rendezvous, where they sold their plews to the first company to reach the appointed gathering place with whiskey and supplies.

Bat became aware that the talk in the kitchen still concerned the days of the mountain men, and the joy Lisa's father had taken in that life.

"I'd of like to known him then," Julius was saying. "Strong as he was when I knew him, he must of been something when he was young."

"Strong?" Bat interrupted. "He could hunt bear with a switch. Liked to hop on the back of a grizzly and make him buck." He winked at Hutch. "Wasn't a man in the mountains could outshine my brother Jed. 'Ceptin' me." He grinned, remembering the look of Jed astride his horse, Hawken rifle across his saddle, always laughing at some foolishness or other.

"That's what Pop always said about you," Lisa said, smiling.

Bat didn't rise to the bait. He just nodded and said, "We was *some* then," the vigor leaving his voice as he felt the loss again. He thought of telling Hutch the story of the dancing bear to keep his own spirits up, but he never told it as well as Meek did, and before he could decide whether or not to start in on it the conversation had passed him by and turned to the weather and the snowpack in the mountains and the chance for a good hay crop. That was all right for them, he guessed. This cattle business might turn out all right, the way Jed had said it would, but such things held little interest for the mountain man. The warmth and the food had made him drowsy, and he had lost any desire to trek through the cold in search of some contrary beast that was almost certainly far away and headed in the wrong direction. Hunting could wait for a while. Just now he wasn't done remembering.

His first year in the mountains hadn't been without its hardships for a sixteen-year-old boy, and as if the natural challenges weren't enough, he had had to suffer the constant gibes and pranks the trappers directed at every greenhorn, until one morning when he and Jed and a few others were camped on Pryor's Fork and a grizzly shambled into camp before anyone was awake. Bat was aroused from his dreams by a soft grunting close at hand and he looked up to see the great bear lifting a youngster named Toussaint right up in the air by the shoulders, bedroll and all. Toussaint was too petrified even to cry out. Almost without thinking, Bat lifted his rifle from his blankets, where it rested at night to keep the powder dry, and let fly at the bear, creasing its brain and waking the rest of the camp just in time for them to see the bear stagger about in a drunken waltz for several moments, still holding the tongue-tied boy, until it keeled over stone dead into the fire pit. "Well, sir, poor Toussaint reckoned old Bat had missed him clean," Joe Meek said later in one of his many recountings of the story, as he imitated the bear's dying waltz. "Wagh! Old Bat cain't miss! He'll make 'em come or I'm a nigger! Toussaint, he figgered his only chance war to give that b'ar a dance, if'n that's what he come fer. Well, sir, he just begun to get the hang of the footwork when down goes old Ephraim, deader'n a hammer. Old Bat he says, "Thar's b'ar fer breakfast, boys,' and lays back in his blankets, ca'm as ca'm."

Old Bat had been all of seventeen when that took place but from then on he was one of the boys, and for the first time in his life he had felt that he was standing on his own two feet, out from under the shadow of his older brothers. "Hooraw fer the mountains!" he would let out occasionally for no apparent reason,

51

and nobody looked twice because they had all felt the same at one time or another.

Bat smiled at the memory, but the smile turned to a frown. The trappers' life had been one a man could glory in and he and Jed had lived that glory to the hilt, never dreaming that their livelihood had been dealt a mortal blow by a humble worm that lived halfway around the world. But Jed had seen the signs, and so had John Jacob Astor.

Bat gave a snort of disgust, which caused Julius and the others to look in his direction, but he paid them no mind.

He held Astor personally responsible for the death of the beaver trade even though he knew there was no truth to support such a grudge. He harbored it because it pleased him to get back in that way for all the trouble Astor had caused Ashley and Henry and the free trappers, but he blamed Astor mostly for his perfidious abandonment of such a splendid life merely because he suspected it would no longer afford him a profit.

Astor had been one of the first Americans to test the waters of the fur trade, long before Ashley and Henry. In 1811 he had sent an expedition to the mouth of the Columbia to establish a post there and challenge the dominance of the Hudson's Bay Company in what was then still British America. The post was called Astoria and its inhabitants Astorians. Astor was a man who did not intend to be forgotten. Astoria was abandoned during the war of 1812, but Astor re-entered the trade with a vengeance a few years after Ashley and Henry. His American Fur Company prospered, and in time he absorbed almost all of the original Ashley-Henry men. But in 1832, when the trade was near its peak, Astor had seen a new kind of top hat on the streets of London during a visit there, one made of silk. He guessed that this product of the China trade was the coming thing, and within a few years he had sold his holdings in American Fur and retired from the trade. The trappers scoffed at his caution, even in the face of falling prices, but Jed Putnam had nodded quietly and started thinking about what he would do next. A man didn't have to look to the streets of London or Boston to see trouble for the fur trade, he said. Right there in the mountains anyone but a fool could see that the best beaver grounds were trapped out and new grounds were as hard to find as virgins at Rendezvous. "Beaver's bound to rise," the others said, but it didn't, and the popularity of silk hats continued to grow.

At the Rendezvous of '37 Jed had bought no supplies, and when the gathering disbanded he had turned his horse toward South Pass. There he had taken a last look back to the Green River and the mountains beyond, where the remaining mountain men, Bat Putnam among them, walked streams in which the old beaver dams now went mostly unrepaired. He knew that some of his friends would linger there for years and some would die there, joining all those who had already gone under at the hands of bears and Blackfeet, winter cold and plain carelessness. He didn't begrudge them that choice, but clinging to the dead past just was not in his makeup, and so he had spurred his horse eastward, hoping to find something to do with the rest of his life

52

that would give him just a small portion of the satisfaction he had felt during his years in the mountains.

"Poor doin's," Bat muttered. He had no liking for the memory of Jed's departure and the demise of the beaver kingdom, but a man needed reminding now and again that the world was something more than dry powder and fat cow.

Realizing he had spoken aloud, Bat looked up to find Hears Twice gazing at him. Bat made signs that said *I am thinking of long ago*, and the Indian nodded. He knew that what lived in memory was just as real as what a man did today. Bat could savor his deeds and pleasures of the past simply by remembering them faithfully or by telling his stories to a friend, just as the Sioux kept their history alive by continual telling and retelling of the great deeds. If the memories died, the past would be gone, for they did not write things down. Only in the winter count did they preserve the barest framework of that living history. The count was kept by the band's rememberer, the historian, on a specially prepared elk or deerhide. He chose a single picture to represent the most significant event of each passing year and drew that picture on the hide. But the winter count was like the poles of a lodge, useless without the memories of the people to cloak it and contain therein the past life of the band. Bat smiled at Hears Twice. The old man knew what it was to remember the past.

Hears Twice had eaten with the others and for the most part he had been content to follow the conversation with his eyes, as was his custom on such occasions. No one was sure just how much English the old Sioux understood, but he laughed along with the rest when something funny was said, and if he didn't it was just as likely that what he had heard didn't fit in with the Sioux notion of what was funny rather than because he hadn't understood. Now and then he made a few signs of his own when the talk turned to something that concerned the Sun Band as well as the settlement in Putnam's Park, such as the sudden snowstorm or the scarcity of game or the passing of the recent thaw. He repeated what he had told Bat earlier—hunters from Sun Horse's village had had little success in the recent moons, bringing in scarcely enough meat to supplement the small resources of jerky and *wasná* from the fall hunt, now almost gone. The Lakota—for so the western Sioux called themselves as well as their language—were hungry. He conveyed the news matter-of-factly, not wishing to dwell on his people's misfortune. The Sun Band lived in the old ways of the Lakota, scorning the domesticated Sioux who lived near the Indian agencies in Dakota and subsisted on handouts of beef and wormy flour from the government. Ridicule would be heaped on any of the Sun Band who lowered himself, even in times of hardship, by begging from the whites. Hears Twice came to visit today because he could bring something to trade; it was only proper that he stayed for a meal when visiting a neighbor's lodge. When the apple pie was served he nodded his thanks with dignity and contained his secret delight.

As the dishes were cleared Julius took his fiddle from its peg on the wall and tuned the strings. Hutch lost no time in reaching for the old banjo. If Julius was content to let the little ranch take care of itself for a while, he would get no argument from Hutch.

Harry Wo finished the last of his coffee and got to his feet. He had grown accustomed to the strange flowing melodies played by the black man and the boy, but he had work to do. The others could stay in the kitchen all afternoon if they wanted. When the snow melted they would want shoes for the horses and sound wheels on the wagons and Harry preferred to set those things in order now at his own steady pace, making a little headway each day on the never-ending list of blacksmithing and carpentry chores he performed so well.

Hears Twice rose as Harry moved to the door, and motioned him to wait. Since their first encounter Harry had instinctively accorded the Indian the deference one properly showed an elderly and wise man and now he waited patiently as Hears Twice stepped to the entryway. He returned with his lance and Harry saw that the blade, which some Indian had made from a large blacksmith's rasp, was bent. Hears Twice handed the lance to Harry and made a few signs in Bat's direction.

"He says straighten the blade and make it hard again with white man's magic."

Harry grunted. "You tell him Harry Wo ain't no white man. I got my own magic. Tell him he must pay." He would temper the blade so the old Indian could split the shoulder bone of a buffalo bull with it, if he had the strength.

Without waiting for a translation from Bat, Hears Twice made signs.

Bat grinned. "He says he already heard how much it'll be. He'll fetch you a couple of rabbits in a day or two."

Harry nodded, and favored Hears Twice with a trace of a smile as he slipped into his canvas coolie's jacket. He liked the trappers' rabbit fricassee that Jed Putnam had taught Ling to make. It was a welcome respite from a diet heavy in beef. Taking the lance with him, he stepped out into the snow.

To Harry, Hears Twice's ability to understand English and his refusal to speak it, except rarely, were unremarkable. Harry too had learned English fairly quickly, at least the understanding of it when it was spoken. But his pride, so insulted by the universal disdain expressed for the natives by the English barbarians who dominated foreign trade with China, absolutely prevented him from speaking in a manner that would encourage feelings of superiority in white listeners. He had shunned the pidgin English used by the British in China, and always chose his words with care. In America he had avoided the ingrown settlements of Orientals, where the prejudice of the surrounding white communities was strongest. He moved in this strange land in his own way, at his own pace, finding places for himself and Ling where they could observe, rather than be observed. It was easy for Harry to respect Hears Twice's silence.

The forge in the blacksmith's shed needed only a little stoking and a few puffs of the bellows Harry had made himself, and soon the fire was glowing warmly. He took off his jacket and threw back the heavy tarpaulin that served to protect the open side of the shed against the worst weather. When it was clear and truly cold, Harry could work in his shirt sleeves with the tarp down, but today the temperature was near freezing and he liked to watch the falling snow as he worked. It took a considerable effort on the part of the weather to make Harry Wo feel a chill. After the winter he had spent in the Sierra Nevada Mountains driving spikes for the Central Pacific Railroad, he regarded any lesser weather with quiet disdain.

In a short time he had the lance blade glowing as he prepared it for the anvil. Outside the shed the flurries thickened and thinned, sometimes revealing the full length of the valley floor down to the cut in the hills where the river trail passed through to the foothills and the plains beyond. Harry was from the mountains of eastern Szechwan province and, despite all the peculiarities of this foreign land, when he was alone with his work and the falling snow he felt at home. He raised his eyes often from his work, appreciating the infinite variety of motion the wind imparted to the white flakes that flew as gracefully as birds, and he was the first to spy the riders approaching on the wagon road.

In the kitchen, the fiddle and banjo sustained the festive mood of the noonday meal. Lisa paused in the washing up to enjoy the rhythms of the music, much as she might have stopped to rest in the penetrating warmth of the first summer's day. She felt a serenity that seemed to have its origins not just in the peaceful atmosphere in the room but outside the house, in the valley beyond, as if the whole of Putnam's Park were wrapped in a mood of tranquillity. She was pleased by the success of her dinnertime conversation. If anything, Julius seemed even more ready than she to get on with the work that lay ahead, and for the first time she felt a growing confidence that they would succeed in fulfilling her father's vision.

The tune came to a close and Julius smiled. Hutch's banjo playing had improved tenfold with almost daily practice during the winter and he now wove the melody so skillfully into his style of playing—"drop-thumb," he called it—that Julius often took a harmony line and left the melody to Hutch.

"Is it true that Hears Twice can hear things before they happen?" Hutch glanced at the Indian. He had been thinking about it as they played.

"You mean like them rabbits he promised Harry?"

Hutch nodded. Julius smiled and shook his head.

"He was funnin' with Harry. He always pays him rabbits when he needs something done."

"Now and again he'll give you a start," Bat put in. "Injuns ain't like white folks. A bird'll look at 'em crosseyed and they'll take it as a sign. Old Hears Twice, he gets his signs afore the rest of 'em now and again."

"You'll fill the boys' head with notions," Lisa chided.

Hears Twice had enjoyed the music, occasionally sipping from a last cup of heavily sweetened coffee, but now his mood grew serious as the men looked in his direction. He had observed the formalities of his visit, making his trade, accepting food when it was offered, discussing matters of interest to all; it was time to state his real reason for coming. He caught Bat's eye and began to make signs.

Bat grew suddenly interested. "He says he heard somethin' last night; that's why he come down today, for a look-see. Somebody's comin', he says. Visitors. They'll be along pretty soon, he says."

"At this time of year?" Lisa found herself growing apprehensive. No casual travelers would be abroad in this region, not for another month or two, and not even then if the rumors of an Indian outbreak persisted.

Bat looked carefully at Hears Twice, seeking an indication that this was a joke springing from some impenetrable area of Lakota humor, but the old Indian met his gaze solemnly.

Julius got to his feet and started for the door that led to the dining hall and saloon. Lisa moved to follow him.

"You let me see who it is," he cautioned her, and he passed through the door, followed by the other men.

The large L-shaped room they entered could seat seventy or more at its long wooden tables and benches. It was dusty from disuse and so cold that the men's breath hung in small trailing clouds behind them. A long bar ran the length of the back wall; in the shorter leg of the L was a small general store whose shelves were now mostly empty. Antlers and horns and stuffed heads hung from the walls, and an immense potbellied stove dominated the middle of the room. Like the great hall of some medieval castle, which it resembled in function if not in construction and scale, the saloon had been used as a banquet room, trading post, dance hall and makeshift theater over the years; but perhaps because of the way the bar confronted anyone who entered through the main door from the porch, or in acknowledgment of the smiling woman who reclined in the obligatory oil painting behind the bar, the room had come to be called simply "the saloon." In deference to the well-bred sensibilities of Lisa's mother, the lady in question was thoroughly draped in a garment that revealed her curves but only hinted at charms that were more freely displayed in similar portraits to be found in countless cowtown taprooms.

The men crossed the cold room to the windows, Hears Twice close on Julius's heels and Hutch trailing along out of curiosity. Outside the snow was falling lightly and they could see halfway down the valley, past the first hay crib, past the clump of pines where the road made its last turn and ran straight for the settlement. Except for the cattle, still searching the feed lines for a mouthful of hay, the valley was deserted.

Julius glared at Hears Twice.

"*Úpelo*, Julius," the Indian said softly. "*Wana úpelo.*" They are coming now.

Bat watched the cattle for a time. They accepted snow or sleet, rain or shine, passively. Unless spooked by some real or imagined anger, they never showed excitement. What was the use of a life like that?

He turned back to the saloon. He had always regarded the cavernous room as a monument to his brother's optimism, but the cattle might serve just as well. The saloon entombed a past that was dead and gone, while the pregnant cows represented Jed's hope for the future.

Jed's ability to accept the dying of one good way of life and then another had always been a source of wonder to Bat. Even when the fur trade, the grandest life a man could wish for, showed signs of turning moribund, Jed had accepted that calamity without complaint and had looked to the future with his eyes full of hope.

At the time, Bat had wondered if Jed might not be something of a fool. Hadn't Jed been Bat's teacher, conveying to his younger brother all his own love and understanding for the mountain life? How could a sensible man turn his back on it all and ride away, never again to see the long crystals of ice forming on a still mountain lake, of an autumn morning?

Well, of course Jed had come back. After a dozen years spent lollygagging about back in the States and riding Putnam-owned ships as far away as China and England, he had heard the mountains' call and he had returned, first to guide the emigrants and then to settle here for good, in Putnam's Park, however unlikely a place it had seemed to set up road ranching.

Jim Bridger had been the first to choose the life, and he had asked Bat to go in with him, but Bat had turned him down. Old Gabe had a right to go soft in the head if he liked, but Bat would have none of it, then or later. Gabe had set himself up on Black's Fork of the Green, back in '42, plunking himself smack next to the Oregon road, where he was subjected to the full force of the human river that flowed westward on the trail. It had been just a trickle at first, meandering to the green valleys of the Oregon country. Politicians had urged the settlement of Oregon for the greater glory of the United States, but most men thought more of self than nation, and it took the cry of "Gold!" to get them going. Then the trickle became a flood of men, scrambling for the diggings in California, and Gabe had had to suffer every nitwit in the bunch, each fool who stood in the light of the setting sun and asked which way was west. Gabe had answered them all and pointed out the road, and he'd done all right too, until the Mormons drove him off in '53.

At least Jed had been sensible enough to realize that he had no wish to weary himself answering foolish questions; what he wanted was someplace to raise a family and live out his days in contentment. And so he picked a place up off the flat, in country that had some shape to it, where there were trees to soothe the eyes and cooling breezes in summer. Nearby was an old Indian trail and a pass through the mountains by which travelers could return to the plains and pick up the Oregon road at South Pass, where it crossed the Divide. The Putnam Cutoff drifted more than sixty miles north from the main trail, and the detour cost a few extra days, but at certain times of the year its advantages were clear to any man with a grain of sense. Four or five days weren't such a price to pay in a journey of four months or more. Not when it meant you could reach the halfway point with stock well fed and feeling fresh.

Bat smiled. Jed was a crafty son of a bitch and nobody's fool; Bat had come to see that in time. Jed had chosen this valley because it suited him, and because in wintertime Bat and Sun Horse were just a couple of hours' ride over the next ridge. He had blazed his cutoff and pointed the way, kind of like laying out bait. But of course what he had really done was pose a challenge for his fellow men, to see what they were made of, and for the most part they had lacked the gumption to pick it up. Taking his cutoff required some courage and wisdom, and Jed was thus protected from the worst fools on the Oregon road, who were in plentiful supply. Take a long way 'round? Nossir, not me. Their business was to get to California, and quick about it. Greed drove a man faster than a whip.

Those that did take the cutoff found no trap at the end of the bait trail. More like the pot of gold lit by the rainbow of promise. When the land along the main trail was grazed bare in midsummer, the experienced scouts and wagon bosses knew they would find good pasture in the broad bottomlands of Putnam's Park and they knew the condition of the stock was paramount. While the horses and mules and oxen browsed placidly on the rich grass, the emigrants ate Eleanor Putnam's cooking, as much of it as they could pay for, conserving their own supplies for the journey ahead. Here, six weeks or more from St. Joe, they knew the demands of the trail all too well, and they could set right mistakes they had made at the start. They might buy some items they were short of or lacked altogether, or unburden themselves of something useless in exchange for what they needed. Before long, Jed had added a small wing to Putnam House, providing a handful of extra beds where the more genteel among the travelers could spend a night away from the cold ground and hard beds of their Murphy wagons. The rooms were clean and free of insect life, the food was good and the company lively, in welcome contrast to the miserable shacks and pigsty conditions that characterized most of the ranches that hovered along the emigrant roads like buzzards waiting to filch the traveler's savings in exchange for a bellyache from bad food, a swollen head from bad whiskey and a host of new reasons to scratch under his longjohns.

In the judgment of those experienced on the trails, Putnam's Park was the best road ranch in the West, if not the most convenient. Those who came here to rest and regather their strength declared it the preferred haven between the jumping-off places in Missouri and the myriad trails' ends where the individual hopes, dreams and greed of the emigrants led them.

Even so, the saloon had been full to capacity only a few dozen times over the years, and not once since the early sixties, but those rare occasions had been enough to satisfy Jed, convincing him that he had done right to build a room big enough to contain high spirits and high jinks without busting at the seams. He had received his guests with an almost baronial propriety, basking in the talk, laughter and many-tongued altercations of the emigrants, who had been glad of the chance to sit with their feet up to the big stove on a cool mountain evening, listening to Jed's tales of a time just twenty or so years before when there were only twelve hundred white men north of Taos, and every one of them a better man than any stuck-in-the-mud hog farmer or city dweller back in the States, sure as God made the beaver swim and the water run clear in the Rocky Mountains.

Bat looked about the saloon, trying to imagine it warm and full of life once more. Nearby, Julius stood with folded arms, looking out a window, "Ca'm as ca'm," Meek would say, waiting for what would come. Hears Twice and Hutch stood beside him, the boy shifting about and peering through the glass panes. The snow had thinned somewhat. From where he stood, Bat could make out the outline of the western ridge.

He had to give it to Jed: he'd picked a good spot and done all right, even if Bat had never thought much of road ranching.

To give himself something to do he ambled the length of the room, counting his paces. Too short for a shooting contest, but broad enough for a person to do a proper job of kicking up his heels to music, as Bat knew from experience. He missed the dancing.

He hadn't set foot in the saloon three times during the winter. He disliked places that were haunted by voices of the past. It seemed to him that the logs and planks sometimes whispered echoes of all they had heard over the years. Bat looked at the broad plank floor that had been trod by so many feet clad in all manner of boots and shoes—and moccasins—every pair of them, save those that belonged to Indians or the people who lived in the park, in that unrelenting hurry to get somewhere else that only a white man with ambition seemed able to muster. Today the planks guarded their tales under the fine mantle of dust that had sifted down since Ling Wo last swept the floor. Just when Bat was ready to confront what the ghosts had to tell him, they fell silent. It irritated him but did not surprise him; he had long ago come to accept the perverse nature of things in general, in the material and spirit worlds alike. Besides, the ghosts held no secrets from him. He knew the sort of men who had passed through this room and why they came no more. They had been noble and base and everything in between, men as different as honest farmers just looking for a chance to start anew and gold seekers hoping to strike it rich without dirtying their hands. Oh, yes, there had been gold seekers. Fortune had played a small joke on Jed Putnam. With the discovery of gold in the Idaho country in 1860 and in Montana three years later, some of the fortune hunters turned north from the Oregon road and Jed found himself playing host to the very same greed-driven men he had come here to escape. They were packers, a lot of them, riding horses and leading mules, able to get over the West Pass earlier in the spring and later in the fall than wagons could. As usual, Jed took the turn of events with good grace and did what he could for them; by then he had more pressing worries than the avoidance of fools. The miners moved to the new gold fields by two roads, one laid out by John Bozeman along the eastern flank of the Big Horns, his route following the Putnam Cutoff for the first seventy miles or more, and the other up the Big Horn River valley to the west, blazed by Jim Bridger, who had returned once again to scouting. Jed advised all and sundry to take Bridger's route. It lay in the country of the friendly Shoshoni, and by then there was trouble with the Sioux.

In the summer of '51, when Jed was still guiding wagons, Bat and Sun Horse had been at Fort Laramie for the great peace council, the first one between the whites and the tribes of the northern plains. The fort had only recently been purchased by the army; before that it had been a trading post under several names, and numerous bands of Sioux had wintered there for twenty years, trading with their white friends. "Loaf-Around-the-Forts" the other Lakotas called them. At the council the white men had sat in chairs and the Indians had sat on the ground—Lakota and Cheyenne, Crow and Blackfoot and Arapaho and Shoshoni, friend and enemy alike—and together they had agreed that the whites could have a single road through the country to get them where they were going. "The Holy Road," the Indians called it, because while on the road the whites could not be touched, not even a few horses run off for sport. Even then some of the tribesmen had felt the first stirrings of concern as they watched the endless procession of whites across their lands, looking for all the world like a column of ants when seen from the distant buttes, all trudging westward, the whole vast tribe moving from the old nest to a new one for reasons known only to themselves. One Shoshoni orator had suggested that his people might move east to the lands the whites were vacating.

Bat shook his head. Fancy notions they all had. It seemed like a long time ago. One road for the whites and everything else for the red men. Sun Horse wasn't even called Sun Horse yet, and the band was led by his father, Branched Horn. They were of the northern bands, those who kept to themselves and scorned the too-easy life of the Loafers. The mountains still held out a high-flown dream and a golden promise to Bat and his Lakota brothers, and it was two more years before Jed started building in Putnam's Park.

And then, after the house was built and the Putnam Cutoff was blazed, even as the first adventurous wagons rolled gratefully into the cool green bottom of the little park—especially grateful then, for the year was dry—Fate had reached out a cold finger and touched the Holy Road and after that nothing was the same.

Down at Fort Laramie a Mormon's cow had wandered away from a party of emigrants. Some said the cow was on her last legs and purposely abandoned, but whatever her condition she had seemed attractive enough to some Sioux camped a few miles from the fort. The animal was taken in hand and butchered, and the Mormon, perhaps seeing a chance to gain more than the cow was worth, reported the loss to the post commander and said the animal had been stolen. The commander designated a young lieutenant to take a squad of men and seize the offending Indians, and it was here that Fate played her malevolent part. The officer chosen for this detail was named Grattan, and he had often expressed a confidence that with thirty men he could cut a swath through the whole Sioux nation. Now he had his chance. Taking his thirty men and all his mammoth ignorance of Indians with him, he went to the heart of the Sioux encampment and demanded the surrender of the thieves. The great Brulé headman Conquering Bear met with Grattan and protested that the warriors who had seized the cow were Minneconjou visiting the camp; guests in camp were inviolate, he explained; no one could lay a hand on them. This custom had the force of law among the Sioux. Let our friend, the agent at Laramie, handle the matter, Conquering Bear asked. Grattan refused. The headman then offered a good mule in exchange for the cow, but again the officer refused, and he was fast growing impatient. The Lakotas who understood the white man's talk knew that the interpreter was not translating properly, but before this could be explained to the officer, he made a move toward Conquering Bear, his soldiers leveled their rifles and from somewhere a shot sounded.

Conquering Bear fell. And then a great noise rose over the encampment, with more shooting, and when the dust blew away on the warm summer winds, Grattan and his thirty men had followed Conquering Bear in death. The Indians struck their lodges and fled.

Thus the fire was lit. At first it had only smoldered, flaring briefly here and there as one side and then the other perpetuated a cycle of misunderstanding, violence and revenge. In time the conflict had burst into full-scale war. The troubles had forced the emigrants to take roads farther to the south, away from the old trails along the North Platte. The telegraph was moved, and when the rails came they too followed the new route. And although it remained where it had always been, Jed's road ranch in Putnam's Park had gradually receded from the narrow thread of civilization that linked the Pacific coast with the eastern states until it was little more than a forgotten outpost. Well before the end of the sixties, the stream of visitors had dwindled until a cannon could have been fired across the saloon in midsummer without endangering a living soul. When new peace treaties pacified the Sioux, the wagons did not return. For almost eight years now, a tentative peace had rested uneasily on the Powder River country, but the few wagons that still followed the western trails found enough fodder along the main road, and only the foolhardy would think of venturing into the last hunting grounds of the Sioux.

And just as he had accepted the death of the fur trade, Jed had accepted the end of his road ranching with equanimity, and he had turned to the future. Bat looked out on that future now. The flakes were falling thick and heavy, fluttering to earth in a dead calm, but he could still make out a few cows plodding through the snow, sniffing for a few bits of hay. And then something else caught his eye.

"*Wana hípelo*," Hears Twice said. They are here.

Bat nodded. "Two of 'em." He glanced at the old Indian and saw that he was smiling. It did not surprise Bat that the prophet was right; he had come to expect it.

The door from the kitchen opened and Lisa stepped into the saloon, wrapped in her wintertime riding coat of mountain goatskin, made with the thick white fur turned in.

"Well?" she asked as she joined those at the windows.

"They're comin' now," Bat said.

"I don't see anything," she said, but she stepped back, moving closer to her uncle. He put his arm around her, feeling her apprehension, the fear of approaching danger. It wouldn't have been so in the old days, before the Indian troubles, he thought. The fear had arisen in recent years as if it had sprung out of the ground. But the seeds had been planted long ago, and the crop had been nourished by the blood of two races.

He separated himself from Lisa and moved closer to the windows, putting all his attention on the dim figures in the snow. He had whiled away much of the day with memories of times long gone. Now it was time to pay mind to the strangers, whoever they might be. Strangers riding into camp brought a change, for good or naught, but they always brought a change.

"I don't see nothing either." Hutch scratched at a pane that was frosted over by his breath. He moved down to the next window, as if moving ten feet to one side might give him a line of sight past the falling snow.

"You ain't been long enough in the mountains," Julius said. "Snow catches your eye. You got to look through it like it wasn't there."

The flurry thinned a little, and now Julius too could see the riders as they appeared like men coming out of a mist on a river bottom. They were white men. The bearded one had a rifle in a boot under his right leg and the butt of another gun showed briefly on the other side. Loaded for bear, that one. A buffalo hunter, maybe. But what was he doing here?

The other rider was clean-shaven and younger.

Julius felt a sudden resentment at this intrusion into the isolation of the park. There was healing going on here, slow work that needed more time. Lisa was getting over the loss of her father, but she was only now ready to look ahead. If old Jed had lasted a few more years, or if Lisa had married and her man had come to live here and take a hand in things, then the loss of Jed Putnam might not have struck so hard. But there was no use iffing. Jed had died when he did and things had to go on without him. Julius had been planning on steering Lisa's thinking toward the days to come and he had made a start at the noon meal, but he wanted more time for slow talk warmed by the kitchen stove, the way Julius's mother and maiden aunt had talked, sitting by the small stove in the cabin when he was a boy. Minutes would pass without

62

either woman saying a word. Then one would break the silence and for a time the soft flow of conversation would reach Julius where he lay in his bed, trying to stay awake. The gentle talk of those two women had been his lullaby, comforting him as it drifted past his bed the way the big river drifted past the plantation wharves. He needed that kind of talk with Lisa while the park was still sealed off from the world by winter, but he had waited too long.

The riders were drawing closer, and Julius made out the carcass of a deer behind the bearded man's saddle. The brim of the younger man's hat was curled slightly in a Texas roll, and a rope hung from the horn of his saddle, which was also Texas-style, made for work, not show. Perhaps they were just a pair of drovers who had kept going north after a drive up the Kansas trails. Their comfort in the saddle, their indifference to the weather, the steady pace of their horses—these things spoke of men at home out of doors. But then Julius noticed how the younger man rode a pace or two behind his companion, glancing constantly from side to side. There was no mistaking it—he was covering the bearded man's rear. Between the two of them they would miss nothing that happened on any side. Julius grew uneasy. If they were only a couple of drovers, what were they doing here in the middle of winter? Visitors, Hears Twice had called them. The old Sioux was right. The riders had a sense of purpose about them. They had the bearing of men set on a destination, and everything about them said it would take more than a half-baked mountain storm to make them seek shelter. Whatever their purpose, it had brought them here.

Julius motioned the others back from the windows and he reached for the double-barreled Richards shotgun that hung above the front door of the saloon.

CHAPTER
FIVE

Hardeman's eyes roamed the settlement, taking in the dormant garden fenced with chicken wire to keep out the deer and rabbits, the chicken coop and icehouse and the woodpile stacked high with split wood even as spring drew near. He saw the lone tipi beyond the house, noted the smoke from the peak, and felt his blood quicken. Close to the barn were new corrals, a pigpen, and three Durham bulls fenced away from the small herd of cows that were still feeding on this morning's hay down in the meadow. Four dairy cows were kept away from the bulls too, in their own paddock. The house and barn were well placed for shelter from the north winds, set on higher ground up away from the creek to avoid the coldest air that hung along the valley floor. A small spring house stood by the stream, where half a dozen geese were paddling about in the water. The little ranch lacked for nothing. It was just what Jed Putnam had seen in his mind's eye when the place was only a dream.

The cattle in the meadow had caught Hardeman's attention as he and Johnny rode past. The cows were a crossbreed, Durham and Longhorn he guessed, confirmed now by the presence of the Durham bulls by the barn. With the cows were three or four mature steers, kept back to provide meat for the settlement, but the herd had been culled in autumn, there was no mistaking that. It was a seed herd with all the pure Longhorn blood weeded out and the proportion of Durham blood about to be raised another step. The bulls were being kept off the cows until summer so no calves would be born during the coldest months of winter. Taken all together, it smacked not of some helter-skelter outfit trying its hand at raising tough and chewy beef, but of a thoughtful and controlled exercise in animal husbandry. It seemed that Jed had turned to raising cattle since the source of his road-ranching business had been sent elsewhere by the railroad and the constant threat of the Indian wars. Like so many others, he had apparently decided that raising beef was the occupation best suited to the Great American Desert.

A rhythmic clanging came from a shed built against the barn, but Hardeman was prepared for the sound; he had seen movement in the shed as he and Johnny rounded the clump of pines at the last turn in the road. Whoever it was had had more than one chance to see the riders coming, when the flurries thinned to allow a view down the valley. The blacksmith's inaction spoke of a place at peace with itself, unsuspecting, and this suited Hardeman perfectly. By the Indian tipi, a dog sat up and faced the newcomers, but it didn't bark. Near the barn, two cats sat on a stump. They too watched the riders placidly. Not even the animals in Jed Putnam's domain were prone to take alarm at the approach of strangers.

The blacksmith's hammer clanged again, beating a steady rhythm. "He's Chinese," Johnny said. They were the first words he had spoken since the two men left their night camp below the river canyon.

Hardeman moved a knee against his horse and the animal turned toward the shed. Johnny's mount shifted course like a shadow to hold position, and Johnny gave a tug on the lead rope to bring the single pack horse along. The boy's lanky body accommodated the movements of his horse with a naturalness not even Hardeman could match. More than one white man had jokingly remarked that there must be horse blood somewhere in Johnny's ancestry.

Johnny's face was pink from the cold. His straight brown hair was cut short at the top of his collar. His neck was protected by a huge blue bandanna wound twice around and tied snugly. The bandanna was long enough to tie his hat down over his ears in a storm. He wore a hip-length blanket coat and wool pants tucked into boots that came to the tops of his calves. He carried no weapons. The blue eyes beneath the wide-brimmed hat had lost their usual calm; they had become unnaturally alert, like those of an animal turned loose in unfamiliar surroundings. Hardeman hadn't seen that look since their first months together, when a much

64

younger Johnny had first explored the white man's world that was so strange to him. In time the look had left him, and over the years the boy had ridden more than once into the face of mortal danger with no change of expression or thought for his own safety, serving as Hardeman's extra pair of eyes without being asked. It wasn't fear in his eyes now, anymore than it was fear that had kept him from ever raising a hand against another man in the seven years they had been together. There was a change in him, but the reason was locked somewhere in the boy who never spoke more than a small part of what was on his mind.

Johnny's unsettled manner puzzled Hardeman, but the confidence he had felt that morning lingered on unshaken. He felt the satisfaction in his stomach and the strength of the deer meat in his body. It was amazing the confidence a man got from a bellyful of fresh meat.

He had been waiting for scarcely an hour when the doe had stepped to the creek to drink, and she had died cleanly from the first shot. When Hardeman had returned to camp, Johnny had a cookfire already made, and there was no trace of the sweat lodge.

"What if I'd missed?" Hardeman had asked.

"You don't miss."

"It could happen."

"Then you would be warm and I'd be hungry," Johnny had said with only a hint of a smile. He had eaten part of the liver raw, seasoned with gall, the way the Indians ate it. Hardeman had chewed in silence as the boy tried a few tentative bites before roasting the rest of the liver over the flames. Johnny had said only what was necessary as they broke camp and since then nothing until now.

As they passed the main building Hardeman noted the unmarked snow on the long porch and the old paint peeling from faded lettering on the wall. The words were almost obscured by the lines of snow that clung to the upper surfaces of the gray logs. "Emigrants Rest," they proclaimed, "Saloon & Gen'l Goods," and lower, "Buy & Trade." Over the door in the middle of the porch a sign hanging from an iron bracket swung in the wind, creaking softly, the eyebolts tired from protesting years of westerlies; "Putnam House," it said, and below that an eagle clutched a banner: "We Owe Allegiance to No Crown." The simple statements on the sign and wall, so inadequate a description of Jed Putnam's self-contained mountain hideaway, evoked for Hardeman an image of the man, complete to the puffery of a patriotism that Jed had always kept cloaked in his abundant dry humor. Hardeman suspected that he had hung the sign as much to declare his independence from any pompous government back east as from those on foreign shores. He urged his mount into a trot. The Chinaman would know where the boss might be found.

The riders were even with the end of the porch, about to pass around the corner of the building, when Johnny reined back suddenly. "The door on your right," he said quietly, as a tall Negro stepped onto the porch with a shotgun in his hands.

Hardeman was glad that Johnny had prevented an armed man from approaching behind them unnoticed. He thought to unbutton his buckskin coat as he reined around to face the porch, but the Negro held the shotgun loosely in one hand, the hammers on half cock.

"Howdy," the man called out, and Hardeman decided against any move that might appear hostile; he kept his hands in plain sight on the saddle horn.

The colored man was about fifty, he guessed; strong and unafraid. His walk through the unbroken snow on the porch revealed the rolling hips of someone who had spent years on horseback. A cowhand, maybe; one man in four on the cattle trails up from Texas was black, former slaves moving about the country trying their luck at different jobs, getting the feel of being free men—but then he noticed the man's trousers, tucked into high army field boots like his own. The wool was light blue, or had been, and the faded strips of facing down the outer seam of each leg had once been yellow. They were sergeant's pants, from before the uniform changed in '72. Hardeman could read details on United States Cavalry uniform as plainly as a regimental chaplain read the Bible.

"It's kind of poor weather for traveling." Julius came to a stop at the corner of the porch, looking down at the riders, the shotgun aimed indifferently at the snow in front of the horses.

Hardeman nodded. "The boss around?"

"Could be." Something flicked across the dark face. Hardeman felt he had done something to be judged for, and the judgment had gone against him. The blood rose to his face.

"It could be we'd like to see him," he said, more sharply than he intended. "We're looking for Jed Putnam."

"This is his outfit. You're welcome to step in out of the cold."

"We're obliged." Hardeman swung his horse toward the long hitching rail in front of the saloon, and Johnny followed close behind him. They dismounted and Hardeman busied himself for a few moments with slacking the cinch and removing his St. Paul coat, which he threw over the saddle and the rifles to protect them from the snow. It wouldn't do to be short-tempered now. He was glad the colored man hadn't taken offense at his tone of voice.

Julius lowered the shotgun further. You made strangers welcome whether you wanted to or not; that was a rule of the frontier as important as not prying into a man's business or his past. If they had known old Jed, his suspicions might be wrong.

As they crossed the deserted saloon Julius found that most of his caution was directed now toward the younger man. He was comfortable with the bearded one; that was a man who had seen and done many things that would be revealed slowly, if at all; he would be dangerous if provoked, but he had left his rifles outside and Julius had hung the shotgun back on its pegs before leading the way to the kitchen. The younger man was twenty, maybe twenty-one, and a little taller than the other, but something about him evaded quick understanding. Maybe it was the slight limp, his body moving in a way long accustomed to an old wound or deformity.

66

It's his walk, Julius thought, but not the limp. The youth wore boots, but he moved across the floor like a man walking barefoot on soft grass. Almost like an Indian.

Julius entered the kitchen first, holding the door open for the two strangers. Only Hutch and Ling were with Lisa now.

"He's looking for the boss," Julius said.

"We're looking for Jed Putnam," said Hardeman.

"He was my father. I'm Lisa Putnam." She offered her hand and the bearded man took it. She had seen the way his eyes swept the kitchen as he entered, pausing in turn on Hutch and Ling before stopping to rest on her. She had met his gaze of frank appraisal longer than he expected, but he did not look away. His hand was strong and warm, recently withdrawn from the glove he held in his other hand.

"Was?" Hardeman was numb, struggling to regain control of his thoughts.

"He died last fall."

"He died?"

"He had a stroke in August. He died a month later." The man was still holding her hand. Lisa withdrew it, feeling an unaccustomed warmth in her face. What was the matter with him? Couldn't he understand a simple thing like that? Her father was dead. For Lisa, the stating of that fact had required an effort of will. Jed Putnam had been felled suddenly on a hot afternoon when the thunderheads stood tall above the mountains; he had lingered for a time, his grip on life tenacious even as an invalid, as he himself remarked. "I'm hanging on," he had whispered to Lisa one day when she asked how he was feeling, never expecting a reply. They were the only words he uttered between his stroke and the day of his death. And throughout that long month Lisa had nursed him and sat with him, watching the remnants of his life ebb steadily away. When the spirit had finally left him, there was no discernible change; his passing was like the fading of the sky at day's end, with no single moment when one could say the light had gone. At the last he had smiled, and the smile had remained when his face grew cold to the touch.

"I'm sorry," Hardeman said, feeling stupid at his inadequacy. He had been on edge ever since entering the warm kitchen. He had glanced briefly at the Chinawoman and the boy—another hired hand by the look of him—and his eyes had come to rest on the young woman in the simple blue dress who said she was Jed Putnam's daughter. She held a coffee cup in her left hand, and in the first moment Hardeman saw her she had the look of someone caught in a secret act.

He glanced around the kitchen, searching for signs. Six chairs were pushed back from the sturdy wooden table; another was occupied by the young hired hand. Three chairs stood squarely in place. On the table there were wet rings made by half a dozen cups. The plates and serving dishes from the recent meal were in the galvanized sink, half washed; the sideboards were wiped clean. This was not a kitchen where things were left out of place. Even now the Chinawoman straightened two of the chairs and wiped the table with a damp rag.

The signs led Hardeman to a certain conclusion. There were only four people

67

in the kitchen now, apart from himself and Johnny, but there had been more here just a short time ago.

He looked again at those present. The Chinawoman was at the sink, back at her washing up. The boy, a few years younger than Johnny, sat where he had been ever since the strangers entered, looking from one to the other and then at the colored man and Lisa Putnam, waiting for someone to speak.

Beneath the stove a large orange cat stepped out of its basket and crouched on the floor, ready to move quickly should the occasion demand it. The cat's wariness heightened Hardeman's sense of hidden danger.

None of those here lived in the Sioux tipi outside. Who did, and where was he?

Hardeman moved a little to one side so he could see the room's three doors—one to the saloon, one to the outside, a third that probably led to the back of the house. "I'm sorry," he said again. "I guess that makes you the boss now."

"Julius was my father's partner. Now he is mine."

Hardeman understood at last what had passed across the Negro's face outside. It was anger at being taken for a hired hand just because he was colored. Still, it was a reasonable guess. Christ, he thought, let there be an end to the surprises here. He contained his annoyance with difficulty. The news of Jed's death had caught him unaware. It was a possibility he had never considered; he had always thought of Jed as immortal.

It was Jed Putnam who had taken young Chris Hardeman in hand in the summer of 1851 and taught him the skills of the frontier, and after Jed had left the emigrant trails to set himself up in Putnam's Park, Hardeman had heard news of him over the years. And now he had finally come to see his old friend. The Putnam Cutoff was right where it should be and Jed's mountain park was just as Hardeman had always imagined it; approaching the settlement with Johnny, he had felt Jed's presence in every building and shed, in each of the cows down in the meadow. To find that Jed was dead had put him off-balance. With an effort he steadied himself now. He would need new allies, and there was no telling which one might prove most valuable. He put out his hand to the colored man.

"I guess I left my manners on the trail. My name is Hardeman; Chris Hardeman. The boy is Johnny Smoker."

Julius hesitated, but he took the hand and shook it. After all, he had concealed old Jed's death for no reason, just some instinct he still didn't understand. "Julius Ingram," he said. "This here is Hutch. The cook is Ling Wo." He saw Hardeman cover a momentary surprise at being introduced to the small Chinese, who nodded politely before turning back to the dishes.

Johnny Smoker scarcely acknowledged Lisa and the others as they glanced in his direction. He stood apart, too far for a handshake. He had seen Chris shift position and had seen too the sign Chris had made with his hand. It was a small movement known only to the two of them. It said *There may be danger*. From his place by the stove, Johnny could watch the three doors, and everyone in the kitchen. The boy named Hutch was looking at him with open interest now, and his face showed no deception or awareness of danger. Perhaps Chris was wrong. Still Johnny did not relax his guard. He stood waiting for whatever might come, his face calm, but he was not calm within. For seven years he and Chris Hardeman had ridden together, from the dry wastes of the Utah Territory in '69, when Chris had hunted meat for the railroad crews and Johnny had carried water to the thirsty Irishmen, to the cattle trails of Texas and Kansas where Chris had risen quickly to trail boss and Johnny had gained a reputation of his own for his uncanny way with horses. From Chris, Johnny had learned the ways of the people who were moving westward across the land, changing everything as they went, and he could have had no better teacher, for Chris saw men for what they were, with strengths and weaknesses, and he knew that the truth was stronger than any pretense. They had ridden a long way together, Johnny absorbing everything but never truly belonging— except with this man, the one who had raised him and taught him and protected him since the Washita. And then this morning when he awoke among the willows, Johnny had felt a change. The feeling had persisted throughout the day, and although he had tried to speak to Chris about it, he had not found the words. Now as he stood quietly by the huge woodstove, Johnny knew he stood truly alone for the first time in his life.

"You must be hungry," Lisa said. "There's plenty left from dinner. Please sit down." She moved toward the stove to see if the stew was hot, glad of something to do.

"We ate today. We'd be grateful for a cup of coffee." Hardeman unbuttoned his coat, clearing the way to the Colt revolver in his waistband. He moved to the head of the table, choosing a seat where he could face the room. "And some whiskey, if you've got it." He saw the hesitation in Lisa Putnam's movement and the shadow of disapproval that crossed her face, which was as he had intended. It was time these people were put off-balance now, while he collected himself and prepared his move.

Julius was about to protest as Hardeman sat down, but Lisa motioned him to silence and nodded in the direction of the cabinet where the whiskey was kept. No one had sat in her father's chair since his death, but there was much to learn about the visitors and she had no wish to entangle them in her painful memories. She handed a cup of coffee to Johnny Smoker and placed another in front of Hardeman as Julius set a bottle on the table. She seated herself, leaving a vacant chair between her and the bearded man, surprised that he rose partway as she joined him. He waited for her to sit before he settled back in his own seat.

"Did you know my father well?"

"It was a long time ago, Miss Putnam. We rode together on the California road, guiding wagons. We were friends."

"Then his death is your loss as well. I'm sorry."

Hardeman remembered himself at seventeen, lost in the teeming streets of Independence, Missouri. He saw the face of Jed Putnam looking down at him from horseback, sizing him up at a glance; the truth of Lisa Putnam's words struck him and he felt the loss sharply then, accepting for the first time that there was to be no reunion with his friend, a man he hadn't seen in more than twenty years. He poured a dollop of whiskey into his coffee and sipped it, feeling the warmth go straight to his core. He had been at loose ends in the spring of '51, arriving in Independence without money to join a train, without horse, without supplies, and in less than an hour he had met Jed Putnam. The trails blazed by the mountain men had become the highways of a booming westward migration and the skills of the mountain men were once more in demand, this time to keep the legions of greenhorns who straggled across the plains and mountains from dying of sheer ignorance along the way. Jed had already delivered two trains safely to Sacramento, and when he decided to hire young Chris Hardeman, no one had argued. Fortune did not often smile that broadly on a wandering youth. But Hardeman had let the friendship lie fallow. He had held it in reserve like money in a bank and now it was gone, stolen away without a sound or a warning by the hand of Death.

Lisa Putnam was watching him as he sipped the coffee. Her blue eyes reminded him of Jed's. Was the hair her mother's? He saw how it gleamed, and noticed for the first time the small lines at the corners of her eyes, the furrow of worry between her brows, and the dryness of her lips. The skin on her face showed the effects of the sun. She wore no rings and her hands were marred by half a dozen small cuts and nicks. She spent long hours out of doors doing the work of the ranch, he guessed, caring for the cattle and horses and looking after the smaller livestock too. She was the boss in more than name.

Uncomfortable under his scrutiny, she moistened her lips with the tip of her tongue and looked away, but she couldn't know what he was thinking. She couldn't guess how good a face so plain and natural looked after six months of keeping company with painted saloon girls and the prim wives of proper Kansas citizens. She was in her thirties and showed it. Any woman who lived out of doors on the frontier grew old before her time, and most looked the worse for it, but not this one. Plain wasn't the word to call her by. The mountains had stamped an imprint of strength and character on her; she bore the marks of time like rewards instead of burdens. If you took in the whole woman, the long legs and slender waist and modest bosom, the eyes like Jed Putnam's and the blood rising again to her cheeks, you saw that she was beautiful and felt like a fool for not seeing it at once.

"Your father was wagon boss and chief scout the first trip I took on the Oregon road," he said, forcing himself to smile, needing to disarm her suspicions at the start. "He took me on as assistant scout. I told him I didn't know the first thing about it. He said he liked the cut of my jib. He'd do that sometimes, use seafaring talk."

"His family were shipowners in Boston," said Lisa, relaxing a little, certain now that the man was telling the truth.

70

Hardeman nodded. "He said if I'd come from Pennsylvania on my own stick, I'd do to cross the mountains with. He gave me a horse." He leaned back, the smile coming more easily now as he remembered the perverse nature of the pinto Jed had innocently offered, knowing the boy would learn much from the hardy Indian pony. He drank again and the warmth began to spread through his body. "He must have looked all over Independence to find a horse that would teach me the most. That one trip was all we made together, that and back through the mountains in the fall. He showed me the beaver country, Horse Creek and Green River and the New Fork Lake. He called it Loch Drummond, after some Scotchman. The next spring he got me a job as chief scout with a big train; they took me on his say-so." In one year with Jed Putnam he had learned more than some men learned in a lifetime, not only about the trail but about the weather and which watering places were dry in spring or fall, and how to talk to the Indians. And then the mountain man had proved himself the best kind of teacher by pushing Chris into the chief scout's job before the youth thought he was ready, making him depend at once on what he had learned and thereby assuring that he would never forget it.

He drained his cup of the last of the coffee and poured it half full of whiskey. Lisa did not entirely disguise her displeasure. Hardeman grew expansive in the telling of his memories. "After that I saw him now and again. Then he quit the road and came up here. I knew about this place before he found it. It's just like he said it would be."

"I'm surprised you never came here, if you were friends."

Hardeman shook his head. "I got my wagons out early in spring, but not too early. Always made good time on the road; no detours. The one year I wanted to take Jed's cutoff the company voted against it." He chuckled. "It was a dry spring and not much grass. I warned them, but they said 'California or bust,' and came pretty near to bust. We lost three animals out of four. They cut their wagons in half in the desert and looked worse'n a bunch of Mormon handcarts rolling into Sacramento, but nobody died." He drank from the cup. "Worst damn bunch of fools I ever rode with." He fell silent, fighting off a surliness that whiskey sometimes brought out in him. This woman disturbed him, looking at him with Jed Putnam's eyes. They had a way of seeming to look past whatever fences you threw up, as if they were saying, "Never mind about that, I know what you are." But she couldn't know the other reason that had kept him from coming by on the trips back from California, when his time was his own and there was no one to vote him down— the notion that he would wait to see Jed until he could measure up to the man and stand beside him as an equal.

For years he had wondered what could give him the sense of satisfaction felt by a Jed Putnam, a man who had been there in the beginning, when the mountains were tracked only by moccasins and buffalo. Scouting had held much promise, and Hardeman had once been confident that in time his own deeds might be written in the history of the West below such names as Jedediah Smith and John Hoback and Kit Carson and Jim Bridger and Sublette and Hickok and Jed Putnam. But the Washita had stolen those hopes away. In the years since then he had been a freight hauler and a hunter, cowhand, trail boss and lawman, enough occupations to satisfy most men for a lifetime, but he took little pride in these accomplishments, viewing the list warily as an accounting of jobs and professions each of which had failed him in some way or another. Now he was a scout once again, sure of himself and set on a course. He had come here to leave his mark on the West in a way that Jed would approve, he thought, and he had planned to ask Jed for his help. But Jed was gone, and there was no longer any measure to meet.

He raised the cup to wet his throat and saw it was empty. He poured again and looked at Johnny by the stove. "You getting warm over there, Johnny Smoker?" A splash of whiskey fell on the table as he righted the bottle.

Johnny nodded.

"You're welcome, of course," Lisa Putnam said, sounding somewhat uncertain. "We have more than enough room nowadays. I'm sorry you came all this way for nothing."

Hardeman smiled, giving her no warning. "It wasn't just to see your father, Miss Putnam. You know how word gets out about one thing and another. We heard, those of us on the trail—back when Jed built this place—we heard he was given the valley by a Sioux chief name of Sun Horse."

At the mention of the name a chill descended on the kitchen. Johnny Smoker looked from face to face, searching for the reason, but Hardeman kept his gaze on Lisa Putnam and saw that she was afraid.

"What do you want with Sun Horse?" Julius was standing at the foot of the table. He had seen the gun in Hardeman's waistband, knew he was meant to see it, and the knowledge made him angry.

"You know him then." Hardeman's tone made it a fact, not a question.

"Mr. Hardeman didn't say he wanted anything," Lisa said, trying unsuccessfully to keep her voice calm.

"He must be an old man by now," Hardeman said blandly.

"Sure," Hutch explained. "Old Sun Horse, he's just—"

Julius cut him off. "You get on out and mend that harness like I told you."

"You said it'll hold till—"

"You hear what I say?"

Reluctantly, the boy got up and went out, taking his coat from its hook in the entryway. Julius had never spoken to him so sharply before.

In the kitchen no one spoke until Hutch was gone.

"It's true that Sun Horse gave my father the valley." Lisa no longer smoothed the edge in her voice.

"We need to find him, Miss Putnam. We have a message for him from General Crook."

The chill deepened.

72

Julius sat down at the far end of the table. "Sun Horse is wintering up north this year. On the Tongue, maybe, or the Rosebud."

Hardeman was growing increasingly wary of the deceptions he sensed growing around him. It was time to break the standoff.

"The way I hear it, Sun Horse has spent every winter for more than twenty years in the next valley over from here." He was careful to keep his tone even.

Anger sparked in Julius's eyes. "Are you saying I'm—"

"I'm just saying what I hear," Hardeman interrupted, before the colored man said something that could not be ignored. "He's a peace chief. He stays clear of the hostile bands."

"That's right, he's a peace chief." Lisa took a short breath and gave ground. "You'll have to forgive us if we're cautious, Mr. Hardeman. Sun Horse is an old friend. My uncle lives with him. It's true they winter near here, but we haven't seen them in some time. The hunting has been very bad. They may have gone north in search of game."

Hardeman paused before answering. How much of the truth was she telling him? It wasn't likely Sun Horse would move his people in winter, nor would he be fooled by a February chinook.

"If Sun Horse is a friend, Miss Putnam, you'll help us. We came to warn him. All the Sioux who weren't back on the Dakota reservation by the end of January have been declared hostile."

"Hostile! There has been no trouble here since Red Cloud's War!" Lisa felt a swift anger and a swifter fear, knowing now that the thing she had hoped would never happen had been inevitable, its coming only a matter of time.

Red Cloud's War, so called for the Oglala warrior who had dominated its battles, had ended in 1868 after two years of fighting, a clear victory for the Sioux and their allies, the Cheyenne and Arapaho. As soon as the Civil War was over, the government began negotiating with the Indians for the right to open John Bozeman's road along the east flank of the Big Horns in order to speed the development of the new gold fields in Montana Territory. The government was in debt following the war and the mineral wealth of the western territories was needed to replenish the national treasury. The Indians balked at this invasion of their favorite hunting grounds, and while the negotiations were still going on, troops were dispatched to begin constructing three forts along the Bozeman Trail, ignoring Jim Bridger's safe route west of the mountains. This effrontery brought down on the troops stationed at the new forts Reno, Phil Kearny and C. F. Smith the unbridled fury of the Sioux and their allies. They harassed the soldiers without letup, inflicting heavy casualties, and in the end Washington yielded, unable to supply the forts reliably, let alone provide safe passage along the Montana road. A new treaty concluded at Fort Laramie created the great Sioux Reservation west of the Missouri River in Dakota Territory and recognized the Powder River country—all the land from the Black Hills in the east to the Big Horn summits in the west and from the Oregon Trail in the south to the Yellowstone in the north—as "unceded Indian territory." Most important, it provided that there could be no more cessions of Sioux land unless three-quarters of the adult male Sioux marked their approval on paper.

With the treaty accepted by both sides, witnessed by more than a hundred headmen who came to Fort Laramie to make their marks upon the pact, the troops were withdrawn from the Montana road and the jubilant Indians burned the forts. Since then, the bands that shunned the agencies and the government beef had continued to live west of the reservation, in the Powder River country, and although there had been some skirmishes along its borders, the region had enjoyed an uneasy peace for almost eight years. Lisa's father had warned that it couldn't last forever, not unless the white man changed his ways.

"It's the Black Hills trouble," Hardeman said now. "The government wants all the Sioux on the reservation where it can keep an eye on them. The army sent out riders in December, Indian riders from the agencies, to all the bands in the country here, giving them until the end of January to come in."

"January?" Lisa was appalled. "Who gave an order like that? Do they know how cold it has been this winter?"

"The order came from Washington." Hardeman left unsaid all the distant ignorance that implied. "It could be some of the riders didn't get through, what with the cold. Crook is giving Sun Horse a chance to go in peaceably."

"The riders may not have gotten through because of the cold and they want women and children to travel three hundred miles in January!" She turned away. "They're going to take it all. They're going to take all the land west of Dakota." She looked at Julius. "They are doing exactly what my father said they would do. The government will move the Sioux out of the Powder River country and then the settlers will come in and that will be an end of it. The Sioux will never get it back." She spun to face Hardeman. "This is treaty land! Sun Horse has lived at peace in this country all his life!"

Hardeman drank off the rest of his coffee. The bite of the whiskey took his breath away and helped him to keep quiet. Everything she said or suspected was true. He couldn't oppose her now or she would get up a head of steam that would vent itself on him and there would be no help from that quarter, not any time soon. Let her get her anger out, but don't provoke her or she would argue herself into taking a stand she couldn't back down from. Jed had taught him that, about dealing with Indians—"You want a man to come around to your way of thinking, don't push him into a corner and don't talk him to death. You handle him right, he'll come along soon enough like it was his own idea."

Julius cleared his throat. "I reckon the soldiers will come when the snow melts."

Hardeman shook his head. "Crook gathered his troops during the thaw. He's got eight hundred men at Fetterman right now. He'll be on the move soon, if he hasn't started already. There will be another column from Fort Abraham Lincoln."

"Damn them!" Lisa rose suddenly. "God damn them!" She walked to the window, struggling to hold back her tears of rage. She held herself tightly, her arms crossed below her breasts as she stared out into the darkening afternoon. It was snowing in earnest once more. She could see the glow of a fire in the tipi by the woods. The wind gusted hard and the tipi vanished in a gray-white cloud.

A log fell in the stove. Ling Wo moved silently to add more wood. She had not understood all that had been said since the two strangers had entered, but she knew that Lisa was worried and afraid, and she sensed that the quiet life she and Harry had enjoyed for almost five years was in danger. She accepted this with an imperceptible shrug. The Western world was mysterious to Ling, who could not fathom the forces that moved it. She trusted in simple things she could experience and believe in. She believed in this kitchen, the most calming room she had found since coming to America. She believed in Lisa and her father, who had taken Ling and Harry in, had shown them the American meaning of the word "friend," for which there was no precise equivalent in the life of their homeland, where the line between friendship and family was a gulf not easily bridged. Here, she and Harry had been accepted as family almost overnight, and to Ling the process had seemed magical. This life had been good to her and she wished it to continue, but if the fate and fortunes of Putnam's Park, all those invisible ruling qualities the Chinese called *joss*, were changing, the change was inevitable and would have to be accepted. Ling did not struggle against the inevitable.

"Sun Horse never raised a hand against a white man." Julius was the first to speak. "He don't allow no one—no other bands—to fight in his country."

"But he turned his back when his young men snuck off to fight in Red Cloud's War." Hardeman had to know where the Negro stood, and Julius's quick anger was his answer.

"He couldn't do nothing else! If you know Injuns, you know that! The chiefs don't give orders like in the white man's army!" Julius sat back in his chair and brought his anger under control, glancing over his shoulder at Lisa, then turning back to glare at Hardeman. "He's been a friend to these folks. He protected them in the war."

Throughout the conflict, Julius had been with the Ninth Cavalry, stationed far away in the Southwest, and had heard only what the army grapevine had to tell about the war. Among the black soldiers of the Ninth, there had been a grim resolve that if they were tested in a similar struggle, they would not add another defeat to the records of the frontier cavalry. But in Putnam's Park he had found attitudes toward the Indians that were new to him. Sun Horse was Jed's friend, and after some initial suspicions, Julius had come to accept the Sun Band, at least, as peaceable neighbors. With Jed gone, he had found himself speaking now as the old mountain man might have replied to inquiries like Hardeman's, sticking up for Sun Horse and concealing his whereabouts, but even as he spoke, Julius wondered at the rightness of his course. If the

75

war should come to Putnam's Park and he were forced to take sides, which would he choose?

"Listen to me, Miss Putnam," Hardeman said. "If Sun Horse goes in to the reservation now it could save the peace. He's Sitting Bull's cousin. The other headmen respect him. It will make them think twice about fighting the army. If they go on fighting, they'll lose, you know that. This is their only hope." The sounds of a recurring dream came to him—cries of triumph and pain, the screams of dying horses...

He locked the memories away. He must give all his attention to the woman or she would see too much. Everything he had said was true, but it was not all of the truth. He had not said what would happen if Sun Horse refused to go in.

He drank again, flushed from the whiskey now. It took an effort to stay alert. He wanted to relax as he might have done among friends, and stop shadowboxing with the truth. What was it the woman feared? There was something more, beyond the danger to Sun Horse and his people. "Take us to Sun Horse," he said bluntly. "Help us persuade him to go in."

Without turning from the window, Lisa slowly shook her head. When she spoke, her voice was far away.

"His people have no meat. They're not strong enough to travel."

"Crook has a beef herd and supply wagons. If Sun Horse will go peaceably, they'll get beef and blankets and grain; and an escort to the reservation." Lisa turned and Hardeman saw the first flicker of hope in her eyes. His whole hand was on the table now, all except the ace up his sleeve. It was time to play that too. "They can keep their horses. And some guns for hunting. Crook will give his word."

Lisa's mind was racing, trying to summon up everything her father had taught her. Jed Putnam had seen much of the world and he had spent many patient hours passing on what he had learned to his daughter, even when she was a young girl, teaching her with stories instead of lessons, holding her attention with skills he had learned years before around winter campfires where a man's ability to entertain his companions was sometimes as important as his grit in a fight. He had shown her how each great force in the world beyond affected her own life, and during her years in Miss Jameson's School, all the politics and history that her teachers had presented as so many dead facts had fallen into living patterns when seen through her father's eyes. Now, she had recognized at once, even before Hardeman explained, that General Crook wanted to use Sun Horse to persuade the other bands to go peacefully to the Dakota Territory, and she knew that the ways in which the white man wanted to use Sun Horse would not stop there. If his people were allowed to keep their guns and horses while the unrepentant "hostiles" were deprived of theirs, there would be jealousy and dissension among the bands, which would suit perfectly the schemes of the politicians and Indian agents. As long as the headmen were set against one another, suspicious and distrustful, there could be no effective resistance, no concerted outbreak or uprising. They would try to make Sun Horse a white man's Indian, like the once mighty Red Cloud of the Oglala, who had been to Washington and now enjoyed strutting about in a top hat and frock coat. "You see," said the agents, "Red Cloud has learned the white man's ways. He is a good friend to the Great Father in Washington." And in the eyes of his own people the great war leader, who had done so much to win the war for the Bozeman road, had fallen from grace and was no longer trusted. But Lisa knew that Sun Horse was nobody's fool and could resist the white man's blandishments, if he were alive to do it. "How long will it take General Crook to get here?" she asked.

"That depends," Hardeman said. "He'll go on north if I don't find him first. He's after the war chiefs—Sitting Bull and Gall and Crazy Horse. He's giving Sun Horse a chance, Miss Putnam. But if Crook finds another band first and the fighting starts, there will be no beef for Sun Horse and no safe escort. It'll be too late then."

"Fort Fetterman is less than a hundred miles away," said Lisa. "General Crook's column could be here in a few days."

Hardeman nodded and poured himself more whiskey. He rose and walked to the stove, where he filled the cup with coffee.

Lisa was thinking hard. Crook could be here soon, or he would proceed north, down the Tongue or the Powder. And even then there might be time. If the Indians had their scouts out they would surely see such a large force. Able to strike camp in thirty minutes and to move thirty miles in a day, the Indian villages were like needles in a vast haymow, while the slow-moving soldier columns resembled a field mouse crawling blindly in the stack. The chance of the mouse coming on one of the moving needles was slight. And so there might still be some time even if General Crook passed by Putnam's Park. But Sun Horse must be warned and the matter set before him at once. And he must be made to see that he should not surrender, for that meant losing his home here forever.

But if Hardeman knew where Sun Horse wintered, why had he not gone there directly? Because he had wanted Jed Putnam's help in persuading Sun Horse to surrender, and now he wanted Lisa's. He seemed honestly to believe that the course he proposed was the best one for Sun Horse, and Lisa was just as certain it was wrong. Sun Horse must not go in now; he must remain free and stay away from the soldiers, and she must find a way to help him do it.

But how? For the moment she did not know. It would take time to find a way, and meanwhile she needed to distract Hardeman from her true intention.

What would my father do? she wondered, and the answer came at once. He would fight. As a trapper he had fought beside his friends against all odds, and on the one occasion when violence had threatened his home in Putnam's Park, he had ridden out alone, ready to die. In the summer of 1865, a time of continuous raiding along the emigrant trails, a war party of Cheyenne had pursued a small wagon train into Putnam's Park. It was the first time trouble had threatened the park, for it was under Sun Horse's protection, and he was a peace man respected not only among the Lokata but among their friends the Cheyenne as well. The sanctuary was known to white travelers, and the knowledge had kept some wagons and pack trains coming despite the Indian raids, particularly those bound for Montana and the gold fields there. Jed Putnam was friendly with the local Indians, everyone said, and they never troubled him. His own brother was married to Otter Skin, daughter of the Sioux Chief Sun Horse, and lived with the heathens. It was said that Sun Horse himself had prepared a potion of herbs and magic that had revived young Lisa Putnam's mother from the fever that struck her not long after Jed brought his wife and child out from Boston to join him, and had restored her to the good health she enjoyed until the day she died some years later of general fragility and a sudden attack of the grippe. Surely there could be no danger in such domesticated savages. Occasionally, the Indians themselves had directed travelers to cross the mountains at this point, by the Putnam Cutoff, or risk their lives if they continued along the eastern slopes.

But on that summer day of 1865 Sun Horse and his people were far to the north on their summer hunt. The Cheyenne had spied the wagons as they entered the river gap and had pursued them into the park, and the travelers had flogged their draft animals while praying with all their might that the tales of sanctuary were true.

After grouping the wagons in the yard between the Big House and the barn and organizing the frightened emigrants for the defense of the settlement, Jed had mounted his horse and ridden out to meet the warriors with his rifle in one hand and the other raised in a sign of peace. The Cheyenne were so impressed with the bravery of the white man who rode down the road alone that they had stopped to hear what he had to say. Lisa had watched the exchange from a second-story window with a trapper's long rifle held steady on the leader of the war party, four hundred yards away.

The Lakota call me the Truthful Whiteman, her father had told them in signs, making the movements broadly so they could be read across the twenty paces that separated him from the Cheyenne. *Sun Horse, the Lakota peace man, gave me this valley. My brother is married to Otter Skin, the daughter of Sun Horse. For twelve winters I have lived here with my family, and in that time there has been no fighting here between red men and white. I first came to the mountains to hunt beaver, and the Shoshoni called me Bear Heart. I fought the Blackfoot and the Crow, the Gros Ventre and the Piegan, and I took their scalps. I have never fought the Cheyenne and I will not be the first to break the peace in this valley, but if you think it is a good day to fight, I will fight. If there must be blood on this ground today, some of that blood will be Cheyenne.*

The warriors had looked at the man who faced them alone, sitting so calmly on his horse. They looked at the settlement and the tight group of wagons, defended by twenty nervous guns, and the Cheyenne leader made signs to Jed. *The Cheyenne respect none more than the true men of peace* he said. He knew of Sun Horse and the one called the Truthful Whiteman. It was not a good day to fight, not here in this place of peace. The war party had turned and ridden away.

I am my father's only child, Lisa thought, and it is time I learned how to fight for what I believe in.

Hardeman had resumed his seat and was looking at her through the rising steam from the cup in his hands, now blowing gently to cool the coffee. Lisa was suddenly glad he had been drinking. It might dull his perceptions. Let him think that I fight for myself, she thought. A white man understands a selfish motive best of all. If he thinks I am afraid only for myself then he may not see what I can do for Sun Horse.

But what can I do?

"The treaty says that no whites can live here," she said. "Did you know that?"

Hardeman nodded. "Sun Horse gave your father this land before the Laramie treaty was made."

"That's right. He even gave him a deed." Her tone was bitter. "It is a piece of deerskin cut square with a bone knife and written with ink made from berries. Sun Horse wrote the deed in pictures. They are called pictographs, I think, the sort of drawings they use to record the winter count. They say, 'The Sun Band of the Lakota gives the valley of the clear water to the Truthful Whiteman, Jedediah Putnam.' My uncle wrote out my father's name and Sun Horse copied it onto the deed himself. The *P* in Putnam is backwards. The gift was recognized in the treaty of 1868 by letters from the peace commissioners to the Secretary of the Interior. Of course, those commissioners have all retired and the secretary went out of office with President Johnson. Tell me, Mr. Hardeman, will the government recognize that deed when the Sioux are living like beggars on the Dakota reservation?"

"I don't know." Hardeman had not expected this, but he seized on it; it explained the woman's fear and gave him the key to her cooperation. "They might if you help us. Take us to Sun Horse, Miss Putnam, and I'll do what I can about the deed." He found himself wanting to help calm her fears, but he knew the impulse came from the whiskey and he stopped himself from promising anything more. All of his promises would be worthless if events turned against him.

"We came to help Sun Horse," said Johnny Smoker.

Everyone in the kitchen turned to look at the young man who had not spoken since entering the room. There was a slight sound and then a door opened, and from a hallway that led to bedrooms in the back of the house, Bat and Hears Twice stepped into the kitchen.

Hardeman relaxed somewhat, the nagging question of the empty chairs answered at last. The Indian had stayed out of sight until he had a chance to

79

learn something about the strangers. He was as old as a rock, if not a day or two more, and it was plain that he lived in the wild; he had none of the signs of a domesticated Sioux and he showed the self-composure that Hardeman knew as the mark of an Indian who still felt sure of his place in creation. The mountain man would be the uncle Lisa had mentioned and the brother Jed had spoken of now and again, the one who had lived with Sun Horse since the end of the fur trade. He might have his own reasons for keeping hidden or he might simply have come to see things from an Indian point of view, regarding all strange whites as possible enemies. The presence of these two meant that Hardeman was close to finding Sun Horse, no matter what Lisa Putnam decided to do.

He relaxed even more when he saw a smile on Johnny's face; it was a smile he bestowed only on a friend.

"It's all right," Bat said to Lisa, his attention on the youth. "Hears Twice says there ain't no danger from these two."

The Indian was aware of nothing except the presence of the young man by the stove. He shuffled across the room, looking Johnny up and down with growing delight. He made a few tentative signs, forming the hand movements more broadly than usual, as he would for a child or another who might be ignorant of the sign talk. Johnny responded with a few signs of his own, quick and sure.

Bat pulled a chair out from the table and sat down hard. "It can't be," he said softly.

Hears Twice was smiling broadly. "*Oyate Tokcha Ichokab' Najin*," he said. He Stands Between the Worlds. And Bat saw it was true.

"It can't be," he said again.

"Uncle Bat?" Lisa looked from Johnny to the Indian to her uncle, seeking some explanation.

"The boy is Sun Horse's grandson," Bat said.

Hears Twice made a single sign, moving his forefinger out from beneath his chin, showing that the words came straight from the heart and tongue— *It is true.*

For a time the measured ticking of the Waltham wall clock was the only sound in the kitchen. Beneath the stove, Rufus stepped back into his basket, curled up, and closed his eyes.

Ling Wo had listened with interest as the identity of the strange boy was revealed, but now she turned back to the stove where she checked the fire, then opened the oven and set the three risen pans of bread dough on the rack before gently closing the door. With the dinner dishes done, it was time for her to start thinking of supper, and she could not allow herself to be distracted for long, no matter what mysteries presented themselves in her kitchen.

"Hmp." Julius broke the silence. "He looks mighty white to me."

"His grandson?" Lisa shook her head. "I don't understand. How could he—"

80

Bat chuckled as he rose from his seat. "I don't understand it all neither, child, but I'm thinkin' we'll hear about it soon enough." He turned to Julius. "He looks pretty white to you, does he? You got a point there. Yessir, you got a point." He could scarcely contain his glee. "And you're just the feller to know if a man's got a touch of the tarbrush, now, ain't you? Or the Indian paintbrush? Well, he is white, as a fool can see, but that don't change the fact. Old Sun Horse is this boy's grandpap, and that's truth. Was took off a wagon train and raised up by Sun Horse's first boy, White Smoke. That was afore your time, I reckon." He stuck out his hand to Johnny Smoker. "How ye be, boy? You're lookin' right pert for a dead man."

"I'm all right," Johnny said, still smiling. "Glad to see my uncle Lodgepole again. Sorry I didn't get here in time to meet your brother."

Bat nodded. "He'd of took a shine to you, I'm thinkin'. You recollect this old coot." He motioned to Hears Twice.

Johnny made signs to say *I am glad to see you again, Uncle,* and he shook Hears Twice's hand.

The Indian touched his left breast, then raised a crooked forefinger in imitation of the rising sun and the warmth it cast into his heart.

Forgotten by the others, Hardeman tipped his chair back against the wall and rested a boot against the edge of the table, the cup of whiskey in his hand. The bottle was almost empty. The whiskey warmth had risen to his head and he no longer fought it off, allowing himself to give in at last to the bone-weariness that had accumulated on the long journey from Kansas like some slow-acting opiate. What was it about a man who drank too much? People thought he was weak, and they dropped their guard. The trick had worked for him more than once, but it had almost failed him today.

"I still don't understand," Lisa was saying. "I'm sure I have never seen him before."

"Of course you ain't," Bat said, still chuckling at the confusion around him. His high spirits were beginning to infect the others, tempered only by their impatience at his slowness in unraveling the youth's kinship to Sun Horse. Bat turned to Hardeman, noting the solid build and the beard cut neat the way a city man would do, but neither the hands nor the eyes belonged to a city man. The eyes met his own steadily, as Hardeman idly stroked a small scar on his cheek with the fingers of one hand, and Bat saw something familiar in the look the man gave him. What was it? The eyes were the window to the soul, it was said. Bat felt a small shock of surprise as he recognized a soul that was kin to his own.

He took the whiskey bottle from the table and raised it to regard the small amount remaining. He gave Hardeman a nod and a wink.

"You play yer cards pretty close. Well, I'll drink to that." He put the bottle to his lips and drained it in an instant.

"Wagh!" he exclaimed, savoring the harsh bite of the whiskey. He wiped his mouth on his buckskin sleeve and turned back to Lisa. "Well now, you recollect White Smoke, the one married a Cheyenne woman and went to live with her folks? Could be you don't. You was just twelve or so when he went south to get hitched, I make it." But Lisa remembered Sun Horse's eldest son, and she nodded. "They lived with Black Kettle's bunch down south. White Smoke, he brought the boy and his ma to see Sun Horse just one time. We was in summer camp on the Little Horn. Sun Horse took to the boy like he was blood kin, and maybe something more besides." He glanced at Johnny. "That was in '64 they come visitin'. Four years later we heard he was dead at the Washita, killed when Long Hair Custer hit Black Kettle's village, may I get that murderin' son of a bitch in my sights just once afore I go under, beggin' your pardon, Lisa honey. Anyways, the boy's folks was killed, White Smoke and Grass Woman both, and the boy plumb disappeared. The Cheyenne figgered he was burned in a tipi, They found some bodies, after, a few the right size; 'course they was burned pretty bad. Sun Horse took the news hard. . . ." He let his voice trail away, looking at Johnny.

"Chris found me in one of the lodges," he said. "I was shot in the leg. I couldn't walk. He took me away from the fight. We've been together since then."

Bat suspected that those few words were the bare bones of a story that could be fleshed out all night over a warm fire in a winter lodge, a story he would dearly like to know, but he would let it pass for now. With the remarkable fact of Johnny's kinship to Sun Horse told in a few words, Bat remained silent, trying to work out what the boy's presence would mean to Sun Horse and the band, coupled as it was with the news of soldiers coming into the country to make war.

Hardeman was looking at Julius. "You were a soldier once yourself."

Julius straightened in his chair. "Regimental sergeant major, Ninth Cavalry. You?"

Hardeman shook his head. "Civilian scout." He sipped his coffee, hoarding it now that the whiskey was gone. The Chinese cook cracked open the oven and peered in quickly, and the comforting smell of baking bread filled the kitchen.

"Then you were one of the men who led General Custer to Black Kettle's village," Lisa said.

Hardeman nodded. It was not an action he would defend. He saw the disapproval plain on her face, but no similar reaction from the others. If anything, the knowledge of Hardeman's scouting seemed to reduce Julius Ingram's suspicions. As a soldier, he knew the scouts for what they were, frontiersmen of one stripe or another, good men and bad, but men who knew the country and the Indians. As for Bat Putnam, he had the greatest reason to be hostile to a man who had led soldiers to a sleeping village of Cheyenne, but his expression revealed no judgment. Most of his attention was still on Johnny.

The young man shifted one foot to another, glancing first at Bat and then at Hardeman. "I'll unsaddle the horses," he announced, and moved for the door to the saloon. That was his way, deciding to do something and setting out to do it all in a moment, the way he had decided to come here to see Sun Horse.

Hardeman got to his feet and drained the last of the spiritous coffee from the cup. "We've got the better part of a deer we took this morning down below the canyon. Might be you folks would like some deer meat for supper." He moved to follow Johnny and as he passed through the saloon door he heard Lisa Putnam call after him.

"You'll find grain in a bin by the horse stalls."

On the porch Johnny was waiting. The snow had stopped and to the north the sky was clearing. Judging by the light, the unseen sun had already gone below the western ridge. The air had lightened and it acted like a tonic on Hardeman, washing away the dullness caused by the whiskey. "It could be we'll see a blue sky tomorrow," he said, and Johnny smiled.

"I can take care of the horses, if you like."

Hardeman shook his head. "We'll do it together." Each cared for his own horse and his own belongings; they treated one another as equals, as much as possible given the difference in age and experience, and Hardeman was not about to change that now after seven years.

He unwrapped his reins from the hitching rail and led his horse toward the barn, enjoying once again the feel of the settlement nestled so snugly at the head of the valley. Back in the kitchen they would have plenty to say right now, about Sun Horse's grandson returned from the dead and the former army scout who rode with him. They could think what they liked. He had quit scouting to care for the boy, that much they could gather from what Johnny had told them, and the rest of the story no one knew, not even Johnny. It was his own affair and none of theirs.

He had signed on with the army during the War Between the States, for the sake of the Union. And he had found himself helping to hold the western mountains not only against the threat of Rebel incursions from the south, but also against the Indians who sortied from every point of the compass, constantly testing the bluecoats, whose reserves were drained off by the white man's war between brothers. Hardeman knew the Indians and their ways, he respected them as warriors and as men, and from time to time he was able to smooth over a misunderstanding and keep the peace. But no quiet words of reason could quell the wave of hostilities that had swept the Colorado border after an incident that took place in November of 1864 on Sand Creek. There a peaceful encampment of southern Cheyenne under Black Kettle was struck and decimated by a ragtag assortment of volunteer militia led by Colonel John M. Chivington, a former preacher. Black Kettle was renowned throughout the Cheyenne nation as a great leader whose efforts to make peace with the whites had been unceasing. Outraged by the unprovoked attack, the Cheyenne sent the war pipe to their allies, the Sioux and Arapaho, and more than a thousand warriors took to the trails, launching a year of unprecedented raiding across the central plains, even as the surrenders of Lee and Johnston brought the white man's fratricide to an end.

With the Rebellion over, the Army of the Plains was strengthened and Hardeman stayed on, offering his knowledge of the aborigines in the hope that the bloodshed here could be brought to an end as well. Unlike most of the men whom he led, Hardeman had known the frontier before the mutual suspicions between red men and white erupted into open conflict. He knew that the Indian leaders were reasonable men, for the most part, willing to talk, even willing to share the land, which they did not imagine they owned, not as a white man understood the notion. But the white man's notion was spreading fast, and in the years immediately following the war, the violence rose to new heights. Goaded by the Homestead Act's offer of free land and the release of thousands of men from the Northern and Southern armies, new settlements spread rapidly from the major rivers in Kansas and Nebraska, and the tribes accustomed to hunt on the central plains reacted by striking at settlers, emigrants and troops whenever the chance arose.

The army officers, fresh from victories in a very different kind of war, were used to set-piece battles and a foe that would stand and fight, but the Indians fought by different rules. They would fade away in the face of a superior force, only to reappear nearby to attack a supply train or steal the soldiers' horses. Time and again the frustrated officers failed to inflict lasting harm on the tribesmen, and in the parleys and councils they did no better. They were impatient with the Indian custom of eating and smoking before important talk; they broke etiquette by interrupting the Indian orators in council; they ordered the proud warriors about and insisted on bringing troops near their villages when they came to parley. On one such occasion, some Sioux and Cheyenne camped on the Pawnee Fork of the Arkansas fled from their lodges, fearing a repetition of the Sand Creek massacre. General Winfield Hancock, then the commander of the Division of the Missouri, felt that he had been tricked, and reacted imprudently. He ordered the village burned, further convincing the Indians that the whites could not be trusted.

Hardeman had quit the government's service in disgust over the incident. It seemed to him that the whites did not want peace at all. They provoked the Indians at every opportunity and seemed determined to push the tribesmen off every decent patch of land on the frontier, or perhaps to exterminate them altogether, and he would have no part of such an undertaking. For a time he sought other scouting jobs but found nothing much to his liking, and in the fall of 1868 he stopped at Fort Lyon, Colorado Territory, to see James Hickok, and old friend who was scouting for the Tenth Cavalry, one of the two Negro cavalry regiments. "Wild Bill," the newspapers had christened Hickok, one of the most famous scouts on the frontier, but he and Hardeman had scouted together for General Smith the year before and had always called each other by their Christian names.

"Christopher," Hickok said, when they had exchanged recent news, "you could do me a good turn, if you were so inclined. General Sully wants me to scout for him down toward the Indian Territory. It's to be a winter campaign, Phil Sheridan's idea. Figgers he might catch hold of the Indians in winter." Hickok had chuckled and Hardeman smiled. The army's inability to come to grips with the Indians was a standing joke among the old hands in the scouting corps. "Now I'll tell you what," Hickok continued. "The army picked the cream of the crop when they chose officers for these darky regiments; they're good fellers, all of 'em. They're quick, and they'll listen what a man tells 'em. The Tenth is goin' on patrol in Kansas while Sully goes south, and I've no mind to leave 'em now."

He had brushed aside the hairs of his moustache with the knuckle of his index finger before he went on, a habitual gesture Hardeman knew well.

"You're the old man in this business," Hickok said, grinning. Hardeman was the older of the two, although by just four years, and Hickok delighted in exaggerating the difference until it seemed to be one of generations. But he turned serious then. "You know Black Kettle from the Medicine Lodge treaty council. Talk is he's been over to Fort Cobb not long ago to find a safe place for his people. Wynkoop was off somewhere, but he'll be back right quick." Edward Wynkoop was a former army officer, now Indian agent for the southern Cheyenne. He had roundly condemned Chivington's attack at Sand Creek and ever since had worked hard to diminish the ill will the massacre had engendered among the Cheyenne. "You go on with Sully. Tell him I sent you. See if you can't set him down with Black Kettle and Wynkoop and pull a treaty out of all this hooraw."

"All this hooraw" was the then-present state of military affairs on the plains. In the north, Red Cloud's War had just been brought to a conclusion with the signing of the new Laramie treaty, while on the central plains the army had suffered two signal defeats in recent months. Sully himself had blundered about the Indian Territory in September, accomplishing little but to convince the warriors there that they could meet and beat him on their own ground, while Major George Forsyth's much-heralded band of frontier scouts had been soundly whipped on their first outing in Kansas, in the fight called the Battle of Beecher's Island.

"There'll be some hotheads want revenge for Beecher's Island before they make peace with the Cheyenne," Hardeman observed.

Hickok nodded. "Sully's no hothead. He ain't Ulysses Grant, neither, but he'll seddown and listen to sense if you make him."

Now, in Lisa Putnam's barn, Hardeman pondered the fateful meeting. Hickok's request had sent him on his way to the Washita and had changed his life.

"There's grain in that bin," he said to Johnny. The three horses were in adjoining stalls, saddles and packs removed, their halter ropes dropped loose through the rings at the feed troughs. Johnny walked to the grain bin and returned with a tinful of oats, then went back for another. Sometimes you hardly noticed the limp, unless you watched for it. Hardeman rolled his shoulder and felt the reminder of the bullet wound there. But for the meeting with Hickok his shoulder might be as good as new. But Johnny would most likely be dead.

On the day when Hardeman and Hickok had talked, Sully's command had already left Fort Dodge and gone south to establish a supply base on the Beaver River. Hardeman had found them there, at the new post they had dubbed Camp Supply, and the state of affairs had not been at all as advertised. Phil Sheridan, eager to observe the progress of the winter campaign, was on hand. He had sent General Sully back to his district headquarters and had given command of the expedition to Brevet Major General George A. Custer of the Seventh Cavalry. Custer had been court-martialed the previous autumn and sentenced to a year's suspension of rank and command over the shooting of some deserters and absenting himself from his command without proper authority. Word had it he had gone to visit his beautiful wife. But Custer was Phil Sheridan's fair-haired boy, and at Sheridan's request the sentence had been remitted by General William Tecumseh Sherman and Custer was returned to his regiment in time to join the winter campaign. When he learned that Hardeman had been sent by Wild Bill Hickok, Custer gladly took him on, and on the morning of November 23 the column left Camp Supply. Hardeman rode at the head of the line with California Joe and the other scouts, full of misgivings. It seemed to him that the Boy General was eager for action and would not listen kindly to suggestions of peacemaking.

For four days the column marched south in half a foot of new snow without finding any trails. As they struck the South Canadian River, Hardeman suggested a turn toward the southeast and Fort Cobb, where the command might refresh their supplies and discover what the men at Cobb knew of the Indians. Privately, he hoped that Agent Wynkoop would be on hand and might know the whereabouts of Black Kettle.

Custer agreed to the suggestion, but even as the last of the supply wagons forded the river, the advance scouts sent word that they had found what appeared to be the trail of a large war party heading south toward the Antelope Hills. Custer took the scent like a hound with his blood up and for the rest of the day the column pressed close on the heels of the scouts. After a short stop for supper, the pursuit continued into the night, and it was nearing midnight when the foremost scouts returned to say that they had found a village close by, on the south side of an oxbow bend in the Washita River.

Custer began immediate preparations for an attack at dawn. He detailed Hardeman to lead Major Elliott and his three companies around to the northeast, to a position across the river from the village. Hardeman protested that the trail the command had been following had been lost in the dark, hours before, and that it was not certain the war party was in the village or even what tribe of Indians was camped there.

"Oh, we shall see them well enough at first light, Mr. Hardeman," Custer said, and he turned away to give further orders to his troop commanders.

The night was cold, fires were forbidden, and sleep was impossible. Before the first glimmer of dawn, Hardeman slipped away from Elliott's position and made his way cautiously down the east side of the river. As the first glow in the east revealed the countryside around him, he discovered a trail made the day before, leading away from the sleeping village. The war party—if in fact it was a war party—had passed through the village but was no longer there. To the west, stars were still visible. He dared to follow the trail a short distance to the southeast, and as he crested a rise he was greeted with the sight of another large village farther down the stream, and thin columns of smoke rising from beyond the next low hills, visible against the growing light of dawn, where yet another village lay hidden. Obviously there were many hundreds, if not thousands, of Indians, probably from several tribes, comfortably settled in winter camps along a short stretch of the Washita. Any one of the villages could have been the war party's home.

Hardeman spurred his horse back toward the command, urging the tired animal into a slow gallop. From more than a mile away he saw that Elliott's men were preparing to cross the river. He stopped against the skyline and raised his arm in a broad wave, not daring to shout or fire a shot. He was heartened to see an answering wave from the command, but even as he whipped his horse in a circle and pointed to show that he had found the enemy downstream, a rifle shot sounded from the village, followed by a bugle calling the attack, and then it was too late.

When Hardeman reached the village, all three elements of Custer's force were among the tipis, and the Indians—Cheyenne, Hardeman saw now— were running for cover in the brush along the river and in the rough ground to the south and west, where they set up an angry fire at the soldiers. His face tight with rage, Hardeman had ridden through the battle, looking for someone who could turn back the clock a quarter of an hour and stop the slaughter. Through the dust and smoke he saw a man lead a woman from a lodge and untie two horses tethered there, and as the man mounted with a nimbleness that belied his years, Hardeman recognized the Cheyenne headman Black Kettle. If he could reach the chief and take him to Custer, there might be a chance. But Black Kettle was wasting no time; waiting only long enough to be sure his wife had mounted, he led off at a dead run for the river, with Hardeman pounding after them, shouting uselessly against the din of battle.

Black Kettle had almost gained the river when a bullet struck him in the back. He fell from his horse into the water at the edge of the stream and lay there, facedown. The woman turned back to go to her husband's aid. She saw Hardeman racing toward her but she disregarded the danger, and she had just dismounted when she too was hit and fell dead in the water.

In that part of the country the Washita cut its channel in a dark reddish soil; where it had been stirred up by the soldiers' crossing and the splashing of escaping Cheyenne, the river ran blood-red.

Later, the Kiowas claimed that the war party Custer had trailed was one of their own, returning from a raid against the Utes in Colorado. They said it had merely passed through Black Kettle's camp on its way home.

Hardeman came out of his reverie suddenly, wondering what was wrong. Something in the barn had changed—a sound... He relaxed and felt a little foolish when he realized it was only the horses. They were done with their grain and had stopped chewing.

Johnny was leaning against the wall of the stall, waiting patiently.

Hardeman put a hand on the youth's shoulder. "We'll turn 'em out now, I guess."

They removed the halters, slapped the horses on the rump and chased them out the back door. Hardeman threw his saddlebags over one shoulder and the deer carcass over the other and waited in front of the barn as Johnny pulled the doors closed behind them. He looked about at the peaceful valley. The sky was clearing quickly now and the cold was growing strong. The lampglow from the windows of the house looked warm and inviting.

In the blood and thunder of the Washita battle, he had managed to save one boy. He had turned from the scene of Black Kettle's death, intending to leave the village, but before he was beyond its confines he had cause to enter a lodge that was as yet untouched by the torch, and there he found a youth of perhaps twelve or thirteen years huddled over a dead man and woman, and despite the boy's Cheyenne garments and his apparent lack of any knowledge of the English tongue, Hardeman had perceived that the boy was white. Over the years he had restored to the boy some of the choices that were taken away on that cold November morning by the soldiers who had killed his adopted parents and scattered his people. Johnny was a reminder of his failure and a measure of his atonement, and now, at Johnny's behest, they had come here.

Once more Hardeman came as a peacemaker. Once more he came to stop a winter campaign, and this time he would not fail. He would do it without Jed Putnam's help, without the help of Jed's daughter Lisa, if it came to that. This time there would be no sleeping village wakened by the sound of gunfire and bugles. He had come to make peace and peace there would be, no matter the cost.

SIX

The next day was clear and very bright. The morning warmed quickly, the temperature rising to the freezing point and beyond before the riders were out of sight of Putnam's Park. They were five, Hardeman and Johnny Smoker, Bat and Lisa Putnam, and Hears Twice, who had accepted the hospitality of Bat's lodge overnight. In the open, the new snow was soft and damp above an old crust, while in the shade of the trees it remained dry and powdery. From time to time a clump of snow on the branch of an evergreen would let go and fall, knocking more snow from the lower branches, occasionally spooking a horse or bathing one of the riders in a sparkling cascade of white. They rode mostly in single file, taking turns breaking a path. Where the creek bottom widened they rode abreast, the order of march changing as the trail narrowed again and forced the horses to fall in one behind the other.

As they reached a rocky defile where the trail curved away from the creek and rose steeply among large boulders to pass by a small waterfall, Lisa dropped back and allowed Hardeman to go ahead of her. She had felt his eyes on her all morning and she let him take the lead now gladly. Over the years she had grown accustomed to the surprise and frequent glances she had received from men and women who were shocked to see a woman riding astride and dressed like a man, but she had become uncomfortable under Hardeman's gaze.

She wore her short coat of mountain goatskin and a gray stockman's hat of five-X beaver. Her riding pants were buckskin, cut close to give her a sure seat in the saddle. Her hair was loose, gathered at the nape of the neck with a dark blue ribbon. Fur-lined moccasins came up to her knees, in the mountain man's style. The trappers had adopted the Indians' winter moccasins, made from buffalo hide. They had thick rawhide soles, and rabbit fur sewn around the foot, and they were comfortable at forty degrees below zero. For ranch work, Lisa wore boots, but on the trail she reverted to trappers' footwear, a custom she had kept since childhood. It was a practical outfit, suited to the requirements of her surroundings, but even on the frontier few white women dared such unconventional attire and the army wives in the western garrisons still clung to their awkward sidesaddles. Victorian habits and manners were as strong among "proper" gentlemen and ladies in the new territories of the American West, seven thousand miles from Victoria's throne, as they were back in the States and among European gentry around the world, where these attitudes were the ramparts that protected

European civilization against the barbarism it encountered on all sides as its empires expanded. Lisa's parents had explained these prejudices to her when she was old enough to understand them, but her father had laughed at such foolishness. He had had no use for customs or behavior that went against common sense, and as a child Lisa had learned to ride astride as a matter of course. When she had returned from four years of finishing school in the East, Jed had been more than a little taken aback to see that his daughter had become a young woman of beauty and considerable refinement. "I always thought a woman sitting on a sidesaddle looked foolish and out of place," he had said, unsure of what to expect from this self-assured stranger. "You do as you please in civilized diggin's, but up here you'd best ride in a sensible manner unless you're plumb set against it." He had never forgotten the bad fall his wife had taken while riding sidesaddle in Putnam's Park, and he had put it partly to blame for Eleanor's early death. His wish had suited Lisa perfectly, for she had felt very foolish and quite out of place whenever she had ridden sidesaddle in the company of her eastern relatives. Her first ride after her return to Putnam's Park had been bareback and astride, full gallop the length of the valley, just as she had ridden to greet incoming wagons when she was a child. As ranch work became part of her life once more, it confirmed her in the habit of wearing men's clothing out of doors. Skirts were a preposterous encumbrance when working with horses or cattle.

Her horse stumbled in the soft snow and she gave him his head. He leaped forward onto firmer footing, crowding Hardeman's mount and causing Hardeman to glance back. He saw how easily she sat, allowing the horse to find its own way, quickly dropping back and falling into step behind his own. She rides as well as a man, he thought.

He committed the land to memory as he rode, noting the lay of the mostly wooded slopes that rose on either side, the evergreens forcing out the aspens more and more as the creek trail climbed higher into the hills, but a part of his mind was still on the night before. "All right," Lisa had finally said. "I'll go with you to see Sun Horse. I won't promise more just now, but I'll go with you." He had expected nothing more. It would take time for her to decide where she stood on the future of the Sioux, but she would come around. Meanwhile, her presence, and Johnny's, would lend weight to what he had to tell Sun Horse.

Hardeman had stayed out of the evening's talk. There were ten of them in the kitchen once the boy Hutch and the Chinese blacksmith came in from their chores and Bat Putnam's Sioux wife joined them for supper. Ling Wo cut steaks from the deer and pan-fried them with onions, and the settlement folk kept up enough idle chatter to be polite, but none of them was the sort to press a stranger to talk when he didn't want to. Then, over a new pot of coffee and the remains of an apple pie, Bat Putnam had found a way to turn the talk to Johnny Smoker again by telling of a summer when there had been heavy traffic on the emigrant trails, and little game, and a white child had been found in an abandoned wagon by a Cheyenne hunting party.

90

"Them wagons put a fright on everything with four legs for a day's ride either side of the trail," Bat said. "White Smoke and some Cheyenne boys, they come on a handful of wagons herdin' some beef cattle, so naturally they allowed as how they'd take it kindly if those folks would give 'em a steer by way of sayin' thanks for safe passage 'cross Cheyenne lands, you might say. I weren't there, o' course, but I got this from White Smoke hisself when he brung the boy to visit, but I'm gettin' to that. The way he told it, them white folks wasn't much for palaver. Never said a word, nary one o' them. Just leveled on the Injuns and let fly, dropped one young feller in his tracks, name of Dog Runs or some such. Well sir, that set the badger loose. White Smoke and the boys, they lit into them wagons and burned a couple, even lifted a little hair. They figgered to teach them folks some manners if it killed 'em, and it did that for a couple. The rest put out for the tall grass right smart, left this youngun by his lonesome." Here Bat had looked at Johnny for the first time. "White Smoke, him and Grass Woman never did have no offspring, so he took the boy and raised him like his own."

Hardeman had wondered if Johnny knew it all—about the Cheyenne killing whites in the wagon train, maybe killing Johnny's real parents. And for the first time he had wondered what else the boy might not know, or might have kept to himself about his childhood, the way he had kept Sun Horse to himself until two weeks ago.

Bat had passed along then to the summer a few years later when White Smoke and his wife had brought Johnny to the Sioux summer encampment, and Bat had glanced frequently at Johnny, as if hoping to draw some response from the silent boy. And then to Hardeman's surprise, Johnny had begun to talk, directing himself to Bat, telling what he remembered of that summer, how the size of the Sioux camp had impressed him, the young friends he had made, and how his grandfather, Sun Horse, had taught him the sign language. Lisa Putnam had seemed fascinated and young Hutch had hung on every word. Hardeman had listened closely, but he had concealed his interest.

Why had Johnny spoken so rarely of his Indian childhood, if, as it now seemed, he remembered those years fondly and in such detail? Hardeman had never inquired overmuch about Johnny's time among the Cheyenne, which he had thought of at first as a long captivity, but later came to see was a way of life the boy had accepted quickly enough, with the adaptability of youth. Johnny scarcely ever mentioned those years, and instead of asking a lot of questions Hardeman had sought to ease the boy's way back into the white world, expecting that his Indian memories would die out in time. But last night, seeing Johnny's eyes bright as he spoke of his childhood, hearing the excitement in his quiet voice as he told of memories he had never revealed before, Hardeman had wanted to get the boy off alone, to discover why those memories had burst forth now, so full of life, and what lay behind the silence Johnny had worn all day like a cloak. But his head ached from the whiskey and he was groggy with fatigue, and when they had finally been alone in a back room with two bunks, made warm and friendly by the fire the Chinawoman had built in the little stove, he had had strength only to roll his blankets out on the bare mattress before falling into bed fully clothed and sleeping like a dead man until an hour after cockcrow.

He urged his horse forward now to overtake Johnny.

"You all right?" he asked as he drew even with the young man. Johnny had hardly spoken a word all morning.

"I'm all right." Johnny's faint smile told him nothing, but the boy spoke again. "I wish there was another way. For Sun Horse, I mean. So he wouldn't have to surrender."

Hardeman's expression was grim. "Burned-out lodges and death scaffolds on the ridgetops, that's the other way."

Johnny made no reply and he kept his thoughts to himself for the rest of the journey, although he remained close to Hardeman.

The riders passed over a divide and began to descend again, soon joining the course of a creek that flowed into a long, narrow valley, whose elevation, Hardeman judged, was probably somewhat lower than Putnam's Park. It was closer to the foothills but well protected nevertheless, walled off on the eastern side by a ridge so sharp and steep it might have been hewn by some giant's axe. The nearer end of the valley was hidden behind a wooded rise; at the far end Hardeman could make out a small lake, frozen and snow-covered. The air was calm here, and warm, as if the valley gathered the sun, and he smelled the scent of the pines on the hillsides.

He wished he and Johnny were alone, riding into the mountains for a day of hunting before moving on to try their luck in the next town or the next territory.

As the small band reached the flat, where the creek curved around the end of the wooded rise and reached the valley floor, Hardeman heard a horse neigh in the distance. He turned his head to locate the sound, seeing at the same time the faint white plumes of smoke rising into the endless blue sky. The Sioux village lay beyond the next grove of trees and still the riders had not been seen. After today, the scouts would guard the approaches better. He cast his mind over the rugged trail from Putnam's Park. Cavalry could follow it easily, but a handful of warriors could hold it against a regiment, and even without opposition it would be hard going for infantry and impossible for wagons. He hoped there was another approach to the Indian camp.

He had left both his rifles in Putnam's Park and now he patted his pistol where it rested in his waistband. Being without the rifles made him uncomfortable; he didn't like leaving his belongings here and there; what he owned he carried with him, ready to move on at any time, but today it was more important to show his peaceful intentions. His slicker was tied behind his saddle and his buckskin jacket hung open in the warmth of the day; he buttoned it now to cover the revolver. He had brought the Colt more out of habit than from any expectation that he might need it. Even if danger threatened, it didn't do to pull a gun in the red man's camp. Grattan had learned that the hard way back in '54. Hardeman had seen the graves.

92

"We best go first," Bat said as he and Hears Twice moved past Hardeman and Johnny. Bat had noticed how Hardeman caught the sound of the horses before he himself had been able to make it out over the noise of the stream, gushing now in the warm sun. Gettin' deef, he thought. At least I ain't goin' blind. He still had the eyes of a young man, for the long distances.

He glanced at Johnny as he passed by and received a small smile in return. Although the youth had been lively for a time the night before, he was silent today. Bat had a hard time reconciling this thoughtful young man with the cheerful boy he remembered from twelve years before. But that was before the Washita. The White Boy of the Cheyenne the Lakota had called him then, before they saw the way the power moved with him; before he was called Empty Hand and He Stands Between the Worlds.

The riders were in the woods now. There were children playing near the creek and they spied the horsemen first. Two of the older boys ran forth to greet Bat, whom they called by his Lakota name, Lodgepole, as Johnny Smoker had done the day before. Through the trees, Bat could see the village, set back from the creek on a flat expanse of higher ground, away from the cold river air. The twenty-four tipis were pitched in the old way of the Lakota, forming a circle with an opening to the east, whence came the first light of day.

Bat leaned down and sent one of the boys to find old Dust, the camp crier, who in turn would tell Sun Horse that visitors came to see him. Nothing more, for there was no way to prepare him for the news these visitors carried, or the sight of Johnny Smoker.

Bat looked at the camp circle as he drew nearer, noticing how the clear day and bright sunshine made even the patched skins of the poorest lodges appear fresher. Many of the people were about, men sitting on robes in front of their lodges, smoking, and children playing in the sun. Here and there a woman scraped at an animal skin stretched tight on a frame of sticks, but he saw nothing larger than a badger and no meat on the drying racks. In summer the long poles on their forked uprights were laden with strips of buffalo meat drying quickly in the sun over smoky fires that kept the flies away. There were feasts after a successful hunt, but the Sun Band had not feasted since autumn. The hunting had been bad all winter and was no better now, with spring on the way. The dogs that came trotting to investigate the newcomers were thin, their noses constantly searching the ground for some scrap that might have been overlooked. Even the ponies moved listlessly within the herd, which had been twice as large twenty years before. The Sun Band was in no condition to fight horse soldiers.

Near the stream an old man sat cross-legged on a rock, facing the sun, which was now at its peak. His eyes were closed and he sang in a thin voice:

> Le anpetu kin washtéyelo
> le anpetu kin washtéyelo
> le anpetu kin washtéyelo
> le anpetu kin washtéyelo

This day is good. This day is good. This day is good. Over and over he sang, the simple melody repeating after the fourth time. Bat breathed deeply. The air was cool and absolutely clean and yet it still carried all the smells of the evergreens and the creek and the village so close at hand. He could smell the horse herd beyond the camp, and the smoke of the lodge fires, and a mixture of new and old hides from the lodges. It was a good day, that was true, but he was nagged by a worry deep within him, a fear that before long he would have to leave the people with whom he had lived since the dying days of the fur trade.

Bat had not greeted the decline of the trade with the same quiet acceptance displayed by his brother Jed. That a change in the preferred style of gentlemen's hats could bring to a halt the way of life most perfectly suited to the exercise of a man's free spirit had seemed to Bat an obscenity. How could a London toff prefer a hat made by a worm to one made from as wily and clever an animal as a beaver? It went against common sense. But then common sense was in short supply wherever white men lived in large numbers. There was nothing like the daily threat of starvation or a sudden and violent end to make a man call forth his full measure of common sense; that was the life Bat had found in the mountains and that was the way he intended to live for the rest of his days. He had never considered any alternative for long. When he finally admitted to himself that beaver would not rise again, he too had left the heart of the beaver kingdom, turning his horse eastward toward the Black Hills. It had not escaped his notice that among the horseback Indians the individual and his right of free choice were as inviolate as among the trappers; a man lived as he wished and followed the leaders he chose. If Bat was to be denied the company of his brother mountain men, most of whom had already trickled out of the mountains to east and west, following the watercourses that they themselves had trapped bare, then he would live with the Indians.

Why he chose the Sioux he had never answered to his own satisfaction. During his trapping years he had had more intercourse with the Shoshoni and the Bannock, but something drew him east across the Divide to the most numerous people of all, who were then still moving gradually westward and adapting themselves to the higher elevations, where they acquired a fondness for wooded slopes and snowy peaks and the buttes where the eagles nested. Perhaps he chose them because they, like the white men, were a people on the move, or because their women were often tall and slender, or because, like the trappers, they were unrelenting foes of the Blackfeet.

At first he had only meant to visit some friends, a small band of Lakota who had come to the Rendezvous on the Popo Agie in '38. He had found them near Bear Butte, a handful of tipis following the aging warrior Branched Horn. Branched Horn's son Stands Alone, later named Sun Horse, was a few years older than Bat; the two had fallen in together at the Rendezvous and now they renewed their friendship. Bat was invited to travel with the band as a guest and he accepted. He observed the Lakota customs, he was a good hunter, he fought the Crows and Blackfeet; he proved himself in the eyes of the people. The visit grew long, covering the passing of the moons, and then a second snow. Stands Alone had a daughter called Otter Skin, and although she was not tall and slender like some of the other women, she found her way into the heart of the gaunt white man her brother Standing Eagle called Lodgepole.

Bat knew what was expected. One day he left camp alone and was seen by no one for ten days. When he returned he had six horses with him, slipped from a Crow pony herd in the cold quiet before dawn. He offered the horses to Stands Alone, and they were accepted.

And then something had happened that made Bat feel at once a fool and a very fortunate man. Like the other trappers, he had always accepted the simple notion that among the Indians a man bought a wife the way he might buy a sack of flour in the settlements. But as Otter Skin was putting up their lodge, the lodgeskins a gift from Branched Horn's wife and the lodgepoles a gift from Stands Alone, Bat saw the horses he had paid to Stands Alone given away to the poor members of the band in Bat's name. From Otter Skin's relatives and other members of the band came more gifts then, backrests and robes and horn bowls and spoons, and porcupine quills and beads and dyes, which Otter Skin would use to decorate shirts and leggings and robes for her husband. And Bat saw that the six horses had started a flow of giving that before long had touched nearly every member of the band either as giver or receiver, and that the "price" he had paid for his wife had been returned to him many times over. As the years went by he observed among the Lakota a continuity of giving that sustained the whole band in times of plenty as well as times of need, and he saw across the gulf that separated these tribal people from the white man; he came to realize that perhaps this life he had chosen was not a poor cousin to his days as a free trapper, that it might contain all the freedom of the mountain men and something more as well, a brotherhood even the mountain men had never known.

As the years became decades he had never found cause to regret his choice, or any cause, until recently, to suspect that he would not live out his days among the Lakota and in the end be wrapped in robes and hoisted on a burial scaffold on some windswept mountainside, there to be taken back to the earth and the elements like any other member of the tribe. But as the hostilities between the plains people and the advancing white men steadily increased, Bat had finally confronted the fact that a time might come when he would have to fight his own kind or return to live among them. As the tribes of the central plains and then even some bands of Sioux were forced onto reservations, Bat heard tales of life in those places and he went to see for himself. He saw the bleakness and broken spirits there, and he resolved that Penelope should never know such a life. When the day of judgment came for the Sioux, he would take her to the settlements, and there, among the people of her husband's race, she would live out her days.

Some trappers had left their Indian wives behind with no more regret than they felt at leaving a pair of worn-out moccasins, but Bat had never considered such a course for a moment. In his marriage robes he had found a comfort and a sharing as profound as that between Jed and Eleanor, if altogether different in substance, and Penelope had proved herself as faithful and true as a woman of any other race or time, even when others whispered that her husband had abandoned her. In the winter of '48, Joe Meek had passed through the mountains. He and his Shoshoni wife, Virginia, lived in the Oregon country then, and Joe was on his way to beg help for the Oregon settlers from the government in Washington City, following the massacre of some white missionaries by the Cayuse Indians. He asked his old companion Bat Putnam to accompany him on the journey, and Bat agreed. He was gone for ten long months. "Your husband will never return," the other women told Otter Skin. "He is a whiteman, and by now he has married a whitewoman." But Otter Skin made no reply to such accusations. She went about her daily tasks, caring for the children, two boys and a girl, and often she sat in front of the lodge, beading a pair of leggings she would give her husband on his return. Young men stopped to speak with her, but she turned them away. When summer died and the snow fell again, her father told her in private that she might consider herself a free woman simply by putting her husband's things outside the lodge. "If he has not returned when the leggings are finished, I will do so," Otter Skin said. But the beadwork grew more and more elaborate until it covered nearly every inch of the leggings, and only when her husband sat in his place at the back of the lodge once more did she declare them finished. It was then that Bat had christened her Penelope, for she had proved herself as constant as Penelope of old.

Bat's daughter had died of an illness before reaching womanhood, and his sons had married girls from other bands. One had been killed by Blackfeet and the other lived with Sitting Bull's Hunkpapas. But he still had Penelope, alone now in their lodge back in Putnam's Park. She had never lived away from the circle of her people before and he wondered if he had done wrong by staying all winter in the settlement. You're a fool, he told himself. When your folks need you, you go. Lisa had needed him, but now her need was ending, and Bat suddenly wished he had thought to pack up the lodge and bring Penelope along with him today. They should return to the Sun Band, to their own people, for whatever time remained.

At the entrance to the circle of lodges—the "horns" of the camp—the riders were greeted by Dust, the crier. He was a spare, wiry man of more than seventy winters, and it was one of his functions to conduct visitors to the headman of the band. He led off to the left, moving around the circle in the formal manner, and a few passers-by stopped to watch. Riders entering in the ceremonial manner meant important visitors or important news, or both. From around the camp many eyes followed the riders' progress.

Halfway around the circle, opposite the opening, Dust halted in front of a tipi whose lodgeskins were bare of any ornamentation save for a single yellow disk, no larger than a man's head, painted near the entrance flap; overlapping the disk, as if riding out of the circle, was the figure of a horse, blue-black with white markings. The other lodges were decorated, some extensively, with symbols depicting the deeds of the owners, and in some cases showing their special relationship with the spirit powers. A lodge's position in the circle bespoke the honor a man had earned, public trust bestowed by the band and its leaders, membership in warrior societies, and more, but the place of greatest honor was occupied by this simple lodge with its lone emblem.

A tall man peered out of a nearby lodge, then stepped out and approached, and Bat hid his displeasure as he climbed down from his saddle. He had hoped it would be possible to meet first with Sun Horse before Standing Eagle made an appearance, but his brother-in-law was war leader and had a right to be there. "How're ye feelin', Eagle?" he said.

"This child's plumb froze fer 'baccy. You bring some?"

"Nope. Plumb forgot."

"Poor doin's."

Bat's annoyance was banished by the surprise he saw on Hardeman's face. He had forgotten the astonishment that could be occasioned in white men by Standing Eagle's notion of what passed for the American language. The Lakota had learned the tongue from the Putnam brothers, and it stood to reason that they had made sure he would speak it like a true man, not some medicine-show Indian or Bible-thumping preacher. He grinned at his brother-in-law. "By God, Eagle, you look like something the dog dragged in. You feelin' poorly, are you?"

Standing Eagle's eyes were red-rimmed and swollen. Probably he had been hunting in recent days and had kept to the dark of his lodge today to recover from a touch of snowblindness.

"Been sleepin'," said the Indian. "Ain't got much to eat, cain't raise no sign. This coon figgers to catch some rest while he can." He gathered his blanket more tightly about him and drew himself up, trying unsuccessfully to make up for the hair that was not combed and the tattered moccasins on his feet, a pair he no longer wore anywhere except in his lodge.

"You're a wuthless dunghead, and that's truth!" Bat exclaimed. "Never could make a raise with a fat cow breathin' down yer neck. " He jerked his thumb at Hardeman and Johnny Smoker. "These boys made meat down below the part yestiddy. A nigger's willin' to shake his bones, 'stead o' lyin' all day abed, he'll make 'em come."

"Wagh!" Standing Eagle coughed, and fell silent. Among the Lakota the relationship between brothers-in-law was unrestrained, permitting practical jokes and teasing without any loss of dignity, but Standing Eagle was the one member of the band who had never fully accepted the white man who had married his sister, and he suffered Bat's insults grudgingly at best.

All the riders had dismounted, and still there was no sign of life from the headman's lodge. Within the camp circle the coming and going that had taken place since the horsemen entered—men and women passing close for a look at the strangers—became now a general gathering as the people came to see their leader greet the whites. From here and there about the camp, groups of men and women approached, led by the older men, the band's councillors. One young boy entered the camp circle at a run and darted among the grown-ups, arriving breathless at Standing Eagle's side.

"Hello, Uncle," he greeted Bat in Lakota. He was Blackbird, Standing Eagle's son, a lad of sixteen or thereabouts; the Lakota placed little importance on birthdays, reckoning a man's age instead by how many winters he had lived through. Blackbird was in his sixteenth winter. Like the rest of the Sun Band, he knew Lisa Putnam by sight. He received a few signs of greeting from Hears Twice, but most of his attention was on Hardeman and Johnny Smoker.

Standing Eagle had glanced at both of the strangers in turn and his eyes had moved on without recognition. Bat smiled inwardly and thought to say something that would whet the war leader's curiosity without giving away the secret, but he held his tongue when he saw the entrance flap of Sun Horse's lodge pulled aside from within.

The first to emerge were the headman's wives, Elk Calf Woman, white-haired, as old as Sun Horse himself, and Sings His Daughter, young and comely, a Crow captive who had been adopted into the band. Bat winked at Sings His Daughter and she repressed a soft giggle. The two women turned, and when Sun Horse appeared, they took him by the arms and assisted him as he stepped through the low entryway. They released him then and moved to one side, joining the other women as the councillors gathered around Sun Horse.

Hardeman needed no one to tell him that this was the headman. He took in the worn buffalo robe held loosely about the almost frail body, the unadorned gray hair combed straight and long, and he felt the man's power.

What was it about some men that commanded such attention? It was in the eyes, he thought. Among white men they reflected the assurance of being obeyed, the knowledge that a man's position guaranteed authority. He had seen more than enough of that look among whites. But some men revealed something more. William Tecumseh Sherman, for a fact, and Ulysses Grant in a different way. And then there were Black Kettle and Roman Nose and Tall Bull of the Cheyenne who came to mind; Satanta of the Kiowa and Ten Bears of the Comanche, and the great Sioux chief Conquering Bear, who had still been alive when Hardeman made his first trip west on the Oregon Trail. Conquering Bear was gone now, and all three of the Cheyenne. Great men led lives of constant danger. And now here was the same look in the eyes of Sun Horse. It was something far removed from the smug self-assurance of high position. It was the look of a man who carried a burden but saw no way to set it down. Perhaps it was no more than doubt, and a willingness to lead on despite the uncertainties that life heaped on all who held the fate of others in their hands.

Hardeman met Sun Horse's gaze and was careful to reveal nothing. The Indians admired self-control above all other qualities. Sun Horse stepped forward now and it seemed to Hardeman that even his shambling gait displayed a contained self-confidence. In Fort Laramie or D. A. Russell, wrapped in his moth-eaten robe, he would have been indistinguishable from any of the old Indians who lived near the forts, giving in to whiskey and despair, but Hardeman had learned long ago to be wary of judging any man by the finery he might or might not have about his person. Even among the proud Sioux, whose great warriors sported eagle-feather bonnets and finely beaded clothing and who judged a man by the size of his horse herd and his lodge, there were men who shunned these things and yet stood above all others in honor and respect. It was said that Crazy Horse, the young warrior whose name struck such fear into the miners in the Black Hills, went into battle with no paint and no feathers and was always retiring among his people.

Hardeman knew how the reception would go: first welcome the visitors into camp, feed them and smoke with them, then listen to what they have to say; always the formalities were observed. If a man brought news of the end of the world in fire and destruction, it would be the same. A white man would just state his business the minute he got within speaking distance, but an Indian didn't work that way.

"*Hau, tunkanshi.*" Bat addressed Sun Horse formally, as the occasion demanded. Greetings, father-in-law.

Sun Horse replied with equal formality and shook Bat's hand. He turned then to Lisa. "Lisaputnam." He said it as one word, holding out his hands and clasping both of hers, smiling broadly. He had seen her only once since her father died.

"I am glad to see my uncle looking so well," Lisa said in fluent Lakota. There was no blood relationship between them, but among the Lakota, relationship was not defined by blood alone, and Jed Putnam had been like a brother to Sun Horse. The word Lisa used was *até*, which meant "father," but was applied to paternal uncles as well. She swallowed against a lump in her throat and was glad she had come. How can I help him? she wondered. Let me find a way.

"You savvy Lakota?" Bat asked Hardeman, and Hardeman shook his head. He did not have the gift of foreign tongues the way Johnny did, and Lisa Putnam too, it seemed.

"This white man is called Christopher Hardeman," Bat said in English. "He brings a message from the soldier chief Crook, the man we call Three Stars."

Standing Eagle had moved close to his father; he talked softly in Sun Horse's ear even as Bat spoke. The translation was a smooth process, perfected by years of practice. It neither slowed nor interrupted Bat's speech. At the mention of Crook's name, Standing Eagle frowned, but he finished what Bat had said, adding nothing. At the same time, Hears Twice had put the few English words into signs, and so even as Bat fell silent, all those present knew what had been said. A murmur of concern moved around the circle.

Bat switched to Lakota then, and he spoke to Sun Horse for a minute or two, gesturing once at Hardeman. When he was done he turned to the scout. "I told him you rode with Jed back in '51. Said you missed meetin' me and Sun Horse both, down at Laramie. We come down for the treaty council, but you and Jed was already gone on to Californy. Sun Horse, him and Jed got along. Knowin' you was Jed's friend puts you up a step or two in his eyes."

Sun Horse spoke to Hardeman, regarding the white man with new interest, and when he was done, Bat conveyed his message. "He says you're welcome. 'A friend of the Truthful Whiteman'—that's what they called Jed—'A friend of the Truthful Whiteman is welcome in this village' was the way he put it. He says he hopes you'll be a friend to the Sun Band, like Jed was. He invites us to eat in his lodge before the council meets to hear the message. He says the huntin' ain't been good, but what the Sun Band has, it will always share with its guests."

Hardeman saw the councillors nod their approval and guessed that he had been honored by the warmth of the headman's greeting.

"Tell him I thank him for his welcome," he said to Bat. "And tell him I hope we will be friends. Tell him Johnny and I come with a message of peace for the Sun Band."

Standing Eagle translated Hardeman's words for his father as the white man spoke, and as Bat gave the scout's response formally in Lakota for the benefit of the others, Sun Horse turned to the young man standing beside Hardeman.

Bat gestured to Johnny as he concluded, and for Hardeman's benefit he added, "I told him the boy's got a special reason for comin', sump'n besides the message."

Sun Horse waited for some further explanation, but none was offered. He looked at Lisaputnam. She glanced at the young man, then back at Sun Horse, and she smiled. The man called Hardeman was watching the youth too, as a father might watch a son. Sun Horse wished to know more about this bearded whiteman who seemed so sure of himself. He noted the man's eyes, set so deep beneath the brows. They were farseeing eyes, the eyes of a scout; this was a man with the vision to lead his people. There was something odd in his expression now, as if he expected something to happen. The young whiteman was looking at Sun Horse, and he too seemed to be waiting—

The sounds of the village grew suddenly faint around Sun Horse as all his attention was brought to bear on the young man. He saw something in the youth's eyes that awakened an image long in disuse, a memory placed carefully in that deep recess of the mind where he stored remembrances of beloved ones who had gone on to the spirit world. He felt a chill despite the warm sunshine, and the fear of death, and the heightened awareness of life that he always felt when the unseen forces of spirit power moved near him.

100

The young man touched his breast and made a few signs. *My heart is glad to see you, Grandfather.*

"Hunhé!" Sun Horse's astonishment escaped him against his will as the young man's signs asked him to believe the impossible. Many called him Grandfather, children of his children and countless more, for it was a term of respect used by children and adults alike, but no whites called him that. There had been one once, a boy now dead...

How is it that a whiteman calls me Grandfather? He made the signs too rapidly for any but an experienced sign talker to follow.

Just as quickly the answer came: *It is true I am a whiteman, but I was raised a son of the Cheyenne.* The hands paused, and then they added, *My father was White Smoke.*

Tears sprang to Sun Horse's eyes. As much as the message they conveyed, the hands themselves had confirmed the identity of the young man who stood before him, as they danced in the air with a life of their own. None spoke the language of the hands with that special grace Sun Horse remembered so well, none but the white grandson he himself had instructed in the sign talk one summer long ago.

From the crowd there were murmurs of surprise, and the older ones explained to those who had joined the band in recent years, and others too young to remember, about the baby White Smoke had adopted, and the belief that the boy had perished with his father at the Washita.

Have you come from the spirit world? Sun Horse asked half seriously and half in jest. He felt light-headed and foolish.

Smiling, Johnny shook his head. *I am a man of flesh and blood, as you are, Grandfather. I did not die at the Washita.*

Wordlessly, the old man stepped forward and placed his hands on Johnny's shoulders, content for the moment not to wonder how this thing came to be, simply glad that it was. After a time he brushed a tear from his cheek and smiled. He made more questioning signs, and gestured in Hardeman's direction. Johnny replied with the sign for *friends* and followed with more, telling only that he and Chris had traveled together since the Washita, where Chris had saved his life.

Sun Horse nodded, satisfied to learn the heart of the youth's story now. Later there would be time to hear it all. He turned to Standing Eagle and spoke a few words.

"Sun Horse asks Standing Eagle how come he don't say howdy to his nephew," Bat translated for Hardeman.

Standing Eagle did not hide the hostility in his voice when he replied.

"He says, 'Your grandson comes to us dressed like a whiteman, bringing word from a white soldier chief. I will hear the message before I welcome him.'" This time Bat translated while Standing Eagle was talking, and Hardeman noticed that the mountain mannerisms disappeared from Bat's speech as he gave the running translation with practiced ease. "Standing Eagle's Sun Horse's boy," Bat added, loud enough for his brother-in-law to overhear. "He's war leader of the band. Not much of a one for polite chitchat."

Standing Eagle's words had caused Sun Horse to grow more serious. Would the gift of his grandson's return be taken from him even before he could fully grasp it? Still, the question must be asked. When he spoke now, it was in Cheyenne.

"Have you come, then, only to carry a message?"

Johnny replied in the same language, his use of it uncertain after seven years, but he looked Sun Horse in the eye and his words brought joy to the old man's heart. "I have come to see my grandfather, as he told me I should in the year of my dream."

CHAPTER
SEVEN

"My brother Jed spoke of you a time or two," Bat said as Hears Twice's daughter Mist passed more of the steaming soup to Hardeman, who sat across the fire next to Lisa. "You the one picked up a gimpy-leg Dutchman on foot in the Humboldt, ain't you? Summer of '52?"

Hardeman nodded. "We called him Dutch John."

They were in the lodge of Little Hand, Hears Twice's son-in-law, and the sun had fallen halfway to the snowbound ridges since the short council session had ended. The band's advisers had met just long enough to hear Hardeman's news and Crook's message before returning to their own lodges to talk over what they had heard. That evening they would meet again to decide what to do. Hears Twice had invited the whites to eat in his daughter's lodge, but Johnny Smoker had remained with Sun Horse at the old man's request, and since then there had been no word from the headman's tipi.

Little Hand was a short man with a pinched face who sat in the back of the lodge beside Hears Twice. He had not spoken to the whites since his initial greeting, which was so curt it had bordered on being impolite. Hears Twice's three grandchildren, two girls and a boy, had sat wide-eyed for a time, staring at the visitors, but they had quickly grown used to the presence of the whites and they had been sent outside when they grew restless. They returned from time to time to peer into the entrance and giggle, covering their mouths with their hands.

"We called him Good Leg John in the mountains," Bat said. "Was a Gros Ventre arrow pulled him up lame and I'm the fella cut it out of him. Son of a bitch never had a grain of sense in his whole family. He stayed in the mountains long after the trade give out, huntin' beaver. And I'll give it to him, he could raise beaver from a dry crick, but he never got more'n powder money for the plews. Finally give it up. Lit out in the dead o' winter. Said he had a mind to see Californy 'fore he went under. I told him that mule of his had died long since and just didn't have the natural sense to lay down and quit, but he slung aboard and that's the last I seen of him. Glad the coon made it even if the mule didn't." The story came easily to him and required little effort in the telling, but he took no pleasure in it. He had spent half the afternoon trying to loosen Hardeman's tongue with gab, to no avail. Get a man talking and sooner or later he'd show how his stick floated, but it would take a stout pole and a good place to pry to get ten words in a row out of Hardeman today. He was drawn up tighter than a Mormon's purse strings, holding himself way off somewhere out of reach, and Bat gave up the effort now, falling into a moody silence, nagged by the persistent feeling that the scout was holding out on him.

Bat had searched his memory long and hard to find the "time or two" Jed had spoken of a young lad he took on as apprentice scout in the summer of 1851. He had found the right tale, and the handful of words Jed had applied to Chris Hardeman, but they bore a significance beyond their number. "I liked the cut of the boy's jib," Jed had told it. "He'd come from Philadelphia—city boy like us—made it clear to Missouri by his lonesome. Threw him on a paint horse that could smell Injun from a mile off and knew solid bottom from quicksand in the middle of the nighttime, dark of the moon. The boy learned quick, 'n' he was as good as his word."

He was as good as his word. If Jed said it, it was true, but Bat still couldn't shake a suspicion that Hardeman was holding something back. Like Stone Bull, he thought, remembering the scalp that had fluttered from his rifle until it had grown so ratty that it offended him and he had thrown it away. He and a few companions had come on Stone Bull up on the brakes of the Gros Ventre; the Crow warrior had been alone, standing over a fresh-killed moose, and my, wasn't he friendly. "Seddown," he says, "heap plenty meat." Crows were always friendly when they were outnumbered. He had fallen all over himself to welcome the little party of trappers into his camp and see that they got fed. But he was forthright, and had a sense of humor that tickled Bat's funny bone, and Bat had found himself liking a man that all experience taught him to regard as his enemy. Sure enough, when a dozen other Crows showed up the next day, Stone Bull and his friends had tried to lift the trappers' hair. "He'd tried it 'fore breakfast, he might be carryin' my topknot today," Bat had later told the story. "But me'n Old Webb, we slept sound and et the rest of that moose for breakfast, and we was up to Crow that day." At this point in the tale he would bring out Stone Bull's scalp to show how the fight had ended. Old Stone Bull, he was a good enough sort, but he held out. He knew them other boys was comin' along and he kept shut. What was Hardeman holding out? Bat had taken a liking to the man, but he wouldn't let that put him off his guard.

Hardeman knew a thing or two about dealing with Indians, that much was plain from the way he had spoken to Sun Horse and the other councillors. He had relayed Crook's message simply and directly, adding his own promise to see that the Sun Band was given all that Crook had agreed to, which was a smart move on his part. The councillors naturally put more faith in the word of a man who sat with them and smoked the pipe than in some soldier chief they had never seen. Hardeman had handled the long-stemmed ceremonial pipe well too, one hand cradling the dark red pipestone bowl while the other grasped the stem as he offered it to the four cardinal points and the sky and the earth. He handled it with respect, and the councillors had noticed. And Bat had been interested to see how calmly he had filled his belly, first in Sun Horse's lodge before the council and now here. It was poor doin's to serve dog to white folks, Bat thought, but Hardeman pitched in like dog soup was about the slickest doin's he could imagine. He knew a thing or two about Indians, all right.

Bat was proud that Lisa had been included in the brief council out of respect for her father and because she was now in charge of the settlement in Putnam's Park. She had sat quietly, saying nothing, and had borne the initial surprise that a woman should be asked to sit in council without showing it. She too had eaten well. Jed had taught her to be grateful for what there was and not to be bound by conventions that stood in the way of getting fed. She'd had dog soup before.

Little Hand belched loudly and set his wooden bowl aside facedown to show that he wanted no more. He turned to Bat and asked in Lakota what he knew of Hardeman, referring to him only as the *washíchun* scout. *Washíchun* was the Lakota term for white man, but it was also the name given to the ceremonial bundle a Lakota wore about his neck, which often contained some small symbol of a man's spirit power. The word meant something that bore spirit power within itself, and at first the Lakota had applied it only to the *shiná sapa*, the black-robe missionaries who were among the first white men they had seen, the ones who spoke of *God* and wanted to hear nothing from the Lakota holy men in return. Before long, all white men came to be called *washíchun*, and the name conveyed, to those who understood its true meaning, a sense of the strange and unpredictable power within the whites. Little Hand spoke the word as if it made a bad taste in his mouth.

Bat told Little Hand what he knew about Hardeman, and how the scout had cared for Johnny since the Washita battle. Little Hand asked more questions then, and when Bat had answered as best he could, Little Hand gave a noncommittal grunt, looked almost contemptuously at Hardeman, rose, and left the lodge.

"Wanted to know all about how Johnny came to stay with a white scout after the Washita fight," Bat told Hardeman. "I said you was like the boy's *hunká-father*. There's no word for it in English, nothing just like it in a white man's life. Means 'relative-by-choice' in Lakota. A *hunká*-father takes over some of the work of a real father in raisin' a boy; teaches him things, tells him stories of the people. But it's a heap more—it keeps the boy from stayin' too long in his mother's tipi, gets him out into the world, teaches him to trust another man like a father, helps him to see he's gotta choose his own way, 'stead o' just followin' in his pa's footsteps. You might say when a boy's with his *hunká*-father he's halfway to bein' on his own. Seems to me that's pretty near what you done for Johnny, ain't it?"

"You could say that," Hardeman replied after a moment, surprised to learn that the Sioux had a word for a relationship he had thought unique. "Little Hand didn't seem any too pleased with the idea."

"Oh, he don't reckon whites know about *hunká*-relatives and such, but don't mind him. He don't unbend much any time when it comes to white folks. Him and Standing Eagle, they're the ones who'll speak for war." He hadn't meant to say it, but it had been on his mind. He wasn't used to watching his words here in camp. The steady stream of talk he had kept up since the council ended had relaxed him after a silent morning in the saddle. It didn't do to talk when it wasn't necessary on the trail. You travel in silence, you'll see your enemy before he sees you, if you're lucky. Years of habit had taught Bat to curb his naturally loquacious tongue beyond the camp circle, but now he would have to watch what he said even here, and remember that neither Hardeman's ears nor Johnny Smoker's were sure to be friendly. In the council the youth had spoken in support of Hardeman, a little reluctantly, perhaps, but he said he could see no way for the Sun Band to survive but by surrender, and that put him across the fence from Bat Putnam, who didn't want to see the free life of the Lakota come to an end.

"Tell me, Mr. Hardeman," Lisa said suddenly, "when you and Johnny were in Texas you must have seen a good deal of the new methods for raising beef."

"Some," Hardeman replied, trying to imagine how Lisa Putnam knew that he and Johnny had been in Texas, until he remembered that Johnny had told her last night, there in the kitchen, when he learned that Julius Ingram had spent time on the cattle trails.

"Are many of the stockmen there experimenting with the new breeds?" Lisa wanted to take Hardeman's mind off what Bat had said, and the chance that the Sun Band would decide to fight rather than surrender.

"Some," Hardeman said again. "There's a lot of them think that the Longhorn is God's gift to the cattleman and shouldn't be tampered with. But there are others who look up to Kansas and see rails moving south. First they were in Abilene, now they're in Dodge and Wichita. Some say before long they'll build across the Indian Territory into Texas, and then there will be no need for a beef as tough as the Longhorn just to get to market."

Lisa nodded. "We used to take our cattle to Cheyenne, but since they built the stockyards at Rawlins, we only have to drive them a hundred miles. My father said a dairy cow could walk a hundred miles."

The talk of beef raising held little interest for Bat and he let his attention wander. The sun filtering through the hides of the tipi cover suffused the interior with a warm and gentle light. The fire in the central pit was small, scarcely needed on the sunny afternoon. He leaned against his backrest and stretched his feet out to the fire, glad of a chance to unbend his legs. The rheumatism was paining him today, a result of years spent setting traps in ice-cold streams, but he suffered the discomfort without resentment; it was a small misery and far less than he was

105

willing to pay for the joy the trapping years had given him.

Outside, the camp was quiet, but it was not a peaceful calm. The news brought by the two *washíchun* had traveled quickly and was now being discussed intently in the tipis of the warrior fraternities. Tonight, when the council met again, the lines would be drawn; they would turn to Bat, the white brother they called Lodgepole, both those who favored surrender and those like Little Hand who wanted to fight the soldiers. What will the whites do if we fight? What will the whites do if we surrender? What does Lodgepole advise?

How could he answer? Could he tell them that before he would take Penelope to live on a reservation he would leave them and go back to his own kind?

Hears Twice began slowly to stoke a pipe. The reddish bowl shone from years of handling and found its way in the old man's palms as if alive. When the pipe was lit and going, Hears Twice handed it to Bat and made signs that said *It is good to smoke with friends*. He always did that, making signs or on rare occasions speaking the words, as if it were part of his medicine to smoke with friends and let them know he thought it was a good thing. Bat nodded, the way he always did, and inhaled deeply, letting the smoke burn his lungs and make him giddy before he blew out slowly, savoring again the tang of the willow bark that was mixed with the shredded trade tobacco. He wondered where among the whites he would ever find for Penelope the hospitality and welcome to match those he had received for thirty years among the Lakota.

Bat didn't like changes, especially those that forced him to give up something he cherished. Where had Jed got the ability to move on from one thing to another over the years with his spirits always high?

The talk of cattle and different breeds and how fast they grew had come to an end and neither Hardeman nor Lisa had found anything new to talk about. Bat turned to Lisa now as if what he had to say were no more than part of an ongoing conversation. "He was smiling at the end? You sure of that?"

"What? I'm sorry, I was thinking."

"I asked about Jed, there at the end. You said he was smiling."

Lisa nodded. "He was smiling, Uncle Bat. There was no pain at the end."

But pain wasn't what worried Bat. He saw something else in that ghost of a smile. The thing had haunted him all through the winter months like some puzzle from his childhood—seemingly simple, but the solution so hard to find. The thought of that dying grin on his brother's face gave him pause. How could a man who had taken such joy in life smile at the loss of it? Right through the fur trade and the road ranching and on into his first efforts at raising cattle, Jed had found an unending kind of glory-be wonder in the simplest things, a wonder that had stayed with him right to the end. That final smile went against nature! Jed should have been battling the shadow of Death with the last breath in his body. But Bat knew that nothing truly went against nature, and all winter he had been trying to shake the suspicion that Jed had learned some secret about life that he himself didn't know, something he would do well to learn before he approached his own end of the trail. He would like to know it now. He had no heart for the life he and Penelope would lead once they left the camp circle of the Sun Band. If only he could divine Jed's secret, it might help him to make the transition with a better will.

He realized that the pipe lay dead in his hand and he passed it back to Hears Twice, who scraped the ashes carefully into the fire and refilled the bowl, lighting it before passing it to Hardeman. It was a social smoke, not ceremonial, all part of an informal ritual that helped to pass the better part of winter in the Lakota lodges, as long as the smoking mixture lasted. It was an accompaniment to the winter tales and the visiting from lodge to lodge, a way to break a silence or prolong it, depending on the moment. Silences were comforting among a people who felt no need to speak when they had nothing to say.

Bat tried to quiet his own thoughts, but the silence here was tense with waiting and he himself broke it again.

"You want to get home by dark, you might think about startin' out pretty soon, Lisa honey," he said. "I'll stay the night, what with the council and all."

"There's a bit of a moon tonight," she said. "We can find our way in the dark if we have to." She hoped for a chance to speak to Sun Horse alone before leaving the Lakota camp. She turned to Hardeman. "Mr. Hardeman?"

"Johnny hasn't seen Sun Horse in a long time. There's no need to rush him. We'll wait a while longer, if you don't mind."

The fact was, now that they were here and Crook's message delivered, Hardeman was in no hurry to leave. It had been a long time since he had sat in an ordinary Indian lodge as a guest. Taking such opportunities when they came along was a lesson Lisa's father had taught him, so many years ago. "What you see in council, that's only one side of an Injun," the mountain man had said. "Injuns got a peculiar notion about a man who leads the people. They figger he oughta be serious where the lives of the people are at stake. So in council, a man sits sober and listens close when another feller speaks his mind. He speaks his own in turn, sober and serious. And that's where a white man's likely to see his first Injun, sittin' down to palaver. So the white feller goes home and he says, 'Boy, them Injuns sure is serious folks,' and that's where the mischief gets started." The mischief Jed had in mind was the mistaken notion that formal speaking was the normal Indian manner. It had led in turn to the equally incorrect idea that all Indians were solemn and emotionless and somewhat methodical not only in their manner of speech but in their manner of thinking as well, and these errors had played their part in preventing a better understanding between the races. It was good to be reminded that the Indians were men and women not so different from white people in many ways; they had children who grew hungry when there was not enough food, and within a small band like this there were men as dissimilar as Bat Putnam and Little Hand. Hardeman trusted Bat, but he wouldn't turn his back on Little Hand. *Him and Standing Eagle, they're the ones who'll speak for war,* Bat had said, and Hardeman remembered now that Little Hand had sat next to Standing Eagle in council and seemed to side with the war leader in everything he said.

It was not necessary for a white man to offer the pipe to the sacred directions in council, but Hardeman had held the stem toward the west, north, east and south before he touched it to his lips, moving it around the horizons as the Sioux prayed and as Jed Putnam had taught him twenty-five years before, when they had sat down to parley with a scouting party of Minneconjou. The pipe swore him to tell the truth, and his display had been calculated to demonstrate to the council that he was aware of the obligation. The smoke rose to the sky, alerting the spirits to the words that followed. The councillors had watched him closely as he smoked, and Johnny had watched too, for he had never before seen Hardeman among Indians. When the pipe had completed its rounds, Hardeman had conveyed General Crook's message, saying that the government's order must be obeyed, the Sioux must go to Dakota, but because Sun Horse was a peace man, Crook would give him an escort, and beef and blankets for his people, if he would go in peacefully. But before Hardeman had finished telling all that Crook would promise, Standing Eagle had interrupted him loudly, his voice full of anger. The war leader had retired to his own lodge to dress for the council while Sun Horse fed the guests; he had reappeared with eagle feathers bound in his hair, which he had combed and braided, and he was togged out in all the finery he could muster. His shirt and leggings were finely beaded and he carried a new trade blanket, brightly striped in red and blue. He wore earrings of silver and bits of feather, and necklaces of shell and bear claws. Even among the other councillors, some of whom wore the feathered headdresses for which the Sioux were famous, with tails that touched the ground, Standing Eagle was an impressive figure.

Throughout the proceedings, Bat had translated for Hardeman, talking softly in his ear, conveying word for word what was said, but he listened to Standing Eagle's outburst in its entirety before turning to the scout. "He says he don't need no promises from a white soldier chief. He don't need no meat from the white man's spotted buffalo neither. He says he'll fight Three Stars if'n he comes near to the Sun Band."

It seemed to Hardeman that there was scorn in Bat's voice for the war leader's lack of good manners.

As soon as Standing Eagle fell silent, Sun Horse rebuked his son sharply. The headman was dressed just as he had been when the whites first arrived, in his worn robe, with no feathers or ornaments in his hair, but his voice carried an authority that sent Standing Eagle back to his seat, his face dark with embarrassment at being scolded before the council.

"He put ol' Eagle in his place, right enough," Bat murmured. "Reminded him that in council each man speaks until he's done. It's time to listen now, he says. The council's gonna meet again tonight, and then Eagle can speak his mind. Now it's time to listen."

108

Hardeman had continued then, directing himself to Sun Horse. "The Sioux can't win this war," he said. "The whites will send one army after another until you surrender. It's time for the peace men to act for peace. Say you will go in, and I'll bring Three Stars here. Sit down and talk with him and you will see that he is not like some of the other officers. He fights to make peace, not to conquer, and he keeps his promises." Here he made a sign, bringing a forefinger out from beneath his chin to show that the soldier chief's words were straight. "When the soldiers have helped your people safely to Dakota," he went on, "then perhaps Sun Horse will do his part to stop this war. Send your men to Sitting Bull and the other headmen. Tell them that Three Stars is an honest man who can be trusted; tell them to make peace while there is still time. Do this, and Three Stars will let you keep your horses, and some guns for hunting."

When Hardeman was done, Sun Horse had asked a single question. "What will Three Stars do if we will not go in?"

"Three Stars is coming here to find the Sioux. When he finds a band, he'll give them a chance to surrender. If they won't surrender, he will fight." Hardeman put it bluntly to emphasize the danger. Sun Horse had merely nodded, but he kept his eyes on Hardeman for what seemed like a long time, as if searching for something else behind the white man's words. At last he had moved his gaze to Johnny Smoker. Hardeman had felt lightheaded, as if a weight had been suddenly removed from him, and only then had he realized that Sun Horse had responded directly to his words. Standing Eagle, silenced by his father's rebuke, had ceased his translating. Sun Horse understood English. Then why did the war leader translate for the old man at all? Hardeman wondered. Probably to give him more time to consider what he had heard and prepare his reply. The old fox was too clever by half.

"I don't mean to pry, Mr. Hardeman," Lisa said now, "but I have wondered why Johnny waited so long to find Sun Horse. Even to let him know that he was alive would have saved an old man some unnecessary suffering."

Hardeman handed the pipe back to Hears Twice before answering. "The boy never wanted to come before, or I would have brought him." His tone was meant to discourage further talk on the subject, but the woman wouldn't take the hint.

"They seem to think a great deal of each other," she said. "What was it that Johnny said about coming here because of a dream?"

I have come to see my grandfather, as he told me I should in the year of my dream, Johnny had said. He had spoken in Cheyenne, but evidently old Hears Twice understood Cheyenne, for he had translated Sun Horse's question and Johnny's answer in signs for the Sioux, and Hardeman could read the sign talk better than most white men. It appeared that Lisa Putnam could read signs too. She seemed to know a good deal about Indians, and missed very little that went on around her. Well, if she wouldn't let it alone, he would tell her enough to satisfy her curiosity and silence the questions that way.

"When Johnny was with the Cheyenne, he had a dream," he said. "It wasn't a dream like white people get; more like one of those special Indian dreams. A spirit dream, he called it. It said he would return to the whites one day, and when he was about to become a man he would choose whether to live with the whites or go back to the Indians. It was the summer Johnny and his folks were visiting Sun Horse." He saw that Bat was listening now. The mountain man nodded as if he were well acquainted with that summer, and the dream. "The old man told Johnny that when he was ready to choose he should come see him. He's ready to choose. He picked the white world, so he came to tell Sun Horse."

"Powerful dream," Bat said more to himself than the others. "Come true too."

It was clear from Lisa's expression that the unexpected revelation had given her more than enough to think about for a while, but Hardeman wished the matter were as cut-and-dried as he had told it. Ever since the moment in front of Sun Horse's tipi when Johnny had told Sun Horse why he had come, the old man had taken on the air of someone whose fondest wish in life had come true. Once he heard the boy's words, he seemed to attach to Johnny's return an importance out of all proportion to what Hardeman had expected.

What more could there be to the dream, beyond what Johnny had told him all those years ago back in Utah?

Shortly after the Washita battle, Hardeman had found the boy a home with an army officer's brother, a St. Louis merchant. The man and his wife were childless, and they had taken Johnny in willingly when Hardeman delivered him there shortly before Christmas. The boy showed none of the wildness sometimes evidenced by other white boys who had lived for a time with the Indians. Those who had grown to manhood among the savages sometimes rejected their white relations completely, slipping away at the first opportunity to rejoin their wild adopted kin. But other children taken by Indians and recovered while still young had reverted to white ways without protest; Johnny's case was not so unusual.

Early in the new year, Hardeman had left St. Louis, thinking to return in a year or two and see how the boy was getting on. He took a job with the Union Pacific, hunting meat for the crews, and as the spring warmed and sent the snowmelt rushing down the rivers and streams, the rails had leaped westward like a quick-growing vine, sometimes advancing fifteen, seventeen, almost twenty miles in one day, in the final sprint to meet the tracks of the Central Pacific, which were rushing eastward across the Utah desert. And there in Utah, two weeks before the golden spike was driven at Promontory, Johnny had found him.

The boy rode up on the same Indian pony Hardeman had picked for him from the captured herd after the battle. He was dressed like a St. Louis schoolboy, with the rest of his belongings tied in a sack behind his saddle. The merchant and his wife had treated him well, he said—his English had improved greatly during the winter—but he had had enough of cities. He would stay with Hardeman, if the scout would have him. It had been so simply put, with Johnny's eyes looking straight at him, that Hardeman had been unable to refuse.

The boy had spoken of the dream for the first time there by the U. P. tracks. Once Hardeman had said that Johnny could ride with him and promised he wouldn't send him back to St. Louis, Johnny had sat the two of them down right on the track and, like a couple of men entering a business arrangement together, they had discussed the terms of their partnership. As they talked, they could feel in their rumps the hammer blows from a quarter mile up the track, where the crew was spiking down a new section of rail.

"I am going to work my own way," Johnny had proclaimed, all of thirteen, maybe, but tall for his age. "I had a talk with the crew boss here. He said I could be water boy. It ain't a job I want to do for long."

"Well, now," Hardeman had said, trying to come to grips with the new self-assured manner of this boy who only a few months before had been wearing Cheyenne clothes and paint, "it's not a job that'll last too long. Rails figure to join up in a few weeks, and that's that."

"What do you reckon to do next?" Johnny had asked, all serious.

"Why, I'm not exactly sure. I never saw Sante Fe and that country down there. I had a thought I might head that way. Maybe drive some freight. Seems like it might be a way to see the Sante Fe Trail."

"That suits me," Johnny had said, and surprised Hardeman by adding, "I can do most anything with horses or mules. I can learn to drive a team quick enough."

"All right then, we'll try her," Hardeman had said. "As a matter of fact, I'll tell you what. Let's say we stay on at one place or one kind of work just as long as we're both satisfied. When one of us wants to put out for someplace else, we go."

Johnny had stuck out his hand and they had shaken on the deal then and there, and they had kept to it ever since.

"There's one thing I ought to say," Johnny had added. "A few years back I had a dream. A spirit dream, the Indians called it. It said I would come back to my own people and live with them for a time. But I don't really belong to this world. Not to the Indians, neither. When I come to be a man, I got to choose. Dunno if you put stock in such things."

"I do if you do" was all Hardeman could say, and Johnny had nodded.

"It said I stand between the worlds, and on account of that I shouldn't fight any man, white or Indian. I don't carry a gun or knife." When Hardeman made no objection to that, he went on. "I reckon I should see as much of the white man's world as I can, so I'll know how to choose when the time comes. Only thing is, how will I know when it's time?"

"You'll know," Hardeman had said then. "You'll feel the need to step out on your own, and you won't need me anymore."

Since then Hardeman had all but forgotten the dream. They had watched the cheering crowds at Promontory Point and seen the two steam engines head to head, all polished and shining, and the high mucky-mucks of the Union Pacific and Central Pacific talking about what the rails meant to the nation, and then Hardeman and Johnny had gone south, but they hadn't stayed long on the Sante Fe Trail. One trip was all it took to convince them that watching the back end of a string of mules was no way to see the country, and before the year had come to an end, Johnny remarked that he'd like to see the Longhorn cattle over in Texas, and the cattle ranges had kept them busy for the better part of six years. Through all that time, Johnny had never mentioned the dream again. But he had never carried a gun, and although he took to carrying a pocketknife he had used it only as a tool; it never seemed to enter his mind that it might be a weapon. Hardeman had looked out for Johnny when trouble threatened, but the boy didn't rub people the wrong way and more often than not it had been Johnny who helped Hardeman out of a touchy situation by watching his back and keeping an eye out for unexpected threats. More than once in the Kansas saloons and bordellos during the winter just past, Johnny had been there when Hardeman needed him.

And then two weeks ago, back in Ellsworth, Johnny had said out of the blue, "I guess it's time."

"Time for what?" Hardeman had asked. They were in the boarding house where they shared a room. Like most trail hands, their jobs had ended in the fall when the cattle were delivered to the railhead. There had been no jobs in Dodge, so they had moved up the U. P. rails until they found work in Ellsworth. Hardeman had passed the winter as a deputy city marshal, and Johnny had worked in a stable, where he had trained and cared for the horses of the town's best citizens.

"Time to choose," Johnny had answered. He was lying on his bed, with his feet propped up on the steel frame that was painted white.

"Choose?"

"Choose between the worlds." Johnny sat up then, grinning. "I'm a white man, I guess, and I reckon to give the white man's world a go." He had seemed pretty pleased with himself. "Like you said," he went on, as if the conversation had been just the other day, instead of nearly seven years before, "I got the notion to put out on my own. Course, there's nothing to say we couldn't get back together in a year or two, like equal partners, so to speak."

"We've always been pretty equal," Hardeman said.

"That's true enough," Johnny agreed. "But I guess we might be even more equal after I've been off on my own, like you've been." He was still smiling to show he meant it all for the best.

"Might be," Hardeman had conceded, a little taken aback by the whole thing. That was Johnny's way, thinking something over on his own and only saying it when he had it all worked out. Johnny must have seen something

112

in his expression, like disappointment, or maybe just surprise at the suddenness of his announcement.

"Oh, I'm not fixing to run off just yet. I've got something to do first, and I'll need your help. It'll mean leaving Ellsworth."

Hardeman hadn't objected. A winter of lawing had been enough to convince him he wasn't suited for the job, although he had earned the respect of both the rougher elements and the gentry, such as it was. But he had never stopped in a town for so long, and he had been ready to move on. Now that he was back in the mountains, he understood the feeling better. As a scout, he led by persuasion; if other men granted him authority it was because they believed in his leadership, not because they feared his badge or his gun. Unlike some men he did not like being feared, or making others do things against their will.

"Where are we headed?" he had asked Johnny then.

"I don't exactly know," the youth had admitted. "I've got to find a Sioux Indian called Sun Horse. He's my grandfather."

"Your grandfather?" This revelation had shocked Hardeman only a little less than hearing Sun Horse's name from Johnny's lips. "You say his name is Sun Horse?"

Johnny had nodded. "He's a peace chief. He's got his own band. They winter somewhere in the Big Horns. The Valley of Flowers, he called it, but I guess that's just an Indian name."

These few words had been enough to convince Hardeman that Johnny was talking of the same Sun Horse who had given Jed Putnam the land for his road ranch, and he had marveled at how the lives of a few men could cross and recross in a land as vast as the western territories. How different his own life would have been if he had never met Jed Putnam, or Hickok, or Johnny, he had thought. It seemed that Sun Horse was destined to join that company.

"It might be I know where to find Sun Horse," he had said, surprising Johnny in turn, and the boy had told him the rest of it then, about how his Cheyenne father wasn't Cheyenne at all, but Sioux, firstborn son of Sun Horse, and how he had met his grandfather at the summer camp of the Sioux nation.

They had left Ellsworth the next day.

Two weeks had passed quickly since then, and it seemed to Hardeman now that Ellsworth was as far away as Philadelphia, and as long ago.

Footsteps approached the lodge and a soft cough announced someone waiting outside.

"That'll be Sun Horse, I'm thinkin'," Bat said, rising stiffly to his feet, but Hardeman was already halfway to the entrance.

Outside, Sun Horse stood next to Johnny, his weathered face struck full on by the afternoon sunshine. Hardeman looked from one to the other and saw that whatever had passed between the old man and the youth over the past few hours had brought them even closer together.

"I'll be staying here," Johnny said, as Lisa and Bat emerged from the lodge. "I'll come down with Sun Horse when he brings word what the council decides. Tomorrow, most likely."

Hardeman nodded. He had expected that Johnny would want more time with Sun Horse, now or later. If the boy handled himself right, he could do much to persuade the old man to surrender.

"I'll fetch the horses," he said to Lisa, and he went to where the animals had been picketed beyond Sun Horse's lodge. As he tightened the girths of his own saddle and Lisa's, he looked back across the camp circle and saw that she had drawn Sun Horse aside. They were walking slowly, her arm linked in his, and she was talking earnestly for his ears alone. But it didn't matter what she said to him; nothing could change how things stood. Sun Horse would see that. He had to think of the women and children. "The helpless ones," the Indians called the women and the young, and the old men who couldn't pull back a bowstring any longer. The first thought of a chief was always for the helpless ones, and there was only one way to protect them now. Hardeman had come to show him the way.

Back in Ellsworth, Hardeman had been astonished to learn that by a round-about circle that passed through Putnam's Park, Jed's dream come true in the Big Horns, Johnny and he were both connected to an old Sioux he had never met. It had seemed fateful, somehow, and yet as they left Kansas, Hardeman had had no more in mind than to accompany Johnny on his quest. When the boy had found Sun Horse and told him of his choice and had bid the old man farewell for a last time, Hardeman would return with Johnny to the settlements and there see him off on his own, and he would know that the obligation he had undertaken back at the Washita had been honorably discharged.

But they had stopped in Cheyenne to buy a few supplies, and they had seen the swarms of miners and the new houses and other buildings springing up everywhere, and heard the talk on every lip about the Black Hills and the Powder River country and how the whole territory would open up for gold and settlement and the fulfillment of any man's dreams once the savages had been pushed out of the way by the military force that was even then gathering at Fort Fetterman. Hardeman had seen at once that the Sioux were doomed, their fate sealed beyond recall; they would be confined where the white government wished them to be confined, or they would be attacked and punished until they bowed to the inevitable. He had felt a new urgency then to find Sun Horse and, with Johnny's help, persuade the peace chief to take his people to the reservation, to safety, before it was too late.

They had bought their supplies and mounted up and started out of town, bundled up against falling temperatures and a strengthening wind, when Hardeman had spied a familiar figure moving along the boardwalk, a man that stood a head above the rest of the crowd, dressed like Sunday-go-to-meeting in a starched collar and frock coat, his long hair oiled and combed. "James!" Hardeman had shouted.

Hickok had turned and peered about with eyes that seemed not to see so well any longer, and only when Hardeman rode over and dismounted did he exclaim, "Why, Christopher, old boy! It's been years! Damned if you don't look the same. And Johnny Smoker too, grown up like a sapling."

Hardeman and Johnny had seen Hickok a few times over the years, first at Fort Hays, Kansas, just a week or two after the Washita fight. It had been Hickok who gave Johnny his name. "What do you call the boy?" he had wanted to know, and Hardeman had shrugged. "He remembers his name's Johnny, but that's all. He doesn't know his family name." But then Johnny had spoken up, the first time he had talked to any white man other than Hardeman. "My father White Smoke!" he had announced, and Hickok had laughed at the boy's proud tone. "Why that'll do, won't it? We'll call him Johnny Smoker!" And the name had stuck.

In the following year Hickok had been badly wounded by some Cheyenne that caught him alone near Fort Lyon and since then he had aged beyond his years. There in Cheyenne, Hardeman had felt that he was looking at an older man.

Hickok had insisted on buying the two of them a beer and they had been unable to refuse.

"Christopher, you old rascal," Hickok had said, wiping the foam from his moustache with the knuckle of his index finger. "You can't fool me. I know what brings you here. You couldn't pass up the chance to get in on one last campaign. You've come to see George Crook."

"Crook?" Hardeman was puzzled. He knew Crook had been given command of the Department of the Platte the year before, but had no idea that Crook was anywhere near Cheyenne.

"He's here, old boy! Don't tell me you didn't know? He's across the street in that very hotel." Hickok pointed out the window of the saloon to a three-story brick building with a false front. "He'll take on another scout. You go find him and see if he won't. One thing for certain, Christopher, the army won't take no for an answer this time. They're going to finish the job, good and proper. There won't be any more scouting for the army in this neck of the woods, not after this. Take the chance while it's there."

"What about you, James?" Hardeman asked, feeling the beginnings of an idea he couldn't quite seem to grasp.

Hickok looked suddenly very tired. "Oh, I've done my scouting. Times aren't what they were, at least not for me. Besides, I'm getting married in a week or two! Going to take the wife to Cincinnati to see her folks. It's past time I settled down. You and I, Christopher, we've done our part."

Hardeman had scarcely heard his old friend's reply, for in that moment all the pieces of the plan had fallen into place as comfortably as hot beans in a hungry man's belly and he saw it whole in an instant. It was work of a master craftsman, all the makings set up one by one over the years and brought together in a single sweep by the hand of luck. If he hadn't known Jed Putnam and heard the story of Sun Horse giving him the little valley in the mountains, if fate hadn't put Johnny Smoker in the hands of Sun Horse's eldest son, if Hardeman hadn't stopped to visit Hickok in the fall of '68 and gone off to scout for General Sully, and—most improbable of all—if he hadn't been the one to enter the tipi in Black Kettle's village on the Washita and find Johnny still alive... And now here was Hickok again, to provide the final piece of the puzzle: the presence of George Crook in Cheyenne as Hardeman and Johnny passed through. Here all the chance encounters over the years were suddenly combined to show Hardeman a way not only to save Sun Horse but perhaps to end the new campaign before it started, and bring to an end twenty years of fighting between the Sioux and the white man.

If only Crook would agree.

Hardeman had left Johnny with Hickok and he crossed the street to the hotel, where he found Crook in the lobby, surrounded by a group of officers and newspapermen. Hardeman identified himself as an army scout, mentioning Hickok and Generals Sully, Custer and Smith all in one breath, and said he wished to speak to General Crook privately. To his surprise, Crook agreed after only a moment's hesitation, and they retired to the dining room, then deserted at mid-morning. There Hardeman had set forth the plan. If he could find the Sioux peace chief Sun Horse and persuade him to go voluntarily to the Dakota reservation with his people, would Crook provide an escort, and beef and blankets for the women and children? Would Crook send riders from the reservation to the other hostile headmen, saying that the peace man Sun Horse had gone in willingly, to see if such news might not bring in the others? Hearing that the soldiers had helped the Sun Band to make the journey safely would surely persuade some bands to surrender, and those in turn might persuade others until the remaining hostiles were so few that they would see no hope in further resistance. He told Crook that he had with him a boy related to Sun Horse, a white youth who had lived with the Indians, and he knew a former mountain man who was friendly with the peace chief. He believed that with the help of these two he could influence Sun Horse to trust General Crook's word.

Crook stroked first one fork of his beard and then the other. "And if Sun Horse will not agree, what then, Mr. Hardeman?" the general wished to know.

Hardeman answered without hesitation, for that eventuality too was part of the plan and even then there was a way to make a peace that would bring the hostiles to Dakota.

Crook had asked more questions then, and Hardeman had answered him, and when there was no more to say, Crook had thought in silence for less than a minute before he agreed the idea was worth a try, and gave it his blessing.

116

"But understand me well, Mr. Hardeman," Crook had said. "I cannot delay this campaign. You must reach Sun Horse and bring me his reply as quickly as you can. If I come upon one of the war leaders first, there may be no way to prevent fighting."

Within an hour of leaving Crook, Hardeman and Johnny had bid farewell to Hickok and left Cheyenne behind them. As they made their way toward the Big Horns, Hardeman had told Johnny what he hoped to do, and asked him for all he knew about Sun Horse, wanting to learn anything that might be useful in dealing with the peace man. Johnny had been a boy of just eight winters or so when he met his grandfather and he didn't remember much, but he did remember that Sun Horse was Sitting Bull's cousin; the Hunkpapa holy man had been in the Sioux camp that same summer and Sun Horse had talked with Sitting Bull about Johnny's dream. Hardeman seized on the relationship as a sign that his hopes were justified, that the plan might really work, and it was then that he had conceived the notion of asking Sun Horse to send word directly to the hostile bands, to plead with them to make peace and go in. The promise that the Sun Band could keep their horses and guns had come from Hardeman, not Crook, but if Sun Horse would take this step for peace, Crook would surely grant him any favor within reason. The horses and guns were a gift from Hardeman to Sun Horse, as the peace man's help would be a gift to Crook. The plan had assumed a life of its own, and Hardeman was the only one who knew the whole of it; by keeping it to himself and offering such unexpected gifts as these at the right moments, he might maneuver them all, red and white alike, into positions from which fighting would be impossible, and with luck the Indian wars on the north plains could be ended forever before the Sioux and Cheyenne ponies had time to grow sleek on the new grass of spring.

Across the camp, Lisa and Sun Horse turned back toward Little Hand's lodge, where Johnny and Bat Putnam were waiting. At even a short distance, Lisa might be taken for a man, another scout perhaps, in buckskin pants and trappers' winter moccasins, come to bring a message to the Indian chief. What had she told him? And how much influence did she have with Sun Horse now that her father was dead? As the old man rejoined Johnny and Bat, Hardeman saw how Johnny positioned himself beside Sun Horse, as if he belonged there.

In that moment he suddenly realized, not as a worry or a suspicion but as an inescapable truth, that he had made a fundamental miscalculation. He had intended Johnny's return to be an unexpected gift too, one that might have a powerful effect on Sun Horse, making him more likely to take Hardeman's advice and join him as a peacemaker, but he had never for a moment considered what effect seeing Sun Horse again might have on Johnny, nor what feelings might arise in the boy when he found himself once more among the Indians. He understood now the doubts he had felt the morning before, down below Putnam's Park, when he saw Johnny building a sweat lodge; even

117

then the boy had seemed to be loosening his hold on white man's ways and remembering the Indian customs he had left behind seven years before. And now, having seen the bond between Sun Horse and Johnny, having heard the talk of the dream, Hardeman knew in his bones that something more was taking place here than a simple reunion between an old Indian and a long-lost grandson. It was as if a promise had been fulfilled.

An Indian had a dream and it changed his life. It gave him strange notions and made him do stranger things. What would Johnny's dream make him do now? Since the Washita, Johnny had moved through the white man's world without objection, regarding it curiously on occasion but never showing a desire to return to the Indians. He could read and write and name the eighteen Presidents of the United States in order. He could eat with a knife and fork and converse with a mule skinner or a banker's wife, and his recent decision to remain permanently in the white world had seemed heartfelt and genuine. But that was back in Kansas, and Kansas was far away. What if he changed his mind and stayed with the Sioux?

And what if the Sun Band would not surrender? Hardeman was prepared for that event, but not for the possibility that Johnny might cast his lot with theirs, nor had he told the boy that part of the plan.

A wolf howled in the timber far away. Much nearer, kiotes on the other side of the village answered, the eerie warbling song of the pack rising and falling and echoing from the hills before dying out. The day was getting on when the kiotes sang for their supper. Time to be getting back to Putnam's Park. He held an arm straight out and measured the height of the sun. The width of two palms separated the blinding disk from the western ridge. Two hours until sunset, three until dark. Above him the sky was still unblemished. The air, which should already have been taking a chill that would deepen quickly as night fell, remained strangely warm. A change was coming, and it could only be a change for the worse after a day like this one. He took a deep breath and wished he could drink in the whole sky.

The next move was up to Sun Horse and the council. Until they gave their answer Hardeman could only wait, but no matter what they decided there could be no turning back now.

He swept his eyes around the narrow valley for a final time to set the picture in his mind. When he first arrived, he had noticed the trail that went away to the north, leaving the valley beyond the little lake at the far end. That would be a better way for the cavalry to approach, so they need not pass through Putnam's Park. If Sun Horse would not surrender, Hardeman would slip away alone to intercept Crook on his march up the old Bozeman road and he would bring the soldiers here to surround the village in the dark of night and capture the horse herd without a shot while the warriors were still groggy with sleep. Sun Horse and his people would be taken to the Red Cloud Agency under guard, and word would be sent to the hostile bands that the great man was on his way to the reservation after a peaceful surrender in which not a man had been harmed. With the right words of persuasion, at least some of the hostiles would go in, and by the time they learned that Sun Horse had been taken by surprise it would be too late for further resistance.

Crook was the key to the plan. Without him the risk would be far too great. He had no love of senseless bloodshed and his reputation was that of a man who made and kept the peace, not one who sought his own glory in battle. In Arizona he had sent riders dashing throughout the department to call an immediate halt to further military actions the instant the proud Apache head-men said they would sit down and talk peace. He knew how to talk to Indians and he had pacified the most feared corner of the Southwest with straight talk and a conviction that if Indians were treated fairly they would come to see the fruits of living in tranquillity side by side with the white men. With Crook in command and Hardeman to lead him, for once there would be a bloodless surrender.

He started across the camp with the two horses, and then he saw the smoke.

From the ridge that formed the eastern boundary of the valley, a column of smoke rose straight into the air, lit by the golden glow of the lowering sun, a white pillar against the spotless blue, growing taller by the moment. Now the smoke was interrupted, and Hardeman made out a figure on the ridge. The man moved, a blanket or robe flying in his hands, and again the smoke puffed up, the signal visible as far as the eye could see.

CHAPTER
EIGHT

Sun Horse stepped out of his lodge into the dark and walked beyond the camp circle to relieve himself. The snow did not squeak beneath his moccasins as it had the night before. The air was damp; perhaps it would snow tomorrow. He was grateful for the relative warmth of the evening; he was in his sixty-ninth winter and no longer shook off the cold as a young man might. He opened his robe and pulled aside his loincloth to urinate in the snow.

To the west the crescent moon lowered its slender blade into a bank of clouds that breathed and moved closer as he watched. This was the Moon of Sore Eyes, the Snowblind Moon, when the sun rose higher each day to shine off the lingering snows and a man's eyes became red and painful from long days spent hunting far from camp.

Delay.

The feeling came over Sun Horse suddenly. Delay. The people and the horses were not strong enough to fight Three Stars' soldiers, but neither were they strong enough to flee to the larger encampments of Crazy Horse and Sitting Bull, nestled somewhere in the river bottoms near the Yellowstone. That afternoon, Sun Horse had directed that a signal should be sent, in the hope that it might be seen and relayed, so the people there should know that soldiers were coming soon. For a moment he had wished that he and his people were with the northern bands, but even with strong horses such a journey would be dangerous now. In the Snowblind Moon the weather changed suddenly and often; a village on the move, lulled into carelessness by springlike warmth, could find itself suddenly enveloped in stinging snow that seemed to leap out of the ground itself, obscuring everything in the space of a few breaths. It was not safe to travel in the Snowblind Moon.

Delay.

Lisaputnam had advised the same thing that afternoon. "Find a way to put Crook off," she had said, her voice full of urgency. "Tell him you will come to the agency in the spring. Tell him anything, but don't leave this country now or you will never get it back!" He could hear her voice still, feel the touch of her hand on his arm, and the strength of this white woman who stood alone, leaning on no man. "Stay here for one more year without fighting the soldiers and there will be a new government in Washington—a new President and men with new ideas. They will have a new Indian policy, I am sure of it."

"And will they leave us in peace?" Sun Horse had asked in English, although she had spoken in Lakota. He had learned the whiteman's tongue long ago, so as to understand them in council and speak to them there. In his own village he used English rarely; it was not a language well suited to expressing Lakota thoughts. But he had used it without thinking, speaking of the *washíchun*, and Lisaputnam had replied in the same tongue.

"My father believed that if the Lakotas could keep this land until President Grant left office, there might be a chance to keep the Powder River country forever."

If a whiteman like her father were the Great Father in *Washing-ton*, then perhaps... But Sun Horse knew the futility of trusting one *washíchun* to right the wrongs done by another. Had not this man Grant proclaimed his respect for the red men when he was raised to power? "The Indians have a right to live," he had said. But his promises had not brought peace to the Lakota, nor the certainty that they would be able to continue living in the way of their grandfathers. Sun Horse had spent much time learning what he could of the whites, and still he understood so little. Only that over the years there was little difference between one President and his successor, or between the men who made up one council of government and the next. In the end they acted as whitemen always acted, like the thunderclouds that roamed the mountains in summer—inconsistent, unpredictable, striking out without warning.

Delay. It was the first certain feeling he had had since hearing Three Stars' message; but as soon as it came, the sureness gave way to questions. How to delay? And to what end?

The winter moons were usually the most contented of the year, women happy

120

because the men were in the lodges instead of off hunting or at war. Winter was a time for storytelling and quiet talk over the shared smoking of a pipe as the men visited from lodge to lodge. But this winter there had been little peaceful talk. There was too much concern for the sacred Black Hills—the *Paha Sapa*—and the thieves' road that the bluecoat chief Long Hair had made two summers before, now crowded with men rushing into the hills to dig for the yellow metal that made whitemen crazy. And there was worry of a more immediate kind, for the children and the old ones, in whose eyes the beginnings of hunger could be seen. The supply of dried meat from the fall hunt had been small, the hunt not very successful, and the meat was almost gone. Daily the hunters went out, but they brought in little meat. Even during the thaw, the buffalo and elk and deer—the four-legged brothers that provided the Lakota with all their needs—had been absent from their accustomed feeding grounds.

The talk in the lodges touched often on these misfortunes and the threat of war with the whites, and the people turned to Sun Horse for counsel and leadership.

But Sun Horse had been silent.

"The Great Mystery perhaps turns away from the Sun Band," Sees Beyond had suggested, but he had spoken the thought softly to Sun Horse, not openly to the people. Like Sun Horse himself, Sees Beyond was a *wichasha wakán*, a man who sought to understand the spirit world, that realm of powers, great and small, that lay all around and within the visible world of living creatures. The younger *wichasha wakán* was a mystic, often retreating to the high places where a man could feel the strength of the earth and sky most strongly. Sees Beyond took no part in the affairs of the band, the decisions about when to move and where to go or what course to take.

"We live as the Lakota have always lived," Sun Horse had answered. "There is no game because there is no game. In some seasons the four-leggeds are not so numerous." Sun Horse had trained Sees Beyond, whose power now grew so different from his own. The younger man seemed almost to dwell in the spirit world, while Sun Horse used all his abilities to guide the people through this life, in harmony with the powers that touched the lives of men. Sees Beyond had surpassed him in some ways, he knew, and he had felt the beginnings of uncertainty about the true reasons for the Sun Band's misfortunes. Perhaps it was true, perhaps *Wakán Tanka*, the Great Mystery at the center of all things, had turned away from the band, but Sun Horse could offer no course that would bring meat to the lodges, not until the snows melted and the new grass was up and the horses grew strong again.

And now came word that a white soldier chief would give meat to the Sun Band if they would go to the Dakota reservation. Soon the council would meet to decide. War or surrender, or hopeless flight. The councillors would speak and express their anger, and they would turn to Sun Horse for guidance.

Perhaps the headmen who had long since gone to the agencies were right. There was no way to fight the overwhelming power of the whites, they said. Red Cloud himself was there now, at the agency that bore his name. He had been twice to *Washing-ton*, traveling the iron road, and it seemed he had become like a whiteman himself. Little Wound was there, and Spotted Tail, the uncle of Crazy Horse. Even Man Afraid of His Horses had gone. He was Oglala of the Hunkpátila band, like Crazy Horse, and once he had been a great leader in peace and war. Make the best bargain with the whitemen, these leaders said, and work hard to see that the whites keep their word.

But how to be sure a whiteman would keep his word? Some were honorable, to be trusted as one might trust a Lakota who gave his promise. But the others... There was a saying among the Lakota: "The promises of the *washíchun* are like the wind in the buffalo grass."

Over the years Sun Horse had watched the advance of the whites, keeping his people removed from the spreading conflict. Like a war leader, he had watched the battle from afar, so as to see all its parts. But now the battle drew near and he could no longer remain aloof.

He straightened his breechcloth. The last fragment of the moon sank into the approaching clouds and the air turned cooler, as if the tiny fingernail of a moon had provided the warmth that Sun Horse had found so pleasant only a moment before.

He turned to look at the camp, taking pleasure in the glow from each tipi, the quiet and the calm. A village at peace. He stretched out his arms to encircle the lodges, seeking to protect them. More than anything else he wanted to preserve the peace he felt in this place. But how? The chill of his indecision was more discomforting than the dank night air. For years he had been preparing himself for this moment, following the power of his vision, and now his power seemed to have left him, leaving him alone, not knowing which way to turn. He was like a tree in a dead calm, seeking any hint of a breeze to sway him one way or another.

Twenty-five snows had fallen since the summer of his vision. It was a warm summer; his name was Stands Alone then, and his father, Branched Horn, was still alive. Branched Horn had led his band of Hunkpapa to the fort called Laramie for a great council with the whites, and there Stands Alone had seen for the first time the stream of whites flowing westward in their wagons, the dust constantly drifting this way and that on the summer breezes. He had been fascinated by this endless journeying, all in one direction. In less time than it took for one moon to grow fat he had seen more whites pass westward before his eyes than all the Lakota who lived in all the lodges of all the bands, and he felt a growing certainty that his destiny was linked to these pale strangers from the east. One day, without telling anyone, he made *inipi*, the cleansing ritual that preceded all ceremonies, and then he went to a little hill overlooking the wagon road to seek a vision. *Hanbléchiyapi*—they cry for a vision—the Lakota called this quest, and it was usually performed when a youth became a man. A young man went alone to some high place for days and nights without food, praying for a promise of power. If the Great Mystery heard, the reply might be borne in a hundred forms, by a

122

cloud or a puff of wind, by an insect, a bird or an animal, some creature that in the years that followed would be a special helper to the man. Stands Alone had performed the ceremony in his sixteenth year, but he had seen nothing; after five nights alone on a rocky butte in the Black Hills he had finally returned to his people weak and ashamed, with no vision to tell. Even so, he had become *pezhuta wichasha*, a man who cured sickness with roots and herbs, and later *wapíye*, a healer. His lack of a vision seemed less important then, for practicing these callings would have been impossible without the favor of the spirits, who were all but separate aspects of the One Spirit at the center of everything—*Wakán Tanka*. Branched Horn was *wichasha wakań*, a holy man, and he gladly instructed his son in matters of the spirit world; he encouraged the young man and urged him to make the vision-quest again when he felt that the time was right.

There at Fort Laramie Stands Alone had been certain that the time for his vision had come. Sitting naked atop the small hill he had prayed continuously to the four quarters, to *Wakán Tanka* above and the earth below, asking for the vision that had been denied him in his youth. And on the morning of the fourth day it had come to him, the horse from which he took his new name, running to him out of the sun, bearing a promise of power. He had followed the vision to this valley where he and his people had wintered for twenty-five years. The band had become his on the day following his vision, as he had become Sun Horse, for on that same day his father had passed the leadership to him. Over the years the band had been strengthened by lodges from other bands, men and women who had heard of Sun Horse's vision and wished to live under his leadership, and for twenty-five years he had brought them to spend each winter here, beyond the corrupting influence of the whites, beyond the reach of their whiskey and diseases, yet close enough to learn their ways with the help of Jed Putnam, a truthful whiteman.

Even before he had walked down off the hilltop to tell his vision to Branched Horn, Sun Horse had understood its meaning. His power was to understand the true nature of the whites, and to lead his people to live in peace with them. Since that day his understanding had increased steadily and his people had remained at peace. Yet now a *washíchun* soldier chief demanded that Sun Horse surrender or prepare to fight, and he could see no other choice before him.

The night had darkened as the moon set. The chill of the snow penetrated to Sun Horse's feet even through the fur-lined moccasins he wore. The clouds were advancing rapidly and only a few stars remained in view above the eastern ridges. Sun Horse gathered his robe tightly about him and made his way back to his lodge.

Inside the tipi a fire burned brightly. Sun Horse's elder wife, Elk Calf Woman, had built it up, knowing he would need to warm himself when he returned. Even as he entered, she was adding more wood, kneeling beside Johnny Smoker where he sat looking into the flames. At the rear of the lodge the younger wife, Sings His Daughter, was working a piece of mountain goatskin between her hands,

123

softening it. She had saved it for more than a year, until Sun Horse should need a pair of summer moccasins that would resist the brambles and thorns when he walked alone on the mountainsides, as he liked to do. Sings His Daughter smiled shyly at her husband, still modest about showing affection in the presence of others.

Sun Horse looked at her kindly, and once again he congratulated himself on his good fortune. With Elk Calf he had enjoyed almost fifty years of contentment, despite their occasional differences, and now that she was getting old he had taken a second wife to help her with the work. Standing Eagle had captured Sings His Daughter from the Crows two years ago, in the autumn, thinking to make her his second wife, but Willow Woman, Blackbird's mother, would have none of it. Standing Eagle had brought the young captive into his lodge, although not into his sleeping robes, but when it became clear that Willow Woman's jealousy would not subside, Sun Horse had arranged to marry the girl to preserve peace within his family and within the band. Sings His Daughter was young and strong, and she was very pretty. The enthusiasm she displayed in the privacy of her sleeping robes and the pleasure she gave Sun Horse were unexpected gifts she had brought to his life.

"You should not stay out so long," Elk Calf chided him, frowning.

"I like to look at the village at night," Sun Horse said, a little petulantly. He would not be scolded in front of his grandson. "It is quiet outside. I can think better there, away from all your talking."

"My talking! Hmp. I have hardly spoken since you returned from the council."

It was true. Elk Calf knew that Sun Horse was concerned about the message from Three Stars, and the second gathering of the council that would begin in a short while. She had motioned to Sings His Daughter to keep quiet as Sun Horse and his white grandson talked through the afternoon and into the evening, and between them the two women had spoken only a handful of words.

"I see the fires in the lodges and I know my people are warm," Sun Horse said, moving his elkhorn backrest a little closer to the fire. He sat back against the robe that covered the horn frame and he reached for his smoking pipe.

"They are warm, but they are hungry," Elk Calf said, taking her place at his left hand. She said it gently. She picked up the legging she was repairing with a new piece of deerskin. Sun Horse would not wear new leggings until his old ones were in tatters.

Sun Horse made no reply. This was his wife's way, reminding him, with a few well-chosen words, that all was not well with the band. Reminding him of his duty. *Let none grow hungry through the actions of a leader.* The Ancient Ones, the wisest Lakotas of past generations, had said this, the wisdom handed down over the years.

Elsewhere around the camp circle other wives were making their concerns known at this very moment. It was the men who met in council, but when they gathered in the council lodge the opinions of the women would be represented there, and no course would be adopted of which the women did not approve.

Sun Horse's people were hungry, and now they were threatened by war. How could he lead them away from both dangers? What would the council decide to do? What should he advise?

He filled his pipe carefully with a mixture of trade tobacco and red willow bark and lit it with a small stick from the fire. He smoked without ceremony, wishing only to calm himself, and while the pipe was still burning he passed it to the youth beside him.

Johnny Smoker was the source of his hope. Hand in hand with the soldier chief's message had come the miraculous return of Sun Horse's grandson, so long given up for dead, and what was more, his coming had been foretold.

Two nights before, Hears Twice had coughed softly outside Sun Horse's lodge. When he was invited in, he had sat quietly for a time, as if listening. Then, in signs, he had told Sun Horse what he heard. *Something comes*, he said. A *power is coming. It is very strong. It can help the Sun Band or destroy us. It grows from the meeting of two people.* That, and no more. This afternoon, at the moment when he had recognized his grandson, Sun Horse had felt sure that the young man was one of those the prophet had heard. But who was the other? Hears Twice did not know. Nor did Sun Horse, but he sensed a hidden power in the return of his grandson, something as yet formless, undirected.

Taku shkanshkan, the wise ones said. Something is moving. Something not of the world of men, and yet a part of it. Something unseen and unseeable, yet it could be felt. Sun Horse felt it now, as if the force that animated all living things had recently grown stronger.

The youth passed the pipe back now and Sun Horse set it aside to cool. He did not know what to call this grandson, even in his thoughts. To all appearances he was a whiteman, a stranger. Yet within him there were the memories of a boy who had lived with the people called *Shahíyela*, a boy Sun Horse had once known. Johnny Smoker, the whites called him, but other names demanded to be heard, names that recalled a young boy's dream, and a promise of power.

That afternoon, Sun Horse had drawn the young man out, seeking to know what he had become in his years among the whites. Johnny had told of the places he had been and the things he had seen, speaking in English at Sun Horse's urging, using the whiteman's language to describe his life in the whiteman's world. His tales had confirmed much of what Sun Horse already knew—the limitless numbers of the *washíchun*, each one alone, without tribe or band, often without even a family, moving from one place to another for no reason that Sun Horse could understand. And although the youth placed no emphasis on such things, Sun Horse saw too the endless cleverness of the whites, and many examples of their power. Through it all, the young man's words revealed the constant presence of the man called Hardeman, guiding him and teaching him, showing him the way in a strange world, but leaving Johnny free to form his own opinions about the whites and their customs. He was fortunate to have had such a teacher.

At length, Sun Horse had turned Johnny's thoughts to his childhood, asking to hear about the years between the young boy's visit with his parents to the Lakota summer camp and Long Hair Custer's attack on Black Kettle's village at the Washita.

"I was proud to be *Tsistsístas*," Johnny had begun. The Cheyenne name for themselves meant the One People, the Real People, the word carrying a meaning that set them apart from other men. *Shahíyela*, the Lakota said, people who speak another tongue. The white name came from the Santee Lakota, who said *Shahíyena*.

"When I was a boy", Johnny said, "I was *Tsistsístas*, and I wished to be nothing else." He fell silent then, making an effort to remember, choosing his words with care, and when he spoke again it was in the Shahíyela language. The words came haltingly at first, and then more freely, the speech and images flowing from the same world. Occasionally he used a word of English or Lakota, or a few signs, when the Shahíyela words failed him.

It had been in the year the whites called 1864 when Johnny and his parents had summered with Sun Horse, and they had stayed on through the autumn, accompanying the band on the fall hunt. At last, late in the Moon of Falling Leaves, when the Sun Band had set out for their wintering place in the Big Horns, White Smoke and Grass Woman had taken their son and returned to Colorado to join the village of their people at Sand Creek.

There they found tragedy. Black Kettle's camp had been attacked by territorial militia and many were dead. Outraged by the attack, the *Tsistsístas* were preparing to take up arms against the whites throughout the eastern part of Colorado Territory, accompanied by their allies the Arapaho and the southern bands of Lakota. But Black Kettle would not fight. His first responsibility as a chief was to keep the peace, no matter what the provocation. He took his band away from the troubles, and in the years that followed, he remained at peace with the whites. White Smoke stood by Black Kettle's side and helped him calm the angry howls of the young men. In the autumn of 1868, Black Kettle and White Smoke went to Fort Cobb, in the Indian Territory, to seek the protection of the army, for there was new trouble following some raiding along the Solomon and the Saline. General Hazen, the officer in charge, denied sanctuary to the Cheyenne, but Black Kettle understood that if he remained south of the Arkansas, he would be safe from the bluecoats' punitive expeditions. He went into winter camp on the Washita, close by the camps of Kiowa and Apache, Comanche and Arapaho, and there Long Hair's soldiers found him on a wintry morning in late November.

Here Johnny had paused, not sure he should continue, but Sun Horse had nodded to encourage him. "I would hear how my son died," the old man had said. Until now there had been none to tell him. Others had been able to say only that the one called White Smoke was gone, not the manner of his going. And so Johnny had told him of the battle.

"The Lakota message-carrier Man Who Rides had come to us that day, bringing word that the war in the Powder River country was over and a new treaty had been signed at Fort Laramie. We were glad that the Lakota and *Tsistsístas* had won the war and the whites had been made to leave our country there. I think even my father was glad that we had won, although he was a man of peace." Throughout the telling, Johnny never spoke his father's name, for it was not good to speak the names of the dead.

"There was a feast that night, and dancing, and while we were dancing, a war party of Kiowas came through the camp and told us they had been raiding against the Utes. They had seen the tracks of many soldiers not far away, but we were south of the Arkansas and we were at peace, and we thought we had nothing to fear.

"In the morning I was still in my robes when I heard a shot. I thought one of the horse guards must have shot a deer by the river, but then I heard many horses approaching camp and someone shouted that soldiers were coming, and then I heard the bugles. My father and I jumped up and ran outside, and we saw soldiers crossing the river and others coming from another side. I saw the horses' breaths make steam in the cold air. 'My friends, do not fight them,' my father called out. 'We are at peace,' he said, but already the fighting was starting, and no one heard him. My father and I were both barefoot and we were hopping from one foot to the other to keep our feet from freezing, and I laughed because we looked foolish, but he told me to be quiet.

"Before long the soldiers were in the village and my father said, 'We must take your mother away where she will be safe.' So we brought my mother out of the lodge and started away to the south, but while we were still among the lodges we saw Black Kettle and his wife come out of their lodge and mount their horses, and we watched, hoping they would get away. But when they reached the river, Black Kettle was shot and his wife was killed when she went to help him. This made my father very angry. 'Now I must fight!' he said, and he ran into a lodge to find a weapon. My mother and I ran in after him. I wanted to fight too. There was no one in the lodge, but there were some weapons there and my father took a rifle and began to load it. I saw a bow and some arrows and I took them, but my father grabbed them from my hands. 'You must not fight,' he said. 'Remember your dream!' 'I am *Tsistsístas*!' I said. 'I will fight to protect the helpless ones!' But he would not let me go, and before I could say anything more there was shooting outside and bullets came into the lodge and struck both my father and my mother. I wanted to fight more than ever then, for my mother was dead and my father was dying, but still he would not let me go. 'Remember your dream,' he told me again, and then he died."

Johnny had fallen silent then and the lodge was very quiet as Sun Horse and the two women had waited for the youth to continue.

After a time he said, "When I saw him die, something inside me changed, and I did not want to fight anymore. I stayed with the bodies of my parents to protect them from the soldiers. When the soldiers attacked the village four winters before, on Sand Creek, they had cut the bodies of the dead, I was told, even the private parts of the women, and I would not let that happen to my parents. I was holding my mother's body when more bullets came into the lodge and struck me in the leg. Then a whiteman came through the entrance with a pistol in one hand and a knife in the other. He was not a soldier. He was dressed in buckskins and I knew he was one of the scouts who had led the soldiers to our camp. I thought he would kill me, but he looked at my mother and father and he saw the wound in my leg, and the fight went out of his eyes. He said something I didn't understand, for I had forgotten the English I knew as a child. Then he made signs, asking if I was white. I wanted to say I was *Tsistsístas*, but I remembered my father's words and I remembered my dream. I signed to him 'yes.' He picked me up and took me out of the lodge, into the whiteman's world."

Again the boy had fallen silent, but then he had looked at Sun Horse, and Sun Horse saw the trouble in his eyes. "My father died because of me," Johnny had said. "If he had not stopped to talk to me he might have gone outside and lived."

Sun Horse had shaken his head. "And he might have died there, fighting the soldiers." He had waited for more than seven years to hear this tale, and the strength of his son as a peace man gave him joy. "Your father was angry when he saw his friend shot down," he had said. "A great peace man dead at the soldiers' hands. But when he saw you prepare to fight he forgot his anger and he reminded you of your dream. And so he died as a man of peace must die, trying to stop fighting with his last breath."

Sun Horse had risen then and suggested to his grandson that he remain for the night, and together they had gone off to Hears Twice's lodge to send Lisaputnam and Hardeman on their way, Sun Horse smiling and enjoying the warmth of the afternoon, keeping to himself the stunning effect of the boy's tale.

It was the manner of telling, rather than the story itself, that gave Sun Horse pause. At first, Johnny had spoken as a whiteman might, making no distinction between things that he knew from his own experience and things he had heard or been told. But soon there had come a change in the way he spoke, and by the time he related the battle and the death of his father, he told the tale exactly as a Lakota or Shahíyela might have done. Both peoples had strict customs that governed how a man conveyed something he knew whenever he spoke of matters that were important to the people, for such events became part of the history of the bands. A man told only what he knew from his personal knowledge, and no more. If possible, one or more witnesses stood by to correct any errors in the telling and to prevent boastful embellishments. For eight winters the youth who was now called Johnny Smoker had been among the whites, speaking only English and hearing only the careless way of talk that was the white custom, yet here in a single afternoon he had fallen naturally into a manner of storytelling that was careful and correct in the Lakota manner, and wherever he had touched on matters Sun Horse had heard told by others, every detail was exact.

Now, sitting beside his grandson once more in the warm lodge, Sun Horse reached again for his pipe. While his hands were busy with the familiar task of filling the bowl with the smoking mixture, he turned to the youth and spoke in Shahíyela.

"Your friend the whiteman. Why has he come here?"

"He came because I asked him to come," Johnny replied. "It was he who went to Three Stars and asked that you be given a chance to surrender. He hopes the other headmen may surrender too when they hear what you have done and know you were not harmed by the soldiers. He came because I asked him to come, but he has also come to make peace."

Sun Horse pondered this for a time, and then he said, "And you. You have come because of your dream?"

Johnny nodded. Except to mention it in telling of his father's death, he had said nothing of his dream, or why he had come.

"I am an old man," Sun Horse said, lighting the pipe. "I do not remember so well anymore. Tell me again of your dream, whatever you remember."

The truth was that Sun Horse remembered his grandson's dream very well. It loomed in his memory as sharp and clear as his own vision from the hill overlooking the Laramie fort. All afternoon he had circled around and around, approaching this thing; above all he wished to hear how well the youth remembered the dream, and what it meant to him.

As he had done that afternoon, Johnny gathered himself for a time, preparing himself to speak. "It was in the summer when we visited the Lakota," he said at last. "We arrived in the Moon of Ripe Cherries, when the young moon still had horns." He located the story in time, as a Lakota would always do when speaking of events long past. "We had been in the camp for four nights, and on the morning of the fifth day I awoke before my parents and I did not know where I was for a little while because I had had a strange dream. I dreamed I was standing alone in the middle of a plain. To one side, at a great distance, stood all the Real People and Lakota, all the men and women of both nations, and they were calling out to me, but I could not understand the words. To the other side, also at a great distance, stood white men and women covering the land as far as I could see. They too were calling to me, but I could not understand the words. Then from far away on the plain, something approached me, walking between the two peoples. As it came near, I saw that it was a white buffalo cow. She spoke to me so that I heard the words not with my ears but only in my thoughts, and she said, 'You are standing between the worlds. You live with the Real People now, but in time you will return to live among the whites. When you are about to become a man you will decide to which people you belong, and until then you shall fight no man, red or white, lest you kill your brother.' I looked to either side and I saw that all the people had disappeared, and when I looked back at the buffalo cow I saw a beautiful young woman standing there. She smiled at me and turned to walk away and then she became a buffalo again and walked until I could see her no more."

Sun Horse was shocked to the center of his being, and it took all of his control to remain calm. A leader of the people must be calm. Only in calm could a leader decide what was best for the people.

The words were the same. The dream had been told now just as the young boy had told it twelve years before. Only the voice had changed, that of a man replacing the voice of a boy, and within the words Sun Horse heard the voice of Little Warrior, the White Boy of the Shahíyela, speak again. Word for word the two tellings were the same.

"Have you lived as the dream said you should?" Sun Horse asked, his voice calm.

"I returned to the white world when my mother and father were killed at the Washita, and since then I have carried no weapons nor fought any man."

Sun Horse nodded calmly, as if this were no more than he expected, but his thoughts were anything but calm. From the dream the boy had been given two names: He Stands Between the Worlds, to remind both peoples, Lakota and Shahíyela, that he did not truly belong to them, and he was also called Empty Hand, so all should know he would fight no man. I gave him names, Sun Horse reminded himself, not one but two, passing on to him the custom of my family that each man shall take a name from his vision-dream if it has sufficient power. But I did not truly believe in the power of this dream. No white child could dream of *Ptésanwin*, the White Buffalo Cow Woman, who brought the sacred pipe to the Lakota and showed us how to use it. *Ptésanwin*, the greatest figure from the old tales, could not come to a white child in a dream. So I believed in my heart.

Why?

Only because the boy was white, and that is why I am a fool. Who is to say that a boy born white shall not have a dream of power if he is raised among the Lakota or Shahíyela, or even among the Pawnee or Crow or Blackfeet? Lakota children raised by the whites do not have dreams of power. They lose touch with the spirit world and become almost like whitemen. Shall a white child living among the Shahíyela or Lakota retain only the powers of a white child? Power is in the life we live.

But I doubted the dream when the boy told it to me, and when I heard he had died, I believed it to be so and I forgot the dream.

There in the Lakota encampment, that summer when the boy was young, Sun Horse had been so moved by the dream that he had gone to tell it to his cousin Sitting Buffalo Bull, himself a spiritual man who dreamed often of what was to be.

130

"If he has truly dreamed this," Sitting Bull had said, "he is Buffalo Dreamer."

Sun Horse had nodded. Already the boy was called by so many names. Little Warrior and White Boy of the Shahíyela, and now Empty Hand and He Stands Between the Worlds. Buffalo Dreamer was not a name, but it was an obligation, more than it seemed a boy of eight winters should have to bear.

"He is white, yet he is Shahíyela," Sitting Bull had continued, very serious. "But if his dream of *Ptésanwin* leads him in time to give up the white world, it will not be to the Shahíyela that he returns. *Ptésanwin* is Lakota. She brought us the pipe and taught us how to live. If the boy chooses to return he will live among the Lakota, and he will bring the power of *Ptésanwin* to help the people."

Sun Horse had told the boy none of what Sitting Bull had said. They had decided this between them, the two holy men. If the boy chose the Lakota world, he would be told then, so he would understand his responsibility to use his power for the good of the people, but first he must make his choice freely, unburdened by any sense of obligation.

In the Moon of Falling Leaves, before White Smoke and Grass Woman and their son had gone off to the south, Sun Horse had made the boy promise to return to see him when it came time for him to choose between the worlds. "I will come, Grandfather," the boy had promised solemnly.

And now he had returned. The prophecy of *Ptésanwin* had come to pass. Which world would the young man choose?

As soon as he asked himself the question, Sun Horse knew that Johnny had already made his choice, and he knew that he had chosen the white world. Surely if he had decided to live with the Lakota he would have said something before now. But he had said nothing of his dream until Sun Horse brought it up, and yet he remembered it perfectly. And Sun Horse recalled now a certain reserve in the young man, an occasional unwillingness to meet his grandfather's eyes, as if he were embarrassed or ashamed. So he had chosen the white world. And he had no reason to be ashamed; he had been among the whites for seven years, while his Shahíyela childhood was far behind him. But even so, Hears Twice had predicted power in the boy's coming! *It is very strong. It grows from the meeting of two people.* . . . Was he, Sun Horse, the one who would join with the young man? Sun Horse the Lakota meeting the One Who Stands Between the Worlds, even though the youth had chosen to remain white? If the power of the Lakota could be joined with that of the *washíchun*, what might then be accomplished? Anything at all . . . !

But Sun Horse felt certain that he was not the one. He sensed no new power in himself, nothing to match that brought by the young man. Who was it then? And would the power from this meeting help Sun Horse's people or destroy them? Could he have a hand in determining that, at least?

For a moment he wished he knew what the future would bring. But it was not his power to foresee what was yet to come. The spirits knew all that had been done and all that would be done, the Ancient Ones said. It was given

131

to some men to hear what the spirits had to tell about events yet to come. Hears Twice was one of these, and Sitting Bull foresaw the future in dreams. But Sun Horse dealt with events of the past and present, with what he knew and what he saw before him, and in this lay his strength as a leader.

He wished his cousin Sitting Bull were nearby now, so they could visit and talk again of the boy's dream. But the Hunkpapa was far to the north, many days' travel, too dangerous in the Snowblind Moon with soldiers riding down the Powder. If Three Stars found Sitting Bull's camp, the soldier chief would attack and Sitting Bull would fight. Perhaps it would be easier that way, not knowing of the approach of the horse soldiers, simply to spring from the lodges and fight, perhaps to die in defense of the camp. It was good to die for the people, the Ancient Ones had said so.

If he were not attacked, Sitting Bull would still choose war. He was of the bands that had fought the whites at every turn, driving them from the soldier forts on the Bozeman road, harassing them along the Yellowstone three summers ago when they came there to mark the ground for an iron road like the one in the south, going in recent moons with Crazy Horse, the strange man of the Oglala, to fight the miners who dug in the sacred *Paha Sapa*. Sitting Bull's young men would demand to fight once they knew that soldiers were coming to the Powder River country. Perhaps they already knew, if the riders from the agencies had found Sitting Bull's camp in the Moon of Popping Trees. A rider had reached Sun Horse's village, but many had believed the message ordering the Lakota to the agencies was false, sent by white traders in the hope that more bands would come to trade for iron pots and colored cloth and *mni wakán*, the burning water that took a man's mind for a time and left him weak and easy to anger.

Now Sun Horse knew the message was true. The hunting bands had not gone in and the soldiers were coming, and so he had ordered the signal sent from the ridgetop to warn others of the bluecoats' approach. Perhaps even now Sitting Bull was preparing to trap them in some wooded draw on the Tongue or on the creeks of the Rosebud. Sooner or later, Sitting Bull would fight, Sun Horse was sure, and he was just as sure that to fight the whites was to fight the whirlwind.

A turning point had been reached and a choice was demanded. What was the power his grandson brought? How could it be used for the good of the people? To these questions Sun Horse could give no answers. Still his only certainty was the need for delay.

The fire fell in on itself, one log rolling up against the ring of stones that lined the pit. Sun Horse prodded it back onto the coals and added more wood. For some time he had been aware of sounds coming from outside the lodge, men moving about the camp, and he had recognized the voices of the principal men as they moved towards the council lodge. Now the camp was quiet. The council awaited him.

He put the clamor of his unresolved thoughts suddenly to rest and rose to his feet. He went quickly around the fire, then bent low and stepped out of the lodge, closing the entrance flap carefully behind him.

Elk Calf Woman rose as Sun Horse left the lodge. Sings His Daughter had already gone to her sleeping robes and the old woman moved to her own pallet now, smiling at Johnny as he glanced at her. Elk Calf's hair was white and her skin was as brown and wrinkled as her husband's. Johnny wished he could speak to her, but she understood no Cheyenne and he remembered little of the Lakota he had learned as a youth.

He had almost called out as Sun Horse left, to make the old man stop and hear what he had to say. Half a dozen times during the afternoon and evening he had tried to tell why he had come, and each time his tongue had failed him. I have chosen the white world, he had wanted to say. It was simple enough, but for the past few days it seemed he couldn't find the words to talk to anyone about what was on his mind, not to Chris, not to his grandfather, the old man he remembered and yet did not know.

This morning, when he and Chris had arrived in the Lakota camp, the decision had seemed right enough. He had seen the hungry dogs and the weakness of the people, and everything so unexpectedly primitive. The tipis that had been spacious for a young boy seemed smaller now, and unpleasantly smoky on such a calm day. Most of all, Sun Horse was not as Johnny had remembered him. Throughout the afternoon he had struggled without success to associate the old man who sat beside him in the lodge with the imposing figure he had approached with such awe as a young boy. He had been about to tell the old man of his choice then, when he judged that enough time had passed for him to tell his true reason for coming, but then a horse had neighed softly somewhere beyond the edge of camp.

The sound had awakened in Johnny's memory a sharp image of his boyhood, from the day when he and his parents had drawn near the great Lakota gathering where he had met his grandfather for the first time. White Smoke had given him his first horse for the trip north and he had ridden it proudly, ranging out in front of his father and mother like a scout, but always keeping within their sight. When he topped a rise and saw the peaks of the Lakota tipis in the river plain below, set among the dense cottonwoods, his pony had neighed, catching the scent of the Lakota horse herds, and he had reined in, awestruck by the size of the encampment. It was not a gathering of all the Lakota bands, but the Cheyenne

133

were few compared with the Lakota and their camps not so large, even in summer. Johnny had kicked his pony's ribs and galloped down the grassy slope; even then he was a better horseman than most boys his age and he was proud of his skill, so highly prized among the Cheyenne. He swung down to peer from beneath his horse's neck, imagining that he was charging on a camp of Crows or Snakes. An *akíchita* rode out to meet him, one of the marshals that guarded the camp. Seeing that the attacking rider was only a boy, the man allowed him to enter the encampment at the run, whooping with glee. The *akíchita* laughed, and called out, "Look, the Shahíyela send their warriors to make war on the Lakota." A few lodges of Real People were with the Lakota and they took the boy for one of their own. He was tanned from years in the sun and covered with dust from the journey. One man had recognized him, but he said only, "This is the son of White Smoke and Grass Woman. He is called Little Warrior," and Johnny had been proud to be a Real Person and a boy who was growing up fast. He had joined the other boys in their rough games and he had held his own, despite his slight build. Even as a small boy he had displayed the same temperament, his father said, always ready to stand up to any challenge. On the day the Cheyenne warriors found him, in a wagon abandoned by the fleeing emigrants, he had pointed his hand at the Indians like a make-believe pistol, and he had shouted "Bam! Bam!" "He is a brave little warrior," White Smoke had observed, and so the boy had received his childhood name.

But within a few days of arriving at the Lakota summer camp, Johnny had given up his childhood name and his life had been changed forever by a dream.

This afternoon the call of a Lakota pony had brought back these memories. The gentle light of the sun filtering through the lodgeskins had become suddenly familiar then, and Johnny had felt a comfort he had not known for a long time.

Now, as he listened to the soft breathing of the two sleeping women and the gentle hiss of a damp log in the fire, the feeling returned as if he had summoned it, familiar and comforting. But as soon as it returned, the sense of belonging abandoned him, leaving him alone once more, and he did not seek to recapture it.

He had not come here to recall his boyhood or to regain a feeling of being at home among the Sioux. Since leaving Kansas he and Chris had talked a great deal about what lay ahead for the Sioux, and Johnny could see no way out for Sun Horse and the hostiles; they would have to go in now, or lose everything if they fought the army. He had told the council as much, reluctantly, wishing he and Chris could have brought some other message. But there was no escaping it. One way or another, the Sioux would all be living on the Dakota reservation before long, with no pleasant wooded camping places and no quiet springs where the buffalo came to drink. By the look of things, there might soon be no buffalo left at all in Dakota or anywhere else. The northern herds were being thinned out fast by the hide hunters, Chris said, and down in Indian Territory you could go from one season to the next without seeing fresh tracks. With the buffalo gone, the life Johnny had known in his childhood would disappear. He had cast his lot with his own race, whose future seemed bright, but the confidence he had felt in his decision back in Kansas eluded him now.

It had all been so clear to him in Ellsworth. He had made up his mind and set out to tell the grandfather he had not seen in twelve years that he had chosen to remain in the white world, where a man could go where he wanted and do as he wished, where Johnny had come to understand what the whites meant when they spoke of freedom and a man's right to choose his own way. He had come to say that he valued that freedom as his own now and could never give it up. It was something that had been growing in him, becoming a part of him, ever since he got his first job breaking horses for a white man.

He and Chris had been together for a year and a half when Chris took a job with a former Confederate major who was about to set out for Abilene with three thousand Texas Longhorns. At first the major hadn't wanted to take Johnny along. The boy wasn't strong like some of the youths he had accepted for the drive, the major said; he was still a tad young for drover's work. Instead the major offered to let Johnny do odd jobs around the ranch until he and Chris Hardeman returned from Kansas.

In a corral nearby, three men were breaking horses that would go into the remuda; the major had the most cattle in the herd and it was up to him to provide the cow horses that all the drovers would ride. The horses in the corral had been halfway broken by the simple methods used by men who had little time to accomplish a job that should have taken months of steady work, but they were sturdy animals and showed promise, Johnny thought. The wranglers were fighting a stubborn horse that had picked today to refuse the saddle or even the blanket, while the major's young son watched from atop the fence. Johnny had walked to the corral and asked, "You mind if I try?"

The wranglers had got a good laugh out of that, but when they saw that Chris Hardeman's quiet young companion was serious they had agreed quickly enough. They didn't mind a chance to sit on the fence and be entertained by this kid who thought he could do a man's job, not if the boss was willing. Johnny had taken the reins and talked softly to the animal in Cheyenne for a time, too softly to be overheard by the others. Then he had led the animal to the gate.

"Don't turn him loose!" one of the wranglers cried out. "He's rope shy! It'll take us all day to fetch him back!"

Johnny paid no attention, opening the gate against the man's protests, leading the horse away from the noise and scents of the corrals, away from the other penned horses stamping nervously, and then he had mounted the animal bareback and ridden him at a gallop around the house and corrals and bunkhouse, slowing him to a lope and finally a trot before coming to a stop by the corral again, where he had saddled him and handed the reins to one of the speechless men.

"All right, son, you've a way with horses," the major had said. "Tell me what you think of that animal there." He pointed to a small corral where two horses were penned apart from the others. The horse in question had one front foot resting toe-down on the ground.

135

"He's got a bruised bone," Johnny said after examining the animal's leg and hoof. "I don't know what it's called. This one here."

"The pastern."

"If you say so. He'll be all right if you don't let anyone ride him for a while. Say eight or ten days."

"What about the other one?"

"You give him to your boy there. He'll be all right around the ranch. No good for long drives. Too narrow in the chest."

"You're a Yankee, I believe. No offense," the major said. "I happened to notice an accent in your speech. It's New England, am I right? Vermont, I'll wager."

"New Hampshire," Chris said, stonefaced, imagining what the major would have said if he had known that Johnny was still more at home speaking Cheyenne.

"Well, no matter if you're both Yankees," the major said. "By God, Hardeman, you must have raised the boy in a stable. He has surely got a way with horses." Chris had said nothing. "Damn it all, man, I can't put the boy in charge of the whole damn cavvyard!" the major had exclaimed, and Chris had grinned. Cavvyard was what Texans called the remuda, which was what the Spaniards called a bunch of horses. The profusion of tongues among the whites had not surprised Johnny, not after living with the Cheyenne and Sioux and Arapaho.

"Just let me work with the horses," Johnny had said, and the major had agreed. From Texas to Kansas five years running, working with horses had been Johnny's doorway into the white world. Wherever he and Chris had gone, there were always horses, draft horses and cattle horses, horses for work of many kinds, and even on the frontier they were sometimes kept purely for pleasure, and a young man who could gentle and train them quicker than most, with no harsh words or brutality, was always in demand. Johnny had marveled that a skill he took for granted was so valued by the whites, and over the years he had come to see that his way with horses could take him wherever he wanted to go. He could stay in any place as long as he liked, and when he wanted to move on he could pack up and leave, sure of finding work in the next place that struck his fancy, and in the end it was this sense of being his own man that had made him choose to remain among the people of his birth, living as one of them.

There had been no single moment when Johnny had made his decision. Rather it was as if it had been made for him some time back and left for him to discover. He had discovered it two weeks ago in Ellsworth and he had told Chris about it the same day. That morning, at the stables where he worked, a cattle buyer from Chicago had offered him a job. The man was raising racehorses and he wanted Johnny to come and work for him as a trainer. Johnny had said he would have to think on it, and as he pondered the offer that afternoon, it struck him that there was no reason he should not take the job. Chris would want nothing to do with a place like Chicago, but Johnny had never seen a big city. Why not go by himself? He had found the thought exhilarating. He could get the feeling of standing on his own two feet with no one to look out for him, and after a time he and Chris could hook up again as equal partners, man to man.

136

With that realization, he had become a free man. The understanding of his independence was simple and strong, like something he should have known long before. "How will I know when it's time?" he had asked Chris when they were first together, and Chris had said, "You'll know. And then you won't need me anymore." He hadn't really intended to say anything to Chris about his new feeling, not until he had more time to be sure of it, but in the evening after supper the words had just come out of him as if they were said by someone else, and the minute they were out, Johnny had felt proud of himself.

But before he could accept a job in Chicago or anywhere else he had an obligation to fulfill, and so he had turned the cattle buyer down and he and Chris had set out for the Big Horns to find Sun Horse. He had thought at first to come alone, but the truth was, he had been a little afraid of that notion. One white man riding by himself into the heart of the Sioux hunting grounds might not get a chance to say who he was or why he had come, if he were taken by surprise. Two men would have a better chance, he had reasoned. Chris was a scout and he knew how to deal with the Indians, and so Johnny had asked him to come along, glad of the chance to make this last journey with his partner before setting out on his own.

And then yesterday morning down in the willows below Putnam's Park, he had awakened with a strong desire for a sweat bath, although he had not had one for more than seven years. The urge had not struck him as strange. It was the simplest ritual of the plains people, practiced in a like manner by the Sioux and Cheyenne and many other tribes as well, a cleansing made in preparation for other ceremonies, before hunting, before any serious undertaking, and Johnny had performed it as a fitting preliminary to seeing his Sioux grandfather again. It had taken him only a short time to build the small structure and warm the rocks on the fire, and when he emerged from the heat and the steam he had felt renewed, ready to confront Sun Horse, ready for whatever might come. But it seemed to him now that he had washed away not only the stink of the towns and saloons but his deeper attachments to the white world as well, leaving himself cut adrift, his confidence in why he had come shaken and his memories of the Kansas town he had left only two weeks before unaccountably remote.

Elk Calf Woman stirred in her sleep. She rolled onto her back and began to snore softly. The wind shook the smoke flaps and blew the rising smoke back into the lodge. Johnny got up quietly and stepped outside to adjust the flaps. It was beginning to snow. Beyond the camp circle, the horses had turned their tails into the wind. To the east a few stars were visible, but the clouds were sending probing fingers out toward the plains, settling lower and snuffing out the stars one by one. It was not a true storm, Johnny knew. The clouds had formed around the mountain peaks in late afternoon and descended to the foothills as night fell. Tomorrow might dawn as clear as today, or the clouds might linger on for a day or two and drop a few inches of new snow on the mountains. Mountain squalls could be severe, even dangerous, while fifty miles away on the plains the sun shone brightly.

As he settled himself by the fire again, Johnny welcomed the warmth and the shelter. Once more the tipi and the fire and the sleeping women were all that was real, and it seemed to him that something deeper inside him than the thoughts a man turned over in his mind had pushed him to make the jump across the gulf that separated whites and Indians so he could feel comfortable once more in a smoky lodge, if only for a few fleeting moments. What was it that could push him so, almost against his will? It was a force beyond his control, something that moved him toward events he couldn't see on his own, something like the spirit power his grandfather had told him about all those years ago on the morning of his dream. "You have been given a promise," Sun Horse had said. "If you remain true to your dream, in time the power will touch you."

Could it be that such things were real after all? Hadn't the dream said he would leave the Cheyenne? And hadn't he left them at the Washita, feeling so rootless and alone at first, just the way he felt now....

It was true! What he felt now was the same thing he had felt seven years ago as Chris Hardeman carried him from the lodge where his parents lay dead and away from the burning ruins of Black Kettle's village!... But he had overcome it then, and he had found a place for himself among the whites. Why did he have to bear it a second time?... Because his grandfather had seen to it that he would come back! "When it comes your time to choose between the worlds, come to see me," Sun Horse had said, making him promise, knowing that to keep his promise he would have to leave the white settlements behind and return to the Lakotas, where all his old memories would be awakened!

He had come back as he had promised, and now he truly stood between the worlds.

In his own lodge Hears Twice sat quietly in his accustomed place, facing the entrance across the fire. It was called *chatkú*, the seat of honor, sometimes given to a guest of high standing, usually occupied by the man of the lodge. It had been offered with unexpected deference to Hears Twice two winters before, a few days after the old man had heard his son-in-law complaining in the night to Mist that her father was worthless. Hears Twice knew that his daughter had demanded this concession in some way Little Hand could not refuse, as a means of asserting her father's place in the lodge. Usually he took pleasure and amusement at Little Hand's continued discomfort in this matter—the warrior was too proud, and devoid of humor—but this evening Hears Twice was as oblivious to such things as he was to the small movements in the lodge as Mist prepared the sleeping robes for her husband's return from the council. In warmer weather Hears Twice would have sat outside the camp circle, free from all distractions, as he did when he listened to those special sounds only he could hear—the sounds of what was to come—but tonight even in the tipi he could sense the approach of something he had first heard before his trip to the white settlement, before the arrival of Sun Horse's grandson and the *washíchun* scout. The meeting he heard had not taken place yet, but it would happen soon, and what was still unseen drew steadily nearer.

The raiders struck in the dead of night when everyone in the camp was asleep, save for the herders and pickets. It was the second night of the march and the expedition was camped on the Dry Fork of the Cheyenne River, less than thirty miles from Fort Fetterman. The beef herder saw the horsemen first and he cried an alarm twice before a shot caught him square in the chest and hurled him from his horse.

Whitcomb was awakened by the herder's warning cries and when the first shots sounded he was already slipping into his buffalo greatcoat. It seemed to him that only moments had passed since he had been lying in his bedroll looking up at the fat crescent moon, which hung in the sky like something almost artificial. It was like a clever creation for a night scene on a theater stage, he had thought, a man-made moon lit from within by a coal-oil lamp. But no lamp ever burned as clear and bright. He realized that he must have dropped off to sleep soon after thinking those whimsical thoughts, for the moon was nearly touching the horizon now, its light silhouetting the fringe of pines on a low ridge ten miles west of the encampment.

Just after dark he had taken a last turn around the E Troop bivouac to see that the horses were picketed properly and the men had their "A" or dog tents set up and sufficient bedding from the wagons. As long as the column was in company with the supply wagons, the men would sleep in tents and there would be extra blankets and robes and even crushed-cork mattresses for some, but Whitcomb had decided to sleep from the start as he would sleep throughout the campaign. Satisfied that everything was in order, he had spread his bedroll out on the ground beyond the company's twin rows of tents as he had done the night before. The canvas strip in which his buffalo robe was wrapped was laid down first, then a double poncho of India rubber to ward off the dampness, and then the robe itself, in which Whitcomb wrapped himself thoroughly. After the trip from Fort Laramie, when he had only the robe, his new accommodations seemed the height of luxury. When the attack came he discovered that there was an important advantage to sleeping under the stars: he was the first man on his feet, his new Army Colt in his hand, ready to repel the attackers, while the rest of the company struggled to escape the confines of their tents.

A shape loomed up beside him. "Report, Mr. Whitcomb?"

He recognized Lieutenant Corwin in the dim moonlight. Corwin was in his field blouse and he too had a pistol in his hand.

"Sorry, sir. I have no idea what caused the alarm."

"What in hell's going on?" came a shout from across the camp.

"Indians!" someone answered.

"Where'd they go?"

"This way," came a cry from the left, and then, "Over here!" from the right.

First Lieutenant Francis Corwin, brevet major, had reddish-brown hair and tired eyes that sparked now with sudden life as the camp erupted in confusion around him. "Find Sergeant Dupré," he said calmly. "Tell him to get eight men mounted up and wait for my orders by the picket line. Tell Polachek to hold the rest of the men in a defensive perimeter and for Christ's sake not to shoot unless they have a clear target. When you've done that, report back to me."

"Yes, sir!" Whitcomb made as if to doff his cap in the traditional salute to a superior officer, but his Colt was in his right hand and he realized that the salute, which was a custom of the service, not a regulation, was a waste of time in battle. He ended the motion awkwardly, embarrassed by his own stupidity, then turned and set off down the tent line at a trot, determined to carry out his first order under fire in record time. He and Corwin had got off on the wrong foot and he was anxious to repair the damage as soon as possible.

Two days ago he had met Corwin in the officers' mess at Fetterman, already eating. "See me in my quarters after dinner," Corwin had said, and an hour later Whitcomb had reported to a tiny room in the Bachelor Officers' Quarters. Three iron bunks had been fitted into the small space in the effort to accommodate Crook's command on the post. The extra beds had displaced the usual folding and rawhide chairs, leaving as additional amenities only a pine washstand, a greenish looking-glass, a chromolithograph of the coast of Maine, and two chintz curtains. When Whitcomb appeared, Corwin had been forced to sit on his own bunk to receive his new subaltern after first pushing aside some books and his folded dress uniform.

"So you're the Rebel cadet" had been his opening words. Whitcomb had heard the hostility in his tone and his heart had fallen.

"Yes, sir," he had replied.

"If I had my way," Corwin had said, looking him in the eye, "no offspring of Rebel officers would be at West Point and sure as hell none would serve in this army. But then I don't have my way, do I?"

Whitcomb had ventured no answer to that question and after a moment Corwin had waved at the opposite bunk. "Sit down, Mr. Reb. Has anyone told you about the situation in this troop?"

Whitcomb nodded. On first hearing of "Major" Corwin from Lieutenant Bourke, Crook's aide, he had assumed that Corwin was E Troop's commander, but as he left the mess hall after the noon meal he had been intercepted by Bourke, who had taken him aside and informed him that Corwin was actually the troop's first lieutenant, although he had been brevetted a major during the war and had

140

commanded a battalion at the time. It seemed that Company E's true commander, one Captain Alexander Sutorius, was under arrest at Fort D. A. Russell, the troop's permanent post, for chronic drunkenness, leaving Corwin in temporary command for the duration of the present campaign.

"Most officers make a great to-do about their brevet ranks," Bourke had said, "but not Boots Corwin. He won't insist you call him Major. I observe the courtesies and refer to him that way in General Crook's presence. I thought you should know what was what before you met him."

"I appreciate your taking the trouble to tell me, Mr. Bourke," Whitcomb had replied, genuinely grateful. Remaining ignorant of Corwin's position could easily have led him to put his foot in his mouth, and once he was there in the tiny room with Corwin he had been careful to give his superior no further cause for annoyance. Corwin seemed to find the mere fact of his Southern birth quite sufficient.

"We're on our own, Mr. Reb, just the two of us," Corwin had said. "But this troop is going to perform as if we had a full complement of officers. You may be a Rebel, but you're my Rebel now, so hear me well. We have good non-coms. First Sergeant Dupré and Sergeant Polachek and Corporal McCaslin are the backbone and the rest are good enough. They're all veterans. When you don't know what to do, and that will be most of the time, ask me or ask one of them. They may be wearing stripes, but they know a hell of a lot more than you do, and don't forget it. I will expect you to think for yourself when you have to, but when you're within reach of my orders you will follow them without question. I want that to be as clear as spring water. Understood?"

"Yes, sir," Whitcomb said again. Corwin had asked him a few questions then, about his duties since leaving West Point and why he wished to be a cavalryman, and finally he had dismissed him brusquely, leaving Whitcomb feeling that he had a black mark on his record before he even began, through no fault of his own.

He came upon a knot of men and made out Sergeant Polachek, the senior line sergeant, in their midst.

"Polachek!" he called out, lowering his voice as he reached the man's side. "Form the men in a defensive line on the camp perimeter and tell them to hold their fire unless they have a definite target. Quick now."

"Yes, Leftenant. I haff already given such orders." Polachek had learned his English in England and his Middle-European accent was strangely tinged with British mannerisms.

"Where is First Sergeant Dupré?" Whitcomb demanded. "I have an order for him from Major Corwin."

The spare form of Corporal McCaslin appeared at his side. "He's took two men and gone to see after the horses, sorr. Just to be certain there's nothin' amiss there."

"Good. You take four more men and bring them to the picket line. You're to get them mounted and await the major's orders. I'll inform Sergeant Dupré."

Without waiting for a reply, Whitcomb turned and started off at a trot toward where the troop's horses were picketed. Each company's mounts covered a fair expanse of ground at the edge of camp. When the column halted for the night, each trooper rushed to stake his horse in the best grass available; planting a picket pin established his claim, which extended the length of a lariat in all directions, and woe to the trooper that staked an overlapping claim. In hostile country the mounts were usually hobbled on picket lines at dark, but no one had expected an attack this close to the Platte.

The camp was growing quiet as officers took control of their men. The campfires had been quickly smothered and the only light on the scene was supplied by the setting moon. Soft calls from one point to the next revealed that no one knew where the shots had come from, and on every side men looked fearfully about with guns held ready.

As Whitcomb approached E Troop's horses he could make out the beef herd beyond. The steers were bawling anxiously and milling about; from somewhere in the darkness came the sound of a man moaning softly. Whitcomb spied the stout form of Sergeant Dupré talking to the horse guards and he quickly conveyed Corwin's instructions. With his orders carried out, he started back for the company's tent line, moving along the edge of camp, when a shift in the breeze brought him the faint sound of hoofbeats and he made out two horsemen streaking for the beef herd. The Indians were clinging low to the necks of their mounts, riding straight for the camp.

"There they are!" he shouted, and even as the warning left his lips he was cocking the Colt, which he had held in his hand all the while. He squeezed off a shot and he knew he would remember the moment forever—the first shot he had fired in anger. But it wasn't anger, or the chaos of battle his father had described. The scene was unnaturally quiet, broken only by the mooing of the frightened steers, and the emotion he felt was little more than a childlike excitement.

The Colt bucked again, brought to bear and fired almost without his conscious effort; he had been taught familiarity with hand and shoulder arms since early boyhood and the actions came automatically to him. There were other shots now, the booming of Springfield rifles from Major Coates's infantry pickets and the crack of a Winchester. The Indians whooped and urged their ponies ahead, darting among the cattle, which scattered at their approach.

Whitcomb lowered his gun and hesitated, uncertain which way to go. He was ordered back to Lieutenant Corwin but the attackers were in the other direction. He saw motion near the horses and made out Corporal MacCaslin and his men arriving to join the horse guards, who were gathering mounts from the picket ground. Sergeant Dupré already had one horse saddled. Beyond the horses, steers were bolting in every direction from the herd, and the milling in the center of the bunch revealed the progress of the Indians, who were hidden in the rising dust. The steers running toward the camp found themselves confronted by men afoot, wagging their hands and shouting, and the frightened animals shied away,

142

turning back into the herd and past it, and from these the leaders took their direction. In the blink of an eye the bunch had form and purpose, stringing out away from the camp, wheeling to the south. Full of all the fear that the uncertain smells of a strange landscape and sudden noises in the night had awakened in them, they turned toward the trail by which they had come to this place, perhaps lured by some dim memory of Fort Fetterman, where they had grazed peacefully for more than a week before being prodded northward against their will. The edge of the herd passed among E Troop's horses, spooking those closest to the frightened steers. Sergeant Dupré's horse shied and broke away from him, cantering off in a snaking path that brought it near Whitcomb, some fifty paces distant.

"Whoa, now," Whitcomb said in a gentling voice that carried through the din of rushing hooves and bawling steers. He held out a hand to the animal. Its eyes were wide, the whites showing; faced with panicked cattle on one side and a man on the other it chose the man, slowing to a walk and allowing him to take the reins. Whitcomb reached his decision almost without thinking. He swung up the on-side stirrup and cinched the girth in a single motion, too fast for the horse to inhale if it were a bloater. With the girth made fast, Whitcomb was in the saddle in an instant and off in pursuit of the herd, which was even then vanishing into the darkness. He was beyond the reach of Corwin's orders and opportunity had presented itself. It was a chance to show his superior what he was made of. "Follow me!" he called out, and then he gave his attention to the rough terrain, keeping an eye on the cattle as they arced in a long curve around the encampment.

There was no sign of the Indian raiders as he gained on the tail end of the stampeding herd. The cattle raised dust on each stretch of bare ground and bawled as they ran, never swerving from the course they had chosen once they completed their sweep around the camp and found the smells of the trail back to the fort.

Behind him, already faint in the distance, he heard the call to boots and saddles from at least one bugle. There would be help on the way soon. Meanwhile he would do what he could. Ahead of him the steers flowed down into a ravine and up the other side with barely any loss of speed. One animal bellowed hideously as it snapped a leg and fell. Whitcomb's horse stumbled once but caught itself, and it struck him that if he were unhorsed out here he would have a long walk back to camp in the dark.

In that moment, with the realization that his life was truly in peril, the campaign became real for him. Until now it had been little more than the fulfillment of a boyhood dream, full of romance and devoid of danger, although since his arrival at Fort Fetterman most of his ideas about what life with the frontier army would be like had been rudely shattered, commencing with the image he had of himself riding to battle in a column of smartly uniformed men. He had greeted with stunned disbelief the garments urged on him by the post trader, to whom Lieutenant Corwin had sent him in response to his embarrassed question about what General Crook might have meant by "proper clothing." Many of the items were unfamiliar to him and he hesitated to don them, but when the expedition had formed up the following morning, he saw that all notions of regulation dress had been thrown to the winds as the command clothed itself for the campaign. Uniforms, what few items a man deigned to keep from his standard issue, were buried under buffalo and bear greatcoats and overblouses of Minnesota blanket. Field boots were discarded in favor of high buckskin moccasins worn over two pairs of heavy woolen stockings and then themselves stuffed into buffalo overboots almost too cumbersome to fit a stirrup. Similarly discarded were the officers' sabers, which were heartily denounced as a "clattering nuisance" in the field. Emblems of rank were dispensed with as well, although General Crook wore a black Kossuth hat with the insignia attached and had replaced his bearskin hunting coat with an army overcoat trimmed with a high collar of wolf fur that came, Whitcomb was assured by Corporal Stiegler, from a wolf Crook himself had shot with a pistol while on foot. Apart from the general and a few others who kept the Kossuth hats, the common headgear was a woolen campaign hat with fur borders that pulled down over the ears. Those who could afford them wore green Arizona goggles as well, so called because they had first been used to protect the eyes in the desert Southwest, where the sun was intense, before being drafted into service for winter campaigns. The post trader had included a pair of the goggles in Whitcomb's kit. Once on the march it had struck Whitcomb that the cavalry bore more resemblance to a raiding party of Cossacks or the Mongol hordes of Genghis Khan than a force of the United States Army, save for the Springfield carbines, which were hung from the shoulder by a sling and rested muzzle down in a socket on the off-side of the saddle, and the coloring of the horses by troop, which was visible from a great distance. This was a custom originated at the instigation of General Custer shortly after the war, whereby all the bay horses were assigned to a single company, all the blacks to the next, and chestnuts, grays, sorrels and the other colors all similarly assigned; the roans, piebalds and other leftovers went to Company M, the last in the military alphabet, giving rise to its designation as the Brindle Troop. Depending on the horses available, a regiment might have two or more troops with mounts of the same color. General Crook's command contained elements of both the Second and Third Cavalry Regiments, and as it happened, there were two bay troops in the column, of which Whitcomb's company was one. At Fetterman he had reluctantly given up the sorrel gelding that had carried him safely from Cheyenne in exchange for a mount of the proper color.

To Whitcomb's surprise, General Crook himself rode not a horse but a mule that had carried him through all his Arizona campaigns, a sturdy specimen called Apache.

Behind the ten companies of cavalry, the men all clothed in motley anonymity and the horses wearing their different colors with pride, came the two companies of infantry, followed by the ambulances, supply wagons, pack train and beef herd. There were eighty-six wagons, four hundred mules and sixty steers. It was an imposing force, and before long Whitcomb had begun to take a perverse pride in the rough appearance of the men. The frontier Cavalry was already an uncommonly hirsute military force, with individually tailored sideburns, mustaches and chin whiskers everywhere in evidence; once on the march the differences began to pale as most of the men allowed their facial hair to grow unhindered as protection against the weather. Within just two days, most visages were darkened by the beginnings of full beards, increasing the column's resemblance to a band of brigands.

From the start, Whitcomb had been impatient with the pace of the march. On the first day the column had gone into camp at one o'clock, after covering just twelve miles. On the second day, sixteen was sufficient. Neither officers nor men seemed put off by the slow progress, but Whitcomb was champing at the bit. The country north of Fetterman was gently rolling, sparsely covered with bunchgrass and small clumps of sagebrush, and it seemed to go on forever. Because of the undulations of the land the command could never see more than a mile or two in any direction, and when some distant landmark, such as the four squat forms of Pumpkin Buttes off to the northeast, was seen first from one rise and then another, it never seemed to grow nearer. It had occured to Whitcomb that in such country a body of armed men, friendly or hostile, could approach close to the column without being detected, and he had placed this lesson in his memory, but until the moment of the attack it had been widely assumed that the hostiles were far to the north. This impression had been reinforced on the first day of march, when the command had encountered a band of Arapaho moving toward the agencies. "Heap plenty Minneconjou," they had told the scouts, pointing north and describing a distance the scouts had interpreted as being about seventy miles or more. Crazy Horse was reported to be up there, and within half an hour his name had been spoken up and down the length of the column.

Now, alone on the prairie, chasing pell-mell through the dark after the fleeing cattle, Whitcomb wondered if the hostiles might not have been watching Fetterman all the time, just waiting for Crook to venture out. The column had marched under a brilliant sun despite Crook's hope for bad weather. It had snowed the night before they left the fort, confirming the scouts' predictions, but since then the entire countryside had been clear, save for the distant Big Horns, which had remained hidden under a low bank of clouds that clung to the mountains like a winter cape. Had the command been shadowed every step of the way? Whitcomb felt a chill, as if someone were watching him from behind.

The Longhorns had found their stride now and even stretched low over his horse's neck he could gain no ground on the herd. He knew next to nothing of beef cattle, but he saw their steady run and fear-driven determination and in a moment of unpleasant comprehension he knew that he had no hope of turning them without help. He looked back over his shoulder. Off to his right the last sliver of the moon was sinking below the horizon. If a party of troopers had been sent out, chances of overtaking the cattle in the thickening gloom were next to nothing. Simply following the trail would be difficult enough. He was on a fool's errand.

145

As soon as the realization came to him, he acted to correct his mistake, slowing his mount to a canter and reining him back in a tight turn. The quick response of the horse to the command of the reins saved Whitcomb's life.

A shot came from very close at hand and a ball tugged at his shoulder, jerking him around in the saddle. Even as he kicked his horse into a gallop once more, he looked about and gasped to see an Indian horseman almost upon him. The sound of the unshod Indian pony had been hidden by the rumbling hooves of the cattle, now rapidly fading into the distance. The Indian fired again and Whitcomb saw that the man was shooting a pistol.

He urged his horse into a flat-out run, but even so the brave drew alongside of him, his arm holding the pistol straight out. There was a loud click as the weapon misfired, clearly audible across the short distance, and Whitcomb thanked a kind Providence for the cap that had fallen off or the powder that had fouled or the brave's carelessness in checking his loads. He drew his own pistol and threw a shot at the Indian, who shied off and lost a little ground but kept coming. Whitcomb leaned low in the saddle, concentrating on goading the horse onward. He wished he had reloaded the Colt back in camp. How many shots had he fired? Two in camp and one now. He had had only five to begin with because the hammer rested on an empty chamber for safety's sake, so he had two left. He had better not waste them.

At home in Virginia, Whitcomb had ridden to hounds and taken part in steeplechases and he prayed now that his unfamiliar mount would prove up to the race. The cavalry horse plunged into the ravine he had crossed with the cattle only moments before and surged up the far side without breaking stride. Whitcomb no longer looked back, concentrating instead on spurring the animal on, signaling in every way he knew that the utmost speed was needed.

And then suddenly he saw a fire in front of him and the tents of the encampment in their neat rows. He cast a look over his shoulder but the Indian was nowhere to be seen.

Ahead of him a frightened trooper raised a rifle. "Hold your fire!" Whitcomb shouted and he reined in his horse as he passed through the sentries. Armed troopers were spaced evenly around the perimeter of the camp and the fires were being rekindled. He kept away from the light, hoping against hope that his absence might not have been noticed and his re-entry into the camp might miraculously go unremarked, but even as he dismounted, Lieutenant Corwin walked through the light of the nearest fire and approached him.

"Are you a born fool, Mr. Reb?" Corwin's voice was heavy with sarcasm.

"The beef herd was getting away, sir. I tried to stop it. I assumed some help would be sent along."

"No help was sent because no one knew you were gone. And we sure as hell wouldn't risk the men just to chase cattle half way through the night. Can you think hard and tell me why not?" Whitcomb said nothing and after

146

a moment Corwin supplied the answer. "General Crook would prefer not to have the next Captain Fetterman come from his command. Now do you understand?"

"Yes, sir." Whitcomb understood. Corwin was referring to the darkest chapter in the annals of the Indian wars. In December of 1866, during Red Cloud's War, Captain William Fetterman had left Fort Phil Kearny with eighty-one men to pursue a small party of Sioux. He had been under strict orders not to go beyond a ridge within sight of the fort, but his column had followed the taunting raiders over the ridgeline and not a man had come back alive. The raiders had been decoys and Fetterman had followed blindly into the trap.

"We heard shots. Were you attacked?"

"Yes, sir." Only now did Whitcomb remember the tug at his shoulder from the Indian's first shot. He felt no trace of a wound. He reached up and found a hole in the buffalo coat where the Indian's ball had torn the leather.

"How many savages were there?"

"Just one, sir. That is, I only saw one."

"I don't imagine you brought him down?"

"No, sir."

"Then it seems you have nothing to redeem your escapade. Now I will say this just once. During this campaign you will be put at risk often enough by the orders of your superior officers. Wait for those orders and don't set out to be a hero."

By the look on Whitcomb's face the young officer had learned his lesson. Corwin hoped it was so, and he hoped that his first impression of Hamilton Whitcomb was not wrong.

Corwin was still angry with himself for revealing to Whitcomb the bitterness that had lingered in him since the end of the Rebellion. Back in his cramped billet at Fetterman he had set a bad example by letting his personal feelings show, and he had sought to cover his mistake by trying to learn a little about his new second-in-command. He had looked at Whitcomb's papers and was surprised to discover that Whitcomb had graduated twelfth in his class.

"You had a good record at the Point," Corwin had remarked. "Good enough to have chosen the artillery or the engineers." Those branches of the army were customarily the first choices of the top graduates of West Point, but Whitcomb had requested duty with the cavalry.

"My people are cavalrymen, sir," Whitcomb had replied stiffly.

Attached to Whitcomb's record was a list of his male relatives who at one time had served in the United States Army. His father and an uncle were both graduates of the military academy, and after each name Corwin had noted the letters C.S.A. appended. Seeing that, his anger had risen again. He had spent two long years in a Rebel prison and he was lucky to have survived. Many of his friends had died of starvation or disease, but he had seen Rebels starving too, after the war, and he had recognized the bitterness of jealousy in his resentment of Whitcomb. In the young officer before him, he had seen someone who might succeed where he had failed.

Boots Corwin was a veteran of fifteen years in the army and his career had nowhere to go. Brevet major was almost certainly the highest rank he would ever attain, and even that was just a vanity with no substance. Brevet ranks were temporary, conferred for heroic service. During the heady days of the Civil War, when mounted officers had been felled like stalks of wheat, and men were promoted in uncounted numbers to meet the needs of command, hundreds of men had risen from the ranks, Corwin among them, and brevet promotions had been doled out freely, enabling junior officers to serve in positions of command higher than that to which their regular ranks entitled them. Before his capture and imprisonment Corwin had commanded a battalion of cavalry, exercising the full authority of a major. But after the war Congress had quickly reduced the army to fifty-four thousand men, then to forty-two thousand, leaving the service overloaded with officers, most of them veterans of the war who were entitled to be addressed by their brevet ranks and to wear the corresponding insignia but reduced again to command positions commensurate with their permanent ranks. To thin the top-heavy officer corps, service records were given a thorough going over by boards of review, which were quickly dubbed "Benzine Boards," after the harsh and ever-present cleanser. Between 1869 and 1872, seven hundred officers with less than commendable records were washed from the service, which still left more than enough men in command after Congress reduced the army in 1874 to a total of twenty-five thousand men.

Boots Corwin had survived the Benzine Boards, and being demoted from commander of a battalion back down to second-in-command of a single company had been no more than he expected. His imprisonment had crippled his career in mid-stride, just when he had become convinced that he was destined for higher things. While the war lasted he had hoped to be exchanged, in order that he might take part in the fighting again and prove that his early recognition was deserved. But when he had finally been exchanged it was in order that he not die in Rebel hands; by the time his unexpected recovery was complete, the war was over. He had applied at once for duty on the frontier, for it was clear even then that the Indians were not going to accept the advance of civilization without complaint, and where there was battle there was the chance of promotion. The only alternative was to take part in the social climbing and politicking that accompanied the quest for permanent promotion in every army post east of the Missouri, and Corwin had no taste for such pastimes, where he felt at a disadvantage to the well-bred and socially polished West Point officers. On the frontier posts the natural aversion between the West Pointers and the Volunteer officers, many of whom had risen from the ranks as Corwin had done, was held in check by the presence of a common enemy and the opportunities every man had to prove his individual worth in demanding circumstances. But promotions were painfully slow and men grew old in the lower grades. Corwin was thirty-five and he had remained a first lieutenant for thirteen years. He no longer wore the insignia of a major and he did not insist that he be addressed as one, unlike some peacocks whose pride was greater than their hopes of advancement. Corwin wanted an honest promotion won on merit, gained in battle, and he had sensed his chances ebbing away as the years passed; the Indian wars could not last much longer.

There in his quarters at Fetterman, in the eyes of the fuzz-faced youth who had not a scratch on his gold class ring, Boots Corwin had seen the same anticipation of glory and excitement that he himself had felt when he first enlisted, and Whitcomb's hopeful countenance had fanned the awareness of his own failed dreams. But he knew it was done without malice, without awareness.

He had given Whitcomb the customary warning about obeying orders without question, and in the youth's simple "Yes, sir," Corwin had detected no resentment or reservation. It had occurred to him then that perhaps Whitcomb was one of the rare ones, an officer still prepared to learn. If he was, Corwin would take him under his wing and bring him along. Such an officer could reflect credit on his immediate superior, and Corwin had high hopes for the present campaign. Suddenly, unexpectedly, his opportunity had come. With Sutorius under post arrest and himself in command of the company, outstanding conduct during the next few weeks could tip the balance in his favor. But he would need some exploit beyond the ordinary to gain the attention of Colonel Reynolds, the expedition's commander, or perhaps even of General Crook himself. He would need a stroke of luck, and all the help he could get.

Whitcomb had done an idiotic thing in chasing after the beef herd, but he hadn't made excuses. He had taken the blame and stood ready to take his medicine if punishment were given out, but Corwin decided to withhold the sting of the lash.

"All right, Mr. Whitcomb. If you're done with your evening constitutional, perhaps you'll resume your duties. We'll keep a double guard for the rest of the night. Reveille is at five o'clock. See that the men get what rest they can."

"Yes, sir." Whitcomb saluted and he watched Corwin walk away, leaving him alone with his shame and embarrassment. He realized now that he was trembling slightly in all his limbs. He shook himself as if to ward off a chill and looked around. Beyond the nearest fire he caught sight of a face he knew, the forked beard stirred by the light breeze, the level eyes looking at him for an instant before the figure turned away and vanished in the darkness that was now complete. His spirits sank even lower, knowing that General Crook had witnessed his dressing down.

"It is not so bad, sair," a voice said, and Whitcomb saw First Sergeant Dupré and Corporal McCaslin standing nearby.

"What did you say, Sergeant?"

The two non-commissioned officers stepped nearer. "It is not so bad, I think,"

Dupré said in a confidential tone. "You 'ave made a shavetail's mistake. So? You are a shavetail. With respect, sair, Major Corwin, he knows that."

Dupré's r's rolled softly in his throat. HIs hair was black and his mustache was waxed and curled upward into two precise points. He looked more Latin than Whitcomb supposed was common in most Frenchmen. Perhaps in his blood he carried a reminder of Caesar's legions—a moment's dalliance with some fetching Gallic lass two millennia in the past.

Whitcomb smiled ruefully. Dupré's offer of comfort, however small, was welcome. "I hope so, Sergeant. I feel the perfect fool. You'll see to the horses, will you? Make sure the picket line is in order? If you'd take this animal along and unsaddle him, I'd be grateful. I'll see Sergeant Polachek about the guard."

Dupré took the reins and set off, not a man for extra words.

"Beggin' yer pahrdon, sorr. Moight I address the lieutenant confidentially?" Corporal McCaslin stood at parade rest, his eyes looking off into the dark, or not on Whitcomb in any event. His brogue was thick enough to cut with a saber and Whitcomb was hard put not to grin whenever he heard it. Just hearing it now improved his spirits. It reminded him of the appalling Irish accents put on by his classmates at the Point in the impromptu skits that had oftentimes convulsed the barracks, with their barbs equally divided between pompous officers and broadly drawn enlisted men. Whitcomb had half expected to find his entire troop composed of strapping Irishmen who burst into song at the slightest opportunity and were forever drunk or sleeping it off in the guardhouse. Here in Crook's command he had found that the skits struck surprisingly true to the mark, although the officers were a far cry from the stuffy martinets satirized by the cadets; but here he had met for the first time the immigrant soldiers of every nationality whom he had seen depicted in caricature back at West Point. There were Frenchmen and Englishmen and Italians and Germans, the latter seemingly doing their best to live up to the common notion, often found in any duty that required a precise mind and strict devotion to the letter of an order. E Troop had more than its share of the immigrants; in the Third Regiment it was known as the "Foreign Legion," for it possessed not a single non-commissioned officer of American birth. Nearly a third of the company was Irish, and although they had no opportunity to drink once the fort was left behind, they enjoyed a few songs around the evening campfires. The sons of Erin loved horses and fighting and they had flocked to the cavalry in great numbers after the completion of the transcontinental railroad, the work that had first brought many of them out of the teeming eastern cities. Whitcomb had been relieved to find that Corporal McCaslin was a dour man of slight build who neither drank nor cursed and had no voice for singing. His chisel face seemed unacquainted with any type of a smile and he rarely spoke unless addressed, but he was steady, and devoted to the army, Corwin had said. He was formal and correct in his dealings with all officers, and in that respect reminded Whitcomb of his father's colored majordomo. His request to speak confidentially now came as a surprise.

150

"What is it, Corporal?"

"Well, sorr, in the cavalry there's an auld sayin'—'Either the captain or the first sahrgint is a son of a bitch, or yez don't have a throop.' Beggin' yer pahrdon, sorr, but that's the words they use. Well, as yez can see, sorr, First Sahrgint Dupree is a kind man, a natural-born gentleman, yez moight say. And Captain Sutorius is not with us but we've still got a throop, yez can bet yer pay on that. I'll leave yez to make yer own conclusions."

"I won't hear any disrespect for Major Corwin, Corporal."

"Och! Meanin' no disrespect atall, sorr!" McCaslin was genuinely shocked at the thought. "The lieutenant is an officer and a gentleman, sorr, wid more years in this army than I have. He'll take the E Throop to the gates of Perdition and I'll be marchin' alongside him, 'cause I know he'll be comin' back directly after thrashin' the Divil. Himself is a *foine* son of a bitch, sorr, that was what I meant to say. Well, good night, sorr."

With that McCaslin saluted and left him. After he had found Sergeant Polachek and inspected the guards along E Troop's section of the perimeter, Whitcomb continued on around the camp, strolling within the outer cordon of pickets. He was certain he would not be able to sleep again tonight, so he used the time to ponder what McCaslin had said. Perhaps there was some truth in the corporal's words. Corwin had been harsh with him from the start and he seemed to have no great love for Southerners, but he had done nothing that was outright unfair. Perhaps if Whitcomb obeyed orders and stayed on his best behavior, Corwin would warm to him. They were the only two officers in the company, and the better the relations between them, the better the campaign would go.

"Duty first, then initiative," his father had often instructed him in days gone by. He would remember that maxim in the days to come. His father had said something else, though, as well: "It is far better to err by doing than by not doing," by which Cleland Whitcomb meant that an officer who arrived ahead of the rest and acted on his own initiative suffered less for his mistakes than one who obeyed only the letter of his instructions and attempted nothing more. Ham now had the opportunity to learn if that were true.

He nearly stumbled over a figure seated on a low rock. The figure started, and asked, "Who's there?"

"It's Lieutenant Whitcomb, E Troop. Who are you? Oh, excuse me, General, I'm sorry I disturbed you." He felt himself blush and was glad of the dark. Crook was the last man he wanted to see just now, with his humiliation fresh in his mind.

"That's all right, Mr. Whitcomb. I couldn't sleep either. It's something I associate with the start of a campaign. After I have seen action I find that I sleep very well. Perhaps action has the opposite effect on you."

"Yes, sir, perhaps it does."

"'In the intoxication of enthusiasm, to fall upon the enemy at the charge,' eh? It stays with you for a time, especially the first time."

"Sir?"

"Pity the warrior, indeed, Mr. Whitcomb, who never knows that intoxication. Just don't let it overcome your judgment."

Whitcomb blushed again to remember himself just two days ago saying "I don't imagine you have read Clausewitz" to the "scout" with whom he had ridden on the road to Fetterman, the same man who now so gently quoted the Prussian strategist back to him. *In the intoxication of enthusiasm, to fall upon the enemy at the charge...*

"Yes, sir, it was something like that. I'm afraid I made a fool of myself."

"Oh, not entirely, Mr. Whitcomb. You followed your instincts. At least you saw your mistake and made your way straight back to camp. I was not so lucky a few years after the war, out in the Oregon country. We were returning from an engagement with the local Indians, approaching a campsite I knew well, when I saw some sheep tracks. I left the command and climbed to the top of a butte to follow them. Well, don't you know a fog set in just as I reached the top. By the time I found my way down to flat land again, night had fallen and it began to sleet. Before long I was soaked through and I had no matches. In fact, I had nothing to rely upon but my instincts, and so I followed them. I started off in what I took to be the right direction and along about midnight I sat down on top of a sagebrush and waited. Along about two or three o'clock in the morning the sky cleared and the moon came out and there was our camp, half a mile off." Crook paused and stroked first one fork of his beard, then the other. "We have not been given instincts merely to confuse us, Mr. Whitcomb. Over the years they become tempered with experience, but we should never ignore them entirely."

"Yes, sir. I understand, sir. Thank you, sir. Good night."

"Good night, Mr. Whitcomb." Crook heard the young officer's footsteps move away and he resumed his seat on the rock. The breeze had freshened from the west. He missed his dog, but two hundred miles of marching over rock and ice would have lacerated the collie's feet and he would not consent to be carried on a pack animal, so the dog had been left at Fetterman to await his master's return.

If young Whitcomb puts himself in harm's way when next we meet the enemy, and is killed, am I to blame? the general wondered. Perhaps. But the boy needed some encouragement, if he was not to lose his spirit. Corwin was wrong; Whitcomb was no Fetterman. He lacked the fatal arrogance of a Fetterman. There was a cautious self-awareness that would hold him in check. With luck and a little urging he might become one of the peacemakers.

Crook's thoughts turned to Hardeman then, and he wondered where the scout was tonight. He had had enough time to reach Sun Horse, if the peace chief was in his accustomed winter camp.

For some reason he felt the cold suddenly and he got to his feet, stamping to bring some warmth to his legs. A sentry turned in his direction, recognized the tall, bearded silhouette, and continued his rounds.

As he made his way toward the headquarters tents, Crook reviewed his conversation with Hardeman. How the scout had found him in Cheyenne he didn't know, but the man had struck him as being straightforward and sincere, and he had decided to trust him. After all, in Arizona the Apaches had been brought to heel by reason, not by the force of arms alone. Might not the same thing be accomplished here? There was everything to gain if Hardeman was successful. A peace that stemmed from Sun Horse's surrender might well be more lasting than one gained on the field of battle, with all the bitterness and lust for revenge that would give rise to among the young men of the Sioux. Somewhere there had to be an end to the cycle of assault and revenge that both sides had perpetuated on the plains for more than twenty years. The end could come in only two ways—in combat, death and blood, or in a peace made quickly and quietly while the bloodhounds on either side were caught napping. If the fighting continued, sooner or later the Sioux would send the war pipe to their allies and then there would be hell to pay. The formal alliance among the Sioux, Cheyenne and Arapaho was believed to be of recent origin, formed after the early hostilities with the whites, and it was unique in the history of the nomadic and fiercely independent western tribes. The three tribes had agreed to come to one another's aid if any one of their many bands were attacked by the soldiers, and the alliance had been invoked only twice, first by the Cheyenne in 1864, after the Sand Creek debacle, and again four years later by the Sioux, in Red Cloud's War in this very country. Each time the three tribes had taken the warpath together the consequences had been dire for the United States. In January of 1865, following Sand Creek, a thousand warriors had attacked Julesburg, Colorado Territory; they had sacked the town, causing few deaths but much damage to property, and then they had carried the war to the surrounding territories. For most of the next year the western trails were all but impassable without armed escort. Red Cloud's War had been worse. The Indians considered it a great victory, and the massacre of Fetterman and his men their greatest triumph. What might be the cost of a new outbreak, with thousands of warriors moving in concert against the much more numerous white settlements that now dotted the frontier states and territories?

The command tent loomed before him and he found his bedroll beside the tent, which he used only as an office. His striker, Andy Peiser, prepared the bed outside except in foul weather. Peiser knew his commander preferred to sleep where he could see the sky and feel a change in the wind.

Once settled comfortably in his robes Crook lay a while on his back, finding the constellations one by one in and around the broad swatch of the Milky Way that arced across the zenith.

Without the hotheads like Fetterman, and Grattan, who had started it all, would there have been the same history of bloodshed and broken promises between the two peoples? Probably. They were too different. One race would have to submit to the ways of the other, and there was no doubt which would

153

ultimately dominate. Only when the Indians surrendered would red man and white live side by side. The question that remained was when the surrender would be obtained, and at what cost.

Crook was glad that Custer had been called to Washington, although the summons boded ill for Custer's career. The quick-tempered Boy General was a paradox. From his headquarters he fired off one salvo after another in defense of the Indians' right to be treated fairly once they had submitted to the white man's will, yet in the field he was careless of which Indians he attacked and merciless in battle. He was like a sputtering fuse attached to a keg of powder, liable to detonate at any time and destroy the best-laid plans of his superiors, oblivious of the cost to the army and the nation. With Custer gone and Terry in command of the Seventh, there was a better chance that the three prongs of the assault on the Powder River country might coordinate their efforts and bring about a swift victory. Only after the victory could there be justice for the Indians.

The fact was, Custer might do more good for the army in Washington City. If his testimony helped to expose the flagrant corruption in the Indian Bureau, Congress might be better disposed to return the control of Indian affairs to the War Department, where it rightfully belonged. But no matter what the effect of his testimony, Custer was sure to suffer for it. His presence at the hearings could only draw more attention to what was already a major embarrassment to the President, and it seemed certain that Grant's wrath would descend on the colorful general. In all probability he could expect no further field command while Grant remained in office. He would most likely become very familiar with some barren desktop in the capital until after the next inauguration. By then, with luck, the Indian wars on the northern plains would be history.

Crook took a last look around the sky. Above him a star lost its moorings in the heavens and fell, flung across the firmament by an invisible hand, streaking to the north where it disappeared in a final winking flash. He sent a prayer for peace after the falling star and dropped at last into a fitful slumber.

Blackbird moved quickly across the snow in the still brightening light of morning, lifting his snowshoes high, being careful not to catch them on some hidden snag. They were Crow snowshoes, taken by Blackbird's father, Standing Eagle, on a raid he had made against the enemy in the Moon of Falling Leaves, before the first snow. Among the Lakota, it was well known that the *Kanghí oyate*—the Crow people—made the best snowshoes of all.

A sudden squall twisted across the wooded slope, lifting snow from the branches of the pines and whipping it among the bare aspens, gusting up the soft new flakes that had been falling since before dawn.

The boy paused as the squall overtook him, pressing his cheek against the cape of raccoon fur that lay over his shoulders. For a moment his ear grew warm as he scanned the snow with eyes that were quick and bright beneath a high forehead. Under the cape he wore a trade blanket belted at the waist, two shirts, leggings and winter moccasins. He wished he had brought his buffalo robe, but the clothing he had would be protection enough if he kept moving. As the squall subsided, he started off again.

Here among the trees the trail was easier to see. On the open slope where he had first caught sight of the faint tracks he had not been sure they were recent enough to pursue. They were drifting over rapidly, perhaps made the day before, he had thought, but where the tracks entered the shelter of the trees he had found the droppings, not yet frozen, and had set off in pursuit. Where the wind could blow close to the ground the tracks were sometimes no more than faint whirls in the snow, seen by letting the eyes roam the surface for the telltale pattern of irregularities, but Blackbird already tracked as well as a man and he could tell now that he was gaining rapidly on the deer. He hurried on, careful to look ahead as well as down—a hunter who looked only at tracks would go hungry, for his prey would see him before it was seen and would run; if the prey were a great bear or another man, the hunter might lose his life with his eyes still on the ground before him. The boy knew this so well that he no longer thought of it as something to remember; he tracked without effort, moving across the snow as naturally as a lynx, and in the back of his mind it was not meat he tracked, but man, imagining that it was a Crow or a Blackfoot, or the hated *washichun*, who had made these marks in the snow. And as always he also stalked his manhood, sensing it drawing nearer every day; he longed to capture this most of all, impatient for the day when he would be a warrior like his father.

But that day might never come. He came to a halt, losing interest in the tracks. Intent upon the chase, he had forgotten for a time the decision of the council.

Two nights before, the band's councillors had reached no decision. Yesterday, under skies that were mostly clear after a dusting of snow in the night, they had met twice more, once in midday and again in the evening, and when Standing Eagle had returned to the lodge at last, his voice had been laden with disappointment and anger.

"The council will not fight," he had said bitterly to Blackbird's mother. "The washíchun come to steal our land and we will not fight. The council will surrender to Three Stars. All we have they will give to the whites, and our children will grow up as white children do!"

Blackbird and his sister, Red Fawn, had been sent to bed as the council began, but Blackbird had lain awake waiting for his father to return. Standing Eagle's anger had frightened him.

"What did your father say?" Blackbird's mother had asked softly, motioning Standing Eagle to speak quietly so his son and daughter would not be disturbed. But Standing Eagle had seen Blackbird's eyes reflecting the firelight from deep in his sleeping robes.

"Let my son hear his grandfather's words," he said. "Sun Horse says the return of his washíchun grandson has reminded him of the strength of the warrior who does not fight. Only that and nothing more. After that he sat silent as the council talked, silent as they decided that we shall accept the meat Three Stars offers and go with him to the Dakota reservation!"

"And the family of Standing Eagle, what will they do?" Blackbird's mother had asked. His sister was awake too, and they all had awaited Standing Eagle's next words.

"We will leave the Sun Band. We will go to Sitting Bull, where the Lakota still know how to fight."

Blackbird felt his anger rise now, directed at the strange young man who had been raised among the Shahíyela by White Smoke, the uncle Blackbird was too young to remember. His uncle had been killed by washíchun horse soldiers at the Washita River, far to the south, that much Blackbird knew, and he knew he wanted to fight those bluecoat soldiers; he wanted to fight them now to rid himself of his anger against this pale cousin he did not know, against his own grandfather for turning away from him that morning. He had gone to Sun Horse's lodge, needing to tell someone that he was going off to hunt for meat. His father was already up and gone to see how much snow lay on the trail to the north, needing to get away from the village on any pretense. Blackbird had scratched softly at the entrance to his grandfather's tipi and had spoken his name, "Blackbird is here," but instead of the cheerful greeting he usually received, there had been only his grandfather's voice, sounding weary and old, saying, "I am speaking with my grandson. Come back tonight when I have returned from the whiteman's lodge in the valley below."

156

Blackbird had told no one where he went then, sneaking away from the village as if it were an enemy camp, angry at the *washíchun* grandson who had taken up all of Sun Horse's time for two days, angry at anyone who threatened to deny him the manhood he wished for so hard. Already he had killed his first buffalo, and in the Moon of Red Plums he had made his vision quest under the guidance of the *wichasha wakán* Sees Beyond, and he had been given his young man's name, Blackbird. He did not like the name. A blackbird was a small thing, clever perhaps, but not strong like *igmú tanka*, the mountain cat that had come to him in his vision together with the blackbird. Following family custom his grandfather had named him, taking the name from the vision. "Your name is Blackbird," he had said, smiling. "*Igmú tanka* has given you strength to be a hunter, or a warrior if you choose, but the blackbird is wise. Your name will remind you that strength used unwisely is more dangerous than weakness."

It was just like Sun Horse to give him a name that contained a lesson. The old man was overflowing with lessons. Blackbird liked to sit at his grandfather's feet and listen to stories of the days when Sun Horse was a young man, before the *washíchun* came to the plains, but somehow the stories always contained a lesson about what it meant to be a man among the Lakota. Blackbird was still enough of a boy to hope that growing up meant only more chances to ride with the men on their hunt for deer and elk and antelope and buffalo, and to fight real enemies when the time came. But this was not manhood as his grandfather described it. "Becoming a man means not only leaving behind the small bow of a child," he had said. "It means taking responsibility for the people. A man of the Lakota thinks always of the people; he acts always for the good of the people, and to be a leader among the people is to carry the heaviest burden of all. We live in troubled times and the people need wise leaders."

And now Blackbird was not sure he would ever know what it meant to be a man of the Lakota, let alone a leader. He would go with his father to Sitting Bull's camp, making the choice for himself, as a man should. And if the *washíchun* came, he would fight them. At least he would know what it was to fight for the people, perhaps to die for them, as a man of the Lakota.

Before his eyes the tracks were vanishing, drifting full and being wiped away by the wind even as he watched. He raised his face to the clouds and cried out silently, praying for a warrior's strength to see him through the storm and a hunter's cunning to find his prey and bring it home to his family. If he brought back fresh meat, his going off without permission would be forgiven. The family needed meat now more than ever, to strengthen them for the trip north to Sitting Bull.

Blackbird thought suddenly of Yellow Leaf, the daughter of Hawk Chaser. Beneath his deerskin shirts he wore an armband of braided leather that Yellow Leaf had made for him. Would Hawk Chaser follow Standing Eagle, the war leader, or would he surrender? Hawk Chaser was Blackbird's *hunká-até*, his father-by-choice, and next to Standing Eagle the boy respected no man more. Was it possible that he would have to leave Hawk Chaser and Yellow Leaf behind?

He took up the pursuit again, moving off as fast as he dared, almost running, as if his haste might help to assure that Hawk Chaser would make the right decision.

The youth was relieved to find the tracks fresh and clear as he passed over the crest of the small ridge he had been climbing, clearer still as he made his way down the more heavily wooded slope on the other side toward a flat bottom where a creek flowed. The snow thickened suddenly around him, obscuring everything until he could see no farther than the distance across the camp circle back at the village, and for a moment he longed for the comfort of his father's lodge and his mother seeing that his bowl was full, if only with dog stew. And then as quickly as it had come the flurry passed and he saw the deer.

It was a doe. She was moving away from him, pausing now to sniff the wind. Satisfied, she moved on and passed behind a cluster of young spruce at the edge of a small clearing. The boy let out the breath he had instinctively held as he froze in position, hoping the deer had not seen him. He moved forward cautiously and drew an arrow from the quiver that hung at his shoulder. With luck he would have a shot from the edge of the clearing.

He crouched low behind the young trees and peered through the branches. The doe was at the far side of the open space, head down, pawing at the base of a tree, seeking a few blades of grass. Blackbird fitted the arrow to the bowstring and arose as Hawk Chaser had taught him, no faster than a shoot of grass arose from the earth on a warm spring day. But now the doe looked up, eyes wide, muscles tensed. Blackbird held himself motionless, his heart pounding. He had done nothing to reveal his presence; he was downwind of the deer and almost completely hidden by the trees, revealing no man-silhouette; he had made no sound that could carry through the storm. The doe looked about, wet black nose sniffing, graceful ears moving. Blackbird waited. He was not yet ready to make his shot, but any further movement might catch her eye. He must do nothing to alarm her.

But it was no action of the boy's that finally released the trembling muscles of the deer. A trumpeting blast of sound broke from near at hand and sent the deer bounding off through the trees in great leaps that carried her out of sight in the space of a few heartbeats. Blackbird spun in the direction of the sound and his jaw dropped, the bow and arrow forgotten in his hands. Not thirty paces away stood a creature for which nothing in his life nor in the tales of his people had prepared him. A hulking gray-brown body, more massive by far than the largest buffalo he had ever seen, was supported by four treelike legs planted firmly in the snow; from the huge head, a snake grew where a nose should be, and two horns many times longer than those of the bighorn sheep sprouted from the bottom of the creature's head and curved up past the snakelike snout, reaching for the sky. Great flaps stood out from the sides of the head, wings perhaps, to carry the beast aloft so it could swoop down like an eagle to rend its prey with its impossible upside-down horns. The flaps waved back and forth now as the creature raised its head and gave forth once again with the noise that had sent the deer fleeing in terror. As it roared, it lumbered forward a few steps, shaking its head from side to side.

Tasting fear strong in his mouth, Blackbird forced his legs to move. He stepped backward, but at once the tail of the snowshoe caught in the snow and he fought to keep his balance. Turning carefully, he started away through the trees, looking back over his shoulder, praying that the thing would be content to let him go. He broke into a shuffling run.

The eyes spaced far apart in the massive head watched him go, keeping him in sight until his small figure disappeared among the trees. Alone now on the windswept mountainside, the elephant raised his trunk and trumpeted again into the blowing snow.

LISA PUTNAM'S JOURNAL

Friday, March 3rd. 5:50 a.m.

Yesterday, as I glanced often at the trail from Sun Horse's village, I grew increasingly angry at the injustice of his threatened removal from this land. Today I awoke early, and in the moments of my waking I realized that my anger on his behalf is partly a lie. It has not been easy for me to admit this, but I must be completely honest in the days that lie ahead. If I should lose all that my father worked to build, I would want my descendants to know how this came about and to judge if any of the fault may have been my own.

In truth, much of my anger is directed at myself, for failing to see until confronted by this new threat to my home just how much it means to me, and how much I long to remain here and continue in the life my father built; I am angry that Julius and I may not have the chance to succeed or fail here on our own, to see if we are up to the work.

I see too that I have blamed Mr. Hardeman unfairly; he has only brought word of events set in motion through no fault of his own. I should be angry at President Grant and his cronies instead of Mr. Hardeman, but he is here and they are not. I thought myself very clever to tell him of the deed, and my fear of losing Putnam's Park, convincing myself that this was merely a ruse to distract him from my real intention—to help Sun Horse. But my fear for the ranch is very real, and now I am angry with myself for letting selfishness cloud my judgment.

These thoughts come tumbling out, and I am not setting them down very clearly. I hope this process may help to calm me, for from this moment forward, the course of events may depend in part on my actions. Until now I do not believe I could have done anything to change what has come about. I cannot sway the President and the Congress by myself. But now that the danger is at our doorstep I will have a hand in determining the outcome, both for Putnam's Park and, if I can find a way, for Sun Horse. I have no parent to turn to for guidance any longer, but they did not rear me to run from danger. (I do not feel

159

nearly as brave as this sounds. I write it to remind myself of my duty to uphold not only the example set by my father, but that of my mother as well.)

On Tuesday I took a look at my father's life; today I will say a few words about my mother and her family, for she too has lessons to offer. Her decision to marry my father, and, even more shocking, to follow him to this wild place, came as a complete surprise to her relatives. The Emersons tend toward intellectual pursuits and look askance at merchants. They pointed at my father's long stay in the western regions and his failure to assume the running of Putnam & Sons on his return as clear evidence of lack of discipline, a failing they scorn above all else. They knew nothing of the disciplines he mastered in order to survive all those years beyond the limiting conventions of proper society. They arrived early in New England and settled down firmly; the land suited them as did the civilization that arose there, and they made a place for themselves. Unlike the more recent immigrants, or those less fortunate than themselves, who saw the opening West as a place in which to escape old troubles and limitations, the Emersons had no need to escape, and they experienced few limitations on their settled lives. They educated themselves, including the women in the family (I must give credit where it is due), and became professionals, although rarely in professions that earned a great deal of money. For the most part, they scorned wealth. Yet daughters were expected to stay close to their native hearths and to bring new blood, and money, into the family. But within my mother's breast there lived a spirit of adventure undreamt of by her closest kinfolk, and a matching strength of will. My father, of course, perceived this. Her relations did not, until she left them. Even then they expected her imminent return, and only after years of receiving cheerful letters from Putnam's Park did they realize that the family tree had sprouted a branch of pioneers. Then, of course, they took full credit for her decision, and accepted it as proof that the Emersons bred hardy stock. When I went east to school they received me graciously and inquired with genuine interest about every aspect of our life here. They are intelligent people, and always willing to learn. She had those qualities, and an exceptional measure of courage.

Most of these perceptions I gathered from my father, for my mother told her story simply. "I wanted a change," she said, and in those few words she explained her willingness to go beyond the settled life in search of a different achievement and perhaps a deeper contentment. Putnam's Park is as much her creation as my father's, for he would not have remained without her. I will keep their examples before me through whatever comes.

We have no idea why Sun Horse did not come yesterday to convey his decision. "It takes Indians some time to talk things over," Mr. Hardeman said, and his simple acceptance of their differences from ourselves reminded me of my father. Mr. Hardeman is about forty-five, I should say, and bears himself well. He has had much experience on the frontier and has that force of character one expects in men who succeed in making their way out here. He knew my father many years ago, and although he does not say so, I believe my father thought highly of him. I have always found my father's judgment of character to be close to the mark, but I feel some caution where Mr. Hardeman is concerned and I will reserve my own judgment for now. He seems to have a genuine concern for Sun Horse's welfare inasmuch as he is Johnny Smoker's grandfather, but he persists in the belief that surrender is the Sun Band's only course. I see surrender as their last resort and cannot believe things have come to that pass.

As for Johnny Smoker, how I wish I could ask him a thousand questions and hear the entire story of his life, most of all his years among the Cheyenne. Certainly the astonishing fact of his relationship with Sun Horse, and Uncle Bat's evident fondness for him, played a part in my decision to lead him and Mr. Hardeman to the Sun Band's valley, but it did not prepare me for the welcome he received. I have never seen Sun Horse so moved as at the moment he recognized the grandson he believed to have been dead for seven years. And from that moment Sun Horse was not himself. He seemed lost in thought and scarcely aware of the immediate danger to his people. He was attentive when I spoke with him before I left the village, and I hope he heeds my advice, but I fear he did not put much faith in my hopes for a new Indian policy.

Johnny, in what little time I saw him, was mostly silent. He is well spoken and polite when he does speak, and he appears to have good intelligence. Yet there is something about him that makes him seem not quite a part of what is taking place around him. I would not be surprised if he was permanently scarred in some way or other than his physical wound by the manner in which he lost his Indian parents and was returned to civilization. I find myself strangely touched by the boy and his story.

Can he truly want his grandfather to surrender and lose everything?

CHAPTER

TWELVE

Hardeman looked out the kitchen window at the snow that now floated down in a dead calm. All morning the mercury in the big thermometer on the back stoop had hovered near the freezing point while the weather had changed in some way every time he had peered out a window or stepped outside to feel the air. He had been up before dawn, stalking the blue-gray darkness of the empty saloon, pacing off the limits of his patience, wishing for a life in which he would never again have to wait for another man to make up his mind. The snow had been falling then, whirling this way and that in the uncertain gusts, and while he roamed the hallways and public rooms of the sleeping house the wind had risen and brought a moan from the flue of the big saloon stove and a chattering in the strongest gusts from a loose storm shutter somewhere upstairs. As the people had stirred and come to breakfast wrapped in thoughts no one wanted to speak out, the flakes had grown smaller and flew across the yard between house and barn without falling at all toward the earth, and then in the time it took a person to drink half a cup of coffee the wind had dropped to nothing; it was resting, in the way of a spring storm, but it would come back and blow again from the other side before long.

The smell of bacon still hung in the close air of the kitchen. Outside by the barn, Hutch buckled the last strap on the team's harness and swung aboard the empty sled where Julius was waiting for him. The sled moved off quickly down the packed trail that sloped away from the barn and was gone from sight.

The day before, Hardeman had passed the morning by staying restlessly on the move about the settlement. Before breakfast he had helped Harry Wo with the milking and later he had ridden with Lisa almost the whole length of the valley to look at the cattle. They had both kept watch on the creek trail, but neither had spoken of Sun Horse or the Indians. During the noon meal, Hardeman had looked often out the kitchen window and afterward he had stood for a time on the kitchen stoop, waiting, but even then he had known Sun Horse would not come. To decide such an important matter, the Sun Band councillors would talk, and talk, then adjourn to go to their lodges and think, and meet to talk some more. Indians preferred to take the time needed to reach a unanimity of opinion rather than risk a majority ruling that would leave a division in the band, which might weaken it at a crucial moment. They might be talking still, but soon the talking would end.

Today Hardeman was a scout once more, dressed in the scout's uniform of the northern territories. He had worn the buckskin shirt and pants occasionally on the Texas trails but they were unsuited to the respectabililty of the Kansas towns, and they had spent the winter deep in his saddlebags. It had seemed only natural to don them here. He was too hot in the warm kitchen and longed to get out of doors where a man could breathe, but he had no wish to weary himself by pointless wandering. He would wait here. Yesterday he had gone to his room and slept the afternoon away, rising for supper, then going back to sleep again until just before dawn. He was thoroughly rested now and ready for what was to come.

"It will come back around from the other side," he said.

Lisa spooned a last measure of coffee into the enameled pot and set it on the stove to boil. She wore a gray dress of homespun today, one that had belonged to her mother. Her hair was once more piled atop her head; a loose strand hung in her eyes and she brushed at it absently from time to time. "What will?" she asked.

They were alone in the kitchen. Ling had not felt well at breakfast and she had finally consented to rest a while and leave the work to Lisa.

"The wind. It will come back and blow again from the other side before it quits. It always does that on this side of the mountains."

Lisa had noticed when she was a child the way the wind backed in the middle

162

of a snowstorm, but it displeased her that Hardeman should know this secret. It was as if he knew which boards in the upstairs hallway creaked, or how to lift the handle of her bedroom door so it would swing open without a sound.

From close outside the back door she could hear the sound of Harry Wo's axe as he split stovewood. Julius and Harry shared the wood-splitting by mutual consent, not as a way of dividing unpleasant labor but because it was work both men enjoyed, and today was Harry's turn. *Chop*, and then a pause as Harry set another log on the block. *Chop*. Like the ticking of a clock that had lost its momentum and might drag to a halt before Sun Horse brought his answer. *Chop*.

The coffeepot began to hiss within itself. Lisa washed a dish idly, irritated by Hardeman's presence. She did not want to make polite conversation. Each word they had spoken seemed stilted and irrelevant. She wanted to be alone, to recapture for a moment the peaceful solitude she had enjoyed so ungratefully just three days earlier, before the strangers came, before the threat to her home. But Hardeman had shown no sign of leaving when breakfast was done, and she had offered to make another pot of coffee as she cleaned up the dishes.

He had found her early that morning in the library, as she was putting the journal away in the drawer of the mahogany secretary where she sat to write. His breath had smelled of whiskey, and she had found it difficult to maintain the dispassion she had achieved while alone with her journal. But her father had always made the library available to guests and so she had let the scout intrude in what had become her private reserve since her father's death. It was her winter retreat, and Hardeman was the first to broach its sanctuary. She had left him there with scarcely a word and had gone outside in the slowly brightening gloom to climb the rise behind the Big Horse and stand by the graves of her parents, to be alone and think. The handful of others who had died in Putnam's Park over the years were buried in a small plot down beside the wagon road, sheltered by the clump of pines; for twelve years Eleanor Putnam had lain in solitary rest where now she was joined by her husband.

It was from this spot that Jed had first seen the valley that became his home. Lisa had climbed the knoll frequently over the years to tend the flowers on her mother's grave, but only in recent months had she taken the habit of going there to think, standing between the graves, rarely glancing at the two wooden markers, one weathered and the other so new; she knew the names and dates by heart and had no need to refresh her memory.

Today the hillock was almost bare, swept clean by the morning winds, and the stalks of last season's flowers stood bent and broken above the thin layer of snow, marking a rectangle around the edge of each mound. Lisa had looked down the valley, not seeing the house and barn and sheds and the twin ruts of the wagon road, but seeing it instead as it had first appeared to her father, remembering his tale of discovery.

When he left the dying fur trade behind him, Jed Putnam had returned to Massachusetts and his family's shipping business. He made a voyage to the Orient to protect the firm's interests against a threatened British monopoly of the China trade and was gone two years; shorter voyages took him to London and the Caribbean. Between these travels he found time to court and marry Eleanor Emerson, a younger cousin of the well-known lecturer and essayist. Their child Elizabeth was born a year later and Jed settled his wife and child on a farm in Lexington, twenty miles from Boston. He took pleasure in his family, but even they failed to quell his restlessness. The politicking of the seafaring merchant trade held no lasting interest for him and the smoky air and rabbit-warren congestion of Boston oppressed him, and while the Massachusetts countryside was pleasant and serene, it lacked the ruggedness and the untamed nature he had become accustomed to in the western mountains.

His pulse quickened whenever he heard news of the West. He whooped with delight and startled the cook half out of her wits when a letter arrived in the spring of '48 from his brother Bat, saying that he had come along with their old friend Joe Meek, who had crossed the continent to plead for making Oregon a territory. They would be in Washington City on such and such a date, Bat guessed. By the time the letter arrived, the date was at hand. Jed was on the next train.

"What's a coon like you do fer fun up Boston way?" Joe Meek greeted him, once he and Bat were through pounding Jed on the back and cursing, to show their delight at seeing him. "Not much," Jed was forced to admit. "I been to China, though. London too. Got myself a farm." "Hell's full o' farmers," Meek said, and ordered brandy all around. To console themselves once more over the passing of the beaver trade and to commemorate bygone friends, the three former mountain men got moderately drunk and managed to astound or terrify almost all the guests in Coleman's Hotel before the night was over.

And then, not long after this joyous reunion, came the word, moving across the land like lightning, that bright flakes of gold had been found in the tailrace of Johann Sutter's sawmill in the foothills of California.

As soon as it was clear that the strike at Sutter's Mill was something more than a flash in the pan, Jed made up his mind. If the country's westward progress had been slow and steady in recent years, it would be hell-for-leather now, and Jed Putnam did not intend to be left behind. He yielded his interest in J. Putnam & Sons to his brother Jacob in exchange for a fixed amount to be paid over a period of twenty years in installments that would not cut deeply into the firm's capital reserves; he made the same arrangement on behalf of his brother Bat, and in the spring of '49, Jed crossed the Missouri for the last time.

He knew what he was looking for and it was not the ephemeral El Dorado that drew thousands of argonauts along the trails to the Pacific coast. He wanted a home in the mountains, a place to put down roots deep enough to sustain those of his descendants and kin who might want to remain in the place he chose long after his own mortal remains had been turned under its soil.

He signed on with a wagon company in St. Joseph and guided the emigrants to Sacramento, crossing the Divide at South Pass, the same spot where he had said goodbye to the mountains twelve years before; the gateway to the fur kingdom had become the gateway to the West. Jed reveled in the hardships of the journey, confident that he would find what he was looking for if he was patient. One look at the teeming settlements of California convinced him that his future did not lie in that place, already as noisy and crowded and beset by greed and contention as the states back east. But he continued to guide wagons west each summer, and on the return trip he would ride alone or with a companion, revisiting his old haunts and exploring familiar byways, trusting his instincts to tell him when he had found his home. Here and there he encountered an old friend—Jim Bridger at his road ranch on Black's Fork, Tom Fitzpatrick at Fort Laramie, where he was Indian agent to the Sioux. In the fall of 1852 he found his brother Bat on the Tongue River, traveling with Sun Horse's band of Hunkpapa and Oglala, and on the spur of the moment he accepted an invitation to winter with them in the new wintering place the band had adopted just the year before, a secluded valley in the Big Horns. "Shinin' country," Bat said, and Jed agreed when he saw it. The big treaty council of '51 had given the Big Horns to the Crows, but Sun Horse's valley was far in the southern end of the range, and Crows rarely came that far south anymore, choosing instead to yield the ground to their numerous enemy the Sioux.

Jed said nothing of his quest until a time when the snow was deep outside the lodges and there was little to do but smoke the pipe and talk. Then he chanced to remark one evening that perhaps Bat and Sun Horse knew of a place where a man might build a house. Bat looked at Sun Horse and after a time Sun Horse had nodded and smiled.

The next day the three of them put on snowshoes and walked over the southern ridge to a small mountain park that Jed had never seen. They came out of the woods on a low rise that commanded a view of the entire valley and in the space of a deep breath Jed knew that he was looking at his home. But he didn't let his excitement show, not yet. He had to be sure.

For days he tramped the mountain heights on snowshoes with Bat as his guide, exploring the two nearby passes by which generations of Indians had crossed the mountains in summer. One was accessible from the valley by the gentle course of a stream. And then for additional days he rode down to the eastern plains and back until he found a way to the park by a grade gentle enough for wagons to ascend. And only then did he return to Sun Horse's lodge and tell the headman what he had in mind. He had a white wife and daughter and he intended to live like a white man, in a proper house, Jed explained. Wagons would come to the valley, and men who were foolish in the ways of the mountains. But Sun Horse brushed these things aside. It did not matter, he said; in winter there would be no wagons, and winter was when Sun Horse and his people were nearby; in summer they moved north to the Powder and the Tongue and the Greasy Grass to hunt buffalo and camp in the circle of the nation. Jed was welcome in this place. He could trade with the wagons in the summer, and in winter he could visit with his brother Bat and the people of the Sun Band. It was good for the whiteman and the Lakota to live side by side in this place, the headman said.

The fact was, Sun Horse seemed downright anxious that Jed should agree, as if he might have had just such a thing in mind from the start. For Jed's part, he had hoped to live where he might have some peaceful contact with the aborigines, and so to experience once again that part of his mountain life. The arrangement was perfect. When Sun Horse filled a ceremonial pipe and passed it around to seal the bargain, Jed solemnly offered it to the four directions and smoked. He had found what he was looking for.

This morning, as she stood beside her father's grave, Lisa had stood in his moccasins, feeling Sun Horse and Bat by her side, seeing the snow of the valley unmarked except for the feed runs of the moose, which had been more numerous then and were now retreating to the higher valleys west of the Divide. And she had felt a tug deep within her, a contraction of the spirit before a swelling that threatened to burst her heart. The only father she had known was the man who had lived here, at home in the country he loved; she had not known the wandering years of the fur trade or the restless exile on New England shores and far-flung seas. Here Jed had transmitted his love of the land to her and a respect that approached that of the Lakota themselves, who called the earth Grandmother and Mother because it brought forth every generation of man and nurtured each one at its breast. Within Lisa, the love of this land, enclosed and sheltered by the arms of the mountains, was almost painful.

Her father had told her the story of his quest for a home, and of his first view of this valley, on the day she turned twenty-one, not asking that she feel the same thing for Putnam's Park, only wanting her to know what it meant to him. On that same day he had given her a small volume of Thoreau, with a stalk of timothy grass marking a particular page:

> *Of thee, O earth,*
> *are my bone and sinew made;*
> *To thee, O sun, I am*
> *brother.*
> *Here I have my habitat.*
> *I am of thee.*

How could a man like Hardeman understand a tie to the land, a sense of what this home meant to her? He could not. She had seen how he came alive on the trail. It was being on the move that he loved. She had seen it—the eyes always roving, the alertness beneath the outward calm, the body so relaxed in the saddle except for the way he occasionally rolled his right shoulder as if to relieve an almost forgotten pain.

She observed him now as she went about her kitchen chores, not giving him cause to notice that she watched. He sat back in his chair—her father's chair—with his feet on the seat of another, staring out the window at nothing. When he looked in her direction his deep-set eyes were impenetrable, revealing nothing. He seemed to belong here now, clad in his leather shirt and pants;

he was no longer the stranger from the settlements who had sat at the table drinking whiskey only three days before. He could have been from another time, a friend from the fur trade come to visit her father or her uncle Bat. It would be easier then to admit to herself that she found him attractive, easier to get him talking, easier to discover what sort of a man there was beneath that guarded look.... But he was a scout, not a mountain man; he had led General Custer to the Washita and he came here now at another general's bidding.... How could he wait so calmly?!

"Is there a chance the storm will slow down General Crook's march?" she asked, grasping at straws.

Hardeman shook his head, his attention returning from far away. "It's the cold that slows down the army. That and all the fool gear they carry. Crook's done away with most of that. He knows how to cover ground." Nothing short of a blizzard would stop him, and this snowfall was just a half-grown mountain storm that probably wouldn't shed a drop of moisture on the Bozeman road.

"What will Sun Horse and his people do?"

"We'll know soon enough."

"What would you do, if you were Sun Horse?"

"I'm not Sun Horse."

Her patience broke. "Is it that easy to send other men to prison?" Suddenly she wanted to loose all her anger on this man who sat so calmly in her father's chair. "That's what the reservation will be for these people, you know. There are no trees, no game, no camping places that aren't fouled—"

She bit off her words and held the anger in. I need it, she thought. I need it to give me strength. I will fight for Sun Horse and when that is done I will fight to save my home.

But how will I fight? Without an answer to that question her resolve seemed impotent and she felt her courage dissolving. If only she could sway Hardeman to her side. If he were her ally...

She poured a cup of coffee from the pot. "I owe you an apology," she said. "I have been blaming you for bringing bad news, but you are not to blame. I'm sorry."

"There's no need to apologize. We weren't invited. You have been kind, under the circumstances." Hardeman had not meant to make her angry; he welcomed the conversation and wished it to continue, both to keep his mind off the waiting and in the hope of bringing Lisa Putnam around to his point of view. He had provoked her carelessly and he sought a way to placate her now. As Lisa leaned across the table and set the steaming cup before him, he caught a delicate odor he had thought was part of the room, coming perhaps from the woodwork of the cabinets or an unfamiliar herb in the dried bouquets hanging by the sideboard, from which the Chinawoman took a small pinch now and then as she cooked. He realized that it came from Lisa herself, from her hair or a scent she used, or just from her skin.

"Wasn't there a king who killed the messenger because he brought bad news?" he said. He blew on the coffee, regarding her through the rising steam.

"Yes. I can't recall his name right now. Was it Solomon?" she smiled. "No, he was too wise."

Hardeman smiled, and Lisa felt better.

"Maybe it was Lear, on one of his darker days," he suggested.

"You seem to have read a good deal." She took a dish towel from the bar on the oven door and began to dry the dishes.

"More than you expected in a man like me?" Hardeman asked, but he smiled to show that he took no offense. "It was your own father who got me in the habit, and mine, before that. It wasn't something I expected to keep up on the western trails, but Jed was always lending me books that year we rode together. He kept them in his saddlebags, more books than you could imagine. I remember when we got to Sacramento there was a mail package waiting for him, full of books. He sent the old ones off."

"We used to send them from home," said Lisa, delighted by the memory. "First to St. Louis or Independence, then to Sacramento. Twice a year he got new books from the library at home. Tell me which were your favorites."

"Dickens," Hardeman replied without hesitation. "And any man who could tell a good story. Scott. And Shakespeare. Jed said that Bill Shakespeare was the best storyteller in the fur trade, and he had plenty of competition. Your father had this little set of all the plays, each one small enough to put in your shirt pocket, and I carried one of them more than once. I found the whole set there in the library this morning. It was like seeing an old friend."

Lisa pulled out a chair opposite him and sat down. She leaned across the table, the dish towel held in both her hands, and he caught her scent again, more subtle than any perfume. "Sun Horse was my father's friend, Mr. Hardeman, just as you were. He is truly a good man; you must have seen that. He has wintered here in peace since before my father came to this valley. A vision brought him here, to avoid the hostilities. His power is to understand the white men and make a lasting peace, my father said." She was twisting the towel unconsciously, as though wrestling with it. "Don't you see? If Sun Horse could just hold on for one more year, it could make all the difference. President Grant will be gone and there will be a new Indian policy..." She let her voice trail off. Her slim hopes seemed too fragile.

"A year's too long. It will be over by then."

"It doesn't have to be. Not if you help him. He's Johnny's grandfather."

"We helped him all we could by coming here, Miss Putnam. We gave him time." Too damn much time and too many uncertainties to take a hand in things. Too much time to think, and who knows what goes on in that old man's mind. Why did she have to spoil the moment by bringing up visions, and Johnny, and his kinship to Sun Horse?

Doubts about Johnny and his dream and what changes might come over the boy up there in the Indian village had wakened Hardeman that morning, making him rise and dress and sending him out to prowl the house to escape

168

them. He had gone to the kitchen in the hope that Ling Wo might have a fire going, but the stove was cold and the room dark. By the light of a candle he had found a full jug of whiskey in a cabinet and he drank from the jug, lighting a fire within himself to ward off the predawn chill. Then to distract himself he had searched the dim rooms, seeking anything that might make immediate and real the late Jedediah Putnam, the boisterous teacher and companion he had known so briefly, so long ago.

In vacant bedrooms built for people who were long gone and would never come again he had found only the influence of Jed's Boston wife, seeing her hand in the curtains hung at each window—some no longer bright and new but always clean and ironed—the washstands and bedspreads and looking glasses in each room, the framed prints of eastern cities and landscapes and ships traversing the high seas under full sail.

In the downstairs hallway he had encountered the house cat, Rufus, prowling silently, but the cat's search, like Hardeman's, seemed to be fruitless.

Then, rounding a corner, Hardeman had seen light beneath a door, and Lisa Putnam's voice had answered "Yes?" at his knock.

There was no welcome in her eyes when he opened the door, but she had left before he could withdraw, and by the light of two brightly polished brass lamps, their green glass shades and yellow light giving a soothing warmth to the cold light of a stormy morning, he had discovered the library, and it was there that he found what he sought.

In his library Jed Putnam had tucked away that portion of his heritage that did not lend itself to the tall tales, the rough-and-tumble, the outrageous hooraw and brag talk of the leather-clad mountain man he had become by choice. There, enclosed by walls that were lined to the ceiling with books, permeated by the aroma of good leather, from both the upholstery of the matched armchairs beneath the reading lamps and the bindings of the volumes set cheek by jowl around the room, another man lived. Mixed with the odor of leather was the scent of paper, old and new, overlaid with a hint of ink and a coating of dust and the quiet calm that pervades rooms where people come to read. It might have been the reading room of the cattlemen's club in Denver, but no cattlemen's club was ever arranged to suit the taste of the Yankee trader who looked down from the portrait above the fireplace, where Lisa's fire had subsided into a pile of glowing coals. It took Hardeman a moment to realize that the sober gentleman in his frock coat and neatly knotted cravat was Jed Putnam. The hair was combed, the beard and moustache trimmed and tamed. As background, the artist had painted the pilings of a wharf and beyond them the sea, with a single clipper ship in the distance. But in the eyes of the subject Hardeman had found his old friend; the painter had captured the trace of humor in Jed's appraising gaze. They were the same eyes that had looked down on young Chris Hardeman all those years ago, and they said the same thing now as then: "All right, friend, let's see if you measure up."

They seemed to ask questions too, about what had brought Hardeman here after so many years, and why he was still a man on the loose, with no home of his own. "Wanderfoot's a young man's disease," Jed had said when he spoke of leaving the emigrant roads and finding a home. "Most fellers get cured of it without any doctoring. Me, I aim to set a spell when I find the right spot. You'll do the same when your time comes, if you got good sense. A young man roams about to see the world, find out what suits him; but there's more to bein' a free man than always movin' on from one place to the next. You pick the life you want and a place to live it, there ain't a man in the world can stand taller'n you. Mark my words, Christopher. Get yourself a grubstake and set it by. When it comes your time to stop, you'll know."

Hardeman had never forgotten Jed's advice. In the years just before the Rebellion, he had scouted twice for government survey parties, which were then trekking everywhere across the western lands with devices that measured the heights of mountains and the distances between points, searching out routes for trails and railroads and mapping the land to make it known. They had paid well; so well that an experienced scout like Hardeman had made more in one day with the government parties than most men earned in a month. He had had no need for such money then, but neither had he frittered it away at gambling or reckless pursuits. Remembering Jed's words he had placed his earnings in a St. Louis bank, and there they remained. He had not yet found the place to call home.

In the library this morning he had answered Jed's questions as best he could, telling him of the money he had set by against the time when he might stop his roaming, and why he had come here now. He told him what he would do if Sun Horse agreed to go in, and what if he did not, and why he was bound to go through with it no matter what Jed might think, and he had asked Jed for his blessing. But he got no answer from the painting, so he raised the bottle and drank to their friendship, and then he turned down the wicks of the lamps and snuffed the flames and saw that the screen was set in front of the fireplace before he left Jed to his books and went off to the kitchen, where breakfast was already on the stove and Julius and Hutch and Harry were sitting down at the table, each of them as close-mouthed as Jed himself, as if they followed his example.

Now, Lisa rose to return to her task and Hardeman watched her as she worked the handle of the iron pump at the sink and filled the huge tinned kettle that lived on the back of the stove. Her Yankee backbone was stiff and straight and the light from the window caught the wisp of loose hair that hung over her forehead and made it shine.

He drank off the rest of his coffee and set the cup on the table. He had made his plans as best he could and nothing remained but to get on with it. He silently cursed the uselessness of his feelings for this woman, the need to help her and the wanting that was stronger than it had been for any woman in a long time.

That was the way of things, to want what you couldn't have. When it was all over and done, he would do what he could to help her and maybe she would keep her valley and her home, but he knew that no matter which way things went for Sun Horse, Lisa would see his part in the old man's fate and she would hold it against him.

He looked out the window and saw that the wind was rising again as he had known it would. Close beside the house, Hary Wo was still splitting wood, untroubled by the gusts that sometimes blew over the logs before his axe could rise and fall. A stubborn log bound together with knots had resisted his first blow. He replaced it on the block, moving with patient deliberateness. He stepped back and swung the double-bitted axe in a full circle, down and around and up and over, with enough force to challenge the chopping block itself. The blade entered precisely in the old cut and cleaved the log cleanly in two, and Hardeman wished that his own doubts could be cut asunder as neatly.

CHAPTER

THIRTEEN

"That's about the last of it," Julius said as he tossed the final straws to the feeding cattle, and Hutch breathed an almost audible sigh of relief. They were the first words Julius had said all morning, apart from what was strictly necessary for getting the work done, and that was precious little. Hutch had been more than a bit concerned about the colored man's silence, for although Julius was sometimes serious he was not given to brooding. But ever since Hardeman and Johnny Smoker had ridden in three days before, things had changed in Putnam's Park. The little group of friends Hutch had taken such pleasure in had broken up and gone their separate ways, at least in their own thoughts. Yesterday, scarcely a word had been said at mealtimes. Hutch couldn't understand it. To him, the strangers were a welcome sight and he hoped he'd get a chance to ask one of them how things were back in Kansas, where they'd been until recently. Just knowing what sort of a winter it had been would make him feel closer to his ma and pa.

"You reckon you could handle this team for a bit?"

"Sure!" Hutch exclaimed, taking the reins Julius offered.

Julius had seen the worry in Hutch's face and he realized he had been off in his own thoughts all morning. The boy needed some cheering up. It had been a hard morning on the sled. The falling snow made for slippery work, trying to handle a fork and keep your footing, and twice they had had to unhitch the team from the sled and ride the doubletree to break a new trail where the wind had drifted in the old one. Julius was angry with himself for not hitching up all four horses today; he'd decided not to take the extra time, and his laziness had cost more time in the end. Through it all, Hutch had kept at his work without complaint, but every boy needed some encouragement now and again. Julius had got his share when he was Hutch's age, from his father and the other men.

He had thought a time or two this morning about saying what was on his mind just for the sake of getting it out and said, and maybe then he wouldn't think on it so much. But how could he tell Hutch what worried him? I'm too old to start over, he would say, and the boy would think, hell, I just started out on my own and it ain't such a big thing. How could he tell a boy who packed a sack and slung it over some mule and lit out with his pap's blessing, more than likely, what it meant to be Julius Ingram? He would have liked to take out like that when he was seventeen, all right, but he had seen what they did to runaway slaves.

I'm too old to start over, he thought again. I was old the first time and I got lucky. I won't find that kind of luck again.

He had come a long way since Georgia. A long way. How do you tell a boy who's just rid out from Kansas because he felt like it what it meant to be a slave for thirty-nine years and have a Union major tell you you're free on a sunny afternoon while the plantation burned to the ground around you? Thirty-nine was a late start at being free. Two days after the major set fire to the big house at the head of the lawn back up from the Altamaha River, Julius had enlisted in the army for the first time. He had served for a year, first as a hospital orderly and then as an infantry soldier, before being mustered out at the end of the war. And when the four black regiments were formed in 1866, he had enlisted again, and spent three more years in uniform in the Southwest. But he had quit the army in '69 because it was still a white man's army and would be for all time, and he had gone as high as a colored man could go: regimental sergeant major; and every man, black or white, knew he was the best soldier in the regiment. But he wasn't through yet finding out what he could make of himself, and so after three years with the Ninth Cavalry, some of the time spent in Texas, where he had seen the huge herds of Longhorns, he had joined the other freed men who were working with the cattle, and he had become a top hand. He already knew horses and he had learned quick about cows, but before very long he had seen the limits to what a hired man could do. All the drovers, black and white alike, talked at one time or another about owning a spread of their own, but it took money to get enough land to run livestock and not just a cowhand's end-of-the-trail money; it was eastern money and English money buying up the range, and bookkeepers running the business end of a cattle outfit. Julius had seen it all in his time on the trails and he didn't see himself getting any closer to what he really wanted, some place of his own, something that belonged to him that no other man could take away. "Forty acres and a mule" was the dream of many a freed man, but Julius wanted something more. He couldn't see himself going back to tilling the soil; he had been a field hand in Georgia.

"You like it here, boy?" he asked Hutch.

"Sure enough," Hutch said, all serious now and feeling important with the

Belgians answering the reins in his hands, plodding steadily toward the clump of tall pines, the only landmark that could be seen in the swirling white. "Get on, Zeke," he said, just to let the lead horse know he was being watched. "It's a good place to winter, all right."

"You reckon you'll move on come summer?"

"Oh, I might."

"Well, I don't blame you, being young and all. You've got a lot to see, I reckon."

"Seen a right smart lot just getting here," Hutch said, and he grinned. "'Bout the time I set eyes on the Big House for the first time, I was seein' Injuns behind every tree and glad for a place to hide. I like to took you for one when you opened the door."

"Took me for an Injun?" Julius chuckled. "There's some get pretty dark, boy, but not as dark as a Georgia nigger." He leaned on the front of the sled to rest the strain in his back and looked for a glimpse of the house through the snow. Hutch was following the tracks they had made that morning coming out from the first crib.

"I imagine there'd be a place here for you, if you had a mind to stay. You might think of it. There's a trip to Rawlins for supplies. More hands hired on come haying. It gets downright lively then." Julius wouldn't blame the boy if he went on. That's what he would have done, kept moving on, if he hadn't met up with Jed Putnam. You couldn't tell a boy that age to pick some place and stick with it. Besides, he wasn't even sure there would be a ranch come haying this year, but there was no sense burdening the boy with that. By August they might all be gone, or dead in an Indian war. Maybe he had best start toting a pistol when he was out away from the house.

"I'll think on it," Hutch said, and he looked to his driving as the heavy sled coasted past the first crib, the one nearest the settlement, and made the turn for home. The hay from the crib had been fed early in the winter and the square log structure stood empty now. It looked like a cabin started by some fainthearted homesteader, abandoned even before he put on the roof.

"I ever tell you how I met Jed Putnam?"

"A time or two. Abilene, you said."

"Yeah, I guess, I did. Seventy-one, it was, late summer. There was half a million beeves drove to Abilene in '71, and that was a sight to see. Grand ideas folks had about raisin' cattle, and they still got 'em. But there'll be a change. Old Jed saw it coming." He turned to look at Hutch. "Folks used to raise cattle for hide 'n' tallow, you know that?" Hutch nodded. "Reason was, there wasn't no way to ship live cattle, no way to ship the meat without it'd spoil. So folks raised hogs and ate hog meat. Then here comes the railroad. Now they haul cattle live, butcher 'em where they please, so folks eat beef." He looked back at the cattle, still snuffling in the snow for the last of the hay, and he grew more serious.

"The railroad put an end to Jed's road ranching, good and proper. But Jed, he always looked ahead, and he seen a way to get some good out of the railroad. He went to raising cattle. But not thousands of head all turned out to hell and gone like the big outfits. Just a handful, five hundred or so when we build the herd up. Few enough we can keep 'em in the park in wintertime and feed 'em when they need it. Old Jed, he seen forty winters in the mountains. Some of 'em all right for a tame critter, he says. Some not. He reckoned to keep his cattle where he could keep an eye on 'em."

He fell silent. There he went setting out all of Jed's ideas about why the herd should be small as if it were gospel, and he himself had often argued that the ideas were wrong. Build up the herd, Julius had said. Turn 'em out down below the park, raise as many as we can while we can. When the homesteaders come, that's time enough to think small. Just the other morning he had been planning on how to persuade Lisa that his ideas were right, and he had believed he had all the time in the world. It would take some years to build up the herd until the park wouldn't hold any more, and over the years Julius had figured to bring Lisa over to his way of thinking. In time he had thought the Sioux might be pushed farther to the north, and then the homesteaders would come, but he had imagined that time to be far in the future.

A lot had changed in three days. Now it was a matter of keep the park or lose it all.

"Old Jed, he seen the changes coming," Julius mused, "but he didn't see this."

"What's that?" Hutch wanted to know.

Julius smiled at the boy. "He was a wild one when I first set eyes on him. Could drink his weight in corn liquor. You ever been to Abilene?"

"I seen it onct. My pa took me to buy a milk cow. Our spread is on the Smoky Hill up above Salina."

Julius wondered how big the boy's pa's "spread" was. A quarter section in that country. They'd let you take a half section out where it was poor land or dry. But a quarter section was a quarter section more than Julius's own pa had ever owned.

"Abilene was good'n lively back in '71. Took a heap o' hands to drive half a million beeves north. Bill Hickok was marshal then. Might be still, for all I know."

Again Julius fell silent. If the supply of Longhorns driven up the Texas trails in '71 hadn't outstripped the need for beef, and if he hadn't run into a lean and gray-haired frontiersman in an Abilene saloon, he wouldn't have a half interest in Putnam's Park today. It was strange how choosing one saloon over another could change a man's life.

Julius had been out of a job, fresh out, when he met Jed Putnam. The half million Longhorns had caused such a glut on the market that the price had gone lower than ever before. Julius's boss, a canny man who was experimenting with a Longhorn-Durham crossbreed, had been forced to hold his herd outside town like many another stockman, waiting for the price to rise. As the weeks passed, he had let most of his men go, paid off at half wages with money he borrowed against the herd. In time, prices rose all right. An early blizzard rolled down out of Canada and froze nearly two hundred thousand head of cattle to death. The price for the surviving animals went sky-high, but by the time the blizzard hit,

174

Julius's former boss was already bankrupt and Julius and Jed Putnam were long gone from Abilene.

He had spotted Jed right off for a frontiersman, taking him at first for a buffalo skinner, one of the hide men who were even then picking the southern plains of the last great herds. The Texas drovers could always tell when the hide men were working upwind. Sometimes it took half a day to ride clear of the stench. Jed had looked restless and edgy, like a Longhorn put in a pen for the first time. He was moving among the rowdy drovers, stopping here and there to listen to the talk and maybe buy a man a drink. He was talking cattle, and Julius learned quick enough that he was no hide man. "Jersey and Guernsey, Holstein, Hereford, Brahma, Longhorn, Angus and Durham, I've had 'em all," he told Julius over the first of several drinks he bought for the tall colored trail hand who seemed to know a thing or two about a cow.

Jed had recently culled his herd and driven all but a handful to Nebraska, where he sold the animals to the army at the Red Cloud Agency before heading south to Kansas with the proceeds in his pocket. He was looking for advice and help, and he limbered Julius up with whiskey and told him what he planned to do. For fifteen years he had traded animals with the emigrants who passed through Putnam's Park, as all the road ranchers on the western trails had done. He had taken a sick or exhausted animal in trade for something an emigrant needed, and when the animal was well and strong again and in fit condition to go on, he would exchange the animal for two more that were worn out. The profits in such a trade were quick, when a man knew animals as well as Jed Putnam, but he was not in the trade just for profit. He was looking for breeds that would thrive in his mountain home. From time to time he would go down to the ranches along the main trail and do some trading there, and for horses he traded with Indians as well as the whites.

Julius smiled, remembering how Jed had loved to barter. He was a fair man, but he had cut his trading teeth on the fur trade in its heyday, and he could spot the gleam of greed in a fool's eye at a quarter mile. Over the years he had kept back the beasts he liked best, stocking Putnam's Park with work and saddle horses, milk cows, chickens and pigs, and a flock of geese, mostly because he liked their ornery and rambunctious nature but also because he was fond of roast goose for Christmas dinner. He couldn't abide goats, and kept none, but he had cared for and doctored just about every breed of cattle known to man. "I've wintered 'em all," he had told Julius in the Abilene saloon, then growing crowded as dusk fell, "and I'll tell you what: with a little care a nigger could raise some beef up my way. No offense. Now I'm thinkin' beef, not legs and bones." He had no great love for Longhorns, but he knew their virtues. "All hoot 'n' holler 'n' bones," he said, but even though he reckoned to feed his cattle in winter, he knew they would need some endurance and something more than the stubby legs of the English breeds to get them to the Union Pacific stockyards at Rawlins, and so for the time being he had settled on half Longhorn blood, maybe to be bred down to a quarter or less later on. He listened with growing interest as Julius told him

175

about the speed with which the newer strains grew to market weight, compared with the four years it took a Longhorn steer to mature, and as the evening wore on and the level in the bottle he had bought ebbed steadily, Jed grew fond of his newfound companion. "Here's a nigger knows poor bull from fat cow!" he whooped, and a dozen colored trail hands had turned in his direction with fire in their eyes, but Julius waved them off and poured the last of the whiskey.

The next day the two men rode out of town to the grasslands the vast herds were grazing down to stubble. Among the Texas cattle were cows and calves as well as steers, breeding stock for the northern plains. Jed bought sixty pair from a man who could afford to wait no longer, and gave him a better price than he would have got elsewhere on that day, and then they went to the stockyards. In a pen by the railroad siding were three Durham bulls ordered by a man who couldn't afford to pay for them until he sold his herd. "I don't like to take advantage of another feller's hard times," Jed said, but the man said "You'll be doing me a favor. I'll have to stick to Longhorns this year to cut my losses." And so when Jed and Julius set off the next day for Wyoming Territory with their little herd, the shorthorn Durhams grumbled along behind.

"One thing you never said," Hutch interrupted Julius's thoughts.

"What's that? About what?"

"You never told me you killed them fellers."

Julius looked at him sharply. "Where'd you hear a thing like that?"

"Miss Lisa. I asked her a week or two back how you come to be a partner. I sure didn't mean to pry. You never told me that part. Is it true?"

"Anything Lisa said, you got the truth of it. You know that." The boy knew it all now. Julius had never told him about Buck and Sweeny because he wasn't one to take pride in killing a man, even if the two of them put together didn't amount to half of Jed Putnam. Even before they crossed from the Solomon to the Republican, Jed had dropped back from where he was riding point to ride beside Julius for a while and tell him to keep an eye on Buck and Sweeny, two of the hands he had hired to move his herd all the way to the Wyoming mountains. "Here's a child as wouldn't want to cut trail in Blackfoot country with them two" was the way he put it.

Three weeks later, when they were pushing the herd across the Platte, a cow had balked in midstream and Jed's horse had lost its footing when he tried to get a rope over the cow's head. The commotion spooked the other animals and before the cattle were all safe on the far bank one had run over Jed in the water and broken his leg. Once Jed was dried out and laid next to the fire and the cattle were settled down, Buck and Sweeny presented Julius with a deal that pleased them both quite a lot. Old Putnam had the papers for the herd on him and there were half a dozen outfits within a hundred miles where a bunch like that could be sold and the sellers disappear back to Kansas or Texas with no one the wiser. Jed Putnam would be just another grave beside the Platte and there were plenty of those already. Julius said the idea didn't seem entirely fair to Jed Putnam, but perhaps because he was a quiet man, or perhaps just because he was black, Buck and Sweeny had shrugged and made a move to put Julius out of the way along with Jed, figuring that Spooner, the other hand and a man who never in his life made up his own mind about a thing, would fall right in line behind them. As things turned out, Spooner was more than willing to help Julius bury Buck and Sweeny and help get the herd moving again, with Jed Putnam carried on a drag behind one of the horses, his leg set and splinted by the tall Negro.

Julius had thought no more about the incident. He had acted according to his own instincts of what was right and had dispatched Buck and Sweeny with his Starr Army .44 only when there didn't seem to be any other way to convince them. But Jed was inclined to be more generous. Julius had been hired on to trail the cattle to Putnam's Park, and before the incident at the Platte he and Jed had already found that they got along sober as well as drunk and Jed had offered him a job as foreman of the Putnam Land and Livestock Company, a creation that existed only on the bill of sale for the sixty pair and in Jed's imagination. Julius had said he would think about it. He wanted to see Putnam's outfit first. When he finally rode up the wagon road into the little valley and saw the hillsides painted in the aspen yellows and pine green and golden grass of early autumn he had been about to take the job when Jed brought out a new offer, one he had been mulling over as he jounced along on his pony drag. He offered the colored man a partnership down the middle, and held up a hand to stop the protests that rose to Julius's lips. It wasn't as if the business was already a going concern, he said; it was nothing more than the two of them would build together. "I'm pert, and that's truth, but I ain't no cub. You'll do half the work and more."

"Well sir, there we are." Hutch reined the team to a halt in front of the barn, pleased with himself.

"You done her slick," Julius said as he swung off to the ground. "Reckon I'll take it easy from now on."

"About them fellers, did they have the drop on you?"

"Not quite."

Hutch hoped for more and got nothing, so he began to unharness the team, his spirits damped down.

Julius hadn't meant to cut the boy off, but he knew he could tell him the whole story from beginning to end, go over it up, down, and sideways, and it wouldn't matter. He could tell him about each day of his life from the time he was born and there was still no way a boy who had just lit out on his own and took his freedom for granted like the hair on his head could ever see what Julius's stake in Putnam's Park meant to him, or what it was that had been bothering him for three days now. The threat was there, plain enough, although it hadn't been said in so many words: help Hardeman find Sun Horse, help him persuade the old Sioux to take his people to Dakota, and the scout would do what he could to see that Lisa and Julius kept Putnam's Park when the country was opened up for settlement. Sit back and do nothing, or worse yet, side with the Indians, and lose everything for sure.

Lisa had taken Hardeman to see Sun Horse, but had she told him to surrender? Had she gone against her true feelings and turned her back on thirty years of friendship between the Putnams and Sun Horse's band? Julius knew better than to think that. And he knew that even Lisa could not put herself in his boots and feel what he felt for Putnam's Park. If she lost her home she could still start over someplace else, but a colored man's opportunity was a different kettle of fish. For Julius, Putnam's Park was a dream come true, and such good fortune did not fall into a colored man's lap twice in the same lifetime.

Bat Putnam's dog got up from where it had been lying in front of the tipi by the woods and trotted down the path to sniff at the team and the two men.

"Hello, dog," Hutch said, scratching the mongrel's ears. "What in hell is this dog's name, anyway?"

"Ain't never heard him called a name." Julius was working at the harness on the other side of the team. "Leastways not in English. They call him *shunká* in Sioux. Just means dog."

The dog seemed to lose interest in Hutch suddenly. Its ears went up and it turned to look down the valley, a low growl rising in its throat. It rarely barked. Sioux dogs learned to be quiet or they went swiftly to the stewpot.

Julius stopped work and turned to follow the dog's steady gaze. The wind was blowing up the valley toward the settlement, but he heard nothing and the snow was falling thickly still, blocking the road from sight. "You hear anything?"

Hutch listened. "I don't hear nothing."

Julius lifted Zeke's collar off. The dog growled again, never taking its eyes from the valley road. Then for a moment the wind shifted, the snow thinned, and Julius could see to the notch where the wagon road passed through the hills. Emerging from the dark of the cut was a line of moving dots—ten, twelve, more still coming—all gone in an instant as the snow dropped again like a curtain.

CHAPTER —————————————————————————
FOURTEEN

"Can't see a thing." Hardeman peered down the wagon road, but the snow continued thick and heavy. He stepped off the saloon porch and walked down the steps to the hitching rail, as if that advantage would make it possible for his eyes to pierce the dense flurries.

Harry Wo approached from the blacksmith shed, his hammer in his hand; Ling was watching wide-eyed from a window of the saloon. Hutch came running from the barn where he had finished turning out the horses and putting away the harness alone while Julius went to alert the settlement to the coming of wagons.

Julius pointed to a long-handled shovel leaning by the saloon door. "Get the porch cleared off, if you would." Hutch was not sure what this chore had to do with the arrival of wagons in the park, but he set to it with a will, glad to have his part in preparing for company. In the last few days, life in Putnam's Park had become halfway exciting.

Lisa glanced at Julius. "Are you sure?" Her mountain goatskin riding coat was thrown over her shoulders and she had donned her hat to protect her hair from the snow. She had slipped her feet into a pair of gum-rubber boots, which appeared incongruous beneath her gray woolen dress.

"I'm sure."

Hardeman held up a hand for silence, but he could hear nothing over the wind, see nothing but the snow that now hid even the clump of tall pines where the road turned for the settlement.

And then he made out the first sounds, carried on a backrush of air that brought the snow straight in his face—whispered memories of his days as a young scout: the soft creaking of wagon wheels. Then, as if they materialized out of the snow itself, riderless horses appeared, walking and trotting, driven by three riders. In the trail broken by the horses came the wagons. They were like small houses on wheels, enclosed with boarded sides and gabled roofs, drawn by teams of oxen and mules and draft horses.

The snowfall thinned suddenly, the gusting wind dropped, and the full length of the strange caravan was revealed. There were twenty-four wagons in a row, and the first impression of tiny houses was confirmed down to the windows in the sides and the tin chimneys protruding from the roofs. The wagons were brightly painted with decorations of wild animals and gilt lettering on each wagon that said *Tatum's Combined Shows*. The unmistakable growl of a large cat came from

179

one of several flat-topped wagons whose sides were covered by lashed-down tarpaulins.

In the pasture by the barn, the draft horses took fright and galloped to the farthest corner of the fence; in their own enclosure, the bulls pawed the snow. Two geese were walking on the bank of the spring pond; they took to the water now, and there were a few honks of alarm from the flock. The group in front of the saloon stood transfixed, none moving or saying a word.

At the head of the caravan rode a large man on a white stallion that stood seventeen hands at the shoulder. Throwing back his full cloak of royal blue, the rider raised a hand in command. As one, the wagons stopped and the draft animals stood still in the traces, clouds of steam puffing from their nostrils.

From the top of his silk hat to the polished tips of the high black boots into which his tight broadcloth riding trousers were tucked, the man bore his tailored finery as if it were the only fitting dress for a solitary mountain fastness. His eyes were wide-set and alert, the tips of his mustache waxed, his muttonchop whiskers neatly trimmed. His hair was dark and his complexion was ruddy from the cold. Without yet acknowledging the people in front of him, he made a slight motion with one hand.

A small figure jumped from the lead wagon and bounded forward, turning cartwheels and somersaults in the snow, bouncing to a stop in front of the hitching rail where Hardeman stood. The settlement group could hardly have been more surprised if Ulysses S. Grant himself had appeared before them in a clap of thunder, dressed up like a cowtown whore. The small figure was garbed in a loose white blouse, multicolored baggy knee-pants and white stockings, red shoes like bedroom slippers and a conical red hat with a blue tassel. The face was painted and powdered a solid white, save for the sharp black star-points radiating out from the eyes that were wide with excitement.

It was a clown.

He smiled at his dumb-struck audience and passed a hand down in front of his face, wiping away the smile and replacing it with the doleful mask of tragedy. Up went the hand and back came the smile. The figure winked at Hardeman, bowed, and swept a hand toward the man on the white horse. With a spring of his legs, the clown turned a backflip and bounded away towards the wagons as the rider cantered forward, the horse prancing with feet lifted high, coming to an abrupt stop twenty feet away. Then, to the amazement of those in front of the saloon, the horse bent delicately to one knee and bowed his head before rising again to stand before them. The rider swept the silk hat off his head and bowed low in the saddle.

"Madam and gentlemen," he said with all the formality of a ringmaster addressing an audience of city gentry, "I am Hachaliah Tatum, proprietor of Tatum's Combined Equestrian and Animal Shows. Our feats have delighted and astonished young and old alike from Philadelphia and Boston to the Black Hills of Dakota; our next intended venue, the mining establishments of Montana Territory. But I fear we have lost our way. May I inquire as to our whereabouts?" His pale blue eyes paused on each person before him, seeking the one whose authority most nearly approached his own.

Julius was the first to recover his voice. "You're in Putnam's Park. The lady is Miss Lisa Putnam. My name is Ingram."

Tatum smiled and bowed to Lisa, ignoring the Negro completely. "Miss Putnam."

Hardeman moved a little to one side so he could see past Tatum to the full length of the caravan, every man of the circus within his view. Two riders had moved away from the wagons and were drawing nearer. They stopped halfway between the wagons and the Big House. One was of middling height, with a full black beard and mustache. Sharp eyes peered from beneath a derby hat. He wore a buffalo coat and carried a rifle across his lap, the barrel cut short at the end of the forestock. The man's high-strung horse shifted about nervously, prancing this way and that. The animal shied at an imagined something in the snow and turned halfway around, and Hardeman saw that the left sleeve of the buffalo coat hung empty; the rider had only one arm. The other man was shorter. He wore a slouch hat and an angry scowl, and Hardeman guessed he was the guide who had blundered off the main trail.

"Hey, mister," Hutch called out from where he leaned on his shovel. "Is that a sure-enough circus show you got here?"

Tatum smiled his thin smile. "We are a troupe of professionals, young man, bringing entertainment to the hinterland." He shifted his gaze to take in all of them. "We encompass the riding of Astley, the clowning of Grimaldi, the talents of a dozen foreign lands making an unparalleled tour of the western provinces before our much heralded appearance at the centennial celebrations this summer in San Francisco. We carry in our ears the applause of all the great eastern cities, the booming metropolis of Chicago, the teeming polyglot of St. Louis. We are the first to pioneer such a spectacle in the wild territories of Dakota, Wyoming and Montana, and we shall give a week of performances for the Mormons in the Salt Lake valley before boarding the train for the golden shores of California."

"I imagine you're looking for the Bridger road," Lisa offered dryly. "You will have to go back the way you came and around the southern end of the mountains."

"I been through here in summer, years back," the rider in the slouch hat called out. "There's a trail out to the west."

"There is, in summertime." Lisa returned her attention to Tatum. "The West Pass won't be open until May or June. This has been a bad winter."

"I see." Beneath his calm exterior, Hachaliah Tatum was containing a growing rage. It had been clear for some time now that the man called Fisk was no scout, despite his boastful claims, but to mistake this goat path for the wagon road to Montana was more than Tatum would bear. It would take a week or more to backtrack, precious time that could not be regained. He would settle with Fisk later, but now he must put his best foot forward, to encourage hospitality and whatever help might be needed to get the circus safely on its way once more. Assuming the proper facade was the essence of showmanship.

181

"At the moment I am afraid we appear somewhat the worse for our travels. If we might encamp for the night or perhaps—" He had spied the sign that creaked softly above the main doors of the Big House and now he read it aloud. "'Putnam House.' Is this by chance a public inn?"

"Yes, it is." Lisa felt an almost forgotten excitement. "My father built it in the fifties for the emigrants."

"You have accommodations then?"

"My goodness. We only have a few rooms, but—"

Tatum held up a hand, refusing any apology. "Only a few of us will need to sleep indoors. The rest will be quite at home in the wagons. We will be on our way in the morning, weather permitting." He threw a cold glance at Fisk.

Lisa's excitement was growing. She found herself calculating how many meals would have to be cooked—she and Ling would need the help of the circus's cook and supplies for that—and how long it would take Julius and Hutch to get the wagons and stock settled while she and Ling made the beds and prepared the saloon as a dining room. These were more wagons than had been in the park for ten years or longer, more than might ever arrive again at one time, and she felt like celebrating. It occurred to her that it might be a celebration to mark the end of her father's dreams, but she refused to let the thought dampen her good spirits. Even if just for one last night, she would welcome her guests in a style her father would have approved. "We will do everything we can to make you comfortable." She favored Tatum with her most hospitable smile. "It will take us a while to warm the rooms and make things ready, but I imagine you will need some time to get your people settled." The circus master returned her smile and she noticed the even white rows of his teeth. He was rather a handsome man.

"You are very kind," Tatum said. "If your man will show us where to make camp?" He glanced at Julius.

"I'm nobody's man, Tatum." Julius felt the blood rush to his face.

"Mr. Ingram is my partner, Mr. Tatum," Lisa explained quickly. She had heard the underlying threat in Julius's tone and she wanted nothing to spoil the occasion.

"Your partner. Indeed. I stand corrected."

Julius imagined that he heard carefully veiled condescension in Tatum's tone, but it appeared that Lisa hadn't noticed it. Ignoring Tatum he turned to Hutch, who had rejoined the others; half the porch was cleared and the way to the saloon doors was shoveled clean. "We'll put 'em out by the barn. Show the wranglers where the hay is at and put the stock west of the fence. See what they need for—"

He was interrupted by a distant sound so alien that it sent a chill through his body. With everyone else he turned to look down the valley in the direction of the sound and for the second time that morning the inhabitants of Putnam's Park were struck speechless by what they saw. Half a mile away, coming up the wagon road at a lumbering run, was an African elephant bull, his trunk raised before him. He trumpeted again as he ran.

The people of the circus poured from the wagons, talking and shouting to one another in a handful of languages as they greeted the astonishing sight with obvious delight.

"Rama!" Tatum exclaimed. He wheeled his horse about and called out, "Chatur!"

"Tatum, *sahib!*" A dark-skinned man with his head encased in a tightly wound white turban was running toward Tatum, baggy white pants flapping beneath his heavy overcoat. He carried a long staff in one hand. "It is Rama coming, *sahib!* Did I not say he would be finding us?" The man pronounced the Hindi honorific as a single syllable: *sa'b*. He was grinning jubilantly.

"Stop him, Chatur! Get him calmed down before you bring him in!"

"Excellent, *sahib!* I am doing so!" Chatur changed course and ran off toward the elephant, stumbling often in the snow, which came halfway to his knees.

On the porch, Hutch managed to find his voice. "What in creation is that critter?"

"It's an elephant," Hardeman answered from the hitching rail. He wished he could have a few moments for his understanding to catch up with the events taking place around him, which seemed to have gotten out of hand.

The elephant stopped as Chatur drew near. The onlookers could see the small turbaned figure gesturing and addressing the beast, looking for all the world like an outraged father lecturing a child who had misbehaved. Suddenly the long trunk snaked out and grasped the little man, raising him into the air and provoking a gasp from Lisa, but in a moment Chatur was deposited gently on the beast's shoulders where he seated himself nimbly and touched the elephant with his staff, turning him toward the settlement at a placid walk.

"I'll be . . ." Hutch could think of nothing more to say.

Tatum turned the stallion back to the porch, obviously pleased. "Don't be alarmed. Our elephant broke loose last night. I was certain we had lost him for good, but—" He was interrupted by cries of surprise and horror from the crowd of circus people who had gathered beyond the wagons. Riding into sight atop a low rise at the edge of the meadow, midway between the settlement and the approaching elephant, were a dozen mounted Indians accompanied by two white men. The Indians carried lances and bows and a handful of rifles, and even over the distance it was possible to make out paint on some of their faces.

A hush fell on the settlement. It was the turn of the circus crowd to stare dumbstruck at the newest arrivals. The snow had thinned to nearly nothing and the wind had dropped, leaving the valley quiet and still beneath a tightly bound covering of clouds that hung motionless, close to the ground.

"Great God in Heaven!" Tatum breathed.

"They're on the warpath, sure!" Hutch's voice trembled with excitement.

"Hush, boy," Julius calmed him. "They're a hunting party."

Hardeman too had seen that the Indians bore none of the round bullhide shields they carried to war, the raw buffalo hide so hard and thick it could stop an arrow or a lance and might even deflect a bullet, except at close range. He recognized

Johnny and Bat among the riders, flanking the gray-haired figure of Sun Horse, but it was Standing Eagle who stood out, with four eagle feathers bound in his hair and a winter cape of grizzly bear covering his shoulders and back.

Why Sun Horse brought so many men with him to carry the council's reply, Hardeman did not know, but he was sure the Indians intended no harm. Close at hand, the circus whites were backing nervously toward their wagons, all eyes fixed on the Indians.

The elephant had come to a stop facing the horsemen across a hundred yards of snow, the huge ears flapping, the great head swaying from side to side. With unnatural clarity across the distance that separated himself from the Indians, Hardeman heard the startled snorts of their horses as they caught the scent of the strange creature.

Aboard the lead circus wagon the driver glanced anxiously from Fisk to Tatum, looking for a sign, painfully aware of the train's exposed position, but no sign came and now he decided to act on his own. He shook the reins and clucked to the oxen and the wagon began to roll. Behind him the other drivers followed his lead and in a moment the whole caravan was on the move. The people on foot started to edge toward the safety of the settlement, some breaking into a run.

"It's all right! They're friendly!" Lisa called out, but her words were lost among the snap of traces and the creaking of wheels, the snorting of animals and the hubbub of nervous chatter among the circus people. Julius unbuttoned his coat and placed a hand on the butt of his holstered pistol, glad now that he had thought to don the gunbelt before stepping out to await the wagons.

On their small hillock, the Sioux were oblivious to the commotion in the settlement. All eyes were on the elephant.

Blackbird sat his horse next to his grandfather, intensely glad that they had found the beast that had frightened him so badly. He had returned to the village as quickly as he could from the mountainside where he had spied the monster, afraid to disturb his grandfather again but certain this was something he should tell as a scout would do, saying only what he had seen and what he knew to be true. To his relief, Sun Horse had been more disposed to receive a visitor then, and had listened patiently. A hunting party had been mounted, led by Sun Horse and Standing Eagle. Let the hunters find this beast, Sun Horse had said, and then we will go to the white settlement to say what the Sun Band has decided. Blackbird's father had not wished to go but Sun Horse had insisted. We will go together, he said, Sun Horse and Standing Eagle, peace man and war leader, to say that the Sun Band agrees to Three Stars' request and will peacefully await his coming.

Sun Horse too was glad they had found the creature his grandson had seen, glad his words were true. The beast was yet another mystery produced by white-men, another sign of their unpredictable power. "What is this thing?" he asked Bat Putnam.

Bat was looking at the unexpected crowd of strangers in the settlement, hiding so fearfully behind the wagons that were tightly bunched in the yard. Before he could form a reply, Blackbird suddenly put his heels to his horse and charged down the gentle slope straight for the elephant.

"That'll set the badger loose or I'm a nigger," Bat muttered, but neither he nor any of the Lakota moved to stop the boy.

Astride Rama's neck, Chatur awaited the attack nervously. He knew that Rama could not outpace the swifter horse, and he resolved that if these were to be his last moments he would die as a true mahout, defending his elephant with every means at his command. Although Rama was African, chosen by Hachaliah Tatum for the imposing spectacle of his gigantic tusks and ears, Chatur had taught him all the maneuvers of an Indian fighting elephant, and now, with signals from his feet and his wooden staff, he readied the leviathan for battle. But the young rider on his fleet pony was too quick.

Blackbird had planned his move before launching his horse off the knoll and it worked as he had hoped. With all his attention fixed on the huge creature before him, he guided the horse effortlessly, using his knees and the single rein of braided buffalo hide that was looped around the pony's lower jaw. Feinting to the right he drew the beast-rider's attention in that direction, but as the giant head began to swing to meet the challenge, Blackbird swerved the pony quickly to the left, darting past the creature's flank, where he turned to the right again, cutting within an arm's length of the hindquarters and striking them sharply with his bow as he passed. The elephant wheeled to his mahout's command, but boy and pony were safely away and the Indian youth turned for the settlement, bow held high, shouting his excitement and his pride. He had avenged himself on the monster that had sent him running for his life that morning and once more he felt himself on the verge of manhood.

Seeing his triumph, the Lakota whooped their approval and rose to follow him. They gave the elephant a wide berth and formed into a line abreast, charging toward the buildings and the milling people, firing their new rifles into the air.

"Hooraw fer the mountains!" Bat cried out, loosing his own shot. With the wind in his face and the scent of gunpowder sharp in his nostrils before it was snatched away by the breeze, he felt more alive than he had all winter.

On the porch, Julius was enjoying the spectacle when the frightened cries of the circus people awoke him to the danger. "They don't know what it means!" he said, and he looked about for the first sign of trouble.

Beyond the hitching rail, Hardeman turned at the sound of Julius's warning. He had let Blackbird's charge distract him, and now, even as he turned back to the circus folk, a shot sounded close at hand. Seeing the Indian boy come within range, Hachaliah Tatum had drawn a nickel-plated Colt and fired, and was now aiming for a second shot. Hardeman's right hand moved to his belt, but Julius had his gun already out and swinging to bear on Tatum.

"Tatum! You leave it be!"

Tatum turned to look down the barrel of Julius's Starr .44, and in a single motion he returned his own revolver to its elaborately tooled holster, but already another shot boomed out nearby, from the short-barrel Winchester in the hand of the rider in the derby hat.

To Hardeman, his own movements seemed slow and leaden as his hand found the grip of his pistol and his eyes took in everything before him in a rush of fragments, like bits of rock hurled outward from a blast of powder set to break up a boulder. He saw the fluid ease with which Tatum handled his weapon and he noted the fancy twirl the unthinking hand gave the gun before returning it to the holster. On the fringes of his vision he took in the chaos of movement from the circus crowd, all running hither and yon, looking for any cover that would hide them from the Indians, who now scattered prudently in all directions and rode back out of range, those with guns beginning to reload them. He saw Blackbird bent in the saddle, gripping his upper arm, and he prayed that the boy was not seriously wounded. Through it all, most of his attention was on the Winchester in the hand on the one-armed rider. The weapon lurched in a short arc as the man cocked it for another shot, then leaped up to the rider's shoulder.

"Hold your fire!" Hardeman shouted, but as the pistol left his belt he saw the barrel of the Winchester start to swing in his direction, the sharp black eyes finding him in the middle of the confusion, and he saw in the rider's eyes an expression he had seen before, the look of a man caught up in a sudden outbreak of gunplay, ready to strike out at any danger, real or imagined.

Every particle of Hardeman's awareness held on the horseback man before him and the feel of the gun in his hand, his thumb pulling back the hammer, the other hand coming up to steady the shot as his body dropped into a slight crouch. It took forever before the hammer fell and the gun bucked in his hands.

The Winchester went off as Hardeman's bullet smashed into the stock. The force of the blow hurled the one-armed man from his saddle, and as the sound of the two shots echoed off the far wall of the valley and came rolling back again, a third shot sounded, a booming explosion from the porch, where Lisa Putnam stood holding a shotgun aimed just over the heads of the men below her. Smoke curled from the black mouth of one barrel as the muzzle swung slowly around to stare at each person in the yard in turn. Beside her, Julius held his pistol high, his eyes never stopping, searching for any sign of movement.

"The next man that moves gets the other barrel!" Lisa warned in a voice that cut across the yard and silenced the murmurings of the circus crowd.

Hardeman didn't doubt that she meant it, but he turned back deliberately, slowly, to look at the one-armed man, who now struggled to a sitting position in the snow, blood dripping from a cut in his wrist where a splinter from the shattered Winchester had pierced him. Beyond the fallen rider a dozen men from the circus were frozen in the act of bringing their own weapons into play, pistols mostly, drawn in panicked fear of the Indians. Lisa's warning had come just in time to prevent a ragged broadside.

Hardeman kept his gun in his hand and his thumb on the hammer, ready to support Lisa and Julius if any of the men thought to follow up his original intention.

"I will have no more fighting on my place!" Lisa ordered. "Not between the two of you"—she gestured with the shotgun at Hardeman and the one-armed man—"not with those Indians." She fixed her gaze on Tatum. "You don't know our customs, Mr. Tatum, but you had better learn. We are all here on the sufferance of the Indians. They are my friends and I will insist that they be treated accordingly." She felt light-headed and curiously elated. With a gun in her hands all her doubts of the past three days had vanished and she knew she had made the only possible choice: take a stand and fight.

"Your friends have a peculiar way of making us welcome." Tatum fought to hold his temper in check. He had no wish to antagonize this woman despite her incomprehensible behavior in defending the savages who had threatened the pride and joy of Tatum's Combined Shows.

His words brought a murmur of angry agreement from the crowd, and one man called out, "They shot at us! You call that friendly?"

"They shot in the air!" Lisa snapped. "It means they are coming into camp with empty guns. Those are one-shot muzzle-loaders! It's a peace sign!"

The circus men lowered their weapons, the first to draw them now the first to melt back into the crowd once the rashness of their impulse was made clear.

"You won't deny that the boy attacked my elephant?" Tatum said with some heat. Rama had cost him five thousand dollars in gold.

Bat Putnam had left the Indians in the meadow and had ridden forward alone. He was near enough to hear Tatum's last remark. "He didn't attack your elephant, y' idjit!" he told the circus man. "He was countin' coup!"

"Counting what?"

"Countin' coup! You touch your enemy with a stick, you get much honor. Takes a brave man to do it. The boy run into that critter this morning and it give him a fright like to turned his hair. Now he's got his honor back, good and proper!" Grinning, he turned to Lisa and Julius, and gave Hutch a wink. "That boy's gonna be famous, and that's truth. By Christ, this nigger'll give a pony to honor what he done. I'll give two!" A cackle of laughter rose in his throat. "Only man in the whole Sioux nation to count coup on a elephant! That's *some*, now!" With a fling of his left arm he threw the barrel of his Leman rifle into the air without warning and let fly. "Ooeee! Won't he stand tall!" The laughter burst forth in a long peal that echoed hand in hand with the booming report.

On the porch, Julius chuckled softly, amused as much by the mountain man's good humor as the notion of the boy who had counted coup on an elephant. Even Lisa softened her expression and lowered the shotgun.

Hutch found himself laughing. He wasn't certain what was so funny, but since the appearance of the elephant he had watched the unfolding events almost gleefully, as if it were all part of some kind of show put on for his particular enjoyment. The notion that he might be in some personal danger didn't occur to him until the sudden gunplay was over, and even then he had felt certain that Julius and Miss Lisa would protect him from harm. The way Miss Lisa had run into the saloon and returned in an instant with the shotgun, even before Hutch knew why she was alarmed, confirmed this feeling. Hardeman too had taken a stand to protect the settlement and the Indians from the stupidity of the circus greenhorns, and even Harry Wo had raised his hammer threateningly, as if he might crack the skull of anyone who dared to approach the porch where Hutch stood all the while, grinning like a fool. By the look of him, the circus boss Tatum figured the whole shebang might have been put on simply to get his goat.

Bat reveled in the uncomprehending annoyance on Tatum's face. He laughed so hard that he doubled over in the saddle, tears streaming down his cheeks. It delighted him beyond words so utterly to bewilder a man who wore a silk hat.

Hardeman stood apart from the others and felt none of their mirth. He returned his gun to his waistband, struggling to control a slight trembling in his hands. He sucked in a deep breath and held it as he looked off down the valley to where the Sioux had regrouped. They were waiting to see how the action in the settlement would be resolved. He could make out Johnny Smoker in their midst and saw the young man move one hand in a sign that told of no trouble from that quarter. Standing Eagle examined Blackbird's arm and dismissed it with a nod; the wound was not serious. Led by Sun Horse the Indians started forward now, keeping a wary eye on the crowd near the circus wagons.

Hardeman let the breath out slowly and began to relax. He spat in the snow, wanting to rid himself of the bitter taste that was the willingness to kill.

He had taken part in the quick gunplay instinctively, siding with Lisa and Julius because they were right and the circus men were fools, and because he could not afford to have the Sioux enraged by some unthinking offense on the part of ignorant whites. Soon he would hear what Sun Horse had to say and the waiting would be over. He felt the lingering anger and heightened awareness the gunplay had brought out in him and he realized that it didn't really matter which answer the old man brought, so long as the last doubts could be laid to rest and things could move forward in a rush that would keep both sides off-balance, for it was then that he would triumph, when events were moving fast and decisions had to be made in an instant, not after days of thought and misgivings.

He remembered the unspoken oath he had made when he smoked the pipe in Sun Horse's council. The smoke bound the one offering the pipe to speak the truth not just in what he said but all the truth he might know about the matter at hand, and while Hardeman had not told the councillors every detail of his plan, he was at peace with his oath. To him, the whole truth was that the Sun Band must submit. If they yielded to the inevitable, that could be the first step to a broader peace.

It struck him then that what he was trying to do was neither more nor less than to make a piece of history single-handed. There was an army marching up-country to impose a peace by different means. But he had seen his chance and he had taken it, and the truth was, he was not trying to oppose the inexorable forces descending on the Sioux, which would be a fool's errand for certain, but only to slip through the gate and change the outcome a little before the gate slammed closed and another section of the past was penned in for good, immutable and permanent. If he succeeded, and no one saw the mark of a former army scout on the final peace, that would suit Chris Hardeman, for he would have paid his debt all the same and he could go to his grave knowing that but for him the terror and killing of the Washita might have been repeated here, among Johnny's last living relatives.

He watched Johnny riding among the Indians, approaching in a walk, his horse next to Sun Horse's, and he saw once again how at home the boy seemed to be with his grandfather. And he forced himself to remember then that Johnny was a boy no longer. If his dream were to be believed, he would cross the threshold to manhood by his own deliberate choice, and once he had chosen between the worlds for good and certain, he would be free of the dream and he could fight if he wanted to. What if he changed his mind and picked the red man's world? The doubt resurfaced in Hardeman's mind. He had not protected Johnny for seven years just to see him go back to the Indians and maybe die in a winter campaign like the one in '68. Meeting Sun Horse and seeing how much he meant to Johnny had given Hardeman pause; now more than ever he had no wish for harm to come to Sun Horse or his people, yet now more than ever he saw that his way was the only way. Willingly or at the point of cavalry carbines, Sun Horse and his people would go in, and then Johnny would see that the free ways of his Cheyenne childhood were gone forever. Faced with life on the reservation if he stayed with the Indians, he would surely keep to his first choice and remain in the white man's world.

Sun Horse and his warriors had reached Bat now, twenty paces beyond the hitching rail, and they gathered around the mountain man. Johnny caught Hardeman's eye and gave him a short nod, but he made no move to leave the Indians and join his companion.

Hardeman's feet were cold. He turned back to the porch and when he reached the top of the steps, where the boards were shoveled clear, he stamped his boots to shake off the snow. He would wait for Johnny here. The youth would come in good time, and Sun Horse would come too. They had no other course.

Surrounded by the Indians, Bat spoke to them in Lakota, gesturing at the elephant and explaining that the fearsome creature came from halfway around the world; "many moons across the great water, brought on a boat blown by the wind" was the way he put it. He added that in their native land, elephants

189

were greatly respected and often used in war, knowing this could only add to Blackbird's glory. When they heard this, the warriors voiced their praise once more, and Blackbird tried to bear his pride with suitable dignity.

The circus crowd was moving closer now, drawn by interest in the Indians. Some paused to welcome Rama's return as Chatur stopped the beast by the wagons, but most were driven by a stronger curiosity; they had never seen wild Indians before and these horseback warriors were a far cry from the drunken beggars they had seen at Fort Laramie, offering their women to passers-by for a drink of firewater. But there was danger mixed with the curiosity, and hands resting near the butts of pistols that were stuffed in pockets and belts. The wagon drivers had been recruited in the Black Hills to replace men who had contacted sudden bouts of gold fever and deserted for the diggings with Hachaliah Tatum's curses ringing in their ears. The replacements had lost their own lust for gold after hard months in the frigid creekbeds, where arrows and gunshots had come often from the nearest timber. They had eagerly accepted Tatum's offer of work that would take them out of the Black Hills, but their memories of Indians were fresh and vivid and their hostility was obvious to the Sioux, who moved their horses to form a line facing the oncoming crowd.

Between the Indians and the men and women of the circus was the mounted figure of Hachaliah Tatum, one hand resting on a hip. He waited until the crowd drew near him, then touched his heels lightly to the stallion's flanks and rode in front of his people, becoming their leader.

On the porch Lisa grew apprehensive and raised her shotgun once more, but before she could issue a new warning, a chorus of titters arose from the crowd and one man gave out a loud guffaw. Puzzled, Tatum looked around to see that the clown was close behind him, mimicking his posture and bearing, one hand on a hip and the other holding invisible reins, the head held high and the haughty expression matching perfectly. Caught in the act, the clown dropped his pose and scurried into the crowd, provoking new laughter as he hid behind a huge man in a purple cape. The man stood head and shoulders above everyone else. Beneath the cape he wore a red shirt and brown wool trousers tucked into floppy boots. He wore no hat, and his flaxen hair hung to his shoulders, moving now as a breeze stirred it. The imposing giant remained silent and solemn, apparently oblivious to the clown, who peered from behind the safety of the cape. Tatum smiled tolerantly, not seeming to mind being the butt of this joke. At once the clown lost interest in the circus master and pretended to see the mounted Indians for the first time. His eyes sprang wide open and his jaw dropped as he ducked back behind the giant, but soon his curiosity drew him out and he darted forward, using the men and women of the circus as cover, finally daring to emerge from the crowd and approach the Indians on tiptoe, as if they might not notice him if only he were quiet.

The warriors watched this new figure with growing fascination. One man tightened his grip on his lance, but Sun Horse put out a restraining hand as the clown broke into a make-believe Indian war dance for a moment and then drew an imaginary arrow and fitted it to an invisible bowstring, which he drew back, releasing the arrow high into the air. With a hand to his brow he watched its flight, growing concerned as it soared directly overhead. He ran about in panic to avoid its fall, then suddenly clutched his breast and fell dead at the feet of the horses. The Indians burst out laughing, joined by the crowd of whites.

Johnny Smoker could scarcely believe his eyes. He was captivated, smiling broadly and laughing along with the rest.

Now the clown sprang to his feet as a gunfighter, his eyes on Julius, who still held his forgotten pistol in his hand. The clown approached the porch, his hand poised over an unseen holster. Julius hesitated, not sure what was expected of him, and then he entered into the spirit of make-believe. He replaced the pistol in its holster and dropped his hand to his side, waiting. At once the clown's face dissolved into abject terror. He backed away, then turned and ran toward the Indians, where he fell on his knees in front of Sun Horse, his hands clasped in supplication. The crowd roared.

Sun Horse smiled, charmed by the small figure. Like the other Lakota, he had been astonished to learn so unexpectedly that the whitemen too had clowns. *Heyoka*, the sacred clowns of the Lakota, wore tattered skins and robes, not brightly colored clothing, and they decorated their faces and bodies with the jagged lightning symbol to show their sacred relationship with the thunder beings from the west. Their power was based on doing everything backward. They said "no" when they meant "yes," they walked backward, they laughed to show sorrow and cried to express joy. They held special ceremonies and sang many songs, and in neither actions nor appearance did they resemble this whitefaced creature, but there was no mistaking the purpose held in common by the *heyoka* and the small figure kneeling before Sun Horse: each sought to bring happiness to people who were troubled or downhearted or angry. Only moments before, the whites from the painted wagons had approached the Lakota as enemies, the hostility on some of their faces plain to see; now the men and women moved closer in ones and twos, unafraid. The white clown had delighted the hearts of everyone present; he had brought two peoples close enough together to share the warmth of laughter. Sun Horse felt a lessening of the gloom that had enveloped him ever since the council meetings, and something akin to hope.

Finding no help from the old Indian, the clown got to his feet, but he slipped in the snow and teetered sideways, grabbing Johnny Smoker's leg with one hand to keep from falling. Johnny reached down and took hold of the clown's arm—too late. The clown's feet shot out from under him and he threw up his free hand in a futile effort to regain his balance, knocking off his tall red cap. A piled mass of long brown hair fell down about the clown's shoulders.

191

Sun Horse drew in a short breath of surprise. He saw at once that the small features now framed by the soft hair belonged to a girl. The *heyoka washíchun* a young woman? Was there no end to the surprises of the whites? The Lakotas murmured in astonishment.

On the porch, Hutch said, "I'll be..." and once again ran out of words.

Johnny still had the girl by the arm, holding her up until she could regain her footing. He was aware only of her, nothing else.

"Thank you," she said, looking up at him for the first time. He loosened his grasp and her arm slipped through his until their hands touched. She held the contact for a moment, clasping his hand in thanks before finally breaking the grip.

The crowd began to disperse now, sensing that the performance was at an end.

"We best get these folks settled," Julius said to Hutch. The two of them descended from the porch and started off toward the wagons, finding the guide Fisk in the crowd and taking him with them.

From the west, beyond the low-hanging clouds, came a soft roll of thunder. Sun Horse felt a chill sweep through his body like the shock of entering a winter stream. Was it real? The sound had been so faint that he wondered if anyone else had heard it, and then he saw that the other Lakota were looking nervously at one another and glancing at the skies. Thunder in winter was a dangerous power, to be pacified by the ceremonies of the *heyoka*.

Had the clown girl heard the voice of *Wakinyan*, the thunder being? Most of the whites were moving off towards the painted wagons now, the clown girl among them. She was walking beside the man on the tall white stallion. She gave no sign of sensing anything out of the ordinary.

Lisaputnam had gone inside the house. Only Hardeman remained on the porch. He was watching Sun Horse, waiting to hear what the council had decided. Johnny Smoker rode towards the house now to join his friend.

Again came the rumbling from far away, fainter still, and again Sun Horse felt the chill of power.

"*Taku shkan*," he murmured. Something is moving. Something *wakán*. He felt his power rising strong within him, comforting and familiar. Why did it return to him now?

He reined his horse around and rode a short distance beyond the wagon road, facing the stream and the valley. There he opened himself completely to what moved about him.

The *heyoka* girl made the people laugh and thunder came to her. Why?

He looked at the sky and saw that the clouds had risen to the ridgetops. Fine flakes still fell, scarcely enough to see, making the air shimmer. A soft breeze blew from the river and still the power moved around him and he felt calm and balanced, as if he touched the spirit world with one hand and the world of men with the other, receiving the strength of each one. Why?

The power came from the west, he was certain. *Heyoka* were of the west,

192

and the thunder beings dwelt there. So rare to hear thunder in winter.... Even in summer the power of the west was not completely benign; it was the power to make things live but also the power to destroy; rain, the symbol of the life-giving force; lightning, the power to destroy.

A power is coming. It is very strong. It can help the band or destroy us....

This was what Hears Twice had heard! The unpredictable strength of the west brought here now, to help the people or to destroy them!... In spring and summer the rains came from the west, and the snows in winter, the water entering the ground to feed the grass, to feed the buffalo, to feed the people, the life-giving chain flowing from the west....

It grows from the meeting of two people....

Sun Horse shivered violently, so strong was the feeling that coursed through him. He had witnessed that meeting! As soon as the thought came to him he was sure. There was no trace of doubt. Here with his own eyes he had seen the coming together, the touching of the *heyoka* girl and his white grandson, and he had felt the power!

The hope rose quickly in him now, but he quieted his rushing thoughts and calmed himself to listen. He must be sure. Again he looked at the sky, the clouds hanging soft above him, enclosing the valley, turning each sound back on itself so it stood out sharp and distinct, carrying undiminished in the cool air. He heard the grunt of a bear from the painted wagons, the snort of a horse in answer, the beating of his own heart, which surely echoed through-out the valley to be heard by all; and then, carried on the breeze, came the short cry of an eagle.

His eyes searched the valley, never pausing, seeking motion.

There. He saw it coasting low above the willow marsh and the winding river, a young golden eagle, the undersides of its wings still flecked with white. It was the bird the Lakota called *wamblí gleshka*, the spotted eagle, the one that flies highest of all living things, closest to *Wakán Tanka*, the Great Mystery. The bird soared on motionless wings far down the valley, now banking, now twisting, following the river towards the cut in the hills. And now the wings moved and *wamblí* rose into a sweeping spiral that grew wider and higher until the bird grew small and vanished into the clouds.

Sun Horse did not search the grayness for the moving speck—*wamblí* had given a sign and would not return. Something in motion here, something felt but unseen, something truly *wakán*; *wamblí gleshka* had said so, rising into the sky with the same sign that a Lakota made with his hand to indicate whatever was *wakán*, a mystery.

Wakán Tanka, I am sending a voice, he sang softly, the words said within his heart. Hear me, Great Mystery, I am sending a voice. A two-legged is sending a voice. In a sacred manner I call. In a sacred manner a nation is calling. Hear me, Great Mystery, I am sending a voice....

He felt his own power stronger than ever before and he raised his eyes to the spot where *wamblí* had disappeared.

193

For the people I sing! In a sacred manner I sing. . . . Four times he hummed the chant and he had to restrain the laughter that rose to his lips, joy in the return of his power.

Delay! The thought returned with new force, and now he was prepared to speak to the council. Delay, that what comes together here today may grow. . . . Here in this valley that has never known war, a power begins. . . .

Delay.

And now a pathway opened before him and he saw the means to delay.

Send a pipe to Three Stars. A pipe of peace from a man of peace. Send a pipe so Three Stars will know our intention is peaceful. Say the Sun Band will not fight. Ask him to leave our country in peace. Say that in summertime Sun Horse will speak to the hostiles, and he will speak for peace. *With hope we can live until summer.* Our ponies are too weak to travel now. . . .

Send Standing Eagle! Send the war leader to bear a pipe of peace to the soldier chief! *With hope the people can live.* Send a pipe to Three Stars.

But also, now while the snows linger around the villages of the Lakota, send another pipe. Send a pipe to Sitting Bull and through him to all the bands. Ask them to remain at peace. Even if Three Stars will not hear the plea of Sun Horse, let the bands avoid fighting now; if the soldiers come near, let the people move away. Soon the bluecoats will tire of fighting *Waziya,* the winter power, and they will go home. In the summer, when the grass is tall, let the bands meet along the Tongue or Rosebud. Let word go to the agencies and call for relatives to slip away and come to this gathering. Let the great hoop of the Lakota nation be raised in the Moon when Buffalo Calves Grow Fat, and there let the people decide if they will go to the Dakota reservation and leave behind forever the grassy streams and wooded hunting grounds of the Powder River country. There in the great circle of the nation, Sun Horse would speak for peace.

Surely all the Lakota gathered together are strong enough to make a peace with the whites, a peace that might include some of the country here?

That was not for Sun Horse to say. Let the people decide, together.

Once more the Sun Band's council would meet, soon, tonight or tomorrow, but now Sun Horse would speak to them. With their leader strong and confident again, the councillors would agree to send the pipes. They would agree to this delay in order to give Sun Horse time to discover the true nature of the power he had seen joined here today, the power that brought him so much joy.

With a gentle pull on the single rein, he turned his horse to face the settlement. The last flakes of snow had ceased to fall and the air was turning cold. The clouds had risen and thinned. From the west came a shaft of sunlight that bathed the buildings and the snowy hillside in a reddish glow, like the light from a fire. The painted wagons were gone from the yard and were arrayed beyond the barn, where the figures of many whites moved this way and that. The Lakota horsemen, all but Lodgepole and Standing Eagle, were moving toward the wagons, a few whites walking beside them, looking curiously at the Indians. Men were rolling up the tarpaulins that covered the flat-topped wagons and Sun Horse could see in one of them the bear he had heard a short time ago. The animal was pacing back and forth in his cage.

On the porch, Hardeman was speaking with Johnny Smoker. They fell silent and looked in Sun Horse's direction when they saw that he was watching them.

What would Hardeman be prepared to do when he heard that the Sun Band would not surrender? Sun Horse could not guess, but he was certain that the white scout had planned for such an event. He would have to be outwitted, and that would be difficult. He must believe there was a better chance for peace with the sending of the pipes, and he could not be left to stand idly about. . . .

Send Hardeman with Standing Eagle! The war leader to bear the pipe and the white scout to carry the message for Three Stars! And send Lodgepole as well! Lodgepole would speak for the Lakota and Hardeman would speak for the *washíchun*, and together they would show Three Stars a way to make peace without more fighting! "Take your soldiers and leave the country so there will be no fighting now; in the summer Sun Horse will speak to the war leaders of the hostile bands, and he will speak for peace."

The message would be true. Hardeman would believe it, and he would not see the true reason for delay.

Sun Horse felt a deep contentment. With his mind composed and his face betraying no trace of emotion, as befitted a headman of the Lakota, he rode forward alone to surround his enemy.

Book Two

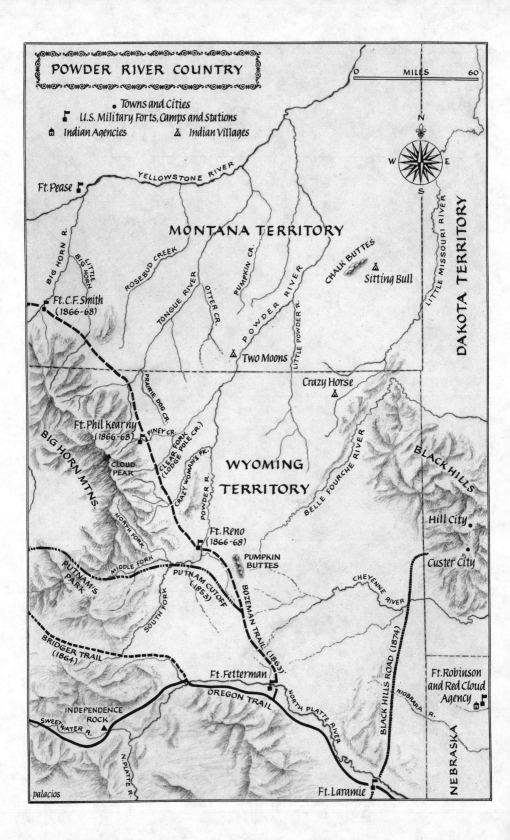

POWDER RIVER COUNTRY

MILES

0   60

• Towns and Cities
♪ U.S. Military Forts, Camps and Stations
⌂ Indian Agencies
△ Indian Villages

Ft. Pease

YELLOWSTONE RIVER

MONTANA TERRITORY

DAKOTA TERRITORY

LITTLE MISSOURI RIVER

BIG HORN R.

LITTLE BIG HORN

ROSEBUD CREEK

TONGUE RIVER

OTTER CR.

PUMPKIN CR.

POWDER RIVER

LITTLE POWDER R.

CHALK BUTTES

Sitting Bull

Ft. C.F. Smith
(1866-68)

△ Two Moons

Crazy Horse

PRAIRIE DOG CR.

Ft. Phil Kearny
(1866-68)

PINEY CR.

CLEAR FORK
(LODGE POLE CR.)

CRAZY WOMAN'S FK.

POWDER R.

BIG HORN MTNS.

CLOUD PEAK

NORTH FORK

WYOMING
TERRITORY

BELLE FOURCHE RIVER

BLACK HILLS

Hill City

Custer City

Ft. Reno
(1866-68)

PUMPKIN BUTTES

PUTNAM'S PARK

MIDDLE FORK

PUTNAM CUTOFF
(1853)

SOUTH FORK

BOZEMAN TRAIL (1863)

CHEYENNE RIVER

BRIDGER TRAIL
(1864)

BLACK HILLS ROAD (1874)

Ft. Fetterman

OREGON TRAIL

NORTH PLATTE RIVER

Ft. Robinson
and Red Cloud
Agency

NIOBRARA R.

INDEPENDENCE ROCK

SWEETWATER R.

N. PLATTE R.

NEBRASKA

palacios

Ft. Laramie

Music and dancers swirled around Bat Putnam. He smiled as he watched the couples spin by, noting the lip rouge and powder on the circus women, their brightly colored clothing, their high spirits. On the makeshift bandstand at the far end of the room, Hutch sat surrounded by musicians from the circus and flailed at his banjo as if his life depended on it, his eyes returning often to a young girl his own age, one of a family of Italian acrobats and aerial gymnasts, who was dancing near at hand with her father. Bat's smile broadened and he sipped again from the glass he held in his hand, taking a special pleasure in the taste of the fiery corn liquor. He danced by himself in a backwater, shuffling a small step suited to a drunken man on rough ground around a Rendezvous campfire, but he wasn't half drunk, not yet. The unlikely arrival of Tatum's Combined Equestrian and Animal Shows offered a natural opportunity for a man to get respectably wall-eyed and Bat intended to make the best of it. He'd already had enough to send most men to their beds, but he was just now oiled and primed for whatever was to follow. Around him, the saloon rang with laughter and life, and the ghosts were banished.

Whooee, some doin's, he thought, but he kept his glee to himself instead of shouting it out as he might have done. He contained it just as he contained the joy he had felt ever since that afternoon, savoring it as a starving man might savor the liver of a fresh-killed deer. There would be time enough later on for shouting out his triumph, if Sun Horse's plan worked. For now he would keep his hopes to himself.

Back this afternoon things had got a mite touchy there for a bit, but he had seen worse happen when a bunch of greenhorns decided that shooting was what you did first off when you set eyes on Indians. Lisa hadn't taken kindly to the shooting. For his own part, Bat felt that burning a little powder had livened up what had been a quiet winter so far and set everyone up just right for tonight's shindig. There was nothing like dancing to work off a hair-raising fright.

The Lakota were gone now. Sun Horse knew that Indians and whites and whiskey were a bad mix. Before they left, the warriors had walked among the circus wagons for a look at the strange animals. Bat and Sun Horse had joined them there when Sun Horse was done talking with Hardeman. They had marveled at the buffalo from Ceylon and the spotted leopard from Africa, the same land the elephant came from. *Igmú gleshka* they called the leopard—spotted cat. There was much excited talk when they saw the bear and the wolves, animals well known to them. A Lakota called Wolf Talker had lingered for a time with the wolves, but they were some foreign kind of wolf and he couldn't understand their language.

199

A small group of the more courageous circus folk had accompanied the Indians on their tour, the mahout Chatur among them, and the Lakota had puzzled for a time over the dark-skinned man when they learned he was also called Indian but came from a faraway land. They seemed satisfied when they learned that this *India* whence he came was ruled by Grandmother England, the same woman who ruled Grandmother Land, which was just six or seven days' hard ride to the north, up beyond the Yellowstone. Several of them had been to Grandmother Land. "Grandmother England, she treats her Injuns pretty good," Standing Eagle had offered.

It had been quite a day for the circus folk too. With the Indians gone, each had his story to tell about the arrival in Putnam's Park and the first sight of wild Indians, and the stories had grown fanciful in the retelling once the strong drink began to flow. Even now, at a nearby table, Chatur was surrounded by circus women eager to hear it all again from the dark little man who spoke in a strangely accented British English. "Oh, I should say, I was most terrified," he was saying. "But Rama was ready for battle!" The women urged him on as Bat moved away to be closer to the music. He would have his own stories to tell about this day.

Lisa had done Jed proud on short notice today. She had put on a feed and a flingding and a celebration that came waist-high to the real thing all those years ago in the Rendezvous camps. After a meal of meat and potatoes and corn pudding and tinned tomatoes and fancy fixings Bat hadn't seen in a dozen years, topped off with pies and breads that little Ling had been the whole afternoon baking, the circus folk had flocked back to the bar for something to wash down the last of their food. And after that there was another glass to wash down the first and before long even the faces of the wagon drivers were downright jolly. From out of the wagons musical instruments were soon fetched, for anyone but a complete fool knows he'd best play for his supper if he's able, and young Hutch had run to get his banjo. It was a fair little band, with some big brass instruments Bat hadn't seen since his Boston youth.

Just now a fat German with nimble fingers stood at the front of the bandstand, which had been made in ten minutes from the bed of an old wagon turned upside down. He played a rollicking polka on an accordion with sweat running down his face. After each song he downed a glass of beer in the time most men took just to draw a breath. Beside him, Hutch kept looking at the man playing the tuba like he might look at a three-legged rooster that had learned how to run. He wasn't quite sure how it did what it did, but you could see by his expression that it tickled him pink.

Bat moved across the floor more quickly now, making his way among the twirling couples as easily as an ermine slipping through a patch of winter willows and feeling just as invisible, for few took notice of him. The quadrilles and reels of earlier in the evening had given way to exuberant polkas and gallops and schottisches, and dancers had their eyes on their partners. The men and women on the floor were breathing hard and sweating freely, their recent hardships forgotten, and Bat could feel the excitement rising around him. The circus folk knew how to enjoy themselves when they found shelter on the trail, that was truth. And if they shouted and laughed and told ribald jokes in French and German and Italian as well as English, that wasn't so different from the old days when the trapper camps heard French on all sides, together with English and Arapaho and Snake and Cheyenne and Lakota.

There had been a time when any chance that brought men together in large numbers had been cause for a boisterous celebration where introductions performed over liberal draughts of forty-rod whiskey led in a short while to oaths of lasting comradeship if affinity was apparent, or mutual avoidance thereafter if it was not. When there were only a few white men in the mountains, it was best to know your comrades well, for your life would certainly depend on them when something set the badger loose. But times had changed. Anymore, the process of getting to know a stranger was slow, from what little Bat knew of current practices in civilized diggin's. The frontier had developed a reserve it lowered so gradually that except in cases of real liking, two parties might meet and talk and go off their own ways with scarcely an inkling about the true nature of the other.

"Wagh!" Bat snorted in disgust at a world where men had so little need to know other men and make a friend where they could. A woman turned, startled by the sound, and shrank back from the mountain man in his greasy leather clothes. Bat saw the rising mounds of her breasts above a low-cut bodice of green satin. He smiled in appreciation and passed on.

Lisa had done her daddy proud, all right, rest his bones. Jed was a mountain man at heart and he had kept to the old ways, even after he planted his stick for good in this valley. Celebrations had been a natural consequence of the arrival in Putnam's Park of any large group, red or white, and today Lisa had put on the show by herself, without Jed at the helm.

Bat saw her now by the kitchen door, looking solemn, and he sidled up close, but she didn't notice him. He slapped her lightly on the rump, then rubbed the spot he had patted, taking an uncle's pride in the shape and feel of his niece.

"Uncle Bat!"

"Won't have you lookin' like that. Not tonight. Don't see a sour puss in this bunch, do you?"

She smiled then and showed her delight. "It's nice, isn't it?"

"What's troublin' you, then?"

"Him."

Bat followed her gaze. Across the room Hardeman was leaning against the wall, watching the dancers. He was wearing the buckskins he had worn all day, but his hair was freshly combed. Johnny Smoker stood beside him. The youth had donned a bright red flannel shirt. A clean bandanna, this one a dark green, was tied loosely around his neck.

"Well?"

"Too close with himself, Father would have said."

"Mebbe."

"What will he do?"

201

"Don't rightly know. He'll go along for now, I'm thinkin'."

"Will he?"

"It's a chance for peace, honey child. If Sun Horse talks to the war chiefs come summertime, might be we'll all come out ahead."

"It's too good to be true. And it's not what he wants. He said over and over again the peace has to be made now or there will be a war." She watched Hardeman through the happy dancers. He stood outside the celebration, watching but not taking part. "I wish I knew what sort of man he really is."

"This nigger knows that fur. Tough like a badger. Don't let much get to him." Bat put an arm around his niece and held her close to comfort her, as he had often done when she was a child. "Happen you come up on his right side, you'd have a longtime friend, I'm thinkin'."

"I'm not so certain."

Bat grinned and released her. "You ain't, but this critter knows. I been told by the bear!" And he danced away with himself, his feet shuffling as gracefully as the dying grizzly bear had shuffled with poor Toussaint. This was the step he danced this evening, not the whiskey stagger of Rendezvous but the bear's dance that had welcomed him into the mountain life, feeling the bear power alive inside him again. Now as then the chance for new life opened before him, at least for a time. New hope was born, given birth by the words Sun Horse had spoken that afternoon.

When Sun Horse returned from his solitary ponderings beyond the wagon road, Hardeman and Johnny had walked to the corner of the porch, near where Bat and Standing Eagle sat their mounts. Sun Horse had joined them there. He spoke in Lakota and Bat translated, and Hardeman listened quietly, never interrupting. Bat had almost laughed aloud to express his glee when he heard Sun Horse's new plan. Like the headman, he had been silent in the council on the previous day, not wanting to urge his brethren to surrender but unable to suggest another course, and now Sun Horse had found one. Bat had been even more elated when Hardeman agreed to go with the pipe carriers, and even Standing Eagle seemed pleased with the scheme.

Why Johnny had picked that moment to tell Sun Horse that he had decided to stay in the white folks' world, Bat didn't know, but even that news hadn't dampened all of the headman's hopes, as if he knew it was coming sooner or later. And when Hardeman and the boy had gone off, and Standing Eagle went to join the other Lakota men among the circus wagons, Sun Horse had motioned Bat to stay behind, and it was then that he had asked Bat to accompany the pipe carriers. Bat had readily agreed. Sending two white men to plead the headman's plan with Crook might just do the trick, but Bat wasn't so sure about having Standing Eagle along. "My brother Standing Eagle does not always keep his temper around the *washíchun*," he had said. "Three Stars will see that he does not want this peace." Sun Horse had nodded. "Three Stars will see, and he will believe all the more in what the pipe tells him. The *washíchun* hear the word of a war leader."

It was true, although from what Bat had heard of George Crook, he knew the difference between a war leader and a headman. Some officers, the best ones, took the trouble to learn the ways of Indian leadership and they saw that a war leader had power only in war, while it was the headmen and the councils that decided the terms for peace, but most soldiers had the arrogance of their kind and figured that a treaty should bear the marks of the warriors. Back in '68 the Oglala had been forced to make Red Cloud a treaty chief because the whites had insisted that the Laramie treaty would be no good until the mighty Red Cloud signed. And so Red Cloud, who was only a war leader of one band, had been given the power to touch the pen at Laramie, but just for that one time.

Bat grinned at the foolishness of the whites. Sun Horse was no fool. He had covered his bets both ways, sending a war leader to carry the proposal of a headman. And the wise old Lakota had remembered best of all the lesson Bat and Jed Putnam had taught him long ago: "Don't treat a white man any different from a Crow or a Pawnee. Don't answer him yes or no. Make him deal."

Sun Horse had found a way to deal; he had found a way to gain some time for the Sun Band, and Bat had hope that the plan might work. In Sun Horse's manner he had seen new confidence, and from that moment Bat's spirits had risen until now he could scarcely contain them. If Crook accepted the terms, there was hope. If Sun Horse could play the peacemaker among the warlike bands, there was hope. Best of all, the summer council might find a way to make a lasting peace and still keep some of the Powder River country, and if that hope was realized, there was hope for Bat to live out his days with the Sioux.

Of course, Sun Horse had said nothing to Hardeman about the call for a summer gathering of the bands; the whites feared any such gathering, sure it could mean only war. "But he may learn of the great council when we give the pipe to Sitting Bull," Bat had said, suddenly concerned. "Perhaps," Sun Horse had replied. "But by then he will have traveled with the pipe carriers for many days and nights. He will eat with you and sleep with you; he will sit in council with my cousin Sitting Bull and he will see that even the famous war leader wishes only to protect his people and save some of his country. Perhaps then the white scout will see that talk of the summer council should be kept from Three Stars." When Crook finally heard of the gathering he might believe he had been tricked, but by then the councillors would have decided what to do; if they offered peace, the offer would be impressive, coming from such an assemblage; if they chose war, it would not matter what Crook thought.

Bat saw Hardeman now, standing on the fringes of the dancing and gaiety. Bat danced the dance of the bear and he saw with the eyes of the bear. Hardeman was a creature of the wild, though perhaps a bit dulled at the edges by too much time in the towns. He moved his eyes like something wild when caught in a crowd like this one, and Bat felt once more a kinship with the scout. He remembered the way Hardeman was at ease on the trail to the Sun Band's village, and he understood the true wisdom of Sun Horse's plan. Together Bat and Hardeman would go to find Crook, and away from this press of people Hardeman would be at ease and they would come to know each other. Bat wondered if Hardeman had ever traveled with Indians in their own country before or if he had always been with white soldiers, ranging out in front of the column, looking for the Indians as enemies. Who was to say what changes might take place in such a man on a journey down the Powder? Who was to say what might happen if such a man should feel in himself the beginnings of kinship with Bat Putnam, or even with the Sioux?

What might be accomplished by a man who had the trust of both sides, a man who could speak for the Sioux as well as the whites?

"Hooraw fer the mountains!" Bat said softly under his breath. He made his way to the bar, where he held out his glass and caught Julius's eye. When the glass was full once more, he moved along, dancing all the while.

The music filled the room and the floor trembled under the rhythmic tread of the dancers. This was the heart of the evening and Bat wanted to share it with his wife. He wanted to hold her in his arms and kick up his heels. They would dance as they had danced when they were young, to celebrate his hope. She wouldn't want to come amongst so many raucous whites, but he would bring her anyway. She was safe with him.

He turned toward the kitchen door to go fetch her from the lodge, but there was no need. There she stood, talking with Lisa, laughing now. Penelope did not often come into the Big House, never having grown accustomed to white men's lodgings or customs, but sometimes she and Lisa sought each other out just for the sake of the hilarity their talk always engendered.

Bat danced close and hooked his arm through his wife's, taking her by surprise, and he swirled her away to the strains of the polka.

Lisa smiled and watched them go, marveling at how well Penelope knew the white man's dance steps.

"We're done cleaning up, ma'am. I'll help to tend the bar, if you like."

She turned to find the circus cook addressing her. He had found her in the kitchen that afternoon not long after the sudden gunplay had ended. Lisa had been wondering how to begin when he had appeared with two women and an angular man named Monty at his side. "Name's Joe Kitchen," he had said. "I'm the cookie." He was round from eating well and short by nature, a white man's counterpart to Harry Wo, and without him the celebration now in full swing around them would have been a poorer thing.

Lisa had not thought twice about how she intended to welcome Tatum's people to Putnam's Park. It was only how to go about it that had stymied her for a time as she struggled to grasp the quantities of food to be prepared; but Joe Kitchen was used to such problems and needed only to know how best to help out, and with his appearance Lisa's uncertainty had vanished. She ordered dusty jugs of whiskey and gin brought from the cellar, and before the afternoon light had turned gray, the bar glasses were wiped clean and a fire made in the stove and the saloon was open for business. And then from Lisa's scanty stores and the circus supply wagons the meal was assembled. Joe Kitchen provided

204

fresh meat the drivers had brought down three days before when the wagons came on a group of winter-poor antelope, and beer to go with the whiskey and gin, and tins of corned beef, even oysters for those that liked them and deviled ham for those that didn't, and together with what Putnam House had to offer from shelves and root cellar the thing was done. The kitchen had grown hot from the heat of two stoves, and fires had been built outside as well, over which the cooking pots of the circus were hung, and before the cries for food grew too loud the platters had been paraded into the saloon where they were greeted with cheers. Through it all Joe Kitchen's sharp tongue and brash manner with the women had enlivened the cooking. He had a way both familiar and respectful, and by the time she finally sat down to eat, Lisa felt she had a new friend.

"You've done enough for one day," she said now. "You deserve to enjoy yourself."

"Oh, I'll have a dance or two later on, right enough. It looks like a run at the watering trough just now."

At the bar a throng of men and women were all clamoring for attention.

"It does, doesn't it. We'll both go, then."

They joined Julius and a gangling roustabout called Ben Long, who were hastening to keep up with the demands for drink. The circus folk were free with their money, and the ring of silver and gold on the worn wood of the bartop was a continuous accompaniment to the music from the band. Lisa filled her glasses and collected coins and half expected to find that her father had joined them behind the bar, so much did the hubbub in the saloon remind her of days gone by.

"What can I get for you?" Lisa asked the question as she turned. She was taken aback to find herself facing a man who rose fully two feet above her head. It was the giant whose bulk had provided shelter for the clown that afternoon. He was no longer wearing his purple cape but he still cut an imposing figure. His hair floated about his head like a mane of straw.

"Well, now. Whatever you think appropriate, I imagine."

He was English, and his manner was anything but imposing. He was diffident, almost shy. Lisa searched her memory for a British drink. Perhaps he would like one of the mixtures her father had learned to make in the British colonies in Asia. "Perhaps a gin and bitters? A Singapore Sling? Or we make a frontier drink called a hailstorm. It's whiskey on crushed ice. It's supposed to have fresh mint too, but we have none, I'm afraid."

"To be quite honest, I have had an astonishing array of concoctions since coming to your country. I think this evening perhaps just some whiskey, if you don't mind." As Lisa poured he offered hesitantly, "This must be a burden for you, being closed for the season as you were."

"I'm very glad to have you, and I wish we were closed only for the season."

"I don't understand. This is a country inn, is it not?"

Lisa laughed. "I have never heard it called that before." She set his glass before him. "My father established himself here to serve the emigrants, but now most travelers take the railroad. Those going to Montana get off at the Salt Lake and go north from there. We're quite off the beaten track now, and most people are afraid of the Indians."

"Ah. I see," he said, not seeing at all. He sampled the whiskey. "Good Lord!" he gasped, and nearly choked. He recovered himself and said, "To quote the monster Caliban, 'I'll swear upon that bottle to be thy true servant, for the liquor is not earthly.'"

Lisa laughed again, liking this huge Englishman very much. "Some call it tanglefoot. I must say, I didn't expect to hear Shakespeare from a circus strongman, even an English one. You are the strongman, aren't you?"

"By an accident of stature, I am. Chalmers. Alfred Chalmers; your humble servant, Miss Putnam." He drank again and appraised the taste thoughtfully. His manner reminded Lisa of the fathers of her Boston friends sampling a glass of new Madeira. She refilled his glass.

"This one is on the house. A courtesy for our foreign guests."

Chalmers raised the glass to her before sipping again, still testing the waters cautiously. He smiled and seemed to relax a little. "'Thou mak'st me merry; I am full of pleasure.'"

"You're an actor, then."

"Would that I could pursue a theatrical career. But there are few roles for one of my, ah, shall we say my standing?" They laughed together and Chalmers drank less cautiously. "I have performed Lear and Macbeth, and once essayed Richard the Third. May I?" His glass was empty. His reticent manner was gone, replaced by a garrulous friendliness. As Lisa poured he grew expansive. "I was consigned to roles, ah, larger than life. But I wished to play them all, Iago and Hamlet and little Puck, and the managers would hear none of it. So I left them to their own devices. Such was the theater's loss. Perhaps in America I shall have better fortune." He drank off half the whiskey in his generous glass and struck a pose, one hand upon the breast. "'Whether 'tis nobler in the mind to suffer the slings and arrows of outrageous fortune,' or to take drink against a sea of troubles, and so in drowning, end them." He chuckled deep within himself and tossed off the remaining liquid. "With apologies to the Bard. And with apologies to our cousins the Scots, I believe a man might grow accustomed to your corn whiskey. It is certainly less spartan than theirs, and—"

He was interrupted by a sudden commotion on the dance floor. An area of quiet spread like a ripple in all directions as eyes sought the cause. Men rose from their seats, others turned, and then all were still.

Lisa reached beneath the bar and found the short-barrel shotgun that was kept there. She brought it up and set it on the bartop, her eyes searching the room. Across from the bar, in the corner farthest from the musicians, a game of cards was in progress, and she saw now that the one-armed man, the one Hardeman had wounded that afternoon, had joined the game. His arm was supported in a sling that Julius had made for him after he had bandaged the man's wrist. The wrist had been sprained by the shock of Hardeman's bullet snatching the Winchester from the man's hand, but no bones were broken and the flesh wound caused by the splintering gunstock was trifling. A young boy from the circus held the one-armed man's cards for him. The man was looking toward the center of the room, but he kept his seat.

On the dance floor, Bat Putnam faced one of the circus men, and when he spoke, his voice threatened violence. "What was it you said, mule driver?"

"I said that squaw's kind of cute and I reckoned to get me a dance." The speaker was no mule driver at all, but the wagon guide Fisk, the man who had led the circus off the beaten track into the wilds. Bearded, florid of face and unsteady of foot, he faced Bat and Penelope across a six-foot clearing of bare planks.

"You're speakin' of my wife, mule driver." Bat had recognized the man, of course, but he would not sully the profession of scouting by including Fisk in its ranks.

"Your wife is it? Jesus Christ, first it's niggers and Injuns, now it's a squaw man!" Fisk's shoulders were muscular and rounded, his eyes dark. Like a badger he moved slowly, but when cornered he was capable of surprising speed. His body was half turned away from Bat as he spoke, one hand groping at his waist. The hand found the haft of a knife and even as the last words left his mouth, Fisk moved, hoping to take the old man off guard. But he failed as others had failed long before him. His knife hand was seized as it came forward, in a grip that threatened to crush his bones, and by means of a movement he could not comprehend even later, when he pondered it long and hard, he found himself spun around and wrapped in the clutch of the old man's arm, while a long skinning knife appeared at his throat.

"That's a loose tongue you got, mule driver. I'm thinkin' you might ought to apologize to my wife."

In the crowd, one of the teamsters, a wiry Ohioan named Morton, his hair prematurely gray, drew a pistol half out of its holster. He was called "Redeye" by the others because of his fondness for forty-rod whiskey, and he had already taken on a respectable load of the cheapest spirits offered by Putnam House, but even drunk he was cautious. He hesitated now, unsure if he should take part, and before he could make up his mind, the decision was made for him.

He felt something cold touch his neck and heard the click of a pistol's hammer being drawn back to full cock. A voice said, "There's time for saloon fighting and there's a time for gunplay. You want to survive in this country, you'd do well to learn the difference."

Morton let his own gun fall back into place. The cold object left his neck. He turned to see the man called Hardeman, the one whose shot had lifted Henry Kinnean out of his saddle and dumped him in the snow that afternoon, already turning away from him. Hardeman's revolver had found its way back into his belt, where he kept it stuffed like a farmer. So confident was he that his warning would be obeyed, he did not bother to look back. Morton flushed red with anger and once again his hand found the butt of his pistol, but the tall Negro, who had been serving at the bar until a moment ago, was nearby in the crowd and his eyes were on Morton. Morton let his hand drop. Even without the colored man's presence, he would have thought twice before drawing again near Hardeman. A short time ago he had been standing by the card table, watching the play. When Kinnean arrived, one of the drivers had remarked that he was lucky to get off with a sprained wrist, but Kinnean had silenced the man with a black look. "Luck was no part of it," Kinnean had said. "He'd of meant to kill me, he'd of done it." His tone allowed for no further treatment of the matter and it had come to rest there. Was it possible that Hardeman had hit what he aimed for, that in the midst of such chaos he had intended all the time to knock the Winchester from Kinnean's hand? Thaddeus Morton would not be the one to find out.

"Say you're sorry, there's a nice fella," Bat Putnam said now. The skinning knife pricked the skin below Fisk's Adam's apple.

"I'm . . . sorry."

"Drop the knife."

The knife fell. Bat released Fisk and picked it up. Without seeming to look where he threw it, he tossed it to Julius. Then he met Julius's eyes and grinned. "You're movin' kind of slow today, ain't you?"

"Didn't want to spoil your fun," Julius said.

And so it ended; no blood had been spilled, not a blow struck. The silence crumbled, then broke asunder as those in the saloon returned to libations and conversations abandoned in mid-glass or midstream, glad of an end to the tension, eager to put behind them the awkward moment that had arisen so suddenly. The band struck up a tune, and in the space of a few measures the floor was filled once again with twirling couples.

Julius found Hardeman in the crowd. "I'm obliged to you for taking a hand," the Negro said.

Hardeman shrugged. "It seemed like you had it under control, you and Bat and Miss Putnam." He nodded toward the bar, where Lisa was replacing the short shotgun beneath the counter. "I didn't mean to step on any toes."

"You didn't. Seems like you've got a way of steppin' in and takin' up the slack no one else sees. I'll stand you to a whiskey, if you're agreeable."

Hardeman nodded, and relaxed enough to favor Julius with a trace of a smile. "I'm agreeable." Together they crossed the room to the bar, where Julius held up two fingers to Lisa.

She nodded in response to the request, but as she reached for a jug of whiskey, part of her attention was still on Alfred Chalmers. The giant had followed Julius to the center of the room where the trouble broke out. Would he have supported Fisk if the fighting had gone further? She had noticed that the men of the troupe—those dressed as performers, not the rough-clad teamsters—had looked in his direction, as if awaiting his move, but he had made

208

none. He was joined now by a rotund woman wearing a silk scarf around her neck, a sash at her waist, a billowing blouse and a skirt that reached to the floor, all in bright colors. She greeted him warmly, but as he spoke to her her expression became serious and she looked darkly at Fisk and the teamsters, now grouped around the card table. She accompanied Chalmers when he returned to the bar and remained by his side. The giant's face was solemn, displaying none of the easy humor the whiskey had brought out in him only moments earlier.

"In Mr. Tatum's absence," he said, addressing Lisa, "I must apologize on behalf of one and all. Such behavior ill repays your hospitality."

"Such things happen, Mr. Chalmers," Lisa said, glad to know where Chalmers stood in the matter. "No real harm was done. Thank you for your concern."

"You are very kind."

Lisa set out two more glasses and poured one half full; before pouring in the last one she raised her eyebrows inquiringly, looking at the brightly clothed woman. The woman's skin was swarthy and her eyes were black and sharp. Her face was framed by dense black curls that fell in ringlets.

"Oh, I beg your pardon," Chalmers exclaimed, putting an arm around the woman and drawing her close. "Forgive me, my dear. Miss Putnam, may I present Lydia Kaslov."

The two women exchanged expressions of greeting and Lydia nodded shyly when Lisa renewed the offer of a drink. Chalmers drank off half of his whiskey in a swallow and addressed Lisa again, keeping his voice low.

"I feel I should warn you, the drivers are rough men, and just now are under scant restraint. The unfortunate Mr. Kinnean showed an uncommon ability to make them mind their behavior, but he is powerless for the time being."

"Kinnean?" Hardeman said.

"The one-armed gentleman with whom you crossed swords, so to speak, this afternoon. He was formerly an army officer, but lost an arm in your recent war, I am told. Mr. Tatum found him in the Black Hills, gambling and down on his luck. He took him on to control the drivers, many of whom were also hired there after our old drivers ran off to try their luck at gold mining. He takes naturally to command and the drivers respect him; but I am afraid a one-armed man with an injured wrist exerts little real authority."

"Might be worth havin' a word with Tatum," Julius said. "Another one of them fellers looks crosseyed at Bat, Tatum won't be leavin' here with all his drivers alive."

As if on cue, the door beyond the bar opened and Hachaliah Tatum stepped into the saloon. Like a child arriving late for school, he became the center of attention for those close at hand. He wore a frock coat and starched collar and a silk brocade vest, and the light of the lamps shone like fireflies in the polished sheen of his boots. His dark hair was precisely parted and brushed back; at the nape of his neck it formed a series of small ringlets. He paused for a moment in the doorway and then stood aside to let the girl who stood behind him enter. He closed the door and ushered her forward, smiling at Lisa.

"Miss Putnam, may I present Miss Amanda Spencer. You know her better as Joey the Clown."

The girl took Lisa's hand briefly with a touch that could barely be felt before she let go.

"I'm pleased to meet you, Amanda." Lisa smiled. "I must admit I had no idea you were a girl until you lost your hat. It's been years since I have seen a clown. It was a great surprise for all of us."

The girl smiled shyly and said nothing. Her hair was combed straight to her shoulders and was held back at the sides with ivory clasps. She wore a simple fawn-colored dress with understated frills at the bodice and cuffs and hem. It's silk, Lisa realized with a start. A real silk dress on a child. How old can she be? Eighteen? Twenty? And so beautiful. "What a lovely dress," she said.

"Thank you. Hachaliah gave it to me." Amanda's voice was as soft and smooth as the fabric of the dress.

"Are your parents with the circus too?"

Amanda dropped her eyes. "My parents are dead."

"A tragic fire," Tatum said, placing a comforting hand on Amanda's shoulder. "It was some years ago. Amanda was just eight at the time. My wife perished in the same fire. We were thrown together by tragedy, you see. It was only natural that I should care for her." A shadow passed across his face, like the remembrance of some nearly forgotten pain, but then he smiled at the girl, regarding her fondly. "She has rewarded me for her care many times over by becoming the star of the show."

Across the room the band ended its breakneck tune, and above the rising rush of voices a man called out: "Amanda!" He waved to her from the bandstand, holding a fiddle above his head.

Lydia smiled at the girl. "You will play for us? Your friends are impatient. Many have requested that you play." She gave her *r*'s a Romany roll.

The fiddler approached them, making his way through the crowd, fiddle in hand. "Come on, now," he said when he reached them. "We've held the fort long enough."

Amanda glanced at Tatum and received an encouraging nod and a smile in reply. She took the violin from the fiddler's hand and was gone, skipping through the crowd like a child turned out to play.

Standing alone in the throng, Johnny Smoker had watched the girl ever since she entered the room. Now, as she passed nearby, she saw him and gave him a hint of a smile. The rhythm of her feather-light steps missed a beat, as if she might stop to say a word, but she passed on.

Amanda. That was what the fiddle player had called out. Amanda. Johnny

210

said the name over in his mind until it fit the girl, who now stood on the bandstand holding the fiddle cocked to her ear as she thumbed the strings one by one and made small adjustments to the pegs. That afternoon he had been struck dumb to discover that the clown was a girl. He could still feel the touch of her hand in his own, the quick squeeze she gave before letting go. Amanda. The name and its owner had entered his life for the first time today, and he would never be the same.

With a nod to the band, Amanda set the fiddle under her chin and began to play. At the end of the first measure, the other musicians joined in and around the room men quickly found partners for the polka.

At the bar, Tatum bowed to Lisa. "May I have the honor?" He held her with authority and led her effortlessly among the dancers until they were close to the bandstand. There was a special quality in the music now and Lisa realized that it came from Amanda. The other fiddler had been content to blend with the band, following rather than leading, but there could be no doubt where the direction of the music came from once the slight girl took the bow in her hand. The others looked to her, and when she nodded to one or the other he stepped forward and took his turn at playing his best. As he stepped back, the sound of the fiddle would rise again smoothly, urging the band onward.

Lisa was flushed and her heart was pounding. How long had it been since a gentleman held her in his arms and guided her through the steps of a polka?

"I want to apologize again for the misunderstanding this afternoon," Tatum said. "Naturally, I had no way of knowing the Indians were peaceful. I must say, you and your man—your partner, Mr. Ingram, took matters in hand very well."

"I'm afraid there was very nearly more trouble this evening, just before you came in. One of your men attacked my uncle. He had made advances toward my uncle's wife." She indicated Bat and Penelope, who were dancing nearby.

Tatum's expression revealed an irritation quickly controlled. "It seems I must apologize again. My men are a rough breed, but such men are necessary in the wilderness. Many of them are veterans of the war; they are familiar with firearms and violence. Mr. Kinnean, the man Mr. Hardeman shot, has organized them for the defense of the circus, should that be necessary. I shall have to take it on myself to control them until his wound is healed."

"I shouldn't like to see any more of your men hurt while you're here."

Tatum seemed about to say something more when the tempo of the dance increased and he gave all his attention to guiding her safely among the careening couples. On the wagon box, Amanda nodded to Hutch and he earned a cheer from musicians and dancers alike as his banjo sang out the melody and moved the polka to a ringing conclusion.

Tatum bowed. "I hope you will honor me with another dance later on. If you will excuse me now, I'll have a word with my men."

Lisa was left alone near the bandstand, where now Julius joined the other

211

musicians, his own fiddle in his hand. Amanda stepped back, yielding the front of the stage, but he declined the offer. "You play whatever you like," he said. "I'll try to find my way."

"Play that waltz," suggested the bassist.

"That's the ticket," said another man. "The one you made up."

The band remained silent as Amanda began a lovely melody in slow waltz time and couples started to move about the floor. As the others joined in softly behind the fiddle, Lisa saw Chalmers making his way towards her, his eyes on her alone as he broached the crowd like a plow horse moving effortlessly through a field of corn, but before he reached her she felt a light touch at her elbow.

"Miss Putnam?"

It was Johnny Smoker. Concealing her surprise, Lisa took the hand he offered and rested her other one on his shoulder as his arm went around her waist. She smiled at Chalmers as they moved away, and nodded when he silently asked, The next one then? She felt like the belle of the ball, sought after from all sides. It was a heady feeling and very pleasant.

She had resolved to take whatever pleasure she could from the circus's unexpected visit. Her success at controlling the crowd this afternoon, her sudden decisiveness when danger threatened, had bolstered her confidence. "Meet trouble when it comes along and don't fret about it beforehand," her father had said. So it would be. She had stood and fought when the moment called for it, and she had put on a meal and an evening's entertainment for a crowd of nearly a hundred on a moment's notice. She would stand and fight again if necessary, for Sun Horse and Putnam's Park, but Sun Horse's plan to send pipes to General Crook and Sitting Bull gave her a breathing space. Tonight she would savor the almost forgotten joy of an evening like this one and tomorrow she would be prepared to face whatever came.

With something close to astonishment, she became aware of the skill with which Johnny was guiding her across the floor. He did not tramp out the beat as many a novice waltzer would do, but glided along with only the gentlest shifting of head and foot and pressure at the small of her back to match the two of them to the lilting rhythm of the dance. And his limp was gone. Lisa's astonishment grew. His gait was perfectly even as he moved to one side and then the other. It was as if the music had effected a miraculous cure. He moved as gracefully as any partner she had ever known. If she closed her eyes she could be back in Boston, at the ball where she had first danced the waltz in public. In school she and the other girls had practiced the forbidden step in secret as soon as one of their number had learned it, but it had taken the daring of an eccentric Boston dowager to bring the waltz into its own in that conservative town. Whatever did they fear? "Too stimulating for young ladies," they warned. And they were right. Waltzing now in her own saloon, Lisa felt the thrill of her first waltz all over again and she hoped the dance would go on forever.

Yet something was missing. Despite Johnny's expert grace, he was not entirely with her. She saw as they turned about the floor that his eyes were often on the bandstand. He is dancing with her music, she realized suddenly. In his mind he was really embracing the notes that Amanda played, as if she were playing just for him.

And then she saw that Amanda's eyes found Johnny too, although they never stayed on him for long. Each pretends not to be entranced by the other, she thought. No wonder young people take so long to find each other. Neither sees the other's feelings.

Tatum passed by the bandstand with one of the circus women in his arms and he smiled at Amanda. Her eyes moved from Tatum to Johnny and back again, but Tatum did not notice. He doesn't see it either, Lisa realized. Why? Because he too has a blindness. He thinks she is still a child.

"May I ask where you learned to waltz so beautifully?" she inquired.

"Oh, it seemed like something worth learning from the white man," Johnny said, a little embarrassed. "Dancing, I mean. I lived in St. Louis for a time. Chris thought I needed a proper home. The man was the brother of an officer Chris knew. His wife taught dancing to young ladies. She used me as a dancing partner for just about every young lady in St. Louis."

"I envy them," she said, and he blushed. "Why ever did you leave?"

"I stayed through the winter. They were good people. In the springtime it just didn't seem right to be in a place like that, all crowded streets and noise day and night. Chris was in Utah Territory, hunting meat for the track crews. I found him there."

So Hardeman had sought a home for the boy, and it had been Johnny's choice to leave that home and rejoin Hardeman in the wandering life. Lisa added this information to what little else she knew of Johnny's companion and protector. He was a puzzling man, but she would leave the solving of the puzzle for another time. She was enjoying herself too much just now to worry about anything. She put her thoughts aside and surrendered completely to the waltz.

On the bandstand, Julius set the fiddle against his chest and moved his fingers silently on the strings, feeling the music. When he was sure of the melody he joined in softly. Amanda heard and turned to face him. She played the tune through with him once from start to finish, and the two fiddles playing the same notes together produced a richness of tone that suffused the room and urged the dancers on.

Joining the waltz late, Bat and Penelope moved onto the floor now, their heads held high, and the onlookers fell back to make more room. They gazed in amusement at the spectacle of the short, bronzed woman and her gaunt mountain man, his otter-wrapped braids swaying in time with the music, as they negotiated the steps of the dance with the confidence of the Astors.

As the melody began again, Amanda moved her fingers up the neck of her fiddle, playing a third above Julius, and together the fiddles sang in harmony.

Amanda and Julius faced each other, the bows dancing in their hands as the room danced around them.

At the bar, Hardeman sipped sparingly from a glass of whiskey as he leaned back against the bartop and watched the dancers. It was his second drink of the evening. He had rationed himself carefully, going against a wish to drink until the whiskey overcame his reticence and propelled him onto the floor to dance with Lisa Putnam or any other woman who caught his fancy. Drink when they don't expect it and don't drink when they do; for now he would remain unpredictable. He felt like celebrating as much as anyone in the saloon, but he hadn't given in to it; he had guarded his feelings. He would keep his wits about him and do what he could to strengthen his hand, now that he knew Johnny would be out of the line of fire if trouble came.

Lisa and Johnny were dancing nearby. She moved lightly in the young man's arms, her toes scarcely seeming to touch the floor. Hardeman had tried several times during the evening to screw up his courage to ask her to dance, but each time he had drawn back. The ballroom was not a place in which he felt at home. He lacked the natural grace displayed by Johnny and the circus master Tatum, who had been the first to take Lisa onto the dance floor. He could perform the steps in a workmanlike manner, but he always felt ill at ease. He half wished he had taken up Johnny's offer to give him lessons, made in jest this past winter in Ellsworth.

The waltz ended and Johnny and Lisa parted. Johnny looked about, spied Hardeman, and picked his way through the crowd.

"Buy you something to wet your whistle?" Hardeman suggested when the youth reached his side.

"A beer maybe." Johnny was flushed from the dancing and breathing hard. He used a corner of his green bandanna to wipe the sweat from his brow.

Hardeman raised a hand to Joe Kitchen. "A beer for a thirsty man."

As Joe delivered the beer, a group of circus men hove up to the bar all in a cluster, calling for a round of drinks. Morton was among them. He glanced down the bar at Hardeman and looked quickly away.

Hardeman raised his glass to Johnny. "When a young man decides to step out on his own, I guess that calls for a toast. Here's to your independence."

A little self-consciously, Johnny touched his glass to Hardeman's and they drank together. Hardeman savored the familiar warmth of the whiskey, but he was pleasantly relaxed without the liquor's assistance. He felt foolish for ever having doubted the boy. Maybe Johnny had sensed his doubts and that was why he had told Sun Horse of his decision this afternoon, in front of Hardeman, there on the porch. When Sun Horse was done laying out his idea about the pipes for Crook and Sitting Bull, and when Hardeman had said he would go along, the boy had waited until it looked like the talk was done and then he had made signs to Sun Horse. *Grandfather*, he had signed without preamble, *I have chosen between the worlds. I am a white man. I will stay with the whites.*

214

Hardeman had found himself taking a deep breath and letting it out slowly. He felt that half his cares had left him in that moment.

Johnny's words had plainly set Sun Horse back a step or two, but he had nodded, smiling slightly, and his hands said *I know. That is what you came to tell me.* Sun Horse had maneuvered his horse close to the edge of the porch and he reached out and took Johnny's hand. It had seemed to Hardeman that he was bidding his grandson farewell. He didn't shake the boy's hand; he just held it. When he let go at last, he had made more signs. *The whiteman's life is always new, always changing. The Lakota life will no longer be the life my father and grandfather knew. It will not be the life you knew as a boy.*

Johnny had stood there awkwardly for a few moments, not knowing what else to say. Finally he made as if to leave, but then he hesitated and turned back. *I am glad you are sending the pipes to Three Stars,* he signed. *I am glad you and your people will remain here, in your own country. I do not want you to go to the reservation.*

Sun Horse had looked at Hardeman as he replied. *My friend has agreed to help us,* he signed. *Together the whiteman and the Lakota will make a peace.*

Hardeman hadn't been sure whether Sun Horse meant himself and one white man together, or all the Sioux and all the whites. Either way, he hoped the old man was right.

He and Johnny had left Bat and the Indians then, and when they were alone, Johnny had said he was glad Hardeman would go with the pipe carriers to see Crook.

"It seems like it gives the Sun Band a better chance, with you there too. At least General Crook will listen to you."

Hardeman had kept his misgivings to himself. When the Indians took their leave he had chosen to stay behind, preferring to spend a last night in Putnam's Park before setting out on what could prove to be a more dangerous journey than Johnny had any reason to imagine. Hardeman intended to give Sun Horse's pipes every chance to work their medicine, but his own plans were still held in reserve. Tomorrow he and Bat Putnam would go to the Indian village, where they would no doubt be obliged to bide their time a while longer. There would be another council to hear about the pipes, then ceremonies to get the pipes ready. All in all another day or two would pass before he could be away and on the trail with the pipe carriers, where actions and choices came easily to him and he wasted no time in fruitless imaginings.

Johnny was sipping his beer as slowly as Hardeman sipped his whiskey, and Hardeman saw how the boy looked over the rim of the glass as he drank, his eyes returning again and again to the bandstand and the girl playing the fiddle.

"Some doings, the circus and all," Hardeman observed.

Johnny smiled, a little embarrassed, as if one of his secrets had been found out.

"They're dead set on moving along tomorrow," Hardeman continued blandly. "They got big doings ahead, up Montana way, then Salt Lake and California.

We always said we'd get to California, you and me."

"I heard them talking," Johnny said. "The big Englishman and a couple of the others. They want a guide to show them out of the mountains and on to the Bridger road. They don't trust that Fisk to find his own boots on a clear day."

Hardeman seemed to ponder this for a moment, but he had heard the same talk. "Well, I've got to be going off with the pipe carriers in a day or two, whenever Sun Horse is ready with the pipes. But you could get them on their way easy enough." He said it as if it were a brand-new idea.

Johnny smiled, suddenly pleased with himself. "Well, I guess I could do that, couldn't I?"

Hardeman was reminded once again of himself when he was much younger, and how Jed Putnam had set him off on his own. He would try to do as good a job for Johnny, and he would do it with a will, now that Johnny was staying in the white man's world for sure. Maybe Johnny would keep on going with the circus and see California. If the two of them had to go their separate ways, now was as good a time as any, and Hardeman would be left here alone to do what he had to do.

"Maybe I'll have a word with Tatum," Johnny said, and then as if Hardeman had spoken his thoughts aloud, he added, "I'd come back up once I got them to where they knew the trail. I'd be here when you get back. I could spend some time with Sun Horse."

Hardeman nodded, showing no surprise. He should have known the boy wouldn't go off for good, not knowing his grandfather's fate. With luck it might all be over before Johnny got back, but Hardeman was still troubled by the memory of Sun Horse's manner, all confident and cocksure like a young man, when he explained to Hardeman about the pipes that afternoon. He had been too confident, maybe, as if he had kept some secret to himself, but Hardeman had looked for a trap in the plan and found none. His mind had worked quickly, and he had agreed to go with the pipe carriers for one reason—Sun Horse's willingness to talk directly with the hostile headmen and plead for peace. He remembered what Lisa Putnam had told him about Sun Horse earlier that same day. *A vision brought him here, to avoid the hostilities. His power is to understand the white men and make a lasting peace.* If that was true, it was a powerful reason for Sun Horse to work hard for surrender. To an Indian, a vision wasn't an assurance of what would be, but a glimpse of what was possible, with all the burden for making the vision come true falling on the one who had it.

Sun Horse's plan was better than sending messengers to the hostiles, and it increased the chance of bringing them all in without trickery. But it meant stalling for time, and that was risky now that the campaign had begun. Custer and Gibbon might both be out by now, and while troops were on the prowl, the war could start at any moment and blow the chance for a truce to smithereens. If Custer came within striking distance of the Indians, there would be

216

hell to pay. And even if Hardeman found Crook and Crook agreed to Sun Horse's offer, there would still be risk; it would take time to send word to the other commanders in the field.

The risks loomed larger in Hardeman's mind now, but a general peace would be worth all the risks if it could be brought about. And if Crook would not accept the pipe, there would still be time to bring him here, with the pipe carriers taken hostage to assure the good behavior of the Sun Band, and even then the peace might be preserved, despite the deception and betrayal.

Hardeman drank the rest of the whiskey down in a gulp and set the glass on the bar. He felt the rush of the liquor rise to his face and the Dutch courage growing strong inside him, but he would drink no more this evening. From now until he and the pipe carriers returned from their journey, he would have to depend on his own inner resources, not the helping hand of John Barleycorn.

The musicians ended their tune and Johnny drained off the last of his beer. "If you don't have the sense to dance with a pretty woman, I sure do," he said. He grinned at Hardeman and slipped away to reach Lisa's side before any other man could beat him to it. Hardeman saw Lisa smile and nod, accepting the young man's invitation, and as he looked around the room he saw the pleasure in the face of each woman as a man presented himself to her. By asking a woman to dance you paid her a compliment, and the compliment was all the more welcome if you were the one who had been watched as only a woman could watch, never looking directly, but always knowing the whereabouts of the man whose attentions she wished for most of all.

Hardeman leaned back against the bar and tapped his foot to the polka, keeping his eyes on Johnny and Lisa as they circled the floor. She was enjoying herself as if she hadn't a care in the world.

When the band slowed and the dance drew to an end, the couple moved closer until they stood before him. They parted and Lisa curtsied. "Mr. Smoker, sir, I haven't enjoyed myself so much in years."

Johnny inclined his head in a small bow and moved off, flashing a quick smile at Hardeman, as if he had brought Lisa here intentionally. She looked at Hardeman and he stepped forward.

"Miss Putnam? I'm not as good as Johnny, I'm afraid, but if it's not too fast—"

"Never apologize for asking a lady to dance, Mr. Hardeman." She smiled, and Hardeman was surprised to see the light of pleasure in her eyes. The band began a waltz and Hardeman started off. Left lead, right lead, *one*-two-three. It really wasn't so hard. If he could make a horse change leads at will, he could certainly manage it himself.

Lisa accommodated herself to his movements effortlessly, even when his balance or timing threatened to desert him. She fit perfectly in his arms, and after a time, he had mastered the rhythm of the dance sufficiently to notice that the back of her waist felt firm beneath his palm, not soft like most women.

217

He could feel her muscles move as she leaned back against his hand and he realized now that she was looking at him, and she was smiling.

"Mr. Hardeman—"

"Miss Putnam—"

They spoke at the same instant and the coincidence forced them to laugh. She moved a little closer and held his shoulder more firmly.

"I wanted to speak to you," she said. "To thank you for agreeing to the peace pipes, and to speak to General Crook for Sun Horse. I feel that we are allies now."

His first impulse was to warn her not to count her chickens, but he restrained it. She saw his hesitation.

"You do think there is a chance for peace?"

He nodded. "If Crook will hold off now and come back in summer. And if Sitting Bull will agree. With the pipe, and the word of a war chief and a peace chief, Crook might be able to persuade Sheridan to stop the campaign, at least for a while. If the War Department will go along; and if Crook thinks it's a good idea in the first place. That's a lot of ifs."

"But if he does, surely his word will carry weight. He is the commander of the Department of the Platte."

"He answers to Sheridan and Sherman. And there's more to it than just the Platte, Miss Putnam. There's an army reduction bill going up to Congress soon, and a bill to give control of the reservations to the army. Sheridan wants to show that he needs the troops and can keep the Indians in line if he has them."

"I see." She considered this soberly for a time, never missing a step of the waltz. "But surely in Congress there are some who favor fair dealing with the Indians. Senator Schurz—"

"It's in the army's hands now. If they want to bring this thing to a close, they'll do it, and they'll take the scalps back and nail them on the wall while Congress is still talking."

"And if General Crook will not accept the pipe?"

"We've got to plan for that, too."

"You sound as if we were truly allies, Mr. Hardeman."

His reply was cautious. "We can be. If Crook won't take the pipe, there'll be just one choice left for Sun Horse. I've already told him he'll have to fight or go in. If you ask him to surrender, he might listen to you. He trusts you."

She drew back. "I have already advised him not to go in."

"So has Johnny. Or at least he told Sun Horse he's glad he found a way to stay out." That surprised her. "It's advice from the gut, not the head, Miss Putnam, if you don't mind my putting it that way. And either one of you can change your mind. Both of you together might be enough to convince him, if it comes down to it."

"I have seen the reservations, Mr. Hardeman. Have you?" Her voice was hard now.

218

Hardeman nodded. "So has Johnny. And Sun Horse knows what's there. But if it's put to him right, he's smart enough to pick the...drawbacks of living on a reservation to a war that might destroy his people."

"Drawbacks? Is that what you call a life barren of all hope?"

"On the reservation they'll still be alive, Miss Putnam. As long as they're alive, they can find a reason to live."

She was silent and very serious for a time, but finally she met his eyes again. "Yes. I believe that."

They danced in silence. Hardeman saw Harry Wo and Ling watching them from where they stood near the kitchen door, smiling in evident approval. Bat Putnam and his Sioux wife danced nearby and he too smiled, as if it mattered not a whit to him that Hardeman and Lisa seemed always to succeed at making each other uncomfortable, or that they ran out of things to say. Hardeman sought a way to raise Lisa's spirits again and bring back the look of pleasure in her eyes, but before he could think of one the dance ended and she curtsied quickly and silently before disappearing into the crowd.

LISA PUTNAM'S JOURNAL

Saturday, March 4th. 6:45 a.m.

Usually my early mornings with this journal are spent in silence, but today I can hear the circus folk up and about, animals being fed, some wagons already moving into line. The stars shone brightly all night and I believe it will be a fair day for the departure of these guests who have brightened our lives so unexpectedly.

Mr. Chalmers ate breakfast in the kitchen this morning, where we fed the early risers in the midst of the preparations to feed the rest of our guests. He was accompanied by Lydia, whom I met only in passing yesterday evening. She is a Gypsy, of "noble" blood, she claims, and my, didn't Hutch's eyes open wide when he saw her bracelets and earrings and lip rouge and her imposing girth. Next to any person of normal stature she would have to be considered a large woman, but next to Mr. Chalmers she manages to appear almost delicate. Each of them put away enough porridge, pork chops and eggs for two workingmen. What an odd couple they are, and what good company. They always seem to be laughing about one thing or another. They are not married, but I do not deceive myself into believing they are merely friends, and so I conclude that not all the tales told of traveling performers, whether in the theater or a circus such as this one, are fanciful or slanderous. And yet while the morals of these folk may not be those professed (if not always practiced) by polite society, and while they take no pains to conceal their informal <u>liaisons</u>, in the short time that I have known the men and women of Mr. Tatum's circus I have found among them some who

219

are as trustworthy and honest as any upright citizen on Beacon Street or Broadway. Certainly morals are one of the standards by which we judge one another; we wish nothing to do with those who lack them entirely; but a breach of common morality, in itself, is not sufficient reason for rejecting someone outright. Such has long been the wisdom of the frontier, where persons are judged according to more universal standards. (Forgive me. Tomorrow is Sunday and I shall keep any further sermons to myself until then. Sometimes I find myself defending our life here, which is difficult to understand in some respects unless one has been forced to live it. I am always mindful of future generations that may read these pages, and I try to set forth the standards by which we judge ourselves, for their standards will surely be different. Today I find myself defending Alfred and Lydia, for whom I have much respect and affection after knowing them for less than a dozen hours.).

Mr. Chalmers thinks it will be mid-morning before the caravan is formed and on its way. He sees in his fellow troupers a reluctance to leave this place of festivity and rest. Usually, he says, they are all up and about before the sun without complaint, and off to the next town or city.

Johnny Smoker will guide the circus out to the plains and south to Mr. Bridger's trail. He will be gone perhaps as long as a week or more. Although it is pure guesswork on my part, I imagine that his feelings for young Amanda played some part in his decision to undertake this job. Last evening they finally did get a dance and a chance to exchange a word or two. Johnny was waiting near the stage when she put her violin aside, and as the rest of the band played on, he gave her a waltz that would have pleased Terpsichore herself. When it was over, Amanda was off like a shot. I fancied I knew something of what she was feeling. How many times did I allow myself to be friendly with some young man passing by and stopping for the night? I might favor him with a dance or two, knowing all the while that in the morning we should part, never to see each other again. Perhaps because of just such knowledge, Amanda gave Johnny little encouragement. Now they will be in company together for some days, but when the train of colorful wagons is safely on its way to Montana, he will retrace his steps to Putnam's Park.

Before the evening was over last night, he asked me most politely if he might remain here while Mr. Hardeman is off with the pipe carriers, and of course I agreed. "I'll lend a hand around the place," he said. "If there's something that needs doing, just point me to it." I am sure he will do more than his share. But during our short conversation I also learned something about him that caused me to alter my first impression of him. When Mr. Hardeman told me Johnny had chosen to remain among white people, I accepted this as only natural. After all, he has been with Mr. Hardeman for seven years and more, and I imagined he wished nothing more from life than to follow Mr. Hardeman wherever he might chance to go. But it seems that when Mr. Hardeman has returned, the two of them will part soon after leaving here. Johnny takes it as a consequence of his choice that he should set out on his own, making his way as a man,

220

looking after himself. He informed me of this very simply, as if it were no more than natural, but to me that decision reveals much courage and independence of mind, and I will see him in a new light from now on.

As for Mr. Hardeman, there too I have learned something new. He came to breakfast this morning just as I was leaving the kitchen, and I saw in his expression an eagerness to be on his way, and something more, something I felt I should recognize. I realize now that I saw that same look on my father's face, many years ago in my childhood, when we lived in Massachusetts. My relatives saw it too, and hadn't the faintest idea what it was. They considered him a good-for-nothing who would drag my "poor suffering mother" to an early grave. But we knew better, she and I. He sought a life that was complete; a home in a place he loved and an active life suited to that place and to his perception of the world at large; this is what he found in Putnam's Park. When my mother and I disembarked at St. Louis and saw him there waiting for us, the searching look was gone, replaced by one of real contentment. Mr. Hardeman's quest is similar, of that I am sure. When his journey on behalf of Sun Horse is done, he will move along and keep moving until he finds what he is looking for. I hope for his sake that he finds his own Putnam's Park, and I regret the somewhat hostile face I have shown him on more than one occasion. Whatever danger he may have brought with him, the government's actions with regard to the Indians are not his doing, and I believe he is motivated by peaceful intentions. Certainly the horrors of the Washita must have had a deep effect on him, to make him leave the service of the army and take under his wing an orphaned boy. Soon he and Uncle Bat will leave here for Sun Horse's village, there to await the preparation of the pipes and the departure of the pipe carriers. I wish him Godspeed.

Ling used the meal gong to summon the circus folk to breakfast. In recent years we have used it only in summer, when the hands may be far from the house as mealtimes approach. I enjoyed the familiar clanging. It sounded a short time ago, and judging by the noise from the saloon, breakfast is in full swing. I must prepare Mr. Tatum's account.

Bat Putnam stepped out onto the kitchen stoop and paused to let his eyes adjust to the brilliant sunshine. In his hand he held a small sack of coffee he had wheedled out of Ling in exchange for a promise of fresh meat when next he made a raise, once he got back. Today Bat needed coffee to keep him alive, and it would be welcome on the trail.

He looked distastefully at the meal gong, hanging from the tree closest to the stoop. It was a three-quarter section of iron wagon-wheel rim, suspended by a rope. Ling had set to thrashing it with her hammer just as Bat staggered towards the house from his tipi that morning, and she had had the gall to laugh when she saw how he cringed and stopped his ears against the noise.

He looked around the yard, savoring the peaceful silence now that the circus wagons had pulled out. The day was clear and warm and the glare of the sunlight off the snow was blinding. He had rubbed some stove soot on his cheekbones to cut the glare, but still the light made his head throb painfully.

In the blacksmith shed, Harry was firing up his forge. There would be clanging and banging from that quarter before long. Bat cast a quick glance in the direction of the sun, squinting hard. It was nearing midday, and high time to be getting along.

Beyond the barn, Penelope had struck the lodge. He could see her packing the last of their belongings onto the pony drags that were lashed to the four sturdy Indian ponies. While the pipe carriers were gone she would live in the circle of her people.

"It won't be the same here without you and Penelope," Lisa said, coming out of the door. She had on her gum boots and she had thrown her mountain goatskin coat over her dress. She was hatless; the light breeze ruffled her hair, which glistened in the sunlight.

"Oh, we'll be back soon enough, one way or t'other," Bat said. He saw the worry in her face and his tone grew stern. "Now don't you set to frettin'. We'll do what we can."

She smiled. "I know you will." She linked her arm in his and they started off together.

Across the yard, Hardeman emerged from the double doors of the barn, leading his saddled horse. Bat felt Lisa hesitate, and saw how she looked in the scout's direction. He patted her rump gently.

222

"You go on now, and remember what I told you. Come up on his right side."

"I can't seem to find it," she said, but she left him and strode off toward the barn with long steps, lifting her boots high in the soft snow that had been turned to mush by wagon wheels and hooves and booted feet.

"You're not leaving without a word, Mr. Hardeman?" she said as she reached him.

"Just coming now to find you, Miss Putnam."

"I wanted to wish you luck."

Hardeman thought to tell her that it would take more than luck, but he saw that she was full of hope and he had no wish to dampen her spirits. Johnny had said the same thing not long before, shaking Hardeman's hand and wishing him luck as the circus wagons began to roll off down the road.

He looked down the valley and saw that the caravan had just reached the clump of pines where the road made its last turn to the settlement. Johnny was somewhere in the long string of wagons and animals, but he would come back before long. "Well, I'll see you soon, then" was all Hardeman had said as the caravan started off. He didn't care for goodbyes.

Lisa had followed his gaze. "It will seem empty here without them," she said.

He heard the loneliness in her voice and turned to look at her, remembering the feel of her lithe body in his arms as he danced with her, and suddenly he wanted to take her in his arms to comfort her. She would permit it; he could see it in her eyes. But the eyes did not ask, as some women's did. They did not invite him. She kept her wants concealed.

"You 'bout set, Christopher?" Bat called. He sat astride his bay mare beyond the yard fence, with Penelope beside him on her paint and the four pack horses in train behind her.

"All set," he called back. "Well, you take care, Miss Putnam." He swung up into the saddle and started off.

"And you, Mr. Hardeman," he heard her say.

When he reached the gate that would let him out of the yard he looked back as he leaned down to open the latch, and he saw that she was still standing there. Maybe when he returned . . .

Such thoughts were useless. He latched the gate carefully from the other side. "Hyup!" he said to his horse, kicking it into a trot to overtake Bat and the Indian woman, who had started on ahead. Today both of Hardeman's rifles were in their scabbards and all his essential belongings were packed in the saddlebags and bedroll. He would come back for Johnny Smoker if he could, but for now he was on his own, self-contained and self-sufficient.

It felt good to be on the move again.

Down in the meadow, Hutch and Julius stopped working to watch the circus pass by a hundred yards away. Hutch spied Johnny Smoker riding beside the wagons and they exchanged waves.

"Never seen the like of it in this valley before," Julius said. "Won't see it again if I live to be a hundred."

Other hands were raised in farewell from some of the wagons. Johnny was riding beside a wagon driven by Chalmers, the English giant, and beside him on the seat Hutch imagined he could make out the much smaller figure of Amanda, the clown girl. He envied Johnny his few additional years and the independence they gave him. The quiet youth was more than a little sweet on Amanda, Hutch was fairly certain, and now he would have at least a few days to get to know her better. All Hutch knew about the acrobat's daughter he had watched throughout the evening, until her father had sent her off to bed, was that her name was Maria Abbruzzi. She was nineteen years old, he had learned from one of the musicians, and the one time she had looked him right in the eye and smiled, Hutch's heart had turned over inside him. But she was gone now, along with the rest of them. He recalled a line from a song he knew, and he hummed it softly, thinking the words without saying them—*There's more pretty girls than one, there's more pretty girls than one*. Just now it didn't seem possible.

"Watch that fork," Julius said. They had begun to feed the cattle again to quiet their bawling, and Hutch had pitched a forkful of hay dangerously close past the colored man's arm.

"Sorry."

From up the valley came a high-pitched cry and they both turned, Hutch a little apprehensive, wondering what crisis might have arisen. Julius saw his worried look and smiled.

"Nothin' to fret about. That's just Lisa moving cattle. Looks like she and Harry are taking the heifers in to the calving lot." The squat outline of Harry Wo was unmistakable at a distance, all the more so when he was on horseback. The heifers had been fed first in the pasture close to the settlement, on the far side of the river, and Lisa and Harry were gathering them now to move them into the lot beside the barn. It was another of Jed's customs, bringing the first-time mothers in to be watched during calving. Dairymen did it, and beef-cattle breeders too, in more settled countries. First births were often difficult and there was no need to lose any more calves than would be lost anyway in the natural course of things, so Jed had reasoned.

"Hooo!" came the cry again. The taller of the two riders raised a hand in the direction of the hay sled, and Julius and Hutch waved in reply.

To Lisa, the two men looked like miniature figures on a toy sled, dwarfed by the vastness of the broad meadows all white with snow and the empty sky above. "Hooo!" she shouted, urging the heifers along. She was glad to be outside and on horseback where she could vent her feelings freely. She wore the smoked goggles her father had used in the springtime to ward off snowblindness. Her goatskin coat hung open and she could smell the scent of pine on the air. The willows were budding already; spring would remain a tantalizing suggestion for another month or more, but the hope was there, and Lisa felt her spirits improving.

After Hardeman and Bat had left, she had thought to help Ling strip the bed

224

linens. Joe Kitchen and his helpers had cleared away the remains of breakfast and left the kitchen spick-and-span before stacking their own pots and pans in the large boxes fixed to the sideboards of the supply wagons. All that was left for Ling and Lisa was to air the rooms and sweep the saloon and wash the linens, but Lisa had been unable to face the suddenly empty house. On an impulse she had decided to move the heifers today. After sending Harry to saddle the horses she had changed her clothes in a moment, and on her way back outside she had told Ling to leave the washing for later.

It's not as if I were shirking, she told herself now, turning her horse aside to bring along a trio of heifers that hoped to avoid the roundup. There is always other work to be done if you don't like one job, and we should have brought the heifers in before now. There's the calving shed to be prepared too. There's always plenty of work to take your mind off other things.

But the other thoughts remained with her, demanding to be heard, as they had been doing ever since Bat and Penelope and Chris Hardeman rode off up the creek trail, and Lisa turned inward to face them now, to get it over with. She felt abandoned, and the feeling brought to mind the summer she had turned twenty-five, when the cavalry lieutenant with the tired eyes rode out of Putnam's Park for the last time. He had been stationed at Fort Reno during the first year of Red Cloud's War, and when he could get away he would ride up to Putnam's Park alone, pitting the bravado of his love against the eyesight of the Sioux. Lisa had returned his love, but when he had asked her to marry him and live the life of a frontier cavalry wife, she had hesitated, and lost him. There, at least, the feelings had been freely spoken and the choice had been clear: choose between Putnam's Park and life in the most tightly bound society west of Chicago. Paradoxically, the officer caste imitated most closely the customs and habits of the very social set that so disdained the army—the proper, inbred, educated classes of the East, the same people from whom Lisa had fled in haste once her schooling was completed. But when the young lieutenant first rode into the park with his troop behind him, such thoughts were far from Lisa's mind. There had been little reasoning involved, only an outrush of feeling that swept them both up and brought him time and again to her door, through the autumn and the winter and on into another summer. She had sensed a hurt in him, a wound the Civil War had caused not in his body but his spirit, and she had done her best to heal him. On a day as perfect as this one in the second summer of their courtship, he had asked her to marry him, and without giving him an answer she had set aside with scarcely any hesitation the virtue she had sternly guarded in the face of advances made in eastern cities. Afterward, when he pressed her for an answer, she had delayed, silencing him with kisses, but from that moment, reasoning and realities had replaced the tide of feelings. In the end, Lisa has been unable to leave her home, although she might have left it safely then in her father's hands. Daughters married and became a part of their husbands' worlds, and fathers were left behind to pass on the estates to their sons. But Jed Putnam had no sons, and he had fed his love of the mountains to his only child; she had consumed his passion as if

225

it were ice cream served on a hot August afternoon on one of the neatly mown lawns her mother's relations maintained around their country homes in the East. She had stayed in Putnam's Park, and it had been her own doing.

There were no other hands to receive it now. In any event, Lisa had made her choice. She would remain. Someday, perhaps, if her tenure here endured, a man would choose to remain with her, to become part of her life and make his own mark here as Jed Putnam had done; as his daughter would do, given time.

"Hooo!" she shouted, louder than was necessary to move the fifteen heifers along. They were in a bunch now, nearing the buildings of the settlement.

Where was it written that she must be drawn only to men who threatened the very fabric of her life? A cavalry lieutenant sent to provoke an Indian war; a scout sent to herald the end of countless centuries of Indian dominion over these lands. The image of Chris Hardeman rose in her mind and she recalled the calm words she had written about him that morning in her journal. As usual, she had kept her feelings veiled, as far as the written record was concerned. In her heart she wished him Godspeed not only to convey him safely through a hazardous journey, not only in the hope that he and the others might succeed in turning back General Crook's expedition against the hostiles, but also to bring him back to Putnam's Park and to her.

A skittish heifer bolted from the bunch suddenly and tried for a third time to return to the meadow, but Harry was there to head her off. He berated her loudly in Chinese, which he was sure would frighten her far worse than anything he might say in English, and Lisa couldn't help smiling at the sight of the stout blacksmith shaking his finger at the wide-eyed bovine. Harry wore a broad-brimmed hat pulled low over his eyes to protect himself against the glare. He was a good enough rider, and always dependable when moving cattle, but he bounced in the saddle. His legs were simply not long enough to grip the horse properly. He was the shortest, fattest cow-boy Lisa had ever seen.

"Hooooop!" she shouted, feeling better. She always felt better when she confronted her fears. For now she would place her fears for the pipe carriers in the part of her mind that was reserved for events whose outcome she could not affect. "If you can't change it, let it be," her father had been fond of saying, and she would try to do just that. Hardeman would return or he would not. If he did . . . He seemed to be as reluctant to show his feelings as she was to reveal her own, but things might be different when he returned. Things were always different when two people parted and came together again.

Meanwhile, there was work to keep her busy. It was always so; others came and went from Putnam's Park, but Lisa remained. The park remained, the work remained, and it sustained her.

The heifers were entering the yard between the house and the barn. They trotted in a contented group now, only occasionally casting a glance back at the two horseback figures behind them. Patches of hay remained here and there where the circus animals had been fed before dawn. Lisa had made a tidy sum on the hay she had sold to Tatum, and still she had more than enough to last out a cold spring, if that were in store. One of the heifers stopped to steal a mouthful of hay and Lisa rode her horse up behind the browsing animal.

"Boo," she said suddenly and the heifer ran to rejoin her companions.

Harry had the gate open and the first heifers were ambling into the buck-fenced lot. Lisa reined her horse aside to recover two animals that were drifting off toward the barn and the bull pasture beyond, and then she saw the cancer-eye cow. She had been cut out and brought to the calving lot two days earlier, when Lisa and Hardeman rode through the meadows to look over the cows. She was standing still and peculiar in the middle of the lot. Her vulva was protruding and her tail was partially raised. She hobbled around in a circle, her back humped up. Two tiny hooves stuck out from beneath her tail.

"Harry! We've got a calf to pull!" Lisa called. She hazed the two heifers toward the gate and left them for Harry to gather in while she hitched her horse to the fence and ran to the barn for the rope and tackle that were sometimes used to pull a backwards calf from inside its mother. Without help the cow would die, and the calf, if it were ever born at all, would be born dead. The calving supplies should have been seen to and put in the calving shed days ago, but she had put it off. First because I was lost in a winter of mourning and reflection that I believed would go on forever, she thought. And then I let the circus distract me. You can't do that when these animals need you.

When she returned from the barn, Harry was already off his horse and in the lot, moving this way and that with his surprisingly quick rolling trot, trying to turn the cow into the calving shed, but she didn't want to go into that dark place. Her nature was to stay outside and give birth in the mud and snow of the corral.

"Come on, mama cow," Lisa said as she climbed the fence, holding the calf tackle in her free hand. "Be a good girl instead of a contrary beast. We're only trying to help."

There was a sound like distant thunder and Lisa looked at the sky all around, but there was not a single cloud. She had removed her goggles in the barn and it took a moment for her eyes to adjust to the glare. In the meadow she made out the hay sled, almost empty now. Julius and Hutch seemed to have heard something too, for they were motionless on the rack. At the foot of the valley the circus wagons were gone from sight. A small white cloud that Lisa hadn't noticed before hung over the river canyon.

Amanda waved for a last time as the circus caravan left the hay sled behind. "I wish we could stay longer," she said. "I'd like to learn all those Negro dance songs Julius knows. Oh, look!"

She pointed suddenly. On the far side of the river a moose and her calf lumbered out of a thicket and headed across the meadow, legs jerking high above the snow. The calf followed in its mother's tracks. As they reached the split-rail fence at the edge of the meadow, the mother paused, then jumped and cleared the top rail with ungainly ease. The calf hesitated before making its way between two of the rails with a lurching leap.

227

"What are they?" Amanda asked in a hushed voice.

"Moose, I believe," Chalmers offered, glancing to Johnny for corroboration. The youth was riding close beside Chalmers' wagon.

"That's right."

The three of them watched as the two dark forms disappeared into the trees.

"I must say, I wish I had time for some hunting hereabouts," Chalmers mused. "Moose is quite good eating, I believe."

"It's all right," Johnny said. "Elk is better, and buffalo is best of all."

"Ah. Then I have already had the best," Chalmers said, pleased with himself. "At Delmonico's, of all places. I had a bison steak. Not at all the same as cooking the fresh-killed beast over a fire in the bush, though. Still, it was excellent."

"I think mooses look as if their hind legs were put on backwards by mistake," Amanda said.

"The plural of moose is moose, dear," Chalmers corrected her.

"That's ridiculous," she said, but she seemed pleased with this bit of information, however odd, just as she seemed pleased with the fine day and everything around her. Ever since the wagons left the settlement she had kept up a bright chatter, asking questions and looking all about. She took a childish delight in the smallest thing, the flight of a raven or the sound of a bull in the bull pasture calling out his springtime feelings to the cows.

"Mr. Springer! Keep up with the rest, if you please!" Hachaliah Tatum had left his place at the head of the caravan to stop by the trailside, and now he called out to a lagging wagon in the middle of the caravan. Chalmers' wagon was fifth in line and the Springer wagon was several more to the rear.

The circus caravan had been late getting off, and Tatum had been in a bad humor by the time the wagons were finally all in line; his farewell to Lisa Putnam and the settlement had been brief. The delay was caused by many small things—packing the cooking pots, capturing half a dozen draft horses that had escaped their pasture during the night to join the cattle in the meadow—but most of all by the general reluctance of one and all to leave Putnam's Park, where they had been welcomed so warmly.

"Everything in order, Mr. Chalmers?" Tatum inquired as Chalmers' wagon drew even with the circus master. Tatum reined his horse in beside Johnny's and rode in tandem with the young man.

"Quite in order, Mr. Tatum," Chalmers replied. "The spirits of the performing artists are excellent. No difficulties of any sort." Chalmers was the unofficial spokesman for the performers; when Tatum wished to convey any general directions to his artists, he spoke to Chalmers and the strongman passed the orders along.

"Very well," said Tatum now. "Be sure to keep up the pace."

"Oh, Hachaliah, that's ridiculous! We can't go any faster than the wagon in front of us!" Amanda smiled to take the sting out of her words.

A small window opened behind Chalmers' head and Lydia's round face appeared.

"Lydia." Tatum tipped his silk hat to the Gypsy woman, then touched his heels to the white stallion's flanks and trotted ahead to resume his place in the lead.

"You mustn't tweak his nose just for the fun of it, my dear," Lydia cautioned Amanda once Tatum was out of hearing.

Amanda smiled, seeming pleased with herself. For a time she was quiet, looking about her at the valley and the snow-covered hills that loomed ahead of the caravan as it approached the river trail.

"What will you do when Mr. Hardeman comes back?" she asked suddenly, speaking to Johnny. "I mean when you leave here."

The question took Johnny by surprise. "I don't know," he said. The uncertainty didn't concern him. He would figure out what to do when the time came. Amanda knew that he would be going off on his own once he and Chris left Putnam's Park; he had told her the night before, when he danced with her, just as he had told Lisa Putnam. Telling others of his plans made them all the more real, and it strengthened his resolve, although his resolve had been in fine shape ever since he had returned to Putnam's Park. Of course knowing Sun Horse was safe for the time being had helped some. At first, the council's decision to surrender had seemed like the only thing for them to do, and Johnny had realized then that he wasn't really standing between the worlds at all. The Indian life was changing, and he no longer had the chance to go back to the life he had known in his boyhood. And then, when he had stood on the porch beside Chris and heard Sun Horse set out his startling new plan, Johnny had seen fresh hope for his grandfather, but the free life that hope might gain belonged to Sun Horse and his band, not to Johnny. Back in the park, seeing the circus and finding himself among white men and women again, the worries he had felt in the Lakota camp had seemed suddenly trifling, and his confidence in his choice had returned. The presence of the circus in the park was a perfect example of the surprises and sudden possibilities that sprang up in the white world when you least expected them, like the job offer from the Chicago cattle buyer, and once again it seemed unthinkable to abandon this world and the freedom it offered. And so when Chris and Sun Horse were through speaking, Johnny had told his grandfather of his decision then, more certain than ever that he was doing the right thing.

Sure, he was a little frightened by the idea of being on his own and not having Chris to depend on, but he knew the rewards to be gained by standing on his own two feet and setting out to get what he wanted. He had done it once before, when he left the Wheelers' home in St. Louis and crossed three states and the whole of Wyoming Territory before he found Chris at last in Utah. After just one winter with the Wheelers he knew he wanted something more from life than growing up as a merchant's ward in St. Louis, and he knew he was too young to find it on his own. Chris Handeman was a man who could help him find what he was after, if Chris was willing, and so Johnny had set out to ask him. The odd thing was how few folks thought it strange that a boy so young should be going all that way on his lonesome. "I'm goin' to find my pa," Johnny had told them. He hadn't said that Chris wasn't his real pa, or that he had lived with the Cheyenne Indians until five months before, and folks had taken him at his word. A lot of them had helped him along his way with a meal or some company on the trail or just a kind word of encouragement. Here and there some of them had offered him a job, and looking back on it now, Johnny saw how even then the white man's world had been reaching out to show him what it had to offer.

He breathed deeply of the cool clean air with its scent of pine and suggestion of spring, and his life opened before him. He was old enough now to find what he wanted on his own, and the time had come to do it. Looking back over his years with Chris, it seemed that Chris might have been preparing him for this moment all the while, making him ready to stand on his own, starting with the bargain they had struck back in the beginning: whenever one of them wanted to move on, they went. In such matters Johnny's wishes had carried as much weight as Chris's, and time after time Chris had forced him to make up his own mind about one thing or another. To hang back now would be to throw away all the lessons Chris had taught him. When he had found what he was looking for, he and Chris could hook up again, and that would suit Johnny just fine, but for now he had some looking around to do. Opportunities were everywhere; all he had to do was pick among them. Why, in just the past few days new ones had arisen. Hadn't Amanda said that Tatum's Combined Shows would be in San Francisco all summer? And hadn't he and Chris always said they would go to California someday? What was to say he couldn't go alone? The job training racehorses in Chicago had slipped by him, but who was to say what chances might come his way if he found himself in San Francisco?

Johnny suddenly wished he could hurry the circus along at a faster clip, and hurry himself back here, and hurry the pipe carriers on to General Crook—where the general would surely listen to reason and grant Sun Horse's request because Chris Hardeman was the one who brought the pipe to him—and hurry Chris back to Putnam's Park, all so Johnny could start off on the adventure that lay before him and find what he was looking for, and hook up with Chris again just so Chris would be proud of him and he could stand beside his old friend as an equal.

But if General Crook accepted Sun Horse's offer to meet with the hostile chiefs in summer, after Sun Horse had talked with them, Johnny would remain near his grandfather until then. He owed the old man that much.

For the first time in his life he felt a duty that threatened to keep him from what he really wanted to do.

"Look how solemn he is," Amanda said, and Johnny saw that she was watching him. She nudged Chalmers and imitated Johnny, slumping in her seat until she was a pitiful figure to behold. She passed one hand up before her face and straightened at the same time, revealing a bright and happy expression. She passed the hand back down and once again assumed the sorrowful face of tragedy, but then she smiled. "Those are the two faces of a clown. You have to be able to change from one to the other in a moment."

Johnny smiled. "Sun Horse says you have *heyoka* power."

"What kind of power?"

"*Heyoka*. It's what the Sioux call a clown."

Amanda was puzzled. "What do they know about clowns?"

"They have clowns of their own. The *heyokas* make the people laugh in hard times, and when times are good they act sad to remind the people that hard times are never far away."

"That's what we do!" Amanda said, delighted.

"*Heyokas* are a good bit different from white clowns, I guess," Johnny said. He had seen a real clown show only once, in St. Louis. "The *heyokas* are sacred beings. They control the power of the west. They dress in ragged clothes, and they're painted all over with sacred symbols. There's more to them than just clowning."

"Do they paint their faces?" Amanda asked. "Like Indians, I mean?"

"*Heyokas* paint their faces in special ways only *heyokas* can use, with lightning and hailstones."

"I wish I could see them!" the girl exclaimed. She looked around at the valley and the mountains. "I wish we could stay here longer. When we're gone all this will seem like a dream. It's already like a dream. No one will believe us when we tell them about the Indians." She was filled with sudden despair and Johnny looked about for anything that might distract her from the thought of leaving Putnam's Park.

The caravan was entering the river canyon, where the air was cooler. The canyon descended directly toward the south, and the late morning sun had just cleared the high cliff across the river on the eastern side. Its rays touched the wagon road for only a short time each day, and the ground here was frozen hard. To the right, bathed in sunlight, rose a steep hillside that ascended for a thousand feet or more to a broken rimrock crowned with smooth cornices of snow sculpted by the winter winds. Close beside the trail the brush grew thicker where it received the runoff from the slope.

"Look there." Johnny pointed to a clump of sagebrush.

"What?" Amanda looked and saw nothing. Chalmers too was peering at the brush.

"It's a snowshoe rabbit. See his tracks? Follow them until they stop."

"Oh! He's beautiful!" Amanda said in a voice that was barely louder than a whisper.

The creature, actually a hare, but called a rabbit throughout the West, crouched motionless in the shadow of a bush, still white in its winter coat, its ears flat against its head. They watched it until they had passed beyond and out of sight.

Four wagons to the rear another pair of eyes spied the tracks, and then the hare against the snow. "Look there." Kinnean gestured with his injured arm, confined in its sling. The driver beside him wrapped his reins around the brake lever and reached slowly for the shotgun that lay at his feet. Just as slowly, he raised the gun to his shoulder.

"Better than chicken, if you ask me." He sighted and fired.

The driver's name was Johansen. He was pale-eyed and blond, a lanky man in his twenties. At home he had shot rabbits and quail and partridges for his mother's table, and at the age of ten he had watched his home burned and both his parents killed in the Sioux uprising of 1862. He had come west to the Black Hills from Minnesota in the autumn and throughout the winter he had kept his shotgun loaded with buckshot against the chance of being surprised by Indians at close range. He fired at the hare instinctively, without thinking to change his load, and reduced the animal to a bloody swatch in the snow.

"Damn," he said unemotionally as he realized his error.

The booming roar of the shotgun rose from the base of the canyon, gaining strength as it echoed between the hillside and the rock face of the cliff across the way. As the echoes rolled away there came another sound.

Up and down the string of wagons, men and women looked to see who had fired. At the head of the column, Tatum looked up. At first he saw nothing more than what seemed to be a small cloud at the base of the rimrock, but it increased rapidly in size and took form as the snow at the top of the slope began to move.

"Avalanche!" someone shouted.

"Turn the wagons!" Tatum cried out. All along the caravan, people shouted in alarm, and in seconds the scene became one of pandemonium.

Three wagons had already reached the narrowest part of the trail, where there was no hope of turning, but still the drivers whipped and shouted at their teams, heaving on reins and cursing in an effort to back or turn the teams in the impossible space. These were supply wagons with broad wheels, hauled by slow-witted oxen, and always placed in the front of the train to make a trail for the rest.

"Jump!" Tatum shouted at the frantic men. "Get away!" He was at the fourth wagon, where he seized the bridle of the lead Clydesdale. He kicked his own horse and heaved the draft horse around, managing to double the team back and pull the wagon in a tight turn. One wheel slipped over the edge of the embankment that fell sharply to the river, but Tatum's urging kept the team pulling and the wheel found purchase on the frozen ground and rolled, bouncing over snow-covered rocks, back to the road surface.

"Hah! Get up!" the driver shouted and the wagon jumped forward as the team hauled in unison. It careened past other wagons still trying to turn, only to find its way blocked fifty yards beyond by a tangle of men and horses and wagons that would take long minutes to undo.

"Amanda!" Johnny shouted. The noise from the animals and wagons and the people of the circus was almost deafening. He kicked his horse close to Chalmers' wagon and reached out as Amanda turned and saw him. She had

232

sat paralyzed throughout the first moments of the growing chaos around her. Now she moved into Johnny's arms without thinking. He lifted her from the seat and placed her before him on the horse as he shouted to Chalmers to get down from the wagon. At the same moment, the back door of the gaily painted little house burst open and Lydia jumped out, screaming. Johnny looked back as he spurred his horse to safety and he saw the avalanche gaining speed close above the road. The road was covered with milling, panicked horses.

The horse herd had been driven in front of the wagons to break a way through the recent snow. At the first shout the wranglers had looked up. They were frontiersmen and did not need to be warned twice of an impending avalanche. They saw the moving snow and without hesitation they reined their horses around and fled back the way they had come, all but Jack Fisk. Fisk was ahead of the horses, leading the way. He too looked up, and even as he grasped the meaning of what he saw, he waved his free arm and shouted "Hyahhh!" to spook the lead horses and turn them back. The herd wheeled and some of the animals bolted, taking their direction from the fleeing wranglers, but the shouts and confusion surrounding the lead wagons checked their flight. They caught the panic of the struggling oxen and refused to pass. As the driver of the first wagon leaped from his seat and ran for safety, the oxen felt the slackening of the reins and lumbered forward, scattering and dividing the horse herd. Those on the side of the trail close to the hillside saw an opening there and took flight back along the line of wagons, but the remaining horses fled in the opposite direction, given impetus by the bellowing oxen and the clatter of the wagon. Once decided on their purpose, the riderless horses flew like thistles on a storm wind, those in the rear overtaking and passing the clumsy wagon and moving now among the leaders, a single rider swept along in their midst.

Back in the tangled caravan the horses that had found the way to safety there ran the length of the train, shying from men and women on foot, conveying their fear to the other animals, even those well out of danger. The mules pulling Joe Kitchen's cookwagon bucked in the harness, kicking out at the air.

"Whoa, now!" Joe hauled on the reins with all his might to keep the mules in line. The leader reared as a panicked horse swerved away from a running man and bumped against the pitching mule; the mule kicked out and the horse kicked back, striking the mule in the hindquarters. The leader lunged into his harness with a force that threw Joe Kitchen off-balance and sent him sprawling to the seat, grabbing for a handhold. The reins slipped from his hands and the team was off and running, careening between Chalmers' abandoned wagon and the hillside.

None but Joe himself had seen the events that caused this sudden flight. Each person in the caravan had his own jumbled impressions of the unnatural moments that followed the first warning shout. Feet seemed weighted down with lead. No action was quick enough to respond to the white danger that gathered force and hurtled down the slope with heart-stopping speed. But soon most saw that they were well beyond the path of the avalanche; they stopped running and turned to watch the spectacle.

The billowing cloud was huge and high above the slope, rising from the leading edge of the avalanche like steam from a rift in the roof of Hell. It bore down on the road with express-train velocity, but as the horrified spectators looked on with mouths agape, the cookwagon raced with equal speed to meet it.

"Jump, Joe!"

"Jump for your life!"

Cookwagon and mules and driver were lost in the rolling cloud of snow as the avalanche poured over the road and into the river beyond, blocking half the stream. A cold gray mist spread to the knot of watchers and beyond, cutting off the sun.

"Joe!"

"He's gone."

"*Gott im Himmel.*"

"I saw him jump!"

"Quiet!" Tatum held up a hand for silence. "Joe! Joe Kitchen!"

They listened. Men and women shivered and hugged themselves and stamped their feet against the sudden chill, but already the sunlight filtered through as the mist settled, like the miraculous clearing of the sky in the middle of a winter storm. The flakes continued to fall, becoming finer and finer and sparkling in the sunlight to lend a numbed enchantment to the scene; the air over the roadway cleared, and the hushed group of onlookers could see where the lead wagons had been. One remained on the trail. There was no trace of the cookwagon.

"There! Look there!"

A figure moved, crawling from beneath the wagon that had been spared. The figure stood and walked toward the onlookers. It was a man, short and round.

"Joe?"

"By Christ, it's him!"

Joe Kitchen wore a strangely satisfied look as he approached them, and to their surprise they could hear him laughing to himself.

"He's come unhinged."

"Like hell I have!" he shouted. "I'm just taking what satisfaction I can from knowing I won't have to fight those muleheaded sonofabitches anymore." He stopped and pointed at those watching him, laughing even harder now. "By God, look at you. You're a bunch of snowmen!"

They looked at one another and saw that he was right. As the snowy mist settled it had covered them all with a layer of white that clung to hair and hats and coats, even to eyebrows and mustaches and beards. They looked like

234

minions of Jack Frost, or a gathering of ghosts. They laughed at themselves, grateful to be alive.

"He's quite right, you know," Chalmers boomed, laughing with the rest. "Look at us all." He slapped the snow off himself and Lydia and clapped Joe Kitchen on the back as the cook joined them.

Amanda and Johnny Smoker still sat astride Johnny's horse a short distance away. Johnny's arms were around the girl, holding her close against him as they stared in awe at the mound of snow that covered the road to five times the height of a wagon.

Others returned their attention to the avalanche now.

"Where is Jack Fisk?" Tatum demanded of the crowd at large.

"He was out in front," someone said.

A wrangler rode toward the jumbled mass of snow and rocks. A horse caught in the soft snow at the edge of the mound struggled to get up but repeatedly slipped and fell, denied the use of its broken leg.

"I saw him," the man said to no one in particular. "He took out the other way." He drew a revolver and shot the horse neatly through the brain, then raised the gun and fired twice more into the air. "Fisk!" he called.

"Stop that, you fool!" Tatum was livid. He cast a worried glance up the slope. "You'll bring down the whole mountain!"

"Seems to me it's already done fell on us. Fisk!" The call echoed in the canyon but there was no reply.

CHAPTER
SEVENTEEN

On the fifth day of March the snow began before dawn and continued throughout the morning, coming from the northeast. The troopers pulled their caps down low and their collars high and turned their faces westward to avoid the stinging pellets that threatened to blind them.

The countryside was dreary, growing rougher as the expedition approached the Powder. The rolling, barren prairie had given way to rills and gullies that had deepened into ravines and arroyos. Whitcomb was amused by the proliferation of terms used by the troopers and packers to describe all the varieties of little canyons that cut the frozen countryside. Thus far, he was certain only that a swale had a rounded bottom, often grass-covered, and a coulee had steep sides. As the soldiers descended the Dry Fork of the Powder they were flanked by treeless bluffs of dull slate and sandstone, occasionally colored by streaks of yellow clay. The Big Horns, which they had first seen two days earlier resplendent in their snow-capped majesty, loomed nearer, gray and forbidding now when the clouds thinned and rose high enough to reveal the presence of the mountain chain. Off to the right, Pumpkin Buttes watched the column's progress like four massive sentinels.

Squads of flankers rode always within sight of the column, usually within a hundred yards. The day before, under a brilliant sun, the flankers had been three hundred yards to the sides and the scouts six hundred or more to the front; now Colonel Stanton kept his scouts in pairs, each in sight of the next as they ranged back and forth in advance of the column. They were the eyes of the expedition, watching for sign, peering into ravines, searching for a footprint or a force of lurking Indians.

Since the night attack on the camp there had been abundant evidence that the hostiles were aware of the column's every movement. Until today the sun had shone almost constantly on the expedition, cheering the men and making it easier to bear the wind that blew steadily in their faces, but the clear air had aided the hostiles as well; looking-glass signals had flashed often from the right flank and once a dark column of smoke had risen from a butte on the northern horizon. Today such signals were made impossible by the storm, but already the column had crossed the tracks left by several small parties of Indians and the troopers had caught their first glimpse of the savage warriors. Several times during the morning horsemen had revealed themselves to the soldiers singly or in small groups, never more than half a dozen, sitting out of rifle shot, watching, first from the right and then from the left, first from the front and then from the rear. The company commanders were under orders to observe these vedettes but under no account to give chase. Nor did the scouts follow any of the trails they saw. The risk of ambuscade was too great and General Crook wanted to conserve the strength of the horses. By his steady progress northward and his refusal to engage small groups such as these, he hoped to confuse the hostiles, so he had told the company commanders. Confusion was his only weapon now; any hope of surprise was futile, thanks to the watchfulness of the Indians.

"Sir, there's another one!" Corporal Atherton called out, raising his voice just enough to carry up the column to Lieutenant Corwin. E Troop was at the tail of the line today; since the night attack one company of cavalry had been placed behind the pack train to guard the expedition's rear. Whitcomb and Corwin were riding together at the head of the troop. They reined aside now to look where Atherton was pointing. Seventy or eighty yards away First Sergeant Dupré and his three flankers had come to a halt. Dupré was pointing to the southeast. Whitcomb slipped off his green goggles and dropped them around his neck and now he saw the Indians, half a mile beyond the flankers, nearly invisible in the thin snow that had stopped falling only twice all morning. There were four. Or five. Or four men with five horses. He shook his head and shielded his eyes with both hands. The movement of the snow made seeing details at long distances nearly impossible.

236

"Are they always the same ones, first in one place and then the next?" he wondered aloud.

"There's no way of knowing," Corwin said. They watched the Indians for a few moments longer and then Corwin trotted on to regain his place in the column. Whitcomb followed close behind. For three days now, ever since the incident with the beef herd, he had been kept under Corwin's constant supervision. For any job that required the least responsibility, Corwin called on Dupré or one of the other non-commissioned officers. Only when a chore was devoid of any risk did he call on Ham Whitcomb.

Two officers were riding back along the column. They touched their caps as they reached Corwin and turned to ride alongside him.

"Good day, Major," said Lieutenant Bourke, Crook's aide. He smiled at Whitcomb. "Lieutenant Whitcomb."

Whitcomb smiled in reply. "Lieutenant Bourke." He recognized the other man as Charles Morton, Colonel Reynolds' adjutant, a second lieutenant like Whitcomb and Bourke. Colonel Joseph J. Reynolds was nominally in charge of the troops, but officers and men alike knew full well that Crook himself was actually giving the orders. Reynolds had been a major general of U.S. Volunteers during the Civil War, and he preferred to be addressed as "General." He had been the commanding officer of the Third Cavalry for the past six years, but while serving as commander of the Department of Texas he had been tainted by some vague scandal and relieved of that duty. The general opinion within the expedition was that Crook had taken Reynolds under his wing and would watch him closely.

"Sir, General Reynolds' compliments," said Morton, addressing Corwin, "and he asks if you will kindly put out two more sets of flankers to the east."

Corwin nodded and turned to Whitcomb. "Mr. Whitcomb, you will go to the rear and relieve Sergeant Polachek as file closer. Instruct him to put out two more sets of flankers to the east and lead one himself."

"Yes, sir." Whitcomb reined around and trotted back along the line, cursing silently. Surely he could be trusted to lead a set of flankers! The Indians were plainly taunting the column and had no intention of attacking! What could be the harm in giving him something to do for once?

When he reached Polachek he passed along Corwin's orders and then took over the tedious chore of "file closer," the man charged with seeing that the end of the column kept closed up. The wind gusted, lashing snow in his face; he put his goggles back in place to protect his eyes and stretched his mouth wide to flex his face against the cold. He felt a small pain and then a chill as a drop of blood oozed from a new crevice in his lower lip. His lips were cracked from drinking the brackish alkali water that was all the country offered. He cursed his forgetfulness and dabbed the blood away with a glove.

Ahead, Morton and Bourke parted company with Corwin. As Morton cantered off to rejoin the front of the column, Bourke rode toward the rear. He raised a hand in greeting as he neared Whitcomb.

237

Whitcomb had made it a point to learn as much as he could about John Bourke since their meetings at Fetterman. Bourke had enlisted in the Union Army when he was only sixteen and had served throughout the war as a private with the Fifteenth Pennsylvania, winning a Medal of Honor before he was twenty. After the war he had attended West Point and then served for some years in Arizona Territory. He had been Crook's aide for five years now, commencing shortly after Crook took command of the Department of Arizona. Next to the general's striker, Andrew Peiser, it was said that Bourke knew the general better than any other man. Three years ago, for reasons unknown, he had turned down a brevet promotion to captain.

"Well, Mr. Whitcomb," Bourke greeted him cheerily, "how are you enjoying our little jaunt? Being from the South, you must feel the cold more than most." Bourke's beard, begun at the start of the campaign to augment his full mustache, already covered his jaw completely. Whitcomb's own sparse chin hairs were an embarrassment to him and afforded no significant shelter from the weather.

"I am more stiff than cold," Whitcomb replied. "I've been saved by an impulsive purchase at Fetterman. The trader sold me a set of underwear made from merino wool sewn to perforated buckskin. He said they were the last pair in my size, and indispensable to a winter campaign. When I was fifty yards from the store I almost went back to demand my money. But I kept them. And glad of it, I must admit."

Bourke nodded. "I have some myself."

"You do? You wouldn't humor me?"

"On my honor. I wouldn't be without them."

Whitcomb smiled, relieved. "I very nearly left them in my saddlebags. I was embarrassed to be seen putting them on. But that second night, after we lost the beef herd, I braved the cold. That was the hardest part, stripping down to put them on."

"I wouldn't worry. You'll probably wear them for the rest of the campaign, and when you see the fort again, they'll stand on their own." The two men laughed together.

"You seem in very good spirits," Whitcomb ventured.

"I am always in good spirits on campaign, Mr. Whitcomb. If my spirits lag, I grow careless and fail to note a change in the wind, or the direction a rabbit is facing; then before I know it, General Crook has wished aloud to know just such a thing and my ignorance is revealed." He smiled.

"The general has a consuming interest in many things, I understand."

"In all things!" Bourke laughed again, and Whitcomb felt the cold less than he had a few moments before. "For example, yesterday when that dust cloud was sighted, it was Little Bat who first saw it and came riding to report to Colonel Stanton. The colonel was riding with General Crook at the time, and the general wanted to know not only the size of the cloud, but also its drift, direction and speed, the color of the dust and a few details I have forgotten. No piece of information is too small to escape his curiosity. And believe me, once he learns something, he never forgets it. He knows more about scouting and signs than

Grouard or any of the rest. When he asks you something, half the time he already knows the answer, and you had better be prepared to answer him thoroughly."

"You have been with him some time. Since he took command of the Department of Arizona, I believe."

Bourke looked at Whitcomb more closely. "Well, I was warned. I had been told that our Mr. Reb was something of a student of the western campaigns, but I had no idea that study included the histories of each general's aides."

Whitcomb stiffened at the use of a name he had hoped not to hear again, and Bourke noticed. "Oh, no offense, none at all, I give you my word. I didn't mean to let it out. It seems you have acquired a nickname. An admiring one at that, at least in part."

"It is hardly admiring to be called a rebel," Whitcomb said coldly.

"Please believe me, Ham— Do they call you Ham or Hamilton?"

"My friends call me Ham."

"And I would be pleased to count myself among your friends. You must believe me when I tell you that having a nickname is a good omen. It's the first step in being accepted by the men. I am afraid Southerners will be called Johnny Rebs for some time to come, and no amount of indignation can change that, but like Yankee or Jayhawker or Paddy, it can be either pejorative or admiring, depending on the use. I've heard the name Patlander a few times, as you can imagine."

"But you're not... Well, not like the others."

"D' yez mean Oi've lost the brogue? Arrah! Oi'm iz Oirish iz inny man in the column." Bourke grinned and dropped the broad accent he had learned from the enlisted men. "My people merely came well ahead of the tide. Even I say 'Irish' meaning the more recent immigrants."

"You said my nickname was admiring only in part."

"Well, the men admired your spunk, going off on your own. What remains to be seen is whether you are brave or merely foolish."

They laughed, and Whitcomb put a glove to his mouth. He inspected a new spot of blood. "Here," Bourke offered, and he pulled a small jar from the pocket of his overcoat. He unscrewed the top clumsily with his gloved hands and extended the jar to Whitcomb. It was filled with a greasy substance. "It's beef tallow. I got it from Colonel Stanton's cook. Rub a little on your lips."

Whitcomb clamped one glove under the other arm and slipped his hand free, quickly dipping a finger in the tallow and applying it to his lips. He rubbed them together to work the tallow into the cracks. At once the chapped skin felt better. "Thanks," he said as he restored his hand to the bulky muskrat gauntlet. In less than a minute he had almost lost the feeling in his fingers, but the temporary discomfort was worth it. How many more bits of lore were there still to learn about staying comfortable in a cold climate? Hundreds, certainly. He would never learn them all.

"May I ask you something?" he inquired of Bourke. "I've heard several of the men refer to Major Corwin as 'Boots.' You said it yourself, back at Fetterman. Do you know how he got the nickname?"

239

"The men will tell you it's short for 'Boots and Saddles,' because he's army through and through, but the real origin is more interesting." He hesitated a moment, glancing at Whitcomb, and then said, "He was taken prisoner during the Rebellion. Did you know that?"

Whitcomb nodded. "That much and little more."

"The day he was captured the Rebels took his boots. From then until he was exchanged, he had only rags to cover his feet. His boots mean more to him than most of us. He always has an extra pair in his kit."

"He sleeps with his boots on too."

"How are you getting along, or shouldn't I ask?"

Whitcomb was about to say something of his treatment at Corwin's hands, but he thought better of it. In the army no one liked a complainer, and complaints about a superior officer were always suspect. "Well enough," he said. "But I must say I find it a little discouraging to see him still in first lieutenant's bars after all his years in the army." He flushed suddenly, realizing Bourke might take this personally. "I'm sorry. I understand you could be a captain now if you'd wanted."

Bourke shrugged. "In the war a brevet rank was good for something in the way of command responsibility, but no longer. I decided I would have a permanent promotion or none at all. Advancement is slow nowadays."

"I'm afraid I'll be old and gray before I ever command a troop."

"Oh, I wouldn't be so sure. You have already come to General Crook's attention. The headquarters staff is tickled pink by that chase after the beef herd."

Whitcomb felt the blood rise to his face again. "That's an incident I would just as soon have forgotten, as you can imagine."

"Let me tell you something," Bourke said in a tone that did not carry far. "That dressing down you got from Boots Corwin is nothing compared to what you would have received from the general if you had succeeded in turning the herd."

Whitcomb frowned. "I don't understand."

"Good Lord, man, you don't imagine Crook wanted that herd along for the whole campaign? If Sheridan had agreed, we never would have had the first steer on this march. The staff officers are joking that Crook himself hired those Indians to run them off."

"You can't be serious!"

"He only brought them because he was ordered to! That raid suited him perfectly!" Bourke was gleeful, his eyes twinkling, although his walrus mustache hid most of his grin. "Cattle always slow you down and they could have been stampeded by a wolf or an Indian on some other night, under much worse circumstances. As it is, they ran off when they still had a chance of getting back to Fetterman and the general is grateful. We're going to cover some ground now, you mark my words."

"We don't seem to be in any great rush just yet."

"He likes to give the men and animals a few days to condition themselves. Before long we'll leave the wagons behind and then you'll see us move right along. The general wants us on an equal footing with the Indians except for one thing—the condition of our horses."

Ahead of them the column was slowing and now they heard the command, passed down the line: "Dismount! Walk your horses." For fifteen minutes of each hour the cavalry walked to warm themselves and give their horses some rest.

"Well, if I listen closely, I can hear my duty calling," Bourke said as Whitcomb reined his horse to a stop. "I had better get back up front. Perhaps I'll see you when we make camp tonight."

He rode off leaving Whitcomb feeling pleased with himself, as if he had done General Crook a personal favor by failing to recover the cattle. I might emerge from this campaign with flying colors after all, he thought, if that chase is not to be held against me.

At mid-afternoon, the column halted suddenly.

Corwin turned to Whitcomb, who was once more riding beside him. After a few hours of file closing he had been relieved by Corporal McCaslin. "Go to the front, Mr. Whitcomb, and find out why we have stopped. If the men can dismount, let me know."

Even as Whitcomb gratefully spurred his horse into a warming canter, the call to dismount was relayed down the column, and he was doubly glad. His orders took him from Corwin's stifling presence, at least for a time, and now there was no reason for him to return quickly.

The reason for the halt was apparent when he reached the head of the column, where officers and scouts were inspecting a trail that had recently been traveled by a large body of Indians crossing the path of the army's advance. A few of the scouts walked along the trail for a few dozen yards to be clear of the gathering and there they examined the tracks closely. Whitcomb saw John Bourke with Generals Crook and Reynolds, who were listening intently to the reports of several scouts. Reynolds was white-haired, with muttonchop whiskers, and he alone of all the officers kept his chin clean-shaven on the march. Whitcomb dismounted and moved a little nearer. It was the closest he had been to the colorful scouts since the start of the expedition. They were dressed for the most part in furs, buckskins and leggings, high boots or moccasins, and hats and caps of every variety. The one man Whitcomb knew by sight was the swarthy Frank Grouard, who was speaking to Crook now, gesturing at the trail. Grouard was a hulking figure standing over six feet tall; his past was a mystery, and the subject of much speculation in the command. Some said he was half Sioux and half Negro, while others maintained that he had been born in the South Seas. All agreed that he had been held captive for some years among the Sioux, in the camp of Crazy Horse himself, it was said. Whitcomb had heard a rumor that Grouard's loyalty to the white man was suspect, and that General Crook had instructed Big Bat and Little Bat—the scouts Pourier and Garnier—to drop Grouard in his tracks if he showed the first sign of betraying the column to the hostiles.

"Mr. Whitcomb, isn't it?"

Whitcomb turned to see Captain Anson Mills addressing him. The twelve companies in the command had been divided at the start into six battalions of two troops each; Mills was commander of the battalion that comprised his own Company M, Third Cavalry, and Corwin's E Company. Mills carried a long-barreled shotgun in the crook of his arm. Many of the officers bore personal weapons instead of the cavalry carbines; Winchester repeaters were a favorite but Mills touted the virtues of double-ought buckshot for dispatching Indians at close quarters.

"Yes, sir." Whitcomb saluted.

"Have you been sent here by Major Corwin?" Mills was always punctilious about referring to Corwin by his brevet rank, a courtesy he himself expected in return. He had been brevetted lieutenant colonel for gallantry in the battle of Nashville, Tennessee. He had black hair, black eyes, a mustache and goatee. His speech was abrupt and his manner excitable, which always made Whitcomb nervous in his presence.

"I'm to find out why we've stopped, sir. Major Corwin wished to know if there was to be a long delay."

"I imagine we'll move along soon," Mills replied. "Quite a trail, this one." He jabbed a hand at the tracks.

The overlapping prints of unshod horses and moccasins of all sizes were plain to see, but Whitcomb was puzzled by the long striations that scored the ground where the Indians had passed. He pointed at the marks. "What makes those tracks, sir?"

Mills looked at him as if he had asked how many legs were to be found on the average horse. "Lodgepoles," he said, and Whitcomb blushed violently, feeling the perfect fool. He knew very well that the Indians transported their belongings on travois, or pony drags, made by crossing two tipi poles across a horse's back and lashing a small framework across the lower ends of the poles to bear whatever might be required, whether the lodge covering, house-hold belongings, or a wounded man. Yet he had not put this knowledge together with the strange marks before him. All his life had been spent in the white man's world, where there were foot and hoof and wheel prints, but nothing such as this.

As he rode back along the column he glanced at the newest mules in the pack train, young animals with their manes roached and tails bobbed short so the packers could tell at a glance which were the inexperienced beasts most likely to cause trouble. No wonder the troopers called fresh young second lieutenants "shavetails." Graduates of the military academy, they were edu-cated men, but they knew nothing at all in the areas that mattered most. It seemed that acquiring knowledge was not enough. Like a new tool, knowledge must be used over and over again until its application became second nature. Whitcomb resolved that before the campaign was over, he would be a shavetail no longer.

242

As the afternoon wore on the snow gradually stopped. Two more vedettes of hostiles were sighted and duly ignored as they attempted to entice a foolish pursuit. Later, shots boomed out far in front and set the column on alert, but one of the scouts returned with the welcome news that his comrades had brought down two buffalo bulls. More shots sounded as the head of the column drew near the wooded valley of the Powder, and again game was the cause of the shooting, antelope this time. The guides chose a crossing through a patch of sluggish, milky water rather than risk the wagons on the treacherous alkali ice; the river bottom was quaggy and the horses lurched about, unhappy not to be able to see their footing, but the crossing was made without incident and as E Troop arrived at the far bank they saw that the companies from the head of the line were already encamped for the night and the men were gathered around the cookfires, watching the butchering of bison and antelope with unconcealed interest.

The valley was broad, more than a mile wide near the crossing, and well timbered with cottonwood. But despite a generous growth of lowland grasses, the horses and mules were picketed in lines together and fed grain from the wagons, and the command was camped near the stream, well removed from the densest stands of trees and any other cover that might provide an avenue of approach for infiltrating Indians.

Visible on higher ground beyond the river bottom were a few jagged timbers and a fragment of a palisade wall.

"Old Fort Reno, I imagine," Whitcomb observed to McCaslin as they dismounted.

"Indayd, sorr. Major Corwin was stationed here once upon a time, durin' Red Cloud's War."

"Oh?"

"Yes, sorr. For him it must be like comin' home to a graveyard."

McCaslin crossed himself, but Whitcomb did not need that sign of the Catholic faith to give him the feeling that there were ghosts about. Fort Reno was ninety miles from Fetterman, and it was the southernmost of the three forts built ten years before to guard the Bozeman Trail. It had been abandoned in 1868 when the Laramie treaty was signed, and before the last trooper was out of sight the gleeful savages had set it alight. This was the first military expedition into the Powder River country since then and suddenly Whitcomb felt that even this bustling camp of eight hundred men was small and trifling compared with the vastness of the terrain they sought to pacify.

By now the matter of making camp had become routine. Major Coates posted his infantry sentries, animals were picketed and fed, tents were erected in rows by company, and the evening meal was prepared. Whitcomb performed his duties and set out his bedroll and when he was done he sauntered in the direction of the headquarters tents, where he found John Bourke writing in a small leatherbound book. Nearby, a gathering of company officers and scouts was just breaking up, the scouts already mounting their horses and starting off to the north to survey the surrounding country.

Bourke closed his book and replaced it in a pocket of his greatcoat. "There. If I don't write in my diary each day when we make camp, I don't get it done at all." He stood up and gestured about the campsite. "Well, this is all right, isn't it? Lots of firewood, at least. I swear, I can feel the cold in my bones. Come along over here; we've a good fire going."

"Rank hath its privileges," Whitcomb muttered, eyeing the commodious tents for the staff officers and the tables set here and there.

"What? Oh, I see, the luxuries of the headquarters mess." Bourke's tone was sarcastic. "Look here, you see the general?" He nodded toward a tent not far away. With the staff meeting over, General Crook was reclining on a buffalo robe outside the tent, his arms crossed beneath his head, gazing skyward as if relaxing on a warm spring day. "That is where he sleeps," Bourke continued. "You see that fellow there? That's his striker, Andy Peiser. He's been with the general as long as I have." Beyond Crook, an enlisted man of fair complexion and middling height sat in a folding canvas chair, reading a small Bible. When Crook shifted position, resting his head on one hand, Peiser looked up, and returned to his reading only when it was clear that Crook required nothing of him. Many officers had strikers, enlisted men hired as personal servants, and many troopers sought the job, for it could earn them something beyond a private soldier's thirteen dollars a month.

"Why does the commanding general sleep on the ground, you ask?" Bourke grinned. "He's got a striker to make his bed for him, you think. He could sleep on a cot, swaddled in a stack of buffalo robes like some traveling British lord. Well, he sleeps like that because he prefers it that way, and once we're clear of the wagons the rest of us will have it no better. You won't find another man on the campaign who can do with fewer comforts or keep up the pace better than George Crook. He's uncanny, boyo, you mind what I say. Once down in Arizona we had marched for twenty-six hours straight, and when we finally stopped, we all fell to the ground like tenpins. Not him. He strolled off to the marsh nearby and shot a dozen reed ducks for the men's supper. Oh, here's a man you should meet." Nearby, an officer was hanging a mercury thermometer from the pole of the medical tent. "Your life may depend on him, although I earnestly hope not. Dr. Munn," Bourke addressed the man, drawing near, "may I present Lieutenant Whitcomb. Lieutenant, Assistant Surgeon Munn, our ranking medical officer. Dr. Munn is preparing to measure the degree of our discomfort."

Whitcomb and Munn shook hands and exchanged pleasantries and the doctor nodded at the thermometer. "Back in Washington they love bits of intelligence such as this. I tell them what temperatures we encountered and they write in their reports that the troops were perfectly comfortable at thus and such a temperature in standard field issue. God help us if anyone believes that. No frostbite in your troop, I trust, Mr. Whitcomb?"

"No, sir, none at all." All the officers in the command had been warned to be on the alert for the first signs of frostbite among the men, and to see that no one exposed himself carelessly to that crippling affliction.

The light on the scene, which until then had been dim and growing steadily dimmer as night approached, now changed dramatically. The camp was illuminated suddenly by a brilliant orange glow and the three men turned to see that the sun had emerged from beneath the clouds, its lower edge already touching the horizon. To the east the slopes of the benches and hills descending to the river were painted in gold and scarlet and for a brief time the camp was almost silent as everywhere men stopped to regard the unexpected beauty.

"Fat lot of good he does us now," Bourke observed irreverently as the fiery sphere slipped below the western hills and left the camp in a gloom that thickened quickly. "I could have used a glimpse of old Sol about noontime today." He moved a few steps closer to the large fire in the middle of the headquarters camp. "If it clears tonight it will be damn cold."

"Mr. Bourke!" A man Whitcomb did not know was approaching, waving to get Bourke's attention. "I have been looking for you. Oh, I don't know your friend. Perhaps you would introduce—"

Shots sounded from the edge of camp, first one and then two more; all were the familiar reports of the infantry's Springfield rifles. Close on the heels of the shots came derisive shouts demanding to know how many trees had been injured. "More jittery nerves," Whitcomb said, joining Bourke and the other man by the fire. Since the first attack on camp there had been some shooting each night, directed at anything that resembled the shape of a man in the uncertain light. At dawn, most of these "Indians" had proved to be stumps or rocks. The night before, three flesh-and-blood Indians had crept up through the brush in the hope of stealing a few horses, but they had been sent running with a brisk flight of lead compliments.

A ragged stuttering of sharp explosions broke out from two sides now, and a bullet passed not far overhead.

"More than nerves, I think," Bourke said, looking around. Men were running toward the edges of camp and a few shouts from the officers were attempting to put order in the soldiers' response to the shooting. A ball struck the fire, sending up a cloud of sparks and causing the three men to jump back. "You might want to join your troop," Bourke observed, and he walked calmly away.

Whitcomb lost no time in following Bourke's suggestion and he reached the tents of E Troop just as Corwin came running through the growing confusion. Ignoring Whitcomb, he addressed Sergeant Dupré.

"Form up the men on foot, Sergeant. General Crook expects the hostiles to go for the horse herd; we're to help protect it."

"Yes, sair." Dupré began to move among the men, passing Corwin's orders along to the other non-commissioned officers and speaking calmly to steady the excited soldiers.

"Mr. Whitcomb." Corwin turned to his second-in-command. "Take Sergeant Duggan and ten men and assist Major Coates."

"Yes, *sir!*" He found Duggan, a lanky Irishman, among the milling troopers and in a few moments they had assembled a squad of ten men, armed with carbines. As he led the way at double time toward the sound of the firing, Whitcomb was smiling. The real brunt of the attack might well come in the vicinity of the horse herd—if the hostiles could put the cavalry afoot they would have won the campaign with a single well-timed stroke—but Corwin hadn't been able to isolate Whitcomb from the fighting entirely. From the sound of it, a lively exchange was in progress between Coates's infantry and a considerable band of concealed attackers.

The cookfires had been kicked to smithereens within minutes of the first shots and the camp was in a dim twilight now, coming in part from the west, where a small orange glow lingered, and in part from the dull gray clouds overhead, lit by the unseen half-moon. Whitcomb nearly bumped into a running man, excused himself, and suddenly found himself among the infantry, who had taken sheltered positions in hastily improvised rifle pits. "Put the men where they'll do the most good, Sergeant," he instructed Duggan, and then worked his way toward the edge of the perimeter to survey the state of affairs.

Muzzle flashes sparked in the dense cluster of cottonwoods immediately to the front and the troopers responded at once, firing at the flashes. Whitcomb discerned the reports of cavalry carbines among those of the infantry's rifles. Good man, Duggan, he thought. The E Troop men were already in position. The return fire was disciplined and brief. The men reloaded quickly to wait for the next flash that would reveal some lurking Indian's position. The trees were sharply silhouetted against the somewhat lighter sky, but no detail at all was visible in the foreground.

Whitcomb found a place behind a stump and drew his revolver. A pistol would be as much use as a carbine here; more use, if the attackers got up their courage to charge.

More shots came from the cottonwoods and there was a cry of pain close in front of Whitcomb. "Ye haythen bastards!" the wounded man shouted. His voice was strangely muffled, as if he spoke with his mouth full of food. A figure rose ten yards beyond and fired at the woods. It was an infantryman; Whitcomb could make out the long shape of the man's rifle. The figure struggled to push another round into the trapdoor breech, but he paused and raised a hand to his head, then slowly toppled to the ground. He fell near the remains of one of the cookfires and the glow from the coals illuminated his still form sufficiently well for the attackers to see; shots began to sound from the cottonwoods and bullets kicked up gouts of dirt near the fallen soldier.

Without forethought, Whitcomb scrambled across the intervening distance, pistol in hand, ignoring the sound of two balls that passed close by, one on either side of him.

"Careful, boys, there's a man to the front!" The return fire from the troopers was lively and Whitcomb was glad to hear the cautionary warning. The voice was calm and forceful, and from those few words Whitcomb recognized a fellow Virginian. Who could it be? He hadn't been aware that there was another Virginian on the campaign. He had reached the wounded man now and he dropped to his knees beside him. The man had been shot through the face. A ragged hole gaped in his left cheek. Small wonder that his voice sounded odd, Whitcomb thought. He holstered his pistol and grabbed the man by the armpits, dragging him quickly away from the fire as more shots struck the ground nearby. He paused in the shelter of a large rock and ducked as a ball struck the boulder and sprayed the two men with flying chips. The wounded soldier groaned.

"It's all right," Whitcomb said, and he wondered if everyone mouthed such platitudes at times like this.

"Covering fire, boys!" came the same voice that had called the warning just moments before. The troopers' Springfields set up a barrage and the muskets in the woods fell silent. Whitcomb heaved on the wounded man and dragged him across the final yards to the troopers' lines. Two men jumped up to help him.

"That were a fine piece o' work, friend. Let's us truck 'im to the doc. Oh, 'scuse me, sir."

How in the devil did the man recognize me? Whitcomb wondered. Is my face known to every man in the command? He looked closely at the soldier who had spoken and he recognized him as one of the privates from his own company. What was his name? Dowdy, that was it. "Thank you, Dowdy. He's out cold, I'm afraid."

"Donnelly here, sir," said the second figure. "If you two lay aholt of his shoulders, I can tote his feet."

Together they carried the unconscious man like some awkward piece of broken-down machinery and found their way to the surgeon's tent.

"What have we here?" Surgeon Munn examined the man quickly by the dim light of a veiled lamp. "Well, it's messy, but not too bad, I think. The ball missed the jawbone but it took out three teeth. It must have given him quite a blow."

"He'd of got more'n that, if Mr. Whitcomb hadn't of pulled his bacon out'n the fire," Donnelly said.

"The ball knocked him out, sir," Whitcomb said quickly. "But he got off a shot at them first. He stood up and let them have it."

"I'm amazed he could stand. Well, I'll patch him up as best I can."

As the three men returned to the line the fire was lessening. Whitcomb found Sergeant Duggan and familiarized himself with the positions of the E Company troopers in case he should need them for some further action, but a silence fell on the encampment and as it lengthened it became apparent that the invisible attackers had withdrawn. After half an hour the cookfires were rekindled, and, with a double guard keeping watch, the troopers finally had their supper. It wasn't until Whitcomb had seated himself on a cottonwood log with a tin plate in his lap that he realized he had come through the brief skirmish without a moment's confusion. From start to finish he had obeyed his orders and done the right thing almost by second nature. He held out a hand and saw it was steady. Perhaps he was born to be a soldier after all.

He was examining this notion with some curiosity when he was approached by the same man who had just joined him and Lieutenant Bourke when the attack began.

"Lieutenant Whitcomb?" Whitcomb nodded. "May I sit down?" Whitcomb nodded again, still trying to force down the last piece of leathery bull meat. The man removed a glove and extended his hand as he seated himself beside Whitcomb on the log. "Bob Strahorn, *Rocky Mountain News.*"

Whitcomb had heard of Robert Strahorn, the only civilian on the campaign, and he realized now that he had seen the man from time to time without knowing who he was. He usually kept close to General Crook and Whitcomb had assumed he was another of the staff officers, for he was clothed like all the rest. He was tall and lean and had straight black hair. The two men shook hands.

"Well," Strahorn said, "you were certainly in the thick of it this evening. I hope you won't mind if I corroborate a few facts?"

"I don't mind." Whitcomb was both flattered and wary at being approached by a member of the press. His wariness was compounded by the professional soldier's reserve in the face of civilian inquiry. Newspapers were seldom kind to the frontier army, but the dispatches Whitcomb had seen in several papers on his journey west all spoke admiringly of General Crook. Strahorn's own paper, the Denver *Rocky Mountain News*, in its February 22 edition, had offered the opinion that General Crook, on his imminent campaign, would "'go through' the Indian country after his usual fashion and will leave things in better shape than he finds them." For all Whitcomb knew, Strahorn might have written the flattering piece himself. Still, he would have to be cautious until he had taken the measure of the man.

"I understand you have been on active duty just a short time." Strahorn's manner was open and curious.

"That's right. I reported to Fort Fetterman on February twenty-ninth. My father has been ill and I was allowed to spend some time at home." Careful. Answer the question; don't volunteer information.

"This was a more serious attack than the others, wouldn't you say? General Crook believes the hostiles wanted to run off our horses."

"The horses are under guard, sir, well within the camp boundaries, and will remain so."

"That's true enough. But once we leave the wagons behind and proceed on our own, it will be necessary to tether the horses individually so they can forage for themselves at least for a few hours each evening."

Whitcomb hesitated. Clearly the man knew a good deal about the workings of a cavalry campaign. Perhaps more than himself. "I don't presume to anticipate the orders of my superiors," he said.

"That was a brave thing you did this evening. Major Coates is grateful for your help in saving Corporal Slavey."

"Who was it?"

"Corporal Slavey, of Captain Ferris's company."

"Well, I was closest to him when he was hit. Anyone else would have done the same thing."

"Perhaps. Your modesty becomes you. Please don't think I am trying to draw you into any boastful statement, Mr. Whitcomb. I am simply trying to get to know you. After all, you have occasioned some notice on the campaign so far, what with your single-handed attempt to retrieve the cattle, and all."

"Oh, Lord, don't write about that, I beg you."

"It may not reflect too badly on your spirit, I should think."

Whitcomb recalled Bourke's comment on that event, and the question of whether it had been brave or merely foolhardy. How would this evening's actions reflect on him? To his benefit, he earnestly hoped. Several of his own men had said a word or two to him as the camp returned to normal, praising him for helping the wounded man. Lieutenant Corwin had distinguished himself by his silence on the matter, although Whitcomb was sure his superior had heard of it by now. Why should a word of encouragement from Corwin be so important to him? He didn't know, but he wished for it still. E Troop's commander was a "foine son of a bitch" indeed, and a harsh judge, unwilling to mete out praise when it was deserved.

"I understand you have a nickname," Strahorn was saying. "I overheard some of the men referring to you as Mr. Reb."

"I wish I had never heard the name."

"Why, you're a young man. The Rebellion was not your responsibility."

"It is not an easy responsibility to set aside."

"Yes, I know life has been hard in the Southern states," Strahorn offered, misunderstanding him. "Many families were ruined. I hope yours was not among them."

"We still have our land, and the British insist on their Virginia tobacco." Whitcomb did not elaborate on the difficulties of Reconstruction, or the great changes the defeat of the Southern cause had imposed on the plantation system of growing tobacco.

"May I ask if your relatives took up arms for the Confederacy?"

"Yes, sir, they did." Whitcomb drew himself up. "My father and uncles fought with the Army of Northern Virginia, as I would have done, had I been old enough. A man must fight when his homeland is threatened."

"True enough. Even now the Indians are fighting for theirs, but they'll lose in the end, of course. I must say I don't see too much future for this country here. There might be some farming in the river bottoms, I suppose, and the scouts say the land is less arid farther north. We have seen several outcroppings of coal, though. That alone may be reason enough to open it up."

"And there's the Black Hills gold. That's why we're here, indirectly."

Whitcomb was scarcely aware of how skillfully Strahorn drew him out. The man was friendly and encouraging, and for his part, Whitcomb was glad of a chance to talk with someone who was neither superior nor inferior in rank, with the attendant difficulties that impeded free expression in those cases. First with Bourke and now with Strahorn, today had offered him his first opportunities to speak freely since the campaign began. The two men sat for a time, discovering common interests and chatting of many things, and before long Strahorn steered the talk back to Whitcomb's family and background. By the time they parted to go to their beds, the newspaperman could have written a concise biography of Second Lieutenant Hamilton Whitcomb and given a thumbnail sketch of his closest relatives.

After bidding Strahorn good night, Whitcomb took a short walk among the sleeping men of Company E, a habit he had already developed as part of his routine before retiring. Corwin was awake, preparing his own bedroll, but he said nothing beyond a curt reply to Whitcomb's good night. Whitcomb could feel Corwin's eyes follow him as he walked along the row of tents. He's always watching me, he thought. Why? To catch me in a mistake.

A figure rose from the ground as he approached his bedroll and he recognized one of the men from Sergeant Duggan's squad, but he didn't know the man's name. The soldier was older than most of the other privates in the company, with graying hair and beard. He was of Whitcomb's height but more solidly built. He stood ramrod straight, almost at attention, as he came to a stop before the young officer.

"Mr. Whitcomb, sir."

He was the Virginian! By those few words, Whitcomb recognized the voice that had called out a warning to protect Whitcomb as he helped the wounded soldier.

"Private—?"

"Gray, sir. John Gray. It's a little joke on the Yankees. I was formerly Captain John Wesley of the Army of Northern Virginia. I knew your uncle Reuben, sir. I just wanted to say it is an honor to serve under you."

The man's complete sincerity moved Whitcomb deeply and for a moment he had trouble finding his voice. Private John Gray, formerly Captain John Wesley of the Army of Northern Virginia. How many other former Confederate officers were to be found in the ranks of the United States Army, enlisted under assumed names, the only way they could continue in uniform? And why had Gray waited until now to present himself? Because of what Whitcomb had done for a fellow soldier this evening? Until he was sure of the young officer whom he himself should be commanding? Whatever the reason, he had come forward now, and Whitcomb felt he had been given rare praise indeed.

"Thank you, Private Gray," he said at last. "The honor is mine." Without thinking, he extended his hand. Gray hesitated, then took it, and they shook hands firmly. "Well, good night," Whitcomb offered, not knowing what else to say.

Private Gray smiled. "Good night, Mr. Reb." He winked one eye almost imperceptibly, then saluted quickly and went off to his bed of buffalo robes.

The command was on the march again shortly after dawn, passing by the ruins of old Fort Reno on the benchland above the river. Little remained of the once proud post: a few chimneys, part of an adobe wall, a fragment of one small building. The site was littered with broken gun carriages, axles, old stoves and other metal debris. Two hundred yards north of the fort there stood a dozen broken and falling headboards to mark the cemetery.

"Eyes right!" Lieutenant Corwin ordered as E Troop passed near the graves, and he held a salute as he rode by.

Once again the column advanced directly against the force of the storm, which had returned before first light to dispel any hope that the glimpse of sun on the previous evening might presage a pleasant day to follow. The men huddled deep within their coverings of fur. Scarves and bandannas were tied across their faces leaving only the eyes exposed. Those who had them wore the green Arizona goggles. The snow descended in a succession of squalls that whipped up the fresh flakes from the ground and enveloped the column in sudden whiteouts, sometimes limiting visibility to less than a hundred yards. In between these intense assaults, patches of blue sky and tantalizing periods of sunshine intervened. At these times the countryside far on all sides was revealed, along with new evidence of hostile eyes watching. No horsemen appeared today but several columns of smoke rose in silent conversation far to the north and looking-glass signals flashed nearer at hand until the clouds returned.

The landscape to the north and west of the Powder River Crossing was a divide of numbing monotony, an alternation of ridge and gulch barren of vegetation, save for an occasional low mesa with a decorative fringe of bunch-grass. For twenty-seven miles the mounted troopers shivered in their saddles or led their horses while flankers and scouts kept watch. As always, the infantry marched the entire way, and both infantryman and cavalryman thought the other had the best of it. As dusk approached they gratefully made camp by Crazy Woman's Fork, the most pleasant stream they had yet encountered. There was ample brush for firewood and sheltered campsites, and the water ran sweet and clear beneath a solid foot of ice. The halfbreed scouts said that the stream took its colorful name from a Sioux squaw who was not content to sport in her sleeping robes with her husband alone, but took herself to two or three other tipis as well while camped on these very banks. Women of the Sioux were expected to be chaste and modest, the scouts said, and the tribe considered such flagrant behavior to be truly demented.

In the morning there was no order to get under way. The soldiers stayed

251

close to the cookfires and ate all that was offered. At midday the storm ceased abruptly, the wind dropped and the sky cleared; the troopers took to strolling beyond the limits of camp to survey the countryside, while keeping an eye on the headquarters tents. They noticed the scouts coming and going from the north, over the next divide.

As the sun dropped below the mountains, which rose stark and majestic fifteen miles to the west, the company officers were gathered in a semicircle around General Crook and Colonel Reynolds. Boots Corwin found a seat beside his friend Teddy Egan, captain of Company K, Second Cavalry.

James Egan, called "Teddy" by his friends for reasons that were lost in the past, had served with Corwin in the Second Cavalry during the Rebellion, and like Corwin he had risen from the ranks. Unlike Corwin he had not been captured by the enemy. He had emerged from the war a first lieutenant and was commissioned captain three years later. In his service on the frontier he had already distinguished himself. He seemed to have a knack for being in the thick of trouble. At the peace conference with the Sioux in the previous autumn there had been a tense moment when one of the chiefs who favored war rather than selling the Black Hills had harangued his fellow tribesmen, saying there was no time like the present to start the fighting. Egan had drawn up his troop between the Indians and the commissioners, with carbines at the ready. Faced by this silent, motionless line of determined men, the Indians, who outnumbered the soldiers ten to one, had backed down.

"A dollar says Reynolds never opens his mouth," Egan said now, too softly for anyone but Corwin to hear.

"Thanks, I'll keep my money."

"Gentlemen," said Crook, calling the meeting to order, "I had thought to bring the wagons a bit farther with us, but General Reynolds and I have decided to return them to Fort Reno to await us there." Reynolds kept his eyes on Crook, and he seemed content to let his superior do the talking. "The many signs of Indians hereabouts have convinced us that we must move quickly if we wish to regain the initiative." A light breeze lifted the twin tails of Crook's beard where they rested against his greatcoat.

The officers glanced at one another. There would be no more crushed-cork mattresses, no extra robes and overgarments thrown into a wagon during the day to be recovered at night when the mercury fell. But their expectations of hardships to come were tempered by a quickening of the blood. At last the real campaign was to begin. The marches had lengthened steadily each day, building endurance in livestock and men, until the limit of the wagon train's capability had been reached.

"We will carry no excess baggage," Crook continued. "Each man, officer and trooper alike, will carry only the clothing he can wear, and one buffalo robe or two blankets. There will be no tents. Officers will mess with the men. Staff officers and others who may be unattached—Mr. Strahorn, that will include yourself—will mess with the pack train. We will expect to remain in the field for fifteen days. Our provisions will be hardtack and coffee, half rations of bacon, and whatever the country may provide. For the horses, one-sixth rations of grain." He paused and looked around the gathering. "Look to your animals, gentlemen, and your men. By now each officer has been informed by Assistant Surgeon Munn regarding the measures necessary to prevent frostbite. Thus far we have had none and I intend that we shall have none. A man with frostbite might as well have been wounded by the enemy." He paused again to let his words take effect before issuing his final pronouncement. "Gentlemen, insofar as it is possible for half a thousand men and horses to disappear, it is my intention that we should do just that. For the next several days we will march only at night, or under cover of the weather."

He opened his greatcoat, revealing a glimpse of red flannel lining, and pulled out a plain Waltham watch of the kind called a "turnip" by the troopers, for its shape and size. He consulted the watch for a moment, then put it away. "We leave at dark. Be prepared for a march of more than thirty miles."

Corwin and Egan walked together back toward their companies when the meeting disbanded. "It's about time!" Egan exclaimed when they were beyond the headquarters area. Corwin shared his friend's enthusiasm and hoped he might have a bit of Egan's fabled luck. He was well aware that both Crook and Reynolds regarded Egan as an up-and-coming officer destined for further promotions. He resented neither Egan's rank nor his achievements, but he earnestly wished for similar opportunities.

"How are your men bearing up?" he asked as they prepared to part.

"Ready to whip their weight in bears. How's your new lieutenant coming along?"

"I'm keeping him on a tight rein."

Egan smiled. "Up to your old tricks?"

"Something like that."

An hour later the cavalrymen bid farewell to the supply train and the infantry, which would escort the wagons back to Fort Reno and remain there to guard them, and set out under clear skies and a gibbous moon that bathed the country in an eerie silver light. The rough prairie soon gave way to sharper bluffs and rising foothills, and the column was compelled to climb steeper and steeper grades. Before long they traveled in a column of twos instead of the standard four abreast. When they reached the divide where the Clear Fork of the Powder originated, they saw that the terrain around them had become thoroughly mountainous. To their left, the Big Horns stood silent and grand in the moonlight.

As the tail of Company E reached the crest of the trail and began the descent into the valley of the Clear Fork, Ham Whitcomb, the troop's file closer once more, found John Bourke sitting his horse beside the trail and he reined aside to join him.

"You look like Hannibal's sentinel," he greeted his friend.

"By God, look at us, Ham!" Bourke whispered in awe. "It's like some monstrous snake." He was almost chuckling from the exhilaration and grandeur of the scene, and Whitcomb saw the aptness of the image at once. The chain of mounted men and pack mules could easily have been a tremendous serpent slithering over the crest of the divide and down the other side in search of a mythic prey. It was an image out of the Arabian Nights, all the more so for being seen by moon and starlight. The creak and slap of leather and steel were the sounds of the reptile's scales, and the glint from burnished holsters and the shining metal of bridles and carbines flashing along the column in the cold light only heightened the impression of sinuous movement. The frosted breath from the mouths of animals and men became puffs of steam or smoke, evidence of the fire within. The serpent had only to open its mouth and tongues of flame would burst forth.

"We better get along before you're missed," Bourke said, breaking the spell.

"There's not much danger of that," said Whitcomb, but as they overtook E Troop he saw Corwin riding in the rear, beside Sergeant Duggan.

"I'll see you later," he muttered to Bourke, and slipped into his place in line.

"Were you lost, Mr. Reb?" Corwin demanded coldly.

"No, sir. I had the troop in sight all the time." He would not defend himself. He had done nothing really wrong, after all.

Corwin said nothing further, but he rode alongside for a time before finally touching his spurs to his horse and moving off toward the head of the troop.

"It's a grand view, sir," observed Sergeant Duggan when Corwin was out of earshot. "Well worth a little stop."

"You'll see nothing like it in Ireland, eh, Sergeant?" Whitcomb had been told that Virginia in the springtime, with its multihued carpets of green, brought some men to mind of the Emerald Isle.

"Oh, no, sir. To be sure."

"You're not suggesting that Mr. Whitcomb stopped merely to take in the countryside?" came the measured tones of Private John Gray, riding near the rear of the troop.

"He were seein' the general's aide 'bout our full rations of bacon, ain't that right, sir?" The moonlight fell on the smiling face of Private Peter Dowdy. "The general knows there ain't no troop in the command what fights like the Foreign Legion, so he's givin' us full rations to keep our strength up. Ain't that right, sir?"

"Quiet in the ranks. You know the orders," said Whitcomb. On a calm night a voice could carry unexpectedly far and the officers had been cautioned to keep their men silent, but his tone softened the mild rebuke. By their words of support, Duggan and the others had confirmed what Whitcomb already had dared to hope—he had made a start at winning the trust of the men. They were coming to like him. They were silent now, but he could feel their high spirits, equal to his own, and he was proud to be in such company.

Everywhere along the line heads were up and looking about and there were soft exclamations of wonder, even from the unlettered among them, at the strangely beautiful landscape. For more than a week now these men had endured constant discomfort, but not of a constant nature; with every change in the weather, with each diurnal change from light to dark, they had had to alter their response to the demands placed upon them; yet if anything they were now a more cohesive force, strengthened by the hardships of the march and the probing of the enemy, more sure of their mission. Equal to any force in the world.

Equal or superior? Given birth by a higher culture than that of the Indians and engaged on the grand enterprise of the white race, they should be more than a match for the barbarous foe, but Whitcomb found a lingering uncertainty within himself. So far from all physical evidence of the "higher culture," the cavalrymen were mounted warriors much like the hostiles. The frontier army and the Indians alike were scattered in small groups across a harsh land, occasionally venturing forth to do combat. He remembered his talk with Strahorn then, and what he himself had said about men defending their homeland, and a few lines from Macaulay's *Lays of Ancient Rome* came to him:

> *For how can man die better*
> *Than facing fearful odds,*
> *For the ashes of his fathers*
> *And the temples of his Gods?*

At the age of ten he had felt a boyish determination to fight and die, if necessary, to prevent the conquest of the South by the Yankee invaders. The Indians were fighting now to protect hunting grounds and loved ones and the burial places of their fathers. Could it be that they too felt a similar resolve? Perhaps any man, high or low, gained an added measure of strength when he fought for his home.

They were equal, then, the two sides. Save for the condition of the horses.

Could it really be reduced to that? he wondered. Equal save for a few handfuls of grain?

Equal save for the use of the wheel. Wagons had transported the grain and so the cavalry horses remained fit and strong; this was the tactical edge, not any superiority of race.

He thought again of the travois tracks two days before, and was struck by the gulf that separated the red men and the white. How could two such different races ever hope to live in harmony? What could you do or say to be understood by a people who saw the wheel and comprehended its purpose, but rejected its adoption?

255

LISA PUTNAM'S JOURNAL

Monday, March 6th. 11:45 a.m.

For the first time since the avalanche I have found a moment to write. There have been no calves born since late yesterday and I came in early to catch my breath before dinner. There has been much to do, what with getting the circus folk settled for a stay of some weeks. Snow has been falling almost continuously since yesterday morning and the foul weather, made worse by wind, has been no help, either in resettling the circus or in keeping an eye on the calves, which now number four.

We who live here are accustomed to the threat of being blocked in the park for a time by an avalanche in winter or a slide in spring or fall whenever the rains are heavy, and I should have warned Mr. Tatum to avoid loud noises in the canyon, but there is no use crying over spilt milk. Harry and I were about to pull a calf when I heard a distant sound. I watched the cloud of snow grow larger and larger over the gap and still I didn't realize what I was seeing until the circus horses came tearing up the valley. Then I was off, and I thought my heart would stop or wear itself out before I reached the river canyon. Harry offered to go with me, of course, but even in that moment of panic I did not wish to lose a calf, and so I left him to tend the cancer-eye cow while I took his horse with me, thinking to pick up Julius on the way. Julius and Hutch had already begun to run towards the river and had very nearly reached the bottom of the valley before I overtook them. When we arrived at the scene we found men and women standing in bunches, staring at what used to be a wagon road, and we soon learned the reason for their benumbed expressions. Jack Fisk and half the circus horses had vanished as the avalanche struck the road; without those animals, many of the most valuable and highly trained performing horses among them, all the planned performances across the western territories and in California were in peril. And then came the miracle. Julius climbed atop the avalanche to survey its extent, when what should he see but a figure coming towards him from the other direction, none other than Jack Fisk, and very much alive. He and all the missing horses, save one that was not quite swift enough to avoid being caught and swept away, had reached safety farther down the road. He had feared that many of those behind him might have suffered a dreadful fate. The reunion was a sight to see. Everyone laughed and embraced, even the usually taciturn teamsters and wranglers. Such was the general relief at seeing Mr. Fisk alive and learning that the horses were well, everyone commenced to tell the others his or her own experiences in the frightening moments as the avalanche tumbled down upon them, and it was not uncommon to see two people relating their individual tales, each to the other, and both speaking at once.

256

There was just time enough left in the day for Julius to go with Mr. Fisk and two wranglers and drive the stranded horses up over the southern ridge to re-enter the park by that route. They would have had hard going in bad weather, but the day remained fair except for the advent of some high clouds, the harbingers of the storm that has been blowing ever since.

I learned that Johnny Smoker had snatched Amanda from Mr. Chalmers' wagon, which he believed to be doomed, and he was generally praised for saving her life, although the wagon survived. Mr. Tatum thanked him most gravely. When I first arrived, Amanda and Johnny were still together on Johnny's horse, but they saw me looking in their direction and Amanda slipped quickly to the ground. How soon the awareness of common proprieties returns once danger is past. Since then they have often been in each other's company, and they, at least, have some reason to welcome this turn of events. When he is not with Amanda, Johnny is helping out with some chore or another. He seems always to know where to lend a hand, and already I think of him as one of the crew. Yesterday morning he went feeding with Julius and Hutch, and Julius says that Johnny handles a team as well as men with twice his age and experience. He suggested it might be possible for Johnny and Hutch to feed alone now and then, freeing Julius to spend more time with the cows and heifers during calving. This may prove to be a great blessing in the weeks to come.

There is no doubt that Mr. Tatum and his wagons are trapped here until warm weather sets in. The avalanche is the worst I can remember. It swept the slope clean. In addition to the mass of snow, which is thirty feet deep in places, the slide is full of rocks and boulders of all sizes. This will make the clearing away very difficult and time-consuming, and there is no sense even beginning until the snow and ice are gone. As we have done before for the worst of these blockages, we shall have to hire men with wagons from Rawlins to help us, and I cannot afford to pay them to haul away ice and snow that will melt of its own accord soon enough. The road is blocked for eighty to one hundred yards and is piled high for most of that distance. The surface is almost too rough for a man on foot, quite unthinkable for a horse. Because of the rocks and earth, which will freeze into the mass as it sets itself and settles, smoothing a way across the top will not be possible, and as my father learned when he first attempted that solution, such a snowy highway becomes treacherous whenever the temperature rises above freezing, and it is unusable in spring until the snow melts away and the rocks are removed.

The circus folk have recovered from the initial shock of finding themselves marooned here and have settled in, apparently determined to use the time to good advantage. Yesterday Mr. Tatum was everywhere, organizing rehearsals and seeing to the animals, Meanwhile, Joe Kitchen and Monty and Ben Long and I went to explore the edge of the avalanche to see what might be saved. We are all grateful that the loss of life and property was not greater, but what was lost has hurt us sorely: in the missing supply wagons was nearly every bit of the circus's food stores. In two hours of hard digging, we salvaged scarcely two crates

257

of tinned goods and felt lucky to find that much. This morning, Joe and I surveyed the contents of cellar, storeroom, pantry and root cellar, and while there are sufficient goods to feed a large group such as the circus for a few days, enough to sustain the park's year-round inhabitants almost indefinitely, there is not enough of anything (except the good Wind River valley potatoes) to feed all these mouths for the month or two the circus will be forced to remain. Beef is our sole resource. We have already butchered old One-Eye and soon we will have to select other cows from the herd; the steers will go first, of course, but they won't last long. Some of the circus animals need meat and I can no more see them starve than I could let these people go hungry. Naturally Mr. Tatum will compensate me, but money cannot immediately restore good mother cows of the same crossed breed, nor their healthy calves. We will lose a calf for every cow that is killed, and we will feel the loss for some time to come.

Today Mr. Tatum has passed the morning in the saloon at a table near the stove, poring over ledgers and notebooks and spending long intervals staring out into the falling snow, according to Ling. Coffee is one thing not in short supply and she came often to refill his cup. When I passed by just now, on my way to come here, he rose and invited me, with his gracious good manners, to eat supper with him this evening. He suggested we might discuss our shared difficulties and perhaps find solutions to some of them, although what more he thinks we can do except wait for spring, I cannot imagine.

The pipe carriers must be well on their way by now. It may be weeks before we learn the outcome of their journey.

CHAPTER _____
EIGHTEEN

Early in the afternoon the snow stopped, but chill winds kept most of those in the settlement indoors.

Beyond the circus wagons, Hutch and Johnny Smoker and the fat German accordionist pitched hay from a wagon to the circus horses, which had been turned into the fenced pasture with the bulls.

"Good grass you haff here," said the German. He rolled a handful of hay between his gloved fingers and held it to his nose, nodding approvingly. His name was Gunther Waldheim and he was the circus's riding master. His two sons, Johann and Willy, were the star equestrians of the troupe, expert at acrobatics performed on horseback as well as the spectacular leaps to and from the saddle at full speed that were known as *voltige*. They brought Teutonic enthusiasm to their athletic stunts and they enjoyed the respect of Hachaliah Tatum, to whom they left the more stately art of High School, the ultimate form of equine training, designed to demonstrate perfect accord between horse and rider. Johann and Willy's father was known to everyone in the circus as Papa Waldheim. He no longer performed, but the care and training of the horses remained in his hands.

"Good grass," he said again, letting the dried stalks fall. He pitched a huge forkful of hay over the fence, spreading it out with a practiced flip of the fork as the hay fell. His girth was deceiving, for beneath a protective layer of fat his muscles were as hard as ever, and he could still demonstrate any of the horseback stunts to his sons when he thought they were not performing up to his standards.

"If we're gonna keep this many horses in here all the time we ought to build a hay crib in the pasture," Hutch said, looking at Johnny to see what he thought of the idea. Then he remembered that the circus horses would be here for only six or eight weeks, and he was afraid Johnny might think the notion foolish, but Johnny just nodded soberly.

"Mm hmm. Might be handy, just for the bulls."

Hutch hadn't thought that a crib might be useful even after the circus was gone; he was pleased once again with the way Johnny was making himself part of the outfit, now that he too was here for an indefinite stay. The presence of the circus had deprived Hutch of the friendly mealtime company around the kitchen table; everyone ate in the saloon now, filing past long serving tables and sitting wherever they pleased. Julius and Miss Lisa were still taken up with their own thoughts, which had something to do with Sun Horse and General Crook's march up-country, and it all confused Hutch a good deal, because up until now he had thought you just naturally raised a cheer when the soldiers set out to chase Indians. Hutch and Johnny had taken to eating together, and Hutch was grateful for the older boy's company. From the first, Johnny had shown a willingness to help out without any trace of presumption, even though he had been on the Texas cattle trails and obviously knew a lot more about working a cow outfit than Hutch did, and it had occurred to Hutch that he might learn a thing or two from Johnny. He eyed the rope hanging from Johnny's saddle every time he was in the barn, and before long he hoped to get Johnny to teach him how to rope. That was one skill a man ought to know before he set out to work on a bigger place.

"You reckon we'll have to haul more hay to that elephant today?" Hutch asked Johnny now.

Johnny shook his head. "Chatur said one load a day'll do him."

"I never did see the like of how that critter eats hay," Hutch said. They had taken a wagonload of hay to Rama that morning after they were done feeding the cattle, and Chatur had demonstrated a few of Rama's tricks for Johnny and Hutch.

"Come, Rama," the little brown man had said, smiling at the elephant and making a motion with his staff. "Show the *sahibs* how you are saying hello."

The elephant had raised his trunk above his head and sat up on his haunches like a dog.

The wagon was nearly empty now and Papa Waldheim leaned on his pitchfork while Hutch and Johnny cleaned up the last forkfuls.

"Good job, boys. It vill be enough today."

A shot sounded nearby and the three of them turned to see Hachaliah Tatum standing at the end of the twin line of painted wagons, a pistol in his hand. He took aim and fired again, and a tin can flew off the fence railing fifty feet away. Without lowering the nickel-plated Colt he fired three more times and each shot knocked another can from the fence.

"That's good shooting," Johnny observed.

"Oh, he iss good," Papa Waldheim said. "In the circus he performs mit pistol and rifle, shooting glass balls in the air. Here, see him now."

Tatum drew something from his pocket. With the Colt held in his left hand he tossed a small round object high in the air. With no apparent haste he transferred the gun back to his right hand and fired without seeming to take aim. The glass ball vanished in a puff of shards.

"By golly, he can't miss, can he," Hutch exclaimed.

"It iss not the best he does," Papa Waldheim said. "In performance he shoots mit mirrors, over the shoulder. Many tricks, all very good. Like this, when he practices, it iss because he iss thinking. It helps him to concentrate, he says. The better he shoots, the harder he iss thinking."

Tatum had reloaded his pistol. Holding it in his left hand once more he reached in his pocket again and this time he threw three balls in the air with a single toss. He fired once, twice, and a third time, catching the last ball just before it hit the ground.

A shrill whistle sounded from the opposite direction, coming from the barn.

"Uh oh," Hutch said as he turned. Julius was waving to them from the barn door. "He seen us lollygagging around. Now he'll have another job for us quick."

"So, ve face the music together," Papa Waldheim said. "You haff helped me, now I help you."

Hutch picked up the reins and clucked to Zeke, who was hitched to the wagon alone. When they neared the barn they heard laughter from within, and Julius was smiling.

"Hop down, boys," he said. "We've got us a clown show."

"Ach, I forget!" Papa Waldheim exclaimed, putting a hand to his head. "I am supposed to invite you. Amanda asked special for you," he said to Johnny. "Come, come, come. She vill never forgiff me."

He clambered to the ground and ushered Johnny and Hutch quickly into the barn, where they were surprised to find nearly everyone in the settlement gathered to watch an impromptu performance.

The barn had been taken over by acrobats and aerialists the day before, and large steamer trunks containing their costumes and equipment stood open in vacant horse stalls. The hayloft had a square opening in the center, so it could be loaded from a wagon driven in the large double doors. Across this opening a tightrope had been strung, and a trapeze hung from one of the roof beams. At the moment, neither of these was in use. The attention of the audience was directed instead to a single improbable figure in the middle of the floor, a gray-haired man dressed as a parody of a British gentleman. He wore a silk top hat and a morning coat with tails so long they trailed on the ground. His formal trousers were baggy and the soles of his shoes were about to part company with the uppers. He stood motionless, or nearly so, yet he managed to give every appearance of being in the final stages of drunkenness, and his efforts to retain both his dignity and his consciousness provoked almost continuous laughter from the audience. His eyes began to droop, his figure to wilt, and in the nick of time he caught himself and stood bolt upright, looking around quickly to see if he had been observed. He clasped his hands atop his ebony walking stick and assumed a dignified pose, but soon he began to lean to one side, and just when he was about to fall he saved himself by taking a step in that direction.

"Ah. Here you are." Alfred Chalmers appeared beside Johnny and Hutch. "Amanda has been saving the best for last. Come along with me; we have a place for you."

He beckoned them to follow him and led them through the crowd to a place near the front rank, where he seated Johnny on a packing crate beside Lisa Putnam. Chatur shifted sideways where he sat cross-legged on the floor and made room for Hutch, smiling a welcome.

Chalmers cleared his throat loudly and waved to Amanda, who was across the way in one of the stalls, dressed in her colorful costume and wearing her makeup. She nodded, waved to Johnny, then clapped her hands twice to signal the man on the floor.

Without turning he raised a hand to acknowledge the signal. The movement overbalanced him to one side; he lurched in that direction and reeled offstage to a round of applause.

"That gentleman is Samuel Higgins, one of Amanda's partners," Chalmers explained to Johnny in a low voice. "You are about to see both of them, and Amanda as well, in a new piece of work they are performing here for the first time."

Amanda was the first to appear. She carried a parasol and she had removed her red clown's cap. Her long brown hair bounced lightly as she strolled along, twirling the parasol, a young lady out taking the air. Now, from opposite sides of the barn, two other figures entered the stage. One was the elderly English gentleman, quite sober now and moving his walking stick jauntily as he stepped along. The other was a French cavalier, a lithe young man scarcely five feet tall, with black hair, pale skin and bright, flashing eyes. He wore a sword at his waist, a huge-brimmed hat adorned with an ostrich feather, and a heavy cape that threatened to envelop him at every stride.

"The young gentleman is Carlos Moro," Charlmers informed Johnny and Lisa. "He is Spanish and he joined us only a year ago. He is quite marvelous. His first training was as an acrobat, but Sam has taken him under his wing and he and Amanda are teaching him the clown's art. I think you'll agree that he is a good pupil."

Both men spied Amanda at the same moment. They approached her from opposite sides and bowed to her. The Englishman inclined slightly at the waist and tipped his silk hat; the cavalier bent almost double and swept his plumed hat across the ground. As they straightened, each eyed the other suspiciously while he endeavored to engage the young lady's attention. Amanda favored first Sam and then Carlos with a smile, a little flustered by all the attention she was receiving. Carlos took her smile as encouragement; he stepped in front of her, giving Sam a gentle shove to one side, at the same time offering his arm to Amanda. Before she could decide whether or not to accept, Sam recovered his balance and stepped hard into Carlos, throwing the small cavalier to one knee. Utterly ignoring the smaller man, Sam tipped his hat to Amanda once more and offered her his own arm. But already Carlos was on his feet again; he placed one booted foot on Sam's posterior and shoved hard, sending the Englishman sprawling facedown on the ground. Carlos smiled to Amanda and bowed low, but Sam was back quick as a flash and he delivered a stinging blow to Carlos's backside with his walking stick. The young cavalier shot upright, his mouth wide in a silent howl of pain. Recovering himself, he advanced on the Englishman, who raised his walking stick in a stern warning. In an instant the cavalier's rapier was drawn, its blade placed across the tip of the walking stick, and still Carlos advanced, forcing the Englishman back.

Now it was Amanda who pleaded for attention. She moved along with the two men, arms outstretched, silently entreating them to stop before the fighting went further, but neither of the men would take his eyes from the other. She touched Carlos's sword arm, tugging at the sleeve, and he glanced at her. With the small man's attention distracted, Sam knocked the cavalier's hat to the ground with a swipe of his walking stick.

There was no restraining Carlos now. He brushed Amanda aside and advanced on the Englishman. His rapier crossed the walking stick once, twice, and then with a flick of the wrist he sent the stick flying, leaving Sam defenseless. The cavalier silently laughed his triumph as he pranced around the Englishman, flicking at him with the rapier. So great was his joy that he spun in a pirouette, whereupon his cape wrapped itself tightly around him, pinning his sword arm against his side.

Seeing his adversary's predicament, the Englishman drew from his morning coat a three-foot length of flexible lath with a handle at one end. Gleefully he struck the cavalier on the backside with a resounding *thwack* that brought a burst of laughter from the crowd and sent Carlos sprawling on the floor, howling silently in pretended pain. As he struggled to his hands and knees the slap-stick fell again, *thwack*, and sent him head over heels in a somersault. *Thwack*, and another somersault, and by expert timing of both blows and somersaults, Sam appeared to be rolling Carlos around the floor like some ungainly ball, to the great delight of the onlookers.

Amanda, meanwhile, was in despair. On her knees, she begged the two men to stop, but they ignored her. Casting about for some way to get their attention, she spied the ladder leading to the hayloft, and now an idea seized her. She sprang to the ladder and scrambled up to the loft, where she put her hands to her mouth and pretended to cry out to the men below. Sam stopped with slap-stick upraised. Carlos untangled himself from his cape and looked up. Amanda stood at the edge of the loft and silently proclaimed her intention of throwing herself into the abyss if they would not stop fighting.

In an instant the two men were on their knees, their animosity forgotten as they begged her to step back from the edge. She took a step back but held up a warning finger. There must be no more fighting. Her suitors' gestures assured her that all was peace and good will between them, and would be forever more.

She smiled, and began to descend the ladder. Sam's attention was all on Amanda, but Carlos had spied the slap-stick, which the Englishman had cast aside. Moving slowly, the cavalier grasped the wide piece of lath, and he struck the kneeling Englishman suddenly from behind without warning, sending Sam in a tumbling somersault.

But Amanda heard the blow, and in a trice she was atop the ladder again. When Carlos saw what he had done he threw the slap-stick aside and begged her to forgive him, but she ignored her suitors now, apparently lost in a profound sorrow. From the floor of the loft she picked up a violin and a bow, and placing the violin beneath her chin she stepped to the edge of the loft. Without hesitation she took another step—onto the tightrope.

Below her, Sam and Carlos placed their hands to their mouths, not daring to make a sound.

As Amanda moved along the rope with measured steps, she began to play a tune that her audience knew well, the lovely waltz that had moved Johnny Smoker to take Lisa Putnam in his arms and glide around the saloon with her on the night of the circus's arrival in Putnam's Park. But the tune had a different quality now. The notes were played lingeringly, in time with Amanda's steps on the tightrope, and the air became plaintive and sad. The clown seemed to be utterly alone, oblivious to her audience. Everything about her attitude and her movements bespoke solitude and loneliness.

Those assembled below watched her progress in utter silence, captivated by the pathos of the scene.

At the edge of the loft, two cats appeared. They looked down at the audience, then at Amanda. The almost feral barn cats had been very little in evidence since their domain had been invaded by the circus folk, keeping instead to the loft and the shadows and the nighttime hours. Encouraged by the stillness and the music, these two ventured forth now to see what was afoot.

When Amanda reached the far end of the rope she stepped lightly to the boards of the loft and turned, sustaining the last note for a long moment before she dropped the bow to her side.

The audience burst out with applause and cheers, but the clown did not acknowledge them. Her attention was on her suitors, and they too were applauding, pausing now to clap each other on the back and embrace, so great was their relief

263

at seeing her complete her journey safely. Eagerly, they beckoned her to come down.

A rope hung from the post to which the end of the tightrope was tied. Setting her fiddle aside, Amanda grasped the rope with hands and feet and slid gently to the barn floor, where her suitors awaited her. They stepped forward, jostling for position, each wishing to have the privilege of greeting her first, and for a moment it seemed that they might resume their hostilities, but Amanda raised a warning finger. At once the gentleman and the cavalier fell all over themselves to protest their innocence; they embraced, bowed to each other, shook hands, and ended by placing their arms across each other's shoulders as evidence of their comradeship. Satisfied, Amanda offered an arm to each of them, which they readily accepted, and together the three clowns walked off the floor in high good spirits, to the cheers of the onlookers.

"Bravo!" Chalmers exclaimed, getting to his feet. Around him the others rose, and as the jubilant trio returned to bow to their public, the audience accorded them a standing ovation.

The clowns bowed several more times, holding hands, evidently quite pleased by their reception. Finally they left the floor as the audience rose from their places to offer individual congratulations or to return to activities that had been set aside when the performance began, but no one was anxious to leave the barn and the festive air the clowns had created.

Hutch spied the blond head of Maria Abbruzzi in the crowd and he moved in her direction as Johnny and Lisa accompanied Alfred Chalmers to the last horse stall at the rear of the barn, which had been provided with a canvas curtain to serve as a makeshift dressing room. Lydia was among the well-wishers there and she had Amanda wrapped in her arms, clutching the girl to her more than ample bosom.

"Ah, how you make me smile, little one. How you lift my spirits."

"Delightful, simply delightful!" Chatur exclaimed, seizing Amanda's hand when Lydia released her, and wringing it between both of his own. "Quite different, and most delightful!"

"Do you really think so?"

"It seems they found it enjoyable," Sam said, standing close beside her. Like Alfred Chalmers, he spoke with an English accent. Carlos kept to the background, smiling and nodding pleasantly.

Amanda noticed Johnny and Lisa now and she smiled, happy to see them.

"You were wonderful," Lisa said, taking the girl by the hands.

"Did you like it, really?" Amanda's eyes moved to Johnny.

"I'm just sorry I didn't get to see the beginning," he said.

"Oh, you can see those routines any time. We'll do them just for you. It was the new piece I wanted you to see. Sam and Carlos and I worked it up ourselves." Amanda seemed more at ease now, comforted by the praise of her friends and colleagues.

264

"It is quite a novelty, my dear," said another voice. "And quite a surprise to me, as you may imagine."

Hachaliah Tatum stepped through the small crowd around the clowns. Everyone had been so intent on the performance that few had noticed when he entered the barn to join the audience.

Concern replaced Amanda's smile. "But you did like it, though?"

"Since you ask, I think it may stray a bit too close to theatricality, and you know how I feel about that."

"It isn't theatricality!" Amanda's tone was both insistent and pleading. "It's the combination of clowning and pantomime. You've always talked about that and now we've done it. And everyone liked it. I thought you'd be pleased." She turned to Chatur. "You liked it, didn't you, Chatur?"

"Oh, exceedingly, I should say."

"My dear, Chatur is hardly your most exacting critic." Tatum smiled with a trace of condescension.

"Well, Alfred liked it too." She turned to the strongman for support.

"Ah. Well, in fact I did. I found it charming."

"There. You see?" Amanda faced Tatum.

"I must question the ending," he said. "Are we to think the young lady can keep both suitors?"

"Oh, for heaven's sake, Hachaliah, don't be so practical! Now you're looking at it as theater. You're not supposed to see a story. It's only supposed to give you a feeling."

Tatum was still dubious. "Perhaps," he said. "Do you intend to perform it without your cap?"

"Of course. The audience has to see that the clown is a girl."

"You think the public is prepared to accept a female clown?"

Chalmers spoke up, taking Amanda's side. "Ah, I think perhaps they may, Mr. Tatum, especially if this is only revealed near the end of the performance. It makes the scene original in more ways than one, you see. It could be quite a triumph."

Tatum considered this for a moment before he replied, looking at Amanda all the while. "Well, we shall see. But I must insist that before you take the time to rehearse a new work, you consult me first."

"But I wanted to surprise you!" Amanda's eyes glistened with tears.

At once, Tatum was conciliatory. "There now," he said, patting her shoulder. "There is no need to upset yourself. You did surprise me indeed. You go and get washed up now and I will see you after supper. We can talk about it then. All right?"

"All right," she conceded a bit sulkily.

Satisfied, Tatum turned to Lisa. "Miss Putnam. I promised to show you the animals. It is their feeding time soon, if you would care to accompany me?"

265

Lisa hesitated, then nodded her assent, and with a parting smile to Amanda, she left with the circus master.

"Oh, he infuriates me!" Amanda exclaimed when Tatum was gone. She stamped her foot in outrage. "Why can't he just accept something new?" She took Johnny's arm. "You did like it, really?"

Johnny nodded, blushing with pleasure. "I've only seen one clown show before, but I don't guess I'll ever see a better one."

"Don't worry, little one," Lydia soothed. "Hachaliah will come around in time. But you mustn't fight him. Charm him instead."

Lisa gave her hair a few finishing strokes and set the silver-handled brush aside before coiling the brown tresses loosely atop her head and fixing the coils in place with two tortoise-shell combs. She stepped back from her dresser to survey the result. She wore her best winter dress of forest-green wool, finely woven on English looms. The neckline revealed the merest hint of bosom. Around her neck was a single strand of perfectly graduated pearls; it had been a gift from her father to her mother, brought from China by his own hand. On the lobe of each ear was another pearl, set in gold. All in all, Lisa was pleased with the effect. She had bought the dress when she was eighteen, before returning to Putnam's Park from Boston, and it still fit her perfectly.

She turned to the window for a look at the sky before going downstairs. Although the sun had peeked through briefly just before it set, the clouds were solid once more as the last light failed, but they were tinged faintly with pink.

Red sky at night, sailor's delight, her father would say. Although he had rejected the seafaring life, he had retained a sailor's eye for the weather, tempered by years of experience in the western mountains.

Lisa hoped the weather would turn fair soon. The circus teamsters had grown restless in just two days of inactivity. They played cards all day and into the evening, and more than once there had been sharp words at the gaming table. In fair weather perhaps they would find something useful to do out of doors. And in fair weather the pipe carriers could travel more quickly and return sooner.

But under clear skies the cavalry would enjoy the same advantage and would more easily spy the telltale smoke from distant lodge fires.

Lisa drew the curtains shut with a jerk, wishing to shut out the world beyond the park as quickly as she shut out the approaching night. The pipe carriers would find General Crook and Sitting Bull and make a peace at least until summer, and they would come safely back. In the meantime, she was safe in her home with Julius and Hutch and Ling and Harry, and her new friends from the circus, Alfred Chalmers and Lydia and Amanda; a gentleman had asked her to dine and he was waiting for her now.

She glanced again in the looking glass on her dressing table and patted a stray strand of hair into place, wondering if she should have dressed more conservatively. She might feel out of place in the saloon, surrounded by so many roughly dressed men.

The devil take them, she thought, turning for the door. I dressed this way for myself, not for them.

She felt elegant and she intended to enjoy herself. She would make the best of this evening and each day that followed, and if unwanted thoughts returned she would banish them with work. There were fences to mend and calves to be helped into the world. She would have another look at the heifers in the lot before going to bed. Tonight they were her responsibility.

"Ah, Miss Putnam." Tatum rose as Lisa entered the saloon. He was dressed as he had been for the celebration on the first night, in tailored trousers and frock coat, polished boots, brocade waistcoat and starched collar. He held out a hand and she hesitated for a moment before realizing what he intended, but she recovered in time and curtsied as he raised her hand to his lips without touching them to her skin. A gentleman did not actually kiss the hand of a young unmarried lady.

"You are the picture of elegance," Tatum said, and Lisa felt her face grow warm. She had found that she enjoyed Hachaliah Tatum's company. He was always the proper gentleman, and although she thought he had been a bit too quick to criticize Amanda that afternoon, he had been very pleasant as he showed Lisa the animals in their barred cages; he knew the needs and moods of each one and his genuine concern for their welfare had impressed her. He seemed to regard them as his children.

He offered her his arm now and to her surprise he led her out of the saloon and down the hallway to the library, where a greater surprise awaited her. A small table had been set before the fire. Candlelight glinted off polished silverware that gleamed against freshly ironed napery. In the center of the table was a small bouquet of Ling's dried flowers and leaves. When Lisa found her voice she said, "Why, Mr. Tatum. You take my breath away. I hadn't expected a formal dinner."

"Quite informal, I assure you. I hope you like oysters. I'm only sorry that they aren't fresh, but we must make do with tinned." There was a *pop* as the cork flew from a bottle of champagne. He deftly allowed the overflowing bubbles to fall into a waiting glass.

"Oysters and champagne? I am overwhelmed."

"Please, sit down." He held her chair and seated her at the table. At the center of each place setting was a small dish of oysters in a reddish sauce.

He seated himself and raised his glass. "I hope you won't mind if I drink to an early and warm spring."

She laughed. "Not at all." They touched glasses and sipped. "I feel utterly spoiled. Wherever did you find champagne?"

"In my private stores. I felt under the circumstances there was no point in hoarding it. Please, try an oyster. The sauce is horseradish and tomato." He said *tomahto* in the New England manner.

As a child, Lisa had never cared for the slippery texture of oysters, but the sauce was pleasantly tangy and the sheer romance of oysters and champagne was more than enough to make up for the strange taste.

"We should really have a squeeze of lemon to make it perfect," Tatum said. He drew a gold watch from his waistcoat and opened the case. "We have a few moments before the main course arrives. I instructed Joe to begin at seven o'clock sharp. Your Chinawoman helped him prepare the meal. I am afraid I took some liberties with your household."

"You must have a way with Ling," Lisa said. "You have charmed her into bringing out the very best silver and linen. I haven't seen these things since my mother died."

"I told her it was a special occasion. And I hope you won't mind, but I have changed my mind about one thing. As I told you, I thought you and I might dine together in order that we could discuss matters of our mutual concern—as the proprietor of Tatum's Combined Shows and proprietress of Putnam's Park, if you see my point. But then it occurred to me that what we both need is precisely the opposite: to forget our concerns for a time and enjoy ourselves. And so I propose that we should do just that, although perhaps over coffee I might touch on a few points of mutual interest, if you do not object."

"Not at all."

"More champagne?"

Lisa was surprised to discover that her glass was nearly empty. "Thank you," she said.

"Before we turn to other things, I do have one additional favor to ask," he said as he poured. "You have already done so much for us, I'm glad that what I ask will be only a small imposition, or so I hope. When the weather improves, I trust you would have no objection if we erect our tent? The acts must be rehearsed in a ring to stay in top form, particularly the riding and animal acts. The performers would be grateful for the shelter."

"By all means," Lisa said at once. "Put it up wherever you can find suitable ground. That's no imposition at all." She smiled. "I must tell you I admire the way you make the best of things. You seem to turn disadvantage to advantage." She ate another oyster and sipped her champagne.

"The truth is, this delay will hurt us," Tatum said, "but the damage will not be irreparable. We will surely give up the journey to Montana, and our stay by the Salt Lake will be shortened. The one thing we cannot delay is our arrival in San Francisco." He was silent for a moment. "A month or more before we can expect warmer weather, you said?"

"I'm afraid there is no way to know. It could come tomorrow or not until May."

"Well, there is nothing to do but wait."

Yes, Lisa thought, we are all waiting. You for the arrival of spring, while Sun Horse and I await the return of the pipe carriers to learn if there will be peace or war. For the time being our fates are out of our hands.

She did not like the helpless feeling this realization aroused in her.

"Forgive me," Tatum said, seeing her troubled expression. "I hadn't meant to bother you with my concerns. Ah, here is Joseph."

Tatum beamed as Joe Kitchen entered the library carrying three serving dishes on a tray. He was followed by Ling, and together they astonished Lisa by serving the meal impeccably, each dish presented in turn, first to Lisa and then to Tatum. The main dish was Ling's rabbit fricassee, which Lisa knew well, but she smelled new spices and a hint of wine in the sauce, and she gained a new respect for Joe. Anyone who could convince Ling to alter her recipes was persuasive indeed. Baked potatoes accompanied the fricassee, with thick cream that had just begun to sour, and what must surely have been the last portions of canned asparagus in Putnam's Park.

Joe winked to Lisa as he and Ling withdrew, as silently as they had come.

"I hope you like Hock," Tatum said, magically producing a second bottle of wine with the cork already drawn but reinserted in the neck. He poured the still wine in the second glass that stood beside the champagne glass at each place setting, and as he poured he regarded Lisa so intently that she dropped her gaze and busied herself with tasting the food.

"Forgive me, Miss Putnam. I didn't mean to stare. But you see, as I suspected, you enjoy the finer things in life. I don't mean to offend you by being too personal, but I can't imagine what it would be like to live here all the time, as you do. You must find it... well, a bit removed? You must long for news of the outside world."

"Sometimes," she acknowledged. "But on the whole I am accustomed to it. And we are not as cut off as you might think. We do manage to keep abreast of the nation and its doings. There is the occasional traveler, except in winter, and we get newspapers and magazines by mail. Of course, our mail is irregular, but that is actually a blessing. Once we hear of them, things of no more than passing importance have come and gone, while significant events are reduced to the essence and we can see them in perspective. For example, I gather that President Grant is beset almost daily by new scandals and accusations, but from here I see his Administration not so much as a den of thieves but more as the imperfect work of a good man who failed, perhaps because he was not suited to the task. With apologies to General Washington, there is no reason that good generals should make good Presidents."

She sipped the wine and remembered one of her Boston suitors who had told her of a voyage down the Rhine from the wine-making country. He was the heir of a banking family and he had promised to take her there.

"A point well taken," Tatum was saying. "I am surprised that you take such an interest in political matters."

"Women have the vote in this territory, Mr. Tatum. It is our duty to stay informed. But I must admit that I have only voted twice. Election day is no time to be leaving Putnam's Park for a long journey. Winter comes early here."

"And if you could vote in the national elections, do you believe the course of the nation would benefit?"

"Perhaps, but I doubt it." Lisa smiled. "I believe women are no wiser in their judgments, as a group, than you men."

"*Touché.*" Tatum laughed politely and refilled her glass.

"Which is not to say that we shouldn't have the vote all the same," Lisa hastened to add. "We have as much right to express our judgments, however mistaken they may be, as men do."

"You may be right," Tatum conceded, although he didn't sound convinced. "But since you have brought up the subject of our national government, let me tell you of an experience I had not long ago. You may find it interesting. I was in New York City, and whom should I chance to encounter at an elegant soirée than General Custer himself. He was quite the catch for the prominent hostesses this season. At any rate, I had the chance to speak with him briefly and I found him most forceful. You may not know that there is talk he may be nominated by the Democrats." Lisa made no immediate reply and he misjudged her silence. "Here I am talking politics and your plate is almost empty. Let me get you something more."

He started to rise, but Lisa was out of her chair in an instant. "I'll get it," she said, and he sat back, more at ease being waited upon than doing the serving himself.

"I told Joseph that we would serve ourselves once each course was delivered. They won't disturb us again until dessert."

Lisa served him and then herself, glad of a chance to marshal her thoughts on a subject about which she felt very strongly.

"I believe General Custer to be ambitious, and therefore dangerous," she said as she resumed her seat, taking Tatum off guard. "To give him his due, I believe he is honest. Like many others he has spoken out to condemn the corruption and mismanagement that plagues Indian affairs. But he is a military man; when he has met the Indians on the battlefield he has dealt with them very harshly, and not always with good reason. Like most people, where elections are concerned I am afraid I would decide the contest on matters of direct interest to me, and there are other men I would prefer to see in charge of Indian affairs. Even last autumn I read rumors that Senator Schurz might propose Governor Hayes, of Ohio, at the convention. I know little of Governor Hayes, but I have read a good deal about Senator Schurz. He is well disposed towards the Indians, and if he were part of a new Administration, I believe their affairs might be better handled."

"You continue to surprise me," Tatum said, and meant it. "You are not only well informed, but astute. I must admit I know little of the Indian problem. All that is clear to me is that they must surely give way so these vast lands can be used to their best advantage." He left her dismissal of General Custer unchallenged. The last thing he wanted was an open disagreement with her. He had planned this meal down to the last detail for the express purpose of putting himself in her good graces.

"Oh, but they do use these lands, Mr. Tatum," Lisa said. "From this somewhat barren region, the Indians gain everything necessary for life."

"Nevertheless, they are few while we are many, and we cannot let a handful of primitives stand in the way of a great civilization."

"Such is the common wisdom," Lisa acknowledged, and Tatum heard the disapproval in her voice.

"You don't agree?"

She thought for a moment, and then said, "If we are a great people, surely one of the signs of our greatness is the principle we have enshrined in our government and laws, the idea that each man will decide for himself his own destiny. The Sioux are not a people of written laws, but they too hold nothing in higher regard than a man's right to choose for himself in all matters. That belief is sacred to them, in the sense that it must not be infringed. Yet now they are moved about and their lives utterly changed by powers they do not recognize as having any hold over them. We fought a revolution to rid ourselves of just such oppression. Is it any wonder that they fight us? And can we call ourselves truly great as long as we deny free choice to a people who were here long before we came? The Sioux lived on this land, much as they do now, while your forefathers and mine were burning witches and torturing heretics."

Tatum brightened. "You have put your foot in the quicksand, Miss Putnam. They must give way to us precisely because we have advanced ourselves while they have not. You don't deny that the Indians still practice torture? The tales are too well known."

"Yes, they torture, but to test physical courage, not to punish wrong beliefs. All torture is evil, but is it not most evil when the body is used merely as an instrument to torture the mind?"

Tatum sipped his wine. "It would seem we have entered the realm of metaphysics. Not at all what I expected when I asked you to dine."

"I'm sorry if I disappoint you."

"Not at all," he said quickly. "I could ask for no more stimulating company. Please don't misunderstand me. But frankly, I don't feel qualified to judge which form of torture is the greatest sin. In any event, we have left torture behind us, have we not? The Christian peoples?"

"Not entirely," Lisa replied. "I could tell you of some evils committed against the Indians in the name of righteous Christianity that would rival anything permitted by the Inquisition. But that would hardly be fit conversation for such an excellent supper, or for such gracious company. Forgive me, I forgot my manners. I didn't mean to be argumentative."

"Please, no apology is called for. I have heard others voice support for the Indian, but never with such passion. Your view is refreshingly unsentimental.

271

Many in the East still proclaim the Indian to be the 'Noble Savage.'"

"They are neither noble savages nor the savage beasts that many others describe," Lisa said softly, inwardly scolding herself for forcing her views on a man who could scarcely share her concerns. Tatum was her host at this supper and she resolved to bring the subject to a close. "The truth lies somewhere in between. At bottom they are men and women with many of the same feelings we have about home and family, yet they lead a very different life, one that has given them a perspective quite different from our own."

The door opened and Ling Wo put her head in the room. "You ready for dessert now?"

"Yes, Ling, come in." Tatum welcomed the interruption. The arrival of dessert gave him an opportunity to collect himself and prepare for the negotiation he would instigate once the meal was done.

Ling cleared the table and served a steaming peach cobbler, using Lisa's mahogany secretary as a sideboard. The cobbler had a crust of crumbs and butter and brown sugar, and the tinned peaches had been enlivened by a dash of brandy, also from Tatum's private stores. Ling set a small coffeepot by Lisa's right hand, and a pitcher of thick cream for the cobbler, the coffee, or both.

"Well, this smells marvelous," Tatum said. "Thank you, Ling."

Ling gave a small bow, smiling, and left them alone.

"Oh, it *is* marvelous," Lisa exclaimed, tasting the cobbler. Her expression revealed her pleasure, and all her seriousness of a moment before had evaporated.

Tatum was glad that he had kept his own opinion of the Indians to himself, and pleased that Lisa had been the one to apologize. It would put her a little further in his debt and he would need every advantage he could muster if he were to emerge from Putnam's Park unscathed when spring finally came.

There must be something more he could do! He could not simply wait here for a fickle Nature to release him. He must act! But for two days he had examined his predicament from every side and he could find no escape.

The effect of being marooned here was potentially far more serious than he had admitted to Lisa Putnam. True, if the circus could be on its way by the start of May there might be time to play an abbreviated engagement at Salt Lake City, but the shows in Carson City and Virginia City and Reno would have to be canceled along with the Montana tour, and Tatum had been counting on those receipts to fund his summer in San Francisco. Colonel Hyde, his sole investor on the west coast, had insisted that they should share the expense of erecting the building where Tatum's Combined Shows would perform throughout the summer months. There could be no thought of performing in the tent all that time. A permanent building offered better shelter from the cold summer fogs, less chance of fire, better lighting, and the necessary supports for the full array of aerial acrobatics that the show offered since Tatum had bid successfully for the services of the Abbruzzi family. Those

272

services had not come cheaply, and Tatum's future depended on a successful summer engagement. It had taken his last available dollar to finance this tour; if the tour failed, hope would be lost for a triumphant return to the East and the engagements in New York, Philadelphia and Boston that would elevate Tatum's Combined Shows to the top rank in American showmanship, above Bailey, even above the Barnum & Coup spectacle that was attracting so much attention.

Tatum found the recent success of Phineas Taylor Barnum particularly galling. Barnum had built his reputation by exhibiting freaks and human oddities, some of them real and some the grossest frauds, which Barnum had readily admitted after the fact. "The public likes to be fooled," he had said, while counting his ample receipts. Only lately had Barnum allied himself with W. C. Coup and entered the business of the traveling circus. Tatum considered Barnum a Johnny-come-lately, and thought his already considerable success unmerited. But Barnum's name attracted crowds, and he had even experimented briefly with two rings exhibiting different acts at the same time. Happily, he had reverted to a single ring, but rumors continued that he was seeking new ways to expand the size of his show and Tatum knew he must make his move now, while the gap between himself and Barnum might be closed by a single brilliant stroke such as the one he had planned.

But now everything he had planned was imperiled, put at risk by a shot fired at the wrong moment and a hundred tons of snow and rock. He had spent the morning going over his books and he had reached an inescapable conclusion: the cost of remaining here even for a single month would consume the lion's share of his remaining cash and he would be unable to meet his payroll. Already, a few of the drivers had approached him, saying they were thinking of riding out of the valley on horseback and asking to be paid. He had put a quick stop to that kind of talk. Wary of losing more drivers along the way, as had happened in the Black Hills, he had hired the replacement teamsters for a flat wage to be paid upon reaching Salt Lake City, not before, no matter how long the journey took. This morning he had reiterated that condition in no uncertain terms and the drivers had withdrawn to the card table, where they muttered among themselves and cast dark looks in the circus master's direction. If they caused trouble he would have to handle it himself; it would be weeks before Kinnean's wrist regained its strength. And all the time the circus remained in Putnam's Park the teamsters would be idle while Tatum was obliged to pay Lisa Putnam for their board; when he reached the Salt Lake at last, he would be unable to pay them, and when he tried to put them off with promises to pay them out of his first receipts, they would complain loudly. Word that Tatum's Combined Shows was in financial straits would spread, and Colonel Hyde might well back out of the summer arrangement even if Tatum managed to find his share of the funds. But if some way could be found to pay off the teamsters, a highly successful engagement in Salt Lake City could provide just enough capital to meet Colonel Hyde's requirements and assure the success of the San Francisco engagement.

The only possible solution was somehow to reduce the cost of the enforced stay in Putnam's Park. The extravagance of the private dinner he had lavished on his hostess, although it had required no outlay of hard cash except for a gold eagle to the Chinawoman for bringing out the linen and silver, was intended to remove from Lisa Putnam's mind any suspicion that he might fear the expense. He intended to take her entirely unaware, hoping to obtain a reduced rate for boarding his men by offering in return something less vital than money, but so far he had been unable to imagine what he might offer, or what the ranch might need. As he searched for the answer he had grown increasingly frustrated, feeling himself thwarted by forces that were alien to him, trapped in a frozen cul-de-sac where the devices he was accustomed to use in civilized surroundings were useless. Years of experience in the highly competitive world of traveling entertainments had made him adept at bending others to his will, but what use were his persuasive powers against an avalanche? Such a phenomenon confounded him.

"You have hardly touched your dessert," Lisa said, and he saw that hers was half gone.

"I beg your pardon. I'm afraid I was lost in my thoughts."

He took a bite of the cobbler. The crust was crisp and the peaches sweet, but he was unable to enjoy it.

"Will you have coffee now?" Lisa reached for the pot.

"Thank you."

"I hope you'll give Amanda a chance to perform the new act," she said as she poured. "I don't mean to interfere in your business, but it certainly seemed to please everyone today."

"Of course she shall have a chance," Tatum said pleasantly. "She took me by surprise, that's all. We ordinarily work out new scenes together. Sometimes old Sam helps as well. He is from the old school and he knows a good deal. In England today, the circus has become corrupted by theatrical influence. Some presentations are no more than plays on horseback. The scenes given in Astley's palace would make him turn in his grave. He was the first to present equestrian exhibitions in a ring, you know, and horsemanship has always been at the heart of the entertainments we call 'circus' now. The juggling and acrobatics and clowning come from medieval fairs, of course. But the theater is a separate art and I have endeavored to keep its influence out of my shows. I have a very particular sort of clowning in mind for Amanda, and I don't want her to take any wrong steps." He leaned forward, warming to his topic. "You see, there have always been two quite different styles of clowning since the earliest times. The Greeks and the Romans had buffoons and medieval kings had their jesters, and there is much buffoonery in clowning still, what with the mock fights and the swordplay and all the rough-and-tumble. And many of these clowns have talked. Grimaldi talked and Dan Rice does little else. But I have always believed there could be a combining of the comic aspects with some higher elements of pure pantomime, more in the spirit of the *commedia dell'arte*. There is room for artistry, and pathos too, don't you think? After all, tears and laughter are not so very far apart."

"Certainly if I had not believed so before, I would have after seeing Amanda today. She made us all aware of that."

"Yes. Yes, she did." Tatum knew he had been foolish to challenge Amanda without thinking, foolish to reveal his wounded pride to her. He had suspected that the secretiveness with which she and Sam and Carlos had developed the new work had been deliberately intended to provoke him. And her manner had provoked him as well. So often she seemed to be trying to break away. In makeup, she could be almost defiant. But it was evening now and the makeup would be gone. He would praise the new work and tell her she might include it in the summer performances, and she would be mollified. He would suggest some small changes, of course. It wouldn't do to let her know that she was on the verge of surpassing him with her own inventiveness. If she suspected that, she would soon see that he had no more to teach her, and his hold over her would diminish.

"You should be proud of her achievements," Lisa said. She leaned back in her chair with the coffee cup in her hand. "Life must have been very hard for her after she lost her parents. You have brought her a long way."

Tatum nodded. "This show is her family now, as it was even before her loss. The Spencers were English. They came to this country before Amanda was born, together with Sam Higgins. They knew Alfred Chalmers as well, although he came over later on. Sam and the Spencers came to work for a circus owned by a family named Cooper, where I was assistant manager. My wife was a Cooper, you see. When she died, I took over things as best I could. Amanda and I were both orphaned by that fire, in a manner of speaking, and since then I have looked to her artistic and personal welfare as best I could." His expression was somber as he recalled his loss.

Hachaliah Tatum's parents had been farmers on land adjoining the Cooper property in Dutchess County, New York. Since before the Revolution, Yankee farmers and innkeepers had occasionally exhibited tropical animals to the curious, but the Coopers were among the first to combine their menagerie with circus and equestrian acts and tour the countryside. The family was large and well-to-do, and as a boy, Tatum had worked for them in the stables where their horses and the other animals were kept. There he had met Helena Cooper; she was his own age, and captivatingly pretty. In time, when he had risen to a position of sufficient responsibility to merit her attention, he had courted her and, to his surprise, won her. Like Hachaliah himself, she was willful, ambitious, an excellent rider and a crack shot. Together they performed feats of marksmanship for an admiring public, and Helena took part in the trick-riding act as well, while Hachaliah honed his skill at dressage, of which High School was only a part, and assisted Helena's brother Aaron in managing the show. From the start there had been friction between them. Aaron had a taste for the sensational, and like Barnum he would present anything that might attract the public, no matter how bizarre; Hachaliah favored a circus of almost classical simplicity, with each act presented in its purest form and no oddities or freaks, no theatricalities. The arguments between them had become more and more heated, and the last months of Helena's life were fraught with contention as she tried to keep the peace between her brother and the husband she loved. But the conflagration that consumed the Coopers' permanent exhibition palace in New York City put an end to the arguments. While the ashes were still warm, Aaron had confronted a heartbroken Hachaliah and informed him that the show would be rebuilt according to his dictates, with or without Hachaliah's help; as Aaron's brother-in-law, Hachaliah had received a share in the profits, but that too would come to an end. Though not intended to do anything of the sort, these pronouncements speeded Hachaliah's recovery. His anger at Aaron's cruelty gave him strength and determination, and with Amanda Spencer, Samuel Higgins and a handful of other performers who shared Tatum's views, he had left Aaron Cooper to his own devices and founded Tatum's Combined Shows. Under his careful management the show survived its rocky beginnings and in time it prospered. He had increased its size gradually, and now, as he prepared to stake his claim among the foremost circuses in the land, he was also preparing to take a measure of revenge on his former brother-in-law. Aaron Cooper had recently joined forces with James A. Bailey and they had announced a tour of the Pacific coast to coincide with the nation's centennial. Tatum had kept his own plans quiet, but in California, Colonel Hyde would launch the planned publicity soon. Tatum would beat Cooper and Bailey to the Golden Gate and steal their thunder, but not unless he came to terms with Lisa Putnam now. And yet other than revealing his predicament and throwing himself on her mercy, he could think of no way to broach the subject. He felt himself grasping at straws.

"I tell you what we shall do," he said, pretending a beneficence he did not feel. "Before we leave here we shall give you a proper performance. You shall see Tatum's Combined Shows in all its glory."

"Hmm?" Lisa was taken by surprise. "A performance? What a wonderful idea! I'm afraid I was quite lost in my thoughts. I was trying to remember when the last slide occurred. It has been some years since we had one, and there have been none worse that I know of. It will be quite a job to clear the road."

Tatum's eyebrows shot up. "You have had these before?"

"Of course. And mudslides at other times of year."

Tatum's heart was pounding. "And so you must clear them away?"

Lisa nodded. "Yes. We hire men and wagons from Rawlins to help us, but there's no use bothering until the snow melts."

Tatum shook his head. "What a fool I've been."

"I don't understand," Lisa said, but Tatum rushed on, suddenly leaning across the table toward her.

"You would have to pay to clear the road eventually?"

"Yes," she admitted, taken aback by his intensity.

"And if you could avoid that expense, if you did not actually have to pay money to have it done, that would be greatly to your benefit?"

"Yes, but—"

"Could it be dug away now?" he demanded. "Without waiting for spring?"

"Why, yes, but the work is difficult. The weight of the mass compresses it nearly to the consistency of ice, and it must be blasted apart. It's much easier to wait for the snow and ice to melt. Then all you have to do is haul away the rocks and restore the roadbed if it has been damaged. If I hired men to dig it away now, it would cost more than twice as much."

Tatum was triumphant. "I wasn't thinking of your men, Miss Putnam, but mine. It would cost you no money at all."

"Oh!" Lisa put a hand to her mouth and her eyes grew wide. "I am so accustomed to dealing with this sort of thing in one manner, I hadn't thought that there might be another way!"

Tatum spoke rapidly now. "The cabins in which my people live can be removed from the wagon beds, so you see we have as many flatbed wagons as we need. And more than enough draft animals. But you said the ice must be blasted away?"

"There is plenty of powder! My father always kept some for clearing rocks and stumps, and for emergencies." She did not add that he had also traded powder to Sun Horse's men for hunting—but never enough for war—despite the ban on trading with the Powder River bands.

Tatum thought hard for a moment, then rose and went to the secretary, where Ling had left a decanter of brandy and two small glasses. He poured and returned to the table with the glasses, setting one in front of Lisa as he resumed his seat.

"If my men and I clear that road now, would you contribute shovels and picks and blasting powder?"

"Of course!" Lisa exclaimed. "That's nothing to ask."

He held up a cautionary hand. "I haven't asked everything yet. Would you board my people while we are here in exchange for this labor?"

"It might take you as long to dig through it as it would for it to melt of its own accord."

Tatum replied without hesitation. "Then the digging will go faster as the melting progresses and we shall be away from here all the sooner, and you will have a clear road that cost you nothing but the food to feed us. The main thing is that we will be doing something for ourselves instead of awaiting the whims of the Almighty!"

He could hardly contain himself. He had been the perfect fool not to see that the answer to his problem was close at hand all the time. The avalanche was something so foreign to his experience that it had not occurred to him that other men routinely confronted such obstacles and found ways to remove them. Once Lisa Putnam made him aware of that simple fact, he had seen at once that he could not only put his teamsters to work and save the expense of boarding them, but he might reach Salt Lake City on the date originally planned. The Nevada engagements might be kept after all and the San Francisco plans were out of danger! If she would agree.

"Is it a bargain?" he asked, struggling to remain calm.

Lisa hesitated briefly, making quick calculations in her mind. She could not afford to feed all the circus people for nothing, and her father had taught her never to yield to the first demand in any bargaining. What should her counter-offer be? Until now only Amanda and Tatum and Joe Kitchen had slept in the house, while the performers slept in their wagons and the teamsters in tents. Others might prefer to sleep indoors for such a prolonged stay. She could afford to make them comfortable and she didn't care if the teamsters slept in the hallways now that they would be kept out of mischief by hard work.

"I will board any man that works on the road and I will give you the rooms in Putnam House as well. You will pay me only to board your performing artists."

"Done!" Tatum said at once, and he raised his glass. "To the success of our endeavors."

Lisa surprised him by tossing down her brandy in a single swallow. The fire was warm on her back and the brandy fueled the rising excitement within her. The true cost of feeding the teamsters might in the end equal or surpass that of paying Rawlins men to clear the road in the spring, but the sooner the circus was gone the fewer of her cows she would have to slaughter, and the value of the lesson she had learned this evening from Hachaliah Tatum would more than cover any small deficit that remained. He had taken charge of his own fate and she must do the same. Like him, she could not be content to await the outcome of events beyond her control. The pipe carriers might succeed and they might not; they might come back safely and they might not. She could no more decree their success and safe return than she could single-handedly change the government in Washington City and establish a more just Indian policy, but by following Tatum's example and acting instead of waiting, she could control her own destiny, and with luck she might help to ensure that Sun Horse, at least, could remain free even if the pipe carriers failed.

LISA PUTNAM'S JOURNAL

Tuesday, March 7th. 5:10 a.m.

Last night I could scarcely get to sleep and this morning I awoke early and came here to sit by the fire and think, and even as I was making the fire I found the answer. I have found a way to help Sun Horse! Whether he will accept my help

I cannot say, but I know now that I must tender the offer. I am impatient for dawn to come and for breakfast to be done so I can talk to Julius and seek his approval. I will ask Harry and Hutch to feed the cows this morning, and if Julius agrees to what I intend, we can be on our way up to Sun Horse's village by mid-morning. But until the house is awake, I shall have to bide my time here. How slowly the clock on the mantel seems to tick today!

As I often do when I am excited, I am getting ahead of myself. As I said yesterday, Mr. Tatum invited me to take supper with him. We had a charming meal in the library, all arranged by Mr. Tatum in collusion with Ling and Joe Kitchen. We ate very well and spoke of many things, and then in the time it took us to drink our coffee, Mr. Tatum found the solution to his own dilemma. He and his men will dig away the avalanche! It is the first such attempt since my father's abortive effort years ago. I took heart from Mr. Tatum's determination and resolved once more to attempt some action on behalf of Sun Horse, so he need not merely wait for his emissaries to General Crook to return, but as before, I could not see the way. My father often cautioned me not to worry a problem the way a dog worries a bone. "Set your cares aside," he said, "and look at them again in the morning," and I tried to do just that, with only moderate success.

After supper, Mr. Tatum and I adjourned to the saloon, where he began at once to issue instructions for the digging efforts, which will begin today. I will say more about these as time goes on, when we have had a chance to gauge their chance of success.

There was music in the saloon, not the lively band tunes of three nights before, but the enchanting sound of two violins played together by two magicians, Julius and Amanda. I joined the small group gathered around the stove to hear them, hoping the music would help me to set my cares aside. Johnny Smoker was there, and Hutch. He seems to have caught the eye of a young girl named Maria, and he sat by her for a time. When she was called away by her rather stern papa, I asked Hutch why he didn't get his banjo, but he said he had "played myself out" the other night and wished only to listen to the violinists. Julius and Amanda were playing for each other, all but oblivious to their audience. One would stop in the midst of a song and ask, "Say, do you know this one?" and begin to play a new strain, and whenever they found one they both knew it was something to hear. When Mr. Tatum was done with the wagon drivers he joined us, and before long he took Amanda away. He was very gentle with her and said in front of everyone that he had enjoyed the new work she performed that afternoon. He promised it would have a place in the show this summer, and this made her happy. They spoke for a time at a secluded table while Mr. Tatum had a nightcap, and soon they both went to their rooms.

Once Amanda set her fiddle aside, Hutch did finally get his banjo and he and Julius played a while longer. Then, in between songs, quite out of the blue, he said to Julius, "There's something I've been meaning to ask about old Sun Horse. If he's a good Injun, like you say, shouldn't he be on some reservation?"

Well, Julius thought for a time and then he gave as good an answer as any I could have come up with. "Say a man came to your pa's farm and told him he'd have to sell his house and land. Say he told your pa he couldn't settle where he pleased, but only where this feller said he could. How would you feel about that?" "Well, I wouldn't like it any too well," Hutch replied. "Anyone tried anything like that with my pa, he'd have himself a fight on his hands, I'll tell you what." Well, the minute the words were out of his mouth he saw what Julius was getting at.

Julius went on to tell him about my father's long friendship with Sun Horse and how Sun Horse has always done his best to keep the peace with the whites and sees no reason he should be moved against his will, but what struck me most of all about this exchange was a sudden awareness that until that moment young Hutch had taken the recurrent warfare between ourselves and the Indians as something completely normal, part of the natural state of things, and what is worse, he saw no end for the Indians other than to be shoved aside and left on whatever bits of land we choose to give them. I found myself wondering, if that is the prevalent attitude across the land, how can there ever be peace? This question reminded me of more basic questions, such as: Could all the tragic fighting between ourselves and the Indians have been avoided in the first place? Was it inevitable that the differences between our way of life and theirs should lead to a generation of hostilities and deplorable barbarities on both sides? My father believed that the answers were, first, no, and second, yes. He placed most of the blame on a single characteristic of the white race. Thanks in large part to his teaching, I understand certain things, such as the force of our numbers and the resulting inevitability of our movement to settle this great continent, that are not plain to the Indians. But there is much about the aborigines that is not plain to us, and as one who has had a chance to know them over a period of years, I can only say that while I have always seen in the Indians a desire to learn about the whites, I see in the whites no such curiosity, beyond a passing interest in the savage and bizarre. It is this unwillingness, and the ignorance that has therefore persisted among the majority of settlers in the mountain region, that my father believed was at fault for the conflicts that have brought so much harm to both races.

Still, there is hope. A fair-minded man like General Crook, one who knows the futility of war, may yet make a just settlement. The pipe carriers may increase the chance that for the Sioux the end will be arrived at through discussion rather than fighting, and the white race may redeem some of its failings by making a peace that sets aside for the Sioux some of their ancestral lands. They too deserve a home they love and an active life suited to that place and to their perceptions of the world around them. But last evening's talk reminded me that I cannot trust the wisdom of white men to guarantee Sun Horse the best hope for the future, and this strengthened my resolve to help him. Throughout a restless night I sought the means, and this morning I saw that I hold them in my hands. It was the talk of blasting powder during supper, and

280

the thought of the cows we will save if the circus leaves soon, that gave me the idea. I realize that nothing I can do will assure Sun Horse's survival, but I may increase his chances of saving himself, if he will let me. Should the pipe carriers' mission fail, I am still convinced that the best hope for Sun Horse (and for all the free-roaming bands) lies in remaining free for at least another year, until cooler heads in Washington may prevail. But to stay free, he must be able to move beyond the soldiers' reach. If he accepts my offer and if the gift becomes known, the government will take a harsh view of my action and the title to Putnam's Park may be in jeopardy. Yet I pray that this one time Sun Horse will accept a gift, for the future of his people.

CHAPTER
NINETEEN

The clouds broke and drifted off to the southeast as the morning progressed and by the time the riders approached the Lakota village the sun stood high above the mountains. They entered the camp two by two, Lisa and Julius in the lead and Johnny and Amanda following close behind. Before leaving the settlement, Lisa had impulsively given Amanda a buffalo coat that had belonged to Eleanor Putnam; the coat fit Amanda perfectly, completely hiding her clown costume, but her red cap and white makeup were plain for all to see and the Indians gathered quickly around the riders; some had heard of the clown girl from those who had been in the white settlement when the circus arrived and they were eager to see her for themselves.

Lisa led the way straight across the camp, making no formal passage around the circle this time. She wanted to give the impression that this was a casual visit undertaken on the spur of the moment. Like the visit, the gift would be casually offered, with no formality, and presented in that way it might be easier for Sun Horse to accept. She had asked Johnny and Amanda to come along because she wanted to miss no opportunity to raise Sun Horse's spirits and increase the chance that he would take what she offered; on the day the circus arrived she had noticed that the old man seemed to be both amused and fascinated by Amanda, and she knew he would be glad to see his white grandson again. The two young people had jumped at the chance to accompany Lisa and Julius, and Amanda had accepted without question Lisa's suggestion that she might put on her costume and prepare a few tricks to amuse the Indians.

Even before she entered the camp, Lisa had noticed the smell of cooking meat and she saw now that iron pots hung from their three-legged supports in front of several lodges. The Sioux preferred to do most of their cooking outside on all but the worst days. In front of Sun Horse's lodge, Elk Calf, Sings His Daughter and Bat's wife, Penelope, were all cutting meat for the stewpot that hung over the fire there. A small rib roast was already propped up near the flames to cook. The women smiled as Lisa dismounted.

She greeted Elk Calf Woman with deference and said, "We have brought the white girl to visit the camp of Sun Horse. Is your husband within?"

"He is there," Elk Calf said, pointing. "He will be glad to see his white friends."

Lisa looked in the direction the old woman pointed and she saw two figures not far beyond the camp circle, walking slowly side by side as if they were deep in conversation. But they had seen the riders arrive. An arm was raised in greeting and Lisa waved in reply. The figures quickened their pace somewhat, one holding the arm of the other.

A burst of laughter close at hand caused Lisa to turn. Julius, Amanda and Johnny had dismounted and Amanda had removed her buffalo coat. The clown was silently scolding her horse, but Lisa couldn't imagine why this amused the Lakotas so.

Amanda turned and bowed slightly to the Indians and at once the horse pushed her with his head, nearly knocking her to the ground and bringing renewed laughter from the onlookers. Amanda shook an angry finger at the horse; he bared his teeth in a mock laugh. With palm upraised she commanded him to stop, and when the horse resumed his normal expression, she turned and led him along by the reins, as if training him to follow a lead. Again he placed his head against her back and shoved, this time sending her sprawling in the snow. The Indians laughed uproariously, plainly delighted by this unexpected behavior from an animal they thought they knew so well. *Shunka tanka*, the Sioux called a horse— big dog. When they had first encountered the horse some generations earlier, in the hands of their southern neighbors, the strange animal had appeared to be a larger version of a dog, and the Lakota soon saw that the new beast was used for some of the same purposes—carrying loads, and pulling even larger loads on a drag made by crossing poles over his back. But far more astonishing was the discovery that a horse would carry a man, and the Lakota understood at once that the swift creature would afford hunters and warriors far greater mobility than they ever had before. By raiding and trade they soon obtained horses of their own; they came to know the animal's nature and they experienced the thrill of mastering him, and they gave the horse a new name, one that revealed a heightened respect: *shunka wakán* they called him, the mysterious dog.

Obviously enraged, Amanda leaped to her feet and raised a hand as if she might slap the horse, but at once he hung his head abjectly, full of genuine remorse, and the laughter welled up even stronger. Taking pity on the dejected animal, the clown cradled his head in her arms and stroked his velvety nose to comfort him. Finally she turned to bow to the crowd, showing that the little performance was at an end, and immediately the horse nudged her backside with his head and sent her face first into the snow once more, to the uncontrolled delight of the Indians.

Sun Horse had joined the gathering in time to see the horse's final prank, and Lisa recognized the young man who accompanied him. It was the blind holy man Sees Beyond. His brown eyes were clear and bright and nothing about his bearing betrayed his sightlessness except for an unusual tilt of the head, the face slightly raised in the manner of a man who listened intently for a faint sound. Sun Horse was speaking softly to him, describing Amanda's antics as she got to her feet and scolded the horse again, and Sees Beyond smiled and laughed along with the rest.

"No time like the present, I guess," Julius said to Lisa. "Looks like Amanda's about done."

They handed their reins to two of the young boys who stood nearby, waiting for the privilege of caring for a guest's horse, and together they approached the two *wichasha wakán*.

"*Hau*, Grandfather," Lisa greeted Sun Horse in Lakota. "We have brought you visitors." She turned to Amanda. "Amanda, come and say hello to Sun Horse. You remember him from the other day."

Leaving her horse where he was, Amanda turned a cartwheel in the snow and bounced to a stop in front of Sun Horse and Sees Beyond. She made as if to bow to them, but suddenly she interrupted the motion and straightened, looking apprehensively over her shoulder at the horse and bringing a final swell of laughter from the crowd. The horse stood placidly where she had left him. Confidently now, Amanda bowed low to Sun Horse, removing her red clown's cap and letting her hair fall free as she swept the cap across the snow with the gesture of a courtier. There were murmurs of surprise from the crowd. Not everyone in the village had known that the clown was a girl.

Johnny Smoker came forward, leading his own horse as well as Amanda's, and Sun Horse shook his hand, smiling. "I am always glad to see my grandson," he said in Cheyenne. Then, changing to Lakota, he welcomed the others. "These friends are always welcome in my village. *Hau*, Julius." He shook the black man's hand. "Lisaputnam." As was his habit, he held both of her hands in his own for a long moment. "And this little one is especially welcome." He stretched out a wrinkled hand to Amanda.

Amanda took the hand in her own and curtsied, forgetting she was dressed as a clown.

Sun Horse smiled and returned his eyes to Lisa. "Stay and eat with us. Our hunters have brought in two deer today. The meat has made the people happy, and the white *heyoka* girl has made them happier still."

Lisa knew that the meat of two deer would not go far in a village this size, and she knew it would all be consumed in a single meal. White men might have conserved some of the meat, trying to stretch it out over a few days, but that was not the Lakota way. They believed in eating when meat was on hand and enjoying the pleasure of a full stomach. When there was no meat, that was the time to go hungry.

If Sun Horse would accept what she offered, his people need not be hungry much longer.

"We will stay, Grandfather. But the women are still cutting the meat. Shall we walk together while it is cooking, you and Julius and I?"

Sun Horse nodded, pleased by the suggestion. "I like to walk in the sun. I am an old man now, and I need the warmth of the sun in my bones." He turned to Sees Beyond, who had followed the conversation with his unseeing eyes, always appearing to look directly at the speaker. "Walk with us, my friend." Sees Beyond inclined his head in assent and Sun Horse turned to Johnny Smoker, speaking now in Cheyenne. "And what of my grandson. Will he too walk with us before we eat?"

"Amanda wishes to meet your sacred clowns and learn something about them," Johnny replied in the same language.

Sun Horse motioned to two men, one old and the other young, who stood nearby, waiting. Around them most of the Lakota were going about their business now that they had seen the *heyoka* girl and heard the visitors welcomed. "They too have wished to see her, and they are here," Sun Horse said. Throughout Amanda's performance these two had watched intently, often talking excitedly to each other. Sun Horse motioned them to approach and when Amanda noticed them her eyes grew wide with astonishment.

"Is that them, Johnny? Are they the clowns?" When he nodded, she said, "Look at them! Don't you see? It's Sam and Carlos. They're just alike!"

And indeed the two were in some respects similar to her companions from the circus. The older man was the taller of the two and he walked with a certain dignified care that recalled the Englishman's gait, while the younger one was compact and wiry, with quick eyes and a smile that flashed now as he saw that the whitefaced clown's attention was on him. Both men were dark-skinned; they had jagged streaks of paint on their foreheads and cheeks and their clothing was in tatters, but taken together they could have been mistaken for the circus clowns, made up for a new and unusual scene in their act.

"They are called Talks Fast and Won't Go Alone," said Sun Horse, indicating first the elder *heyoka* and then the younger. "Talks Fast speaks almost as little as Hears Twice," he added; he and Sees Beyond chuckled softly at the joke. The power of *heyoka* lay in doing everything in a manner contrary to the normal one, and even in his name, Talks Fast represented a notion that was the opposite of his true nature.

Hears Twice had appeared beside Julius as the crowd dispersed and the two of them were speaking together now. Sees Beyond turned in that direction as he laughed, as if he could sense the prophet's presence.

"Won't Go Alone is of the Real People," Sun Horse said to Johnny. "He married Half Moon, the elder daughter of Walks Bent Over. You can talk with him in the tongue of the Real People and translate for the clown girl."

284

Johnny brightened, and spoke a few words to the young *heyoka*. Equally surprised, Won't Go Alone responded with a torrent of Cheyenne so rapid that Johnny smiled and held up a hand, making signs to say that the young man would have to speak more slowly.

"Tell me what you're saying," Amanda insisted, taking Johnny's arm and looking from one *heyoka* to the other with open curiosity. "I can't stand it when I don't know what people are saying."

"This one is called Won't Go Alone, and he's Cheyenne. I was just telling him it's good to find a Cheyenne here among the Sioux. I asked what band he was from and he said he's northern Cheyenne. His band is led by Little Wolf now; Sun Horse and his people see Little Wolf in the summer, when they go north to hunt."

Sun Horse watched the four of them with benign interest for a few moments, the two *heyoka* and the two young whites, and then he nodded to Lisa and touched Sees Beyond's arm. Sees Beyond took Sun Horse by the elbow and together they started off, Lisa walking with the two Indians. Julius left Hears Twice and joined them as they moved out of the camp circle, following an often-used pathway to the creek.

"I am happy to see that the Sun Band's hunters have brought meat," Lisa said. The presence of fresh meat in the village today was a blessing, she realized now, for it served to remind Sun Horse of the raised spirits and renewed sense of well-being that having meat in camp produced among the people.

"Wolf Talker heard the wolves last night," Sun Horse explained. "They told of a kill the pack had made, and more deer to be found there. Wolf Talker left the village early this morning with Rib Bone and Crooked Horn, and they found two deer near where the wolves had eaten."

"Your hunters might bring in more meat if the horses were strong enough to carry them farther from the village," Lisa said. As soon as the words were out she realized her mistake, but she gave no sign that anything was wrong. To emphasize the usefulness of a gift increased its value and she wanted to do just the opposite. She would have to be more careful. She was careful to keep her tone casual when she continued, as if referring to something of little importance. "My father kept much grain, more than we need. We have brought a little for your horses. And some gunpowder too, for the hunters," she added as if it were an afterthought.

"Always in the past I have traded with your father for gunpowder," Sun Horse said. "What may I give you in exchange for these things?"

Lisa made a gesture with her hand, politely brushing aside any thought of an exchange. "Sometimes the Lakota make gifts in the name of another," she said. "I have seen you give horses and other things away to honor a brave man, or a boy who has received a new name. Whitemen too make gifts to honor one another. We give gifts to honor a good man who has died." She hoped her father, if he were listening, would forgive her this small lie in a good cause. "Julius and I wish to give you these things to honor my father. He always shared what he had with his friends. The grain and gunpowder are only part of what we bring you today."

They had arrived at a large boulder overlooking the creek. The top of the rock was flat and clear of snow, and nearly twice as large as the kitchen table in Putnam House. Sun Horse placed his foot in a natural step in the side of the rock and clambered to the top. "Come," he said. "Let us sit."

Sees Beyond patted the boulder lightly to orient himself and then without hesitation his foot found the same step and he joined Sun Horse atop the rock. Lisa and Julius sat cross-legged like the Indians, and they discovered that the dark stone was pleasantly warm from the sun.

Once they were settled, Julius brought from a pocket in his heavy corduroy overcoat ten pieces of willow stick, equal in length. The Lakota often used sticks to represent gifts that were too large to be passed easily from one man to another. One by one he set the sticks in a row in front of Sun Horse.

"Each stick represents one of our spotted buffalo," Lisa explained, using the Lakota term *pte gleshka* for the white man's cattle. She said nothing about the value of the cows to the Sun Band, nothing about the poor hunting all winter or the gaunt faces of the men and women who had gathered to watch Amanda perform, nothing of the fact that with these three things, grain, gunpowder and beef, the Sun Band would be strong enough to move whenever they wished.

Sees Beyond reached out a hand, finding the sticks and counting them, but he made no comment.

Julius found that he was breathing easier now that the sticks were out of his hands. He felt almost light-headed, and unaccountably pleased with himself.

The sticks had been his idea, as had the grain. Lisa's first impulse had been to bring the cows along today, and she had planned to offer hay for the ponies. She had looked at the loft in the barn, still half full with winter nearly over, and she knew there were two cribs still full in the west meadow, and she had imagined the Lakota driving their horses over to feed in the park, but Julius had improved on Lisa's ideas and at the same time made it less likely that the circus whites would learn of the help the settlement was offering to the Indians.

From the first, he had been in no doubt about which side his own bread was buttered on, or where the best chance for Putnam's Park lay. Keep the hell out of it, let the army and the Indians work things out between them, and hope when the dust settled that Putnam's Park could go on like before. Sun Horse sending a pipe to Crook had raised his hopes, and when Hardeman had agreed to go along with the pipe carriers and speak to Crook, Julius had figured that wrapped it up; however things turned out, Lisa's deed would have as much chance as ever of withstanding the changes that followed, whether the Indians' title to the Powder River country was reaffirmed or whether they were all removed from the country forever and hauled away to Dakota. But every time he entertained such hopes he had felt mean and small, and last night when Hutch had asked him about Sun Horse he had thought for a time and found that he could give only one answer. After all, if a man lived at peace in his own home, who had the right to move him against his will? Julius Ingram had lived for thirty-nine of his fifty years without the right to his own home or any hope of having it, and now he saw the

286

matter of a man's rights as standing pretty high on the list of things he might fight for. But even so, it was one thing to speak up for Sun Horse and another thing to fight for him, and Julius had hoped he wouldn't have to choose between Putnam's Park and helping the Indians, because he wasn't sure which way he would jump when his own future hung in the balance. And then this morning when Lisa had asked Hutch and Harry to feed the cattle and told Julius she had to talk with him, he had known what was coming, and once again he had found there was only one answer he could give. He knew what Jed's wishes would be and he couldn't go against them, and even leaving Jed and his wishes aside, if that were possible, he couldn't stand against Lisa, not when he saw that her heart was set on helping Sun Horse.

"We have hay and beef and gunpowder," Lisa had said right off, once they were alone in the library. "With those three things Sun Horse and his people can move if they have to. They can go now if they want. Farther north they might find better hunting. The main thing is to keep away from the soldiers."

They had sat in front of the fire holding cups of coffee in their hands and Lisa had clutched hers tightly, as if only the heat from the cup gave her the courage to talk of what she planned to do.

"Not the hay," Julius had said. "That's not the way." He had seen the sudden worry in her expression and he held up a hand to calm her. "We've got plenty of hay, but them Indian ponies will burn all the good they'll get from it just walkin' over the mountain and back, and you start bringin' a bunch o' young bucks into the park with them wagon drivers here, there's gonna be trouble. Besides, if all these folks see us feedin' Injun horses, there's gonna be someone hear of it 'fore long. It ain't that I grudge them the hay," he had added. "It's just that a forty-pound sack of oats is a sight more use to a hungry horse than a forkful of hay. We can tote grain over the mountains easy enough."

They had plenty of grain, stored in tin-lined bins in the hayloft, safe from mice and other rodents, kept for the draft horses in winter and the riding horses in summer; it was a far greater reserve than the little ranch needed, but Jed had kept the bins full ever since the road-ranching days, and the cost of replenishing what they used each year was one he had judged prudent.

Lisa had agreed to the change at once, and then for a while they had worried together about what the circus folk would think if they saw ten cows driven out of the park toward the mountains, but Julius had remembered the gift sticks the Lakota used to transfer horses in naming ceremonies, and that had solved that problem. "There'll be time enough to bring the cows along later," he had said. "We can move 'em into the lot with the heifers and none o' these folks will think twice about it, and the next day when no one's about we can drive 'em up the crick. Do it before breakfast, we'll get out without a soul around."

Together with the cows they would lose to provide meat for the circus even if Tatum and his people stayed for just another month, the herd would be reduced by nearly a third, but Lisa had been quick to point out that they wouldn't have to pay men from Rawlins to clear the road, which meant they would have more cash in the fall when the steer calves were shipped. They might buy another bull, she suggested; they might keep more heifers back too, to expand the herd faster. Somehow they would make it up, if they kept the ranch.

"It will mean we're risking everything," Lisa had said. "You know that. If the government learns we helped a band of hostiles there will be no hope at all that they'll recognize the deed when this is all over."

Julius had shrugged, and he had surprised himself with the simplicity of his answer. "Might be we'd lose it all anyway, if we sit tight. Be a shame to hang on to all we got for no good reason, not if we could help some other folks."

But as they went ahead with their preparations and set out for the Indian village, he couldn't help asking himself what he would have left if he lost Putnam's Park. I'll have my fiddle, he thought, and he had remembered Old Will, the slave who had taught him to play. He remembered as if it were yesterday the first time Will had showed him how to rest the fiddle against his chest and hold the neck with his left hand. "Let you body feel the music," the old man had said. "You body sway, the fiddle she sway too. Tha's the way to make the fiddle sing."

Old Will had died years before the Union major set fire to the plantation. He had lived his life as a slave and his fiddle was all he had ever owned. If Julius had to start over again, he would still have his fiddle and his music, and he would still be a free man. That was more than Old Will ever had, even in his most fanciful dreams.

And the truth was, Julius had his own reason for helping Sun Horse. In four years of working hand in hand with Jed Putnam, talking while they worked, he had learned that everywhere else in the world the white man had enslaved the natives as he spread his empires around the globe, but not in America. In Africa and India and Mexico and South America it had always been the same, but in America Julius and his ancestors had been held in slavery for two hundred years and all that time the Indians had stayed free, those that survived. They had chosen to stay free or die. The whites had brought their own slaves to America because the red men resisted enslavement, and Julius wondered if it might be that he had something to learn from the Indians. He hadn't found the answer to that puzzle yet, and all along the trail from Putnam's Park he had been nagged by the fear that he was risking his life's dream to help folks who could do their own fighting, but here on the boulder beside the stream, as he had set out the ten sticks in a neat row he had felt the fear leave him, and it was as if a great weight had been lifted from his shoulders. He felt like doing a jig.

Sun Horse gazed throughtfully at the sticks, but he did not touch them. Finally he smiled at Lisa. "It is good to honor the dead. And it is true that the Lakota make gifts to honor a good man, but in time there are other gifts that follow, and the circle is complete. The things you bring are of great value to the Lakota. We would give you something in return, but we have little to offer."

Lisa felt a surge of hope. She imagined that she sensed in Sun Horse a desire to accept the gifts. Was he bargaining with her? He spoke of gifts returned in time...

"When you return in the fall you can bring us some meat from the hunt," she said, feeling her heart pounding in her breast. Like the notion of making the gifts to honor her father, this one had come to her at the last moment.

It was Sees Beyond who spoke now. "*Wakán Tanka* has given the *pte* to the Lakota to provide us with meat and covering for our lodges, and many other things. Like the Lakota, the *pte* roam the prairie, going where they wish. We do not keep animals for meat. When we need meat, we hunt. This is the Lakota way."

"The *washíchun* keep the spotted *pte* so that when hunting is bad there will still be meat," Lisa said, hoping to turn the holy man's argument back on him. "It is our custom to share what we have with our friends, just as it is yours. Today we will eat the deer your hunters have brought; tomorrow you will eat the meat from my cattle; in the fall you will bring us meat from the hunt and we too will share the strength of *pte*."

Sees Beyond shook his head. "Our strength is in the Lakota way. If we change our way of life, if we eat the meat of the whiteman's spotted buffalo, we are Lakota no longer."

"And if the soldiers come here and take you to Dakota, to the reservation, will you be Lakota then?"

Sees Beyond shrugged. "It may be that the Lakota life is not strong enough to stand against the *washíchun*."

"But if you take the meat and grain, your people and your horses will be strong enough to travel, and you can stay away from the soldiers." Lisa threw caution to the winds, speaking the value of the gift out loud. They must find a way to accept!

"And yet it will be the strength of the *washíchun* that allows us to move on, and the people will see this," Sees Beyond said, his sharp eyes fixed on Lisa. She could not escape the power of that sightless stare and she looked away.

"No spotted buffalo then," Julius said suddenly in his crude Lakota. He had not understood everything that was said, but he caught enough of the words to follow the conversation. Both Sun Horse and Sees Beyond spoke more distinctly when talking with Lisa, and that was a help. He too had seen that the Lakota were bargaining. "Take grain, take gunpowder," he said. "Lakota hunt. With strong horses, maybe find meat. Hunt in Lakota way, live in Lakota way. Grain makes horses strong; meat makes people strong. If hunting is good, you can move when soldiers come."

Sun Horse knew that what the black whiteman said was true, and he knew just as surely that he could not accept. The Sun Band used iron pots and steel sewing needles and glass beads; they used flintlock and percussion rifles, and the newer guns that took metal cartridges, when they could get them; but each of these things replaced something that the Lakota had used previously, something that served the same purpose; none had changed the Lakota life in a fundamental way. And never had they accepted outright gifts from the whites. To do so would make them no better than the Loaf-Around-the-Forts. As always, Sees Beyond had reminded Sun Horse of a vital principle at the proper moment. It was to preserve the Lakota way of life that he had led his people here to this wintering place; that way of life could not be abandoned carelessly now to protect the band against a danger that might or might not come. If the pipe carriers succeeded, there would be no need to move until the grass was up. But if they failed...

"Still it will be the gifts that give us strength," Sun Horse said. "If the hunting is bad in the warm moons, we will have no way to repay you."

"Then take the grain and gunpowder and hunt now, and hunt for us as well!" Lisa said, speaking the thought as soon as it exploded in her mind. It took all her will to remain calm. "We will hunt with you! *Washíchun* and Lakota will hunt together. Take the grain and gunpowder to honor my father, and as long as we hunt we will bring you more. In return, share your knowledge with us. The Lakota are great hunters and great trackers. Lead us and we will follow. We will share the hunting and we will share the meat!" Her mind was racing. Perhaps some of the circus men could hunt too! The teamsters were busy with their digging, but if some of the performers could join the hunt and bring in meat, that would further reduce Tatum's costs and he would certainly give his consent.

She picked up the ten willow sticks in her gloved hand and held them up triumphantly for Sun Horse to see. "This is another gift you make to us. These cows are mothers. There is new life within them. To honor my father I would kill them for you, and to feed the people in my valley I will kill some anyway, but if you will hunt with us they may live; for every deer we bring in, for every elk, a cow will live and her calf will grow strong. This is something of great value to me, a gift far greater than anything I offer you in return, but I ask it all the same. Say you will accept the grain and gunpowder, and say you will hunt with us."

Sees Beyond turned to Sun Horse, his head held at its habitual upraised angle, his eyes on Sun Horse's face and the fleeing hint of a smile playing about his lips. "The coming together of two people," he said. "It can bring strength to each one."

Lisa did not know what the younger holy man meant by these words, but Sun Horse seemed to consider them very seriously. Finally he nodded.

"To honor my friend Jedediah we accept the grain and the gunpowder. The hunters of the Sun Band will lead the white hunters; we will share the hunt and we will share the meat."

290

As they walked back toward the circle of lodges Sun Horse was at peace with himself. His white grandson and the clown girl had brought their power to the village today, and he was certain now that it was a power to benefit the people. *It may help us or destroy us*, Hears Twice had said, but seeing the meeting between Johnny Smoker and the clown girl had given Sun Horse the idea of sending the pipes, and now yet another choice opened for the Sun Band; for a time, at least, the horses would eat grain from the white settlement, and if the hunt succeeded, the people would have meat. If war threatened, the village could move. Much had changed in just a few days, and no longer was it necessary to choose only between fighting or surrender.

He had been puzzled for a time, when he realized that the clown girl would be leaving right away with the rest of the Strange-Animal People. How could the power grow if she and Johnny Smoker were apart? he had wondered. He had delayed sending the pipe carriers on their way, pondering this mystery, and then had come the news of the avalanche. Blackbird and three other boys had been off hunting and they had tried to pass through the river canyon below the white settlement. They had returned to say that the road was blocked by a huge snowslide and the Strange-Animal People were trapped in the park, and Sun Horse's hopes had soared once more. The bright sun had shone on the hillside above the river, the snow had fallen to block the trail, and the clown girl would stay. So simple. *Okaga*, the power of the south, had done this, and *Okaga* was a life-giving power; the color of the south was yellow because the warm summer sun was yellow, and the sun was the power that nurtured all life. Thus the life-giving power had worked to reaffirm the promise that *wamblí* had made, by blocking the road and assuring that the clown girl would remain.

And here today, Sun Horse had understood something more: the meeting Hears Twice had predicted was not only the meeting of two individuals, but the coming together of two peoples, the Lakota and the *washichun*. The presence of his white grandson and the clown girl in the village, the way they had sought out the *heyoka*, the way the people accepted them, these were the signs that had alerted Sun Horse to the truth; when Lisaputnam proposed the hunt, showing how the two races could work together for the benefit of both, he was sure. These were but the first steps to a wider coming together, and a wider peace.

Within the camp circle a performance by the *heyoka* was in progress, and once more some of the people had gathered to watch. Won't Go Alone was seated on the ground, furiously working a firebow while Talks Fast heaped snow instead of tinder around the base of the spinning stick on its hardwood base. Amanda knelt beside them, blowing hard to encourage an imaginary spark into flame. The performance was well known to the people; they enjoyed the seriousness with which the *heyoka* applied themselves to this futile effort, and the natural way the clown girl had taken part.

Won't Go Alone stopped spinning the firebow now, greatly saddened by his failure. Amanda hung her head, out of breath and exhausted. But then she brightened as if she had a sudden idea. She motioned Johnny Smoker to join her and she took a small box from his hands. With more motions she instructed him to shield the mound of snow with his hands. She took a sulphur match from the box and lit it, then held it carefully against the snow. She blew gently at first, then harder and harder, and the match went out. The expression of drop-jawed disbelief that she assumed at this new failure brought a burst of laughter from the onlookers. She lit another match and shielded it even more carefully with her own hands and Johnny's, and she blew it out even sooner. By now even the two *heyoka* were laughing.

Lisa Putnam's Journal

Wednesday, March 8th. 6:25 p.m.

We got back from Sun Horse's village a little before one o'clock today, having accepted an invitation to spend the night. I have never liked making that ride twice in one day, although it can be done. It seems like a proper journey, and when you reach journey's end you want to stay a while. And so we did. There was dancing after the feast and it was a sight to see, the whole village gathered around an enormous bonfire in the center of camp under the much colder light of a brilliant three-quarter moon. Amanda was worn out after a long day by the time the dancing started, but Sun Horse provided her with a good buffalo robe and she sat by his side, swaddled to her chin in her coat and robe, and she stayed awake through the dancing. She liked the buffalo dancers best of all; she listened with interest as Johnny translated Sun Horse's explanation of the meaning—all about invoking the power of the buffalo for the hunt—but it was the dancer's uncanny buffalo-like movements that really fascinated her. She insists she is going to try to learn them and to use them somehow in the circus act. When the dancing was over we all slept in Uncle Bat's lodge and Penelope was glad of our company. The pipe carriers only left the village on Monday, but she already misses her husband as if he had been gone a long time. I assured her he would come safely back to her, and didn't show my own concern.

By this morning the snow was falling again and our ride home was not as pleasant as the ride over yesterday. We arrived here to find Mr. Tatum in a proper state. When we left yesterday, he was off with his men surveying the avalanche, planning their attack; I left word with Alfred Chalmers that Amanda had gone with us and would be well looked-after. Well, you would think we had abducted her by force and delivered her into the hands of Barbary pirates. How he carried on! He scolded us the minute we showed our faces in the saloon, it being midday and everyone being there for dinner, and later he took me aside to apologize for his tone, but then he scolded me all over again. "Had your father not known them for years, and did not your uncle live among them, they might have killed you all," he said darkly, and then he added, "or worse." There it is again, the supposed ever-present threat of unmentionable outrages against white womanhood. That fear seems to grow in the minds of our people like a weed. There have been such cases, of course; the tribulations of Mrs. Kelly and Mrs. Eubanks are well known. When the Indians outrage a white woman the newspapers call them "brutal savages," as if they were less than human, and men gather in the taprooms to talk of bloody revenge. But is this not just one more way we incite ourselves to hate against a people whose land we covet, whose way of life seems strange to us and therefore hateful? We point at the crime all good people abhor and using it as an excuse we attack the red men wherever we find them. I am a woman, and therefore vulnerable to the violence of men, but everyone speaks of the Indians as if they were the only ones guilty of such abominations. Should I not fear the same thing if I were a Frenchwoman in the Prussians' path? And how did Southern ladies feel when they saw General Sherman's armies bearing down on them? In every war to rend the heart of Europe or England or America such outrages have occured. Among the aboriginal people of this continent these acts are expected, even accepted, when female captives are taken. It is the way of things here. The Indians are in a primitive state and act in accord with their harsh beliefs, but "Christian" people profess a higher standard, and our own savageries carry the added burden of hypocrisy.

I contained myself and did not loose this outburst on Mr. Tatum, nor did I intend to set it down here, but I feel better for having done so. I reminded Mr. Tatum that my father did know Sun Horse for Years and that Uncle Bat does live with the band, and I assured him there was never the slightest danger. He made me promise not to take Amanda off again without speaking to him first.

The circus tent was erected while we were gone! It is a gay affair, the alternating sections of canvas painted white and red and the whole of it waterproofed with paraffin. Other work was done as well. Several of the circus cabins rest on the ground now, while the wagons are used to help clear the road. More on this as the work progresses.

This afternoon the bulls broke out of their pasture and raced down to pay their respects to the cows; we drove them back quickly enough, but I am afraid there may be one or two early calves next year. Harry and Hutch and Johnny Smoker spent the rest of the afternoon repairing the fence, work they will carry ahead in coming days. It has been too long neglected.

The best news of all is that Alfred Chalmers tells me several of the men among the performers have experience with sporting arms; the Waldheims have hunted at home in Bavaria, and Alfred assures me that we can mount competent hunting parties to do our part. We are going to hunt with the Sun Band! I offered Sun Horse beef and grain and gunpowder, and to put the outcome in a nutshell, he refused the beef but accepted the grain and gunpowder on the condition that we hunt together. I don't have the time now to *set forth how we arrived at this plan; I will save that for tomorrow morning when I am a bit more collected. Now I will only say that I am full of hope. We may save a few cows, but the hunt has far greater importance for Sun Horse and his people. With meat and strong horses, they can flee to safety if danger threatens. Julius shares my excitement and tomorrow he will lead the first party of hunters from the settlement. They will meet the Lakotas atop the ridge and set out from there in smaller groups.*

Good hunting to us all!

CHAPTER
TWENTY

The scout watched the approaching rider for a time to be sure he was white. The scout's name was Speed Stagner and he had been the post guide at Fort Fetterman for several years; he had been detailed to remain behind with Major Coates and the supply train when General Crook and the cavalry left them the previous evening and now he was leading the wagons back to old Fort Reno. Falling snow obscured all detail in the landscape beyond a quarter mile, and he had experienced the eerie feeling of seeing the rider appear out of nothing. There was something sinister about the way someone could approach the small column of wagons and infantry so closely without being seen. In clear weather the rider would have been spotted when he first appeared on the horizon and his coming could have been prepared for. Stagner knew all the scouts on Crook's present expedition and most of the other men who had scouted for the army of the Platte in recent years, but he did not recognize this man. He reined his horse around and rode back toward the wagons at a brisk canter.

Major Coates was the first to spy the returning scout and he raised a hand to halt the column. His own company of Fourth Infantry led the way, followed by the supply wagons; Captain Ferris's company brought up the rear. Without any further sign from Coates, three squads of his company fanned out ahead and to the sides of the column. These were their standing orders, and he knew that other squads were taking positions to guard the column's flanks and rear. The knowledge comforted him but did not entirely quell a feeling of vulnerability. They were a much smaller force since the cavalry had left them.

Coates was from New York. He had fought through the whole of the Civil War, including the Battles of the Wilderness, where Grant's and Lee's armies had stumbled about in dense forests and infantrymen had fared far better than cavalry. He had been on the frontier since '69, but he had never grown used to

294

the exposed feeling that always came over him on the empty intermountain plains.

The encampment on Crazy Woman's Fork had been filled with murmured farewells the evening before as the cavalry made ready to depart, and when the last rider was out of sight the campsite had seemed deserted. Coates had drawn his companies into a tight defensive perimeter with their backs to the stream, using the wagons as barricades, but the night had stayed calm and quiet and the men not on guard had slept peacefully. It was mid-morning now, and they had made six miles back toward Fort Reno when Coates last checked the odometer on the lead wagon.

"One man coming up the road, Major," Stagner said as he joined Coates. "White man. I make him to be a guide. Don't know him, though."

"Not one of ours?"

"I ha'n't set eyes on him, best I can make out."

They were joined by Captain Ferris and Lieutenant Mason and the four men watched together as the rider came into sight at an unhurried trot and drew near. The man raised a hand to the soldiers who covered his approach with rifles at the ready, and rode through their lines.

Hardeman glanced at the length of the column, noting the absence of cavalry. He dismounted when he reached the officers, looking for rank insignia and seeing none. He looked at the man standing slightly in front of the others.

"Are you the officer in command?"

"Major E. M. Coates, Fourth Infantry." Coates took in the man's field boots, and the buckskin beneath his St. Paul coat.

"Christopher Hardeman, Major. I'm a special scout for General Crook, sent on ahead of the expedition. It's urgent that I find the general."

"General Crook is not here."

"I see that, sir." Hardeman heard the wariness in the major's voice and he tried to curb his impatience. He was out of practice at talking to a man who considered himself a scout's superior. "I have a message for the general from Sun Horse, the Sioux peace chief."

"I have not heard your name before in connection with this command, Mr. . . . Hartman, is it?"

"Hardeman, Major. I saw the general in Cheyenne and he sent me to find Sun Horse. If you'll just tell me where you left the general, I'll be on my way."

Coates mulled this over for a time, searching his memory. "Hardeman. Christopher Hardeman. No, the name is unknown to me. At what fort are you employed?"

"I haven't scouted for the army in some years, not since I was at the Washita with General Custer."

Coates's eyebrows raised slightly. "Indeed. Did you know Major Joel Elliott?"

Hardeman nodded. "I led his troop to its attack position."

"But you did not remain with him during the battle?"

"When the battle started I was scouting off beyond the village. Once I got back it was every man for himself." This Major Coates knew very well. He knew too that scouts were often not expected to take part in the fighting. With army officers the questions were always the same: Did you know Elliott? Could Custer have saved him? During the battle, Elliott and seventeen men had pursued some escaping Cheyenne out of sight of the village and they had never returned. Custer had made one halfhearted attempt to learn Elliott's whereabouts, sending a scout and a few men to search for him, but that party had been yet two miles from the village and driven back by bands of Kiowa and Arapaho coming from the villages downstream to help their Cheyenne friends. More than a week later, Custer had returned to the battleground with Phil Sheridan and only then had the bodies of Elliott and his men been found, all horribly mutilated. Hardeman had not known Elliott well, but he believed him to have been a decent man, and the news of his death had only served to raise Hardeman's suspicions about George A. Custer's trustworthiness as a field commander.

"Why is it you need to find General Crook so urgently, Mr. Hardeman?" Coates wished to know.

"There's a chance to end this war without a fight, Major. But I'll have to find the general as soon as I can."

"Do you believe it should be ended without a fight?"

"If it's possible. Yes, I do." Hardeman met Coates's eyes straight on as he said this. He gathered his reins and made ready to mount. He really didn't need the major's help to find Crook. The wagons would be easy to backtrack even in the storm, and the trail would lead to the place where Crook had parted company with his supply train. What Hardeman really wanted to know from Coates was how long ago that had been. Was it yesterday? The day before? If it was last night or this morning, Crook was less than a day ahead, but each additional day the wagons had been returning south doubled the distance between Hardeman and the cavalry and made overtaking Crook all the more difficult.

The pipe carriers had left the Sun Band's village two days before, not as soon as Hardeman would have liked, but you couldn't hurry the endless palaver in an Indian council lodge. The Sun Band's councillors had taken nearly an entire day to work out all the fine points of the pipe carriers' mission, and then there had been another day and a half of ceremonies to prepare the pipes. Hardeman hadn't been invited to attend the council and Bat Putnam had told him little about it, except to say that some of the talk had to do with whether the pipe carriers should try to find Crook or Sitting Bull first, and that they had settled on Crook. They knew the soldier chief was more likely to agree to leave the country now if Sitting Bull's participation in the peace plan were already assured, but they were even more certain that the Hunkpapa headman would never consent to remain peaceful until summer unless he first received Crook's promise to withdraw from the Powder River country. His young men were hot for war and he could not go against them without a strong hand. So the pipe carriers would find Crook, and if he were sympathetic to Sun Horse's proposal he would remain where he was while the Sun Band's messengers went on to find Sitting Bull and return with his answer. It was a sound plan and it might work, but Hardeman was anxious to overtake the cavalry before they stumbled on some village and started a war that might be prevented.

"I'll have to move along if I want to catch up with the general today," he said now, hoping to elicit some response that would tell him of Crook's whereabouts. He put one foot in the stirrup. One of the other officers opened his mouth to say something, but Major Coates spoke quickly to keep him quiet.

"A moment, Mr. Hardeman. It occurs to me that some might think it peculiar to find a solitary white man roaming free in a countryside crawling with hostiles."

"The country's big enough. A man keeps out of sight if he knows his way."

"But there might be another explanation. If the man were known to the Indians, he would be allowed to come and go as he pleased. Especially if the Indians knew he was friendly to them."

"What are you saying, Major? Speak plain."

"I am saying that a number of renegade whites are known to be living with the Sioux. Some have been observed fighting against our troops."

"You think I'm such a man?"

"Perhaps. Perhaps not. I am simply saying that such a man who fell into my hands would not be likely to reach a post stockade alive. Just so we understand each other, Mr. Hardeman. I would be most unwise to permit such a man to tell the Indians that General Crook has detached his supply train and is moving up-country with only a mounted column."

"And if I'm telling the truth, Major, you would be unwise to keep me here." He dropped his foot back to the ground. The horse was between himself and the cluster of troops who were listening to the conversation from a short distance away, but the outlying squads were behind him.

"Nevertheless, I would prefer we talk a while longer before I make a final decision about what to do with you," Coates said. "Captain Ferris, will you get Mr. Hardeman's weapons and search him for a side arm?"

Hardeman sighed inwardly. He had prepared himself for this eventuality long since. Why was it that soldiers were so bad at hiding their intentions? They were used to facing the enemy in a bunch; they didn't know how to handle a man who might be either friend or foe. Even this major, who probably had years of service on the frontier, was as open as a book. It took living in the mountains, a man on his own, to read such things, but once you knew the signs they were plain enough. Hardeman had guessed what Coates would do even before the major himself was settled on his course, and as Coates spoke, Hardeman was moving. He dropped the reins and his pistol appeared in his hand as he covered the three steps to the side of the nearest officer. He placed the gun in the man's side. "What's your name?" he demanded.

"Mason, Mr. Hardeman. Lieutenant Mason."

Good man; not too nervous. Forty years old if he was a day, and still a lieutenant. Well, that wasn't so unusual. The man Coates had addressed as Captain Ferris was only now opening his holster, too late.

"Mr. Mason and I will be leaving together, Major," Hardeman said. "I'll turn

297

him loose half a mile from the road. You just hold your water a bit and you'll have him back."

"You men! Cover this man!" Captain Ferris barked. He drew his Remington Army .44 and aimed it uncertainly in Hardeman's direction, but Coates put out a restraining hand.

"Easy, Captain. It seems we have a stalemate, Mr. Hardeman." Several soldiers on both sides of Hardeman had him covered.

"I don't think so, Major. You might get me, but you'll lose Lieutenant Mason here, and I don't think you'll risk that. I'm sorry I don't have more time for talk, but you just say my name to the general when you see him and he'll set you straight. We'll be getting along now, Lieutenant." He reached out to recover his horse's reins and prodded Mason with the pistol to start him moving. It wouldn't do to give anyone much time to think.

"Hardeman! Wait now, just a moment." Coates held out a hand as if to pull Hardeman back, but the scout kept going. "Look here, if I am wrong, I apologize. Surely you can understand my concern." He hoped to detain Hardeman with conversation while he tried to decide what to do.

"I understand, Major, but I have concerns of my own, and staying here half the day to satisfy you isn't one of them." The two men continued on, through the scattering of pickets surrounding the column, Mason in the lead with Hardeman close behind him and the horse coming last to shield them.

Coates raised a reluctant hand to indicate that the scout and his hostage should be allowed to pass unhindered.

"Major, you can't let him leave!" Ferris brandished his pistol again but Coates forced his arm down. "He'll kill Mason himself if he's a renegade!" Ferris protested.

"Then his death will be on Mr. Hardeman's hands." Coates raised his voice so Hardeman would be sure to hear.

Hardeman and Mason walked steadily away from the supply column until it disappeared behind them. Hardeman kept up the pace for perhaps another five minutes and then brought his hostage to a halt.

"Sorry to inconvenience you, Lieutenant." He took Mason's pistol from its holster and removed the percussion caps from their nipples. The gun was a Remington, like Ferris's. Apparently the infantry had a low priority for the new metal-cartridge Colts. Hardeman had bought his own three years ago when they first appeared. The cavalry would certainly have the Colts by now. He threw the caps into the snow, which was deepening among the sparse stubble of the prairie grass. Until this storm, the ground here had been almost bare.

"Can you find your way back to the wagons?"

"Yes, sir," Mason replied. "I'll just follow our tracks."

Hardeman mounted his horse.

"Excuse me, Mr. Hardeman. Was that the truth about a chance to stop the war without a fight?"

"I hope so."

"You may not believe this, but I wish you luck."

298

Hardeman raised a hand in thanks and started off, but he reined in almost at once and called back to Mason. "It will help me if I know where you left General Crook."

"I'm sorry; I shouldn't tell you that. In case I am wrong about you."

Hardeman nodded and kicked his horse into a canter. He had led Mason straight away from the wagon road, due west, and he continued in that direction now. When he looked back a few moments later, Mason was barely visible, already walking back toward the wagons. Once the dim figure was gone from sight, Hardeman reined to the right, turning north to circle around and regain the road a mile or two beyond, where Bat and the others would be waiting for him. Despite his impatience he allowed the horse to slow to a trot. There was no sense wearing out the roan now; he might have a long journey ahead of him. Since leaving the Sun Band's village two days ago, the pipe carriers had not made good time, and they had lost more ground by coming out onto the plain to the Bozeman road only to find that Crook had already come and gone. Hardeman's horse and Bat Putnam's could have made twice the distance they were covering each day; the bay mare had eaten grain all winter in Putnam's Park and Hardeman's roan had been similarly pampered for four days, and more grain had been in their saddlebags when they left the settlement, forced on them by Lisa as a parting gift. But the Indian horses were weak, although the pipe carriers had been given the strongest mounts in the Sun Band's herd. The grain was gone now, the last of it doled out this morning to the Indian ponies to fortify them for a long day's ride over barren lands with little or no natural forage and no time to stop for browsing what there was. From now on all of the pipe carriers' horses would have to live off the land.

"We might ought t' ride all night, if Three Stars's got more'n a day start on us," Bat said once Hardeman had found the little band and told them that he had learned nothing, save that Crook and his cavalry had left the supply train behind and could move across the country now as fast as an Indian war party. In recent moments the wind had strengthened. Bat peered into the storm from within the heavy blanket hood of his Hudson's Bay capote. He wore a trade blanket outside the capote, belted at the waist. The Indians too wore their robes and blankets belted against the cold, and fur coverings on their heads, from which the feet and heads of the former owners dangled. Standing Eagle's winter cape of grizzly-bear fur was pulled up high and held in place at the neck by a rawhide thong, permitting it to serve as both cap and cloak. All the men but Hardeman wore winter moccasins made of buffalo hide, laced to the knee.

"Horses ain't up to night ridin'," Standing Eagle said. He looked about at the sky, which told him nothing. "We best make tracks while we can." He led off with Little Hand beside him. Standing Eagle was the leader of the group because he was war leader of the Sun Band, although he carried no weapons now. The bearer of a peace pipe could not touch a weapon until the pipe was accepted by the one for whom it was intended, and Standing Eagle carried the pipe for General Crook. Nor was Little Hand armed, for he was related in a roundabout manner to Sitting Bull and carried the pipe for the Hunkpapa holy man.

The others moved off behind the leaders. They were six in all and they rode two by two here on the wagon road. Blackbird followed close behind Standing Eagle; beside him rode his *hunká*-father, Hawk Chaser, a middle-aged warrior whose hair was just beginning to gray. Hawk Chaser's exploits in battle were unequaled in the Sun Band. His eyes, set on either side of a nose as straight and sharp as an arrowhead, were constantly on the move, taking in everything. It was Hawk Chaser who had seen the army scout before the whiteman could spy the pipe carriers. He smiled now as Blackbird fell in beside him. The bond between the warrier and his son-by-choice was strong. The boy was silent most of the time but his eyes shone with pride at having been picked to go along. It was Hawk Chaser who had put forth his name, and Sun Horse had agreed. Blackbird was the moccasin carrier; to him fell the responsibility for looking after the bundles of spare moccasins and winter garments for the men, holding their horses when they stopped, caring for the single pack horse, gathering firewood and making the sleeping shelter for the night, and more. It was an important position, and a large step toward manhood for a boy who did his duty without unnecessary talk and performed bravely if the opportunity arose.

Hardeman and Bat brought up the rear, willing to let the Indians lead the way. A man found his natural companions on the trail, Hardeman had learned in his years as a scout. The man you were comfortable riding next to all day usually proved to be the man you could count on in a fight, or when the trail grew difficult. At the Sun Band's village Hardeman had slept in Bat's lodge, and he felt a growing liking for this mountain man who had lived so long with the Sioux. The old man's humor masked a sharp mind; the jokes and mountain tales were the means by which that mind stayed limber and showed its enjoyment of life, but the jokes and tales had been few since they had been on the trail. *You are quiet today*, Bat had signed to Hardeman the day before. Hardeman had merely nodded in reply, causing Bat to break his silence. "Good thing to keep shut on the trail. I'm becoming a gabby cuss in my old age," he had said, after which he was quiet again.

In other circumstances they could have been friends. But friends told one another something of what they guarded in the secret places of the mind, or at least they revealed such things in time even if they said nothing in words, and it seemed to Hardeman, judging by the cautious way he and Bat talked on the rare occasions when the silence of their journey was broken, that both of them were keeping back things they could not reveal, at least not until the pipe was delivered to General Crook and the outcome of Sun Horse's proposal was known.

But even at the start, Bat had been allied with Hardeman against Standing Eagle. What with the delay in getting off, Hardeman had argued for striking north as fast as they could travel once they reached the foothills, and sending just one man out to look for wagon tracks on the Bozeman road. Bat had supported Hardeman, seeing that as the best way to overtake Crook if he had already passed by or to head him off if he had not yet come this far. But Standing Eagle had said that the bluecoats always moved slowly, especially with wagons; the pipe carriers would go east to the wagon road, he insisted, and if they found no tracks there, as seemed likely, they would turn south to await Three Stars at Fort Reno and the Powder River Crossing. The war leader had shown no remorse when he learned that he had underestimated the white soldier chief. He had merely grunted and turned north, following the tracks until the army scout was seen and Hardeman rode forward alone.

Now the six horsemen pressed forward into the strengthing storm and for the rest of the afternoon they had no rest and no food except a few pieces of jerky from the bundles each man packed behind his saddle. As the light dimmed, giving the first indication of approaching night, they arrived at Crazy Woman's Fork and discovered the soldiers' campground. A short examination revealed that the wagon tracks went no farther.

"The cavalry left here before today," Hardeman said, looking at the faint tracks. "Yesterday, maybe. Can't be sure." Three inches of new snow covered the tracks.

Standing Eagle broke a stout branch from a clump of willows and dug in the remains of one of the campfires. When he had excavated a few inches into the ground beneath the ashes he felt the earth with his bare hand and then spoke in Lakota to Little Hand and Hawk Chaser, gesturing about the campsite.

"He says the wagons left here this morning," Bat translated for Hardeman. "He don't know how long they were here. Might be one day, might be more." Bat had examined the campsite for himself, as each of the others had done while Blackbird held the horses. Now the mountain man walked away from the frozen stream to one of the fire pits farthest from the bank, and he brushed the ashes aside to feel the ground. "These fires here are a mite older," he observed. "Ground's plumb frozen. Let's say the pony soldiers left yestiddy and the wagons stayed the night. That puts the cavalry a day ahead of us."

"Or more," Hardeman added.

Bat nodded, looking in the direction the cavalry had taken.

Standing Eagle had been talking with Little Hand and now he switched to trapper's English in midstream. "Ain't much light left. We'll cache here for the night. This child's got a powerful hunger." He pointed to the grass that grew thick beyond the campsite. "Pony sojers kept their horses in close." He grinned. "Must be 'feared o' wild Injuns. Our critters'll eat good tonight."

Hardeman looked at the gloomy sky. "There's an hour of light, maybe more. We might go on a way."

Bat shook his head. "Eagle's right. We best stay put. The country up yonder's rough goin'. No forage and less water. 'Sides," he added, giving Hardeman a wink, "old Eagle feels his belly rappin' on his backbone, he cain't think of nothin' else. 'Bout as much use as powder with no flint till he gets hisself fed." He gave Standing Eagle a hard look then. "Come first light, we'll move along right smart."

301

Standing Eagle's expression revealed nothing as he led his horse away to look for the best grass. Blackbird was already gathering firewood without a word said.

Hardeman too led his own horse away, apparently willing to accept Bat's judgment in the matter. Bat rummaged in his saddlebags for his hobbles. He would picket his mare on a long tether of braided rawhide so she could eat well. A horse was like a tipi, with a hide covering and a fire inside; if you wanted to keep her warm in winter, you had to build a bigger fire. Grass was the fuel, and here on the banks of the Crazy Woman it stood thick and tall above the thin layer of snow.

As he went about the tasks of seeing to his horse and making camp, Bat mulled over a growing certainty that Standing Eagle was dragging his feet every chance he got. First that notion to go east to the Bozeman road, now the solicitous care he lavished on the horses every step of the way. That his brother-in-law was right about the horses' need to eat didn't lessen Bat's suspicions. Eagle was an admirer of good horseflesh, but he would push a pony until it dropped if he had a good enough reason for covering ground. He's holding back, Bat thought. Wants Crook to find a village and set the badger loose. Standing Eagle was as inflexible as a dried beaver hide when it came to seeking any accommodation with the whites and he would rather die than surrender. He had said so in the council.

The Sun Band's councillors had agreed quickly enough to Sun Horse's plan, and then the talk had turned to what would be done if Three Stars would not accept the pipe. Most of the men reaffirmed their earlier decision to go to the Dakota agencies rather than fight. They would permit Crook to escort the band if he still offered that choice, or they would go as best they could if left to their own devices.

"I will not go to that place!" Standing Eagle had interrupted, nearly shouting, and his bad manners had not set well with the councillors, but he had bulled ahead. "I will go to my cousin Sitting Bull and I will fight the *washíchun* by his side! I have seen the agencies. The people there fight among themselves and wait outside the agent's lodge for food like soldier mules sniffing for a few grains of corn! They are no longer Lakota! A Lakota fights for what is his and he lets no man tell him where to go or where to stop!"

"The war leader forgets his first duty!" Walks Bent Over had said with some heat. "Think of the helpless ones!" It was an unprecedented rebuke from the misshapen, thoughtful man who was the head scout of the band. The first duty of a war leader was to protect the helpless ones, the women and children and the elderly, and it had seemed to Bat, as it must have seemed to Walks Bent Over, that Standing Eagle was thinking only of the glory of war and his own honors, but the war leader had defended himself with impassioned eloquence.

"I do think of them!" he had thrown back at his accuser. "They are helpless in war but I am not!" He had brought himself under control then, and as he continued he had looked around the council, demanding with his eyes that his listeners hear the truth of what he said. "If we go to the agencies and place ourselves in the hands of the whites, we will all be helpless. Last year in the cold moons hunting was bad, as it is now, but life was bad at the agencies too. You have heard the tales told by our relatives there. There was not enough food, and only one blanket for three Lakota. Only the robes brought in from the hunting bands saved many from freezing. Tell me, my friends, if all the hunting bands surrender, who then will see to the good of the people? The *washíchun?* Will you place your trust in the *washíchun?* I will not. I will fight now, for the helpless ones, for as long as I have the strength. I will die before I will surrender!"

His reasoning had swayed some of the councillors but even so they had held to their decision to send the pipes. Sun Horse had recommended a course of action and it must be given a chance. There was time enough to think and talk about what to do later.

Standing Eagle had come close to refusing the pipe for Three Stars, but when he saw that he stood alone he had offered his participation in the venture as a conciliating gesture. "It is right that the people should decide these things. All the people, gathered together. If Three Stars will receive the pipe my father sends, there will be peace until the hoop of the nation is raised in the Moon of Fat Calves. Then the Lakota nation will decide on peace or war. My father will speak for peace and I will listen. But I will speak for war."

He had said this calmly and with the dignity a man was expected to show in council, and there had been a few soft *hau's* of approval for the way he spoke his change of heart. But Bat knew his wife's brother better than most. Standing Eagle might have swallowed his pride, but he hadn't swallowed it whole. He would carry out the wishes of the council, but if Three Stars should happen to stay out ahead of the pipe carriers and find some small village in the Tongue River bottom before they caught him, that was out of the war leader's hands.

Bat watched Standing Eagle now as the man tethered his horse. He had chosen his best hunter for the journey and the animal hardly seemed tired at all after what had been a pretty good day's ride. The other horses too were growing accustomed to the trail. A horse could be a contrary animal sometimes; you let him run free all winter without asking too much of him, and he wasn't in a hurry to submit to saddle and rein, but if you kept after him for a few days and made him mind his manners, pretty soon he'd put his whole heart into whatever you asked of him. Standing Eagle was right about one thing: the horses would eat well tonight. Come morning they might not be up to grain-fed mounts, but they'd be fit to travel and Standing Eagle would have one less reason to go slow.

The wind was stiffening and night was coming on fast. The men helped Blackbird build the sleeping shelter and in no time it was done. The night before, they had slept wrapped in their blankets under a bright gibbous moon, but tonight a shelter was needed. It was much the same as a small sweat lodge; willow poles were bent over and lashed together to form a low oval frame, then blankets and robes were spread over it and tied down for a covering, leaving a small smoke hole. A man had to get on his knees to enter and it was impossible to sit fully upright, but the fire was quickly started with one of Hardeman's sulphur matches and in no time the shelter was warm. He had brought the matches out the first night on the trail, when he saw Little Hand begin the slow process of striking flint and steel into a small handful of tinder. None of the Lakota had objected to using the white man's way of making fire.

"Snug as a trader in his lodge," Bat said now, wiping at his watering eyes. There were no flaps to control the venting and when the wind gusted it was smoky inside the shelter, but it was a comforting place for a cold night.

The men chewed slowly on pieces of jerky as they watched Blackbird break small pieces of the trail food the Lakota called *wasná* into a horn bowl filled with water. As moccasin carrier, it was the boy's job to do the cooking. He dropped small hot stones from the fire pit into the bowl and the water began to warm. The cavalry had chopped through the foot-thick ice on the stream to get water for their horses and the thin new ice on the holes had been easy to break. Blackbird added a handful of dried wild onions to the water, then shredded bits of jerky and more *wasná*. Pemmican, the whites called it, using a word from an eastern tribe. It was made from dried meat, usually buffalo, pounded together with dried chokecherries or serviceberries and mixed with tallow. The mixture was sealed in lengths of intestine, with more tallow poured over it to keep out the air, and was carried on hunting and war parties as well as when the village itself was on the move. A man could live indefinitely on *wasná* and the pipe carriers had been given a supply sufficient to last them until the next moon grew horns and lingered in the western sky after the sun had set.

Blackbird removed cool stones and added hot ones and the water began to steam. He patiently stirred the mixture with a wooden spoon and when he judged it ready the bowl was passed from man to man until the weak stew was all gone and the bowl wiped clean with fingers, leaving no scrap behind.

In what seemed like no time at all, Standing Eagle and Little Hand were in their blankets and fast asleep, feet to the fire. Standing Eagle's slumber was marked by a rhythmic snoring. Hawk Chaser took out a pipe and smoked it, speaking low to Blackbird, who never lay down until the last of the men was asleep. The warrior told tales of other journeys he had been on as boy and man, and Blackbird listened with rapt attention, his eyes bright with excitement. It seemed to him that each breath he took was charged with the power of manhood.

Bat followed Hawk Chaser's example and took out his own pipe for casual smoking, a Missouri corncob he had bought the summer before from a trader who had defied the ban on trading in the Powder River country. The man had brought gunpowder too. Bat stoked the pipe with a generous pinch of

Lakota smoking mixture and lit it, smoking just one pinch at a time in the Lakota manner. Outside the shelter the storm blew, buffeting the thin covering.

"Well, you reckon we'll get Crook to swallow the bargain?" Bat's question took Hardeman unaware.

"The bargain?"

"Let the Sun Band be now, in exchange for Sun Horse talking to the other chiefs come summer?"

"I don't know. Washington wants it settled now," Hardeman said. The government's impatience might be cooled for a while if Crook would plead Sun Horse's cause, but at best the hope was precarious. Back in the Sun Band's village, Hardeman had talked to Sun Horse before the council, with Bat translating, trying one last time to make the headman say yes or no and settle it all now, but Sun Horse had merely smiled and shaken his head.

"I have heard what Three Stars wishes," the old chief had said. "Now he will hear what I wish for my people and all the Lakota. Often men must talk for a time before they can agree, and when Lakota talks with *washichun*, they must talk for a long time."

"I can bring Three Stars here," Hardeman had offered, taking an enormous risk by planting that possibility in Sun Horse's mind. "You can speak with him yourself. If you believe he's a truthful man, take your people to the reservation. Then you can ride to speak to the hostiles when the grass is up."

But Sun Horse had shaken his head again. "It is not good to travel in the Snowblind Moon. Tell Three Stars that if my cousin Sitting Bull agrees, the Lakota will remain at peace until the grass is green and then we will meet to talk. Say that to Three Stars, and give him the pipe so he will know the words are true."

Sun Horse had been subdued, as if he himself might have doubts about the plan's chance for success, and strangely, he had been in no great hurry to send the pipe carriers on their way. Even Bat had commented that the headman seemed to be stalling for time. "Been time enough to prepare a dozen pipes," the mountain man grumped on Hardeman's second evening in Bat and Penelope's lodge. But then the next day there had come the news of the avalanche, and the change in Sun Horse had been remarkable to see. He looked as if someone had just handed him title to the whole of the Powder River country, signed by President Grant himself, and then he had produced the pipes at last and given leave for the emissaries to go, sending them on their way with a hail and farewell after a series of trivial delays had kept them in the village for another half day when they should already have been off and gone.

Recalling the scene now made Hardeman uneasy. The old man had stood there in his ratty robe, waving goodbye in evident high spirits, and somehow Hardeman had been left with the feeling that Sun Horse was one up on him. Since then he had found no way to explain the headman's singular changes of mood, but neither had he found any room for deception in the pipe carriers' mission. Besides, Sun Horse was Johnny's grandfather; it was unlikely that he would betray the boy's trust. What was more, he was a peace man with a vision of bringing an end to the conflict with the whites, and Hardeman had come to feel a commonness of purpose with the old man. *My friend has agreed to help us,* Sun Horse had told Johnny. *Together the whiteman and the Lakota will make peace.* The words had reminded Hardeman that his own efforts to make peace over the years had all come about because Jed Putnam had taught him long ago that it was possible to be friends with the Indians, even while both red man and white kept to his own nature and his own ways. If he and Sun Horse could act in good faith, like true friends, they might just pull it off.

"Them politicians are in an all-fired hurry to get this thing settled," Bat said now, setting another pinch of smoke in his pipe. He said the word "politicians" like a curse. "They done got it settled already, three times. I went with Sun Horse in '68, down at Laramie. Him and a hundred more made their marks on the paper that give 'em this country here forever."

"The government needs gold," Hardeman replied. "Needs gold and wants land."

"Hell, the Injuns don't want the gold. Let the politicians have the gold." Bat spat into the fire as if to rid his mouth of the distasteful word. "I'll tell you what, gold's one o' the things got the Injuns plumb convinced that we're all as crazy as a bunch o' loons. That first black-robe in the country here, the one called De Smet? Wasn't half crazy, him. He told all the Injuns he preached at never to let on to a white man that they knew where there was a drop of gold. Forget you seen it, he says, it makes white men crazy." He lit the pipe with a glowing stick and puffed twice. "Let 'em have the gold. What these boys want is the *Paha Sapa.* The Black Hills is the spirit center of the nation. That's the place the souls of the young men fly with the eagles." He looked at Hardeman. "I made the vision quest myself. When I was forty-five years old. Don't imagine you can know what that's like."

Hardeman shook his head.

"Big medicine. Heap big. White man laughs at the red man's medicine and calls him a superstitious heathen. Might as well laugh at a tree. It's something that exists. Stands right there as tall as a mountain, real as a rock, and they laugh at it. It don't pay to mess with Lakota medicine." Again he stoked his pipe and relit it, and Hardeman waited, sensing that the mountain man was working up to something.

"Sun Horse, he figgers there's medicine in Johnny Smoker," Bat continued once the pipe was going. "They call him Stands Between the Worlds, but that ain't all. He's got a heap o' names. The Boy with Many Names, they say. Buffalo Dreamer's one o' them." He watched Hardeman closely and saw no reaction. "Seems like you might not know that part of it. The boy dreamed of White Buffalo Cow Woman. *Ptésanwin,* we call her." He said the name

306

with an unmistakable reverence. "It ain't every boy dreams of *Ptésanwin*."

Hardeman had heard of the White Buffalo Cow Woman. Legend said that she had brought the sacred pipe to the Sioux and instructed them in its use, and to this day a white buffalo was among the most sacred of animals to the tribe. But Johnny had never mentioned *Ptésanwin*.

"'Course that don't mean nothin' now, seein' as the boy picked the white man's trail. That like to took the stuffin' out o' Sun Horse." Bat was staring into the fire, but now he turned again to Hardeman and fixed the scout with his gaze. "See, Sun Horse figgered if'n the boy picked the Injun life, he'd come back to the Lakotas, his pa's folks, not the Cheyenne. *Ptésanwin*, she belongs to the Lakota myths." He used his pipe to make a sign close to his head, indicating matters of the spirit world. "She brought the ceremonies and the ceremonies are the life of the people. They're the heart of the Lakota way, you might say. A buffalo dreamer comin' to the Sun Band would bring life to the people; might even bring the power to save them in troubled times." Bat sucked hard on the pipe, but it was out. He took it from his mouth and held it in both hands, his eyes still on Hardeman. "Young Johnny don't know none o' this. Sun Horse never told him. Reckoned the boy oughta make his choice free and clear, for his own reasons."

The mountain man fell silent. With slow care he scraped the bowl of the pipe clean and dropped the ashes into the fire before returning the pipe to the elkskin sack he had carried slung from his shoulder since leaving the village. A "possibles sack" the fur trappers had called it, and most had carried one. They kept therein their smallest and most essential belongings.

"Big medicine in dreams," Bat said. "Reckon I'll catch me some. We can use all the medicine we got."

He curled in his robe like a bear settling in for the winter, and pulled it over his face. In a short time his breathing slowed and fell into rhythm with the other sleepers.

Hardeman lay back on his bedroll and stretched out, listening to the wind and Standing Eagle's soft snoring, remembering other nights on the trail. The shelter reminded him a good deal of the Cheyenne hunting shelters Johnny had often built for the two of them when they traveled in bad weather; this one was not much bigger, although it held six.

He thought of Sun Horse then, and he realized that he owed him a great debt of gratitude. No wonder it had been a blow to the old man when Johnny told him he had picked the white world! It meant the loss of any spirit power the boy might have brought to the Sun Band. And yet when the boy had the dream, Sun Horse had kept the full import from him, leaving Johnny free to choose. Hardeman wondered if he himself could have kept from trying to influence the boy's decision if he believed the survival of his people might depend on it.

In the end, Johnny had picked the white world and that was that. Back in Putnam's Park on the day they had parted, Johnny had sat astride his horse next to Alfred Chalmers' wagon and Amanda Spencer was there on the driver's seat next to the Englishman, smiling down at Johnny. Johnny had returned her smile before leaning down to shake Chris's hand and wish him good luck, and there had been something in Johnny's expression that Hardeman hadn't seen before, as if the youth had lately discovered one of life's great secrets, the kind that seemed so obvious once you got hold of it, and you felt like a blind man for not seeing it sooner. He was set on his path, and neither his Cheyenne childhood nor Sun Horse's failed hopes for the boy and his dream would affect the outcome now.

Hardeman removed his buckskin coat and spread it over the blankets and the oilskin before crawling into the bedroll. What mattered now was to get on and find Crook, and see if he would risk as much as Sun Horse to make a lasting peace.

Hardeman lay back with his head on his hands. The cavalry was pushing northward, leaving the Sun Band's village farther behind each day, and he was secretly glad. There could be no thought any longer of leading Crook to Sun Horse. Even if the pipe carriers overtook the expedition tomorrow, Crook would not want to turn back and retrace his steps, not while there were other troops in the field and a hostile village perhaps around the next bend in the river. If he would not accept the pipe... Hardeman would cross that bridge when he came to it. But from now on he would sleep easier knowing that the Sun Band, and the people in Putnam's Park, were out of immediate danger.

Hawk Chaser and Blackbird were readying themselves for sleep. As Hawk Chaser wrapped himself in his robe, he cast a glance at Hardeman and it struck the scout that there had been more than a few times in the past two days when he had caught the warrior keeping an eye on him, but there was nothing so unusual in that. In a small group traveling together each man liked to know what the others were doing, especially when one was a stranger. Hardeman gave it no more thought and dropped quickly into a sound slumber.

In the morning the pipe carriers were on their way as soon as the light permitted, moving once more into the face of the storm. Throughout the day the trail left by the cavalry grew fainter as the snow filled in the tracks. When nightfall forced the men to camp once more, in a shallow ravine with no water near, they had not found the soldiers' next stopping place.

TWENTY-ONE

"Jesus H. Christ and twenty-three names of Lucifer! Will yez look at my bleeding bacon! It's frozen harder than a corporal's heart!"

Boots Corwin was wakened by the cursing of the cook. Huddled deep within his robes with even his face covered, he was almost warm enough. He lifted the corner of the robe and sniffed the air. No hint of breakfast greeted him but a gust of snow blew in his face. He dropped the robe and settled back in his lair. Whether or not the command moved today, there would be no orders before breakfast.

They were only five miles from where they had first made camp the day before, after the exhilarating thirty-mile night march. The going had become dangerous at times as the trail wound around steep rock faces where a bad fall awaited any misstep, but no obstacle had seemed to daunt men or beasts and the brilliant moonlight had guided all hands to safety. At five o'clock in the morning of the eighth of March the command had made camp on the Clear Fork of the Powder and had turned into their robes for some much needed rest. Three hours later they woke to find that the clear skies had vanished behind new onslaughts of clouds, and snow was falling again harder than ever, propelled by renewed winds from the north. With black looks at the sky and much cursing, the column had been formed and put under way, but just five miles down the broad valley they had come on this sheltered cove and here they had passed the rest of the day. The men had improvised added protection from the weather as best they could, making crude lean-tos from the abundant willow and cottonwood brush, and they had sought what humor there was to be found in their own discomfort.

Corwin had seen General Crook walking through the encampment more than once and he had noted the concern on the commander's face. The reason was not hard to imagine. The men were just over a week away from Fetterman, scarcely three days from the supply wagons. The campaign was still high adventure. Neither the real danger nor the real fatigue had yet been felt. How would the men hold up?

As evening fell, the storm had not slackened, although the temperature dropped sharply, approaching zero on Dr. Munn's thermometer. A blanket was ordered to be placed on each of the horses, and the men had slept stacked like cordwood, sharing every scrap of available covering.

Corwin raised the corner of his robe again. "Mr. Whitcomb!" he called out.

"Yes, Major?" came an immediate reply from close at hand. The voice had the habitual tone of good spirits Corwin had come to expect from his second lieutenant. The boy rebounded quickly from any disappointment.

Corwin threw the robe off his head and shoulders and squinted against the driving snow. Whitcomb stood a few yards away, cloaked in fur hat and buffalo coat and bulky overboots. He looked entirely comfortable. Beyond the young officer the cook continued to swear inventively as he tried to cut up the frozen bacon with a hand axe. By now the cooks had learned that if they did not want to be hindered in their endeavors by men clustering around the cookfires, they must provide some alternative source of warmth. Some had adopted the practice of building large bonfires for the men, and such a blaze was burning now in Company E's bivouac, but even so, nearly half the troop was gathered around the cook, offering words of advice and encouragement.

"The God damn bacon! Will yez look at that? The God damn bacon broke my axe!" The angry cook pointed to a fresh chip in the blade.

"It ain't the bacon's fault, cookie," said Sergeant Rossi. "The cold makes the steel brittle, see? You could chip it on the ice, even on a log." Rossi spoke American like a native New Yorker. He had been born in Italy but brought to the New World as an infant. He knew more about everything than the next man and had a cheerful way of telling him so.

"All I know is the God damn bacon broke my axe. Give me some room to work here, boys." The cook turned to his small fire and tried to encourage it to more vigorous life. He propped the slab of bacon close to the flames and set the axe beside it.

"Are there any orders yet, Mr. Whitcomb?" Corwin pushed the robe aside and rose to a sitting position. Except for his overcoat, which he had removed and placed atop himself beneath his robe, he had slept fully clothed.

"Nothing yet, sir. It doesn't seem to be snowing quite so hard today."

Corwin looked about at the snow, which flew nearly horizontally across the stream and swirled thickly in the recesses of the cove. It seemed to him that Boreas had returned with new vitality, but he said nothing.

Around him the camp was fully awake, although the light was still dim. As usual, he was among the last up. It was a bad example for the men, but he hated getting up in the morning when he hadn't slept well. It was the one failing as a commander that he recognized in himself, but fifteen years of army life hadn't changed his habits.

Sergeant Rossi suddenly left the group at the cookfire and walked quickly toward Corwin, looking over his shoulder. "Sir, Dr. Munn is making his morning rounds and General Crook is with him."

"Thanks, Rossi." Corwin arose quickly and was folding his robe into a tight roll when the surgeon reached E Troop's bivouac. In addition to Crook, he was accompanied by Lieutenant Bourke and the correspondent Strahorn. Corwin greeted them.

"Good morning, General. Dr. Munn. Mr. Bourke." There were nods and perfunctory salutes all around. Each man's gestures were reduced by the cold to the minimum necessary motions.

310

"No frostbite, I trust, Lieutenant?" Munn inquired of Corwin. "Everyone can feel his toes this morning?" The surgeon had become more visible each day as the weather turned colder and more severe, keeping watch for frostbite and pneumonitic ailments.

Corwin hesitated. He should already have made his own morning rounds, looking for the telltale white spots on noses or ears or fingers. He didn't want to be caught in an incorrect report.

"Sir, I have inspected the troop on Major Corwin's orders. There is no sign of frostbite." Whitcomb gave this intelligence looking straight ahead, standing nearly at attention in the expedition commander's presence, although Crook did not require such formalities on campaign.

"Excellent," said Munn.

Corwin had given no such orders, but if his subaltern had the initiative to perform routine chores without instruction, he would not protest.

"You certainly have the weather you wanted, General," Strahorn observed. He swung his arms in circles to warm himself, looking somewhat like an ungainly bird attempting flight.

"I think the general might have settled for a less severe blizzard than this one, Mr. Strahorn," said Bourke with a wink at Whitcomb.

"Oh, this will serve nicely, Mr. Bourke," said Crook. His beard twitched as he repressed a smile. Since the moment of his arrival he had occupied himself in looking about the campsite, where at last the smell of bacon was beginning to make itself known. The men watched the cook like a pack of hungry coyotes. Icicles hung from mustaches and beards and droplets of ice had formed even on their eyebrows. Collars grew misted with rime as breath froze to the fur. But if they were well fed and kept in tight discipline they would do well enough, Corwin thought. He no longer grew nervous when General Crook took an occasion to inspect E Company. Crook observed everything and he forgot nothing, but he rarely meddled in the responsibilities of his subordinates and never reprimanded his officers in the presence of others except under extreme provocation.

"I don't believe the men will benefit from another day of idleness, Major," Crook said to Corwin. "We will take advantage of the weather to move along under its protection once the men have eaten."

"Yes, sir. As you see, General, there is some delay here. It seems the bacon was frozen too hard to cut."

"All the cooks are having the same problem," Surgeon Munn put in. "Warn the men that forks and spoons should be run through hot water or ashes before using them, or the flesh will freeze to the metal."

"The same precaution applies to the horses' bits; they must be warmed before bridling," Crook added, with a farewell wave of his hand.

With the bacon finally thawed and the men fed, the command formed up and started off, turning west from the Clear Fork and ascending Piney Creek, a small tributary.

"What is the hour, Mr. Reb?" Corwin inquired once they were under way.

311

His horse was tossing its head and prancing a little, urging a faster pace, but Corwin held him in.

With a motion that had become almost second nature by now, Whitcomb ungloved his right hand and reached through the opening of his buffalo greatcoat and then the hip-length coat of Minnesota blanket beneath and brought forth his pocket watch. The case was gold and the inside of the cover bore a miniature portrait of the family mansion in Virginia. By a miracle, both the watch and the ancestral home had survived the war.

"A quarter to seven, sir." He snapped the cover closed and replaced the watch in its interior pocket, surprised at the early hour. All his instincts told him that they were traveling a far northern country in the dead of winter, but the equinox was less than two weeks away and the days were steadily lengthening.

Before long the column left the small watercourse and entered broken country that rapidly grew rougher as it ascended the southern slopes of the next divide. The ground was covered with six inches or more of new snow and on the lee side of the ridges it was drifted as deep as a horse's belly. Once atop the divide the column made its way across an enormous plateau, moving northeast toward the valley of the Tongue River. Ravines cut the trail every hundred yards or so, and the difficulties encountered in descending and ascending the steep and slippery banks of these obstacles slowed the command's advance to the pace of a slow walk. As each troop and each division of pack mules reached the edge of a ravine, that entire section of the column would halt while the horses or mules crossed one by one until they were reassembled on the other side. E Troop was once more serving as rear guard and its progress was painfully slow as the head of the column stretched out farther and farther ahead of it.

At mid-morning, while the troop was halted waiting for the last division of pack mules to cross a particularly deep ravine, word was passed back along the column instructing each company commander to bring his flankers in to a distance of fifty yards. The scouts had found buffalo droppings and recent Indian sign.

"Sergeant Polachek!" Corwin called out above the sound of the wind and the braying of the mules nearby, "you bring in the squads to the east; I'll take the west side! Mr. Reb, you see to crossing the troop. And keep the line closed up as best you can."

"Yes, sir." Whitcomb's disappointment at being passed over yet again for the more hazardous duty was only somewhat mollified by the knowledge that crossing the ravine posed a certain degree of danger to horse and rider and the responsibility for getting the troop safely across now rested with him. The ravine was made by runoff at the edge of the plateau and one mule had already been killed that morning when it panicked at the bottom of a ravine and bolted down the gully and over a cliff.

"A'right now, thet's his turn, y' blackguard!" There was a sudden commotion among the mule packers at the edge of the chasm, and a shifting away from three of the men, two of them holding a single mule and glaring at a lone packer who held another of the beasts. The mules had their ears laid back and they were shifting about nervously.

"That's 'ank 'ewitt, sir," said Corporal Atherton, the only non-commissioned officer remaining at the head of the troop. He was a stocky Englishman with bad teeth. "The man with 'im is Yank Bartlett. ''ank 'n' Yank,' they call 'em. They're like two peas in a pod, always together. The other man is called Chileno John. Watch his left, 'and, on the knife."

"*Lo siento mucho, viejo cabrón,*" the Spanish American said with elaborate hostility, one hand grasping the haft of his large skinning knife. For the moment, the blade remained in its scabbard at his belt. "*Tu te equivocas, sin duda a causa de tu edad avanzada.* It is my turn!"

"Call me an old goat, y' Papist beaner? Why, I'll slit yer from gut t' gullet soon 's look at yer!"

"Try it, *gringo!*"

The packers, all of whom had served with General Crook in Arizona before being brought north at his insistence for the present campaign, were a disparate lot, the two largest contingents being Yankee forty-niners who had learned their trade by packing their own supplies into the California foothills during the gold rush and Mexicans who had grown tired of being drafted to pack arms and ammunition for every revolutionary bandit king that fancied the Mexican presidency. They were separated now into two groups, backing their respective champions.

Whatever the cause of the quarrel, Whitcomb's immediate concern was to end it and resume the chore of crossing the ravine. He dismounted and led his horse forward as Chileno John whacked his mule with a heavy glove and shouted, "*Vaya,* Pinto Jim!"

Yank Bartlett grabbed Pinto Jim's halter and held the mule back. "This animule waits his turn or he's deader'n thet mush you call brains. Keno goes first this time!"

Chileno John's knife began to rise in its scabbard, but Whitcomb stepped quickly in front of the irate Mexican. "Gentlemen," he pleaded with all the firmness of tone he could muster. "I beg you, stand not on the order of your going, but go!"

"Cain't do it, General," said Hank Hewitt, brevetting Whitcomb six grades in rank. "Thar's a double eagle on this here deal. Each mule got to go on his lonesome, 'n the one t' make the crossin' gets the gold."

"Thet's God's truth, General," Yank agreed, and his face brightened with an idea. "Now ef'n you'd be the jedge, why I reckon we c'd be off an' runnin' 'fore y' c'd say 'Old Jack Long's dead 'n' gone.'"

"Corporal Atherton? You know more of this sort of thing than I do."

"Forgive me, sir. I would sooner carry both their packs to the Yellowstone than get in a dispute between Keno and Pinto Jim."

By now most of E Troop was gathered at the edge of the ravine, waiting to see what Whitcomb would do. He took a deep breath and turned back to the packers. "Very well, gentlemen, if you will accept me as sole judge you must also agree that my decision is final and not subject to argument. Understood?" There were no objections. "Very well. How are we to decide who goes first?"

Another of the Mexican packers drew a silver dollar from a pocket and flipped it to the young officer. "*Qué dices, Juan,*" the man said to Chileno John. "*Cabeza o culo?*"

"*Culo,*" Chileno John replied at once, smiling broadly. "*Culo para mi amigo Hank!*" The other Spanish-speaking packers roared, and even the Americans laughed.

"That means 'e picks tails, sir," Atherton explained. "Well, it don't exactly mean tails. It's an impolite term, sir, if you take my meaning."

Whitcomb flipped the coin and caught it, and slapped it atop his other hand. "Heads," he announced.

Hank 'n' Yank smiled, pleased at this small victory, and together they led Keno to the edge of the ravine. Hank patted the mule's neck and stroked his long ears and then he spoke in tones usually reserved for expressing the fondest feelings close to the ear of a loved one. "Y'r a miserable bastard," he began, "'n' some day when I'm starvin' 'n' cold I'll shoot yer dead 'n' feast on yer meat, 'n' when I'm done I'll sleep tight in thet moth-eaten coat y' call yer skin. But fer now, you jest slip down here slick as a beaver, 'n' there'll be oats on yer *sudera* tonight." He hit the mule a sudden blow on the rump and shouted, "Now *git*, y' wuthless hunk o' meat."

As if the blow had been no more than a fleabite, Keno sauntered forth and cocked his head to look at the trail. Without more than a moment's hesitation he stepped down the slope, made slick by the passage of nine companies of cavalry and all the other mules that had already crossed ahead of him. His front feet began to slide, and at once he set his hind legs in a half crouch, keeping his back and his load level as he coasted calmly to the bottom, where he recommenced walking as soon as he had come to a stop, and quickly scrambled up the far slope.

A cheer went up from the onlookers, but Chileno John shrugged. Removing one glove he reached deep into a pocket of his overcoat. He withdrew his hand and offered something to Pinto Jim. The mule flapped his lips greedily and ate the offering, nudging the Mexican's coat for more, but Chileno John shook his head. He pointed at the ravine. "*Ande, pues,*" he said simply.

If a mule can look disappointed, such was the look Pinto Jim gave his master before setting off down the icy slope, but he turned to his business willingly enough and displayed his own preferred method of navigating the obstacle. Disdaining Keno's caution, he kept walking even after the footing became treacherous, slipping and sliding and resigning himself to coasting only when he appeared likely to lose his control entirely and roll headlong to the bottom. Before he came to a stop he leaped for the upslope, giving a small crowhop and a kick of his heels, and lurched to the top as surefooted as a mountain goat, though scarcely as gracefully. No sooner had he reached level ground among the crowd waiting there than he stopped, planted his feet, raised his tail and broke wind loudly, looking back over his shoulder at his master.

314

The onlookers went wild, packers and troopers alike slapping one another on the back and pointing across the way at the insolent mule. Gradually the cheers subsided and all eyes came to rest on the young lieutenant, awaiting his decision. Whitcomb noted that Chileno John still had his hand on the haft of his knife, and he realized that his own hands were sweating within his heavy muskrat gloves.

"Gentlemen," he began, "mine has not been an easy task. But I have been given a duty, and as an officer in the service of our country, I will never shirk a duty." This brought a derisive cheer from the soldiers, many of them welcoming the chance to add insulting comments about the officer class from within the anonymity of the crowd. Whitcomb feigned not to hear them. When it was quiet again, he continued. "It is my decision that in the matter of *style*, Keno is clearly the winner—"

At this, Hank 'n' Yank let out whoops of victory and began to do a jig on the frozen ground to the cheers of a small group of supporters while Chileno John and the Mexicans raised an even louder cry of protest. Chileno John advanced on Whitcomb, but he stopped as the officer raised a hand for silence.

"Quiet, please, gentlemen!" When he had their attention once again, he said, "As I was about to say, I have not been called solely to judge style. I have been asked to judge *mules*. And gentlemen, if ever I have seen behavior more mulish than Pinto Jim's, I can't remember the occasion. I declare Pinto Jim the winner!"

The uproar was deafening now, and even Hank 'n' Yank and their supporters could find no fault with the judge's ruling, although they made token protests for form's sake.

There was a sudden lessening of the general merriment and Whitcomb turned to see Lieutenant Corwin making his way through the gathering on horseback. Behind him were four groups of flankers led by Sergeants Dupré, Duggan and Rossi and Corporal Stiegler.

"Did you order the men to break formation and dismount, Mr. Whitcomb?"

"Not exactly, sir. The packers were having a dispute and we've just now got it settled." Whitcomb noticed that someone had thought to post a few pickets, men with carbines at the ready who were watching the troop's flanks and rear.

"I leave you in charge of the troop for a quarter of an hour and you have let yourself become separated from the command. God help you if the Indians attack while you're cut off like this."

The snow had thinned somewhat and Whitcomb saw that the rest of the column had already crossed the next ravine a quarter of a mile away.

"Sergeant Dupré!" Corwin called out to the first sergeant. "Let's get the men across quickly and get after the column. Mr. Reb, you will bring up the rear with Corporal McCaslin. When you reach the other side you will join me at the head of the troop."

From the moment of Corwin's appearance the packers had become very busy getting the remaining mules across the ravine and on their way, and the trail was clear now for E Troop to cross. Corwin dismounted and led the way, followed by Sergeant Dupré. In what seemed a short time, after the delay for mule judging,

315

Whitcomb and McCaslin were following the last of the men down the icy trail.

"I don't know whom I have to thank for putting out the pickets while I was occupied with those mules," Whitcomb said. "I am grateful to whomever thought of it."

"Routine precaution, sorr. No need for yez to concern yerself. The boys had themselves a good laugh. Does 'em a world o' good, 'specially when they see an officer joinin' in the spirit o' things."

"I'm afraid I got another black mark in Major Corwin's book."

"Don't concern yerself, sorr. Y'r learnin', that's what counts. We all begin like babes in the woods; it's how quick we learn that matters."

As they remounted their horses on level ground, Whitcomb turned to McCaslin again. "By the way, what was it that Chileno John fed his mule back there?"

"That's how he gets his name, sorr. That mule's favorite treat is pinto beans."

Smiling to himself, Whitcomb cantered past the troop, which was moving along at a brisk trot, and took his place beside Corwin in the lead, ready to receive the further reprimand he was certain was coming. But Corwin remained silent until the company had crossed the next ravine and overtaken the rest of the column, and when he did speak his tone was pleasant, as if the morning had passed without incident.

"Look at those mules, Mr. Whitcomb," he said, waving a hand to take in the pack train ahead of them. "Look at the size of those packs. The army says a mule will carry one hundred and seventy-five pounds. At that rate, our train could carry enough to keep us on maneuvers for just seven or eight days, but we're out for fifteen. Our mules carry three hundred and twenty pounds on the average, and they can march twice as far as any other mules in the army on a standard ration of feed. Those pack cushions are called *aparejos*, and every *aparejo* in this train has been made especially for one particular mule, so he can carry a heavy load in comfort. There isn't a department commander west of the Missouri who wouldn't kill General Crook in his sleep if he thought he could make off with this pack train."

He paused for a moment to let this information sink in. "Now look at the men. There are men in this troop, in all the troops, who have started out on winter campaigns where only the officers wore fur coats, while the soldiers were dressed in army blue. But these men are dressed as well as you and I. They're ready to carry a load as well. Before the campaign is over they will have hardships to bear, and they'll carry on because that's their duty." Again he paused, glancing at Whitcomb. "Officers are prepared to carry something called the burden of command, Mr. Whitcomb. In an expedition led by George Crook that responsibility bears an added weight. Just as the mules and the men are expected to carry their loads, so are you. You're not here to entertain the men, or to wipe their noses, or to hold their hands. You're here to lead and command. The more intimate you become with them, the harder that job will be. If you remember nothing else, remember that."

316

Even this last injunction was said without rancor. It was passed along in much the same manner as Whitcomb's own father had sometimes passed along useful observations about life in general to young Ham, back before the war.

The command encamped that night beside Prairie Dog Creek, having made just fourteen miles from the Clear Fork in a long day of hard marching. During the evening meal the men remained unusally quiet and once they had eaten most went soon to their blankets and robes and little shelters instead of spending the usual time around the cookfires for warmth and conversation. It seemed a somber camp, as if the weather had succeeded at last in smothering the good cheer of the men even as it smothered the landscape in a layer of deadening white, but as Whitcomb climbed into his robes, one of the last to do so, he heard a voice raised from a bedroll nearby to address the troop at large. He thought at first it was McCaslin, but the voice was younger and it gave a sardonic lilt to the words.

"Oh, this soldierin' under Gineral Crook is mighty foine, boys. No odds how hard we tramp over this blasted country all day, when we come to camp at night we get all the comforts and convaniences the land affords. Jist think of it—hardtack and coffee for supper, picket pine for mattresses and lariats for coverin', an' the fun of it is, the gineral gets it all the same!"

Whitcomb thought of what Corwin had said that day, about the provisions made for the comfort of the mules and men, and he saw that Corwin was right. The men knew that Crook had outfitted them well and would ask nothing of them that he would not endure himself, and so they would carry an extra burden willingly. But he felt that Corwin was wrong too; such mutual trust and respect need not be put in jeopardy by a moment's man-to-man contact between officer and enlisted men, especially if such moments bred a camaraderie that transcended rank. Until the incident with the wounded trooper during the second attack on camp, Whitcomb had felt like an outsider, and he had begun to despair of ever being accepted. But that moment had proved to be a turning point. John Bourke had said that chasing after the cattle had shown he had pluck; perhaps rescuing the wounded corporal in the fight at the Powder had proved that he had something more than a fool's courage. And if the mule judging today helped to show that he could be a regular fellow, what harm was there in that? None of his actions had been planned to impress the enlisted men, but their attitude toward him had changed nevertheless. Now he felt that he belonged. Such a feeling could benefit both himself and the troop, for it strengthened the bonds between them. The men needed to know that their officers were able and took their welfare to heart. It was as simple as that. Secure in that knowledge they would do anything asked of them. There must be respect for one's superiors, of course, but that did not rule out companionship, even a kind of friendship as well. He understood that, even if Corwin did not. Perhaps it was Corwin and not he who was truly the outsider.

The next day, in the face of continued snow and a persistent wind that lashed the stinging crystals into the faces of the men, the command moved down Prairie Dog Creek toward its confluence with the Tongue River. The animals that gave the stream its name were very much in evidence, running hither and yon on ground and snowbank, perching by the entrances of their burrows to give their shrill warning chatter, unperturbed by the storm. Finally, in late afternoon the strength of the winds dropped and blue skies appeared to the west. As camp was made for the night a party of guides returned from a scout of several days, which had taken them through the country to the north and west, to the banks of the Rosebud. They had killed three deer on the return journey and this venison was quickly distributed to the grateful cooks. Around the fires there was laughter and even a few songs.

Some of the men had adopted the custom of General Crook and the packers, beginning preparations for their beds as soon as the column halted. When the horses had been seen to, each man who followed this method brushed a flat area of ground clear of snow and started a small fire that he would maintain throughout supper and the postprandial conversations around the cookfires. Then, shortly before going to sleep he would sweep away the last coals of his private fire and spread his robes, wherein he would sleep warm and comfortable all night on the heat stored by the ground beneath him. Tonight, with the clouds evaporating, the air took on a threatening chill, and as night fell and the moon rose, nearly full, scores of these bed-ground fires twinkled throughout the encampment, as if in answer to the more austere and distant sparkling of the stars overhead.

Before supper the company officers were called to the headquarters fire to hear the reports of the scouts, and once again Boots Corwin and Teddy Egan sought each other out.

"The damn Indians have skedaddled, Boots," Egan said in greeting. "I got it from Louis Richaud. Lots of villages, plenty of sign, and not a live one in a hundred miles. I'm beginning to catch the odor of wild geese."

And indeed, the first piece of intelligence the scouts reported was the discovery of an abandoned village of sixty tipis. They had found every indication that the Indians who had lived there were well supplied with all the necessities of life.

"They strip cottonwood bark, plenty bark, General. Horses strong, I bet," said Frank Grouard, his dark skin emphasizing the whiteness of his eyes in the firelight. The scouts and officers were gathered in a circle around the fire. Some of the men squatted on their hams while others sat cross-legged on robes or India-rubber ponchos. Corwin was struck by how much the gathering resembled an Indian council. "People strong too," Grouard continued. "Plenty meat. More game close to the Yellowstone. Deer, I think. Elk too, maybe buffalo. Good hunting. We find this in a tree, hung up." He nodded to one of the other guides and the man dropped something at Crook's feet. The general turned it over with the toe of his boot and those around the fire could see that it was the body of a young dog, with the cord that had been used to strangle it still tied around its neck.

Crook looked at the small body curiously, without surprise. "What does it mean, Frank?"

Grouard shrugged and looked at Big Bat Pourier and Little Bat Garnier, who squatted beside him. "Me, I reckon some squaw fixin' dog to eat."

Big Bat spoke up. He was not significantly larger than Little Bat, although he was several years older than the younger man, who was perhaps twenty-two. "They use dogs in ceremonies, General. 'Specially ceremonies for war."

"Plenty Crows in that country," Little Bat put in. "Sioux got their horses in corral. I think they worry about Crows come steal their horses, General. Mebbe make war on Crows." Garnier was half Sioux himself, his skin darker than a white man's, but without the tropical features and duskiness that distinguished Grouard.

"Could be," said Grouard with another shrug. "Could be it's just dog stew. That village they move quick, but not scared, General. These people strong."

"And the other village you found," Crook wanted to know, "that one had been abandoned how long?"

"Hard to say." It was Big Bat who answered. The scouts had been divided into two groups in order to cover more country; his group had found the second village. "Everything's froze up pretty good. Might be a couple weeks back, in the thaw. They was Oglala, General. Maybe went over to the Powder, maybe in to the agency. Might be they got the word and went in peaceful, like they're supposed to."

"Sir, isn't it possible that the large village also decided to go in?" The speaker was Captain Alexander Moore, brevet colonel, commander of the Fifth Battalion. "Isn't it even possible that there was a general movement to the agencies in the good weather? After all, the order was perfectly clear about what would happen to those who remained here."

"It's possible, Colonel," said Crook. He did not sound as if he thought it likely. "Frank, what do you think?"

"Sioux don't go to the reservation when he got good hunting," Grouard said. "I reckon they go over Powder River."

"But there were no Hunkpapa among them? No sign of Sitting Bull?"

"No Hunkpapa. Small village Oglala. Maybe Crazy Horse."

"Too small for Crazy Horse," said Big Bat, and Little Bat nodded. "Big medicine, Crazy Horse. He's getting plenty strong, General. Lots of lodges in his village, I'll bet."

Crook digested these differences of opinion as he did all information that his guides or officers brought to him—as worthy of consideration, something to be thought on seriously. He nodded slowly, looking into the fire, and Corwin glanced around the circle of faces gathered there. Colonel Reynolds and his adjutant, Lieutenant Morton, sat beside Crook, and it seemed to

Corwin that Reynolds awaited Crook's decision about their immediate course with some trepidation.

He's worried about the beef herd still, Corwin thought. That incident had reflected badly on Reynolds. It was his responsibility to post adequate guards and he had failed to do so. Rumor had it that Crook was sympathetic toward Reynolds, who had once commanded the Department of Texas. He had been relieved of that post and returned to his regiment after a small scandal involving irregularities in military supply contracts, and rumors of bribery. Lieutenant Bourke had told Lieutenant Sibley, who had told Lieutenant Rawolle, who had mentioned it to Corwin, that Crook hoped this campaign would help to restore Reynolds' good reputation. The loss of the beef herd, which had actually hurt the campaign very little, was an error that would easily be overlooked if Reynolds later distinguished himself. But if Reynolds made further mistakes, the running off of the herd would be seen as the first in a series of events for which he would be called to account.

Crook cleared his throat and looked up like a man who had been lost in his own thoughts and suddenly realized that others were awaiting his words. "We will continue down the Tongue, gentlemen. If General Terry and Colonel Gibbon are in the field we should rendezvous with them near the Yellowstone. Are there any questions?"

"General?" It was Reynolds.

"General Reynolds?"

"Mightn't it be best to cross to the Powder now and follow its course to the Yellowstone? It would seem that there must be some hostiles there. Any major village will do, as you yourself have said. A swift defeat, and the spirit of resistance broken?"

"Perhaps," Crook replied, "but if there are any hostiles remaining on the Tongue, it wouldn't do to have them at our backs when we turn east. If we find them here we can pivot to the right and force them towards Dakota even if the first engagement is not successful. But we need not go all the way to the Yellowstone ourselves. In a few more days we can send the scouts ahead and if they find no hostiles, and no sign of General Terry, I will gladly turn towards the Powder then." He looked around patiently, but there were no further questions. Corwin expected the council to end then, but Crook addressed them again.

"Gentlemen, battle is part of a soldier's life, but his job is to end battle. This is the inherent paradox of our calling. We steel ourselves for the charge; our hearts beat faster and our excitement grows until we actually look forward to the release that battle provides. But we must not forget that our job here is to enforce a peace on this region. If it can be made without bloodshed, the peace will come faster and will sit easier on the shoulders of both peoples. As many of you know, in Arizona we pursued a vigorous campaign against the Apaches until their headmen showed a willingness to sit down and speak peacefully with us. And since that time that region has enjoyed the fruits of

320

peace. In time there will be peace here too, but whether won with quiet words or by the sword remains to be seen. The difference between the two methods is the amount of blood that may be shed in the meantime and the nature of the peace that follows, whether full of a lingering hatred or blessed by a growing mutual understanding. Without the bitterness of a battlefield defeat in their hearts, the Sioux will learn all the sooner that their future lies in living peacefully beside the white men and adopting the industrious ways of the higher civilization." He looked up and his calm blue-gray eyes swept the circle. "And so, as we prepared for war, I sent out an emissary of peace. If he is successful, we may obtain the surrender of Sitting Bull and Crazy Horse without bloodshed."

There was a rustling of small movements around the circle as the men shifted about and glanced at one another.

"Four bits says that's news to Reynolds," Corwin said to Egan under his breath.

"Thanks, I'll keep my money."

"Perhaps there are indeed no villages remaining on the Tongue," Crook continued. "But by taking the militarily sound course of completing our sweep to the Yellowstone and assuring that there is no danger to our rear, we may delay the first encounter for a day or two and give my man a little more time to find us if he has been successful. But make no mistake, gentlemen. If we come upon the hostiles before he finds us, we will not hesitate. If a military solution presents itself, that is the course we will follow. We are soldiers, after all. The choice will have been made for us by fate and we will do our duty as soldiers, knowing we did our best to win over the enemy by entreaty and persuasion."

Crook stood and the others rose with him. The officers dispersed quietly, but when they reached their own bivouacs they gathered in small knots to talk over the general's surprising news. Corwin got his dinner from the cook and ate by himself, shocked by what he had heard. Crook was deliberately slowing the pace of the campaign! If the mysterious peace emissary were successful, the fact would reflect more honor on the reputation of General George Crook, but the officers and men who had gone hunting wild geese through the bitter blasts of a northern winter would be no more than motes in the residual dust of history. Nor would their participation be recognized by the bureaucrats who inscribed and filed the army's records in Washington City, and Corwin would have lost yet another chance for further promotion, the one thing he wanted most of all. He had a good record, but the pages were yellowing with age. The deeds that shone brightest were in the time of the Rebellion, before his capture and imprisonment. Ever since his release from prison he had felt the need to prove himself again. He was young enough to have another ten years of service ahead of him, but he did not want to serve out his days as a lieutenant. Advancement won in the closing days of the Sioux wars would assure him posts of increasing responsibility and op-

321

portunities that would stand him in good stead when he retired.

He had had other opportunities in his lifetime, but he had passed them by for the sake of the army.

As a youth he had wanted to go to sea in a whaling ship. His father, a textile worker in the burgeoning mill town of Lawrence, Massachusetts, had given his consent, and young Francis had been apprenticed to a firm of New Bedford whaling merchants. But one voyage had been enough to reveal the folly of his dream, for he was seasick the whole time. On his return to port he learned that the guns of rebellion were being unlimbered in the South, and he enlisted in the army after being assured he would be required to serve only on dry land. He had learned his new trade quickly and shown an aptitude for leadership, and he had been rewarded beyond his expectations with decorations and rapid promotion. After the war he had spent the last months of his recovery at home, where he saw the new mills lining the river. There was opportunity there, but his mother urged him not to stay. "Look at yer father, Frankie," she said to him one night when the rest of the household was asleep. "He's forty-five years old and his health is gone. Maybe in the army ye can make somethin' better for yerself." Young Boots Corwin was already an officer, and therefore a gentleman, and so he had stayed in uniform.

A few years later, on the frontier, he had met a girl for whom he might have turned his back on the army if he had been wiser and less ambitious. They could make a life together, she said, but not in the army. The Indian wars had been in full swing and Boots had his sights set on captain's bars, and so he had passed that fork in the road without turning aside. Not long after that he had met another girl, one more willing to suffer the hardships of an army wife, and he had married her. With the northern plains temporarily quieted he was transferred to Arizona and she followed him there, where their daughter Elizabeth was born. And then in a move from one post to another the ambulance carrying his wife and daughter had failed to arrive. When their bodies were found, Boots was not permitted to see them.

He had survived by rededicating himself to his profession, at first for no other reason than to take revenge on the savages who had shattered his life, but when he had occasion to view the bodies of some Apache women and children, he found that he had no taste for revenge. He put his hatred aside and his tragedy behind him, and neither he nor those who knew him had spoken of it since. Occasionally he could forget for days at a time that it was something real, something that had happened to him.

He wondered now if he had made the wrong choices at every step of the way. There were fewer opportunities left to him now, and less time, and still the greatest chance for success seemed to him to lie on the path he had chosen.

How great was the probability that Crook's peace mission would succeed? One man, alone? Not much, he thought, and found himself impatient for the dawn, when the command would be on the march again downriver, down to the Tongue and north toward the Yellowstone to scour the country there

322

and find a village if there was one, and if not, to turn to the Powder. When they reached the Powder they would go south, upriver, in a flanking movement that would turn east again toward the Black Hills until the whole country was swept clean, or until it was clear that the hostiles had abandoned their defiance and had scurried off to Dakota when they heard that soldiers were in their country in the dead of winter.

They couldn't all be gone, could they? The memory of the scouts' reports fueled his hope. A strong enemy, well supplied and feeling their oats, that was the enemy Corwin wanted to face. And by a daring winter stroke the plains Indian wars would be won with a bang, not a whimper. The campaign would be studied at West Point and Boots Corwin would be a part of it.

Give me the opportunity and I'll come out of it a captain. That's all I ask.

Fleeting clouds scudded across the face of a round moon that lit the landscape brilliantly when it shone freely. Corwin returned his plate to the cook and the snow creaked beneath his overboots like the flooring in an old house as he made his way to his bedroll. The skin on his face was drawn up tight from the cold and he was grateful for the thick growth of beard he had acquired during ten days of marching. As he settled himself in his robe he noticed the slight figure of Lieutenant Whitcomb moving among the sleeping forms of E Troop's men as placidly as if it were a summer night. He always seemed to prowl about the camp before he went to sleep.

Whitcomb showed promise of becoming a competent officer, but it was far too early to lessen the pressure on him. High spirits and a benign nature were poor armor for the Indian wars. The young officer was too familiar with the men and he needed to acquire a modicum of caution in all things, a suspicion that the world did not mean him well. So far, he had shown himself capable of bearing up under strict discipline and harsh conditions, but he had not yet faced the test of battle, where his good nature would have to be set aside.

CHAPTER
TWENTY-TWO

Once again the pipe carriers examined a place where the cavalry had spent the night, this one on the Clear Fork of the Powder. The morning was not yet half gone and they had already come ten miles since dawn. It was their fifth day on the trail and the third day of the storm, which was blowing still as if it meant to blow forever. By Hardeman's calculation it was the tenth of March, and with every hour that Crook moved northward the risk of war increased.

The valley of the Clear Fork was several hundred yards wide at this point, the bottomland stretching broad and flat to the west of the river. Low peaked hills rose on either side, displaying an occasional streak of reddish clay; the vivid color was startling in the otherwise uniform grayness the storm imposed on the landscape. There were growths of cottonwood and willow along the course of the stream, the first trees the pipe carriers had seen since the Big Horn foothills and the first willow brush since Crazy Woman's Fork. As they moved north the land was becoming less arid. The river bottom was grassy, and Blackbird permitted the horses to crop what they might while the men examined the bluecoats' camp for signs.

Hardeman had looked at the campsite only briefly. He stood now with Blackbird and the horses, waiting for the others to satisfy themselves. As he waited he worked out times and distances, trying to force the cavalry closer by willpower. The signs said the cavalry had been here longer ago than one night. If they were ahead of the pipe carriers by two days, it might as well be two weeks. Crook was moving his troops up-country with a speed Hardeman would not have believed possible under such trying conditions; if he kept up the pace, the pipe carriers would never catch him. Unless Hardeman pushed on alone while his roan was still strong.

"Let's get moving," he said curtly, and the other men paused in their searching to look at him. "They were here and now they're gone. What else do you need to know?" He climbed aboard his horse. "The trail goes downstream." He started off without waiting to see if they would come now or waste more time.

Standing Eagle and Little Hand exchanged a glance. Many of the northern bands were said to be on the lower Powder. If the bluecoat chief descended the Clear Fork to the larger stream, he might mean to continue on the Powder all the way to the Yellowstone, and before long he would come on one village or another. The two men mounted their horses and moved off behind Hardeman, with Bat and Hawk Chaser and Blackbird close on their heels.

The soldiers' trail was easy to follow in the relative shelter of the river bottom, and in what seemed to Hardeman an impossibly short time, certainly it was less than two hours, he came upon a small cove where there were many fire pits and evidence of some cooking.

"They laid over," he said to Bat as he dismounted. He led his horse down the bank into the cove and looked about, his spirits rising. "Must have spent all day here, or a long night, waiting out the storm. They might be just a day ahead." He remounted and gave the horse a sharp tap with his bootheels, urging the roan up the bank to where Bat was waiting. The mountain man had not bothered to dismount.

"Could be we're gettin' lucky," Bat said. "We'll press on. Eagle! Quit yer dawdlin' and climb onto that piece o' wolf meat y' call a horse!"

Standing Eagle insisted on digging in the largest of the fire pits, but the earth was frozen hard and yielded nothing.

Almost at once the cavalry's trail left the Clear Fork and turned to the northwest, following a smaller stream that flowed down from that direction. The stream led into rougher country and finally petered out on the lee slope of a rugged divide.

From atop the ridge, squinting against the full force of the wind and snow, the pipe carriers looked across a broad plateau to the valley of the Tongue River.

"Looks like Three Stars ain't goin' down the Powder after all," Bat remarked, and got a sour look from Standing Eagle.

Through the middle part of the day the riders made good time, despite the steady resistance of the storm. The going was hard in the broken country of the divide, but the unshod Indian horses were nimble-footed and Hardeman's roan seemed at home in any terrain; he negotiated ravines and steep hillsides without complaint. The going was easier when the cavalry's trail descended to a stream Bat believed to be Prairie Dog Creek, and at mid-afternoon the pipe carriers found the soldiers' next night camp.

The riders dismounted from their grateful horses, which Blackbird led to a thick patch of grass close at hand. The stalks of last year's growth rose through the thin covering of snow everywhere hereabouts, carpeting the land even far from the watercourses.

The men chewed jerky and *wasná* as they poked about the camp and here it was Hardeman who dug in one of the fire pits. Six inches down, the earth was still warm. He grinned in triumph, feeling a growing excitement. "Bat!" he called. "They were here last night."

"Still a ways ahead and movin' quick," Bat said, stooping to press his bare hand to the warm earth. "We'll move on a bit, but we best find some shelter and some feed for the ponies afore dark."

Hardeman nodded, knowing Bat was right. The horses had eaten poorly the night before, and the strength they had gained back at Crazy Woman was gone now. Much as he would have liked to forge on through the night, hoping to close on Crook by dawn or soon thereafter, he knew such a course was foolhardy. The trail might easily be lost in the storm, and it was reckless to chance stumbling on the cavalry in the dark, possibly provoking a deadly reaction from the sentries before Hardeman could identify himself. The little band would have to find a good place to camp and start out again at first light. With luck they would catch Crook tomorrow.

"We ain't makin' tracks settin' here," Bat said, rising to his feet and moving toward the horses. In the last two days the mountain man had taken a controlling hand in deciding the pace of the march. There had been some grumbling from Standing Eagle but no open opposition, and Bat and Hardeman often rode in the lead now.

Bat's horse started and shied sideways as he mounted, throwing her head and rolling her eyes, her nostrils flaring. The mare made a soft *huh-huh-huh* and her ears flicked this way and that. "Grizzly, maybe," Bat said, calming the horse and looking about. "Early yet, less'n he went to bed hungry."

The others mounted up and drew closer together as their eyes looked all about, trying to penetrate the ever-shifting clouds of snow.

"Might be nothin', or could be she seen a spook," Standing Eagle said, but his own eyes kept moving.

"It was sump'n," Bat said. The wind covered all sounds a man could hear, but the other horses showed signs of nervousness now, snorting the air and turning their heads as if they were as anxious as the men to know what lay beyond the obscuring snowfall.

"There," Hardeman said softly.

"I see 'im," said Bat.

A single rider materialized in the snow and drew near, a lance held ready, his mount moving at a cautious walk.

"Kanghí wichasha," hissed Little Hand, and Bat muttered "He's a Crow," to Hardeman. *Absaroka* the Crows called themselves in their own language; they were the Children of the Raven, but the white men came from the east, where crows were more common than ravens, and the mistranslation had stuck.

Blackbird kicked his horse to move closer to his father. He reached for one of his boyish arrows that hung in the quiver at his shoulder, but Standing Eagle made a curt motion and the boy dropped his hand.

More horsemen appeared now, all in a line abreast, walking slowly. They stopped when they were a dozen paces behind the lone man in the lead. There were eighteen of them all told.

"Here's wet powder and no fire to dry it," Bat said for Hardeman's ears alone, and he withdrew his Leman rifle from the fringed and beaded case that rested in his lap. Still the Lakota sat silently on their horses and still the Crow rider in the center made no motion, spoke no word.

He's sizing us up, Hardeman thought. Doesn't know what to make of Sioux and white men traveling together in these parts. He wondered whether to clear the way to his pistol. It would be pistol against bow and lance at this distance. Bat might get off a shot but there would be no time for reloading, and none of the Lakotas carried firearms. Apart from Blackbird, only Hawk Chaser was armed at all. He had both lance and bow, but the bow was slung across his back with his quiver and he had only the lance in his hand. Christ, Standing Eagle must feel as naked as a babe about now, Hardeman thought. Eighteen against six. This bunch isn't up to a fight with eighteen Crows. He thought of Johnny Smoker, who, like the two men carrying the pipes, did not go armed, and hadn't done for seven years now, and he missed having Johnny to keep an eye on his back when a fight was in the offing.

He unfastened three buttons on the St. Paul coat, moving slowly. Winter was a poor time for fighting; the clothing got in the way.

Now Standing Eagle raised a hand, moving slowly. He moved the hand in broad sweeps, making the-signs-that-are-seen-across-a-distance, so all the Crows could understand him. *You are far from the camps of the Crow.*

The lone rider responded. *We have come to hunt. The four-leggeds are few in the country of the Crow.*

The four-leggeds have left the Lakota as well, signed Standing Eagle.

You are not hunters, the Crow said.

"And he's a lyin' Injun," Bat said softly. "Ain't no eighteen Crows out huntin' this far south o' the Yellowstone. Them's young bloods out huntin' coup."

I am Standing Eagle, war leader of Sun Horse's band, signed Standing Eagle. *Today I carry a pipe of peace to the white soldier chief Three Stars.*

This statement caused a stir among the other Crows and there was some brief talk among them. The leader listened for a time before returning his attention to the party in front of him. He motioned at the campfires and the tracks leading away to the north. *There have been many horse soldiers here,* he signed.

Standing Eagle nodded. *They are led by Three Stars. We follow their trail.*

The Crow smiled. *The horse soldiers do not come to the land of the Crow. We are at peace with our white brothers.*

Standing Eagle's expression did not change, but his motions became more emphatic. *We will live at peace with the whites when they leave our land and let us live like men!* He made the last motion sharply, the index finger of his right hand thrust erect before him, like the erect organ of a virile man.

The Crow leader's face grew dark at the insult and from the others there were a few angry words, but the leader cut them off with a quick sign.

Hardeman changed his mind about the pistol. Moving no more purposefully than he might have done to scratch his ear, he slipped the Winchester out of its scabbard and rested it across his lap, in the same position as Bat's muzzle-loader. The pistol would be more use if the Crows decide to fight, but they didn't even know he had a pistol yet, and they feared the reputation of the many-shots-fast lever gun.

The Crow leader noted the motion, and the way the six riders sat quietly before him, their eyes meeting his. *Does it take four Lakota and two whitemen to carry one pipe?* he asked.

We have two pipes, Standing Eagle signed. *This man, Little Hand, carries a pipe to my cousin, who winters nearby.* He did not name Sitting Bull, who was a bitter enemy of the *Kanghí,* but he hoped that the Crow might temper their bravado with caution if they thought there were more Lakota close at hand. *The old whiteman is my brother,* he signed. *The other carries a message for Three Stars from Sun Horse, my father.*

"Old man! I oughta pin yer ears back for ye," Bat muttered. "If'n I live long enough."

There was more talk among the Crows and this time the leader was not quick to end it. Finally he turned back to the Lakotas and whites. *The Crow do not make war on those who carry pipes of peace,* he signed. *We will go now. Another day we will meet again.*

As silently as they had appeared, the Crows turned and rode away, quickly disappearing in the snow.

"I'll be dogged," Bat breathed. "I give it to ye, Eagle, you done that slicker'n dog shit on a wet rock."

Standing Eagle grunted and favored his brother-in-law with a rare smile. "Felt nekkid as a child, and that's truth. Figgered us for gone beaver."

"Oh, I'd of thrown that nigger cold, all right," Bat grinned. "It war the others

I worried on. But I reckoned Christopher here and old Hawk and young Blackbird was up to Crow today."

"I will fight the Crow," Blackbird said, and grinned at Hardeman. "But I would rather fight *washíchun*."

Hardeman did not entirely conceal his surprise. It seemed every member of Sun Horse's male line had been studying on the English tongue.

"You notice he speaks a mite better'n Eagle here," Bat observed. "I'm teachin' him different. Figger when he's full growed there won't be many left that savvy trapper talk."

He laughed, joined by Blackbird and Standing Eagle, and Hardeman laughed too, enjoying the high spirits that followed a brush with danger, but he wondered if Blackbird would have time to get full grown. He was Standing Eagle's son, there was no mistaking that. The boy watched his father closely and imitated him in many small mannerisms and gestures. He wanted to be just like his father, and Hardeman wondered how much chance he would have. If war came, Bat had said that Standing Eagle and Little Hand would take their families and join the fighting bands. Blackbird could easily find himself confronting army troops before the month was out. But his initial hostility toward Hardeman had given way in the course of five days together to guarded curiosity. Probably he had never had much chance to see a white man close up over a period of time, except for Bat Putnam, his uncle Lodgepole. Hardeman had noted the respect with which the boy always addressed Bat and the considerate good humor Bat bestowed on Blackbird.

"We better put some country between us and those bucks before they change their minds and decide to raise a little hair after all," Hardeman said.

Bat nodded. "We'll move on till dark. Won't be easy to cut trail tonight. I reckon we'll shake 'em."

But even before nightfall the sky cleared rapidly from the west. As the clouds receded toward the eastern horizon the moon rose above them, its rounded face a welcome sight after so many stormy nights. The air turned frigid and the pipe carriers kept a close watch on their back trail, with an eye always to the front as well, searching there for the glow of campfires or a glimpse of moonlit smoke that might betray the presence of the army camp ahead. The valley of the Prairie Dog widened gradually until it grew as large as the Clear Fork had been, where the trail had left that stream. As the moon rose higher its light grew brilliant; the Big Horns, all cloaked in snow, loomed so close in the west that it seemed the men might reach out and touch them. Finally, with no sign of pursuit and the horses breathing hard, unwilling to go faster than a slow trot, the riders stopped in a grove of cottonwoods by the creekbank. They stripped bark from the trees by moonlight and fed it to the horses and tethered them, hobbled, amidst what grass there was, close by the shelter they built for themselves against the numbing cold.

As he drifted toward sleep Hardeman could hear the regular working of the horses' jaws, and he felt pleasantly contented. The rich grass would restore the animals' strength somewhat, and a few hours of sleep would restore the men. Tomorrow they would catch Crook for certain. They couldn't be far behind him now. Hardeman was almost sorry the pipe carriers' solitary journey was nearing an end. How long was it since he had been this far from any settlement, moving through the country with a small band of companions who knew the land and had the skills needed for any emergency? When he set out from Kansas with Johnny he had never imagined for a moment that he would end up traveling with Sioux warriors and an old mountain man who had gone Injun years before. The Indians smelled different, from the animal grease they rubbed in their hair and from the leathers they wore, brain-tanned and cured in the smoke of many lodge fires, but he had been with white men who smelled worse.

His mind went back to the encounter with the Crows and he almost smiled. How many whites would meet a group of their enemies and look them over and say, "It's not a good day to fight. We'll meet again another time."? If it had been a squad of Crook's cavalry instead of Crows, they would have fired first and maybe not even bothered to ask questions later. The Indians didn't practice war the way the white men did, relentlessly. And so in the end the Indians would lose.

He awoke suddenly, with no idea how long he might have slept. It was still night, but from somewhere came enough light for him to make out the painted face of a Crow warrior inches from his own. The man was smiling broadly and Hardeman recognized the leader of the Crow war party.

A knife rested against Hardeman's throat. He could feel the razor-sharp blade and the pounding of his heart. Beneath his blankets his hand closed around the Colt but he dared not cock the weapon for fear the Crow would sense the movement. Ever so slowly, the Crow drew the knife across Hardeman's throat, the touch feather-light. Hardeman felt a drop of blood run down his skin to the collar of his wool shirt. The Crow removed the knife blade and tapped it lightly on Hardeman's forehead, taking his coup gleefully. A man's honor was greatest of all if he moved close among his enemies, to touch them without doing harm and escape with his own life.

Fairly certain now that the Crow did not intend to harm him immediately, Hardeman's awareness expanded. He saw that the lashings holding down the covers of the shelter had been cut, the robes raised on one side, admitting the moonlight. The moon was still high. He heard the stamping of horses and their soft snorting. The sound came from too far away. Blackbird had gone to sleep as he did each night, with his own pony's lead rope tied to his wrist and passing out beneath the coverings of the shelter. As far as Hardeman could tell, the boy and everyone else in the shelter were still asleep. He heard the horses again, still farther away. Most likely that was what the Crows wanted. Steal the horses and count coup on the sleeping men they had left afoot. A good joke on the little party of Sioux and whites.

Because of the encounter with the Crows that day, Hardeman had brought both his rifles into the shelter for the night. They lay beside him now. The Crow picked up the Winchester and admired it briefly, then passed it to a second warrior standing outside the shelter. The leader whispered something to the other man, who nodded and disappeared from sight. The Crow picked up the Sharps then and prodded the sleeping form of Bat Putnam with the muzzle of the buffalo gun. Bat rolled over, his eyes opening. The Crow rested the barrel of the Sharps on Bat's forehead. Bat's eyes widened.

Hardeman waited no longer. With the Colt's trigger pulled back to disengage the hammer from the sear, he thumbed back the hammer and fired from beneath his blankets, hoping the layers of bedding wouldn't deflect the bullet. The two-hundred-grain lead projectile struck the Crow in the side, lifting him from his knees and dropping him dead across Bat Putnam. The muffled roar of the Colt broke the soft night sounds and released a bedlam of reactions within the small shelter.

"Christ almighty, Christopher!"

"He's not alone! They've got the horses!"

Standing Eagle leaped to his feet, stumbled, and fell against the side of the shelter, pulling away the last of the covering and most of the supporting poles. Bat threw off the dead Crow and stood up as Hawk Chaser and Little Hand struggled to free themselves from their robes.

As Blackbird jerked awake he reached instinctively for his bow even as he pulled on the buffalo-hair rein tied to his wrist. The moccasin carrier was the horse guard, and no duty was more important than that one. To his horror he found that his rein had been cut, leaving only a short piece attached to his arm. The horses were neighing now, somewhere off among the cottonwoods. In an instant, Blackbird was on his feet and running, bow in hand, racing for the trees without stopping to see if anyone followed. The theft of the horses was his fault; he would rather die alone trying to get them back than live with the shame of letting the hated *Kanghí* put the pipe carriers afoot.

He was among the trees now and the sounds of the horses were nearer. If only the other *Kanghí* would wait for their companion!

There! Two men were mounting, trying to control the excited animals. He saw no others. Had there been just three of the enemy? He heard his father call his name from somewhere behind him, but the men would not reach the horses in time. He was closest.

He ran silently, bending low so the *Kanghí* would not see him until he was upon them. The moonlight made it easy to avoid the obstacles in his path. How could they not see him now?

Each of the enemy held four horses. The brazen *Kanghí* had ridden or led their own mounts right up to the pipe carriers' tethered animals! They had them all, even the pack horse. If they got away...

One man started off downstream, leading his four horses, but the other was having trouble with Lodgepole's little bay mare. She crossed behind the *Kanghí*, pulling him around by the arm that held the lead ropes, twisting him in the saddle. He tried to shift the mare's rope to his other hand, the one that held

330

his own rein, but the mare's rope slipped from his grasp. He grabbed for it, missed, and in that moment Blackbird leaped at the man and knocked him from his horse.

They landed on the ground and rolled apart, but the stocky Crow was quick, already reaching for the lithe boy and seizing him by the ankle, the other hand raising a knife. The Crow's horse reared, whinnying and pawing the air as the two men struggled on the ground at his feet. The Crow looked up and Blackbird struck out wildly with his bow, catching the Crow on the side of the head and stunning him, making him lose his hold. In an instant Blackbird was on his feet. He seized the horse's rein and vaulted into the saddle, urging the frightened animal into flight. Ahead of him, three of the remaining horses were running downstream after the fleeing *Kanghí* and the horses he led, but Lodgepole's mare was circling and slowing. The men would catch her easily enough, and they would deal with the remaining *Kanghí*, who was alone and horseless now. Blackbird was concerned with only one thing, the horses that were getting away. They were gone from sight now around a curve in the riverbed. He leaned low over his mount's neck, using his bow as a quirt, straining to hear any sound beyond the clatter of the horse's hooves on the gravel and ice of the river bottom. What if the rest of the *Kanghí* awaited the horse stealing party nearby? What could one boy do against the entire war party?

He could die.

The thought chilled Blackbird but it also hardened his determination. He was the only one with a chance to recover the stolen horses. If the pipe carriers were left afoot they could never catch Three Stars and it would be Blackbird's fault.

The moonlight illuminated the valley and low hills around him with cold white light, every feature standing out stark and motionless. As Blackbird rounded the bend in the river the stream ran straight before him; there too everything was still and for a heart-stopping moment he feared he had lost the enemy, but then...Yes! There was the *Kanghí* now, emerging from behind a clump of cottonwoods, still leading the four horses and followed by the other three.

At once Blackbird slowed his own mount and looked at the ground ahead carefully, trying to match his pace to that of the *Kanghí wichasha* so the man would not hear him.

Now the Crow turned aside, leaving the valley bottom and ascending a gentle slope to the west. Blackbird reined in within the shadow of a low bluff until the man had crested the rise and was gone from sight. The loose horses continued down the stream and slowed to a trot. They could be found later. This was Blackbird's chance to overtake and surprise the *Kanghí*.

He kicked his mount and raced up the slope where the Crow had gone, fitting an arrow to his bowstring as he rode. He counted on the softer ground, covered with grass and barely a dusting of snow, to muffle the sounds of his approach. He raced headlong now, over the low crest and down a grassy swale, and then he was upon the enemy.

The arrow was in flight as the Crow turned and saw Blackbird for the first time, but his turn protected his body and the iron-tipped shaft pierced the flesh of his underarm through his fur cape and winter shirt. He seized the shaft and ripped it away, keeping his grip on the captured horses all the while. He reined to a stop and turned to face Blackbird, who pulled his horse around to return to the attack.

"Come, Lakotah boy! Shoot again!" the Crow called out in crude Lakota, and Blackbird saw that the man was laughing at him. In a fury he kicked his horse, urging him into a reckless charge, and as he controlled the animal with his knees he let fly a second arrow just before he swerved aside. The *Kanghí* leaned calmly away from the arrow and it flew past him harmlessly as the man laughed aloud.

Blackbird wheeled again and drove in between the Crow and the four horses, determined to break them free. He swung his bow with all his strength at the man's head but hit his shoulder instead. The Crow grabbed the bow and pulled sharply, drawing Blackbird closer. A knife flashed in the moonlight as the *Kanghí's* free hand swung down and Blackbird felt a deep pain in his thigh, followed by a warm rush as the blood poured down his leg. With a wrench of his arm the Crow jerked Blackbird from his horse and jumped off his own mount to land on top of the boy, knocking the wind out of him.

"You brave Lakotah boy. Die brave now." The man stradled Blackbird, gripping his hair. He reached out with his knife and placed it at Blackbird's temple.

Blackbird closed his eyes and clenched his teeth, determined not to make any sound as the blade circled his head to free the edges of the scalp. He felt the knife begin to move, the man taking his time, in no hurry now, and then suddenly there was a sharp tug at his hair and the weight of the *Kanghí* left him, as if he had been jerked away by unseen hands. As Blackbird opened his eyes he heard a booming explosion that came from far away, and yet it filled the air around him. He sat up, struggling to regain his breath. Far off on the last rise, well beyond bowshot, he saw a man wearing a *washíchun* hat, mounting a horse.

Where was the *Kanghí?* Blackbird turned and saw his enemy lying still, just out of reach. A dark stain was spreading slowly on the man's shirt. Blackbird picked up his bow and struck a blow on the *Kanghí's* body with all his might, taking his coup, but the effort seemed to exhaust him and the bow slipped from his fingers. He put out a hand to steady himself as his head reeled. He heard hoofbeats and turned to see a rider close at hand, and he recognized the *washíchun* Hardeman, holding a long-shooting buffalo gun in his hand.

Blackbird tried to stand but his legs buckled before he was upright and he fell back to the ground, which felt strangely soft as he struck it. Why did his leg hurt so? He seemed unable to raise his head now, or even to keep his eyes open. He heard the *washíchun's* voice as if from a great distance, and someone touched him, but then he knew nothing more.

"Watch out, he's hurt bad." Hardeman lowered Blackbird's unconscious form to the waiting hands. He had come upon the other men a mile downstream from the night camp, carrying the robes and bundles. They had already caught the three horses that had panicked and run after the fleeing Crow. He himself was on Bat's mare; she had run into the trees and stopped, and he had been the first to reach her.

"If that feller got away, might be he'll bring his friends," Bat said as he helped lower Blackbird to the ground. Hawk Chaser had brought coals from the old fire and was already feeding twigs to a small blaze.

"He didn't get away." Hardeman had dismounted to shoot the Crow from seven hundred yards away when he saw it was his only chance to save the boy. It wasn't bad for night shooting, but well within the range of the Sharps. When he reached Blackbird he had covered the wounded youth with the dead man's cape and his own coat, and had left him just long enough to catch the horses before starting back. Little Hand took the horses now as Hardeman dismounted; he handed the white man his Winchester, which had been recovered from the third dead Crow.

Standing Eagle looked up from where he knelt by his son. "You just seen the one? No others?"

"No others."

"The others was around, they'd of been on us by now," Bat said. "Them three bucks just couldn't pass up a chance to steal Lakota horses, I reckon."

With all the men helping, a shelter was built in short order, a crude lean-to facing the fire, which now blazed high. The night air was clear and bitterly cold. The moon had moved to the western part of the sky and in the east the stars shone brightly, revealing no hint of dawn.

Blackbird was placed close to the fire and covered with several robes, leaving only his wounded leg exposed. Hawk Chaser pulled aside the boy's legging, which Hardeman had slit with his knife in his haste to expose the wound and stop the bleeding. He had bound a bandanna over the deep gash, and above the wound he had placed a tourniquet to stanch the bleeding, which had pulsed from a severed artery. Revealed again now, the wound glistened wetly in the firelight. Hawk Chaser looked at Hardeman and nodded his approval of the measures the scout had taken. He loosened the tourniquet cautiously, and retightened it as blood began to surge from the wound.

Bat picked up the lance that Hawk Chaser had laid close at hand and he set the blade in the fire. Standing Eagle bent low to listen to Blackbird's shallow breathing. He placed his ear on his son's chest for a moment, then felt the boy's face and hands, and finally he made a sign, passing his right forefinger under his left hand, which was held on edge in front of him.

"He'll go under for sure if'n we don't do nothin' fer him!" Bat said angrily.

"The boy's gone beaver," Standing Eagle said, and Hardeman marveled at

333

the man's control. He revealed no emotion at all and might as well have been talking about a wounded horse. "His fault anyway. He'd of been lookin' t' the horses like he was supposed to, none o' this would of happened."

"He's your son!" Hardeman said, shocked by the war leader's attitude.

"Takes his chances on the trail, same's any coon."

Hawk Chaser spoke in Lakota then, and Standing Eagle replied in that language. Bat joined the conversation and Little Hand said a word or two, and when the talk died, Bat turned to Hardeman. "Eagle says even if the boy lives he'll slow us down. We'll have to take him on a pony drag and we'll never catch Three Stars. He says the council sent him to deliver a pipe to Three Stars and that's what he aims to do."

"He'll leave the boy here?"

Bat nodded. "Hawk Chaser'll stay with him. Ol' Hawk's a bone setter; he's got some experience with wounds. If'n the boy lives, he'll bring him along."

"If we move out now, we'll catch Crook today, even with the boy on a pony drag," Hardeman said. "The cavalry will have a doctor with them."

Bat told Hawk Chaser what the white man had said, and the warrior replied, plainly disagreeing.

"Hawk won't have it," Bat explained. "He says the white medicine men are nothin' but bone cutters. They'll lop off the boy's leg quicker'n you can spit. Don't know nothin' about healin', he says. Don't know but what I agree with him, but that's neither here ner there. What I do know is, we ain't certain to find Three Stars today, ner tomorrow neither. He's movin' along right quick. Could be marchin' now. Hawk says there's another way. We cross country to the Powder and go downstream till we find a village where they can care for the boy. We move quick's we can, we won't lose much time."

"And if Crook finds a village in the meantime?"

"Tell the truth, we reckon there ain't no villages left on the Tongue. Word is they've all gone to the Powder. We had a news rider not long ago. We go down the Powder, we might find Sittin' Bull. We can give him the pipe, have a parley, then go on to Three Stars, and it's all wrapped up, slick's you please."

While Bat was talking with Hardeman, Hawk Chaser was speaking to Standing Eagle, arguing forcefully, gesturing often at Blackbird, and in the end Standing Eagle nodded his assent, although with apparent reluctance.

Hardeman was not surprised to learn about the news rider. He wondered what else the Sun Band council knew that he didn't. But the change in plan made sense. If there were no villages on the Tongue, Crook was on a wild goose chase for the time being and the pipe carriers might accomplish their goal by a different route. Hardeman had wanted to go to Sitting Bull first, before the council decided against him. It wouldn't be easy to persuade the famous Hunkpapa, who had a reputation as an obstinate foe of the whites, but he didn't have to agree to everything at once. If he would just promise to stay at peace once Crook was gone from the country, that would be enough to take to Crook, and the general's assent would be all the more likely. Still, the thought of soldiers loose in the land made Hardeman uneasy. He had told no one in Putnam's Park or Sun Horse's village about Custer and Gibbon, nor did Johnny know. Hardeman had learned about the other prongs of the expedition from Crook, and he had kept the knowledge to himself. If the Sioux knew that Long Hair was on the move, they would see a chance to avenge themselves on Custer for opening the Black Hills to miners, and there would be no more talk of peace. But to reach the hostile villages the troops coming from Forts Shaw and Abraham Lincoln would have to march twice as far as Crook had come, and they wouldn't cover ground the way he was doing. For now, Crook was the only general in the field. There was a little time to spare. The pipe carriers would need that time, and luck as well.

"We better see to the boy," Hardeman said.

Each man knew what had to be done. They took positions at Blackbird's legs and shoulders, preparing to hold him down. There was only one way to heal such a wound. The tourniquet couldn't be left in place for long or the limb would freeze and gangrene would soon follow, but before the blood could be freed to flow again, the gash would have to be cauterized.

Hawk Chaser took the lance from the fire. The blade glowed a dull red. The men took hold of Blackbird and leaned over his body, placing most of their weight on his limbs. As the hot metal seared his flesh, Blackbird opened his eyes and screamed, but he remained unconscious; he saw nothing and felt only pain.

When the boy was covered again, the men huddled together in the shelter to await the dawn. The wounded youth needed time to recover his strength after the shock of his treatment. If he still breathed in the morning, they would build him a pony drag and set out for the Powder. Bat and Little Hand took the opportunity to curl in their robes and get some sleep, but the others remained awake, looking at the fire, which was heaped high with new wood.

Standing Eagle's expression revealed nothing of his thoughts, but he was secretly pleased. The threat to abandon his wounded son had brought about a change of course, and the idea had not come from him. He had been certain that Hawk Chaser would propose some way to save Blackbird's life without leaving him behind. It was the responsibility of a *hunká* to do everything he could to protect the life of his relative-by-choice, even at the cost of his own. And indeed, everything had worked out exactly as the war leader had expected.

Standing Eagle placed little faith in his father's hopes of finding a way to lasting peace with the whites. Sun Horse was a wise leader but he took too much on himself. It was madness for any one man to think that he could save the entire Lakota nation, no matter how strong a vision he had been given. As it was, the change in the pipe carriers' course made it all the more likely that Three Stars would come upon some group of Lakota and begin the war, and then the warriors would show the bluecoats how to fight! It was true that the news rider had said that many bands were camped on the Powder, but the hunting bands were spread far and wide across the land, each in its

335

preferred place for the winter. They moved or stayed according to the decisions of each band's council, not by any concerted plan. There might be a small village anywhere.

The *washíchun* Hardeman would have to be closely watched now. Even Sun Horse had seen the need for that, and so Hawk Chaser had come along to guard the whiteman. Hardeman knew the location of the Sun Band's village and now he knew more, because Lodgepole had foolishly told him about the villages on the Powder.

"You will watch him carefully," Sun Horse had told Hawk Chaser in the council. "As long as he is with you and does not betray our trust in him, you will protect him. I wish no harm to come to him. But if he tries to leave you or does anything that might bring danger to the helpless ones of our people or any band of Lakota, you must stop him. If you must kill him to stop him, you will kill him."

CHAPTER

TWENTY-THREE

At midday on the fourth day since the attack by the Crows, the pipe carriers smelled smoke. They were in the valley of the Powder, which narrowed ahead of them where a pointed bluff intruded from the left like an outstretched arm of the rugged, wooded hills that lay to the west. Since Blackbird's wounding, travel had been slowed by the pony drag that bore the wounded boy and by the failing strength of the horses, even though the addition of the three Crow horses to the band's mounts allowed the weakest animals to go unburdened much of the time. The travelers had made their way due east from Prairie Dog Creek until they struck the Clear Fork, which they had followed down to the Powder. By Hardeman's guess they had covered less than twenty miles a day, despite clear weather and pleasant sunshine, which had eased their going. They had seen no recent sign of man—Indian or white—since leaving the trail of Crook's cavalry behind.

The little band came to a halt. It was snowing for the first time since before the night attack, big wet flakes that gathered on their blankets and robes and even clung to Hardeman's oilskin. The wind gusted the smoke smell away, then.brought it back stronger.

Hardeman sniffed the air as the others were doing. It was the clean smell of dry wood burning, with a hint of cooking meat.

On his travois Blackbird groaned and opened his eyes. Hawk Chaser was off his horse and beside the youth in an instant, placing a hand gently over Blackbird's mouth and motioning for silence with the other. Blackbird's eyes asked a question and the warrior made quick signs to say they had smelled smoke and must keep quiet until they knew whence it came. The boy tested the air, then signed that he smelled meat cooking. He passed the edge of his hand across his midsection to indicate his hunger, and he smiled.

At first the boy had lain as still as death on the pony drag the men had made for him, but on the second day he had opened his eyes for a time, though he scarcely seemed to know the men who bent low to speak to him. On the third day he had rested comfortably in the warm sunshine, sleeping most of the time, but once, when Hardeman was riding near him, he had spoken to the white man.

"Why did you come with us?" the boy had asked.

Hardeman had not been sure that the boy knew him, or his own whereabouts, but he had answered, "I came because Sun Horse asked me to."

Blackbird had looked at him steadily from his jouncing bed. "Yes, but why did you . . . want . . . to come?"

"There's been enough fighting," Hardeman had said. "It's time for the Sioux and the white men to make peace."

"My father says if we surrender, the whites will take our land," the boy had said. Hardeman made no reply and before long the youth had dropped off to sleep again.

"I'll go have a look," Hardeman said now. It was snowing thickly, although the morning had been bright and sunny. It would be good to investigate the source of the smoke while the weather offered some protection. By now the soldiers could be anywhere; they too might have crossed to the Powder.

Standing Eagle made a sign to Hawk Chaser, motioning him to accompany the white scout. The warrior nodded, rising from Blackbird's pony drag.

Leaving their horses with the others, the two men went forward on foot, Hardeman carrying his Winchester, while those remaining behind moved themselves and the horses to cover in the cottonwoods, which grew densely here. For the most part since reaching the Powder, the pipe carriers had been able to travel its broad valley under cover of the trees, only occasionally being compelled to cross an open space from one stand of cottonwoods to the next.

The two scouts kept to the brush along the bank of the stream and in a short time they were picking their way through dense willows at the end of the pointed bluff, where the river ran close beneath it. Beyond the bluff, the valley broadened considerably, although its boundaries were concealed by the falling snow. From the left, a sloping benchland reached out onto the valley bottom, created by outwash from the hills. The two men moved along the base of this intrusion, making their way among the bushes that grew there. As they went, the snow began to thin, and in a short time it had ceased entirely, leaving the air clear beneath wispy, thinning clouds that moved gently from the northeast. The wind brought the smoke again, stronger still, and Hardeman thought he caught a hint of horse smell too. The smoke heralded something more than a solitary campfire: there was a gathering of men and animals ahead.

They rounded a small point of rocks where the bench extended farthest onto the bottomland; all the valley beyond lay exposed before them, and there they saw the village.

The tipis were set among the cottonwoods where the river swept close to the western side of the valley perhaps a mile away, beneath broken bluffs that rose sharply for hundreds of feet, offering good protection from the winter storms. A few lodges were in full view but most were hidden by the trees, only their peaks visible. There were dozens, perhaps fifty or sixty, Hardeman guessed. Between the village and the two men, hundreds of horses browsed for grass in the few inches of snow that covered the valley bottom.

Hawk Chaser smiled and said a single word. "Shahíyela."

As the pipe carriers drew near they could see the whole camp, closer to a hundred tipis. There was no single camp circle as in the Sun Band village, but clusters of lodges wherever there were open spaces among the trees. While Hardeman had returned to get Bat and the others, Hawk Chaser had gone ahead on foot to announce the pipe carriers' coming and prepare the Cheyenne for the presence of two white men among the emissaries from the Sun Band. The crier was moving through the village, and from the more distant lodges men and women were still emerging, moving toward the center of camp to see the visitors arrive. Children and dogs were everywhere. As the riders emerged from the dense plum bushes that girdled the upstream end of the camp, the children pointed at the white men and stared with mouths agape at Blackbird on his pony drag. The youth was awake and looking about him with interest. There were many fresh hides in evidence and the smell of cooking meat pervaded the camp; apparently the hunting had been good. Hardeman's stomach rumbled. Since the day of Blackbird's wounding, the pipe carriers had killed just two rabbits and otherwise had subsisted on *wasná*.

"Lakota lodges yonder," Standing Eagle observed, motioning toward the downstream end of the village, where newcomers traditionally placed their tipis. "Oglala, I'm thinkin'. Some just out from the reservation." He grinned at Hardeman.

Among the farthest lodges, Hardeman saw some that were bright and new, made from the heavy canvas trade cloth the reservation bands used instead of animal hides. The rumors that agency Indians were coming west to join the hostiles were true.

Hawk Chaser stepped forward to meet the riders as they reached the first grouping of tipis and dismounted. He addressed himself to Standing Eagle, speaking as a scout who had gone ahead of the party, reporting what he had learned to the man in charge.

"Cheyenne, all right," Bat said for Hardeman's benefit. "The old-man chiefs is Old Bear and Little Wolf, but the day-to-day business is took care of by Two Moons. He's a young feller, but good 'n' steady; I've seen him a few times. This bunch was on the Tongue most of the winter. Got the order to go in to the agencies and come this far. They'll go on when the weather gets warm again." He listened for a few moments and then spoke again. "The Lakota lodges is Last

338

Bull's, the new ones. Come out from the agency durin' the thaw. The others belong to He Dog. They're goin' in with Two Moons. He Dog's *hunká*-relative to Crazy Horse. His brother-friend. Them two been through thick and thicker. He Dog's Crazy Horse's best friend in the world." The disappointment was plain in Bat's tones and Hardeman wondered what had caused it. Was it because the Cheyenne and Sioux here were going in without a fight? Bat had never said what he thought the hostiles should do, or the Sun Band either, for that matter.

Hardeman was pleased by the news. The government's order had said only that the free-roaming bands of Sioux must go to Dakota; there had been no mention of the Cheyenne, and yet Two Moons was going in. If a village this large showed such prudence, there might be others, both Sioux and Cheyenne, that felt the same. It would be worth a little time to learn what Two Moons might know of other bands nearby. If he and the other headmen here were willing to join Sun Horse's call for peace, it might be possible to promise Crook a general movement toward the reservation, and more than one chief to speak for an end to hostilities, if only he would give them time until the weather warmed.

The crier approached the pipe carriers now; he was missing one eye and wore no covering to conceal his loss. He invited the newcomers to follow him to Two Moons' lodge, where the headman awaited them. The horses, all but Blackbird's, were led away by young boys to be unsaddled and picketed until it was learned if the strangers would be continuing on their way that day. Hawk Chaser led Blackbird's horse as the pipe carriers moved off behind the crier, and the wounded youth motioned to one small child to sit beside him on the pony drag and ride with him, but the child was too bashful to accept. The curious crowd followed along, and Hardeman tried to estimate how many Indians there might be in Two Moons' village. Usually there were four or five in a lodge, but here there were many small lodges, scarcely more than wickiups, most likely inhabited by single men. Still, there would be upward of four hundred souls in the camp, about a quarter of them warriors.

"That's Two Moons, now," Bat said softly. They were approaching a prominent tipi in the middle of the largest cluster of lodges, set back against the bluffs. The man standing in front of the tipi had taken the time to don his ceremonial headdress; he wore a fresh buffalo robe with a white band of beadwork around the border and in his right hand he held an eagle wing, his badge of office. His face was round, the skin dark, the eyes clear.

If you took a dime-novel picture of an Indian chief, that's what he'd look like, Hardeman thought. Young to be a headman. He stood straight and proud and patient, waiting for his guests to come to him as if he had no curiosity at all and all the time in the world. Around his neck he wore a bone-and-bead choker, the red beads bright against the white bones. His braids were wrapped in what looked to be lynx fur. He could have been a Sioux, for all that his garments and ornaments revealed. The differences between the two peoples had diminished over the years as they received similar goods from white traders and adopted similar styles of beadwork and personal ornamentation. They were different in language and some

339

customs, and a glance at the arrows of either tribe was enough to distinguish one from the other, but both were horse-riding, buffalo-hunting people. The northern Cheyenne had shared many of the victories and defeats as the Sioux came increasingly into conflict with the whites, and many of the southern bands had come north after Black Kettle's death at the Washita, to live in the Powder River country with their more numerous ally.

Even as Hardeman surveyed the people, many eyes were looking at him, and in one pair recognition sparked. A man turned away and went quickly to his lodge, which stood nearby. Moments later he re-emerged, carrying something in his hand.

The pipe carriers halted a few paces in front of Two Moons, and around them the crowd flowed into a half circle before it too came to rest, joined at the last by a contingent of Lakota from the farthest lodges. Two Moons prepared to speak, but there came a sudden movement—one man, his arm raised, cutting through the people like a buffalo through the tall grass, rushing toward the strangers. His quarry was looking the other way, and so the man gave a short cry of warning.

Hardeman felt someone approaching rapidly from behind, heard the cry, and acted without thinking. Only the speed of his reaction saved his life. As he turned, his body dropped into a crouch, the right hand going for the pistol in his waistband and the left raised against something striking down from above. The Cheyenne war club in the hand of the attacker was deflected by Hardeman's arm and it glanced off the white man's head, a blow that left Hardeman stunned and reeling, but still on his feet, his right hand fumbling at the buttons of his coat where it blocked the way to his pistol. Before the Cheyenne could strike again, a man stepped between Hardeman and the attacker. It was Hawk Chaser, his lance held ready.

Bat took Hardeman by the arm to steady him. "I'd leave that six-gun be, hoss," he said softly. "What're ye feelin' like?"

The wound on Hardeman's head was beginning to bleed and his left arm was numb where the club had struck it. He shook his head to clear his vision. Bat wiped the blood from Hardeman's forehead with a finger and Hardeman winced.

The mountain man grinned. "It don't look too bad, but I reckon it'll swell up some."

Two Moons left the front of his lodge and moved through the crowd, which had clustered around the pipe carriers. Men and women made way for him and gathered behind him as he advanced. Two other men stepped forward more quickly and spoke harshly to the attacker. They were Cheyenne *akíchita*, camp marshals charged with keeping the peace. The pipe carriers had not been formally welcomed into the camp but they were guests nevertheless, their identities and purpose known and announced by the crier, and an attack on them was a serious breach of custom.

Hardeman's attacker replied angrily to the marshals, gesturing at Hardeman, drawing aside his blanket to show a scar of twisted skin in the muscle' of his shoulder above the collarbone. As they heard his words some of the other Chey-

340

enne grew angry, but none moved toward Hardeman, who was protected by Hawk Chaser.

Hardeman was standing straight now, his composure regained. He neither looked at his attacker nor moved toward him. Instead, all his attention was on Two Moons. He wanted the headman's good will. By choosing to go to Dakota peacefully, Two Moons had become Hardeman's ally, albeit unknowingly.

Two Moons spoke at some length with Hardeman's attacker, and while the two men talked, the pipe carriers were joined by one of the camp marshals, who took a place beside Hawk Chaser, his stance indicating clearly that he too would protect the white man. When the talk was done, the marshal turned to the visitors and addressed them in Lakota, gesturing at the man with the war club.

"This is Kills Fox. He knows this white man." Bat put the translator's words into English as the Cheyenne spoke. "He is one of the scouts who brought the soldier chief Long Hair to the village of Black Kettle at the Washita, eight snows ago. Kills Fox was wounded there; he shows you the scar." Again the attacker drew aside his blanket, his face dark with anger. "The wife of Kills Fox died there, and one of his sons."

Two Moons and the rest of the crowd were waiting for some kind of reply from the pipe carriers.

"It is true," Bat said in Lakota. Many in the crowd understood that language, and for those that did not, he made signs as he talked, translating his own words for all to see. The crowding warriors surged forward like wolves toward a wounded buffalo, but Hawk Chaser raised his lance again and now even Standing Eagle and Little Hand closed ranks in front of Hardeman, together with the Cheyenne marshal. Hardeman remained where he was, showing no fear. He felt blood trickling down his cheek.

"It is true that this man was a scout for Long Hair," Bat said, directing himself to Two Moons. "It is also true that after the Washita battle he left the bluecoats and has not scouted for them since. He came to my father-in-law Sun Horse bearing a message of peace from the soldier chief Three Stars; he travels with us to seek Three Stars now, carrying Sun Horse's reply. Two Moons knows that among those who scout for the bluecoats there are many who were once our friends, men who lived among us, traders' sons with Shahíyela and Lakota mothers. Friends become enemies and enemies become friends. We judge a man by what he does now, by whether he behaves as a friend or an enemy. This whiteman has proved himself our friend. When we were attacked by *Kanghí*, he fought them with us and helped to recover our horses. He saved a young man's life." Here Bat gestured at Blackbird, who lay quietly on the pony drag. There were murmurs of surprise in the crowd and some nods of approval. The anger vanished from many faces to be replaced by a new curiosity and respect. Bat waited for the surprise to subside before he turned back to Two Moons. "We come to you tired and hungry, our horses worn out. We need your help to continue on our way. Will our brothers the Shahíyela refuse help to those who carry pipes of peace?"

Two Moons had listened politely as Bat spoke, showing no reaction. Bat had

341

chosen his words with care, framing his appeal in terms that the headman could not refuse, not if he expected to live up to the traditions of his position. More than any other people of the plains, the Cheyenne revered the peace men. Keeping the peace had been the first duty of their chiefs ever since those positions of tribal authority had first been created by Sweet Medicine, the legendary hero of the Cheyenne. A Cheyenne chief must be a man of peace before all else, as well as brave, and generous to friend and stranger alike. "When a stranger comes to your tipi asking for something, give it to him," Sweet Medicine had said. Bat had asked for help in a way that reminded Two Moons of his obligations, and he admired the skill with which the young Cheyenne headman concealed his embarrassment.

"You are the son-in-law of Sun Horse?" Two Moons inquired with no more than polite interest.

Bat nodded. "My wife is Otter Skin, daughter of Sun Horse." He indicated Standing Eagle, at his right hand. "My brother Standing Eagle is war leader of Sun Horse's camp. It is he who carries the pipe for Three Stars. My cousin Little Hand carries a pipe for Sitting Bull."

There was a sound from the crowd at the mention of the Hunkpapa war man, but Two Moons pretended not to notice. He turned to Kills Fox and spoke to him quietly for a time. The angry fire had left the warrior's eyes as Bat talked, and his manner had become subdued. He nodded now, submitting to his leader, then turned and spoke briefly, keeping his eyes averted from the pipe carriers.

"Kills Fox offers a horse to Ice, who knows the secrets of healing," Bat said to Hardeman once the man's words had been put into Lakota by the camp marshal. "He asks Ice to treat your wounds. Old Ice, he's about as famous a medicine man as the Cheyenne got."

A white-haired man stepped out of the crowd and joined Kills Fox. With his short nose, round face and dark skin, he might have been a much older version of Two Moons.

Hardeman touched his forehead and found that the blood there was beginning to dry. His head still throbbed and the pain made it difficult for him to organize his thoughts, but he had no wish to place himself under the healer's care and miss the conference with Two Moons. He made signs to say that the wound was not serious and required no treatment, inclining his head to Kills Fox to acknowledge the courtesy; he was willing to meet the warrior more than halfway if the man wanted to let bygones be bygones.

Kills Fox seemed less than pleased by Hardeman's reply and he spoke again, gesturing now in Blackbird's direction.

"He's offerin' to have Ice look at the boy," Bat explained. "We best accept this time, to let him off the hook."

Bat spoke briefly to Standing Eagle in Lakota and Hardeman inwardly cursed his own stupidity. By refusing to let the healer at least look at his wound, he had denied Kills Fox a chance to atone for his offense against a guest. He would have to find some other way to accept the warrior's apology.

With a show of good will, Standing Eagle agreed to let Ice care for Blackbird's wound. The old healer came forward to kneel beside the pony drag, where he spoke softly to the boy and made signs to inquire about the wound, and Hardeman imagined that he saw a trace of satisfaction on Two Moons' face as the headman welcomed his guests at last.

"All men of peace are welcome in the camps of the *Tsistsístas*. Our brothers the Lakota are always welcome. People of Sun Horse's camp are most welcome, for it is known that Sun Horse is a great man of peace. His sons and their friends are welcome in this village. The whiteman who accompanies them is welcome. Come to my lodge and eat."

The last of the tension dissipated now, evidenced by the soft buzz of conversation in the crowd and the smiles that appeared on many faces. Peace had been restored to the village.

Two Moons motioned his guests toward his lodge, but paused as an ancient man stepped out of the throng and hobbled slowly forward, aided by a younger man who himself was gray-haired and bent. The gathering fell silent. The aged warrior made straight for Hardeman with one arm extended, and when he reached the white man, he seized Hardeman's coat and pulled with surprising strength, forcing Hardeman's face down close to his own. He peered through rheumy eyes, blinking often, and Hardeman saw that the man was nearly blind. With a hand as brown and wrinkled as a dried-up leaf he touched Hardeman's face lightly, the fingers brushing the scar on his cheekbone.

The old man spoke a few words, which had to be put into Lakota and then English before Hardeman knew their meaning.

"Where did they give you this scar?"

"I was shot at the Washita battle."

The old man nodded, smiling, and he laughed. His laughter was strong and clean like a young man's. "I am the one who shot you," he said. "I fired from the entrance of my lodge. If you had not moved, I would have killed you." He sounded disappointed that this had not been the case, but then he became very serious and he seized Hardeman's coat again. "You shot into a lodge and then went inside. When you came out you had a boy in your arms." Here the old man held out a hand to indicate the boy's height. "Tell me what became of him."

"The boy is alive," Hardeman said. "He's with Sun Horse now."

"Is this true?" The old man turned to the other pipe carriers, holding out his hands as if he would grab the words from their mouths. "I wish to hear another say this is true! One of you Lakota! Tell me!"

"It is true," said Hawk Chaser, and the old man did not need to hear the words translated into Cheyenne. He raised his face to the sky and held out his arms as he sang his song of power, a high keening wail of joy.

"What is he called, this boy?" Two Moons wished to know, and now it was Bat Putnam who answered.

"He is known by many names among the Lakota. First we called him the

343

White Boy of the Shahíyela, but later we gave him other names. His father was White Smoke, son of Sun Horse, and after his dream we called him the One Who Stands Between the Worlds."

Translations were taking place all through the crowd and now a murmur arose among the onlookers, rapidly growing to an excited buzz of talk as the southern Cheyenne told their northern cousins the meaning of what they had heard. Kills Fox was speaking to Two Moons, explaining what he knew of White Smoke's adopted son. Above it all rose the old man's cry of joy, which stopped suddenly now as he turned again to Hardeman, who was more than a little taken aback by the reaction to his news.

"I thought you took him away to kill him," the old man said. "The bluecoats shot some women and children in a ravine behind the camp and I thought you would take him there. That is why I believed he had died, but I always hoped he might still live." Tears rolled down the old man's wrinkled cheeks, but he smiled as he spoke. "I made his first bow. I was an arrowmaker then. I made his first bow and his arrows. He was a good boy, and he could follow a trail like a wolf. And with horses..." The old man shook his head. "He had great power with horses. He was a good boy. I am glad he is alive." Then a new thought occurred to him. "Has he chosen between the worlds?"

Hardeman was considering how to reply to this when Bat answered for him. The old man nodded, apparently satisfied, and started away, led by the second man, who had remained silent all the while.

"Quite a stir it makes whenever folks find out Johnny's alive," Hardeman observed.

"Mmm," Bat nodded, watching the old man move off among the other Cheyenne, who were still talking among themselves with much animation. "Like I said, these folks set a heap o' store by dreams."

Blackbird was lifted from his pony drag by three men, directed with sharp words from Ice, the old healer. As the boy was carried off, the crowd began to disperse, and the pipe carriers followed Two Moons to his lodge.

The headman preceded the others into the tipi and took his seat at the back, facing the entrance. He motioned his guests to sit to his left, leaving it to them to work out their positions according to each man's importance. Standing Eagle took the place of honor next to the host and motioned Little Hand to sit beside him. Bat was next, then Hawk Chaser and Hardeman. When they were all seated, another man entered the lodge. It was Kills Fox, who seated himself across the fire from Two Moons, close to the door, in the place of least honor.

The fire was built up high and the tipi was warm and comfortable. The men formed a half circle around the fire, and Hardeman expected that the two women who sat across it in the family's side of the lodge would begin to bring the food at once. The odor of cooking meat filled the tipi, coming from the pot set astraddle of the small cooking fire there. Juices began to flow in

344

Hardeman's mouth, but the women remained where they were, apparently waiting for some sign from Two Moons.

To Hardeman's surprise, the headman began to load a pipe with great care. From the way the smoking mixture was cut and placed in the bowl, Hardeman knew a ceremonial smoke was in the offing, but he could not imagine its purpose. First you fed the guests, then you smoked before the talking began.

Two Moons took a coal from the fire and lit the pipe, and he surprised Hardeman once more by offering it to the directions in the Sioux manner, although the Cheyenne custom differed but little. Honoring his guests, Hardeman thought. When the offering was completed, Two Moons puffed again to be sure the pipe was burning well, and then, partly rising, he passed it with his right hand around the fire to Kills Fox.

At last Hardeman understood the meaning of this smoke. Normally, a ceremonial pipe was passed from right hand to left hand, then to the man on the left, and so around the circle, as the sun traveled around the hoop of the world, as both Lakota and Cheyenne prayed. There was good power in the sun and in the motion it followed through the sky, and men did many things in this way to remind themselves of that power and to partake of it. These things Hardeman knew from his earliest days among the plains peoples, but he had seen the pipe passed in the opposite direction too, on rare occasions. It was a smoke of reconciliation, an apology offered where there had been an argument or open dispute. Here, the village had been dishonored because a visitor had been attacked within the camp; the headman had been embarrassed, although the feeling had to be read from the smallest details in Two Moons' otherwise impassive bearing—a nervous flicking of the eyes, unwilling to meet Hardeman's straight on until the one who had been wronged accepted the pipe.

Kills Fox offered the pipe solemnly and smoked it, and when he passed it to Hardeman his hand trembled slightly.

Hardeman made nothing special of the ceremony. To do so would only call more attention to the wrong and further discomfort his host. He pointed the pipestem to the four directions, then to the sky and the earth, touching it to the ground in front of him before smoking and passing it on. The mixture of red willow bark and trade tobacco went to his head at once and set his wound to throbbing again. His head felt fuzzy, as if he had a fever, and his stomach rumbled.

Kills Fox was smiling as the pipe made its way back to Two Moons. The group was joined in friendship, the apology offered and accepted. Two Moons also was visibly relieved; he became the expansive host now, speaking grandly to the women. At once they served up bowls of hot broth, accompanied by chunks of buffalo rib roast that dripped with juice and blood. It took no awareness of good manners to make the guests fall to with a will.

"These folks been havin' a shinin' winter by the looks of it," Bat observed.

345

He ate noisily, nodding happily at Two Moons. He belched as the food hit his belly and began to calm the giddy feeling the pipe had caused. "Ain't seen so much buffler ner so many hides a-workin' in a heap o' moons."

"Shinin' times," Standing Eagle agreed, his mood improving now that he had a handful of meat in his mouth. With his skinning knife he cut off a piece close to his lips and chewed it vigorously, wiping away the juices on his chin with the back of his sleeve. Bat ate in the same manner, as all the mountain men had eaten, adopting the technique of hands and knife from the Indians. Afterwards, hands were wiped free of grease on leggings, keeping them supple and waterproof.

While the guests were still fully occupied with pieces of roast, the women brought forth an offering that made Bat's eyes light up. *Boudin blanc* the trappers had called this sausage-like creation. It was made by stuffing buffalo intestine with hump meat, tying off the ends and roasting it over hot coals, then finally boiling it for a short time. The trappers had considered it a rare delicacy and Bat ate it now until he belched loudly and could hold no more. "Shinin' times," he sighed contentedly.

When the meal was done at last, another pipe was offered, this one passed sunwise around the lodge and smoked contentedly by all, with a minimum of ceremony, and when Two Moons had set the pipe aside, Standing Eagle told the Cheyenne headman the details of the pipe carriers' mission—the exact nature of Sun Horse's message to Three Stars and why there was a second pipe for Sitting Bull. Two Moons listened attentively. When Standing Eagle was through, he spoke at some length in slow but correct Lakota, to accommodate his guests, who took an immediate interest in his words. At last Bat turned to Hardeman.

"Seems like Sittin' Bull's up by Chalk Buttes, sixty miles or so northeast; more'n a day's ride on a fast horse, anyways. Ol' Two Moons, he's been thinkin' on his feet. Even afore we was in camp, he sent off a couple of young fellers on strong horses to fetch Sit here. Hawk Chaser told him we had a pipe for Sittin' Bull, he jest sent them boys off lickety-split." Bat snapped his fingers and winked at Standing Eagle, who scowled, for he had never been able to master this white man's trick. "Now, Two Moons'll give us fresh horses if'n we're plumb determined to move on, but he says we might's well stay put and rest our horses, get ourselves fattened up. He told Sittin' Bull we've come far and got a man wounded. He reckons Ol' Sit'll be along in two, three days."

Once more, Hardeman totted up the risks of delay. The truth was, he would prefer to council with Sitting Bull here, where Two Moons and He Dog were preparing to go in and there were Oglalas with fresh canvas lodges from the agency, to show that life in that place wasn't so bad. If the pipe carriers pressed on now, they might see Sitting Bull a day sooner, but it was worth waiting an extra day to increase the chance of winning Sitting Bull over to Sun Horse's plan.

Two Moons spoke again, as if adding an afterthought, and Bat smiled. "Two Moons says he'd be just tickled to host a big talkfest. Says he'll speak fer peace, and come spring he'll ride with Sun Horse to talk to the other headmen."

Hardeman's hopes rose like water in a spring, but he revealed nothing. Instead he signed a question to the Cheyenne: *Have your scouts seen Three Stars?*

Two Moons made a sign of negation. *Before the moon was full we saw signals saying the soldiers were coming. Since then we have seen nothing.* He showed little aptitude for the sign talk and he added something in words, speaking to Bat.

"Same time as he sent the boys off to Sittin' Bull, he sent more young men down the Powder to warn the villages to keep their scouts out. It ain't likely the pony soldiers'll catch anyone nappin'."

Hardeman nodded, greatly relieved. "We might as well wait here."

Hawk Chaser spoke to Standing Eagle then, saying that with a few days of rest, Blackbird might be able to sit a horse and go with the men when they left to find Crook. Standing Eagle shrugged and gave his consent to the arrangement with a few words, his expression unreadable.

Bat contained his own satisfaction with difficulty. Events could scarcely have gone more to his liking. He too had seen that there was a better chance of bringing Sitting Bull into the plan if the pipe was presented here, but he had another reason for wishing to remain among the Cheyenne. From the first, he had seen that it would be far safer for Hardeman to meet Sitting Bull here in a peaceful village of Cheyenne than in Sitting Bull's own camp, with his young warriors howling for war, or even out on the trail, where there were the other pipe carriers to be considered. Standing Eagle and Little Hand were blinded by their stubborn distrust of all *washíchun*, and Hawk Chaser had instructions to kill the scout if he acted in a way that could endanger any Lakota, and so Bat had sought any means to protect the white man from his own foolishness, if it came to that, and to increase the chance that he might live out the next couple of days. Wherever Sitting Bull was met, Hardeman would almost certainly learn the full extent of Sun Horse's message and he would hear of the call for a summer meeting of the bands. Even if Sitting Bull refused the pipe, the Hunkpapa was still asked to join in convoking a great gathering of all the Lakota in summer so the issues of peace and war could be decided there in the hoop of the nation. Hardeman knew nothing of this, and how he might react to the news Bat couldn't guess, but here, at least, the white scout had a measure of protection. The sudden attack by Kills Fox, followed by the revelation of Hardeman's role in saving Johnny Smoker at the Washita and the news that Johnny was even now safe with Sun Horse, could not have happened better if Bat had planned it all himself. And when the old man had asked if Johnny had yet chosen between the worlds, Bat had answered only, "His time to choose is now." Let the people here think that Johnny might still choose the red man's world; it would give them hope, and they would value the miracle of the boy's return even more.

By Bat's reckoning, Hardeman was safer in this village now than Two Moons himself. In a few moments, he had been transformed from a white man viewed with suspicion to an important guest in camp, one who would be talked about and watched wherever he went. In the end that might help to keep him alive. If he acted rashly and perhaps tried to go off by himself to find Crook, he would be stopped, by force if need be, but Bat wanted no harm to come to him, and not just for Johnny Smoker's sake. On the trail up-country from the Sun Band's village his liking for the scout had grown, and he thought he had come to understand the man. As surely as Sun Horse, Hardeman sought peace at any cost between the Lakota and the whites, but with the bullheadedness of a *washíchun* he did not see that his way might cost the Lakota more than they could afford to pay. Still, his heart was good, and if he could only be made to see things from the Lakota viewpoint, he could be of help to the Sun Band. With help, the Sun Band might stay free for a time, and that was what Bat hoped for above all.

CHAPTER

TWENTY-FOUR

For several days the soldiers had marched in the daytime beneath bright skies. Since the three days of forced marches under cover of storm and night, which had brought them from Crazy Woman's Fork to Prairie Dog Creek, they had seen no Indians, no signals, and no recent sign. It was as if they traveled in an abandoned land. Among the troopers there were confident proclamations that the hostiles had all fled the country, and rumors that General Crook was persisting in his course down the Tongue even though he knew there were no Indians to be found there. The pace of the march was leisurely now, covering only ten or twelve miles a day.

On the fourth day of sunshine, the seventh since leaving the supply train, the fourteenth of the campaign, John Bourke came to ride in company with his friend Ham Whitcomb for a time. E Troop was at the front of the column today. Whitcomb rode in the lead, flanked by Sergeant Dupré and Corporal McCaslin. Lieutenant Corwin had been summoned forward a short time before and he rode now with Crook and Reynolds and their staffs, and Captain Mills, thirty yards in advance of the troop.

The day was springlike. Greatcoats were open to the breeze and collars were unbuttoned as the men basked in the cheering warmth of the sun. Recent nights had been shockingly cold. More than once the mercury in the surgeon's thermometer had dropped past the lowest reading at twenty-six degrees below zero and continued to fall until the silver liquid had shrunk down into the bowl, where it solidified and remained quiescent until the sun rose the next morning.

"Your beard is making great progress," Bourke greeted Whitcomb, regarding his wispy growth with a smile. Bourke's own beard was in full flower now.

"You must get tired of eating all that hair," Whitcomb replied soberly.

Bourke laughed. "I won't starve on this campaign, Ham. I'm growing my own hay crop."

"I understand our rations are already half gone." Whitcomb hoped by this observation to elicit from Bourke some hint of Crook's plans, but he was disappointed. The general's aide merely shrugged and kept his own counsel. One thing that was clear to Whitcomb without need of confirmation was that the command could not go much farther north if they expected to return to the supply train before their provisions were exhausted.

"Corporal McCaslin tells me that the men think we are here for a look at the country," he told Bourke. "This whole campaign is nothing more than an entertainment for the troops, they claim."

"An extended constitutional, yez moight say, sorr," McCaslin added. "Some of the wagerin' kind—and I add that I never wager, sorr—but some of them as does 're givin' odds that Mr. Lo has taken his wife and kiddies and gone to the reservation, hearin' that we was in the country and all."

"Mr. Lo?" Whitcomb was puzzled.

"From the poet," Bourke explained. "'Lo, the poor Indian, whose untutored mind sees God in everything, and hears Him in the wind.'" He turned to McCaslin. "And what about you, Corporal? Do you think General Crook has brought us here for our health?"

"No, sorr, I do not."

"Well, then?"

"Well, sorr, I'll not be denyin' that I've benefited from the exercise. I'm proper fit, sorr, and that's a fact. And the lads have color in their cheeks. But for meself, sorr, I believe we are here by the grace of the good general, and not forgettin' the Almighty, for one reason."

"Which is?"

"To smite the haythen, sorr."

"As simple as that?"

"As simple as that. The Bible tells us that our Lord Jaysus said to his disciples, 'Go yez forth and teach the haythen.' And that's why we're here, sorr. To teach them haythen redskins a lesson. And I have no doubt that the Almighty will provide haythens enough for the teachin'."

Whitcomb held back the laughter that rose within him. It wouldn't do to embarrass such a firm and simple faith. But he said, "Are you sure that smiting the heathen is the sort of teaching that Jesus had in mind?"

"We're soldiers, sorr. A soldier teaches by the sword. Of course, we have the modern convanience of the Springfield carbine."

"This is true, Walter," Sergeant Dupré said. "But before we can smite the heathen, we must find him. This is a big country, the Powder River country. As big as *la belle France*, but not so *belle*. Eight hundred thousand Prussian pigs could not occupy France, and we are only six hundred men. If the Indians wish to play cat and rat with us, we never see them."

It startled Whitcomb to think of the Powder River country as France. In a civilized land the little army would have followed roads and passed often through small villages and larger towns, fighting battles every step of the way if the land were hostile, but here they had seen only vast areas of unpopulated wilderness. On the first day after the storm, descending Prairie Dog Creek, they had had frequent views of the country far and wide, dropping gently away in front of them toward the valley of the Tongue; then once they had reached the Tongue itself they had traveled for a time in a deep canyon where they could see nothing at all except the valley floor; they had imagined the land above swarming with Indians just waiting to rain down arrows and rocks on the helpless soldiers, but when they emerged from the canyon they had found the countryside peaceful and unthreatening once more. They had followed the twisting course of the river, crossing the ice repeatedly, traveling at first in a valley much like that of the Clear Fork, with broad bottomland contained by low hills. Today the hills had dropped away on either side, revealing a valley several miles wide with gently sloping terraces composed of fine, arable earth. Off to the west stood majestic red-walled buttes, thoroughly timbered on the top. It was an impressive country, beautiful in its own way, and much more hospitable than the barren land along the Platte. The hills were well wooded with mesquite, juniper, pine and spruce, while the bottomland was thick with plum and cherry bushes, ash and box elder, as well as the ubiquitous cottonwood. Firewood had been plentiful at all the night camps and the horses and mules had been glad to forgo their evening ration of grain while they browsed instead on the thick black grama grass and a plant the scouts called "black sage," which they swore was as nutritious as oats. With each passing day, game had become more plentiful. It was a region that could comfortably support both men and their beasts of burden even in winter, but the many village sites found by the scouts, and both of those through which the column itself had passed in recent days, were deserted. The Indian villages were not permanent like those built by white men of all nationalities. They were movable, and what Dupré said was true: in a country as large as France, how could six hundred men hope to find, much less subdue, the Indians?

Whitcomb was pondering the apparent hopelessness of this task when the head of the column rounded a curve in the river and came upon a dense growth of cottonwoods covering dozens of acres, and he saw that it was yet another place of recent habitation. The village was by far the largest seen by the main body of the command and a halt was called while the scouts went ahead to look for signs that would tell them how long ago the Indians had left. There was widespread devastation in the cottonwoods, many of the trees, some of them huge, having been cut down for firewood and for the tender inner bark of the upper limbs, which the Indians fed to their ponies. By the freshness of the plentiful horse manure as well as the reddish shreds of meat that still clung to the bones of elk, deer and bison that were piled high near the drying racks, even the unpracticed eye could see that the village had been occupied not long before.

Captain Mills and Lieutenant Corwin left the generals and their staffs and as they approached the head of E Troop a rider came trotting from the rear of the column. It was Captain Egan.

"What's it to be, Anson?" he demanded of Mills. "We could make another ten miles today if we push on."

Mills shook his head. "We're going to camp here and wait for the scouts." The day before, a small party of the most experienced scouts had been sent off to the north, to explore the country to the Yellowstone.

The words were scarcely out of his mouth when six shots sounded rapidly from the direction of the village site. The officers looked around in alarm, but they relaxed when they saw General Crook's party halted among the cottonwoods, apparently unconcerned. The general himself had dismounted and was walking among some low bushes. Here and there he bent to pick something up and at last he turned and raised one hand high, holding up six pin-tailed pheasants. In his other hand was his Winchester rifle.

"My God," Egan exclaimed. "I've never seen the like of it. Shooting pheasants with a rifle! Even if they took off in a flock, that's damn good."

Crook's coat with its high collar of wolf fur was unbuttoned and it flapped as he walked back to his horse, revealing the red flannel lining in narrow flashes of bright color. Beneath the coat gleamed a row of forty or fifty brass cartridges in the cartridge belt he habitually wore around his waist. Together with his Kossuth hat, the top of the crown open to the air, and the ragged and burned corduroy trousers that flapped about his field boots, the overall impression was distinctly unmilitary.

"He looks like a bandit on the Mexican trails," Corwin said with a trace of awe.

Egan laughed. "God, Boots, have you had a look at yourself recently?" With his unkempt reddish beard, buffalo coat and fur cap, Corwin might have intimidated any run-of-the-mill border ruffian.

When the scouts had completed their examination of the site, the command was permitted to advance. With camp made in short order and supper not yet ready, the men occupied themselves with the curiosities the Indians had left behind. On many of the cottonwood trunks the savages had drawn varied scenes in bright colors, and on the far side of the river there were a number of Indian "graves" among the trees. Although the Indians did not bury their dead, there was no other term by which to call these final resting places. The bodies were raised six to ten feet above the ground on scaffolds or placed in the branches of the trees, wrapped in the best blankets and robes and, in the case of the warriors, accompanied by their weapons, and there they were left to desiccate slowly in the dry climate. The Irish glanced sideways at these eerie remains and did not linger long among the scaffolds.

Throughout the evening, eyes glanced often to the north and heads were raised whenever a horse stamped or whinnied, but the scouts sent off to the Yellowstone did not return that night.

Nor were they in camp the following morning, and word was passed from company to company that the command would remain here for a day of rest. Some of the soldiers amused themselves by hacking through the river ice, which was nearly three feet thick, and trying to coax a somnolent trout up to a simple hook baited with a morsel of jerky, but the trout apparently knew the season as well as the men and refused to be lured into this premature sport. Other men were content to find a warm rock and lie in the sun, or to stroll along the banks of the river. In the E Troop bivouac, Corporal Walter McCaslin stayed close to the cookfires whenever his duties did not take him elsewhere. He had noted Whitcomb's remark about the too-rapid depletion of the expedition's provisions. On the march there was no midday meal, but today the cooks offered up a hot dinner at noontime, and McCaslin was among the first in line. The tough buffalo bull meat that had been the steady diet of recent days was enlivened by a welcome addition, a hot gruel of hominy grits and Indian corn that had cooked throughout the morning on beds of coals. McCaslin ate all he was allowed with methodical care. If there were to be even shorter rations later on, he would do his best to prepare himself by building up his reserves.

By mid-afternoon, a solid front of clouds, thin at first but rapidly thickening, blocked off the sun. The mercury began to drop in the thermometer that hung outside Dr. Munn's improvised shelter and an ungentle wind gusted down the river from the north. As the men buttoned their greatcoats and began to move toward the cookfires for warmth, the scouts returned from the Yellowstone.

"Vell, Frank," a grisled sergeant called out, "haff you find vork for de boys, or are ve bound for de poorhouse?"

"Plenty sign, no Injuns," Little Bat Garnier replied.

"We'll find 'em pretty soon," Grouard said, and went on with the others to report to General Crook. At once, rumors began to circulate throught the camp, and if they were to be trusted equally, elements of the command were to strike off in all directions as soon as the horses could be saddled. After an hour or two, when the scouts had left the headquarters fire and gone off to their own mess for a hot meal, one story came to dominate the rest: the command would set out under cover of dark and march all night. The direction of the march was hotly argued and several disputes came close to fisticuffs, but as evening approached there were no orders to break camp.

The guides had brought in the carcasses of six black-tail deer and at supper the remains of the last buffalo were scorned.

"Whaddya think, Corp? Should we be packin' our truck after supper?" Private Dowdy inquired of McCaslin as they left the cookfire with their plates in hand.

"Boyo, when the officers in their wisdom tell me what's to be done, I'll be lettin' yez know. Until then, eat hearty."

He chewed long and hard at his buffalo meat, savoring the flavor so close to

352

beef but indefinably richer. He had traded his share of the deer to Private Dowdy for a much larger serving of buffalo the poor man had received by the chance of the draw. Walter McCaslin was not one to fuss over the quality of his meat so much as the quantity. He was a spare man and had been lean for all his thirty-eight years, and he missed no opportunity to eat his fill against the chance that he might have to do without on short notice. In his youth he had survived the Famine, and it was his most oft-repeated prayer that if ever he were brought close to death again before his natural time, it would not be through starvation.

After supper the long-awaited order came down the chain of command, passed from the headquarters staff to the battalion and company officers and thence to the men, and the rumors were laid to rest at last. Reveille would be at four o'clock in the morning; the command was leaving the Tongue and crossing to the Powder. The scouts had found no recent Indian sign in the open valley of the Yellowstone and no trace of General Terry or Colonel Gibbon. The trails from all the abandoned village sites on the Tongue led to the east, and it was now the consensus among guides and officers alike that if any hostiles remained in the Powder River country they would be found in the sheltered bottoms of the Powder itself.

Lieutenant Corwin found Corporal McCaslin at the cookfire, accepting the last scrapings of the stewpot from the cook. "What do you think, Walter? Is he ready?" Corwin nodded toward Whitcomb, who was brushing aside the remains of his bed-warming fire not far away, preparing his robes for the night.

"Oh, I think so, sorr."

"I hope you're right."

"He looks to his superiors as well as the men, and the soldier's life is in his blood."

"We'll see soon enough."

At dawn the column was already threading its way into the wooded hills east of the river. E Troop was at the front once more, and responsible for flankers to protect the head of the column. As he gave out the assignments that morning Corwin had looked at Whitcomb as if following a routine that had been established for weeks. "Mr. Whitcomb, you will take charge of the flankers. Set them at three hundred yards but tell them to keep in sight of the column as much as possible. There will be no bugle calls today, so warn them to keep an eye on the guidons."

Now, as the column passed over a low hill and left the Tongue behind, Whitcomb struggled to contain his excitement. He had placed two sets of flankers on either side of the column, each in the care of a non-commissioned officer, and then he had ridden a hundred yards beyond the foremost squad on the southern flank, assigning to himself the position of lone outrider, utterly unfettered by restrictions of any kind. Ahead, the first rays of the sun glinted among the trees atop the next hill, and it seemed to him that he had never seen a day or a landscape so beautiful.

Throughout the morning he kept his position, now and then dropping back and drifting closer to the column to check the positions of his flankers. During a brief nooning stop he checked his squads on the northern flank and then rode in to report to Corwin, fully prepared to be relieved of his position and kept once more under close watch, but Corwin merely accepted his report and turned to some other business, and Whitcomb cantered away with joy in his heart. What had caused the sudden change in his commander's behavior he did not know, but he would neither inquire nor complain.

As the command got under way again he resumed his solitary post, even with the head of the line and well behind the scouts, who were fanned out in a broad arc several hundred yards to the front as they had been in the opening days of the campaign. Occasionally a rise or depression would cut off his view of the column, but usually he could see all or part of it and he was struck once more by the ragtag look of the expedition. Only the coloring of the horses by troop and the close order maintained throughout the march revealed the fully trained soldiery beneath the tatterdemalion garb. He swelled with pride at having been chosen to protect such a noble force, so confident and battle-ready, but he reminded himself quickly that the Indians were a capable foe, often rated as the finest light cavalry in the world, and he examined his surroundings minutely, seeking any movement, any trace of color that did not belong among grass, trees, snow and rock. He glanced often at the guidons, watching for any signal of danger or change of direction. These swallow-tailed miniatures of the national flag were carried at the head of each troop, and in hostile countryside, where bugle calls might forewarn an enemy, they could be used to make silent signals up and down the column and to the outriders on either side. As the afternoon grew long, the guidons fluttered in the breeze but said nothing.

Whitcomb was out of sight of the column, riding through a patch of trees, when he saw the two horsemen. They were a hundred yards or more to his right, standing in the light of the lowering sun, and for an instant he thought they might be others like himself, soldiers who relished the danger and solitude of riding beyond the protection of the command, but as he watched them curiously, one man dropped lightly off his horse and knelt to examine something on the ground before him, and by his clothing and movements Whitcomb knew he was an Indian.

His first thought was to alert the column so it might escape detection. He urged his horse into a trot and made his way toward the top of the low hill that separated him from the command. He reined in before topping the rise, not wanting to present his silhouette against the sky for the Indians to see, and he looked back. The two men were as before, one still examining the ground for tracks or other signs, when suddenly the mounted man extended an arm, pointing to Whitcomb's rear. The brave on the ground leaped to his horse and the two of them were away and into the trees and gone from sight in the twinkling of an eye.

Without waiting to see where the Indians might reappear, Whitcomb spurred his horse over the hill and down the other side at a gallop. "Indians!" he shouted as he passed by Corporal Atherton and his set of four troopers. "Come in to a hundred yards!" To his right he saw another man riding in to report, one of the guides from the front positions. It was Louis Richaud, by the look of him. Whitcomb knew half of the scouts by sight now. He raced for the cluster of officers at the head of the column and he arrived seconds before Richaud. Lieutenant Corwin was there with Crook, Reynolds, Mills, Bourke and several others, and it was to his own troop commander that Whitcomb directed his report. "Indians, sir! Two of them, a quarter mile to the south!" he said as his horse hunched down on its hind legs and skidded to a stop, raising dust on the bare patch of ground.

"Hunters, I make 'em," said Richaud as he drew in beside the young officer. "No war shields." Whitcomb noticed that the laconic frontiersman was breathing easily. His own breathing was loud and rapid, as if he had run the whole distance on foot. The guide's simple confidence in his identification of the two braves, made at a distance of several hundred yards, reminded Whitcomb forcefully of the yawning caverns in his own knowledge.

"Hadn't caught sight of us yet," Richaud added, speaking to Crook, "but they'll make our dust, sure."

"They have already seen it, sir," Whitcomb said, glad he knew something that the scout did not. "When I first saw them one was dismounted. He seemed to be reading sign. Then the other one pointed in our direction and they both rode into the timber."

Crook nodded thoughtfully. "It may be a futile exercise, Mr. Richaud, but you might try to head them off. Take half a dozen men and try to take them alive."

Richaud acknowledged the order with a wave of his hand and he was gone, waving to the other scouts to follow him.

"I think we might bring in the flankers somewhat, if you agree, General," Reynolds said to Crook. "Perhaps Lieutenant—" He hesitated, glancing at Whitcomb.

"Whitcomb, General," Crook said. "Lieutenant Whitcomb. This is our famous Mr. Reb."

"Indeed. Well, Lieutenant Whitcomb, perhaps you would bring the flankers in to a hundred yards. In an orderly fashion, please. We want the hostiles to know we are alert but have nothing to fear."

"Place yourself with the lead set on the southern flank when you're done, Mr. Whitcomb," Corwin added.

Whitcomb snapped a salute. "Yes, sir. I have already brought those men in, sir. I'll notify the others."

As he galloped off to the north, to the lead flankers there, the command resumed its march. He recrossed the column to the south and there, as he had done on the other side, he instructed the flankers to send one man back to bring in the next set; they in turn would send one man to the rear, and so on down the length of the column. In this way all the flankers would be brought in in the least possible time; Whitcomb was pleased with the ingenuity of the plan, which allowed him to rejoin Corporal Atherton and his set of four within a few minutes of receiving his orders. The column was in an open plain among the hills and buttes now, and he could see its full length clearly. One by one the flanking squads were moving in, while the measured progress of the mounted force demonstrated a serene self-confidence, exactly as Reynolds had wished.

Whitcomb kept his eyes on the wooded areas to the south, expecting at any moment to see the scouts return with or without the two Indians, but half an hour passed, and then another, and the column left the open plain to enter a wooded draw between two hills. With each passing moment his impatience for action grew stronger. What could have become of the scouts?

Overhead, the scattered clouds that had sent shadows scudding across the land throughout the day were thickening now, becoming a solid cover, and a little snow was beginning to fall. New snow could help the scouts track the two braves, he realized. How far away might their village be? Richaud had said the men were hunters, and the hunting was good in these regions. Already that day the command had startled twenty or more deer and once they had seen a group of six elk moving off through the trees at a leisurely pace. The abundance of game meant that there was no need for the Indian hunters to range far, no need for them to spend cold nights away from the comfort of their lodges. The village would be within half a day's ride.

This quick analysis of the situation, made without conscious effort, startled him. He examined his conclusions again and found them sound, and he smiled. He was learning! Just two weeks before, such reasoning had been beyond his experience, yet today it came to him as naturally as adjusting himself to the movements of his horse.

"Look there, sir!" Private Dowdy was pointing to a ridge ahead and to the right of the column's line of advance. The expedition was out of the trees now, entering a shallow valley where a creek flowed off to the north. Two riders sat atop the ridge, unmistakably the Indians. Even at the distance, Whitcomb could see the blankets flapping in the wind and the horses' tails blowing. One pony stamped and shook his head.

"Cheeky devils," said Private Gwynn; he was a barrel-chested Irishman and the regiment's champion boxer.

"Countin' our noses, I'll warrant, sir," said Corporal Atherton.

"Come on, y' spalpeens! Man t' man! What d' ye say? Gwynn's the name and boxin's me game!"

"You'll have a chance at them soon enough," Whitcomb said, but he wished he were as certain as he sounded. What was Crook planning? And where were the scouts?

His consternation deepened as the command reached the frozen creekbed. A bugle call sounded and the head of the column turned left, downstream, away from the silent watchers who sat their horses as immobile as statues.

When the entire command had reached the creek and completed the turn to the north, the bugle sounded the order to halt, the notes clean and clear, whipped down the column by the wind, straight toward the Indian lookouts, and now Whitcomb saw the scouts riding in from the southeast. What had they been doing off there? Couldn't they see the Indians sitting brazenly in plain sight?

The scouts joined the clump of officers at the head of the column and long moments passed while they talked, gesturing to the southeast, at the Indians, and to other points seemingly at random. And then to Whitcomb's astonishment the flankers were ordered in from their posts as the command dismounted and cookfires were started. In a short time the smell of coffee and beans filled the air.

It was a quiet bivouac. Horses were not tethered individually to browse, but were kept on picket lines by troop. The men clustered in bunches around the fires and talked in low tones, glancing often from their officers to the Indians and back again. Was it possible that General Crook was not going to give chase?

Lieutenant Corwin paced nervously by E Troop's fire, drawing near to warm himself for a few moments, then spinning abruptly on his heel and striding off to stare at the headquarters fire and the ranking officers gathered there, breaking this routine only when someone noticed that the Indian sentinels were gone.

"They was there a minute ago!"

"I was watchin', and I swear t' God they didn't move. Just disappeared."

"Dey are nott human," muttered Willy Stiegler, E Troop's Austrian corporal. "Deffils, dot's vot dey are!"

Some of the Irish crossed themselves.

Corwin's pacing increased in tempo now and once he seemed to start off toward the headquarters fire, but he thought better of it and turned back.

The day darkened, although it was hard to tell if the loss of light was due to the setting of the invisible sun or merely the thickening of the clouds that rolled overhead from the northwest. The wind picked up and snow flurries fell here and there about the landscape, dropping from the clouds like wispy beards and occasionally sending a handful of flakes to sting the faces of the men and melt in the steam from their coffee.

LISA PUTNAM'S JOURNAL

Wednesday, March 15th. 5:40 a.m.

I have been up and about since just after two o'clock and I am already drinking my fourth cup of coffee. Our heifers delight in making a great fuss and commotion just when one thinks all is quiet and there may be a little sleep to be had. Out I go, which requires a thorough job of dressing (it was just below zero at two-thirty), only to find one heifer that had given birth as efficiently as if she had been at it for a number of years, and another that regarded me with her liquid brown eyes quite placidly and waited until an hour ago to produce her calf. Both are healthy and took quickly to nourishing themselves in the proper manner. One bull, one heifer calf. We now have eight bulls and ten heifers. Not quite half done. I discovered yesterday afternoon that my father forgot to order more of the patent remedy for scours last summer; we have a small supply of the medicine left, but if many calves develop scours this spring I will have to fall back on the old folk treatment.

Hutch and Johnny do most of the feeding now, leaving Julius free to hunt. Yesterday we finished the last of the hay in the east meadow, but we have plenty in the cribs in the west meadow to last until the grass is green. Yesterday afternoon we moved the herd across the river.

The friendship between Hutch and Johnny Smoker continues to grow apace. Johnny has been giving Hutch some instruction in roping, and whenever Hutch isn't trying to spend a few moments with Maria Abbruzzi he is roping fenceposts or farm implements or some unlucky calf in the heifer lot. When he and Johnny are together Amanda is often with them, and where Amanda is, there Chatur is sure to be found. He dotes on her, and although he is nearly twice as old as any of them, I cannot help thinking of him as one of "the young people," perhaps because of his short stature and the delight he takes in all things. They are quite a quartet. I fancy that I am beginning to know Amanda well enough to perceive a change in her just in the short time she has been here. As a violinist or clown she is completely in command, yet when she is simply Amanda Spencer she is often somewhat timid and unsure of herself. But it seems to me that since she has been in company with Johnny she has begun to reveal some of that same confidence and spirit she otherwise reserves for her music and clowning. Love (if I can so dignify her youthful infatuation for Johnny) works wonders on one's self-confidence. Clearly the least of her concerns is how soon the road will be clear and the circus free to leave.

The same cannot be said of Mr. Tatum. He and I have dined together twice more (without the luxuries of that first occasion) and he was pleasant company as always, but I can sense his impatience with the pace of his work. Yesterday there was another slide at the avalanche site, some of the recent snow falling down to replace what had already been dug away. Many of the teamsters have experience with blasting powder but they tend to use too much. This is the second time they have created a larger mess than the one they sought to remove. And still Mr. Tatum persists. Each morning he accompanies his men and oversees the start of their work before returning for his daily riding practice. He works with his white stallion for an hour or longer in the tent, then inspects the other animals. For the rest of the morning he watches the clowns or practices his pistol shooting, and after dinner he returns to the avalanche with the men to spend the rest of the day there. By his disciplined work habits, he certainly sets a good example for all those who work for him.

358

I must get to breakfast and away with Julius into the hills. We promised Mr. Chalmers that we would take him hunting with us and we hope to do better than we have done thus far by going lower into the foothills and moving northward through the valleys there, gradually working around and coming back by way of Sun Horse's village. It will be a long day for me; I feel about all in now, but I imagine I will survive. Mr. Chalmers and the three Waldheims and a few others provide the core of the circus hunting parties. What tales they will have to tell when they leave here, all about being led through the wilds by Sioux guides! I only wish our collective efforts would produce better results. We have been hunting in earnest for a week now, but I am afraid that Sun Horse has made little progress toward preparing himself for a move. There is some improvement in the Indian horses and the hunters are able to range a little farther afield, but what little meat has been brought in is consumed at once and he has put up no jerky at all yet. Still, I have every hope of greater success soon, and that is why I continue to push myself through days like this one. (But how I look forward to my bed tonight!)

Sun Horse has lookouts on the ridges but they have seen no signals in many days. For some time the whereabouts of the soldiers have been unknown.

CHAPTER —————————————————————————

TWENTY-FIVE

The afternoon was well along when the hunting party reached the Lakota village. After a morning of brisk, chill winds and occasional flurries of snow the day had cleared and now the sun stood bright and alone above the western ridge. Willy Waldheim had joined the hunters at the last moment, bringing their number to four. Lisa and Julius led the way while Alfred Chalmers brought up the rear, looking all around as they entered the camp.

"Extraordinary," he said, and Willy nodded. The younger Waldheim brother was fair of skin and hair, with the same well-muscled build as his brother Johann. His sporting rifle, made by Manton of England, was held tightly in his hands and he had checked his load twice as the riders neared the village. He was prepared for anything—except the apparent indifference that greeted their appearance. Here and there a man or woman made a sign of greeting to Lisa and some glanced curiously at the huge Englishman, but otherwise the whites occasioned no more interest in the village than a returning group of Sioux might have done.

Lisa had noticed that the horses in the herd looked a little sleeker and here among the tipis a few women were working at the hides of deer and elk, but the village still had a listless feeling about it; the hunting had not yet had the revitalizing effect she had hoped for. She caught herself slumping from fatigue and she sat up straight, dreading the long ride home.

They found Sun Horse sitting on a robe in front of his lodge, enjoying the warm sunshine. As they dismounted he rose to greet the hunters. He took Lisa's hands in his own and he smiled, but it seemed to her that he was tired.

"We saw two elk, Grandfather," she said in Lakota. "They were far away and we could not get close enough to shoot."

"The Lakota hunters have found no meat today," he replied. Recent days had been clear and bright, and snowblindness was affecting nearly all the hunters now. For two days Rib Bone had been confined to his lodge with pieces of trade cloth soaked in melted snow water resting on his eyes. Early in the afternoon Sun Horse had seen Crooked Horn return to the village alone, with no meat hanging from his saddle, and now he too kept to the darkness of his lodge. For seven days Lakota and *washichun* had hunted together, and as the days passed and so little meat was brought to the kettles, Sun Horse had felt his bright hope fade like the leaves of autumn once the golden glory was past.

"Stay and eat with us," he invited the whites, but Lisa shook her head. Groups of white hunters passed through the village often enough now that they were no longer obliged to observe the courtesies of formal visits, and she had no wish to eat the meat that others needed.

"We cannot stay, Grandfather. We must get home by dark. We came to give you more grain and gunpowder. Tomorrow if you send a few men to the park, we will hunt in the afternoon down below the river canyon."

She turned to take the sacks of grain and powder that Julius had already removed from the saddles, but Sun Horse held up a hand in refusal.

"Already you have given us much and we have given little in return. For a time, both our hunters and our horses will rest. We will make ceremonies to call our four-legged brothers, to remind them that we are hungry and need their help. When the power of the hunters returns, we will hunt again."

Lisa had half expected something like this. Lakotas did not persist in fruitless endeavors, either in war or peace. Instead they sought the reasons for their difficulties, and those reasons lay always in the realm of spirit power. If hunting was bad, the four-leggeds were displeased with the Lakotas; if war went badly, some warrior had broken a taboo or a ceremony had been performed incorrectly or the enemy's medicine was stronger. Seeking spiritual reasons for difficulties and failure was so deeply ingrained in the Lakota way of thinking that she knew there was no use in arguing. She had heard the finality in Sun Horse's tone; he spoke in the manner of one whose mind was made up. It reminded her of the way her own father had spoken when he had reached a difficult decision.

"Take these," Julius said in Lakota, holding out the sacks, and before Sun Horse could refuse again he added, "Our horses tired. Too much to carry back to lodge." He set the sacks beside the entrance to the tipi, on the robe where Sun Horse had been sitting. "We go now," he announced, turning his back on the gifts and remounting his horse. Once he was in the saddle he said, "Your friends ready to hunt again when you say."

Lisa was grateful that Julius had found a way to leave these last offerings. It was little enough, and far less than she had wanted to give. She wished she could find something to say, something to show how disappointed she was that the joint efforts of whites and Lakotas had come to naught, but her fatigue was overwhelming. She could find no way to encourage Sun Horse or brighten his spirits while her own discouragement was so profound, and she knew her exhaustion was mostly at fault. After a good night's rest she might see things differently, but now the future seemed dark and forbidding.

She took Sun Horse's hands in her own once again and met his gaze, trying to say with her eyes what she could not put in words, and as if he understood her thoughts perfectly, he nodded and favored her with another wan smile.

She left him quickly then, remounting her horse and kicking it into a trot that carried her beyond the village before the others overtook her.

"No sense taking it hard," Julius said gently as his horse fell into step with hers. "We done what we could. He's a sight better off now than before."

"I know," she said. "I just don't like to see him give up."

"I dunno that he has. Seems to me more like he's waitin' on somethin'."

When the whites were gone from the village Sun Horse resumed his seat on his robe. The sun was still some distance above the ridge and the warmth eased his aching joints. In the first days of hunting with the whites the moonlit nights had been so cold that the trees had popped just as they did in the true winter moons. *Waziya*, the winter power, remained strong. The Ancient Ones said that *Okaga*, the life-giving power of the south, battled *Waziya*, in time driving him back to the north so the warmth could return to the land, setting free the spirits of all living things. Many spoke of *Waziya* as a fearsome and evil power because he opposed *Okaga*, but Sun Horse saw the balance between the two. The cold of winter prepared the way for new life, cleansing and healing the earth. In time *Okaga* would return and the balance would be restored. He reviewed in his mind these most basic tenets, seeking something that would show him the way to realize the power of his vision. He had believed the hunt with the whites to be the beginning of that power, but the hunt had failed.

When the women lose their virtue, the buffalo go away, said the Ancient Ones. But no woman of the Sun Band had acted badly or thrown her man away without reason. None had gone to the plum bushes with a man not her husband. These things happened in other bands, the tales told behind raised hands at the summer gatherings, but the Sun Band kept to the old ceremonies and the old ways, and the women in Sun Horse's camp were not responsible for the absence of *pte*.

It had been a fleeting thought, not a serious concern. He knew that he was like a one-eyed wolf circling the herd with his blind eye towards the old sick bull that would be easy prey. He was seeking to avoid the reason that stood so plainly before him: the fault was his own. He had seen a promise of power but the promise had not been fulfilled.

Where had he failed?

He arose from the robe and lifted it from the snow to wrap it around him. Chunks of snow stuck to the coarse hair, making him resemble the old bulls in summer, the fur shedding in patches until mighty *tatanka* looked as ragged as a robe that was cut up to make moccasins after many years of use. The thought amused Sun Horse and he wrapped the robe tighter about him and swung his head low, snuffling like *tatanka* testing the wind. He moved across the camp slowly like an old bull, and the people saw him and wondered why he imitated the buffalo. Perhaps there would be another buffalo dance to summon the four-legged creature that gave so much to man.

Outside the lodge of Sees Beyond, Sun Horse coughed lightly, the *chuff* of the buffalo bull, and he stamped his feet to shake the snow off his moccasins, making the sound of *tatanka* stamping the ground.

"My lodge welcomes a visitor," came the voice of Elk Leggings, Sees Beyond's father. Sun Horse entered.

Sees Beyond and his father were eating. Elk Leggings sat at the place of honor across the fire from the entrance. Sees Beyond sat beside him. Sun Horse moved around the lodge to the left, moving as the sun passed around the sky, stepping behind the men, not coming between them and the fire. A gust of wind shook the lodgeskins and gusted smoke downward from the smoke hole. Elk Leggings' wife stepped outside to adjust the flaps as Sun Horse seated himself in the guest's place at Elk Leggings' left hand.

Sees Beyond had listened carefully to the visitor's progress and now he smiled. "*Hau, tunkáshila,*" he said, and Sun Horse wondered what it was that had allowed the blind man to know him with such certainty. Was it the way he walked? Or perhaps some smell? Or was it simply that Sees Beyond could see his spirit with the inner eye that saw the real world?

"Eat with us," said the old man. Elk Leggings was the band's rememberer and one of the old-man chiefs of the band, the four principal councillors who walked at the head of the village when it was on the move. The old chiefs carried the fire and chose where to smoke and where to camp.

"I have eaten," Sun Horse said. He knew there was little to spare, but when the wife returned she passed him a spoon made from the horn of the mountain sheep and he ate a little, making the polite sounds. When the men had finished eating, a pipe was lit and passed around, and as the bowl cooled, Sun Horse spoke. "I have had a vision. *Wamblí gleshka* has told me of a power that comes from the meeting of two people. It is a power that can bring the Lakota and the *washíchun* together in peace. Hears Twice told me of its coming, before the Strange-Animal People entered the whiteman's valley, before the *washíchun* Hardeman and my grandson, the One Who Stands Between the Worlds, came here. Hears Twice says this is a power that can help the band or destroy us."

362

"Where does the power of peace come from, Grandfather?" Sees Beyond smiled slightly as he spoke the question. It was a question a *wichasha wakán* might ask a very young man who sought to understand the spirit world, but Sun Horse didn't mind. This was Sees Beyond's way, asking simple questions, and this had become almost a game that the two holy men enjoyed together.

"It comes from the east," Sun Horse replied seriously. "We pray to the morning star, which ushers in the light, and this is the light of true understanding. Without true understanding there can be no peace. Not within a man, not among the people, not between two peoples. The morning light is red and so the color of the east is red, and red is the most sacred color, in part because it symbolizes the peace that comes from true understanding."

Sees Beyond nodded. "And even this is not the whole truth of the power of the east. The whole truth is more than one man can ever see, but still each man seeks it."

Not so many years ago they had spoken nearly identical words, during Sees Beyond's apprenticeship, but then it had been Sun Horse who taught and Sees Beyond who learned. They did not need to repeat all the words now, for both knew them well. Recognize that what you see is only a part of the whole. No matter how much you see, you cannot see the whole. Do not ask that something be only that which you perceive, for this is to deny the whole, limiting it to a lesser existence.

There was a soft sound from Elk Leggings and they saw that he had allowed his head to drop to his chest and was snoring lightly, his eyes closed. The old man's wife sat in the back of the lodge repairing torn beadwork on a ceremonial shirt, leaving the men to speak alone.

"My father seeks the truth more and more often in dreams," Sees Beyond said, smiling, and then, "You know that Crooked Horn has returned?"

Sun Horse nodded, then grunted his acknowledgment, remembering Sees Beyond's blindness. Crooked Horn was the best hunter in the band, yet after six days of hunting with the whites he had brought no meat to the kettles, not even a snowshoe hare. Yesterday he had gone out alone to the high places to seek the reason for his failure, as a man often did when his power left him. He sought inside himself, to know if he had broken some condition of his power, an agreement with his spirit helper made at the time of his becoming-a-man vision. Sometimes a man forgot these obligations and his power waned. If he found no reason within himself, the man might speak to the spirits, addressing his spirit helper, or even the Great Mystery, to know if the invisible powers might have forgotten their obligations to the two-leggeds.

The Lakota respected the spirits but they did not bow down to them as the *washichun* did; the spirits too might be at fault, and a good man was not afraid to stand strong before them and remind them of their obligations.

"He spoke to the *pte*," Sees Beyond said, "but they told him nothing."

It was like Sees Beyond to know what was in a man's mind before he had spoken it. Sun Horse had said nothing about the hunt, nothing to show his

363

fear that the hunting was bad because the power he had felt so strongly at the white settlement when the Snowblind Moon was young seemed to have slipped away from him. He had felt the power and he had waited for it to be revealed to him instead of seeking it out. A vision was not a gift but a possibility, something that would come about only if the man to whom it was given fulfilled the promise.

The fault is mine, not Crooked Horn's, Sun Horse thought. I have done nothing. I felt the promise of power and I have waited, doing nothing.

I was so sure! And here in the camp circle I saw the power begin to grow, the *heyoka* of the Lakota joining with the white clown girl, making the people laugh. Lisaputnam and the black whiteman asked that Lakota and *washíchun* hunt together and I saw the power of the white world joined with that of the Lakota; I believed the power I had felt was growing, and I did nothing.

Like Crooked Horn I must look within myself.

"I will make *inipi*," he said to Sees Beyond. "Will you help me?"

Sees Beyond seemed to think very hard for a time. Finally he nodded and reached for his ceremonial pipe. In his own lodge he knew the place of every object and his hands found the pipe and tobacco pouch and then the smoldering stick placed between the rocks of the fire pit, filling and lighting the pipe as easily as a seeing person might have done. As he passed the pipe to Sun Horse, his sightless eyes found the older man's face and he said "Look beyond the symbol!"

He said it sternly, forcefully, almost like an order.

Sun Horse felt a chill as he in turn offered the pipe to the sacred points and smoked, and he knew he was feeling the strength of this *wichasha wakán* whose power grew so strong, and so different from his own. Sun Horse used his knowledge of the spirit world to guide his people through this life, walking with feet placed on the solid earth, yet always acting with proper awareness of the real world behind the world of solid objects, never losing touch with the great spirit power that was available to all men. Sees Beyond seemed to be a part of that real world ordinary men could not see, keeping just a part of his awareness in the living world of men. Never until now had he spoken to Sun Horse of *wakán* things except in questions, always questions; yet now he said *Look beyond the symbol!*

When the pipe was smoked and the ashes emptied carefully into the fire, the two holy men rose together and left the lodge, Sees Beyond holding Sun Horse's arm at the crook of the elbow. There was no need to make special preparations for the *inipi* ceremony; it was the ceremony that preceded all others, and some members of the band performed it daily merely for relaxation and cleaning the body.

The men went first to Sun Horse's lodge, where they found Elk Calf Woman asleep. She often slept away the short winter afternoons and they left her resting, asking Sings His Daughter to come and assist them. Near the aspen grove by the creek, the young woman helped Sun Horse gather the materials while Sees Beyond supervised the building of the *ini ti*, the house where *ni*, the life force, was to be purified. The whites called it a sweat lodge, but the purpose was to cleanse the inner being. Nearby there were several of the small structures set along the bank of the stream and Sun Horse had used one or another of them at various times, but today only a new *ini ti* would suit his purpose. Today he made a new beginning.

The grove was bright with sunlight and shadows. A few small clouds floated past now, coming from the mountains, and to the north the clouds were thicker, but the winds stayed high above the ground and the valley was quiet. The sounds of the village carried to the grove, where they mingled with the sound of the water running beneath the new ice that had covered the stream during the recent nights of deep cold. Sings His Daughter broke the ice with an iron hand-axe and brought a bowl of water for the ceremony.

Nothing in the preparation of the *ini ti* was overlooked, nothing done carelessly, but from the first, Sun Horse noticed that Sees Beyond did not pause as he would have done on other occasions to remind the participants of the meaning in each step of its construction, nor did he sing the usual prayers, and Sun Horse understood his intention at once: they were both *wichasha wakán* and they had no need to be reminded of the symbols; today they sought the deeper meanings.

Working silently together, they placed four willow poles on each of the four sides, marking the four quarters of the universe, bending the poles toward the center, where they were lashed together by Sees Beyond's quick fingers. The surface of the ground had thawed in the afternoon sun, allowing the men to dig a shallow pit for the hot rocks that would be placed there. They covered the floor of the lodge with sage, and strewed the earth from the rock pit in a straight line from the small entrance, forming a path leading eastward to where they would build *peta owíhankeshni*, the fire that does not go out. As Sun Horse built the fire in the sacred manner, Sees Beyond took the rocks that Sings His Daughter handed him one at a time and he placed them at the four corners of the fireplace to mark the corners of the universe, finding their proper positions with his hands, and all the while the two men were silent. Only when Sun Horse lit the fire did Sees Beyond pray aloud for the first time, calling to *Wakán Tanka*, who gave men fire and all other things. "*Peta owíhankeshni* burns forever," he chanted. "It shall make us pure and bring us close to your powers."

When all the preparations were done, Sun Horse stood at the entrance of the *ini ti*. Here too the ceremony might have been shortened. He and Sees Beyond knew all the meanings of the lodge and the pathway and the fire; they might simply enter the *ini ti* now. But something compelled him to add to the ceremony today.

He removed his ceremonial pouch from the cord that held it around his neck. He opened it with difficulty, for the rawhide thongs that held it closed had not been untied for twenty-five years; he had to use his teeth to loosen the knots, but finally the pouch was open and he reached within. He took out a pinch of dust and dropped it on the pathway, and he prayed to *Unchi*, Grandmother Earth, from whom all generations of man were descended.

"Upon you, oh Grandmother, I build a sacred path," he prayed. "I purify myself for the people, that they may walk this path with firm steps. There are four sacred steps on this path, which leads to *Wakán Tanka*. Let me be pure that the people may live!"

He took a step and there he dropped another pinch of dust from the pouch, the dust he had carried for twenty-five winters, the pouch never opened since then. Sees Beyond waited silently as Sun Horse took another step. Another pinch of dust, the prayer said again, and another step, until Sun Horse had placed a pinch of dust on each of the four steps to *peta owíhankeshni* and said the prayer four times, and then he prayed to *Wakán Tanka*. "I place myself on this sacred path for my people. I send my voice to you through the four directions, which we know are but one direction, and that leading always to you. *Ho Tunkáshila, Wakán Tanka*, help my people to live in the sacred manner! Help my people to live!"

A band of clouds dropped a little snow on the grove and Sun Horse breathed deeply of the cool air and tasted the snow of his tongue, clean and pure.

He touched Sees Beyond and together the two *wichasha wakán* removed their robes and entered the *ini ti*. Custom told that the one who led the ceremony should enter alone with the pipe to purify himself and the lodge before those who made the *inipi* ceremony joined him, but here the two holy men combined their powers for the quest that Sun Horse undertook. Over coals that were brought from the fire and placed in the center of the lodge, they burned a dried twist of sweetgrass to purify the little house and invoke the presence of the spirits. After the sweetgrass they burned sage, for all spirits loved the fragrance of sweetgrass but only the most benevolent powers liked sage, and these remained while the others were driven out. Now pinches of *chanshasha*, the red willow bark smoking mixture, were offered to the four directions and to the sky and the earth, and as each pinch was offered to the sacred points it was placed in Sees Beyond's ceremonial pipe. The men did not pray aloud as was usually done, but each prayed within himself. When the pipe was filled, Sun Horse stooped low and left the *ini ti* to place the pipe on the mound of earth at the end of the pathway to the fire, where he left it with the bowl to the west and the stem pointing east. He re-entered the lodge, closing the entrance flap behind him, and sat across from Sees Beyond.

The inside of the *ini ti* was as dark as night. In the center of the floor, where the rocks would soon be placed, a few coals still glowed. Even the darkness had meaning; it symbolized ignorance, the receptive emptiness that was the proper state of one who sought to purify his inner being.

So many symbols in this and all ceremonies, Sun Horse thought. The people were constantly reminded of the spirit powers and the meaning of each one, all truly part of one spirit, called *Wakán Tanka* and *Taku Wakán, Taku*

Shkanshkan, and other names known only to the holy men. *Wakán*, a mystery, that which is not to be understood. Not by one man, nor by all men. Yet each experienced and understood some part of the mystery, not only holy men but all men and women of the tribe. Grown people constantly reminded children of the meanings of each act that sought to propitiate the powers, until the sight or mention of a symbol brought forth a host of the deeper meanings. And yet even the holy men retained the symbols, and perhaps could never reach a true understanding while the symbols remained.

Look beyond the symbol.

Was this what Sees Beyond meant? Cast the symbols aside as he had done today, making the *ini ti* but leaving out so many rituals, so many pauses for prayer; not to say that prayers were unimportant but to cut through obstacles that impeded understanding, knowing that Sun Horse sought the path to peace. . . . The peace that came only from true understanding.

Over the years Sun Horse had sought to understand so much. Perhaps too much? How could a Lakota understand the essence of the *washíchun* nation? Yet this was the promise of Sun Horse's vision and for twenty-five winters he had sought to fulfill the promise.

The little flap covering the entrance opened now and Sings His Daughter passed in a hot rock held on a forked stick, the first of the rocks from the fire-without-end. Each should be touched by the pipe, each standing for one of the directions, a symbol for the boundaries of the universe, but Sun Horse merely took the forked stick and deposited the rock in the center of the lodge without ceremony, passing the stick back to Sings His Daughter. More rocks were brought until the ground was piled high with rocks that carried the strength of the fire within them, cracking and popping as they touched the cold ground, hissing as Sun Horse sprinkled water over them and filled the little house with steam. He threw sage leaves on the stones and the scent of the sage was carried on the steam and the men tasted it as they breathed and felt it tingle on their skin.

Again Sun Horse opened the sack at his throat and reached within, this time withdrawing a perfectly round stone, which he placed among the hot rocks. *Tunkán*, the stone that has fallen from the sky, *tunkán*, the round stone that represents the earth, the whole universe; *tunkán*, part of the word *Tunkáshila*, Grandfather, the one who encompasses the universe, one of the names of *Wakán Tanka*.

Now the holy pouch hung loosely at Sun Horse's neck, only a little dust left, the symbols gone, made part of the *inipi* ceremony. Today he had thrown away the symbols of his own vision, carried with him for twenty-five years; it was time to look beyond the symbols and realize the full power of what he had been given.

There on the small butte overlooking the Laramie fort all those years ago he had watched the few wagons he could see on the wagon road and he had felt the power of the *washíchun*, like the threat of a storm that was heralded far in advance by a few black clouds on the horizon. He had prayed to *Wakán Tanka* to help him understand these strangers who brought such change, such power, to the lands of the Lakota and their allies, and *Wakán Tanka* had sent him a helper.

One day, two, then three days he had prayed, and in his heart he had feared that he would fail again as he had failed to find a vision in his youth, but on the morning of the fourth day the horse had come, running out of the sun. The sun had just come up and the morning star stood in the sky above it. Stands Alone had been praying to the morning star, asking for the light of understanding, when he heard a horse neigh. At first he thought perhaps a friend had come to seek him but he could see no one on the hilltop, and no horse. Again the horse neighed and he realized then that the sound came from the sky. He turned towards the sun and saw that something was partially blocking the light. The shape grew rapidly, shutting out the fiery disk altogether now, and he saw that it was a horse, galloping in the sky, coming straight toward the hilltop. The horse was black, so sleek and shiny that it reflected the deep blue of the sky. It reminded Stands Alone of his favorite mount, his black hunter, but he knew this was a spirit horse, and not of this world. When the horse drew closer he gasped, for there on the hindquarters were the jagged streaks of lightning and dotted hailstones with which he marked his hunter; the other markings were the same too, all but the eyes, which glowed with an inner light like the shine of the morning star.

Nearer and nearer the horse came, galloping silently on the air, and when it reached the hilltop it raced around him four times, moving sunwise, its feet never touching the grass. When it completed the fourth circle it came to a stop beside him, facing to the south. Stands Alone gazed in wonder at the horse, but suddenly there arose a great commotion from the direction the horse was facing, coming from the Lakota encampment by the soldier fort. There were guns firing and a great cloud of smoke and dust, and then he saw the people, white soldiers and Lakota men, rising through the smoke and dust until they were floating in the air at the level of the hilltop. A chief was standing between the white soldiers and the Lakota warriors, his hands empty, and he was talking to them, pleading that they should not fight, but one of the soldier guns fired and the chief fell and then the soldiers vanished in a cloud of warriors that drifted over them like a thunderstorm moving over the peaks of *Pahá Sapa*. When the dust blew away, the *washíchun* soldiers were gone and only Lakota were left, their lodges falling like leaves in autumn and the people floating off in a long line to the north, until Stands Alone could see them no more.

He looked back to the south and to his surprise he saw that the Lakota camp was as it had been before, peaceful and unchanged. The other camps were peaceful too, all the tribes that had been called there by the whites for the great council that would begin soon, traditional enemies camped side by side in peace.

The horse neighed now and pranced about, inviting Stands Alone to mount. He grabbed a handful of mane and leaped to the horse's back, and the horse soared away from the hilltop into the sky, going north and west toward the Snowy Mountains, which the whites called the Big Horns. The mountains grew quickly and in no time at all the horse was descending, approaching a small valley. Suddenly there was a great crying and shouting, and Stands Alone saw *washíchun* ringing the valley, all angry, and some soldiers among them, but as the horse descended to the valley floor the whites disappeared and their voices grew silent.

Stands Alone dismounted and walked by the clear stream and the small lake among the grasses and flowers of summer. He saw the bushes that would soon be heavy with berries, the straight pines for lodgepoles, the deer and elk tracks and the droppings of buffalo. The horse moved with him, whickering joyfully, prancing in the air just above the tops of the grass. Stands Alone lay in the grass, the sun warm on his face, and he felt a great contentment.

Now the horse nuzzled him, danced away and returned, away and back, and he understood that he should mount again. Grasping the black's mane he swung up onto the strong back and together the horse and rider flew up and away, going south and east now, and Stands Alone laughed to feel the wind as they flew. When they reached the hilltop where the horse had come to him, he was surprised to see someone sitting there waiting for him. As he drew closer, he caught his breath, for the man on the hilltop was himself, sitting cross-legged with eyes closed, as if asleep or dead.

Then his vision clouded and for a moment he was afraid, but the horse whickered near at hand and he opened his eyes to find himself sitting on the hilltop, the black prancing in the air before him. The horse neighed a final time, then turned away and galloped off, disappearing into the sun.

At his feet Stands Alone saw a small round stone; he picked it up together with some of the earth from the hilltop and carried it with him when he returned to the encampment by the Holy Road. There he found a camp at peace; nothing bad had happened while he was gone.

In his lodge he found his father waiting for him. With his father was a blind youth called Sees Beyond, his father's apprentice and already *wichasha wakán*.

"I have had a vision," Stands Alone said, and he told them of his vision in as much detail as he could remember, but he did not ask them to interpret it for him. Instead, he explained his own understanding of the vision, the power it offered him and the obligation it imposed, and when he was done each of the holy men in turn spoke his approval, agreeing that Stands Alone's understanding was complete.

"But is it a true vision?" Stands Alone had asked then, voicing his one doubt. "It is said that in true visions only those four-footeds known to the Ancient Ones appear."

Branched Horn shrugged. "Others have had visions of horses."

"Do we not call them *shunka wakán*?" Sees Beyond asked. "If the *shunka wakán* had appeared to the Ancient Ones, would they not have tamed them as we do? Next to *pte*, what four-legged is a greater helper to the Lakota? Shall he have such power in our lives and none in our visions?"

Reassured by this final confirmation, Stands Alone had sent a crier through the camp to say that he would give a feast the next day, inviting all to come, and when the people gathered on the following day they found the kettles full of meat that Stands Alone had provided, and Stands Alone waiting there with robes and moccasins piled beside him and gift sticks in his hand, each stick representing a horse to be given away. When all had eaten, he stood and spoke to them.

"My friends," he said, "we have come here for a great council with the *washíchun*. They say this council will make peace between the whites and all the peoples of the plains, but I have had a vision. In time there will be trouble between the Lakota and the whites, and a great leader killed. I will stay for the council and I will work always for peace, but when I leave this place I will travel to the Snowy Mountains. In the warm moons I will camp with the hoop of the nation, but in the Moon of Falling Leaves I will return each year to the Snowy Mountains to a place I have seen in my vision. I will no longer go east to the Muddy River and I will not winter near the *washíchun*. I go to live in the old way, the Lakota way, and I will welcome any who choose to go with me, for I no longer stand alone. Today I take a new name. Now I am called *Tashunke Mashté Wi Etan Hínape*." And then his relatives passed among the crowd, giving the gift sticks to those who were poor and had few horses, meat to families that had no one to hunt for them, and robes and moccasins and other things where they were most needed.

When the gift giving was done, Branched Horn surprised the gathering by announcing that he was no longer the headman of the band. "From this day forward my son will lead our people," the old man proclaimed, "and I will follow him, for I believe in the power of his vision. He has been given the power to lead us to peace, and so long as I live I will follow in his footsteps."

And so when the great council was done and the tribes broke camp to return to their own lands, the little band of Hunkpapa had grown, some Oglala and Brulé joining the new leader who seemed so sure of his power.

Tashunke Mashté Wi Etan Hínape. It meant His Horse Comes From the Summer Sun. It was a long name, and the people took to calling him *Tashunke Mashté Wi*—His Horse is the Summer Sun. Because it had truly been the spirit power of the summer sun that had come to Sun Horse in his vision and taken him on his journey to the Snowy Mountains, the contraction preserved the deeper meaning of the name, and he did not object. It was Lodgepole who christened him Sun Horse in English. The band was known simply as Sun Horse's camp, or band. Among themselves the people sometimes called it the Sun Camp, or Sun Band, but they always used the full name when speaking with other Lakota; it would have been arrogant to imply that they were People of the Sun, for *Wi*, the sun, was one of the most powerful manifestations of *Wakán Tanka*.

The inside of the *ini ti* was black as night, and dense with fragrant steam. Sun Horse was sweating freely. He breathed deeply, tasting the sage, remembering the day of his vision and the early years of his leadership as if he lived through that time again.

He had not told the people of the other things he had felt, the certainty of great changes coming. The soldier fort and the Holy Road were little islands in a river of Lakota, but he knew there would come a time when the numberless whites would become the river and the Lakota bands would be the islands, and the troubles between the two peoples would grow. His vision had given him the power to lead his people and to find peace with the whites, a peace that came from true understanding. He knew he must perceive the nature of the *washichun* and at the same time preserve the Lakota way, not by retreating far from the whites and imagining they would go away, nor by living close to them where their strange powers could overwhelm the people before they understood how to resist the destructive influences that had made the Loaf-Around-the-Forts less than Lakota.

Keep the Lakota way. Be strong in the old ways and at the same time seek to understand the whites. This was what Sun Horse had set out to do, and before long the strength of his vision had been confirmed. Scarcely a year later the band had been joined by Jed Putnam, the brother of Lodgepole, searching for a home in the mountains. Sun Horse had led him to a valley not far from the band's wintering place and there Jed Putnam had settled with his family. From the two brothers, one living like a *washichun* and the other like a Lakota, Sun Horse had learned much of the white world, and as two more winters passed peacefully Sun Horse thought perhaps he had already discovered the pathway to peace. But then came a second confirmation of his vision, this one terrible and frightening.

It was summer in the year the whites called 1854. Sun Horse and his people were camped with a few other bands on the Powder when riders on sweating horses found them, bearing news of bad trouble at Fort Laramie. An emigrant's cow had strayed and been killed, and Conquering Bear, the great chief of the Brulé, had been shot by soldiers while trying to preserve the peace. Thirty soldiers had been killed and the Lakota had struck their lodges and fled to the north, just as Sun Horse had seen in his vision.

More lodges joined the Sun Band then, and that winter fifty tipis stood in the camp in the Snowy Mountains.

In the next year the soldiers struck back, a large group of them attacking the Brulé of Little Thunder. Little Thunder worked hard to keep the peace; he smoked with the soldier chief Harney and explained that his was not the same band that had killed the soldiers at Laramie, but Harney was an angry man and hot for revenge. After the smoke he attacked, leaving many women and children dead and a hundred of the people taken off in chains to the whiteman's iron house, where they were kept for more than a year.

From that time the troubles grew, a few years of quiet followed by more fighting and new treaties, and then more fighting. Lakota and whites both had their victories, and white scalps hung from Lakota lances. But something else happened, something Sun Horse had not seen in his vision: the Lakota grew stronger, like the point of a wooden lance held in the fire to make it hard. After the first troubles the whites stopped all trading at Laramie and said the Lakota must trade only at new agencies in Nebraska, farther from the hunting grounds. No traders might enter Lakota lands, they said. These words made the Lakota angry, and fewer and fewer went to the new trading places. Only the weakest of the Loafers stayed, while the others kept to the buffalo country along the Powder and the Tongue and learned to do without many of the trade goods they had depended on for so long, finding instead the strength of the old Lakota way. "We do not need the *washíchun* things," they said proudly. "Let him keep them, and his new trading places. Let him roll his wagons on the Holy Road, but he must not come here. If he comes here, we will fight him!" But still there was some trading with the halfbreed sons of former traders, who brought wagons to the hunting grounds despite the ban. Beneath loads of blankets and trinkets they brought good percussion rifles and powder and lead, for these were things the newly defiant Lakota did not wish to do without.

In the summer the Sun Band joined with the other bands to experience the strength of the Lakota nation and in winter they returned to their valley in the Snowy Mountains, and through the growing troubles they did not fight the whites. "To fight the *washíchun* is to fight the whirlwind," Sun Horse counseled his young men, and all the while he sought the path to peace—a peace without surrender, one that preserved the Lakota way.

As more winters passed, the number of lodges in the circle of the Sun Band declined as young warriors left for the bands that fought the whites. But other good men remained with Sun Horse, for there was fighting here too, with the traditional enemies—the hated Blackfeet, the Crows, the Snakes and the Gros Ventres. The Sun Band had its share of hunters and sharp-eyed scouts, and warriors too, not as many as other bands but just as brave. In the summer camp the Sun Band occupied a place of honor in the circle of the nation, and from their men *akíchita* were chosen to police the camp and the buffalo hunts, and men from the Sun Band sat with those who decided matters of importance for all Lakota. Among the bands Sun Horse was respected as a peace man, and at the great summer gathering of 1857, the Lakota headmen bestowed on him the highest honor they could give: they gave him the shirt-for-life, the symbolic shirt made of mountain sheepskin that recognized the wearer as a man to whom everyone looked up, a man who thought always of the good of the people.

When the fighting was the worst, on the two occasions when the war pipes were sent out and the Lakota and their allies the Shahíyela and Arapaho had fought together, Sun Horse journeyed to the peace councils that were called to stop the fighting and there he listened to the whites and spoke to them. During Red Cloud's War he was unable to keep some of his own young men from riding off to join their brothers who swarmed like hornets around the soldier forts, and when the Laramie treaty was made, Sun Horse touched the pen to this new paper even though he had not approved the fighting and had used all his persuasion to keep his warriors home.

The entrance flap of the *ini ti* was pulled aside, admitting the light, and a hand passed in a bowl of cold water. Sun Horse drank a little and handed the bowl to Sees Beyond. He felt the water cold within him and hot without; it was the same water, hot where it had been dripped on the rocks to hiss and steam, breathing throughout the tiny lodge, cold within his stomach. The same water, flowing from the west, falling from the thunderclouds, bringing the life-giving power to make things grow.

A *power is coming. It can help the Sun Band or destroy us,* Hears Twice had said. Sun Horse had seen the power joined, or so he thought. His grandson returned from the dead after eight winters, meeting the clown girl of the whites. Johnny's power, like Sun Horse's, touched the worlds of both red men and white. And the clown girl as well had a two-sided power, the *heyoka* power to make life or to destroy. Together, they created a force that could help the Sun Band or destroy it; it was up to Sun Horse to turn that power to the good and to apply it to his larger task: to understand the *washichun*. He must grasp their essence! How could they be persuaded to make a peace that would leave the Lakota strong?

Peace without surrender.

He shook his head, feeling unequal to the task. For twenty-five years he had sought to understand the whites and through all that time something had eluded him. He could not find the center of the white nation, the core of its spirit. The *washichun* spoke always with many voices; the more of them in one place, the more voices that spoke. Always they seemed to be scattered. Sun Horse was sure he lacked some insight, something he had not yet seen that would make plain to him the whole. Surely such limitless power could not come from people who were broken and scattered?

The *washichun*, not at peace with themselves.

The thought came to him as if it had been spoken clearly by someone close at hand. The lodge was dark again. Had Sees Beyond spoken aloud? Sun Horse felt sure the words had not come from the world of man. He felt a chill of power, despite the warmth of the little lodge.

Not at peace with themselves...That would explain the turmoil of the spirit Sun Horse had always sensed around whites—except a few, such as Lodgepole, who was Lakota now, and his brother Jed Putnam.

If spiritual calm came from true understanding, how then to make peace with a people who had not reached that understanding, that inner calm?

Sees Beyond moved. He poured the rest of the water in the bowl onto the rocks, which sent up a cloud of steam. Sun Horse felt a wave of new warmth envelop him. Droplets of warm water gathered on the bent willow poles and dripped on Sun Horse's back and shoulders.

"Soon the helper will open the entrance for the last time," Sees Beyond said. "And we will see the light."

Hearing this signal, Sings His Daughter opened the flap and the steam poured forth, carrying away everything that had been cleansed from the two that had participated in the ritual, leaving the men fresh and new, as if reborn. As the steam dispersed and the soft light of evening entered the little hut, Sun Horse saw across the creek to the snow-covered slopes where the last rays of the sun were turning the snow red, a warm red like the first light of a new day.

The light that entered the *ini ti* at the end of the ritual symbolized the light of the east, the light of true understanding, which should be the first thing seen by one who has just purified himself. But here it was truly the light of day's end, coming from the west. Sun Horse felt a chill course along his backbone, but this time it was a chill of fear. Could this be the end of the day for the Lakota? Were they to be swept away by the flood of whites?

Twenty-five winters had passed since his vision and still the whites came, moving always from east to west. In Lakota symbolism there were two roads that ran across the hoop of the world. One began in the east, where all the days of man began, and went to the west, where all the days of man ended, and that road was black, for it was the road of worldly difficulties. But there was another road, one that began in the south, where dwelt the power to grow, and ended in the north, the realm of white hairs and the cold of death, and that was the good red road of spiritual understanding. Only by walking that road could a man grow spiritually throughout his lifetime, and so acquire the wisdom to withstand the difficulties he would surely encounter. But it seemed to Sun Horse that the black road was the only one the *washíchun* knew. Was that what he sensed? Was there some vital part missing from the *washíchun* spirit? Could it be that they did not know the red road at all?

The implications of this troubling thought rose in Sun Horse's mind and swirled around him, confusing him, but he put them aside with an effort of will. Later he would return to them, but now he looked once again out the entrance of the *ini ti* to the sun-red hills across the river. The light had reminded him of the two roads all men must walk; that was enough for now.

Moving out of the cross-legged position he had kept for so long, Sun Horse left the *ini ti*. Outside he stood up straight. There was no stiffness in his body. He moved like a young man.

He prayed as he walked the path to the fire, feeling the cool air on his naked body. "*Wakán Tanka*, I place my feet on the sacred path. With joy in my heart I walk the sacred earth. For my people I walk in a sacred manner. Let the generations to come also walk in this sacred way. *Waníktelo!*" The word meant "I will live," but in his heart Sun Horse said, I will live that my people may live.

He squatted and rubbed handfuls of snow all over his body, feeling the shock as he rubbed between his legs, but he laughed at the feeling and stood again, rubbing the snow on his face last of all.

Sings His Daughter held out his robe. As he wrapped it around him he wished for a moment that it were a newer robe, thicker, with good winter fur. The air found its way through a small hole and he felt a cool spot on his leg. He slipped into his old moccasins.

He had not found the answers he sought, but *inipi* was not a ceremony for providing answers; it was a beginning, a cleansing, an opening up.

He looked around and saw the smoke from the lodges rising straight into the dark blue that was spotted with slow-moving clouds. The clouds still showed sunlight on their bellies, but the sun had left the eastern ridge now, and even as Sun Horse watched, the fire-glow died in the clouds and one by one they turned gray.

Inipi—a beginning. The real task lay ahead of him. Now the true search began. On his shoulders lay the burden of fulfilling the promise that *wamblí* had given so recently, and the older promise as well, the promise his spirit horse—his sun horse—had given, all those snows past. Still he sought the way to peace, but now the time was short.

Sees Beyond had also come out of the *ini ti* and was standing beside him now, taking his own robe from Sings His Daughter's hands. Sun Horse looked to the ridges surrounding the valley. For the task before him he should seek out a place of solitude, a high place where he could speak to the spirits and look within himself, as Crooked Horn had done. If the answers to his questions lay within his grasp, they were within himself. It was there he would look.

Already the warmth of the *ini ti* had left his body and he could feel the chill air rising from the creek. With the sun gone, the cold grew quickly stronger. He knew he could not spend a cold night on some lonely ridge like a young man seeking a vision.

Sees Beyond laughed. "Look beyond the symbol," he said, chuckling.

Sun Horse wondered why the young holy man repeated these words now, but then he understood. He took Sees Beyond's right hand and shook it once, firmly, and then he smiled. "*Ho hechetu aloh. Lila pilámayayelo!*" he said, thanking the young *wichasha wakán* for making *inipi* with him and for reminding him of this most important lesson. He took Sings His Daughter's arm and they started together for the camp circle.

Look beyond the symbol. The high ridge was a symbol, one very helpful to a young man on his vision quest. The high places are closer to *Wakán Tanka*, the young were taught, and so they sought the solitude of the high lonely places where the winged ones flew with dignity and where it was easy for a man to look inside himself and find his pathway to power.

But the ridge was only a symbol. A man could find his power anywhere, and so Sun Horse and his young wife made their way toward his warm lodge. The woman leaned against him as they walked. He felt the warmth of her body through the robes and something stirred in his loins. He chuckled and shook his head, and she glanced at him, her face asking a question, but he only smiled. He would like to enjoy this young wife tonight. She knew how to move, and how to give a man much pleasure by showing her own. But he would not go to her robes tonight, although he knew that she wanted him. A warrior did not enjoy a woman on the night before a battle, and Sun Horse's task demanded all the strength a man brought to war.

Inside the cheerful lodge Elk Calf awaited them with the fire built up strong and a little soup warmed, but Sun Horse refused the soup and said nothing as he seated himself in front of the fire. He filled his pipe and smoked, once again offering the pipe to the directions, and his wives knew he thought of matters that concerned the spirit world. Sings His Daughter took up an old deerskin to rub between her hands and make soft again while Elk Calf worked slowly with sinew and awl at the goatskin moccasins, and the three sat together in silent peace with Sun Horse's thoughts undisturbed.

Peace. A word used in so many ways—the peace of a few moons between the Lakota and their enemies; the peace among allies of long standing; the peace of a happy lodge; a man at peace with himself.

For a time Sun Horse put aside all thoughts, his mind at rest like the plain under the summer sun, the swaying of the buffalo grass the only movement.

Then he returned to the question at the center of his task and now a certainty came to him: the Lakota must continue to walk the good red spirit road, whatever the form of the final peace with the whites. Few men could walk only the spirit road; Sees Beyond was one who seemed to tread there almost exclusively, but most men walked both the red and the black roads. To walk only the road of worldly troubles meant to be like the *washichun*, with no inner calm, no understanding. There must be a balance. The Lakota symbols recognized this; where the red road of spiritual understanding crossed the black road of worldly difficulties, there stood the tree of life; its branches were filled with singing birds and it shielded all creatures. There the Lakota nation dwelt, surrounded now by the swirling rivers of *washichun* that threatened to uproot the tree and sweep the Lakota people away forever.

Washichun, a people not at peace with themselves. How then to make peace with them?

LISA PUTNAM'S JOURNAL

Thursday, March 16th. 11:50 a.m.

I am ashamed to admit that I have been up and about for only half an hour, but I do feel greatly improved. Yesterday when we arrived back here just before suppertime I could barely walk, I was so tired. But I thought a bite of supper would do me good and would give me enough strength to help with cleaning up the dishes before going to bed. Ling insisted that I should have a bath and change into fresh clothes before supper, which I see now was part of a conspiracy she hatched with Harry. They had already placed the tub in my room and filled it with hot water, and of course I couldn't resist. I got out of the bath and lay on my bed for what I thought would be only a few moments, and that was the last thing I knew until waking a short time ago to discover that Ling had tucked me in all warm and comfortable and left me to sleep away the night and half of today.

Our dinner this noontime will be quieter than usual. Mr. Tatum has come up with an arrangement which will allow his teamsters even more time at the avalanche. Until now they have been returning here for the midday meal, but beginning today Joe Kitchen's helper Monty will take their dinner to them in a wagon, saving them the time of riding back and forth. Despite the setbacks caused by a too-liberal use of blasting powder, Mr. Tatum is apparently making some progress and is intent on making more.

After feeding the cows this morning Johnny and Hutch spent another two hours mending fence, and they told me just now that they have inspected and repaired all the fence in the park during the past week. What a pair of workers they are. In recognition of their efforts I gave them the afternoon off, which took them quite by surprise. They looked at each other as if to say "What on earth shall we do with an afternoon free?" but Hutch found the solution at once. "You said I was about ready to learn to rope from horseback," he suggested, and I even agreed that they might cut out a sturdy calf from the herd to practice on, if they don't run him ragged.

They say they observed some scours among the calves in the meadow. Julius and I will ride down this afternoon to see for ourselves, and we may stop at the avalanche to have a look at the work going on there.

Well, try as I may to keep my mind on the ranch and its demands, I cannot escape the discouragement I feel over the end of hunting. Our lack of conspicuous success thus far has apparently convinced Sun Horse that the spirit powers do not view our efforts kindly, and yesterday when Julius and Alfred and Willy Waldheim and I passed through the village on our way home, he informed us of his decision to suspend the hunt. We, of course, can continue our own efforts, but Sun Horse's resignation to an unkind fate fills me once more with a fear that he and his people will ultimately surrender or be taken by soldiers, or be otherwise compelled to go to Dakota. As I thought of the Lakotas and their predicament upon first waking this morning, I grew angry all over again at this clear violation of the Fort Laramie treaty, and then I found cause for a new fear, one that makes me wonder if even the most peaceful delegation of headmen can obtain the right to continue living in the Powder River country, for I believe I know now the true reason for the government's efforts to gather all the Sioux in Dakota. It may not be simply "to keep an eye on them" during the Black

Hills troubles, as Mr. Hardeman suggested. The Laramie treaty says in no uncertain terms that there shall be no further cessions of land unless agreed to by three-fourths of the adult male members of the tribe. In a nation of some thirty thousand souls, close to ten thousand may be grown men, and surely the required degree of consent will never be obtained unless the Sioux are all gathered in one place! As long ago as last summer I recall some mention in the newspapers of needing to have the Sioux come to the agencies <u>to be counted</u>. Once there, confined on the reservation, stripped of their freedom and possessions and hope, they might be coerced into ceding not only the precious Black Hills but the Powder River country as well, thus putting a stamp of legality on the theft after the fact!

How much depends on the pipe carriers! If they succeed, the hunting bands will remain free at least until summer, and the government can never obtain any cession—whether of the Black Hills or this country here—without coming to terms with the bands in the Powder River country. And so the hopes I had placed in the hunting are now vested in Mr. Hardeman and Uncle Bat and the others, and my concerns, which until now have been mainly for the Sun Band, have broadened to embrace the whole Sioux nation, for I see now that the fates of all the bands are inescapably intertwined. Such thoughts make my own efforts on Sun Horse's behalf seem small indeed, and I feel helpless once more. It is my hope that by recording these feelings here I may enable myself to set them aside; here in Putnam's Park life must go on, and we can only await the outcome of the momentous events taking place beyond these hills.

The weather continues to be changeable. It is snowing lightly now, but when I first sat down with my journal the sun was shining. Harry tells me last night was clear, and the mercury was below zero when he went to look at the heifers.

CHAPTER
TWENTY-SIX

The cow's sides heaved with a final contraction and the calf's hindquarters slipped onto the straw that was scattered six inches deep all along the fence by the barn wall. Lisa and Julius sat atop the fence, watching the birth. Normal births took place here, out of doors; the calving shed was for pulling calves and caring for the sick ones.

"Pretty big calf," Julius ventured.

Lisa nodded, smiling. "She might be a keeper." Each spring her father had surveyed the new calves from the moment of birth, watching for the ones that stood best and sucked soonest, the ones that kept close to their mothers and the mothers that took best care of their offspring, and from these bloodlines he had chosen the heifer calves he would keep when the steers and the rest of the heifers were sold. Now the responsibility for this selection had passed to Lisa and Julius. Together they would decide the fate of each calf born, and already the process was under way.

The two of them had saddled their horses and started off to look over the calves in the meadow when they had noticed that one of the heifers was about to give birth, and they had stopped to watch. The inspection of the young animals was a pressing task if there was scours in the herd. Scours was a form of bovine diarrhea that could weaken a calf and leave it susceptible to pneumonia or some other fatal ailment, and the affected animals, if any, would have to be treated promptly. But the birth of each new calf was important too, and so Lisa and Julius lingered to watch the most recent arrival while their horses shifted about and stamped, impatient to be off.

The new mother rose now and turned to sniff at the wet bundle she had delivered. Streamers of thick mucus and strands of membrane hung from the cow's organs. Tentatively at first and then with growing confidence she began to lick the whitish birth sac off the newborn calf. The calf's eyes were open and its nostrils flared as it grew accustomed to the experience of breathing. After a first small cry it had remained silent.

"Natural mother," Julius said, pleased.

"Smarter than that other one," Lisa agreed sourly, nodding toward a nearby chute where a cow and calf were confined together. Two nights before, the cow had slept on top of her perfectly healthy calf and killed it. Lisa had been so infuriated that she had wanted to slaughter the cow, but Julius had calmed her down and made her see reason. Another cow with an incurably rotten hoof had a good calf that would need a mother to get him through the summer, but his own mother would not last that long. Crippled, barely able to walk, she would not get enough to eat to sustain both herself and the calf. And so the cow with the bad foot had been slaughtered and her calf was now being grafted on the careless cow that had killed her own offspring. The calf had a section of the dead calf's hide tied to its back so it would smell familiar to the mother, but still the cow was not satisfied with the arrangement. She was haltered and tied to limit her movement in the chute, but as the calf tried to nurse she shied away and kicked at it.

"Quit that!" Lisa said sharply. The cow rolled her eyes and sighed and allowed the calf to suck for a time, but when it butted her udder to release more milk, she kicked again.

"That's enough now!" Lisa jumped down from the fence and climbed over into the chute with the cow and calf. When the cow kicked at the calf again, Lisa kneed her sharply in the side. Again the cow kicked and again she was kneed. After a few repetitions it began to penetrate the cow's dim imagination that there might be some connection between the two actions, and she stopped kicking. Lisa stroked her neck and spoke to her softly as the calf sucked and butted at the udder. Pacified by this attention, the cow settled down and continued to allow the eager calf to nurse even when Lisa left the chute and rejoined Julius on the fence.

"There goes Alfred," Julius said. He was looking off past the circus wagons to where two figures with rifles over their shoulders were walking across the meadow toward the woods.

"Who's that with him?"

"One of those acrobat fellers. Not Abbruzzi; that other bunch from Connecticut."

"Alfred enjoys the out-of-doors more than any of them," Lisa said. "He's to the manor born, I guess. They hunted a good deal in his family." She had been surprised to learn that Alfred Chalmers was descended from English gentry. He was the third of three sons and his eldest brother was now the lord of the manor. With no expectation of ever inheriting it himself unless both of his brothers should die before him, Alfred had turned first to the theater and then to circus life for his livelihood. His tale had reminded Lisa of her own father, the eldest of three sons, and the family business he might have managed had he been a less adventuresome man.

"He don't give up easy," Julius said. "Wish I could say the same for old Sun Horse." Neither he nor Lisa had spoken of Sun Horse or the end of hunting since leaving the Sioux village.

"We mustn't give up hope," Lisa said. "We may hunt together again. And meantime we can save some of our cows by bringing in game meat."

Julius nodded, but he felt no enthusiasm for hunting now that the Indians had abandoned the effort. The good feeling that had come over him back when he and Lisa had first offered the cows to Sun Horse along with the powder and grain had grown even stronger as the hunting got under way. Out in the hills with parties of circus men and Indians, Julius had experienced an elation like nothing he had known since the Rebellion, when he was given a uniform and a chance to fight to preserve his own freedom. Could taking a stand for another man's freedom make him feel just as good as fighting for his own? It didn't seem possible. But when Sun Horse had told Lisa that he was quitting the hunt, Julius had felt betrayed.

A light snow was beginning to fall as a band of clouds passed low over the park. There was a sudden clanging from the blacksmith shed and Julius heard the sounds echo off the west side of the valley. Harry had his forge hot and he was getting down to his afternoon's work. He was forging spikes from an old tooth harrow into improvised pick heads, which he would attach to any tool handle he could fashion. All the picks and shovels in the park were already in use at the avalanche and Tatum wanted more. The circus master was digging himself out of his predicament, but Sun Horse was just waiting. For what?

Willy and Johann Waldheim came out of the barn leading two horses apiece, making for the candy-striped tent. The animals all wore brightly colored woolen warming blankets woven in a tartan pattern. Scotch blankets on English thoroughbreds led by Germans who came here with a New York man, Julius thought. The white man isn't sitting around waiting. He's on the move. The Indians best stir themselves or they'll get left in the dust.

"Look at that," Lisa said softly.

In the heifer lot, the newborn calf had its front legs propped on the ground and was trying to get to its feet in a tiny imitation of the peculiar heave an adult cow used to rise from a lying position. The calf jerked upright, nearly overbalanced, then caught itself and remained standing, legs splayed, looking curiously about. It didn't stay still for long. The mother cow was close at hand, sniffing and licking, and now the calf turned its head toward the hindquarters of this large and attentive beast that smelled so familiar. With a few unpracticed lurches and hops it reached its goal, head probing the udder and finding a teat, beginning to suckle.

"That a girl!" Julius encouraged the calf.

"Will you look at her?" Lisa exclaimed. "If they were all like that..." She shook her head in wonder. "We can turn them out tomorrow if they keep on like that."

"Good mother, good calf," said Julius. "Looks like a keeper for sure."

"Oh, Johnny, look!" came a voice, and they turned to see Amanda and Johnny Smoker approaching, followed by Hutch and Chatur. The quartet of "young people" had taken the midday meal together, and there had been much animated talk and laughter from their end of the table. By custom, Amanda ate with Hachaliah Tatum, but with her guardian off at the avalanche she had joined her friends today.

Amanda ran to the fence and stared at the mother and calf. "He's beautiful! How old is he?"

"It's a she," Lisa said, smiling, "and she was born about fifteen minutes ago."

Hutch turned to Chatur. "Say, how big is an elephant calf when it's born?"

"Oh, very much bigger than that," Chatur replied. "He is approximately this high"—he held a hand about three feet off the ground—"and he is weighing, I should say, two hundred pounds."

Hutch's eyes opened wide. "Say now, you cross one of those with a shorthorn cow and you'd bring up the weight of your calves pretty quick."

Julius grinned. "What you gonna do with a calf's got a trunk and maybe tusks and horns both?"

"Well, I hadn't thought much about it. You don't reckon it's a good idea?" Hutch gave Julius a wink and glanced quickly at Chatur as if to say the little Indian man was buying the whole thing and let's keep it going a while longer.

Julius swung himself down from the fence and untied his horse. "Oh, I don't know." He looked at Chatur. "You suppose old Rama'd like to have a go at one of our cows?"

Chatur appeared dubious. "He has had no company of lady elephants for a long time. I will ask him, certainly. If he is willing, I will turn him loose."

"Don't you dare," Lisa said as she got off the fence and took her own horse's reins. "I won't have some foreign creature terrifying my cows."

As Julius mounted up, Hutch could see that the colored man was laughing softly; Johnny and Miss Lisa were smiling and Chatur was grinning like he knew the whole thing was a joke from start to finish, and Hutch wasn't quite sure who the joke was on but he was grinning too. At moments like this he felt that Putnam's Park was a pretty special place and he was a part of it, and the thought of ever leaving made him uncomfortable. Well, who said he had to leave? It wasn't even spring yet and he still had a lot to learn. There was no great rush about it all, was there? Just now he and Johnny had the afternoon off and they would do as they pleased and take their time about it, and he was darned if he was going to worry about what he might or might not do three or four months from now.

The snow kept up for a time and Hutch and Johnny followed Amanda to the barn and lingered to watch the acrobats and the clowns work. Hutch managed to catch a few words with Maria Abbruzzi and she squeezed his hand and gave him a quick kiss when her father wasn't looking. Johnny seemed content just to sit and watch Amanda even when she wasn't doing a thing. When the snow stopped they saddled a couple of horses and went outside to teach Hutch how to rope from horseback. Lisa had said that Hutch could use any horse he wanted and he saddled a nice sorrel he fancied. He had thought of using his own mule but he gave up that idea without a fight. Old Joe, as he called the mule, was willing enough to be saddled and ridden wherever Hutch wanted to go, but that was the extent of it. He wouldn't haul a wagon or tote a pack or do a lick of serious work and today Hutch didn't feel like fighting a stubborn mule that was set in his ways.

They cut a calf out of the herd and drove him into the big pasture where the circus horses and the bulls were kept. It took Hutch the better part of an hour to master the skill of handling the reins and the rope at the same time and not get anything tangled after the loop was thrown, and then it took him a while longer to get the horse right on the calf and place his loop anywhere near the calf's head. The first time the loop sailed neatly into place around the calf's neck Hutch got so excited that he dallied his reins to the saddle horn and dropped the rope and the calf led the two of them a merry chase to get it back. By then the three Waldheim men were done work for the day and they had come to sit on the fence and watch Hutch's lessons, and Amanda came from the barn in her clown suit and buffalo coat, but Hutch was enjoying himself so much that he didn't mind making a bit of a fool of himself in front of his friends. After all, none of them could even rope on foot, and Johnny said Hutch was learning quick and would be a top roper in no time.

But when he finally roped the calf and got the rope dallied right, his sorrel wouldn't hold the rope tight.

"Let me get on him for a minute," Johnny said, and Hutch dismounted and turned the calf loose. Johnny took out after the calf and roped him again before he even had a chance to get up to full speed. Johnny brought the sorrel to a quick stop and showed him how to keep the rope tight. "Back now. Back," he said, pulling gently on the reins whenever the rope slackened for a moment. After a minute or two he got off and moved hand over hand along the rope to the calf to take off the loop.

Julius and Lisa were passing by on their way back from the meadow. "You been ropin' off that horse?" Julius wanted to know.

"Oh, he's all right," Johnny said, "but he ain't never been taught to back right."

Julius laughed. "He ain't never been roped off before. He's doin' pretty good, considerin'."

The Waldheims seemed to think this was one of the funniest things they had heard all day. "Oh, ho!" they exclaimed, and they clapped one another on the back and pointed at Johnny and the sorrel and talked back and forth in German, which Hutch thought sounded like a string of the fanciest cuss words he'd ever heard.

Johnny just said, "He takes to it quick enough. He'll make a good roper if you keep after him." He turned the calf loose and gave the sorrel back to Hutch. "Here, you try him once."

With Julius and Lisa watching, Hutch chased after the calf and dropped the loop as neat as you please and the sorrel hunched down and jerked the calf clean off his feet when he hit the end of the rope, and he kept the rope tight as a string of barb wire while Hutch got off to set the calf free.

"So, you are a cow-boy now!" Papa Waldheim called out to Hutch.

"Oh, I got a ways to go," the youth replied, not wanting to sound too puffed up in front of Julius and Johnny and Miss Lisa, but he was pleased with himself all the same.

"So, ve buy the cow-boy a beer before supper. What do you say?"

"You go on," Johnny told Hutch. "I'll take care of the horses. We better let that calf go find his mama anyway. He's lost a couple of pounds by now. He's gettin' rope shy too."

The day was getting on and it was beginning to snow again. People were leaving the barn by twos and threes and making for the main house.

Amanda followed Johnny to the barn and as he unsaddled his own mount she took on herself the unsaddling of the sorrel. She brushed his back where the hair was matted from the saddle and when she was done Lisa and Julius had unsaddled their horses and gone, and she and Johnny were alone in the barn.

"You seem right at home around horses," Johnny said. Like everything else he said to Amanda it sounded awkward and inappropriate in his ears.

She smiled. "You can't spend your whole life in the circus without knowing something abour horses. I thought I wanted to be a trick rider once."

They turned the horses out and Johnny said, "I guess it's almost suppertime."

"Will you wait for me while I change?" Amanda did not draw the curtain in the dressing-room stall, where the steamer trunks stood open and overflowing with costumes. She slipped out of her buffalo coat and drew her clown's blouse over her head, followed by the thick woolen jersey she wore beneath it to practice in the cold barn, and Johnny saw her bare back, smooth and white. She held the jersey clutched to her chest, covering her bosom, as she half turned to him.

383

"Would you hand me my petticoat? It's there on the vaulting horse."

He saw the frilled satin garment on the padded top of the wooden vaulting horse and he handed it to her, feeling like an intruder in her dressing room. As she turned away to don the petticoat she dropped the jersey and one small breast was revealed in silhouette. The blood rose to Johnny's face and he walked off to absorb himself in inspecting other parts of the barn, wondering how in the world he would ever be able to express the emotions that were so strange and new to him. For two weeks now he had been searching his past life for some signpost that would point the way he should follow with Amanda, but his knowledge of courting was sharply divided between distant memories of his Cheyenne boyhood and recent years in the cattle towns of Kansas, and neither way seemed suited to his present feelings. Among the Cheyenne, courting procedures, like all other relations between men and women, were circumspect and strictly prescribed by custom. As a small boy, Little Warrior had seen the older boys waiting outside the lodge of a girl who was approaching womanhood. By the lodge or along the trail to wood or water the young man who arrived first was given first chance to speak to the girl when she came along; each made his feelings known and in time the girl did the choosing. As for the physical joining of man and woman, that was no mystery to Cheyenne children. The Cheyenne had a different set of taboos from the white man, and frank discussion of what took place between a man and a woman at night in the warmth of the buffalo robes was not among them. The old women told stories that would have been unthinkable in a St. Louis ladies' sewing circle, and when he entered the white world Johnny had found that he was far better informed in these matters than other boys his age. But although talk had been frank among the Cheyenne, behavior was anything but loose; no women were more respected among the plains people for their chaste comportment than the women of the *Tsistsístas*. A maiden who allowed herself to be seduced was disgraced, and no man would think of marrying her. Courtship was long and young men and women came to know each other well before marrying and starting life together as husband and wife.

It was with this purity of intent that Johnny wished to approach Amanda, but he did not see how such alien customs could have a place here in Putnam's Park. He could not stand outside her bedroom in the Big House and wrap her in his blanket when she came out, or play the courting flute beneath her window. Nor did the courting rituals of the white world provide the answer. It seemed to Johnny that everyone from preachers to stable hands proclaimed their admiration for one sort of woman while chasing after another, and his own experience with both whores and well-bred young ladies had only served to confuse him further.

He had crossed the tracks to McCoy's Addition in Abilene just once, five years ago at the end of his first trail drive. That part of town, which was also called "the Beer Garden," was named for the then-mayor and father of the Kansas cattle trade, Joseph G. McCoy. It housed saloons, gambling dens, houses of ill-repute, and other diversions for the trail hands. Johnny had been in the company of a dozen other young drovers and like them he had been a little drunk, but he hadn't shared their enthusiasm for exploring the fabled pleasures of the brothels. He had almost backed out at the last minute, remembering Sammy Tadich and his refusal to go along. Just a bath and a night's sleep in a real bed was all that Sammy had wanted after two months on the trail. He had met a girl before leaving Texas and he was keeping himself pure for her, although he had set eyes on her just once and for less than an hour. "I met me a girl, Johnny," he had said. "Hair like spun sunbeams." And there had been a look in his eyes that Johnny couldn't fathom. But the other drovers were thirsty for a drink stronger than water and eager to mount something softer than a saddle, and Johnny had no girl back in Texas so he had tagged along. The girl he ended up with was nearly as shy as he was and scarcely older, a sad little thing that had tugged at his heart. He had chosen her more to protect her from the others than to have her for himself, but her shyness hadn't kept her from showing him, gently and expertly, some of the pleasure to be had with a woman. She had instructed him with patience and no trace of condescension, and Johnny liked to think she had shown him more of herself than she did with other men. He had wanted to help her but it seemed that nothing could shake her out of that sadness; she clutched it like it was the only thing anyone had ever let her keep.

There had been another girl too, as different from the first as day from night, just a few months ago in Ellsworth. Johnny had avoided the advances of the whores in Ellsworth, but he had been taken completely by surprise after a proper dance attended only by the town's respectable citizens and their offspring when a very cheerful girl of good family had charmed the pants right off him in the loft of her father's barn. For a time Johnny thought she had her sights set on marrying him and he was giving it some consideration, but she had gently disabused him of the notion. What they had done together seemed to mean about the same thing to her as sharing a beer with a good friend meant to Johnny, and he later found out that she had similarly charmed several of the other boys in town, but never the ones that boasted of their conquests. In late winter her engagement to the son of the town's foremost banking family had been announced, and Johnny had come to see that it wasn't only men who had to sow their wild oats before settling down.

From his two experiences with women, Johnny could draw no useful lessons about courtship in the white world. The stories he heard had led him to believe that it was the whores who were cheerful and gave you a moment's pleasure and sent you on your way with a smile, and the little sad girl that tugged your heart was the one you got in trouble and had to marry with her father's eyes boring hard into your back as you stood up before the preacher. It had happened the other way around with Johnny and he considered himself lucky that things had come out that way, for now at last he figured he knew what Sammy Tadich had felt for the girl back in Texas. Amanda was the girl for him. He would do anything for her, sacrifice anything to win her, but he was walking a trail he had never set foot on before and he felt less sure of himself than a blind man might.

"Johnny? I'm ready." Amanda stepped out of the stall. She had put on a plain gray woolen dress and her feet were clad in small boots with a fringe of fur on the top. She looked altogether as proper as any of the bankers' and stockmen's daughters at that dance in Ellsworth and for the moment at least Johnny was not at a loss. He offered her his arm and she took it, and they left the barn together like any young couple out for a stroll, their bearing measured and correct, only the closeness of their bodies and the bright look in their eyes revealing the pleasure they took from simply walking arm in arm.

A light snow was still falling and down on the wagon road they could see Tatum and the teamsters making for home after a long day's work, the horsemen in a tight bunch and moving briskly, just rounding the turn at the clump of pines. Farther to the rear came the wagons, drawn by mules and oxen. The meal gong broke the silence of the deserted yard and Amanda quickened her pace, hurrying Johnny along. "Come on," she said, holding him tightly against her. "I'm hungry."

But in the saloon they did not find the usual jostling at the serving tables. There was a large group around a table near the stove and a cheer went up as Amanda and Johnny entered. They made their way through the crowd and discovered that an arm-wrestling contest was in progress.

"So, Papa, you think you will do better?" Johann Waldheim rose from the table and ushered his father into the seat opposite Harry Wo.

"I kind of got this deal started," Hutch said as he joined Amanda and Johnny. "I got to wrestling with Johann and Willy and I beat them both, and then Papa Waldheim beat me and I told 'em how nobody'd ever beat Harry, and nothing would do but they all had to have a go at him."

Papa Waldheim set his elbow on the table and clasped Harry's hand and braced himself, smiling confidently, but his expression changed to one of surprise as the signal was given for the contest to start. For a moment the two hands remained motionless and then Papa Waldheim's was borne inexorably backwards. He grunted and frowned and put all his might into stopping the motion, but after a moment it resumed and soon his arm was forced to the tabletop.

"Perhaps you were not ready?" Harry inquired politely, once Papa Waldheim had signaled his surrender.

"Ready? Oh, I vass ready!" He looked up at Julius and Lisa, who stood in the forefront of the crowd. "Ha ha! So you haff a champion? Vell, so do ve! Alfred, a moment of your time, if you please!"

Looking almost reluctant, Alfred Chalmers made his way through the crowd.

"Uh oh, I think I got Harry in trouble," said Hutch.

Harry shrugged and gave Hutch a wink.

As soon as Chalmers seated himself it was apparent to one and all that there was a problem. Chalmers' forearm was nearly twice as long as Harry's and there was no way the squat Chinese could grasp Chalmers' hand.

"Put Harry's arm on a crate," Julius suggested.

"That'd give him an advantage, wouldn't it?" Ben Long protested.

"Oh, I certainly don't object," Chalmers said. "It seems quite the sensible thing to do."

"You don't eat pretty soon, I take the food back," Ling Wo warned the gathering, but no one moved as Joe Kitchen ran off and returned with an Arbuckles' coffee crate, which he set on the table. Harry stood and propped his elbow on the crate and his hand met Chalmers' perfectly.

"All right now," said Papa Waldheim, appointing himself the referee. "On three you begin. One, two...three!"

As had been the case with Papa Waldheim, Chalmers' first reaction was one of surprise, which transformed itself into renewed determination. Harry's face changed very little except for a slight raising of the eyebrows.

"Look at that!" Hutch whispered.

The clasped hands were trembling. The trembling grew in intensity until the table itself shuddered slightly and one leg rattled on the floor. And then the hands moved, swaying first to Harry's side, then to Chalmers', then back to Harry's, and this time the movement was not reversed. At the last, Harry conceded defeat by ceasing his resistance. At once he bowed deeply to the victor as the crowd cheered.

Chalmers rose and bowed just as deeply and then offered his hand, which Harry pumped in vigorous congratulations. When his hand was returned to him, Chalmers flexed his wrist, regarding it as if it were a foreign object. "Extraordinary. Truly extraordinary."

"Never before haff I see Alfred's hand move backwards!" Papa Waldheim exclaimed.

Harry was chuckling. "He got trouble now. He got to stay here until someone beats him. That's the rules. That's what Julius tell me when I come here. Ain't that right?" He looked at Julius and Julius nodded seriously.

"That's the rules."

"Ah. Oh dear." Chalmers was nonplussed. "Perhaps we might have another go? You never know, the first time may have been a fluke."

The onlookers laughed and Harry clapped Chalmers on the back with a blow that staggered the strongman. "You beat me fair and square but maybe we let you go. Come on now, Ling's pretty mad we're late to eat. Lydia!" He waved the Gypsy woman over to join them. "You and Alfred go first." He led the way across the room and there was a general movement toward the serving tables. As Harry loaded a plate with immense portions for Chalmers, the teamsters arrived in a group and hastened to take their places in line. Lisa and Joe Kitchen joined the servers and the line began to move quickly along.

Hachaliah Tatum was the last to enter the saloon. As usual he had stopped in his room to change for supper; his hair was combed and his clothes were as neat as if he had spent the day reading in the library. He spied Amanda near the end of the serving line, chatting with her friends, and he raised a hand to get her attention. He started forward, smiling, but he was intercepted by half a dozen teamsters, headed by Fisk and a man named Tanner.

"We'd like a word with you, Mr. Tatum," Tanner said. He was a bear of a man and the unofficial leader of the Black Hills crowd. He had none of Kinnean's quiet menace but he held a rough authority over the men and he had kept them in line, save for the first night's party and Fisk's bungled attack on Bat Putnam, since Kinnean's injury had rendered the one-armed man's authority impotent. Tanner's voice was deep and resonant and his words were set in place deliberately, like the feet of the oxen he drove.

Tatum waited silently for the man to speak his piece.

"Well now," Tanner said, shifting from one foot to the other and never meeting Tatum's steady gaze for more than a moment. "There's some talk among us, and I'm not sayin' I'm of the same mind, you understand, just to say there's talk. What it is, we signed on to drive wagons, you see. That's what we're paid for, not for all this diggin'. There's some as feels we oughta be gettin' extra for the diggin'."

"I'll drive a team right enough," said Tom Johansen, the lean Minnesota youth who had caused the avalanche by his ill-considered shot, "but I ain't no Paddy to be digging all day with my hands."

"Too proud are yez?" An Irishman named Gimp turned to face Johansen. "We wouldn't be diggin' atall if it wasn't for you and yer shotgun, ye Scandihoovian vagabond! I oughta—" Gimp raised his fists but Tanner stepped between them and brushed the Irishman aside like a cobweb.

"You two keep shut."

Tatum remained silent, content to let the teamsters fight among themselves.

"The fact is, Mr. Tatum, we ain't gonna dig no more for you unless you double our wage." The speaker was Thaddeus Morton, the gray-haired Ohioan who had run afoul of Hardeman that first night. "This here trip's takin' a good bit longer than we figured it would, but we're in no hurry, long's we're gettin' fed good. You want to get out of here, you say you'll double our wage and we'll hold you to it when we get to the Salt Lake."

"You dug quick enough when you thought there was gold at the end of it," said a new voice, and the teamsters turned to see Kinnean close behind them.

"You keep out of this, Kinnean," said Morton. "It's no affair of your'n."

Kinnean stepped closer. "You want to get paid at all, you'll dig."

"I ain't afraid of you."

Kinnean's arm shot out of its sling and the hand seized Morton's wrist, twisting it up behind his back until the driver doubled over with pain. "You just get on to your dinner, Redeye, like a good fellow, and I'll be along to stand you a glass of whiskey." He released the man with a shove, sending him reeling among the tables. Kinnean looked at the rest of the group. "Go on now, Jack," he said to Fisk, and Fisk turned away. The remaining drivers backed off, all except Tanner. "I've no quarrel with you, Tanner. The sooner we get out of here the sooner we all get paid."

Tanner hesitated. "I wasn't much for this deal to start with," he said, and

388

he lumbered off, ignoring the other drivers, who looked once more at Kinnean and Tatum, then turned and followed Tanner.

"I'm glad to see your arm is better, Mr. Kinnean," Tatum said, pleased with how the matter had been settled.

"This arm does the work of two and it heals quick. I thought it was about time I started earning my keep again."

"Can you hold a gun?"

Kinnean nodded. "I'll be ready for Mr. High-and-Mighty Hardeman when he gets back."

"We may well be gone before he returns."

"You may, but not me. I've a score to settle."

Tatum gave a small shrug. "Suit yourself. Just keep an eye on the men until the road is clear and I'll pay you off before we leave." Kinnean nodded and moved off toward the serving tables. Tatum watched him go. It wouldn't matter if the one-armed man remained behind when the circus left, but Tatum needed him now. There was a week or more of hard work left to clear the road and there might be other quarrels to settle. But once the way was clear the circus would reach the railroad in a week and Salt Lake City the day after that, and he would need Kinnean no longer.

At the serving line Amanda was just receiving her plate from Lisa Putnam. Once again Tatum raised a hand and started forward. Amanda looked in his direction, hesitated, then turned away to follow Johnny Smoker and the Waldheims. Tatum stopped in his tracks, frowning.

The silent exchange had not gone unobserved.

"There is trouble there, you mark my words," Lydia said in a low voice. She and Chalmers were seated alone at an out-of-the-way table.

"He seems to bide his time." Chalmers' tone was noncommittal, but he had seen the almost defiant look Amanda had given Tatum. All the same, he saw no good in raising speculation about what might or might not happen because of the youth's interest in Amanda and hers in him.

Lydia fixed him with her sharp black eyes. "He bides his time like a badger in its hole. Come. We will eat with them so there are no empty chairs at the table. If she wishes to eat without Hachaliah watching over her, that is how she shall eat."

Chalmers made no protest. He gathered up both plates in his huge hands and followed Lydia to the table where Johnny and Amanda sat with Hutch and Chatur and the Waldheims. The German equestrian family was made complete by the presence of Greta Waldheim, the mother of Johann and Willy. She was as slight as her husband and sons were robust.

"So, you teach tricks to horses," Papa Waldheim was saying to Johnny.

"Oh, I never had much call to teach a horse tricks," Johnny said. "Not like you do. But a horse'll learn most anything if you treat him right."

"Ja, and you know how to treat him right. Ve been vatching you, Johann and Villy and me. What do you say you come vork for us? Ve got some new horses to train. Ve train them, you and me, and Johann and Villy got more time to practice the act."

The unexpected offer took Johnny aback. "Well, I don't know," he said uncertainly. "I got to wait here for Chris to get back."

"Don't vorry about that. Maybe ve are all here when he gets back, maybe not. Maybe you come join us in Salt Lake City. What do you say?"

"I guess I'd have to think about it. What would Mr. Tatum say?"

"Don't you worry about Hachaliah Tatum." Papa Waldheim lowered his voice as he noticed Tatum standing in the supper line not far away. The circus master was looking at the table. "You vork for me, not him. Ve hire who ve like. So, you think about it. You see San Francisco, plenty of other places. You talk about it to Amanda. Maybe she thinks it's not such a bad idea you should join the show." He gave Amanda a wink.

"Gunther!" Greta Waldheim chided. "Don't tease her."

Amanda blushed and dropped her eyes. Johann and Willy chuckled at her embarrassment. She heard the hard edge in their laughter, not unkind, but knowing. They thought they understood why she had encouraged Johnny's attentions, but they were wrong.

It was true that at first she had led him on for the same reason she had led many others on, the young men in the cities and towns, the ones who flocked to her like butterflies to a bright flower, for this was how she retained a measure of control over Hachaliah Tatum. If he feared that some young man might whisk her out of his life forever he was more easily swayed, and by the frequent exercise of just this threat Amanda obtained from him whatever favor or gift she wished at the moment. It was a game they played, she and Hachaliah, but she had no doubt which of them held the stronger hand. Hachaliah was her protector and he knew her too well; she could never deceive him for long. He knew how much the circus meant to her, the performing most of all, and he knew she depended on him for guidance.

But here in Putnam's Park something had changed. The understanding that she was approaching a turning point had come to Amanda slowly; only in recent days had she realized what it meant, and what she must do.

Until now Hachaliah had supervised her art together with all other aspects of her life. He never interfered with the details of movement or technique in the clown routines but still he exercised overall control, and Amanda had welcomed his advice, for she shared his dream of blending the best of pantomime with the belly laughs of the slap-stick and pratfall. It had shocked her to realize quite suddenly that she had learned all she could from Hachaliah and from now on his continued supervision would only hold her in check. This awareness had begun just a week ago, on the day when she and Sam and Carlos had performed the English gentleman and Spanish cavalier routine for the first time. Hachaliah's first reaction to the new act had infuriated her, and her anger had helped her to see clearly. Later that evening he had taken her aside and he had tried to soothe her with words of praise, but at the same time he had suggested small changes in the act and she had seen that they were meaningless changes, and she had remembered something her father had said to her long ago, when he had been instructing her in clowning for less than a year. Even as a child she had been an apt pupil and her father's delight in her progress had been her greatest reward. One day after she had done some small thing to exceed his expectations he had taken her on his knee and he had said, "Many clowns can learn the old acts and perform them well, but you are one of the rare ones, Amanda. You can dream the new acts. Follow your dreams and never let anyone hold you back." Now at last she had learned how to bring her dreams to life. She and Sam and Carlos had worked out the act together but the vision had been hers, and Hachaliah had tried to change it solely to retain his control over her.

He would never give up that control willingly, of that she was certain, and she had begun to cast about for some means of breaking free. To her astonishment, she had discovered a growing conviction that the key to her freedom lay somewhere within Johnny Smoker.

From the first she had been fascinated by this strange boy who had lived in two worlds, the Indian and the white, if for no other reason than that his life had been so different from her own. She had given him encouragement, using all the small signals she knew how to use to such good effect, thinking only to keep Hachaliah on edge while the circus was trapped in Putnam's Park. Over the past two weeks Johnny had told her the remarkable story of his life bit by bit until she knew it all, and her fascination had grown. He was utterly different from the young men of the cities and towns. Sometimes there in the background, beyond her fawning admirers, she had noticed a shy youth hanging back; she had ignored those, imagining that she could find no attraction in one who lacked the courage to step forward and press his suit. Yet Johnny reminded her of the boys who had watched from a distance. He was hesitant and shy and he did not force his attentions on her, but in him she had discovered another kind of courage and she suspected that she could learn something vital from him, if only there were enough time. He seemed to be without fear. He accepted as natural and right that he should set out on his own, leaving behind the man who had protected him and guided him during all the years since he had been rescued from the Indians. She had felt herself reaching out to him, drawing him closer and closer to her, as if she might absorb his fearlessness along with his tales of adventure on the frontier, and as she saw the willingness, even the eagerness with which he looked forward to his new life, she had realized that she too must make a break with her own protector.

But how? Hachaliah was the circus master; he had the final say about every act of every performer. Could there be a way to remain under his authority and still escape the restraints he would try to impose on her art? Clowning was everything to her; it allowed her to express feelings she could reveal in no other way.

The Waldheims' offer of employment for Johnny had given her sudden hope. It was a possibility she had never considered. If Johnny were a part of the circus, could she use him as a way of controlling Hachaliah and preventing him from interfering in her work? Would Hachaliah stand for it? What if Johnny refused the offer?

He must accept. She would make him accept, and she was glad that she had already taken the first steps to draw him out of his shyness. She had not planned to change her clothes in front of him in the barn, or to defy Hachaliah by sitting with Johnny and the others tonight instead of joining Hachaliah for supper as usual. Both decisions had been made suddenly, on impulse. She was following her instincts and she felt both exhilarated and afraid, sure of only one thing—she must awaken Johnny's desire and bind him to her while the circus was still in Putnam's Park, and she must play on Hachaliah's feelings as she had never done before.

The circus master was leaving the serving table now and as he glanced again in her direction she favored him with a quick smile. It wouldn't do to have him think she was rebelling. She would soothe his suspicions for a time, until she was sure of Johnny; until she was sure of the course she would follow to assert her independence.

After supper Gunther Waldheim took up his accordion and played songs from the mountains of Germany and Austria, and a few couples danced. Johnny led Amanda through two waltzes, but as the second tune ended, Hachaliah Tatum appeared at his side to cut in politely, and when the next song was done Tatum said he was worn out from the day's work at the avalanche and he offered to escort Amanda to her room if she was ready to retire. She accepted with a small nod and he led her off on his arm.

Lisa had come from the kitchen to hear the music and she saw Johnny's disappointment as Tatum took Amanda away.

He'll have to speak up soon or he'll lose her, Lisa thought. The young never see how much they may lose until it's already gone. I knew no better at that age.

She stayed for a time, listening to the accordion and Papa Waldheim's pleasant tenor, but she found herself nodding and she slipped away to go to her own bed.

In the morning she awoke early. She felt fully rested, but not dulled by too much sleep as she had been the morning before, when she had slept past eleven o'clock. She sat up and stretched, her tousled hair falling over her face. As she brushed it away with a hand she heard the rooster crow faintly two or three times. Outside, the wind was up and snow was falling. She arose from the bed and crossed to the window, walking on tiptoes on the cold floor, and she saw that the fainthearted rooster had announced the day from the shelter of the henhouse door rather than take his accustomed perch on the gable.

There was no one stirring among the circus wagons and tents. The rest of the settlement was still asleep, it seemed. But as she turned from the window to dress, a movement caught her eye. The side door of the barn opened and a head emerged, looking first one way and then the other. The head retreated and the door opened wide as Hutch stepped out, but he turned back as someone took his arm. A glimpse of blond hair and the tilt of the boy's head told Lisa that he was being kissed farewell. Suddenly, Hutch ducked back into the barn and closed the door.

The reason became apparent a moment later as Harry Wo came into Lisa's view carrying a milk pail in one hand and a bucket of hog slop in the other. He emptied the slop into the trough in the pigpen and moved on to the barn, entering by the same door and closing it behind him. After another moment the door opened yet again and Maria Abbruzzi scampered away toward the wagons, clutching her cape around her.

Lisa smiled, imagining the mutual embarrassment of Harry and the young couple, and she blushed at her own tacit approval of Hutch's early-morning rendezvous. She knew she should scold him, but that would only embarrass him further and it would have no effect on his virtue. And how should she counsel young Hutch on virtue, when she had abandoned her own?

None of her own family, not even her father, knew the truth of her interlude with the cavalry lieutenant. The Emersons would have been scandalized, no doubt, but what did they know about the frontier? It was to escape the genteel restrictions of the East that Lisa's mother had married Jedediah Putnam while she had the opportunity, and Lisa had felt herself acting with the same courage and abandon.

She thought of Chris Hardeman then and wondered what she might dare in order to hold him, if she thought she could succeed.

She crouched by the stove to throw in a few sticks of split pine kindling, and as it began to crackle, ignited by last night's coals, she slipped out of her nightgown and into her underthings. She took her gray dress from the wardrobe, but then she remembered that this was St. Patrick's Day, and she exchanged the gray dress for the dark green one.

She sat at her dressing table and held her head straight and high as she brushed her hair. There was no Irish blood among the Putnams or the Emersons, at least none that those proud families would admit, but in Lisa's childhood the holiday had grown steadily more boisterous as more and more Irish reached the shores of the New World, and it symbolized for her the joyous spirit of the Irish in America, out from under the British yoke. Today she claimed it for her own to assert her freedom from the distant social conventions that condemned any risks a young lady might take to test the paces of her heart before submitting it to a single set of reins. St. Patrick himself might not have approved, but his Catholic judgment held no sway over Lisa Putnam.

With her hair tied at the nape of her neck by a bright ribbon of green satin, Lisa lifted lightly on the handle of the bedroom door and opened it silently. As she stepped into the second-floor hallway, lit only by one window that admitted the soft gray light of early morning from the landing by the stairs, another door opened and Amanda Spencer tiptoed out of a room that was not her own. She wore a flannel dressing gown over her nightdress and she was barefoot. She did not see Lisa. With great care she closed the door behind her, but not before Lisa had seen through the open doorway to the bed where Hachaliah Tatum was sleeping soundly.

TWENTY-SEVEN

Hardeman awoke. The lodgeskins glowed with daylight and the Cheyenne camp was alive around him. He was warm and comfortable. He allowed his eyes to close again and he lay listening to the sounds of the village and the pleasant crackling of the fire in the lodge. He was in Kills Fox's tipi, where he had slept for two nights. On the day of the pipe carriers' arrival Two Moons had invited them to sleep in his own spacious lodge, once they had decided to wait here for Sitting Bull, but Kills Fox had spoken up quickly to say that while the headman's hospitality was well known, he himself would be proud to have the white scout Hardeman sleep in his lodge, and inasmuch as Blackbird would remain there while he was under Ice's care, would not the war leader of the Sun Band like to sleep by his son? Standing Eagle had accepted the invitation, as had Hardeman, pleased to do anything he could to assure that the hostility between himself and Kills Fox would be completely forgotten.

The Cheyenne warrior had proved himself a generous host. The pipe carriers had been reeling with fatigue when Kills Fox had finally shown them to his lodge, but he had roused his wife and insisted the guests be fed before he would hear of sleeping, and so they had eaten together again and conversed, and Kills Fox had asked to hear of the pipe carriers' journey. Nothing in his manner then or since suggested that there had ever been anything but the greatest good will between himself and Hardeman. Now, lying in the comforting warmth of two of Kills Fox's buffalo robes, Hardeman reflected on the way hostility was allowed to linger like a festering sore between white men who had fought for any reason, or no reason at all. Here it had been erased. Kills Fox had had every reason to attack him, seeing his enemy delivered providentially into his hands after so many years, but when the error of his ways was made plain to him, he put his anger away as if it had never existed and banished any thought of revenge.

Hardeman put a hand to his forehead and was surprised to discover that the swelling of his wound was reduced to almost nothing and the skin there was much less tender to the touch. On the day before, the effects of the head wound had grown worse. He had had no appetite in the morning and had suffered from recurring bouts of dizziness. When Kills Fox had insisted that Ice should treat the wound, Hardeman submitted gladly. The old healer had placed an odd-smelling poultice on Hardeman's forehead and instructed him to spend the afternoon flat on his back without moving. Since then, he had spent most of the time asleep.

He heard a small noise and opened his eyes. He was on one of the sleeping pallets in the family's portion of the lodge to the left of the entrance, behind the backrests that surrounded the fire. Not far away, Ice knelt beside the still form of Blackbird, and Hardeman saw that the boy's leg was exposed once more to the old man's ministrations. Even by the soft daylight filtering through the lodgeskins, it was obvious that the wound was healing.

Hardeman swung his feet off the pallet and sat up, feeling more stupefied than refreshed by the long night's rest. Ice turned at the sound and nodded. No one else was in the lodge. Kills Fox had a comely daughter and a young son; they had been instructed to make themselves scarce while the wounded boy was recovering.

The boy is sleeping, Ice made in signs, putting a finger to his lips. Blackbird had remained unconscious throughout the previous day and Hawk Chaser had expressed renewed concern for his *hunká*-relative, but Ice said he had given the boy a potion to help him rest and he assured the pipe carriers that all was well. The medicine man made more signs now, inquiring about Hardeman's head, and Hardeman indicated that he was much improved. Ice smiled with satisfaction before returning to his work over the boy.

Hardeman stretched and looked about the lodge. The weapons and medicine bundles hanging behind the host's seat, and the skin hangings that lined the inside of the tipi from the ground cloth to a point above the height of a standing man, these decorated with many paintings of the owner's deeds, showed that Kills Fox was a prominent man among the Cheyenne. Two nights ago, entering the lodge for the first time, Hardeman had noticed none of this. It was careless to get so tired that you missed things like that.

Ice began a soft chanting. He took a clump of moss with earth still clinging to the roots and applied it to Blackbird's leg with hands as gentle as a mother's, pressing it carefully into place until no part of the wound showed. With a few motions over the wound he ended the chant, and began to wrap the boy's leg with fresh strips of hide to hold the moss in place.

The entrance flap was pulled aside and Bat Putnam's head appeared. Seeing Hardeman awake he stepped into the lodge, followed by Standing Eagle and Hawk Chaser. "'Bout time you decided to jine the livin'," Bat said. "I reckoned you to sleep plumb through to supper. What're ye feelin' like?"

Hardeman shook his head. "Can't wake up."

At the sounds of the voices, Blackbird's eyes opened.

"*Hau, chinkshí*," Bat said. Hello, son. Among the Lakota, the use of a kinship term closer than that warranted by the actual relationship was a deliberate way of expressing affinity and friendship. Bat did it now to show his concern for Blackbird.

"*"Hau, até,"* the boy replied. Hello, father. His gaze moved from Bat to Standing Eagle, then on to Hawk Chaser and Hardeman, recognizing each in turn. His face was flushed and his eyes were feverish. He struggled to sit up but Ice held him down with a firm hand. Blackbird asked a question and Standing Eagle replied at some length, saying where he was and how long he had been there. Blackbird said something else then, and Bat laughed.

"He says he's only sorry he didn't take the scalp off'n that Crow feller you shot," he explained to Hardeman.

"Was his fault the horses got took," Standing Eagle said. "His job to fetch 'em back too, not lollagag about to count coup and lift topknots." But he was smiling at his son, who lay back now while Ice finished wrapping the wound.

Kills Fox's wife put her head into the tipi and her mouth dropped open to see Hardeman awake and the other men there too. She vanished, and returned a moment later with her daughter, carrying a steaming pot. The woman spoke rapidly in Cheyenne and motioned the men to sit. In no time at all they were provided with bowls of broth and chunks of meat, elk this time, and Ice joined them in the meal while Kills Fox's wife spooned broth to Blackbird, who swallowed the first bowl without saying a word, and then asked for more, causing the men to laugh.

Hardeman found that the meal acted like a tonic. It restored his strength and sent him out to walk about the camp under blustery skies with small patches of blue, feeling immune to the cold. Children played on the snowy banks and ice of the river and the dogs ran between their legs and bowled them over. Despite the freezing temperatures and gusting winds, men and women were everywhere about the camp, the women hard at their daily tasks. Several of the men beckoned to Hardeman and invited him with signs to eat in their lodges, but he declined these invitations, saying that he had only recently eaten and that the Cheyenne cared for their guests as no other people did, remembering the polite refusals Jed Putnam had taught him as the only defense against being compelled to pass the entire day in eating when visiting friendly Indians.

Before long, he noticed Hawk Chaser walking among the lodges, stopping here and there to exchange a word or two, seemingly concerned only with his own affairs and moving at his own pace, but somehow always within sight of Hardeman. Hardeman hadn't missed the protective stance the warrior had taken on the day they arrived; he had put himself in danger to protect the white man, and it occurred to Hardeman now that perhaps this was why the extra man had been sent along: it might be Sun Horse's way of safeguarding Johnny Smoker's longtime protector and companion.

He motioned to the Sioux and made signs to say that he had a mind to climb up the bluffs and have a look at the countryside. Would Hawk Chaser like to come along?

The warrior agreed willingly and together the two men found a trail that climbed to the benchland close behind the village and wound its way along the base of the massive bluffs that overlooked the camp. The men left the trail to climb a small butte whose slopes were strewn with slabs of reddish rock. With some difficulty they scrambled to the top, which, like the rim of the bluffs that stood more than twice as high above the valley floor, was fringed with small pine trees.

The little butte afforded a good view of the village and the valley beyond. A few flakes of snow were falling now but the clouds remained high and there were still some small patches of blue. Bright shafts of sunlight touched the valley here and there, glowing pillars that supported the clouds above. The white landscape was touched with brown and yellow and red where grass and earth and rock showed through the thin mantle of snow. To the east, the hills were covered with trees.

It's a good land, Hardeman thought. Good for elk and deer and buffalo. Good for the Indians. Small wonder they don't want to leave it.

He felt no impatience today, no urge to rush on to find Sitting Bull and then Crook and set matters to rest one way or the other. These things would take place in good time; there was just so much a man could do to force the pace of events.

He looked at the village below him. No one there was in a hurry either. There was a great deal being done among the clustered lodges—robes and clothing made and repaired, arrows straightened and fitted with new heads, torn lodgeskins replaced, wood cut for fires and bark stripped for the horses, meat butchered and cooked and fat rendered and a hundred other things all done every day—but none of it forced or rushed. In a white settlement it seemed that half the people were forever hurrying from one place to another as if each moment were their last one on earth. The scene Hardeman saw from his vantage point was so full of life, yet so calm and peaceful, it was hard to imagine that Crook's column was anywhere within a hundred miles, hard to feel any danger at all.

"Le anpetu lila washté," Hawk Chaser said, He made signs to say, *this day is good*, and then he made a gesture that took in the Cheyenne village below, the river and the country beyond, everything between earth and heaven. "Iyuha washtéyelo." It is all good.

"Washté," Hardeman agreed. "Lila washté." It is very good. He had expended half his vocabulary of Sioux words. To an onlooker it might seem like a conversation of the feeble minded, the two of them standing there and agreeing that the day was good, the village was good, it was good to be alive, but each knew what the other meant, despite the differences between them.

"Washtéyelo," Hawk Chaser repeated. He opened his blanket and drew aside his loin cover and began to urinate, urging the steaming stream into a high arc, to fall as far as possible down the face of the butte. Hardeman realized that he had not relieved himself since awakening. He unbuttoned his buckskin trousers and joined the Indian, the two streams competing for height and distance, dispersing in the air and mingling as a fine rain of drops that showered the reddish rocks and melted the snow. The flow of Hawk Chaser's urine began to jerk and shake and Hardeman saw that the Indian was laughing. He didn't know what was so funny, but his own laughter rose inside him and the two men laughed together as they finished, urging out the final drops, and they kept on laughing as they rearranged their clothing and stood once more side by side atop the butte.

Hardeman felt the pleasure of an empty bladder and a new surge of hope. Surely there must be a chance for these unhurried people, living at peace in their own country, to keep that peace in some way other than the one laid down by the white man—a way they chose for themselves. If Crook should chance to come near this place, Hardeman would go out to meet him. He would take Bat and Standing Eagle with him and they would give Crook Sun Horse's pipe. Hardeman would explain that the village was peaceful and Two Moons was only waiting for the weather to warm again before moving to take his people to the reservation. He would tell Crook that Two Moons was willing to join Sun Horse in speaking to the hostile headmen, and Crook would understand. He would let these people remain here, glad of a Cheyenne ally in his quest for a peaceful settlement.

"Wan!" Hawk Chaser let out a sudden exclamation of surprise, pointing to the north, downstream. A dozen riders were approaching along the west bank of the river, now reining their horses in to a walk to let them breathe and collect themselves before they reached the village. Already children at the edge of the stream had seen the approaching riders and were running to spread the news.

Hardeman could see that the riders were Indian, but Hawk Chaser was trying to discern something more. The warrior shaded his eyes with one hand and peered long and hard, and his face split in a broad grin. He spoke rapidly in Lakota, and then in response to Hardeman's blank look he made the signs for a buffalo bull, the curved index fingers raised beside the head to evoke the horns of a buffalo, then the right hand held close to the waist with the index finger extended to signify the male organ. Finally he raised his right hand in a fist before him and brought it sharply down for a short distance in the sign for sitting or stopping.

Now it was Hardeman's turn to be surprised. "Sitting Bull?" Two Moons' messengers had been sent off less than two full days ago; it seemed impossible that they could return so soon with the famous war leader.

"Tatanka Iyotake." Hawk Chaser nodded enthusiastically. "Tatanka Iyotake. Sit-ting Bull." He began to look for a way down off the little butte, but he paused and offered his hand to Hardeman. They shook hands firmly, sealing some unspoken compact they had made by coming here to enjoy the day together, and then they helped each other down over the sheer lip of the butte and made their way quickly to the village.

Once more the Cheyenne turned out to welcome important visitors. Already, several women were moving off among the cottonwoods to gather wood for the council lodge, where the men would meet once Sitting Bull had been properly greeted and fed by Two Moons.

Bat spied Hawk Chaser and Hardeman approaching, and he moved quickly through the crowd to meet them. "Piece o' good luck here," he said. "Ol' Sit was already on his way, comin' to see Last Bull and get the news from the reservation. Two Moons' boys met him on the trail and brought him along quick."

As the riders drew near it was plain to see that their horses had been ridden hard. The animals were streaked with sweat, which steamed in the cold air. A group of men on foot accompanied the newcomers as they moved through the camp, Oglala from the downstream lodges, led by He Dog and Last Bull, the one muscular and tall, the other shorter and older but also walking straight and proud, honored by this visit from the great Hunkpapa. The day before, Bat and Standing Eagle and Little Hand had visited with the Oglala headmen to speak with them and hear their news.

Only the eagle-wing fan in Sitting Bull's hand showed that it was he who led this band. His hair was combed straight and he wore no feathers, no paint. He was barrel-chested and thick-legged and his eyes were piercing, his face round and sharply lined at the corners of the eyes and mouth. He rode a palomino horse that stood several hands above the shorter Indian mounts. With him were three of his councillors and six younger men, and the two Cheyenne messengers that had ridden to bring him here.

"Well I'll be," Bat exclaimed suddenly. "That's my boy there. Hey, Bear!"

One of Sitting Bull's young men turned at the shout and, spying Bat in the crowd, leaped off his horse and ran to greet his father. The two men embraced, and then Bat's son slapped his father on the back in a gesture remarkably like a white man's.

"Howdy, Pop," he said. "Didn't look to find you here." His English was more heavily accented than Standing Eagle's.

"Big doin's," Bat explained, growing serious. "We got pipes for Sittin' Bull and Three Stars. You know Three Stars is in the country?"

The younger man nodded. "We heerd tell. Ain't seen hide ner hair of him."

Bat turned to Hardeman. "Christopher, shake hands with my boy, Bear. Full moniker's Bear Doesn't Sleep, but you can call him Bear. This here's Christopher Hardeman. Used to scout for the bluecoats but he seen the error of his ways." Bat flashed a grin. "He come along to help us out."

Bear was about thirty, Hardeman judged. He was shorter than Bat and he had the black hair, roundish face and prominent cheekbones of his mother, but his skin was lighter than the average Sioux's and his eyes were gray. As the eyes appraised Hardeman, the scout was reminded of Jed Putnam, and Lisa, and the way they looked a man over when meeting him for the first time.

"Glad to know you, Christopher," Bear said, and then he recognized Hawk Chaser. His face broadened in a smile of pleasure and without pause he switched to voluble Lakota and moved on to the warrior, offering Hawk Chaser both his hands, the forearms crossed in a handshake of special respect.

As they talked, the men moved along with Sitting Bull and his escort, who were being conducted to the village headman's lodge. For these visitors, Two Moons did not delay his appearance. Already he was standing in front of his tipi and he raised a hand in greeting as the riders came to a halt before him. Young boys gathered around the newcomers as they dismounted, vying for the honor of unsaddling the horses and leading them to water. Sitting Bull dismounted with the movements of a man glad to quit his saddle after a long ride. He handed his braided rein to one of the boys and stepped forward to meet Two Moons, walking with a pronounced limp. There was a soft rustle of comments from the onlookers, like a breeze passing through a grove of trees. Those who had not recognized the Lakota holy man at first were sure now, for the tale of this limp was well known. It came from a wound received on the Hunkpapa's first war party, made in his fourteenth year. He had been shot in the foot by a Crow, but that evening Sitting Bull had danced the Crow's scalp around the victory fire.

Hardeman watched the solid, rolling gait, and he was reminded of another limp, also caused by a wound. He took in the Springfield carbine in Sitting Bull's hand, the stock decorated with brass studs, but only four of the others in the war man's party carried rifles and all of those were muzzle-loaders, no two alike. Hardeman had noted a similar shortage of modern weapons in Two Moons' village, belying the rumors that the hostiles were equipped with repeating arms.

Like any visitors to a friendly camp, Sitting Bull and his men were invited to eat, but it seemed to Hardeman that he detected an almost imperceptible urgency behind the brief but courteous greeting Two Moons extended and the promptness with which he ushered his guests into his lodge. The pipe carriers retired to Kills Fox's tipi while Sitting Bull ate, and Bear accompanied his father, taking this opportunity to exchange news of relatives and friends; Hardeman was uncomfortable at being shut away from the sight of the camp and he stepped outside after a short time to wander among the lodges, always keeping an eye on the headman's tipi. Not far from Two Moons' lodge was the council lodge, standing nearly twice as tall. A fire was burning there now, the thick plume of smoke rising into the air that never stopped moving today. A hush had descended on the camp and the calm that had pervaded the scene earlier that morning was gone. Conversations were conducted in lowered tones and many eyes kept watch on the entrance of Two Moons' tipi. Great matters would be decided here today; the village was waiting, anxious for the council to begin.

Long before he expected it, Hardeman saw Sitting Bull and his men emerge from the headman's lodge with Two Moons in their midst. They moved slowly toward the council lodge, giving all that were summoned there time to gather. For Indians, the brevity of the newcomers' welcoming meal amounted to bolting a bite of *wasná* on the run. It seemed that Sitting Bull himself was impatient to hear Three Stars' message to Sun Horse, and the peace man's reply.

Each of the Sun Band pipe carriers had received a stick of specially marked ashwood from the camp marshals, a formal summons to the council. Even Blackbird was carried from Kills Fox's lodge with Ice walking close by his side to see that he was made comfortable in the council lodge and placed close to the fire. The boy was speechless with pride at this honor done him, for he had never sat in council before, but the details of the pipe carriers' fight with the *Kanghí* had been told throughout the village and none doubted that the youth had earned the right to sit with his companions and face the great war leader and holy man of the Hunkpapa. Blackbird had eaten for a second time that morning, a piece of liver from a deer killed the day before, offered to Ice by the wife of Kills Fox. The boy felt new strength in his body and his heart and he had wanted to walk to the council lodge, but Ice insisted that he be carried.

In full regalia the councillors came. Those who were entitled to wear them had donned their feathered headdresses, all except Sitting Bull, and each man had chosen his best robe or blanket for the occasion. They wore breastplates of bone and shell, armbands of silver and copper and bronze. Their cheeks and foreheads were daubed with symbolic paint and around their necks hung necklaces and silver crosses, and presidential medallions presented in Washington by the Great Father of the whites. Beneath fringed leggings they wore brightly beaded moccasins, some hung with little silver bells that jingled as the men walked in stately parade to the council lodge.

The old-man chiefs of the Cheyenne village entered the lodge first. Old Bear was as venerable as his title implied, but Little Wolf was a much younger man, in his forties, his position of trust earned by a combination of selfless concern for his people and great courage in war. Three years before, he had been to Washington, and only his eloquent plea had prevented the northern Cheyenne from being ordered south to the Indian Territory with the remnants of the southern bands. In the fall of 1875 he had attended the council at the Red Cloud Agency, where the Lakota had refused to sell the Black Hills. Little Wolf knew the whites and his words would carry much weight here today. It was he who sat in the place the Lakota called *chatkú*, the place of honor across the fire from the entrance, with Old Bear at his right hand and Two Moons at his left.

The Lakota pipe carriers were seated to the right of Old Bear, Standing Eagle and Little Hand first, then Bat Putnam and Hardeman and Hawk Chaser. Standing Eagle had the feathers of his namesake bound in his hair and Little Hand was similarly adorned. Blackbird was brought to the last place among them, but Hawk Chaser moved, indicating that those carrying the litter should place it between himself and Hardeman. The boy flushed with embarrassment at this new honor done him by the warrior he so admired. Standing Eagle smiled at his son and Little Hand greeted him warmly, "*Hau, misúnkala.*" Greetings, little brother.

Sitting Bull and his three councillors sat at Two Moons' left, completing the circle closest to the fire. Outside this one a second circle was begun by the other councillors of Two Moons' band and the leaders of the warrior societies. Warriors always had a place in council, more so than ever when matters of war and peace were to be discussed, but the *Tsistsístas* were merely hosts here and had no real part to play in what would take place, and so the men of Two Moons' village had yielded the seats of greatest importance to their Lakota guests. Others came, Sitting Bull's young men and more Cheyenne, until more than fifty men were seated in three concentric rings within the lodge that stood higher than any other in the Cheyenne camp. In summer, the lodgeskins would have been rolled up so the villagers might gather outside to hear the deliberations, but today, because of the cold, the coverings were lashed to the ground; despite this, many men and women grouped around the entrance once the councillors had entered, to hear what they might.

As Sitting Bull took his place he spoke briefly with Standing Eagle and greeted Little Hand formally. Sun Horse and his descendants were Hunkpapa, as were others of the Sun Band, and although the band contained many Oglala, even some Brulé and Minneconjou, when the Lakota nation gathered together in summer the Sun Band camped with the Hunkpapa council fire. Little Hand was related to Sitting Bull through Hears Twice's bloodline, and it had been Sitting Bull who interpreted the vision Hears Twice received late in life, and confirmed his status as a prophet.

The Hunkpapa looked at each of the pipe carriers in turn and Hardeman met his gaze calmly, feeling equal measures of curiosity and caution in the man's expression. Sitting Bull's distrust of the whites was legendary. He looked away then, and only the frequency with which his glance returned briefly to Hardeman revealed his interest in the white man who sat with the Sun Band's messengers.

Strips of fat were placed on the fire and as they melted they sent the flames leaping high, filling the lodge with bright light and reminding the pipe carriers of the richness of the northern bands; in the Sun Band village all the fat was added to soups for extra nourishment or used in the making of *wasná*. There was no surplus for brightening lodge fires.

As always, the council began with a ceremonial pipe, which Two Moons filled and offered in the Cheyenne manner—to sky and earth, to east, south, west and north—before lighting it and passing it sunwise to Sitting Bull. The Hunkpapa offered the pipe and raised it to his lips slowly and deliberately, as he seemed to do everything in life, even the most ordinary actions. As a child his name had been Slow, for even when offered fresh berries he would always consider them gravely before reaching out.

The pipe was filled and offered and passed again and again until every man in the lodge had smoked it, uniting them in one spirit, and when the last man had smoked and the ashes had been emptied carefully into the fire, Two Moons was the first to speak. He welcomed all the visitors once again and briefly stated the pipe carriers' purpose in coming. The measured tones of his oratory signaled to those present that the formal talk of the council had begun and that the truth of his words was guaranteed by his honor, an obligation that would be binding on every man who spoke after him. His words were translated into Lakota by a man who sat directly behind him, the same camp marshal that had translated for the pipe carriers on the day they arrived.

After the short welcoming speech, Two Moons nodded to Standing Eagle, who turned to Little Hand. From within his buffalo robe Little Hand drew a beaverskin sack that contained the pipe he had carried ever since it was handed to him by Sun Horse. Sees Beyond had prepared the pipe with Sun Horse, lending his power to Sun Horse's plea for peace. Little Hand opened the sack and withdrew the pipe and a small pouch containing shredded inner bark from the red willow. With careful movements he fueled the pipe and then, holding it in both hands, he offered it to Sitting Bull.

The elongated bowl of red pipestone gleamed in the firelight. It had been shaped and polished patiently and given a final rubbing with buffalo tallow to seal the porous stone. The stem was a straight shaft of ashwood as long as a man's forearm, split in half and hollowed out and bound back together again, the mouthpiece wrapped in the raw hide of buffalo, which had been allowed to shrink and dry there until it was as hard as wood. Near the bowl four strips of colored buffalo hide hung from the stem, black, white, red and yellow, the colors of the four directions. Tied near the mouthpiece were braided strands of horsehair, also dyed in the sacred colors. A stripe of red paint ran along the top of the stem, following the path of smoke from the bowl to the mouthpiece, symbolizing the good red road of spiritual understanding that was sought by all who smoked the pipe. Around the stem was a small circle of black, and a green spot where the black line crossed the red one, green for the tree of life, which flowered where the road of worldly cares met the path of true understanding.

The lodge was silent. In his slow, methodical way, Sitting Bull leaned forward and took the pipe from the outstretched hands, and there was a slight rustling among the councillors as they relaxed. By accepting the pipe, Sitting Bull agreed to hear Sun Horse's request; if he lit it and smoked, that would mean he undertook the obligation that was requested of him.

Now Standing Eagle spoke and Bat talked low in Hardeman's ear, conveying the essence of the war leader's words as he told Sitting Bull how Hardeman had come to the Sun Band, and of the message from Crook and Sun Horse's reply to the soldier chief. The message to Sitting Bull would not be put forth just yet; first the surrounding circumstances would be explained so the origins of the request were fully known.

Standing Eagle turned to Bat, and now there was no one to translate for Hardeman as Bat spoke in Lakota, but he saw new interest on Sitting Bull's face, and obvious surprise when Bat spoke the name Hardeman had heard for the first time in Lisa Putnam's kitchen and often since then when he was among the Sun Band—*Oyate Tokcha Ichokab' Najin*—He Stands Between the Worlds.

When Bat was done, Sitting Bull fixed Hardeman with his gaze and spoke to him for the first time, his voice strong and rough, yet almost melodious.

"The White Boy of the Shahíyela lives..." Bat translated as soon as Sitting Bull began to speak, and then he paused as the squat warrior paused. "He is in the lodge of my cousin Sun Horse, and my cousin believes that a power has come to him with the return of his grandson. A power to make peace with the whitemen. A just peace for both Lakota and whites..." Again the words trailed off and Hardeman felt a certainty that the news of Johnny Smoker's return to Sun Horse had put the Hunkpapa off-balance. Which was just as well, for he himself was brought up short by the war man's words. *My cousin believes that a power has come to him with the return of his grandson,* he had said. *A power to make peace with the whitemen.* What had Bat told Sitting Bull? Did Sun Horse still believe that Johnny had brought him some miraculous power even though the boy had chosen the white world? Was the old man grasping at straws?

Sitting Bull spoke again. "Since the Washita the boy has lived among the whites?"

Hardeman nodded, offering nothing.

"And still he remembers his dream?"

There it was again, always the talk of the dream and a strange power it gave the boy, these things as remote from Hardeman's understanding as the particular beliefs of the white man's many religions. Hadn't Bat told the Hunkpapa that Johnny had at long last chosen between the worlds, that he brought no new hope for the Sioux? Hardeman had no answers for the questions that came to his mind and no time to ponder them. He saw one chance to strengthen his hand and he took it. "The boy has returned as Sun Horse told him he should, because of his dream."

He Dog spoke now, directing a question at Sitting Bull. Sitting Bull seemed to gather his thoughts for a moment and then he replied, obviously intending to speak for some time. Bat listened for a while and then turned to Hardeman. "He Dog wants to know about the dream. Ol' Sit's tellin' him, but he'll make it short. Short's he's able. He was in the summer camp the year young Johnny come a-visitin' with his folks. Sun Horse and Sittin' Bull had themselves quite a talk about that dream."

The Cheyenne knew of the dream and He Dog had heard of it briefly when the pipe carriers arrived, but he and his men listened thoughtfully to the tale Sitting Bull told, some blowing softly through the smoking pipes they had lit after the passing of the ceremonial pipe, the sound conveying wonder and concern at this thing they heard.

Hardeman no longer tried to imagine what was passing through the minds of the Indians. To him the whole thing was unreal. In Washington City, senators and congressmen and the President's ministers decided not only the fate of these bands but of all the western tribes with strokes of pen and ink on pieces of paper, motivated by gold and railroads and land and visions of a union that stretched from Canada to Mexico and sea to sea, while the headmen of the Sioux and Cheyenne sat here as sober as a bunch of Mormon judges pondering a dream a white boy had a dozen years ago, as if the fate of their people hung in the balance.

404

But if the dream made it more likely that the men assembled here would agree to Sun Horse's plan for peace, so much the better.

When Sitting Bull was done no one spoke right away. The Hunkpapa fanned himself slowly with his eagle wing, dispersing a puff of smoke that had drifted his way from the fire, and after a short while it was he that broke the silence, turning once more to Hardeman.

"You have scouted for the bluecoats. You have led men to war. They say you come here now to speak for peace. Why does the soldier scout wish an end to war?"

Hardeman framed his reply with care. "When I was a young man I traveled the Holy Road, guiding the wagons, and often I stopped in the camps of the Sioux and Cheyenne. I rode with one you call the Truthful Whiteman, the brother of my friend Lodgepole. He taught me the ways of the plains people. Much of what he knew, he had learned from you, and he taught these things to me." He paused, looking around the circle of faces that revealed so little. "One year in the Moon of Changing Seasons I returned from the great water in the west and I found the Sioux gone from Fort Laramie. I learned there had been trouble, a great chief killed and some white soldiers killed too. Since then I have fought for my people as you have fought for yours. But there has been too much fighting. I would like to see our people live side by side as we did before the trouble began."

Sitting Bull sucked on his own pipe thoughtfully for a time before looking up again at Hardeman. "And Three Stars, what does he want?"

"He wants peace."

"Yet he comes to our country with soldiers, and he says we must surrender or fight!" Sitting Bull spoke sharply now, and there were sounds of agreement from around the lodge.

"I believe there is another way," Hardeman said, keeping his tone even and firm. "If he will accept the pipe Sun Horse offers."

Sitting Bull was noncommittal. "I would hear what our friends the Shahíyela will do."

The eyes of the Cheyenne found Little Wolf now, and the man who sat in the place of most honor prepared to speak for the first time. He drew himself up and looked around the lodge, the firelight shining off the bright streaks of vermilion that lined his cheekbones, and then he addressed the Lakotas.

"My friends," he said, "I have heard the white scout's words. I too wish peace with the whiteman, so our people may live side by side again. In my village there are many who have seen the bluecoats come to make war on us, at Sand Creek and the Washita, and on the Platte and the Arkansas. The women are frightened by this talk of soldiers in our land. They cry out in the night, seeing the soldiers again while they sleep. The Tsistsístas are at peace with the whites, and yet the messengers came to us in the Moon of Strong Cold and said that we too must go to the agency. Old Bear said perhaps it was only the white traders who sent this message, wanting us to come and buy their blankets and whiskey." He glanced at the gray-haired man by his side and Old Bear nodded. "When Last Bull came, he told us that soldiers were coming soon to make us all go to the reservation, and some say the whites will take our country here and never let us return. I do not know what the whites truly want; it is hard to know the heart of a whiteman." He looked at Hardeman and then his eyes moved to Sitting Bull. "If Sitting Bull will accept the pipe from Sun Horse, I will wait to hear what the soldier chief says. If he will leave us in peace, we will stay here. But if Three Stars says we must surrender, we will go to Dakota, for the sake of the helpless ones."

Sitting Bull waited a decent interval to be sure Little Wolf was finished; when he spoke again he looked at Hardeman. "In the time you speak of," the Hunkpapa said, "when there was peace between us, the whites were few in this country, surrounded by the lodges of Lakota and Shahíyela. You came to our land and you learned our ways, and we accepted you among us." There were a few soft *hau*'s from the Sioux, and the Cheyenne made their own sounds of agreement. Sitting Bull kept his eyes on Hardeman, and as he continued, Hardeman felt the rising rhythms draw the listeners along.

"At the great council in the year the whites call 1851, you asked only that we should permit the Holy Road through our lands. We are going to the great water in the west, you said, and we will not return. Each year more whites went along the road and soon the soldiers came to the Laramie fort. Why do you need soldiers here? we asked. To protect our people, you said. Protect them from whom? we asked; we are at peace with the whites. Why do you need soldiers? The whites did not answer and soon we saw that the soldiers were like *akíchita*, but not good like our *akíchita*. They came to speak loudly to the people and tell them what they may and may not do."

The sounds of agreement were stronger now. Hardeman kept his eyes on Sitting Bull's, unwilling to be the first to break the contact.

"And so there was trouble. Men on both sides died and the Lakota moved away from the Holy Road. Still we wished to live at peace with the *washíchun*, but General Harney came; he smoked the pipe with Little Thunder, and then he killed Little Thunder's women and children and took the men away to the iron house." An angry sound filled the lodge. Sitting Bull waited for it to die away and then he continued, guiding the emotions of his listeners as easily as a Lakota warrior controlled his best war horse.

"Before long, some of the wagons did not follow the setting sun, but stopped in our lands. A few of our people wish to stay here, you said. The land is good. The Lakota and Shahíyela agreed to share the land, and some signed the new treaty you made to stop the fighting that you yourselves had begun."

At last his eyes left Hardeman and he addressed himself to the council at large. "Tell me, my friends, which of the treaties have the Lakota broken?" He paused just for a moment and then answered his own question. "Not one. Always the whites broke them first. I signed none of them and yet I kept each one until the *washíchun* broke it!"

"*Hau, hau!*" the Lakota chorused, and the swell of assent from the Cheyenne lagged only a moment behind as the running translations caught up with Sitting Bull's words.

"Each time the whites want a new treaty, and then before long they want more land. Always we give more and each time they promise that what remains is ours forever." Sitting Bull looked once around the circle and then back at Hardeman. "I have signed no treaties. The land is already mine. It was given to my people by *Wakán Tanka*. The whiteman cannot give me that which is already mine." Here the sounds of approval filled the lodge again. "Once before the bluecoats came to this country. They built forts and they said the wagons of the whites would pass along the road to the lands of the *Kanghí*." He looked around him. "My friends, we fought those soldiers and we whipped them! The forts are like the black stumps that remain after a forest fire. Now the soldiers come again and they want even more than before. They want this country here. They want the *Paha Sapa*. They want all the Lakota living at the agencies. They want to count us, they say. But we are not the spotted *pte* of the whiteman, to be counted and placed in pens! We are men!"

Now the *hau*'s were deafening, and outside the lodge the voices of the men and women gathered there to listen in the cold joined those in the council lodge. Sitting Bull waited until the approving sounds died away and then he drew something from within his robe and unfolded it. He held it up and Hardeman was surprised to see that it was an edition of the Denver *Rocky Mountain News*.

"My friends," Sitting Bull said, "Last Bull has brought me the whiteman's talking leaves from the agency. It is called a *newspaper*." He used the English word, and Hardeman was even more surprised when the Hunkpapa held the paper to catch the light from the fire and began to read aloud in English from the front page. He read slowly, pausing before the longer words and then pronouncing them with precision, all in a flat tone that made Hardeman wonder if he understood what he read.

"*Lying north and northwest of Fort Fetterman is a vast scope of country, known as the 'unceded lands,' to which the Indians have no right or title, but in which the most warlike of them have sought refuge, ever since the general abandonment of that region during the massacre of 1866. Since that date, those bands of Sioux who bid defiance to all attempts at reconciliation have marauded north, south and east from this, their natural stronghold, and then, with the swiftness of an Indian in retreat, have plunged back and regaled themselves on their plunder, thoughts of their isolation, and plans for future incursions.*"

Sitting Bull lowered the paper and spoke once more in Lakota. "My friends, it says that this land does not belong to us. It says we raid the whites and then come here to hide, and it says we do not want peace. But it is the whites who make this war!" He raised the paper and shook it. "The talking leaves say much more. They speak of opening the land to whites the way a man opens

407

the entrance to his lodge, and they speak of opening it with guns. They call us *heathens* and *savages*." Here he spoke the English words. "We do not have words for these things, but they are bad things. A *heathen* is one who does not believe in the *Christian* spirit called *God*, and a *savage* is less than a man."

There was a buzz of disapproval, and angry scowls on many faces, and Sitting Bull waited for the silence to return. When all attention was on him once more, he held the newspaper out before him and allowed it to drop at the edge of the fire, within the ring of stones that lined the pit. The pages curled and turned black and burst suddenly into flame. He waited until the whole sheaf of pages was burning brightly before he spoke, and now his voice was low, almost soft.

"My friends, the whites see only the wrongs another man does to them, never the wrongs they have done themselves, and so they are strong for revenge. They want to fight us, and I believe if they do not fight us now, they will fight us soon. The treaty they made at Fort Laramie says this land is ours, yet now they would deny their own treaty as they have done before. They want this land and if we do not give it to them they will try to take it." He drew himself up and his voice grew stronger. "We have given enough. We can give no more. The game is almost gone from the lands along the Muddy River, the one the whites call Missouri, but this country is still strong. Here there is meat for our kettles. Perhaps the buffalo will stay here with us, their two-legged brothers, when the whites have killed the buffalo everywhere else." The firelight reflected brightly in his eyes as they moved about the lodge, sweeping the faces there, making sure he had their full attention. "This country is our home. I will not give it away nor will I share it with the whites. I have fought them for a long time and I have killed many *washíchun*. They will never let me live beside them in peace." Here he turned to Little Wolf. "I too worry for the helpless ones, but I cannot take them to Dakota. Others may live at the agencies if they wish. Each man must choose for himself. I will stay here. When friends wish to visit me, my village will welcome them, but if the white soldiers come to steal my land, I will fight!"

Sounds of approval swept the gathering, almost every man there adding his voice. After a time the chorus waned, then swelled again as it became clear that Sitting Bull was done speaking for now. When the sounds of assent died out, they were replaced by a soft hum of conversation that gradually came to an end as all waited to see who would speak next.

To Hardeman it seemed that the council might as well end then and there. As long as Sitting Bull held the gathering in the palm of his hand, there would be no dealing with Crook, no chance to delay until summer so the Indians could talk among themselves and agree to the white man's terms. The stumbling block had been reached: if the Indians insisted on keeping the Powder River country, there could be no peace without fighting. But the Hunkpapa had not refused Sun Horse's pipe outright. He still held it in his hand. And he had not said what he would do if Crook left the country now and managed to delay the campaign. Could there still be a chance?

The silence deepened. No one wanted to follow the spellbinding oratory of Sitting Bull. From outside the lodge there was a rustle of movement and a few words exchanged, and then a soft cough at the entrance, followed by a polite scratching on the lodgeskin.

Two Moons spoke a few curt words, wishing to know who it was that would interrupt the council.

The entrance flap was pulled aside and a man entered. He was slender and not very tall, and his hair was much lighter than an Indian's—almost sandy at the ends. His nose was straight and thin, and a dark scar at the corner of one nostril spread a little onto the cheek.

Hardeman's first thought was that the newcomer must be a trader's son, one of the halfbreeds who moved between the northern bands and the agencies, offspring of the men who used to trade with the Sioux along the Holy Road and in their camps, bringing wagonloads of goods to trade for furs. In recent years the army had limited trade to the government agencies, where no guns or powder would be included with the goods. As long as the Indians could get the things that enabled them to lead a nomadic life, they would remain free, but once their supplies came only from the official agency post, that, together with the diminishing numbers of the buffalo, would soon compel them to live where the white man wished them to be. Denied the occupation of their fathers and mostly raised among their mothers' people, many of the traders' sons now rode with the hostile bands.

Hardeman looked at the man's eyes, seeking the trace of blue or gray that would tell him he was right, but the eyes were soft and brown, and in his dress the newcomer was Sioux from the fringes of his winter moccasins to the mountain lion fur that wrapped his braids. He wore blue leggings and a red breechcloth, beaded modestly with a single stripe along the lower edge. His blanket too, which he now folded and placed over his left arm, was bordered with a band of beadwork, but otherwise his clothing lacked the ornamentations the young men of the Sioux loved so well; no copper or silver disks hung from his hair, no quill or beadwork adorned his simple buckskin shirt; he wore no paint or feathers.

The man's eyes moved around the lodge, pausing on the white men, and Hardeman felt as if the eyes looked right through him.

Two Moons spoke, his voice utterly changed, all cordial welcome now and revealing a trace of deference. To Hardeman's astonishment the Cheyenne chief moved a little to one side, making room for this strange man between himself and Sitting Bull, who offered no objection. The man moved through the outer rings of the council, those seated there moving with alacrity to permit his passage, but he made a sign of polite negation and seated himself in a vacant spot next to Hawk Chaser, close to the bottom of the inner circle.

Hawk Chaser shifted himself slightly to make more room for the newcomer, and by a slight inclination of his head and a small movement of his hand he indicated both welcome and respect. "*Hau,*" he greeted the slim man as he settled himself.

"*Hau,*" the stranger replied, his eyes taking in the warrior's erect bearing, quiet dignity, and the single eagle feather bound in the graying hair.

"*Tashunka Witko,*" one of Sitting Bull's young men whispered to his neighbor. Hardeman caught the words and it seemed there was something familiar there, but he couldn't put his finger on it. Was it the man's name? He cursed his own ineptness at languages. Who was this stranger that caught everyone's attention so completely? Since he had entered the council lodge all eyes had followed him. The councillors didn't stare, which would have been impolite, but if the light-haired man had turned his head or raised a finger, every man in the lodge would have been aware of the motion.

Hardeman forced himself to hear the words again in his mind and search them for some hint of meaning. *Tashunka Witko.* That was it! *Shunka* meant a dog, or a horse. The full name for horse in Lakota was *shunka wakán*; it meant sacred dog, but horses were sometimes just called *shunka* if the meaning was clear. *Tashunka* would be "his horse" or "his dog," but what was the rest of it? *Witko?* It seemed he had heard the word before, if he could just...

A chill enveloped his body so completely that he had to struggle to keep from shuddering. The hair on the back of his neck felt like crawling insects. Was there so much power in a name? Realizing at last who it was nearly paralyzed him. He feared that his efforts to regain control of himself would be noticed, but he saw that all the others were looking from the newcomer to Two Moons and Sitting Bull, waiting for one of them to speak. On Hardeman's left, Bat Putnam was smiling.

Bat needed no one to tell him the identity of the stranger. He had first met Crazy Horse when the young man was just twenty-two, in the Lakota summer camp the same year Johnny Smoker and White Smoke and Grass Woman had come to visit Sun Horse, and he had seen him occasionally since then when the bands gathered together. The people spoke of Crazy Horse as they spoke of no other, and Bat felt the man's power now, grown so strong in the intervening years. He might sit at the bottom of the lodge or go about with no feathers in his hair, but he would never just melt into the people and be one of them as it often seemed he wished to do.

Our Strange Man, the Oglala called him. As a child his hair had been almost yellow and the other children had teased him. His people had been among those that camped at Fort Laramie until the death of Conquering Bear, and white women traveling along the Holy Road had often asked if he was a white child held captive by the Sioux, but Crazy Horse's parentage was known beyond a doubt, his mother a Brulé, the sister of Spotted Tail, and his father an Oglala of the northern band called Hunkpátila.

Bat had heard nothing of a messenger sent to find Crazy Horse, but he was not surprised that the warrior should show up like this. He was always sent for whenever Lakotas met to discuss important matters, although he held no formal position that entitled him to sit in high councils. Probably He Dog had sent a rider. His arrival here just two days after the pipe carriers meant that he was camped not far away.

Once again Two Moons prepared the ceremonial pipe and once again it was passed, just around the inner circle now, to include Crazy Horse in the proceedings. When the pipe had returned to Two Moons' hands and was emptied and set aside, Crazy Horse took out his own smoking pipe and loaded it in an unhurried way from his pouch, seemingly intent on this little task as the silence deepened around him. Many noticed this pipe and knew what it meant. It was the short pipe of a man who had been brought down from high position. Crazy Horse had once been a shirt wearer of the Oglala, one of just four young men chosen for this honor when the ceremony was revived a dozen years before. The shirt wearers were named by the Big Bellies, the chiefs' society, and the giving of the special shirt meant that the ones chosen were men of the people, placed above the *akíchita* in camp and on the trail, men who guarded all the people, great and small, and set aside their own passions even when wronged. But Crazy Horse's shirt had been taken away in bad trouble over a woman. A Lakota woman had the right to leave her husband and go with another man if she chose, and Black Buffalo Woman had gone with Crazy Horse openly, in the light of day, but the husband had chased the couple and had shot Crazy Horse in the face, the scar still plain to see, and because Crazy Horse was a shirt man, he had sent the woman back to her husband to prevent trouble among the people. He wanted the woman and she wanted him, but he thought of the people before his own happiness and in the quiet of the lodges the people praised him. But then one day, weakened by another grief, the death of his younger brother at the hands of the Snakes, Crazy Horse had spied the woman's husband and in a fit of rage and sorrow he had taken a gun and chased the man all the way to the Yellowstone, and for this the Big Bellies had taken away his shirt.

The chiefs had the right to do this thing, but the people did not approve the act. Crazy Horse is still a man of the people, they said; always he counsels the young men to think of the people in war, not to spoil an ambush or let the enemy escape because a foolish warrior could not wait to count coup; he does not sing his own deeds, they said, and always he thinks of the people first. But Crazy Horse accepted the Big Bellies' judgment without protest. The people said that taking the shirt was a shameful act that had broken the power of the Big Bellies. The chiefs' society had never met again and now its members were scattered among the agencies, holding out their bowls for the white man's rotten meat and wormy flour, while Crazy Horse, although no longer a shirt man, was honored still, for the people believed in his power and they looked to him for guidance. In his becoming-a-man vision he had seen his horse floating above the ground, carrying him safely through the ranks of his enemies and leading his people to victory. The name he was given after this vision did not mean his horse was crazy, as a white man understood the word. It meant something closer to enchanted. In the vision the horse had behaved strangely because it was a creature of the spirit world, bringing him a promise of power. As long as the power stayed with him, Crazy Horse could not be hurt by his enemies, and that was strong medicine in the eyes of the people. In the years since the taking of the shirt, he had been made lance carrier for the Raven Owners warrior society and more recently lance carrier for all the Oglala, this honor not given to anyone for many years.

"Well, my friends," Crazy Horse said when the pipe was lit and going, "they say that pipe carriers have come from Sun Horse, and they say a whiteman brings a message from the soldier chief Three Stars."

As if these few words had broken a beaver dam and released the waters of a stream, the silence of the lodge was broken and one voice followed another, first Two Moons and then Standing Eagle and then Bat Putnam, telling why the pipe carriers came and what had been said up to now, and when Bat spoke of Hardeman and Johnny Smoker, Sitting Bull joined in, and he and Bat between them, aided by the southern Cheyenne, told of the boy and his dream. The name He Stands Between the Worlds was mentioned often, along with the word *wakán*, to touch on the mysterious powers of dreams and prophecies.

At length a silence fell as Crazy Horse absorbed what he had heard, rocking slowly back and forth as he sucked on the pipe that had grown cold in his hand.

He looked up at Bat Putnam and he smiled. "Perhaps my friend Lodgepole carries the pipe to Three Stars?"

Bat motioned to Standing Eagle. "My brother-in-law carries the pipe. I will go with him to Three Stars and I too will speak with him."

"Then Three Stars will hear the words of Sun Horse as if they came from his own lips."

There were a few soft *hau*'s from the Lakotas. Bat was embarrassed by this quiet expression of praise and trust from the great Oglala. He had translated Crazy Horse's words for Hardeman automatically, before he absorbed their meaning.

The soft brown eyes of the light-haired man shifted to Hardeman. "They say Three Stars keeps his promises. If he takes the pipe will he go in peace?"

Hardeman knew it was time to talk straight; there would be no deceiving this gathering. "Three Stars is a soldier," he said. "If he has to, he'll make peace in the way a soldier knows best, but he's a man who thinks for himself, like the men of the Sioux and Cheyenne. Show him a way to a lasting peace without fighting and he'll listen. If he takes the pipe, he'll keep his word."

"They say Three Stars sent you to Sun Horse," Crazy Horse said, and here he made a gesture that took in the lodge and all he had been told. "They say you told Sun Horse he must surrender or there will be war."

"Three Stars didn't send me," Hardeman said, meeting the steady gaze. "I

412

went on my own. Johnny Smoker, the one you call He Stands Between the Worlds, wanted to see his grandfather. He told me about Sun Horse and I saw a way to make peace. We found Three Stars and talked with him and then we found Sun Horse. Three Stars gets his orders from Washington. They think the only way to make peace is to get all the Sioux onto the Dakota reservation now. But if you show Three Stars a new way, one he can believe in, he'll take it." He didn't say that both he and Crook had planned on Sun Horse's surrender as the first step to peace, or that both of them believed the hostiles would have to give up the Powder River country. If there were many as stubborn as Sitting Bull, unwilling even to consider leaving these pleasant, wooded hills, there would be fighting in the end, despite all the efforts of the peacemakers.

Hardeman fought off a chill of foreboding. Sitting Bull had fired up the council with his carefully chosen words, but still Two Moons and Little Wolf intended to take their people to Dakota unless a deal could be struck with Crook, and it remained to be seen where Crazy Horse stood.

"It is said that Three Stars is a quiet man who listens," Two Moons said now. "Perhaps if the soldier chief hears words of peace from the war leader of Sun Horse's people, he will—"

"It is my father who speaks of peace!" Standing Eagle burst out. "His words are not mine! I would fight Three Stars now and leave his bones for the wolves to chew! I would carry the pipe of war, not peace! Let us fight him now, any who are brave enough. Let others run away like the camp dogs before the sticks of the old women! I will not run away! If Three Stars must fight, I will fight him!"

There was a heavy quiet in the lodge. Many of the men covered their mouths and looked away, everyone there embarrassed by this shocking breach of good manners. Several of the Cheyenne glared angrily at Standing Eagle and one man put his hand on his skinning knife. Standing Eagle reddened, but he continued to sit straight. He had spoken against his own father and come near to calling his host a coward, but to show weakness now would only bring more scorn on him.

From the head of the second circle of councillors, He Dog spoke to Standing Eagle, his voice heavy with sarcasm.

"Has the camp of Sun Horse enough guns and powder to fight the soldier chief now? It is well known that Sun Horse's people do not trade with the whites often. It is said they have few guns. The pipe carriers say that the people are hungry and the horses weak. Would the war leader fight the bluecoats even before the new grass is up?" He paused for effect and then continued. "The winter has been hard. My own horses are well. They found good grass on the Tongue and the Rosebud and we gave them much cotton-wood bark, but still I would not entrust them with the safety of my helpless ones if the soldiers came to chase us day and night as they like to do. Are your horses so much stronger than mine?" After another pause he looked across the inner circle at Crazy Horse. "My brother-friend has fought the bluecoats often. He tells of many guns, all of them the back-loading kind now, and some the many-shooting kind. Let my brother-friend say if he believes we can fight the bluecoats in the Snowblind Moon."

Once again the eyes in the lodge turned to the light-haired man. He Dog had stated the risks of fighting, but it seemed he was asking Crazy Horse if there might be hope in such a course. There were others here who might permit themselves to be swayed if the great Oglala encouraged them.

It was a moment before Crazy Horse replied. "It is true the soldiers have many guns," he said, and his eyes moved to Standing Eagle. "Some will go to Dakota rather than fight and they do this because of concern for the helpless ones." He glanced at Sitting Bull, who held himself aloof from the proceedings. "Sitting Bull says he will not go. He will stay here and fight the bluecoats if he must, and he too does what he thinks is best for the people. Each man must choose for himself. Standing Eagle carries pipes from Sun Horse, a true peace man. Sun Horse wears the shirt-for-life and always he thinks of the helpless ones. The war leader of Sun Horse's people knows this and perhaps that is why he bears a pipe of peace instead of war."

There was an easing of tension. Anger faded from the Cheyenne faces. Crazy Horse had offered Standing Eagle a way to atone for his outburst if he would acknowledge his responsibility for the helpless ones. And by emphasizing that each man must choose for himself, the Hunkpátila had told He Dog to follow his own conscience.

Hardeman felt a glimmer of hope. If Crazy Horse came out on the side of peace, that might bring Sitting Bull around.

Standing Eagle kept his head high. His face was set and hard, and he did not meet Crazy Horse's eyes. "The hunting has not been good for my people. It is true our ponies are weak, but no weaker than the whitemen who live in wooden houses and hide away from the coldest days of winter. Who has known the bluecoats to remain for long where snow covers the ground and the wind blows cold? Even on weak horses we can fight them and send them running with their tails between their legs."

"It is said that Three Stars rides always at the head of his men," Crazy Horse said evenly. "They say he sleeps on the ground, under the stars, like the war men of the Lakota. They say he is at the front of battle, never the rear. They say his men fight hard for him and will follow where he leads them."

Standing Eagle saw that bravado would not get him through this moment; he would have to yield. "Perhaps Three Stars is not like the others. When a leader is strong, the warriors fight harder." He turned to Crazy Horse as he said this and those present knew he was acknowledging the Hunkpátila's great skill as a war leader. Standing Eagle's head was no longer held so high and his voice had softened. "If Three Stars comes to fight the camp of Sun Horse, I will fight him, but the helpless ones will suffer. To save the helpless ones, our councillors would have us go to Dakota if there is no other way, but my

414

father hopes to make a peace with the whites that will let us keep our country here. A peace not only for Sun Horse's people but for all the Lakota. It is for this reason that he sends pipes to Sitting Bull and Three Stars, so there will be no fighting now; so he may have time to find another way. I will take the pipe to Three Stars and with my brother-in-law and the white scout I will tell him my father's words." Here he gestured at Bat and Hardeman, sitting near him.

The last of the tension dissipated. Standing Eagle had retreated from his angry call for war and had restated his responsibility as a pipe carrier. Within the customs of a Lakota council, he had apologized for forgetting himself.

Hardeman was struggling with the realization that Sun Horse had tricked him. From the start, the old man had said he would speak for peace, but he had never said outright that he would take his people to Dakota or encourage others to do so. All along Sun Horse had been just like the others, intent on keeping the Powder River country! Was it possible that the whole business with the pipes was nothing more than a trick? Hardeman couldn't believe that. Sun Horse's desire for peace was real, he was sure of it. But how could there be a settlement if the hostiles wouldn't go in? Like the men in Washington, Hardeman had always believed that giving up the unceded lands was a precondition for peace. Until now. Suddenly he felt that belief weakening. Could there be another way? Only this morning, looking down on the tranquil Cheyenne village, he had felt that the Indians might find peace on their own terms, but then he had imagined only a short delay in submitting, not counter proposals that flew in the face of everything the white men wanted.

One of Two Moons' councillors broke the silence, and his eyes were sad. "The whites are more numerous than the buffalo," he said. "More numerous than the blades of grass on the prairie, so they say. To speak of fighting them is useless. Perhaps we should take the whiteman's hand and accept what he offers us, rather than fight him and risk losing everything."

"They *want* everything!" Crazy Horse snapped, his eyes flashing with sudden anger, and Hardeman felt the shock of this change in the light-haired man like a slap in the face. "They always want more! They want the *Paha Sapa*; they want this country here; they want everything! We can give no more!" And then as suddenly as it had come, Crazy Horse's anger was gone and the fire left his eyes. He looked at the Cheyenne councillor kindly. "Each man must choose for himself what to do," he repeated, and for a time he seemed lost in thought. Finally he drew himself up and looked around him.

"My friends," he said, and his voice was calm now, "the Lakota and the whiteman walk different trails. Each man is good in the sight of *Wakán Tanka*, but the *washíchun* do not see this. They wish to make us like them, only poor and weak beside them. They call us wild and they do not like wild things. They kill the buffalo and bring the tame spotted kind in his place. They wish to tame us as well. They do not like to stand beside one who is strong in a way different from their own." His eyes looked around the inner circle. "They

415

even seek to tame the earth, the mother who gives them life. They claim the land for their own and fence their neighbors away, and love of possessions is a sickness among them."

There were some *hau*'s and other sounds of approval, but a few men looked away in embarrassment. Like the whites, the Lakota and the Cheyenne sometimes measured a man by his possessions, by the number of horses he had or the hides he brought in as a hunter, hides his women made into robes and shirts and leggings he wore with perhaps too much pride. Crazy Horse spoke often against these things, giving his own horses away to the needy and wearing none of the finery some men admired. "Do not become like the whites," he often said, "seeking power and possessions."

"My friends," he said now, "we cannot live beside the whites. I do not wish to make the *washíchun* into a Lakota, nor will I let him make me into a *washíchun*. We have given them some land and they have taken more. They are all around us now, as once we were around them. Let them keep the land they have and live there in their own manner, but I will not live beside them."

As Sitting Bull had done earlier, Crazy Horse held the gathering in his hands, but unlike the Hunkpapa he did not dominate them with fiery rhetoric; instead he showed them his reasoning, revealing the workings of his heart. He glanced at Sitting Bull now, and the war leader nodded, revealing just a trace of a smile.

"If I must choose between surrender and fighting"—Crazy Horse paused, and he gave a little sigh before he said the next words—"I will fight. I will not go to Dakota. I will stay here. If the soldiers come, I will fight them."

He picked up a handful of earth from the edge of the fire pit, where it was dry and warm from the heat of the fire, and let the sandy soil trickle from one hand into the palm of the other; he reversed the position of his hands and repeated the action as he spoke again.

"I have signed none of the whiteman's treaties, but after we whipped them when they built forts in our country, I kept that treaty and I have fought them only when they broke it."

There were murmurs of assent now, for all knew the deeds of Crazy Horse. Since Red Cloud's War he had fought the soldiers when they came along the Yellowstone to find a way for an iron road there, and he had fought in the Black Hills when the miners came to dig for gold. Each one present knew the truth of these things.

"The Ancient Ones say that a young man must know war so he can understand peace. I have seen much fighting, and I will fight again if the whites try to take what is mine. But I do not wish to fight forever. I like to see the little children play unafraid and I like to hear the women sing with happy hearts. Sun Horse is *wichasha wakán*; he has great power for the good of the people and now he seeks the path to a lasting peace. If the soldiers will go away now, I will stay at peace until the grass is tall, and when Sun Horse comes to speak to us, I will listen." The sounds of approval were strong

416

now, and Crazy Horse turned to Hardeman. "Tell this to Three Stars. Tell him he must leave our country now. Tell him to speak to the Great Father in *Washing-ton* and say that the Lakota want peace. But we cannot live side by side with the whites. If there is to be peace, we must each live in our own country, in our own way."

Hardeman allowed himself to betray no reaction to the Oglala's words, but his mind was working furiously. The lines were clearly drawn now: on one side were Crazy Horse, Sitting Bull and Sun Horse, all determined to keep the Powder River country, and on the other was mustered the limitless power of the white nation. Sun Horse might not fight to keep his land, but Crazy Horse and Sitting Bull would, and between them they could sway the majority of the hostiles. If there were any way left to avoid war, it would have to be found now.

From the start, Hardeman's own goal had been to prevent fighting by any means, but he had not planned to help the Indians defy the government's order, and yet if they remained adamant about keeping the Powder River country, there would be war . . . unless there were some way for them to remain here and still satisfy the white man's demands. It seemed a futile hope. Crazy Horse was willing to hold in his warriors if Crook would leave the country now, and that was a start, but the hostiles would have to give up much more. If the whites didn't get what they wanted, they would fight for it. . . . But what if the hostiles yielded everything the whites truly wanted? What if they appeared to surrender? Whites were often shortsighted. If they believed they had won, the hostiles might secure for themselves the one thing they demanded without conditions—a part of the Powder River country to keep forever! Not all of it, for there too they must yield, but they might keep a part!

But as quickly as they had risen, his hopes fell again as he realized the whites would never strike such a bargain. In their minds, the Powder River country represented a hiding place for the "warlike" bands, those that defied "all attempts at reconciliation," in the newspaper's words. Such views were widespread on the frontier, where the unceded lands were seen as a place where the hostiles could perpetuate their wild way of life and gird themselves for repeated outbreaks, and that was what the whites feared most, failing as they did to see their own role in maintaining the hostilities.

Hardeman looked at the rings of seated figures around him. Say the word "Indian," and most whites imagined just such men as these—the painted and befeathered warriors of the Sioux and Cheyenne. Illustrations in dime novels and magazines and newspapers alike depicted all Indians in a similar manner, whether they were plains Indians or not, and they were usually shown brandishing tomahawks and rifles, threatening peaceful settlers. And always there were white women cowering in terror in the foreground; that was how the fear was kept alive.

Hardeman looked at Crazy Horse and Sitting Bull, leaders who shunned the finery for which their people were famous across the land. Newspapers

417

imagined them plotting rapine and bloodshed; their names were spoken with fear in the taprooms of Custer City in the Black Hills; mothers invoked them to frighten children into nightmares. Yet here they sat before him, giving no orders, commanding no legions except by respect, strong personalities and greatly admired by their own kind, but so different from the popular notion among the whites. Men of the people, the Lakotas called them, and it was true; they were natural leaders who had risen from the people. As the words spoken here made plain, they were not afraid to fight, even against superior weapons and bad odds, but they fought for their people. They were portrayed as constantly seeking war, yet here they sat discussing ways to end it forever, willing to fight only if war came to them. And in that they were no different from other men. What man would not fight if his home were attacked?

If only the whites could be made to see these men as they truly were. . . .

There were soft conversations going on here and there about the lodge, but Little Wolf cleared his throat now and the others fell silent. The Cheyenne chief glanced at Sitting Bull, who remained as expressionless as a chunk of rock, and then moved his gaze to Hardeman.

"If the pipes Sun Horse sends are accepted, and if Three Stars goes from our lands, when will he come again to speak with the headmen of the Lakota?"

It was Crazy Horse who answered, before Hardeman could frame a reply.

"In the first moon of summer, when the wild turnips are ripe," the Oglala said. "But we will not meet him at the Laramie fort or the one called Fetterman. Too often in the past our headmen have gone to the forts when the whites called them. They sat under the guns of the soldiers and they signed the talking leaves full of promises the whites never kept. This time the bluecoat chief must come to sit among the Lakota, to be heard by our women, our men and our children."

"He must not bring his horse soldiers," one of Sitting Bull's councillors put in, his eyes flashing. "He must come alone."

The idea came to Hardeman then in a rush. He began to speak even before he was certain what he would say, but he knew he could not yield on the first specific demand or he would win nothing. It was important for Crook's prestige that he have an escort. Of course, no one yet knew if Crook would agree to the plan at all, but when the pipe carriers met with him they must know all of the Indians' demands. First secure Crook's escort, then broach the new thought that Hardeman felt would surely burst him at the seams if he did not voice it soon.

"When the Lakotas go to council with the whites, they always take their young men," he said. "Red Cloud took his young men to Laramie, so did Spotted Tail. Every chief who has gone to council with the whites took his young men. Three Stars must bring his young men when he comes to council with the Lakotas, but he needn't bring them all. One company. Forty or fifty men."

Crazy Horse nodded. "It is true that our headmen take young warriors to

418

council. Three Stars may bring one *troop*." He used the English word, surprising Hardeman, but the scout merely nodded and was careful to keep his face calm and his voice even when he spoke again, as if bringing up a matter of only passing interest.

"It may be that Three Stars will want to bring other men with him, some white men who are not soldiers. You know that much trouble has been made when the men who sit in the Great Father's council in Washington don't understand what the soldiers and the Lakotas have agreed. If some men from Washington come with Three Stars, you'll know that they hear you with their own ears and will take your words truthfully to the Great Father. They will come here and they will see that you want peace." Then, as if it were only an afterthought, he added, "And perhaps some of the men who write for the talking leaves will come, so they will write the truth about Crazy Horse and Sitting Bull."

Sitting Bull gave a small shrug and attempted to conceal his interest, but Hardeman knew he had the Hunkpapa's attention.

Two Moons spoke briefly with Little Wolf and then exchanged a word or two with Crazy Horse before he turned to Hardeman. "Three Stars may bring some men from *Washing-ton*. The Great Father may come himself if he wishes, but at least he must send some of his advisers to hear our words."

Crazy Horse nodded. "They say that Three Stars speaks the truth. It may be that he would carry our words truthfully to the Great Father, but it is good that his advisers should come here to see us at peace in our own country."

"Let Three Stars bring the men who make the talking leaves," one of Sitting Bull's councillors added, his voice edged with sarcasm. "Perhaps then they will tell no more lies about us."

There was a chorus of agreement from the gathering and even a little laughter, and Hardeman felt hope growing strong within him. In a moment he had changed the very nature of the summer meeting. No longer would Crook come alone, accompanied only by soldiers; instead he would bring a peace commission to treat with the hostiles. The Indians believed Crook was trustworthy and as long as he led the commission they would not object. Alone, Crook might have reached an agreement with the hostile bands, but a full peace commission might achieve something far more important. Received here, in the hostile camps, the officials and the newspapermen could see the true state of affairs for themselves. They would see that Crazy Horse and Sitting Bull were defenders, not attackers, and that could be the start of changing white opinion on the frontier and beyond. Such a change was vital if these brave men were to keep some portion of their hunting grounds.

There was a chance it might work. If Sitting Bull would agree, the chance became almost a certainty. With a pipe from Sun Horse and the agreement not only of Sitting Bull and the Cheyenne, but also of Crazy Horse, the most feared warrior of all, and an invitation to bring a new peace commission in summer, Crook might be willing to order the army from the field and take

419

the part of the Sioux against the likes of Phil Sheridan. "It is preposterous to speak of keeping faith with the Sioux," Sheridan had once said, but Crook knew the value of bargaining with the Indians in good faith, and for the sake of a real peace that gave the whites what they wanted, cooler heads than Phil Sheridan's might make a pact and keep it.

As if he sensed Hardeman's hopes and wished to caution the white man, Crazy Horse turned to him now. "Tell Three Stars one thing more," he said. "Tell him we will hear no more talk of selling *Paha Sapa* or leaving our country here. He must know this, so he will understand what is in our hearts."

Hardeman took a deep breath. If the whites were denied the Black Hills gold there would be no peace commission, no new treaty. But here in this council the speeches were done and the bargaining had started, and as long as there was room to bargain there was still hope.

"The whites don't want the hills," he said, new ideas coming fast to him now. "They want the gold. Do the Lakota and Cheyenne want the gold too?"

Sitting Bull broke his long silence. "We have no use for the soft shining metal. Sometimes we cast it into bullets." He smiled, but the expression was out of place beneath the eyes that were as hard as ever.

"Let the whites have the gold, then," Hardeman suggested as if this were nothing more than good sense. "Say they can go to the Black Hills and mine the gold, and when the gold is gone the hills will be yours. In a few years the miners will be gone, just as they have gone from the diggings in Colorado, and over in South Pass in the land of the Snakes."

"The whites say they want the land," Crazy Horse said. "They do not give up what they want without a fight."

"How do you get a bone away from a dog?" Hardeman asked. "Offer him another bone, one he might like better."

Crazy Horse's expression revealed a new interest. "What bone should we offer the whites instead of *Paha Sapa?*"

"The whites want an iron road along the Yellowstone. Let them build it, but not in your country. Say they can build it north of the river in the land of the Crows."

Crazy Horse pondered this for a moment, then nodded. "If it is north of the river, that is not our country, so we give away nothing. Will the dog let go of *Paha Sapa* for that?"

For this too Hardeman had an answer. "Give him more. Offer him the land north of the Platte up to the place where the Dry Fork joins the Powder, at old Fort Reno." It was the last card he had conjured out of his sleeve in recent moments. His whole hand was on the table now. If there were ways around the obstacles that remained, others would have to find them.

There were rumblings of discontent when the white scout's words were translated, but Old Bear leaned forward, fixing Hardeman with his gaze. "What will the whites do with the land?"

Hardeman shrugged. "They'll farm, or raise cattle."

420

Old Bear shook his head. "The land there is dry. The water is bitter. There are no trees and little grass."

Hardeman didn't argue the facts. "You've seen in other places how the whites dig ditches to bring water to dry land. Let them do that along the Platte. There are men who will bring cattle or try to farm anywhere they feel safe from attack by Indians. Give them the land along the Holy Road so they feel safe there. This country here is better for the Lakota and Cheyenne."

Little Wolf nodded. "And when the country there is full of whites, they will look here and they will say, 'That land looks good to me,' and they will wish to take it away."

There it was. Someone had seen the weakness. How could even a new treaty erase that fear?

"They'll do that right enough," Bat observed in English, and Hardeman was surprised to hear the mountain man speak for himself. For what seemed like hours, Bat had said nothing except to translate the words of others; his voice had been the voices of Crazy Horse and Little Wolf and Sitting Bull and each of the others, conveying both their words and emotions; now there was a triumphant spark in his eye as he added his own thoughts to the council for the first time. "Leastways if it's still 'unceded Injun territory' like it is now, they'll try to get it for sure. To a white man, 'unceded' means he ain't got 'round to takin' it yet." He stroked his beard thoughtfully. "'Course now, it'd be a mite harder to steal if'n it was reservation land all official and proper. Say it was called the Western Sioux Reservation, and say in exchange for what you reckon we oughta give the white man, he give us one thing a heap o' folks been wantin' fer a long time. Say they build us an agency in this country, a reservation post where we can trade peaceful-like without goin' off to the Red Cloud Agency or clear to the Missouri."

Without waiting for a reply from Hardeman, Bat repeated his proposal in Lakota to the councillors, who received it with a rising buzz of approval. Men spoke to their neighbors, nodding, and in the inner circle Hawk Chaser smiled and said a few words to Blackbird, who had followed the proceedings raptly with eyes and ears, never making a sound. Even Standing Eagle looked pleased.

When quiet returned, Crazy Horse spoke to Hardeman, and it seemed he might be suppressing a new excitement. "Many times we have asked for an agency here, but it must not be on the Powder River or anywhere in the middle of our country. Always before, when the *washichun* build a trader fort, soon the bluecoats come with their guns. If there is to be an agency for us, it must be on the Yellowstone. The whites may bring their fireboats with goods to trade, but the agency must be there, at the edge of our land, not in the middle."

The council expressed approval of these conditions and Hardeman fought to remain outwardly calm. Why not? An agency might be just what was needed to seal the bargain and make it stick with both sides. The whites would know that the former hostiles were being closely watched, and with the northern part of the Powder River country a proper reservation, the western bands might keep some of the land they cherished most. Crook could make it work! He would see where the road to peace lay: not in demanding that all the hostiles go to Dakota, to give up the Black Hills and everything else they held dear, but by offering the one thing the Indians wanted above all else—part of the Powder River country—and getting in return not only the Black Hills gold but an end of opposition to the Yellowstone railroad and a gift of land along the Platte into the bargain! Such an exchange might appear lopsided enough to please even the greediest whites.

One by one each pair of eyes in the lodge came to rest on the solid figure of Sitting Bull. It was time for his decision. The bargaining had gone ahead as if the Hunkpapa had already smoked Sun Horse's pipe, which still rested cold in his hands; Crazy Horse had agreed to the peace man's request, although there was no pipe for him, but without the cooperation of Sitting Bull, all the talk might be for naught.

With deliberate slowness, Sitting Bull turned to look at Standing Eagle. "Sun Horse asks me to hold back my young men and stay at peace if Three Stars will leave our country now. Is that all he asks?" Before binding himself to grant a favor that was asked by the sending of a pipe, a man naturally wished to know the exact nature of the terms.

Standing Eagle cast a short glance at Bat Putnam before answering, but as the war leader began to talk, Bat put his words faithfully into English for Hardeman. There could be no question of keeping back anything now. Hardeman had contributed as much as anyone to the success of the council. He had brought Crazy Horse into the bargain, and if anything would convince Sitting Bull, that would do it. The scout deserved to know the whole truth of what was going on.

"Sun Horse asks that the seven council fires of the Lakota meet in the Moon of Fat Calves, together with our friends the Shahíyela and Arapaho. He asks Sitting Bull to join in calling for this great gathering, where my father will speak to the headmen of all the bands."

"What will Sun Horse say to the council?" Sitting Bull asked softly.

"He will speak for peace between white and Lakota," Standing Eagle replied. "Surely, my father says, all the Lakota gathered together are strong enough to make a peace with the *washíchun*, one that includes our country here." He hesitated for a moment and then continued. "If Three Stars will take my father's pipe and agree to return in summer to talk of peace, I too will speak to the council. I will ask them to give the whites the gold from *Paha Sapa* and the land along the Platte, and to let them make their iron road on the Yellowstone in the land of the *Kanghí*."

Throughout the lodge there were murmurs of approval. If the terms reached here today could win over the angry war leader of the Sun Band, they were fair indeed.

Silence returned, and once again all attention was on Sitting Bull, but he did not acknowledge it. For a long time he sat staring into the fire. Just when it seemed that Little Wolf might speak to the Hunkpapa, Sitting Bull moved. In his careful way he reached out and took a burning stick from the fire. He blew out the flame and touched the glowing end to the bowl of the pipe that he had held for so long in his hands. He puffed once, twice, then drew in a little smoke and let it out at once, watching it as it rose up and dispersed in the updraft from the fire. The others watched it too, for they knew that the smoke taken through this pipe, or any pipe so consecrated, had the force of a prayer.

The quiet in the lodge was complete but for the sounds of the fire. With the measured movements of ceremony, Sitting Bull offered the pipe to the west, the north, the east and the south; he raised it high toward the heavens, then touched it to the earth. "My friends," he said, "I accept the pipe sent by Sun Horse. If Three Stars takes his soldiers and goes out of our country I will keep the peace until the great council. I will send a pipe among the bands and ask that all come together in the Moon of Fat Calves, which the whites call *June* and my people call the Prairie-Turnip Moon." He looked at the faces around him, wishing none to misunderstand. "I do this because my cousin Sun Horse is a man to respect, a man of peace. It may be that by sending this pipe here today he has already set us on the path to a peace that will last. It may be that the whites will take what we offer and leave us alone, here in our own country. I too want peace, but I will not sell our country here. The bones of my fathers lie among these hills, and before I give this country to the whites, my own bones will join them." The sounds of agreement filled the lodge again and Two Moons and Little Wolf and He Dog gave their own approval to Sitting Bull's words of defiance. It seemed that the councillors had found not only the terms to present to Crook, but a new strength as well, born of this gathering. When the voices died away, Sitting Bull continued. "In the hoop of the nation I will make the Sun Dance to ask for power to help my people. After the Sun Dance the great council will meet, and when it has ended, then we will meet with Three Stars and the men from *Washington*."

Once more the Hunkpapa holy man touched the glowing brand to the pipe and puffed, and then he handed it to the man on his left, sending it sunwise around the inner circle. As the pipe was passed, the smoke rose into the air, mixing with the smoke of the council fire and finally wafting out the smoke hole at the peak of the lodge. It rose into the sky to signify that each man who smoked was witness to what had been said, joined in a spiritual commitment to the promises made here today.

TWENTY-EIGHT

The council had taken up the greater part of the day. When it ended at last, some men remained around the large fire, talking among themselves, but finally even they left the lodge and stepped into the bleak light of late afternoon. The clouds were breaking and the air was turning colder, but there was no promise of a general improvement of the weather. The winds still gusted fitfully and to the west a new bank of clouds loomed high, cutting off the light of the sinking sun.

Here and there about the village, men and women were grouped around individual councillors to hear what had been said and decided in the long meeting. Beyond the central cluster of lodges, Sitting Bull and his men were already mounted on fresh horses given them by Two Moons. Ordinarily the visitors would have accepted the hospitality of a friendly camp; as it was, they would travel in the dark of what promised to be a bitter cold night. Sitting Bull wished to return to his own band without delay. When he left the Powder to make for Chalk Buttes, his young men would continue down the river to spread the news of today's council and to warn the villages there to keep watch for Three Stars and his soldiers. No one wanted to risk war now, just as the hope of a strong peace was born.

Crazy Horse too would leave soon. He had lingered for a time in the council lodge, talking to He Dog, but now he was at the bottom of the camp among the Oglala lodges, changing his saddle over to the horse He Dog had given him in exchange for his own tired mount. Soon he would be gone off to the southeast, riding alone.

There was a clatter of hooves as Sitting Bull and his party set off. Bat Putnam waved a last farewell to his son and watched until the riders were across the river and on their way; then he turned and rejoined the rest of the pipe carriers, who stood in a group near Two Moons' tipi.

"You reckon Three Stars will talk turkey?" Standing Eagle asked Hardeman.

"Not all white men are fools," Hardeman replied, trying to sound hopeful. He couldn't let the others suspect what he was thinking. Stay hopeful and keep calm, that was his best chance now. "They're bullheaded, but not all fools. There was strong talk here this afternoon. He'll listen."

"Mebbe," Bat said. "Most white folks don't put much stock in Injun talk. They'll just go on to get what they want, regardless."

"Crook wants peace. If the whites stick to that order pushing all the hunting bands to Dakota, there'll be a war."

424

"That's truth." Standing Eagle grinned. "This coon smells the war paint." He seemed to think it was a pretty good smell.

Two Moons passed by and stopped to say a few words to Standing Eagle before going on towards his lodge.

"He invites us to come eat," Bat said.

Hardeman smiled in spite of himself. "I could have guessed that. They don't let a person work up much of a hunger."

"A man gets honor by feeding his guests." Bat grinned.

"Do this child good to fill his belly," Standing Eagle said. "We'll have a long day tomorrow, I'm thinkin'." He started off after Two Moons and the others followed along; you ate when the opportunity presented itself, for you could never be sure when you might eat again.

The pipe carriers would not leave the Cheyenne village until morning. Darkness was only an hour or two away and there was no reasonable cause to rush off into the gathering night, not when the whole countryside would be alive with sharp eyes by morning, all watching for Crook and his cavalry. The pipe carriers would be accompanied by Cheyenne riders and some of He Dog's Oglalas, to keep them in touch with the scouts from the Powder River villages and bring word to the messengers as soon as Three Stars was found.

Hardeman couldn't wait until morning, but as the daylight waned and the night gathered force, the snow creaking beneath the feet of those who moved about the camp, it seemed to him that not only Hawk Chaser but Standing Eagle and Little Hand and even Bat Putnam watched his every move. When they had all eaten their fill and smoked and talked for a time with their host, Hardeman stretched and yawned and said he guessed he would turn in, and at this Standing Eagle was suddenly very tired and he rose to accompany Hardeman to Kills Fox's lodge, where Blackbird was already asleep and the Cheyenne were preparing to go to their robes. As the fire burned down and the lodge darkened, Hardeman let his breathing become deep and long as he listened for Standing Eagle's familiar snoring, but it didn't come. He waited for what he thought was an hour or more and then he raised himself on one elbow.

By the dull red glow of the fire he saw Standing Eagle's eyes open. Hardeman nodded and smiled, as if he couldn't sleep, and remained for a time with his head propped on one arm, watching the glowing coals. Finally he lay back and pretended to sleep, but he sensed Standing Eagle's wakefulness. He decided that there would be no getting away tonight and he tried to doze off, but his mind would grant him no rest and in the middle of the night, long before dawn, he heard the sounds of horsemen entering camp.

In moments there was movement in the lodge. Kills Fox put a few sticks on the fire to make light and Hardeman wondered if the Cheyenne too had been feigning sleep. Kills Fox's family was awake, and only Blackbird remained unaware of the movements both inside the lodge and without.

"Big party, sounds like," Hardeman said softly, pulling on his boots.

"Twenty horses or more, I make it," Standing Eagle said as he threw back his robes and sat up. "Hunters comin' home, I reckon. They had a party out."

There was an undercurrent of excitement in the voices that could be heard from beyond the lodge. Kills Fox slipped into his winter moccasins and pulled a heavy robe around him, then stepped through the entrance with Hardeman and Standing Eagle close on his heels.

In the center of camp, women were already bringing fire from their lodges and adding new sticks to make a blaze. The men from Kills Fox's lodge encountered Bat, Hawk Chaser and Little Hand in company with Two Moons, all moving toward the fire. Bat glanced at the dark sky overhead.

"Solid cloud," he said. "Dark's a white man's soul. 'Scuse the expression." He smiled, and Hardeman could see the mountain man's teeth in the gloom.

Men from many lodges were gathered around a group of Cheyenne horsemen near the growing bonfire. A rime of ice coated the hairs of the horses' noses and the sweat was frozen to their flanks. They had been ridden hard. Already, young men were leading some of the horses away to be unsaddled and turned out with the rest. Some cuts of buffalo and the carcasses of three deer were unpacked from behind the saddles and carried off.

"They been huntin' the land between the Tongue and the Powder," Bat said when he had listened to the talk for a time. "Two o' their boys seen Crook."

"Where?!" Hardeman was buttoning his St. Paul coat against the cutting cold and now he slipped his hands quickly back into his heavy fleece-lined gloves, flexing fingers that had grown stiff from the chill in a few short moments.

"There ain't no rush. They was headed east, then hit a crick at sundown and turned north to the Yellowstone. Otter Crick, I make it. Thirty miles off and headed the wrong way. There ain't no villages up there."

"What time do you make it?" Hardeman asked.

"Oh, 'bout a good snooze to first light, Injun time. White man time, some past midnight, I reckon."

"We put out at first light, we'll find 'em by 'n' by," Standing Eagle said.

"Suits me." Hardeman wrapped his arms around himself and shivered. "Too cold to put out now." He turned back toward Kills Fox's lodge. His shoulders were hunched against the cold and he shuffled along like a man still half asleep and anxious to get back to bed. He did not look back until he reached the lodge. As he hoped, Bat and the others had remained with the hunters to hear more of what they had to say. With luck the talk would go on for some time, in one lodge or another. They might even sit down with Two Moons and make a formal report on the hunt and what the scouts had seen. Half the camp was awake now.

Hardeman's guns were inside the tipi, all except his Colt, which he had stuck into his waistband when he arose. He had slept fully clothed and had put on his hat and jacket and St. Paul coat before stepping outside, but his saddlebags were in the lodge with his rifles. The cardigan and extra cartridges and other odds and ends would have to be left behind. He couldn't risk going inside, where Kills Fox's wife and children were awake.

He moved around the lodge and slipped into the cottonwoods that surrounded

426

the cluster of tipis. Some light came from the cloudy sky now, brighter when the clouds thinned in the east, and once he caught a brief glimpse of the waning moon rising there over the hills across the river. He had no trouble making his way among the trees to the horses. The pipe carriers' mounts had been cut out of the herd the evening before, and were tethered close to camp. The saddles were in an unoccupied lodge nearby, used to store bales of buffalo hides and dried meat and kegs of gunpowder placed atop the hides so the powder would stay dry.

In moments he had his roan bridled and saddled. Before mounting, he turned the other horses loose and watched them amble off toward the river. After drinking they would drift upstream to the main herd.

Once on his own horse's back, Hardeman leaned low and guided the animal downriver at a slow walk. To a casual observer, the horse might seem to be moving at random, looking for forage.

His chance had come along and he had taken it. He might not get much of a lead, but a man traveling alone at night was hard to find. If he got clear of the village safely, he could be anywhere by morning.

The clouds were thickening now and the way was dark and difficult. Hardeman gave the roan his head and kept the river on his right. While he was still within hearing of the village he strained to catch any alarm, but none came. On a night as cold as this even the sentries stayed close to the warmth of the lodge fires.

When he judged it safe, Hardeman straightened in the saddle and urged the horse into a trot. Bat had said there was a trail that left the Powder some miles north of the Cheyenne camp, one that avoided the roughest land due west of the village. The going was faster that way, Bat said, and the pipe carriers had planned to take that route in the morning. The cross-country trail went straight to Otter Creek, heading west and a little north. Even if Crook broke camp an hour after dawn, Hardeman would be nearly upon him by then.

When he had ridden for perhaps an hour he saw a fork to the left and took it, following the new trail up a long shallow ravine and into the hills beyond. Once up out of the confinement of the Powder River bottom and alone in the open country, his fear of pursuit diminished and he gave most of his attention to what lay before him. His senses were fully alert, his eyes seeking anything the gray-shrouded night would reveal. He was glad to be on the move again, using old familiar skills to find the way and follow it. As the moon rose higher above the clouds the night brightened somewhat, allowing him to move faster, alternating between a trot and a lope, and the country fell away behind him.

At the moment when Standing Eagle had told Sitting Bull of the call for a great summer council, Hardeman's brief surge of hope had died like a lone candle blown out by a storm wind and he had known at once what he must do. Why hadn't they told him, Sun Horse or Bat or one of the others?! If he had known, he could have tried to make them see the fatal folly of the notion, and maybe talked them out of it.

It was plain why they had kept the knowledge from him. They knew the whites feared any gathering of the tribes, but they didn't see just how strong and deep

427

that fear ran. In the camps of the Sioux and their allies, counting the reservation bands and those scattered across the Powder River country, there might be as many as ten thousand men of fighting age, while the entire army of the United States, stretched thin across a vast continent, numbered only twenty-five thousand. After a generation of bloodshed, the whites saw in any massing of the tribes but one possible consequence: the long-feared uprising that might overwhelm the sparsely garrisoned frontier posts and set back a final peace for years. Hardeman had heard these fears voiced during the long winter months in Kansas by towns-people and farmers, citizens and soldiers. Now, with such a gathering in the offing, the whites would howl for war, and any talk of new peace negotiations would be swept away like thistledown in a thunderstorm.

And on the Indian side it was far from certain that the terms agreed upon at the council in Two Moons' camp would survive once the bands were assembled in all their strength. The council had foreshadowed the change that might come about then—the defiance growing stronger and stronger as one man after another recalled the history of injustice at the hands of the whites and stated his willingness to fight before he would yield anything more. Sun Horse would speak for peace and some like Two Moons might support him, but others would speak as well, men who were hot for war, and in the end it might not be the words in council that would decide them, but the sight of hundreds, maybe thousands of lodges arrayed along some stream, the grass tall for the pony herds and the young men feeling the flow of new life and courage that all young men felt in springtime. They would imagine themselves invincible. "Let the *washichun* come," they would say. "Let them bring as many soldiers as they wish. We will fight them!" The terms from yesterday's council would grow in proportion to the Indians' confidence until the demands were as unreasonable as those of the whites; until there was nothing left to say and only war remained.

Even if by some miracle the great union of the tribes did not result in war, the whites would never accept any new treaty that sprang from such a gathering. It would seem that the Indians were dictating terms from a position of overwhelming strength, and no matter how reasonable the terms might be, the white man's pride would make him refuse any settlement offered in such conditions.

No, there could be no summer council for the Sioux. If fighting were to be prevented, the peace must come now, swiftly and with no further talk, and Hardeman could see only one way to bring it about, using the same tactics by which he had originally planned to force a bloodless surrender on Sun Horse if all else failed, only now the prize would be the most famous of the hostile chiefs. With Sitting Bull taken to Dakota unharmed, there might be no summer gathering after all, and then there was a chance to salvage some of the good from the council at Two Moons' village. White politicians had been known to listen to a general who brought peace to a troubled region. If Crook could force a peace on the north plains while the country was still in the grip of winter, there was a chance that the things Crook believed in could be implemented here as they had been in the deserts of Apachería—justice for the Indian; promises made and promises kept. It would mean night marches and great caution if Crook's column were to reach Chalk Buttes and locate Sitting Bull's camp without being discovered by the hostile scouts. There was much risk in the plan, but nothing was gained without risk. On the way, Hardeman would tell Crook what had taken place at Two Moons' council, what had been said by Sitting Bull and Crazy Horse and the others. Without new fighting and bloodshed to arouse a new wave of hostility, Crook might persuade the men in Washington to be magnanimous in victory by granting some of what the Sioux asked, including a western Sioux reservation and an agency on the Yellowstone. With luck, and with white fears calmed by a victory, the terms reached in the council still might come to pass, although at the point of a gun.

The trail was following down the bed of a frozen creek and now the curving swale widened abruptly and ended, opening into the valley of a larger stream, which Hardeman guessed must be Otter Creek. Here the trail left the little rivulet and made straight for the larger watercourse. The wind had dropped and a few patches of moonlight shone through the clouds. As he neared the banks of the creek, Hardeman saw that the trail met a larger pathway there and he reined in sharply, looking to left and right at a swath of fresh tracks in the shallow snow.

He dismounted and led his horse along, his eyes on the ground, until he found what he sought. He squatted beside a dark clump on the trail and with his gloved hand he picked up a round ball of frozen horse manure. It seemed solid enough, but as he applied more force it suddenly broke and fell apart in his hand. He removed a glove and tested the road apple with his bare finger to be sure. The center was not frozen.

How long would it take horse dung to freeze solid on a night like this? One hour? Two? Not more than that. The clumps of droppings were scattered over a distance of fifteen or twenty feet. The horse was ridden. A horse on its own would stop to move its bowels.

Someone had passed this way recently. The Cheyenne hunting party? They had been only thirty; this group was larger, fifty or a hundred or more. It was hard to say how many, after a certain number of horses had passed along in a narrow row. It might have been a band of Sioux—Hunkpapas or Oglalas returning to another camp after a day of hunting. . . .

The new snow had been scattered by the many hooves and the older snow beneath had been broken up until it was as soft as sand; it shifted about underfoot and did not hold tracks well, but here and there on the edges of the trail were a few clear imprints. Hardeman took from the pocket of his jacket the tin box that contained his sulphur matches. He struck a light and saw the sharp outline of a shod hoof. Captured American horses?

A sudden fear chilled him. He returned to the dung and broke open another partially frozen dropping. He lit a second match and his fear was confirmed. The dung was not composed solely of digested grass. In the soft center of the road apple were the hulls of oats.

429

TWENTY-NINE

A weary soldier leaned against his horse to rest. Gradually his body relaxed and he dropped into the snow at the animal's feet, but the fall did not wake him. A form appeared out of the gloom of the ravine and leaned over the exhausted trooper.

"Luttner! Get up, man! You'll freeze to death!" Lieutenant Whitcomb shook the sleeping private harshly and hauled him to his feet. "Luttner? Do you hear me? You've got to stay awake! Here, Private Gray, Donnelly, keep an eye on him."

"We'll watch him, Mr. Reb," Gray said softly. "Come on, Heinie, snap out of it. There's a good fellow."

"Quietly, Mr. Reb, we don't want to advertise our presence." Whitcomb heard Corwin's voice before he saw his commander coming along the line. Somewhere above the clouds a half-moon shone down, but little of its light managed to penetrate the frozen gulch where the expedition had halted an hour before to allow the scouts to survey the land in front. Whitcomb thought the warning ridiculous. The horses were making enough noise to wake the dead, stamping and snorting from thirst. They had had nothing to drink since the previous afternoon. All the water encountered on the night march had been locked away under thick ice, and the axes were back with the cooks and the pack train.

"I'll be at the head of the column for a few moments," Corwin said. "See that the men are kept awake, but do it quietly."

"Yes, sir." Whitcomb continued on his way along the length of the troop, encountering first Dupré and then McCaslin. Sergeants Polachek and Duggan were on the move too. It seemed that a man fell to the ground every few moments only to be hauled to his feet by his comrades or one of his superiors.

After what had seemed an interminable delay at the stopping place of the afternoon before, the company officers had finally been summoned to the headquarters fire and there were given their instructions by General Crook. Colonel Reynolds and six companies had been detailed to leave at once on a forced march through the night. The scouts had discovered the back trail of the two Indian braves and were confident they could follow it to the hostile village. Fifteen scouts led by Big Bat, Little Bat and Frank Grouard had been sent along to guide the expedition.

They had marched for nine hours up the drainage of the winding creek, through rugged hill country frozen as solid as glass and just as treacherous under foot. The night had been pitch-dark until the waning moon rose at last; the clouds were broken for a time but then they regathered to drop new showers of snow on the soldiers, and even with the dim light afforded by the moon the going had been slow. The ground was cut everywhere with ravines, each of which had to be scouted on foot before a crossing was attempted. The men had traveled under the constant threat of being thrown when they were mounted or of losing their own footing when they led their horses over the worst obstacles. Miraculously, neither man nor horse had been seriously injured, but there had been many falls.

As the night lengthened, the temperature had plunged, and now, in the frigid arroyo, the waiting was almost unendurable, but few of the men complained. The entire campaign up to this moment, the sixteen days of marching through storms and sleeping through sub-zero nights, had had but a single goal — to launch a striking force against the hostiles. And now that force was on its way, following a recent trail, ready to do battle at a moment's notice. They were unencumbered by packers or mules or extra equipment. Each man carried the clothing he wore and a lunch, nothing more. Even the pistols had been left with the companies that remained behind. Only Captain Egan's Company K still had their Army Colts, for they would lead the charge when the Indian village was found.

Whitcomb thanked his lucky stars that E Troop hd been one of the companies chosen for the night march. The four companies that had stayed with General Crook would start in the morning by a direct route for the juncture of the Powder and Lodgepole Creek, where the command would reunite within twenty-four hours, it was hoped. If there was to be a battle, they would miss it.

He stumbled on the rough ground and nearly fell, but someone caught his arm.

"Good God, Ham, have a care." It was John Bourke.

"Thanks, John. I haven't much feeling left in my feet, I'm afraid." He hopped from one foot to the other, hoping to stimulate the circulation.

"We're all having tough going. You'll see it through."

"I should say both horses and men are doing very well," said another voice, and Whitcomb made out Strahorn, the newspaperman, behind Bourke. Crook's aide was unattached, sent along on the march at his own request, free to go where he wished; he and Strahorn and Hospital Steward Bryan had formed a compact to stay close to one another and to be in the thick of the action if a fight came about. Throughout the night they had traveled in company with E Troop. "This is a difficult march under difficult circumstances," Strahorn said. "Your first campaign is turning out to be more than you bargained for, Mr. Reb."

"Not at all, Mr. Strahorn," Whitcomb replied with what he hoped was a convincing nonchalance. "It's everything I expected."

"Perhaps Mr. Bourke has seen worse?"

"I have marched about Arizona on nights just as dark, Robert, but none as cold as this."

From the head of the ravine a general rustling of equipment and a renewed stamping from the horses revealed that the waiting was over at last and the command was getting under way. The three men lost no time in reaching the head of the troop, where Steward Bryan was holding Bourke's and Strahorn's mounts. As they rose out of the ravine, following Company K, they found Captain Egan waiting there beside Lieutenant Corwin, and the two troop commanders fell in beside them. There had been no order to mount and the men were glad to walk for a time to stir some warmth into their limbs.

Egan was swinging his arms and bouncing about as he walked, and his teeth chattered as he spoke. "This is it, John," he said to Bourke. "A village, the scouts say."

"Where?! How far?"

"Oh, they haven't found it yet, but they will. Those two bucks we've been tracking are ahead of us now. Fresh tracks came in on their back trail and they joined up with some of their friends. Twenty or thirty of them, Grouard says, a big hunting party, all heading for home. 'Are you sure, Frank?' Reynolds asks. He's a cautious bastard, John, and you can tell Crook that for me when you see him. I wish old George was here. Anyway, Big Bat spits in the snow and he says 'You bet on it, General. Huntin' party goes out, they split up in threes and fours. When they come back together, they're makin' fer the lodge fires.'" Egan's mimicry of the scout's speech was close to perfect.

Being on the move once again quieted the horses, although they continued to shake their heads and snort, both from excitement and thirst. The gray horses of K Troop looked like ghostly shadows in the darkness, while E Troop's bays were all but invisible. Whitcomb's senses were sharpened by the anticipation of battle and the fear of premature discovery, and the rattle of the bridles and the whispered soothings of the troopers seemed to him a cacophony that could not fail to alert the hostiles, if any were near.

The attack force appeared to be on the apex of the entire region, having reached the headwaters of the creek they had followed all night and passed at last into another drainage that sloped away to the east. If anything, the land ahead of them was rougher than that behind. For an hour they stumbled along in silence and then Corwin raised a hand and pointed to the front. "Look there, Teddy. That's the bluffs of the Powder. I'll bet four bits."

"No, I think you're right. Damn, it's getting light already."

Not far ahead there was a perceptible bulging of the horizon. Between the land and the cloud bank above, a thin band of sky was visible, and it seemed to glow. The moon was high overhead and it could not account for the hint of brightness in the east. Dawn was approaching, and Whitcomb imagined that he knew what the two troop commanders must be thinking. If the scouts failed to find the end of the hunters' trail soon, the chance for a dawn attack would be lost. There could be no thought of a daylight assault unless conditions were perfect for achieving surprise; lacking that, the column would have to go to ground. Could the six companies of cavalry still fight effectively after a cold day in hiding with nothing but jerky and hardtack to eat? The horses needed water badly, and heavy demands had been put on them since the ration of grain they had received before parting company with Crook and the others. They had no large reserves of strength. Water and a day of rest might change that, but no fires could be made to melt snow and ice for drinking water, not this close to the hostiles.

Whitcomb could feel his heart pounding in his chest and he breathed deeply of the cold air to calm himself. There was nothing he could do to speed the column along, nothing to conjure an Indian village up out of the frozen ground.

But if there were a camp anywhere along the stretch of the Powder that lay just ahead, shouldn't there be a sign of smoke against the first light in the east? . . . Yes!

"John! Look there!" He nudged Bourke, who was walking beside him.

Bourke had been half asleep on his feet but now he jolted fully awake. Directly ahead, where Whitcomb was pointing, there was a dense column of smoke that had been hidden until now by a dark cloud far on the horizon. Others had seen it too, for the column halted now and Bourke and Whitcomb could make out the horseborne figures of several scouts moving off to investigate.

While the expediton waited once more, excited whispers flew up and down the column, but Bourke held himself apart from the others, watching the place where the scouts had disappeared, praying that they would find a village so General Crook's hopes for the attack force might be realized.

"Gentlemen," Crook had said once the company officers were gathered around him the afternoon before on the banks of the icebound creek. "I hope those Indians have taken the bait and believe we are proceeding towards the Yellowstone with no interest in pursuing them. But pursuing them is precisely my intention. The scouts have found their back trail and Frank is confident he can follow it in the dark." Here he had looked at the swarthy scout and Grouard had nodded, a little cautiously it had seemed to Bourke.

"The expediton will consist of the First, Third and Fifth Battalions," Crook had continued. "General Reynolds will be in command."

Bourke had been stunned. In each department where he had been stationed, George Crook was known as a commander who led his men into battle personally. He was always in the front, never in the rear. In Arizona he had eaten as much trail dust and smelled as much powder burned in anger as any man in the department. There could be only one explanation, Bourke had decided; Crook was giving Colonel J. J. Reynolds a chance to vindicate himself and burnish his reputation by making a good showing here. And it was not as if Crook himself would be safely in the rear; with only Hawley's and Dewees' four companies left to him he would have to protect the pack train, which would be a great temptation to any other hostiles who might happen upon the reduced command. He would have to make his way with that small force across some fifty miles of broken country to the appointed rendezvous with the attack force. But for Reynolds' sake he had given up the chance to be in at the kill.

When the officers' council was done, Bourke had asked Crook's permission to go with Reynolds and it had been granted at once. No doubt the general would be glad to hear a detailed report on the action, if any, and how Reynolds conducted himself throughout, although no such request had been made. Crook did not use Bourke as so many lesser men employed their aides, to follow them about like servants, awaiting any indication of their masters' pleasure. Bourke served as an extra pair of eyes and ears, an extension of his general, to be where he could not and to learn what the presence of a general officer would have prevented learning.

Already he had seen that Crook's faith in his scouts was justified. More than once during the night Grouard and the others had had to get down on their hands and knees to follow the faint signs, and more than once the trail had been lost, but never for long. They had proved themselves the equals of any scouts Bourke had known in Arizona, and the smoke rising so plainly in the east gave every indication that they had led Reynolds to the long-hoped-for goal: an unsuspecting village of hostiles.

Like those around him, Bourke was bitterly disappointed when the scouts returned.

"Coal measure!" came the whispered word. "Burning coal!"

The disappointment was general as the column got under way once more. They mounted their horses now and set off at a faster pace.

"I don't know if I can stand another false alarm like that," Whitcomb muttered.

"It's going to ruin my story if the whole campaign turns out to be a false alarm," said Strahorn.

They passed near the burning coal deposit and regarded the thick black smoke with hostile glances. It was not the first one they had seen and they felt they should have known better than to be taken in. They smelled the burning lignite and there seemed to be a sulphurous taint to the smoke, like a suggestion of hellfire. The Montana and Wyoming countryside abounded with such outcroppings, a surprising number of them on fire, set alight by some savage's campfire or by lightning. How long did they burn? Bourke wondered idly. Until they consumed the coal, or enough of it to deny air to the fire. The scouts said that one bed they had passed had burned for more than forty years.

The cloudy skies were brightening now and it was apparent that dawn was not far off, but scarcely a quarter of an hour later the alarm came again, "Smoke ahead!" and once again the cavalrymen came fully alert in an instant, all their senses straining to gather whatever they might have missed in a moment's inattention. The column halted and the three rearmost troops were brought up beside those in front so they stood in a double column, and all the officers were ordered to join Colonel Reynolds as he waited for the scouts to return.

"I think we will not be disappointed this time, gentlemen," he said. "Smell the air."

They did, and it was not the burning of coal they recognized, but wood-smoke. When the scouts returned, appearing silently out of the misty air, Frank Grouard was grinning.

434

"Big village, Colonel! Plenty horses! Down in the bottom. We find a way down, one here, one there."

He pointed, and aided by the other scouts, he conveyed what they had learned. Two rocky gorges led down to the river, hundreds of feet below. One emerged south of the village, they believed, and the other to the north. The village was west of the Powder, between the frozen stream and the mesa on which the command now stood. Its location had had to be judged by the situation of the large pony herds on the bottomland, but there was no doubt that a village was there and that it was a large one.

"We shall have to move without delay, gentlemen," Reynolds said after hearing the scouts out, and he gave his orders quickly. Captain Henry Noyes's Third Battalion, composed of his Company I and Egan's K Troop, would descend the southern gorge, led by Big and Little Bat and three other scouts. They would attack from that side as soon as they reached the bottom, with Egan's gray-horse company charging the village while Noyes himself secured the horse herd and drove it away upstream. Capturing the Indian horses and leaving the warriors afoot was a vital part of the scheme. Meanwhile, Captain Moore's Fifth Battalion, after being led to the valley floor by Frank Grouard and Louis Richaud, would advance from the bottom of the northern ravine to prevent escape in that direction; thus Moore would be the anvil against which Egan's hammer would strike. Mills's and Corwin's companies, the First Battalion, were to follow behind Moore and be kept in reserve, to be used as needed as the battle developed. Both of these battalions would lead their horses as far as possible and leave them in a safe location, going the rest of the way on foot. Reynolds was to accompany Moore and Mills; he wished Noyes and Egan Godspeed with a firm handshake to each one.

"Well, Ham old fellow, this is where we part company, I'm afraid," Bourke said to Whitcomb. "Mr. Strahorn, Steward Bryan, I propose we accompany Captain Egan."

"You lucky bastard!" said Whitcomb, but he was grinning and he shook Bourke's hand fervently.

"It's the luck of the Irish, boyo. Happy Saint Paddy's day!" With a farewell wave, Bourke moved to join Egan, whose soldiers were already starting off behind Noyes's company. With Strahorn and Bryan close on his heels he joined Egan at the head of K Troop and in a short time the other elements of the attack force were left behind.

When the two companies reached the boulder-strewn defile that the guides had chosen for the descent, Bourke was aghast. It seemed impossible that men, let alone horses, could make their way down the eroded gorge, which was cluttered with fallen trees and undergrowth. Leading their mounts, the battalion entered the gorge in single file and immediately their progress was marked by the snapping of twigs and limbs as the guides forced a way through the brush. Saddles creaked in the cold and the men cursed as their horses stumbled repeatedly. Bourke winced at each stone overturned, every clatter of hoof against rock or frozen ground, but he soon ceased worrying about the noise and concentrated instead on getting himself to the bottom in one piece. There were frequent halts as one horse at a time was helped past the worst obstacles, and when the column emerged at last into a gentle vale that sloped away to the valley floor, the sky was bright overhead. The descent had taken more than an hour.

The vale was bordered on the left by an uneven ridge that intruded into the valley like an arm. Ahead, in the narrow width of valley bottom that was all they could see, there was no sign either of an Indian village or of the expected horse herd.

"Is this where we're supposed to be?" Noyes wondered aloud. Neither four years at West Point nor fifteen years of army service since then had erased his strong Maine accent.

Egan nodded to Big and Little Bat. "You boys have a look-see over that ridge."

The two scouts mounted their horses and raced off to a low saddle that was fringed with pines. They were out of sight for only a few moments and when they returned they brought shocking news. "We ain't nowhere close to the village, Cap'n," Big Bat said to Noyes. "You best see for yourself. We can cross the ridge up yonder."

The battalion mounted, and followed the scouts over the saddle and into the much broader valley beyond, where they halted again. To their right was the Powder. Ahead of them lay a wide benchland divided roughly in two by a small creek that flowed from the west. Beyond the benchland, over a mile away, where the river swept close to steep, rugged bluffs that overlooked the valley, the peaks of many tipis were visible in a sizable stand of cottonwoods. Nearer at hand in the valley bottom, which was ten or twenty feet lower than the edge of the benchland, hundreds of ponies were grazing in plain view.

"My God, we've botched it!" Noyes exclaimed.

"Couldn't be helped, Cap'n," Big Bat said. "Frank, he reckoned the village was down about there." He pointed to the foot of the ridge behind them. "It was there, we'd be sittin' pretty."

"Look!" cried Bourke, pointing across the benchland. There, on the southern end of the bluffs, was a line of men on foot advancing toward the slopes overlooking the village. Below and behind these small figures was another group, probably Mills's command, descending the edge of the benchland beyond the creek. Noyes's battalion, which had confidently expected to be the first into battle, was in danger now of being the last.

"That must be Moore up on the bluff," Eagan said. "It looks like he's trying to work his way along to the north end of the village. He might still cut off their retreat."

"But the Indians will see him!" Strahorn objected.

"They can't yet but they will soon enough," said Egan. "The quicker we get into the village, the better." This last remark was directed at Noyes.

"You don't think the mix-up calls for any change of plan?" Noyes seemed perplexed by the discovery that Reynolds' plan of attack could not be executed as originally given.

"Good God, Henry!" Egan exploded. "We're the only ones who still have a chance to do what were supposed to! Let's get on with it!" He yanked his horse around and started off with his troop following behind, placing Noyes in the awkward position of hastening to overtake his nominal subordinate.

"These animals don't have much spunk left," Egan said to Bourke, reining in from a trot to a fast walk. "Damn the luck, anyway! I just pray to God we get close to that village before some young buck decides it's time for a look around the countryside."

In a double column the battalion crossed the benchland. Once down off the low ridge they were out of sight of the village, and the danger of sudden discovery lessened for a time. As they crossed the little creek they saw Mills's battalion emerge from a gully not far ahead, and Egan sent one of the scouts to tell Mills to hold back until the attack began, then to come in and support him from behind.

"I can't see Moore," said Bourke, searching the bluff that now rose close above them.

"I hope to hell he keeps out of sight until we get into the village," Egan muttered. "If the Indians see us now and set up a defense, we'll be in hot water."

The battalion was approaching the northern edge of the benchland, and once more the peaks of tipis could be seen among the cottonwoods on the river plain below. The scouts, who had been moving ahead of the column to watch for gullies that might impede its advance, now returned.

"Injuns wakin' up, Cap'n," said Little Bat. "Boys 're takin' the horses to water."

"Better yet," said Egan, pleased. "The ponies will be that much farther from the village. Where do we get down off this bench?"

"Go down here," Little Bat replied, gesturing to a gully nearby. "Ain't many trails good for horses up ahead."

"Dismount. Pass it back," Noyes called out in a soft voice as he swung out of his own saddle.

Like dominoes toppling in a row, the mounted men leaned over one by one and stepped to the ground. Overhead, two ravens floated on motionless wings and one of the birds croaked twice; otherwise the valley was silent but for the soft rush of the wind and the small stampings and whuffings of the horses.

Egan glanced at Noyes, who nodded. "You go ahead, Teddy. We'll follow you. I'll separate to the right when you form into line."

Egan moved part-way down the short column of troopers and addressed his company in a tone just loud enough for all to hear. "Once we're down below, mount up when I do. Forward by twos and left front into line on my signal.

437

Trot until we're seen. Buglers will then sound the charge, and forward at the gallop." He grinned. "From then on it's Murphy's saloon, boys. Don't be afraid to let them hear you coming."

As they descended the gully the soldiers were hidden from the village and when they gathered on the bottomland only a few tipis were visible at the edge of the cottonwoods. There was no movement there.

The scouts drew aside as the soldiers formed up by company. The attack was up to the troopers. For now, the scouts' job was done. Together with the men who had guided the other companies to the valley floor, they would join Colonels Stanton and Reynolds, to be reassigned as needed during the fighting.

"Good luck, John," Egan said to Bourke as he set his foot in his stirrup. As one the troop mounted behind him and the riders moved out two by two, straight toward the river. Bourke rode beside Egan, with Strahorn and Bryan right behind. When the company was formed in a straight column, Egan raised his arm and swung it to the left. In the space of a few heartbeats the troop had executed a letter-perfect left front into line, and the forty-seven horses and riders advanced in a company front, breaking into a trot. Behind them, Noyes's black-horse troop moved away from the gully in a column and swung off to the right, toward the pony herd. K Troop's grays strutted as they advanced, sensing the repressed excitement of their riders, but the line remained as straight as if they were on parade, and still, ahead of them, the village was silent.

CHAPTER
THIRTY

Blackbird came awake with a start. Daylight showed through the lodgeskins; the winds were gentle and the camp was quiet. It was early then, if the women were not yet up and about.

The fits of sweating that had kept him in a feverish haze for most of the day before were gone now and his leg no longer throbbed beneath the tight wrappings the Shahíyela *wapíye* had placed around the wound. He felt much better, and unusually alert.

What had wakened him? It was as if he had heard a distant calling or a strange sound, but everything was quiet; unnaturally so, it seemed.

That was it! He raised himself on his elbows to see the pallet where his father had slept each night since they had been in the Shahíyela camp. His father was gone! And so was his uncle Lodgepole and the *washíchun* Hardeman! All his life

Blackbird had slept with his father's soft snoring close at hand. He had been awakened not by a sound but by the absence of one so familiar he scarcely noticed it until it was gone.

He sat up and reached for his moccasins, grunting slightly as the movements awakened a pain deep in his leg. Ignoring the pain he struggled into the tall winter moccasins and laced them tightly.

A voice said something in Shahíyela and he saw that Kills Fox was awake.

"Where is my father?" Blackbird asked.

"The *washíchun* scout runs away," Kills Fox replied in crude Lakota. "He go to bring the horse soldiers, your father say. Your father, your *washíchun* uncle, Hawk Chaser, they go after him. They find him, they kill him."

The *washíchun* Hardeman a traitor? His father and Lodgepole gone? They had left him here! Blackbird struggled to his feet, but he fell back as pain shot through his leg.

"They come back for you!" Kills Fox said, motioning Blackbird to stay. "Stay here. Get better. They come back."

"I am the moccasin carrier!" Blackbird protested. He looked about desperately and saw the poles that had been used to carry his makeshift litter to the council lodge. He seized one and used it as a crutch to heave himself to his feet. If he could only get to his horse he might be able to ride. He threw his lionskin cape over his shoulders and struggled awkwardly to belt his robe around him.

Kills Fox's wife and children were awake now. The woman spoke to her husband, and although Blackbird could not understand her words, he knew by her tone and the concerned expression on her face that she was urging Kills Fox to make him stay.

Kills Fox merely shrugged in reply. The boy was not his son, nor even of his tribe. He was moccasin carrier to the Lakota messengers and he had his own responsibilities. It was not for Kills Fox to tell him what to do. He made a gesture wishing the boy well.

Blackbird smiled gratefully and with a few words of thanks he slipped out of the lodge.

It was well past sunrise but still the village slept. In winter there was no rush to leave the warmth of the buffalo robes. The day was cloudy and cold and there was a thin mist in the valley bottom. Blackbird shivered. He wondered how he would ever find his horse and then he remembered that the pipe carriers' horses had been taken to the bottom of the camp after the council of the day before, so the little band could leave early in the morning. He started hobbling in that direction, but even with the help of his makeshift crutch, pain shot through his wounded leg at every step. If the wound began to bleed he would grow weak, and what use would he be to his father then?

He saw a fur-clad youth riding among the tipis and he recognized him as Lakota, a nephew of He Dog. He waved to get the boy's attention.

"*Hau*, cousin! Will you take me to my horse? I have to go after my father and the other pipe carriers."

"You're Standing Eagle's son, aren't you? I'm glad your wound is better. Does it hurt much?"

"Not much," Blackbird lied. "Will you take me to my horse?"

"Come, I'll help you." The youth held out a hand and hoisted Blackbird up behind him. At once some of the pain left Blackbird's leg. Sitting on the horse was much better than walking.

"I'm going after our horses now," the youth said. "Many scouts are going out to watch for the bluecoats. My uncle He Dog is going with them."

"Bluecoats? Where are the bluecoats? Has someone seen them?"

"The hunters saw them. Didn't you hear?"

"I've been asleep since yesterday after the council."

"Shahíyela hunters came back in the night. They saw the bluecoats half a day's ride to the north, going toward the Yellowstone."

"Wait, you're going the wrong way! Our horses are over there." Blackbird pointed toward the downstream end of camp but the boy shook his head.

"The *washíchun* turned them loose. Your father and the others found their horses with the herd. I hope they catch the *washíchun* and come back with his scalp." The youth kicked the pony into a trot and Blackbird held on to the other boy, bouncing painfully. He felt an increased sense of urgency now. If the soldiers were going toward the Yellowstone there might be no immediate danger, but why had Hardeman gone off alone? Why hadn't he waited so the pipe carriers could all go together and take the pipe to Three Stars? Had the white scout really gone to betray them? Hardeman was his uncle Lodgepole's friend. "Not all white men are bad," Lodgepole had said to Blackbird one afternoon on the trail north, before the attack by the *Kanghí*. "This one has been like a *hunká*-father to your cousin, the One Who Stands Between the Worlds. He is a good man and he speaks the truth." But Blackbird remembered other words as well, words his father often said: "Do not go to the hilltop for water nor to a white man for the truth." It seemed his father was right.

There were a few other boys among the trees, gathering the horses to drive them to water, and Blackbird looked everywhere for the familiar coloring and three white moccasins of his own horse. The ponies moved among the plum bushes and cottonwoods, appearing and disappearing, and he began to fear that it would take all morning to find the sturdy pinto when suddenly he saw the half-white, half-black face that he knew so well.

"There he is! That one!"

"I see him. You go on foot and I'll bring him to you."

Blackbird slipped to the ground, forgetting his wound in his excitement and grunting as a jolt of pain reminded him. The Lakota youth trotted off, placing himself between Blackbird's horse and the others, guiding him out of the trees and away from the river.

As the pinto drew near Blackbird he caught the boy's scent and whickered softly. Blackbird said a few words to calm the animal and he stood still as the pinto stepped close to sniff his outstretched hand to see if it held some sweetgrass or perhaps some dried buffaloberries. The rawhide rein slipped easily over the pony's lower jaw and Blackbird fastened his braided war rope around the horse's middle. His injured leg would not grip the horse properly, but the war rope would hold him in place.

"Thank you, cousin," he said to the Lakota youth. He realized he didn't know the young man's name.

"Ride quickly!" the youth encouraged him. "Maybe you can count coup on the whiteman's body!" He trotted off after the other boys.

Blackbird tried to jump to his pony's back but his wounded leg buckled and he nearly fell. He needed something to stand on. He was in a wide, flat-bottomed wash that led from the base of the bluff to the river. It was deeper than the height of a man and twenty or thirty paces across. Not far away there was a short stump. He started toward it, supporting himself with one hand on the pony's withers. He realized now that he was thirsty and very hungry. In the village, smoke was puffing up from a few lodges as the women built up the fires. He thought of stopping to get a little *wasná* or jerky from Kills Fox's wife. But someone might ask where he was going. The scouting party might want him to wait and go with them, and he didn't want to wait for anyone. He was moccasin carrier for the Sun Band's pipe carriers and it was his duty to catch up with them as soon as he could. Worse yet, someone not as understanding as Kills Fox might insist that he remain in camp and not go out at all. The *akíchita* could keep a young man in camp if a scouting party was planned.

No, he would not risk stopping in the village. He would follow the broad channel to the bluff and ride around the back of the camp to the downstream end. He would find the pipe carriers' tracks and start out on their trail at once.

The thought of setting out alone frightened him a little, but he had been given another chance to prove himself a man and he must take every opportunity he got. Besides, there was really no reason to be afraid. Hadn't he saved the pipe carriers' horses? Hadn't he counted coup on a *Kanghí* enemy? And hadn't he sat in council with Sitting Bull and Little Wolf and Crazy Horse? The recollection of his recent deeds and the honors they had won him bolstered his courage and he felt himself well along the path to manhood.

He had nearly reached the stump when a fluttering in the corner of his eye caught his attention. He turned to see that the branches of an old cottonwood not far away were filled with black specks; here and there a head cocked or a wing flashed, revealing a bright red patch. The tree was alive with blackbirds. They were the first he had seen since autumn and their arrival was a sure sign of spring.

He felt a chill, and tightened the thong that held his robe belted at the waist. There was nothing springlike about the day. Riding would warm him. He climbed atop the stump and was about to mount his pony when he felt the chill again, not truly a chill of the body but more of the senses.

Taku shkanshkan. Something is moving.

It was as if he heard his grandfather's voice. How often had the old man told him to be aware of the motion of spirit power, of *shkán*, the life force that pervaded all things?

Taku shkanshkan, Sun Horse said whenever Blackbird tried to explain some inexplicable feeling he had had, some sense of the mysterious powers that moved invisibly through the world. Something sacred is moving, the old man would say, as if that explained anything to a boy of fifteen winters.

With a shock of recognition he realized that this was the feeling that had awakened him that morning, not simply the absence of his father's snoring but this sense of power moving about him, calling him from sleep. The feeling had brought him out of the lodge and here to this place, where he found a tree full of blackbirds, his spirit helpers, the messengers from the vision that had given him his young man's name.

Had they come here today as messengers? He watched them intently, as if they might tell him something of great import, when suddenly they took to the air as one, clucking a *chk, chk, chk* of alarm, and flew off in a tight cloud down the river.

And now Blackbird felt the hair on the back of his neck rise as he made out other sounds that seemed to come from all around him. He heard the sound of many feet stepping in the cold snow and something like the bells on the sticks the Lakota horse dancers carried in their ceremonies, but not so sharp and clear; it was the clink of metal on metal; he heard leather creaking, and beneath these noises he heard breathing, tens of mouths breathing, the spirit world breathing in his ear.

He could not move. His skin seemed to have become rigid, as if he were encased in a coating of ice.

His eyes saw motion on his left and suddenly all the sounds came from there. Fur hats were the first thing he saw, rising above the bank of the wide channel all in a row. Then faces came in sight, eyes almost hidden beneath the fur caps pulled low. The faces were covered with hair.

The heads rose higher, supported on shoulders and bodies that sat, that did not move, but still they jogged up and down and drew nearer, looming above him all in a row. The men were cloaked in furs and dark colors. They were whitemen. Now he saw the horses, all gray. Every horse a gray horse but for three on the near end of the line. Eyes swung in Blackbird's direction and found him.

No man made a sound and each held a pistol in his hand. All in a line on their gray horses they reached the edge of the bank and rode down into the wash.

The behavior of the riders was otherworldly. Were they spirit riders or men?

It didn't matter. They were upon him now. The end of the line would pass within ten paces of his stump. The breath puffed from the horses' nostrils and steam rose from their coats. He could see the breathing of the men too.

Blackbird inhaled deeply, noticing the clean taste of the air. It filled him until he felt light enough to rise up and float away. He would fly away like the blackbirds.

The second man from the end of the line pointed his pistol at Blackbird and the boy heard a *chk* as the hammer was drawn back. The sound was unnaturally loud and seemed to echo in the wide ravine. *Chk, chk, chk, chk.* All along the line came the sounds now, like the warning of the blackbirds.

CHAPTER

THIRTY-ONE

"Let him alone, John."

Bourke lowered his Colt, grateful that Egan had spoken. He hadn't really wanted to shoot the boy, whose courage in the face of certain death was impressive. He had aimed instinctively to prevent the boy from giving an alarm but then he had realized that a shot would wake the village just as surely.

Keeping to its steady, unhurried trot, the company was across the wash and up the far bank in a few moments. Bourke looked back. The boy stood as before, motionless atop the stump, but as Bourke watched he leaped to his pony's back, giving a whoop that sounded almost joyful, and galloped away toward the river where he disappeared among the trees. Bourke saw another rider there, then two more, youths pushing a few horses to the river to drink. They looked up, startled by the cry, and saw the cavalry. It was a miracle that they had not seen the soldiers before now. The first boy's exultant whoop sounded again from among the trees.

"Easy now," Egan said calmly. The troop was nearing the plum bushes that girdled the near end of the village. Egan slipped out of his greatcoat and let it drop to the ground, and along the line others followed his example, freeing themselves for action. In the village, dogs began to bark.

The riders threaded their way among the bushes and emerged in a ragged but ` unbroken line on the far side just as the entrance flap of the nearest lodge was raised from within. A woman looked out and her eyes and mouth opened wide. For a moment she made no sound; then she took a sharp breath that Bourke could hear from thirty feet away and she let out a frightened cry. Her head vanished and the flap fell closed, and for a heartbeat the village was as it had been before. Then came a shot from the far end of the line, answered at once by the distinctive report of a cavalry carbine; the two shots echoed off the face of the bluff, and as the sound rolled away, Egan raised his voice and ordered the charge.

The K Troop bugler had been holding his instrument to his lips for several moments, nervously awaiting the order. His first notes overlapped Egan's shout and the line broke into a gallop, splitting into fragments as it reached the lodges. Some of the men fired at random into the tipis and then suddenly the camp erupted in chaos. Men, women and children poured from the lodges like sparks from a hundred fires and running figures were everywhere, many lightly clothed or partially naked, as they had slept. The men had weapons and they began to use them at once as others ushered the women and children toward the brush and boulders at the base of the bluffs.

The troop was in the midst of the thickest grouping of tipis now, and they began to hear the sound of bullets ripping the air around them. A horse screamed and went down, blood and intestines pouring from its stomach as if from a burst balloon. The troop farrier called out "Help me, boys, I'm stuck!" as he struggled to free his leg from the weight of the writhing animal. The stark panic in the cry of the mortally wounded horse sent a chill through Bourke. He raised his pistol, looking for a target, but he seemed to see nothing but women and children running every which way around him, all glancing at the soldiers as if they were devils incarnate.

"There's something wrong with my horse," Hospital Steward Bryan said, and Bourke looked over to see only a wet bulge of bloody flesh where the animal's right eye should have been. The horse pitched forward, throwing Bryan clear. A single shot had pierced both of the animal's eyes, killing it so suddenly that its heart continued to pump, its muscles to work, carrying it a dozen paces beyond where it had been struck before it finally fell.

"Are you all right?" Bourke reined in beside Bryan and he realized that he had shouted at the top of his lungs although the stunned youth was only an arm's length away. The din of battle was growing around them, shouts of anger and fear making more noise than the scattering of shots exchanged between the soldiers and the fleeing Indians.

"That's the one!" Bryan shouted suddenly, pointing at a warrior kneeling behind a nearby lodge, hastening to reload his flintlock. "He killed my horse!" He leaped to his feet and raced toward the Indian, holding his pistol aloft as if he intended to bash the murderer over the head with it. The Indian ran off toward the bluffs with Bryan hot on his heels. Realizing that he was in danger of running straight into the arms of the hostiles, Bryan suddenly reversed direction and scampered back as quickly as he had gone.

"That boy can run," Egan observed. "I'd like to have him on my team for the regimental foot races. Oh, look out, John!" He swerved his mount as a brave jumped from a tipi and fired in their direction. Bourke's horse jerked his head as the right rein fell loose, cut neatly by the bullet just inches from the bit. The animal reared and Bourke nearly lost his seat. He brought the horse under control with pressure from his legs, leaning forward in the saddle and pulling on the left rein, wheeling the frightened beast in a tight circle until it came to a stop, panting, and allowed Bourke to dismount. Egan leveled his Colt at the now defenseless brave, but the Indian flung his ancient musket at Egan, and as the troop commander ducked to avoid it, the brave sprinted off, leaping a fallen cavalry horse as lithely as a deer and vanishing into the brush.

"I wish Mills would get in here!" Egan reined his horse around, trying to make some sense of the sporadic action around him. The advance had stalled in the center of the village. With their women and children shepherded to safety, some

444

of the warriors were working their way back among the lodges.

"We'd better—" As Egan started to speak, a ball struck his horse in the neck and the animal dropped dead in its tracks, barely giving Egan time to throw a leg out of the stirrup to avoid being pinned, as the farrier had been. The fall knocked the wind out of him and he was gasping for breath as Bourke helped him up from the ground.

"They're not stupid, you know," Egan said when he could speak again. "They're shooting at the horses."

The handful of troopers who had overrun their commanding officer and advanced farther into the village were falling back now, firing as they retreated. Bourke realized that he was panting as if from hard physical exertion. He forced himself to breathe slowly as he sighted at an Indian darting among the lodges, working his way towards the soldiers, but his shot went wild as a horseman galloped up, causing Bourke's own horse to shy and jostle him. The rider was the bugler from Noyes's company. He jerked back on his reins, dropping the horse to his haunches; the skidding hooves sprayed dirt and snow around Egan's feet.

"Major Noyes's compliments, sir, and he begs to inform the captain that he is having some difficulty gathering all the Indian horses. Major Corwin has gone to help us and Major Noyes expects to have them in hand soon enough. He inquires to know what your situation is."

"He'll have them in hand, will he? I wish to Christ I had something in hand. Do me a favor, will you? Sound dismount. I haven't seen my bugler since we started the charge."

As the call to dismount sounded through the village it was picked up by another bugle not far away, and K Troop's bugler came riding to rejoin his captain.

"You stick by me, dammit!" Egan barked, and he turned back to Noyes's man. "You can tell Major Noyes I am holding my ground but I would appreciate some reinforcement as soon as possible. If you see Captain Mills on your way back, give him my compliments and tell him to get his ass in here!"

Noyes's bugler saluted and rode away. The men of the troop were grouping on Egan now, leading their horses. One man held a shattered elbow. Another cried out suddenly and fell to the ground spewing blood, shot through the neck.

"Someone help that man, and follow me!" Egan called out. "Sergeant McGregor! Defensive line along the river!" He led the way toward the thick growth of trees and bushes along the river, on the east side of the village. A riderless horse galloped past, stirrups pounding its flanks, reins trailing.

Once among the brush, Egan and his non-commissioned officers dispersed the company in a line facing the village and the bluffs beyond. One man in eight gathered the horses and led them away to a cluster of cottonwoods at the southern edge of the village. The cavalry bridle included a link-strap, a fifteen-inch piece of leather clipped to the bit ring and throatlatch. Whenever the troop dismounted, the horse handler in each set of four unclipped the link-straps from the throat-latches and hooked them to the bit ring of the next horse until he had four horses on a single lead. In battle, one man in eight held the horses, freeing all the rest

445

to fight without concerning themselves for the safety of their mounts.

"It's a big village," Bourke observed when Egan was satisfied with the placement of his men and returned to take a position between Bourke and Strahorn. Nearby, Steward Bryan was tending the unhorsed farrier, who had been shot through the shoulder.

Egan nodded. "Bigger than it looked at first. There must be a hundred lodges here."

"We still outnumber the braves two to one, I should think."

"Not with this troop on its own, we don't. Reynolds has got five other companies out there and I'd like to know what in Christ's name he's doing with them." He turned to Steward Bryan. "Do you know how many wounded we have?"

"Three at least, sir, probably more. Your Private Schneider isn't likely to make it. Another man is shot through the stomach but he may survive."

"There are six horses dead too, sir." A sergeant threw himself to the ground beside Egan as bullets clipped the brush above his head. "Three more wounded. As best I can make out, the wounded men are not the ones whose horses are shot, with Private Goings the only exception."

"Which means a quarter of the troop is either wounded or unhorsed," Egan said dryly. "That's a hell of a score for—How long would you say, John? I looked at my watch when we came through the bushes."

Bourke thought for a moment. In battle, time was notoriously hard to judge, but he had some experience. "Thirty minutes," he guessed. "Thirty-five."

"Well, which is it? Thirty or thirty-five. A dollar if you're within five minutes."

"Thirty-five."

Egan rolled on his side to reach through his blanket coat and withdraw a pocket Waltham. "Forty minutes even! You lucky so-and-so. Another minute and I'd have won. I owe you, if we get out of here alive." He grinned.

"You're not serious, are you, Captain?" They were the first words Strahorn had spoken since the battle began, although he had never strayed more than a few yards from Bourke and Bryan.

"Oh, we'll try to get you out of here in one piece, Mr. Strahorn," Egan said good-naturedly. "But just so your notes are accurate, I should point out that the attack is not going exactly according to plan."

"Where the hell is Moore, that's what I want to know," Bourke said. He rose to his feet in a crouch and fired three quick shots with his Colt.

"Find a target, John," Egan cautioned. Several bullets cut the brush nearby, forcing the men to duck down. Egan raised his head slowly. "Look at that, dammit!" he exclaimed. "The red bastards are all up and down the bluffs!" He pointed at the rugged slopes, where puffs of smoke came from concealed positions that commanded excellent views of the village. In addition, fire came from warriors who were moving among the lodges, threatening to retake the ground K Troop had abandoned as it withdrew to cover along the river.

Egan aimed his carbine at a brave climbing the bluff face and he fired. A puff of dust to the Indian's right showed where he had missed. "Son of a bitch. I'll tell you one place Moore isn't. He isn't where he ought to be. What in Christ's name is so hard about moving along those bluffs and getting in position to cover us?"

"Good God!" Bourke exclaimed suddenly. "Look there! You don't suppose that's him over there?" He pointed to a place low on the southern flank of the bluffs, where a few clouds of white smoke revealed an uncertain fire from a more removed position.

"He can't even see the Indians from there! He's shooting at us! Jesus!"

"It's a good thing he's too far away to do much damage," Bourke observed. He reloaded his pistol and holstered it, then looked to the load of his carbine. Unlike the officers that preferred to purchase their own side arms, he had always kept the cavalry's standard issue. He fired a round at an Indian high on the bluff.

"Here's some help, sir," said the sergeant, pointing through the trees. "It must be Captain Mills."

Off to the left, where K Troop had first entered the village, men on foot were advancing close to the base of the bluffs, pushing the Indians before them as they came.

"It's about time," said Egan. "Sergeant Fisher, I want you to go down the line and instruct the men to concentrate their fire on the Indians on the hillside. Mills will need some cover."

The sergeant disappeared in the brush and a moment later the rate of fire from Egan's troopers increased.

Hoofbeats sounded to the front. A lone warrior raced through the village straight at the advancing soldiers, shooting with a revolver. When the gun was empty he threw it at them, then wheeled and galloped back the way he had come, hanging on the side of his horse. Shots from Mills's men chased him and K Troop set up a deafening fusillade, but as the Indian disappeared from sight in the trees he raised himself upright and shouted his triumph.

"By God, they've got courage, you have to give them that." It was Strahorn who spoke, standing to get a last look at the horseman. A ball snapped twigs a handsbreadth from his shoulder and he dropped to the ground.

"Some of them can shoot, too, Robert." Bourke grinned.

"Here's some more o' the boys, sorr." Private Goings, the wounded farrier, had joined the officers, together with Steward Bryan. Goings gestured with a pistol. Another line of men on foot was coming along behind Mills, this one extending from the middle of the village almost to the river. Their advance would bring them close in front of K Troop.

"This is more like it," Egan said. "I wonder who it is."

"It's Boots Corwin!" cried Bourke. "I know that red beard. And there's Ham Whitcomb."

"All right, boys!" Egan shouted down the line. "We'll move out when they reach us. This time we're going to clear the camp. Covering fire!" He fired at the

447

hillside and flipped up the trapdoor in the carbine's breech as he dropped it to his waist to reload. Around him the bushes sprouted fire and smoke as the men of Company K peppered the face of the bluffs.

The firing continued for several minutes and there were cheers from Corwin's men as they advanced. The Indians in the village were falling back, firing hastily and then dashing to a new hiding place before they stopped to reload. With repeating rifles they'd be a match for us, Bourke thought. His fingers were almost too cold to hold his carbine firmly and he thought wistfully of his greatcoat, discarded with the others back at the southern end of the village.

E Troop's line was coming on fast. They had passed by Mills's men and were nearly at Egan's positon. Egan fired a last time and stepped out of the brush, struggling with his carbine.

"Someday I'm going to meet the man who designed this extractor," he said to no one in particular. He pulled out a pocketknife and pried at the base of the jammed cartridge with the blade until at last it popped free. "Boots! Over here!" He waved to Corwin.

"John!" Ham Whitcomb came running up to Bourke and seized him by the hand. "My gosh it's good to see you! What a morning we've had! We brought the horses all the way down and I'm damn glad we did. Mills's are still up on top of the mesa. First we got sent off to help Noyes and I thought we'd never get to see any fighting, but then Reynolds heard you wanted reinforcements and here we are! Our horses are back there with yours now."

As the words gushed out of him he was pumping Bourke's hand all the while and now he noticed that Bourke was wincing in pain.

"What's the matter, John? You're not hurt?"

"No, nothing like that. But there's something not right with my hand." He slipped off his right glove. The tips of three of his fingers were a stark, lifeless white.

Steward Bryan appeared at Bourke's side. "Here, let me have a look, sir." He took the hand and inspected it. "That's frostbite, sir. You'll have to come along with me." He led Bourke off toward the river holding him by the arm, and Bourke raised his carbine in farewell to Whitcomb.

"I'll see you later, Ham! We'll catch up with you."

"Mr. Whitcomb!"

Whitcomb turned to see Corwin beckoning him. Captain Egan and his men were moving off toward the center of the village, joining up with Mills's line. There seemed to be a lull in the firing.

"You will be responsible for this end of the line," Corwin said when Whitcomb joined him. "I want you to take twenty men and get to the far end of the village as quickly as you can. You shouldn't find any resistance there just now. Take Polachek and McCaslin and Stiegler. Put the men in cover and watch out the Indians don't try to flank us by moving up across the river. I'll join up on your left as soon as I can."

"Major Corwin!" First Sergeant Dupré came running up at a lumbering trot,

448

breathing hard. As he ran, the waxed points of his mustache bounced like curls of wire spring. "General Reynolds, sair, he has given orders to burn the village. In my opinion this is a mistake. We 'ave found meat, sair, a great deal of meat. And robes, and much gunpowder in kegs, enough to supply us until summertime. If we can hold the village and send a *courrier* to General Crook, I think maybe he will wish to use this as a base camp."

Corwin nodded. "I'll have a word with Captain Mills. Maybe we can both speak to Reynolds. Lieutenant Whitcomb, you will take your position and hold it until you hear further from me, understood?"

"Understood, sir." Whitcomb saluted and they parted, Corwin going off with Dupré and Whitcomb trotting to overtake the troop, which was still in a line but advancing more slowly now, as the sergeants and corporals awaited further orders.

"Polachek! McCaslin!" The two men turned at the sound of their names and waited for Whitcomb to overtake them. A few troopers drew near to hear what was in store. "We're to establish a perimeter at the far edge of the village and prevent the Indians from flanking us on the right." He gave the orders crisply. It had taken him a moment to understand that Corwin had given him command of nearly half the troop. There would be no hesitation here, no reason to find fault now or later. Orders would be obeyed at once and to the letter. When the battle was done Boots Corwin might invent some reprimand if he wished, but there would be no good cause for one.

There was a sound like a ripe melon breaking on the ground, and something wet spattered Whitcomb's face and coat. A few feet away, Private Peter Dowdy slumped to the ground. A bullet had struck him in the head.

Whitcomb wiped his face and saw blood on his glove. He stared dumbly at the body. Dowdy looked up at him with eyes that no longer saw. The youth was sprawled awkwardly, half twisted on his side.

During the war Whitcomb had seen dead men in Petersburg, some of them stacked like firewood, but they had been stiff impersonal things. He had never seen the spark of life snuffed out before. Already the frigid air was glazing over Dowdy's eyeballs, making them dull and lifeless, while the grisly wound continued to ooze blood. Whitcomb knelt by the corpse and closed the eyes. He looked up at Corporal McCaslin. "It would seem the heathen does some smiting of his own." He rolled the body onto its back and arranged the limbs, folding the arms on the chest. "Do we just leave him here?" he asked.

"There isn't much else we can do, sorr," said McCaslin. "He won't mind."

Whitcomb became aware that Polachek and the others were watching him. He saw his own shock mirrored in the troopers' faces, but the expression of Private John Gray revealed only a sad acceptance.

"You have your orders, Sergeant. Quickly, now."

"Yes, sir. Chentlemen, if you please." Polachek addressed the soldiers like a schoolmaster. He herded them away from the body and they spread out in a line once more, but McCaslin remained with Whitcomb.

Whitcomb got to his feet. "I'll be all right, Walter."

"Yes, sorr. I'm sure of that."

McCaslin left him then. Whitcomb felt a little dizzy, although whether from hunger or fatigue or the shock of Dowdy's death, he wasn't sure. He bent over and removed Dowdy's cartridge belt and then he started after his men.

The village immediately around him was quiet, although there was some firing farther away. Once the village was securely in the hands of the cavalry, the hostiles would no doubt melt into the hills.

He had gone perhaps fifty yards when he came on Private Donnelly kneeling beside a fallen Indian. As Whitcomb drew near, the Indian screamed and his legs jerked.

"What are you doing?" Whitcomb demanded.

"None o' your affair, friend," Donnelly replied without looking up. "I done for this one meself and he's all mine."

"I asked what you were doing, Private."

Now Donnelly glanced up. "Oh, sorry, sir. Just getting a souvenir." He held up the Indian's penis and testicles, dripping blood.

"God damn it!" Whitcomb leveled his carbine at Donnelly. "God damn you! If I ever see you doing this again, if I even hear you have mutilated another Indian, I'll kill you myself! Now get away from me!"

Donnelly fled, but he kept hold of his souvenir. Whitcomb looked down at the dying Indian. The man's loin cover was raised and the bloody damage between his legs had made a pool of blood on the snow. The man had his hands clutched to his stomach, where Whitcomb could see intestines and more blood between the fingers. The Indian was looking steadily at Whitcomb. His breathing was shallow and rasping.

"Damn you too," Whitcomb gasped. He shot the Indian in the heart and turned away, swallowing hard, fighting to choke back his rising gorge.

I will not be sick, he told himself. In the space of a few minutes he had seen the first of his own men die and he had killed his first man, but it was not an honorable victory, not as if he had faced an equal foe in open combat. His mouth tasted of bile. He paused to lean against a tree, breathing deeply, hoping that the chill air would cleanse him.

A bullet struck the ground five yeards away but he did not move. He would live or he would die. He would do what he could to survive, but he no longer felt a trembling fear like the one that had come over him after he had chased the beef herd and been pursued by the lone Indian. What he felt now was a sickness in the heart; it was deep within him, leaving him free to think and act, but he knew it had changed him forever. He would never be the same.

He became aware of hoofbeats approaching rapidly and he was surprised to see a white man on horseback coming from the north end of the village. The rider held no weapon in his hands and the rifle scabbard that hung on the near side of his saddle was empty. Whitcomb was sure he was not one of the expedition's scouts, although he wore buckskins and a long brown oilskin slicker whose tails flapped behind him as he leaned low over his horse's neck and darted among the trees, apparently making for a group of horsemen near a central cluster of tipis. Whitcomb recognized Colonel Reynolds among them.

"Get the renegade!" came a cry of alarm from among the men of K Troop.

"He's after General Reynolds!" another voice shouted.

A volley of shots chased the rider and he seemed suddenly to lose interest in his goal. The reins dropped from his hands and he slumped in the saddle; the horse slowed and veered toward the base of the cliffs. Two troopers sprinted after him. The rider rolled from the saddle and fell to the ground.

"Lookit, will yez! The sonofabitch is wearin' army boots!" The first trooper knelt by the fallen man and pulled off one of the man's boots, then struggled with the other.

"Look out, Liam!" the second man cried out, stopping in his tracks and starting to back away. "The sonofabitch is still alive!"

The second boot came off in the trooper's hands and he fell back hard on the frozen ground, looking into the muzzle of a revolver as the renegade heaved himself up on his elbow. "God damn it, this is a peaceful village!" the man shouted, blinking to clear his vision. Blood dripped from a wound on his scalp.

An arrow sprouted suddenly from the trooper's shoulder and he regarded it with mild curiosity for a moment before he let out a howl of pain and leaped to his feet. As he ran pell-mell for safety, still clutching the renegade's boot, two Indians darted from the brush at the base of the bluff and helped the wounded white man to his feet. Half carrying, half dragging, they took the man away amidst a scattering of shots that failed to stop them from regaining the cover of the brush.

Whitcomb had watched the entire scene distractedly, like a spectator at some curious entertainment, but his attention was seized now by a thunderous detonation behind him. He turned to see that several lodges at the southern end of the village had been set afire and one of these had exploded. The force of the blast had sent lodgepoles into the air like jackstraws, some spinning end over end, others arcing up cleanly for a hundred feet or more before they plumeted back to earth. Close on the heels of the first explosion came a second, sending the troopers among the burning tipis running for cover.

What the Indians' reaction to this destruction would be, Whitcomb did not know, but he knew that he had been away from his men for too long. He set out at a jog trot in the direction Polachek and the others had taken. He could see no Indians remaining among the lodges now. Faced with the advancing troops of Egan's, Mills's and Corwin's companies, they had withdrawn to regroup at the base of the bluffs, but with none of their number remaining in the village, the hostiles on the slope had no further need to be careful with their aim, and fire from that quarter had resumed, heavier than before. As he ran, Whitcomb surveyed the positions there. The pace of firing from

451

individual Indians revealed that most of their weapons were muzzle-loading pieces but here and there a single weapon spoke more rapidly—one of the trapdoor Springfields or perhaps a lever gun used carefully. It was plain that the Indians had no shortage of powder, and it was equally plain that as long as they held their elevated positions, the soldiers in the village were in danger. Why hadn't Moore dislodged them? Before the attack began, Whitcomb had seen Moore start off along the bluffs.

When he reached the bottom of the camp he was relieved to find that most of the fighting seemed to be concentrated elsewhere. His platoon was in good cover in a dense stand of trees and brush that faced a narrow stretch of uneven bottomland lying between the river and the base of the bluffs north of the village. Without the cover of the bushes, some of which stood three or four feet above a man's head, the position would have been untenable. For the moment, the Indians on the slopes above the village were directing most of their fire at Egan's and Mills's men, but an occasional ball reminded the men of E Troop that they must keep well concealed. On the right, across the icebound river, there were more trees, willows and brush, and Whitcomb saw that the danger of being flanked on that side was very real.

"Corporal Stiegler!" he called out, spying the man nearby. "I want three or four men on this end of the line to devote their full attention to the brush across the river. If they see any movement there, I want to be notified at once."

"Yes, sir." Stiegler moved off and vanished.

"Leftenant!"

Whitcomb turned to see Polachek waving to catch his attention, pointing down the line to the left, where Dupré was bringing more of E Troop forward and extending the line in that direction. Dupré saw Whitcomb and waved.

"Step this way, if you please, sir." Polachek joined Whitcomb and led him forward to a concealed vantage point from which they could see across the open ground beyond. "The savages haff a stronghold there." Polachek pointed to a place where the river had scooped out a section of the hillside long ago. The little cove was protected by a fringe of brush and boulders. "I haff no idea how many savages are there, sir. We haff been keeping them pinned down."

"Well, with Dupré and the rest of the men on the line now, we shouldn't have any trouble with them."

"Even so, sir, there is a considerable gap on our left. We are not in contact with any of the other companies."

"There should be someone along soon enough up above, to push the Indians off the hillside. One of the other companies will join up with us then, I imagine."

"Perhaps, Leftenant. I hope so." Polachek sounded uncertain.

"Don't worry, Sergeant. We'll do all right until someone comes along. Carry on."

As Polachek disappeared among the bushes, Whitcomb tried to envision his present position as if it were drawn on a blackboard at West Point. There was an enemy strongpoint to the front, strength unknown. No danger from the rear, no sign of any on the right. Men posted to watch for any flanking movement. But there was a gap on the left and the enemy held the high ground. What could go wrong? One of Whitcomb's instructors in tactics had asked that question repeatedly. "Try to imagine what may go wrong before it does, gentlemen," the major had said. "Because it almost certainly will." Whitcomb was trying to determine what might go wrong here when Steward Bryan appeared suddenly at his side.

"How many of your men have frostbite, sir?"

"Frostbite? I have no idea."

"You had better find out quickly. Many of the men in the other troops are affected because they left their coats behind. The sooner it's treated, the less likely the tissue will be permanently damaged. Find an air hole in the river ice and put the frozen part in the water if you can—if it's a hand or a foot. Then rub it hard with some rough cloth; a piece of saddle blanket or gunnysack or anything like that. Then bathe it with this—it's iodine. Bandage it cleanly if you can and for God's sake try to keep the man warm." He handed Whitcomb a small bottle.

Whitcomb was glad he had kept his own buffalo coat, despite the occasional inconvenience of moving in such a heavy garment. Lieutenant Corwin had called out harshly as some of the men had thrown their outer garments to the ground when the troop prepared to enter the village, and there had been a brief delay as all the discarded coats were made fast to the saddles before the horses were led away to be held with K Troop's. Whitcomb had thought the delay foolish then; he had thought the Indians would be quickly vanquished and the garments could be easily recovered while the mopping up was under way. Now he saw the order in a different light. If the present stalemate continued for long at least E Troop knew where their greatcoats were to be found; he remembered that none of Captain Mills's men had been wearing coats as they advanced into the village. All their coats had been left up on the mesa.

"Thanks," he managed to reply as Bryan hurried away. "McCaslin!" he called out, and was relieved to see the hatchetfaced Irishman scramble through the brush a moment later. "How much frostbite have we got?" He noticed that McCaslin too had chosen to keep his coat.

"Fingers and toes, sorr, and Gwynn's ears."

"Get the affected men to the river." He handed McCaslin the bottle and repeated Steward Bryan's instructions, adding, "Two or three men at a time, mind you, and don't leave a hole in the line."

"Understood, sorr." McCaslin nodded, and was gone.

There was a sudden outbreak of shooting on Whitcomb's left, and a curse. "Watch out! The bastards are behind that bank!"

Whitcomb ducked out of the brush to the rear and ran along the line to where the firing was heaviest. He made his way forward there and came suddenly upon Lieutenant Corwin and Sergeant Dupré. Dupré was reloading a smoking carbine. He fired again across the open ground to the front. Fifty yards away the Indians had advanced to a natural breastwork, a ridge of earth and rocks and driftwood left behind by the river in spring flood. Behind the warriors, among the trees at the base of the hillside, women and children were fleeing on foot along a trail that led off downstream.

Corwin glanced up at Whitcomb. "No cause for alarm, Mr. Reb. They're just covering the retreat of their women. They're going to slip out of the trap, it would seem."

"Should we fire on them, sir?" inquired Corporal Atherton from his position to Corwin's right.

"Fire on the women, Corporal?" Corwin's tone was edged with contempt. "No, I think not. We've done our job. It's Captain Moore who failed to do his. Report, Mr. Whitcomb."

"There are no new injuries, sir. No wounds, at least. Several of the men have minor frostbite. Corporal McCaslin is taking them to the river a few at a time for treatment as instructed by Hospital Steward Bryan. We're in position to the bank of the river."

"All right. If there's enough cover, I want you to bring the right flank forward and have them increase their firing to hold these Indians down. Twenty of our men were requisitioned to help burn the lodges. If the Indians suspect how few of us are holding this line they'll attack for real."

As he said the last words there was a deafening explosion from quite nearby, and another tipi disintegrated in smoke and flames and flying debris. A lodgepole crashed into the brush ten yards away, causing one soldier to jump for his life.

"It's the powder kegs going up," Corwin explained. "They've got enough powder for an army."

"I take it you had no luck with General Reynolds?" Whitcomb ventured.

"Luck? You'll need more than luck to get a sound decision out of old Muttonchop. God, he's a pompous ass! "We must deny these supplies to the savages,' he says, but he doesn't think we might need them ourselves. Do you know how much meat these people have got? Tons of it. I mean that literally. All nicely jerked and baled. And there are hundreds of buffalo robes. We could all eat well and sleep warm tonight, if we ever manage to chase the bastards off. Noyes took seven hundred horses and I hope to God he holds on to them, because it looks like Reynolds is going to burn everything else. He's a damned fool."

"I'll move the men, sir," Whitcomb said, and he moved off, deeply shocked by this blasphemous indictment of a superior officer. Surely Reynolds knew the overall situation better than Corwin. He must know what he was doing.

Whitcomb found Stiegler and McCaslin and passed on Corwin's orders, and as he made his way back along the line he inspected each man briefly for frostbite. He found it often, but none was serious. One man was struggling with a jammed carbine with his bare hands. The extractor had ripped the base off a spent round and the soldier was prying at the remains of the casing with a knife.

"Keep your gloves on, Private!" Whitcomb said sharply. "You're no good to me with frozen hands."

"Sorry, Mr. Reb. I'm sorry, sir, I mean Mr. Whitcomb."

As he moved to rejoin Corwin and Dupré, it seemed to Whitcomb that the firing from the bluffs had increased, but when he paused to listen more closely there was a new outbreak of shooting from E Troop's front and someone shouted, "Here they come!"

Whitcomb darted through the brush in time to see several Indians running forward shooting as they came, and more still leaping from behind the breastwork. He dropped to his knee and fired once, twice, and brought down a brave who had almost reached the soldiers' line. Two of the others met similar fates and the remaining Indians turned and ran for cover, carrying away their wounded comrades.

"Major Corwin! You are hurt?"

Dupré's voice came from close at hand and Whitcomb turned to see Corwin cutting his uniform trouser and woolen underwear with a pocketknife. Dupré removed his commander's overboot and peeled back the flexible upper of the buckskin moccasin. With the layers of clothing drawn aside, a fresh wound was revealed in Corwin's calf. Bright blood spurted from the injury. "Put a tourniquet on it, Sergeant, if you will." Corwin's voice was strained and his face was pale.

Dupré pulled a large bandanna from his pocket and quickly wrapped it around Corwin's leg above the wound. As he was breaking a stick to use in tightening the tourniquet, Lieutenant Paul, from Mills's company, appeared through the brush with three men behind him.

"Lieutenant Corwin? Captain Mills's compliments. He sent us to make contact with you. He regrets he has been unable to advance to join up with you, but half our troop is burning the lodges and the rest of them are trying to make the hostiles on the slope keep their heads down. Captain Mills is in contact with Captain Moore, but Moore refuses to come up and support our left flank."

"He's in contact with Moore! Where in hell is Moore?"

"On the benchland just at the upper end of the village. He was driven off the slope by the Indians. They're up top now, on the summit. I have to get back fairly soon, Boots, but I can lend you a hand for a little while if you need it."

"Damn Moore anyhow! Yes, by God, I can use your help. Mr. Whitcomb, find Sergeant Polachek, tell him to grab fifteen men, and bring them all back with you."

When Whitcomb returned a few minutes later with Polachek, Corwin's trouser was tied back in place and Dupré was pushing the buffalo overboot back over the moccasin. Corwin grunted as the movement in his ankle flexed the wounded calf muscle.

"What in hell's Rawolle doing?" he demanded of Lieutenant Paul. Lieutenant W. W. Rawolle commanded the other company in Moore's battalion. "Moore may be chicken-hearted but that Prussian bastard is always spoiling for a fight. Can't Reynolds find something useful for him and his men to do?"

"There's some movement to the rear, but I couldn't make it out. Our company's horses are being brought down off the mesa. That's all I know. I've got no idea what Reynolds has in mind."

"Let's see if we can't at least push those Indians back from that breastwork. I'd like them to think there's half a regiment on this line. Sergeant Polachek, you go with Mr. Paul and see if you can't work far enough to the left to smoke the hostiles out. Watch out for Mr. Reb here; he's going to be on the opposite flank. Mr. Reb, take a dozen men across the ice and move up under the cover of that brush. Smoke those bastards out and then get back here quick. The center of the line will support you when you open fire."

As Whitcomb and Paul moved off in opposite directions, another lodge exploded nearby and strips of dried buffalo meat rained from the sky like confetti.

Corwin looked at Dupré. "Well, Sergeant, what do you think?"

Dupré arched his eyebrows, shrugged, and waggled one hand in a gesture of uncertainty.

Corwin smiled. "That's what I thought you thought."

"I get the men ready, sair." Dupré disappeared.

A few moments later a steady firing began from the left and right as Paul and Whitcomb reached their positions. "Supporting fire!" Sergeant Dupré's voice shouted, and the brush on either side of Corwin came alive. The Indians saw at once that they were outflanked; they abandoned their breastwork and retreated to the rocks and brush closer to the hillside, where their comrades set up a brief but fierce covering fire. When the last of the retreating Indians was out of sight, the din of gunfire lessened, but it remained strong from off to the left. Judging by the sound, Corwin guessed that the Indians on the slope had seen Lieutenant Paul and Sergeant Polachek's new position and were doing their best to drive the soldiers back. Polachek would have the sense to withdraw slowly so the hostiles wouldn't think the line was weak. The illusion of a strong force on this side of the village would last a while longer, with luck.

Sergeant Dupré came through the bushes and squatted once more beside Corwin. He pointed off to the right across the river. Only by watching very closely was it possible to discern Whitcomb's men moving in ones and twos from cover to cover, retreating toward the company's line. Occasional fire

456

came from several positions along the riverbank, giving the impression that at least a full platoon was in position there.

"He is doing well, sair," said Dupré.

Corwin grunted noncommittally. "I want you to take two men and bring up the horses. Bring them along the river ice and stay out of sight of the bluffs, if you can. And tell McCaslin to have some men gather up as much of that jerked meat as they can find."

When Dupré was gone Corwin let out a long sigh that was almost a moan. He tried to shift himself about to favor his wounded leg. He was certain the ball had struck the bone, but he had said nothing of this to Dupré. There was nothing more Dupré could do for him now. He wanted to lie down and rest, but he knew that once he closed his eyes he would think only of the pain in his leg, so he propped himself against a tree trunk and threw a shot at the bluffs so the Indians wouldn't think this part of the line was deserted. He reached out to gather up a few cartridges that had dropped from his belt when he fell to the ground after being shot. The belt was new. He had had the post saddler at D. A. Russell make it for him to replace his old one, which had finally worn out. Almost every man on the campaign and a great majority of the soldiers up and down the frontier wore similar belts, which they made for themselves or had made by saddlers. The leather loop cartridge belt had been invented by Anson Mills ten years before and it was a great improvement on the standard cartridge box worn at the waist, which allowed the metal cartridges to clatter about in a manner that was always annoying and could be dangerous in the presence of the enemy, but in cold weather the leather loops of the Mills belts were too stiff to hold the cartridges properly. It occurred to Corwin that canvas loops might do better. He would speak to Mills about it.

Another tipi exploded nearby and Corwin jerked his head up. He had been drifting off. He would have to watch that.

He straightened to a more upright position and peered through the brush around him. He could make out McCaslin and another man gathering pieces of jerky not far away. To the rear there was no sign of Dupré or the horses.

Hardeman was half conscious, struggling to comprehend where he was and what had happened to him. Someone touched his feet. He shook his head to clear his vision and the sudden pain reminded him that he had been shot. The bullet had creased his forehead almost exactly where Kills Fox had hit him with the war club three days earlier. He held his head in his hands to steady it, pressing hard. The pain diminished somewhat and he could make out his surroundings.

He was in some sort of cove at the base of the bluffs. The cove was close to the northern end of the Cheyenne camp; it was screened from the village by a strip of brush and rocks. An old woman knelt by Hardeman's side. She had hold of his stockinged feet and was rubbing them vigorously, causing him to feel a dull pain there as well. That was good. If he could still feel anything at all, his feet were not completely frozen. There was a small fire nearby. Apparently someone had placed him by the fire to warm his feet. Around him, two dozen or more Indian women were busy reloading the motley collection of muzzle-loading rifles that were the Indians' only defense against the steady fire from the cavalry carbines. What was holding the soldiers back?

He let go of his head and his vision remained clear, but any movement caused it to reel before it steadied again. He moved his head cautiously and looked around him. Above, he saw that there were warriors in protected positions on the face of the bluffs, firing down into the village. Closer at hand there were men behind the rocks and brush, facing the troopers who had advanced to the near end of the camp. The redoubt was well protected by warriors and was a fair defensive position, so long as the cavalry didn't gain the heights above. Hardeman seemed to remember that there had been more women here a short while ago, and some children too; they were gone now but he didn't know where.

Under the old woman's steady massaging he could feel warmth beginning to return to his toes. He made signs that his feet were all right, and the woman spoke soothingly in words he did not understand. He saw now that she had a pair of high winter moccasins which she clearly intended for him. He helped her to pull them on one foot and then the other, but his fingers were numb, so he left for her the job of lacing them tight and tying them. His feet might be all right, he supposed. It really didn't matter. His head ached and it was difficult to think clearly, but the understanding of his failure was sharp and finely drawn in his mind. Once again he had arrived too late.

In his mind's eye he could see the scene as it must have been just a few hours earlier—cavalry approaching the still-sleeping village, warriors roused by the bugles, leaping out to defend their women and children with no time to put on their paint, no time to dance for courage and spirit power, no time to dress properly; no time to do all the things an Indian usually did before he went to war. Hardeman had seen it all seven years ago, on the banks of another stream far away. And now it had happened again, just as before, down to his own belated entry into the battle and his failure to stop it. The one thing he had tried above all to prevent had happened; the war had begun and where it would end he could not imagine.

From the moment he had seen the oats in the horse droppings, he had known in his heart where the soldiers were going. He had pushed his horse as fast as he dared through the cold night, hoping against hope that the cavalry tracks would turn aside to aim anywhere but at Two Moons' village. But they had kept on, straight as an arrow. They led through country that was rugged and broken, much rougher than the way he had come, and finally, when he grew certain that the army scouts must be following the tracks of the returning Cheyenne hunting party, Hardeman had left the trail and struck off to the east, back to the Powder, praying that he would reach the village before Crook's cavalry.

But when he was still a mile or two distant he had heard the firing. Yet even then he had hoped by some miracle to stop the attack and restore the broken peace. As he entered the village he had looked frantically for gray horses—buglers always rode grays and kept close to the ranking officer in each troop—but as luck would have it he saw a cluster of grays off to the cavalry's rear and realized that an entire troop of grays must be present. He looked for the tall form of General Crook, mounted or on foot, but he saw him nowhere, and then at last he had seen a man he knew. It was Louis Richaud, who had scouted for General Smith in '67 together with Hardeman and Hickok. He and some other men were sitting their horses near Two Moons' lodge. One man with muttonchop whiskers wore an officer's Kossuth hat. "Louis!" Hardeman had shouted. "Louis Richaud!" But his words were drowned in the din of battle. He had ridden pell-mell for the horsemen but a trooper's bullet had knocked him from his roan and he remembered little of what had taken place between that time and this. He didn't know what had become of his boots.

The old woman was done lacing the moccasins. His feet were still cold but he could feel his toes when he wiggled them and already the warmth of the fire was beginning to penetrate the thick rawhide soles. He made signs to thank her, and she answered with signs of her own, saying that soon the warriors would drive the bluecoats away and he would come eat in her husband's lodge. Hardeman nodded and smiled as she turned away, but he thought the outcome would be very different. He had heard the explosions from the village and had guessed what they meant. The soldiers were burning the lodges and the kegs of powder were blowing up as the flames reached them. How much powder had the Indians managed to bring away with them as they fled? Probably not enough.

He listened to the sounds of fighting beyond the cove. He judged the battle to be fairly even now, but it couldn't stay even for long. Soon the Indians would begin to run low on powder or lead and then the soldiers would move in and surround them, and finally they would have to surrender. And what would Crook say to find Hardeman in their midst, wounded and wearing moccasins? Would he believe the improbable tale of the scout's travels and the events that had brought him here? If he would listen, Hardeman would do what he could. He would see what terms he could make for the vanquished tribesmen.

His thoughts were interrupted by a hand that knocked his hat off his head and jerked him up by the hair, making his head throb with excruciating pain. He was helpless to resist.

The Cheyenne who held Hardeman's head raised a knife in his other hand, but he hesitated when the old woman who had given the white man the moccasins shouted from across the fire. A few men came running up, Kills Fox and He Dog among them.

"He led the bluecoats to us!" Hardeman's attacker said, preparing to take the white man's scalp.

"He came from that way!" Kills Fox pointed downstream. "He came after the soldiers attacked us."

"It is true," said another Cheyenne. "I saw him come from the north. We were already fighting the soldiers."

He Dog demanded to know what the Cheyenne were saying, and when one man explained to him in Lakota, he held out a warning hand to Hardeman's attacker. "I did not see the *washichun* come into the fight, but I have seen the man who led the bluecoats here. He is the Grabber, the one the whites call *Grouard*. He came with the second group of soldiers, the ones on foot. I tried to get near him to kill him, but he saw me, and now he stays behind the soldiers, hiding."

"Ahhhhh!" Some of the women were Lakota and they made a sound of wonder and understanding. They remembered the Grabber. When he was just a boy he had been found, naked and alone, by a hunting party of Lakota. When the Lakota approached him, he had held his arms in the air, as if trying to grab something above his head. He spoke a little Lakota, and said his father was a halfbreed trader and his mother an Oglala who lived among the whites. He was given shelter in Sitting Bull's camp and lived there for some years, but when he was a young man he got in trouble with the Hunkpapas and came to live with He Dog, in Crazy Horse's camp. But it seemed that he caused trouble and fighting wherever he went, and in time he had gone back to the whites to live with them. Now he led the soldiers against the Lakota and Shahíyela. Was this how he repaid them for the kindness they had shown him when he was in need?

The Lakota women told the Cheyenne about the Grabber, and one of the Cheyenne nodded. "I have seen him before, in the camp of Sitting Bull long ago, and I saw him here today. This one tried to stop the fighting." Here he gestured at Hardeman, whose hair was still gripped by the other Cheyenne warrior.

460

"I know some of the whiteman's words. He told the bluecoat who shot him that we were at peace."

"He came with the pipe carriers from Sun Horse," said another. "He is a guest in our village."

"We should kill him anyway," said the angry man, but he let go of Hardeman's hair and accepted a loaded rifle from one of the women. He trotted away, back to the fighting.

Hardeman had understood none of what was said, but he gathered that he had Kills Fox and He Dog to thank for saving his life. He wondered what they would have done if they knew that he had run off to find Crook and lead him to Sitting Bull.

"Thought that was you," said a familiar voice, and he turned to see Bat Putnam approaching him with his Leman rifle in his hands. Bat saw the wound on Hardeman's head. "Who done that? Injun or white man?"

"White man. I got into the village but not in time. Couldn't stop the fighting." Hardeman told it in as few words as possible.

"I reckoned you'd try. Glad I was right. Eagle, he didn't believe it, but the tracks told the story. You was on the soldier boys' trail to stop 'em, I said. Bet a horse on it, not that it makes any difference now. 'Course I didn't reckon that's what you had in mind to do when you first lit out. Took us some time to take up yer tracks, what with havin' to catch the horses, and all."

So the other pipe carriers had noticed his absence after all, and they had set out on his trail. How close had they been behind him? If they had caught him they might have killed him, but that wouldn't have changed a thing. The soldiers would still be fighting the Cheyenne and the Sioux and the only thing that would be different was that he would be dead. One man more or less wouldn't matter much. He still might die before the day was done.

"You should have told me about the summer council," he said.

"Sun Horse reckoned you wouldn't come with us if'n you knew. He figgered when you heard about it up here, you might see things our way by then. Guess he was wrong."

Hardeman shrugged. It didn't matter now.

Bat retrieved Hardeman's hat and handed it to him, then brushed aside the hair on his forehead to inspect the wound. He wiped away some fresh blood brought out by the Cheyenne's manhandling, and Hardeman winced. "Hmmp. Looks like you was lucky," Bat said. "'Bout a whisker closer and we'd be buildin' you a scaffold. Well here's somethin' to make you set up and take notice: we got 'em stopped up above." He pointed to the tops of the bluffs. "Two Moons is up there now with some of his boys. Me'n the fellers, we seen where you turned off the soldier boys' trail, 'n' we figgered like you did—take the quick way back to camp 'n' see could we head 'em off. When we seen the fat was in the fire, we made fer the tops of the bluffs on foot. Eagle and Little Hand, they got a good position and slowed down one bunch of soldiers till some of the Cheyenne come up to help 'em. There's a bunch o' Cheyenne and Lakotas in good cover now, got them bluecoats pushed down off the hill and held to the south end of camp. Hawk 'n' me come down to see could we help some here. He's off yonder." Bat pointed and Hardeman saw Hawk Chaser among the warriors in the brush nearby. The Lakota fired an old musket and passed it to a woman to reload.

Hardeman was surprised to discover that he took encouragement from Bat's words. For good or bad he was on the side of the Indians now, and their fate might be his own. With a helping hand from Bat he got to his feet and found that his head was somewhat improved. It felt peculiarly swollen and his hat seemed too small; his hearing was muffled and strange and his eyes worked best when he kept his head still, but his strength was returning.

"Dunno how much longer we'll hold out here," Bat said. "Might be we'll have to skedaddle. Women and kids're mostly off and gone." He pointed at the trail that led downstream. "They'll circle 'round and head for Crazy Horse. He's the closest. I don't guess I should tell you that. Wouldn't do if the soldier boys should hear where the helpless ones've gone to."

Hardeman didn't resent the suspicion. He deserved it. He had tried to fool them all to make peace at any cost. He had kept his cards close to his vest, and in the end, Fate had dealt from the bottom of the deck and walked off with the winnings.

"Horses are coming!" a woman cried, and some men rushed to face the trail from downriver in case soldiers were attacking from this new direction, but they saw the horses now, a bunch of ten or fifteen driven by two Lakota boys and a Cheyenne, and they fell back to open a way into the cove.

Blackbird was the first boy to enter the redoubt, leading the way for the horses. He saw Bat Putnam and cried out joyfully, "*Hau*, Uncle! I am glad to see you! We have brought horses!"

"We bring horses for the helpless ones!" the Cheyenne youth called out in that language, and the women set up a trilling sound, praising this bravery on the part of those so young. The men caught the horses as they slowed and milled about. The last youth paused on a section of old riverbank in full view of the soldiers and made a defiant gesture at the whites, smiling proudly. A bullet struck him square in the breastbone and hurled him from his horse like a rag doll. His body fell on the near side of the brush, behind the warriors crouching there.

Blackbird jumped off his horse and knelt beside the young Lakota. It was the youth who had helped him catch his horse that morning. He had found the boy again when he was crying the alarm, fleeing from the soldiers, although he knew that they could not hurt him. From the moment when the *washichun* had looked down his pistol at him and lowered it without shooting, Blackbird had known that he would survive the day. His spirit helpers, the blackbirds, had warned him of the soldiers' coming and had shown him the way to safety. Feeling brave and confident, knowing his spirit helpers were watching over him, Blackbird had flown away to the river as they had done, crying the alarm, warning the horse guards to save the horses. But already another group of soldiers, these on black horses,

462

were cutting off the herd and the horse guards were riding for their lives. Blackbird had found the Lakota boy and together they had rounded up a few horses the soldiers had missed and drove them downstream, below the camp.

A Cheyenne boy had found them there and together the three youths had waited until they could see where their small bunch of good horses would be needed the most. They had seen the warriors climbing the bluffs to keep back the soldiers, and they had seen the women and children streaming away to the north on the river trail. Finally they had decided to take the horses to the protected cove at the near end of the village, where the last of the women remained. If the soldiers attacked, at least the women would be able to get safely away.

And now Blackbird's new friend was dead. He reached out to touch the face of the one who had been so happy just moments before, so proud to be doing something brave for his people, and the feeling of the flesh told Blackbird that the spirit was gone.

The father of the dead boy, one of He Dog's men, stared incredulously at the twisted body. His joy at seeing his son, who had been missing since the start of the fighting, had been turned to grief in the blink of an eye. "Hókahe, Lakotas!" he cried out suddenly, freeing himself from his shock. "Let us show the bluecoats we know how to fight!" He ran to the exposed piece of old riverbank and fired his rifle at the soldiers' positions. With bullets striking all around him, he began to reload. He poured powder from a flask down the barrel, then dropped in a bullet from a pouch at his waist, and was drawing out the ramrod to tamp the load home when two bullets struck him at once. The rusty flintlock flew into the air as the Lakota threw up his arms and dropped back, badly wounded. Two warriors pulled the man to safety while all along the front of the redoubt other men moved forward through the rocks and brush and set up a brisk return fire, Bat Putnam among them. He sighted his plains rifle carefully and fired, and a cry of pain answered his shot.

Behind the line of defenders, Blackbird was astride his horse once more, the tears already drying on his cheeks. "Hókahe!" he shouted. "Come, my brothers, it is a good day to die!" He kicked the pony into a gallop and raced through the brush, making straight for the soldiers' lines.

"Come back, little brother!" Bat cried out when he saw Blackbird, but it was too late. A flurry of shots came from the troopers and Blackbird fell.

Within the cove, a Cheyenne dropped the jaw rein of the horse he was holding and seized a musket from one of the women. Without thinking, Hardeman grabbed the startled pony and swung himself onto the bare back, praying that the animal would respond to knees and heels without the control of a bit. Leaning close to the pony's neck he kicked it into a run and out across the open ground beyond the brush, heading for Blackbird's motionless form.

Bullets flew around him and one nipped at the shoulder of his slicker. His hat flew off his head and he felt the wind in his hair. And now Blackbird moved. Good boy! Playing possum all that time! An arm was raised and Blackbird managed to lift himself high enough so Hardeman would be able to take the arm. He hoped he could lift the boy up behind him. His head still throbbed and his vision blurred, causing him to blink hard and shake his head to clear his eyes.

He was almost there. Careful now, don't want to fall off the damn horse . . . Reach down . . . It's going to work . . . Oh, God! . . .

A searing pain like the touch of a firebrand exploded in his left shoulder. He was knocked backward, off-balance and unable to see his surroundings through a red haze of pain that rose before him. He struggled to stay on the horse's back. His ears were filled with the pounding of his heart and a roaring cry of anger that he realized came from his own throat as he looked about for his attacker. He felt rather than saw his pistol in his hand, and felt the recoil as he fired aimlessly. The horse wheeled in a tight turn, then shied and reared, and Hardeman fell.

He fought off a black cloud that threatened to envelop him and he saw the Indian pony galloping away. Blackbird was nearby, crawling slowly toward him, one arm outstretched. The boy's wounded leg trailed behind him, and there was a new wound in his side, where the shirt and cape were soaked with blood. A bullet ricocheted off the ground between them, throwing shards of rock in Blackbird's face and making him duck back and cling to the earth.

Hardeman's vision was strangely clear, but fragmentary, as if he saw through the eyes of a dream. He and the boy were in a shallow depression, sheltered somewhat from the troopers' fire. Perhaps if they didn't move . . . He let his head drop back and he looked up at the gray sky. In a moment he would do something, but right now he needed to rest. His whole left side was numb and he could feel a wetness soaking his shirt. Where was he wounded? . . . . He heard a bugle sound in the village, and horses neighing. The soldiers would advance on horseback now, and that would be that. . . . Nearby, the gunfire had increased . . .

He became aware of hoofbeats close at hand, approaching fast. He looked up and saw two mounted men bearing down on him, soldiers on large cavalry horses, one chestnut and one dapple-gray. He saw every movement of the men and horses, the wide eyes and heaving chests of the animals, the open mouths of the men, shouting wordlessly. One brandished a revolver; the other held a carbine.

And now there were more hoofbeats, from behind. Hardeman managed to turn his head, although the effort seemed enormous. From the base of the bluffs, Hawk Chaser was riding to meet the troopers, carrying only a lance.

Hardeman returned his attention to the soldiers and he saw now that his own pistol was still in his hand. How many shots had he fired? It could have been just one or half a dozen. He wasn't sure. Too much effort to check his load, and not enough time. The ground trembled from the hoofbeats of the approaching horses. He rolled on his right side and raised the Colt, supporting his elbow on the ground. His thumb brought the hammer back and he watched it as if it belonged to someone else. Force of habit. . . . Good habit too. . . . He sighted on the gray horse. . . .

There was a deafening explosion that seemed to come from everywhere around him and his arm jerked from the recoil. Through the smoke he saw the gray buckle at the knees and fall head over heels, throwing the rider clear. The man sprang to his feet and scurried off, favoring one leg. Hardeman sighted at the other horse but the soldier swerved and the shot missed, and the soldier's Springfield boomed harmlessly in reply. Against Hardeman's will, the arm holding the Colt dropped to the ground. He saw the trooper rein in sharply and leap from the horse; the man was going to shoot from the ground this time. Hardeman tried to raise the Colt again but his arm refused to move. He was condemned to watch, unable to interfere.

The soldier gauged the time left to him. Up went the trapdoor at the carbine's breech. The partially extracted cartridge was stuck, but the trooper yanked it free and found a new cartridge at his belt. In went the cartridge, down went the trapdoor. The man sighted, and suddenly Hawk Chaser was upon him, charging into Hardeman's vision like an avenging apparition, his lance raised high, now starting downward as the arm launched it.

The soldier ducked sideways, but not quickly enough. The lance struck his shoulder and glanced off, leaving a deep gash. The trooper cried out in rage and pain and he fired the carbine one-handed at the retreating Indian. Hawk Chaser seemed to sway in the saddle but his horse carried him out of Hardeman's vision and Hardeman could see only the soldier, who had one foot in his stirrup now. With a lurch he was up and away, managing to haul himself into the saddle only after the chestnut had reached a gallop. Cheers came from the watching troopers, accompanied by a ragged volley to keep the Indians pinned down.

Hardeman found the strength to move his head. Blackbird lay where he had been before, unmoving, his eyes closed. From the direction of the village the bugle call sounded again. Hardeman heaved himself up with his good arm and managed to hold himself in a sitting position. There was much activity among the tipis, horses moving about and men mounting. The troopers were preparing to advance.

But they were not advancing! There was no firing from the village now, while from the Indian positions came a renewed barrage of fire and a few triumphant shouts. Three huge explosions drowned out the other sounds for a time, coming one on top of the other as the fires found more powder, and then through the echoes of the blasts came the notes of the bugle once more, repeated over and over, from farther away now. With a shock, Hardeman recognized the rallying call. The soldiers were withdrawing! He couldn't believe his ears, but it was true. The mounted cavalry were milling about beyond the burning lodges, forming up, and now they were off, moving out of the village to the south, upstream, away from the Indians, who swarmed out of the rocks shouting jubilantly.

Hardeman saw movement in the corner of his eye and he looked to the dense brush at the bottom of camp, beyond where the Oglala lodges stood abandoned. There. A man on foot crouched low. Another behind him was helping a third man with a wounded leg, and he caught a glimpse of a horse being led downstream. There were still some troopers there. If they didn't

465

move quickly they would be cut off. Did the Indians see them? It didn't seem so.

A sudden dizziness made Hardeman drop his head until the spinning sensation slowed and stopped. Something was nagging at him. There was something he wanted to do. He raised his head and looked around. The wounded trooper had dropped his Springfield when he fled. Hardeman crawled over to the carbine and used it for a crutch as he struggled to his feet. His left arm hung useless at his side. Nearby, the village burned. No more than a handful of lodges had escaped the torch. Where the kegs of powder had exploded there were smoking craters, as if the Indian camp had been bombarded by artillery. Upstream, the cavalry were streaming across the open land of the valley bottom. Some riders were driving the huge pony herd along behind the column of troopers. A handful of Cheyenne started off on foot after the cavalry. Scouts. They would keep an eye on the soldiers and report back.

Hardeman shook his head. What was it he had meant to do? There was something he needed to know. Someone . . . He looked around seeking some reminder, and then he saw Hawk Chaser.

That was it.

The Indian lay sprawled on his side not far away. Hardeman moved unsteadily across the intervening space, aiding himself with the carbine. When he reached Hawk Chaser he touched the man with the Springfield and rolled him onto his back, and then he saw the wound. Half of the warrior's head was blown away, yet on what remained of his face there was no anger or fear. Just peace.

Men had reached Hardeman's side now. Nearby, one helped Blackbird to his feet. The boy was conscious, but unable to stand on his own. Hardeman looked back down at Hawk Chaser, then turned and stumbled away, searching the ground.

"Easy, Christopher." Bat Putnam put an arm around his waist to help support him.

"It's over here," Hardeman muttered. He pulled the mountain man along, driven by a need he couldn't put words to. He saw what he wanted; he bent over and nearly fell, held up only by the surprising strength in Bat's skinny arms. His hand closed around the feathered shaft of Hawk Chaser's lance.

He shook Bat off and started back, clutching both the lance and carbine in his good hand and using them to help himself along until he stood once again beside the fallen warrior. He dropped the carbine next to the body and then with most of his remaining strength he raised the lance and planted it in the ground. The Indians might not understand, but he knew what it meant. A lance against a Springfield carbine, model 1873. An iron blade made from the rim of some emigrant's wagon wheel against four hundred grains of lead propelled by fifty-five grains of powder. But Hawk Chaser hadn't seen the inequity. Hawk Chaser was a warrior. To him it was just one man against another.

466

Bat had followed Hardeman closely, ready to catch him if he keeled over. Hardeman turned to him now, searching for something to say, needing an explanation.

"It's good to die for the people," Bat said.

Yes, it's good to die for the people. Hawk Chaser had believed that. And he did a good job of dying. Hardeman wondered if he would die as well when his time came. He had no people to die for. His parents were gone and he had never stayed long enough in one place to acquire a family. Except for Johnny. And now Johnny was on his own and free to fight for himself.

He saw Blackbird watching him. The boy was leaning on Standing Eagle, who had appeared from somewhere. Blood was oozing from the wrapping on Blackbird's leg and from the new wound in his side. His lionskin cape had fallen from one shoulder and the shirt was torn there. Hardeman could see the fresh scar from the small wound the boy had received in Putnam's Park, from Tatum's shot. More wounds in a few weeks than most men received in a lifetime.

A peculiar sound came from the village. Men and women were moving among the shattered lodges, picking up the few items that might still be of some use. In the center of camp a knot of women were gathered around something that moved along the ground. They followed it, arms lifting and falling. It was a man. He rolled onto his back and for a moment Hardeman saw the dark-blue field blouse and bearded face, and then the women closed in on him again and there was a muffled scream. After a time one woman stood and raised a severed arm above her head, making the high trilling sound of joy.

Hardeman looked away. He removed his St. Paul coat with difficulty and some pain on account of his useless left arm. Using Hawk Chaser's lance to steady himself, he dropped to his knees and sat down beside the body. He covered it with the oilskin to hide the horrible wound and the expression of peaceful acceptance, which was no less unsettling.

"I'll stay here with him," he said to no one in particular. "You fix up something to carry him on."

The wind was stretching its legs again, whipping the willows this way and that, but Hardeman no longer felt the cold. A gust brought smoke from the village and he smelled the odor of destruction. He shrugged off the attempts of one man and then another to see to his wound. Men and women spoke to him in Indian tongues and hands touched his shoulder in attempts to comfort him, but he paid them no mind and soon they left him alone. Before Bat and the other men returned with a pony drag to bear Hawk Chaser's body away, Hardeman had lain down beside the body and gone fast to sleep.

When he awoke, he did not know where he was. It was dark, and there was firelight coming from somewhere out of sight. An Indian bent over him, a man he didn't know. The man's face was painted white and his hands and arms were red. He was dressing the wound in Hardeman's shoulder.

Why was the Indian helping him? He had led the soldiers here. . . . No, that was another time. This time he had tried to make peace and he had failed. . . .

He was in a small shelter made from scraps of old tipi coverings. The smell of smoke, heavy and fresh, came from the hides. The pieces of lodgeskin must have been salvaged from the village. There was another smell as well, one more pleasant, though pungent and strong, and he saw now that the floor of the shelter was covered with small branches of sagebrush. Next to him, so close he could have reached out and touched him, Blackbird lay asleep, with new bindings of cloth and hide around his leg and midsection. Once again the two of them were sheltered together while their wounds were treated. But where were they?. . . . Hardeman felt at his waist and relaxed a little when he found his Colt there where it belonged.

There was a loud gasp outside the shelter, a sound not quite human, and then the murmuring of several voices, followed by a hideous scream.

Hardeman tried to get up on his elbows. The medicine man said something and pushed him back down, tying a ragged piece of buckskin in place. Hardeman realized that his left arm was bound against his chest as a white doctor might have positioned it for a sling. There was an ache deep in his shoulder that throbbed in time with his heartbeat. With his good hand he touched his left shoulder cautiously, probing to test the extent of the wound. No broken bones? That was a piece of luck. And the bullet had missed his lung. Maybe God was merciful after all.

He laughed, and the medicine man smiled. Hardeman shook his head, trying to make the Indian understand that there was nothing to smile about. "God isn't merciful," he said. "He's a cruel son of a bitch who lets his children maim and kill each other. He sends young boys to war and lets good men die for no reason."

The medicine man nodded, still smiling, and picked up a small round drum. He began to sing a song, drumming a steady accompaniment. From somewhere outside the little lodge came a short screech, followed by a liquid blubbering sound, and then a few words, "Please! Oh, God, please don't kill me!"

Hardeman rolled off his low pallet of robes and crawled to the entrance of the shelter, ignoring the medicine man's efforts to stop him. He pulled aside the crude flap and looked out.

He stared at the scene before him, unbelieving. They were skinning a young soldier.

"Best you go back and lay down, Christopher." Bat Putnam was seated just outside the shelter, taking no part, just watching. There was no trace of his habitual humor in his expression.

Hardeman crawled out of the shelter and sat on the ground beside Bat. A large fire was burning nearby and he could feel its warmth. On the other side of the fire stood a second shelter; Hardeman could see the wide-eyed faces of three young children peering from the entrance. Beyond the firelight the night was dark, and there was no hint of moon in the cloudy sky. The little camp was close below the benchland at the edge of the Cheyenne village, which was now utterly abandoned but for the small group here. Besides Standing Eagle and Little Hand and Bat there were six others, two men and four women, all presently watching the unfortunate soldier. Just at the edge of the firelight, ten or a dozen horses were tethered and hobbled. Closer to the Indians, a few dogs sat watching the spectacle.

The trooper was made fast to a young cottonwood near the fire. He was naked. His lips had been cut away, and his eyelids too, so he could not close his eyes. Little Hand was working on the soldier with a skinning knife, trying to separate the skin from the chest muscles, but the young white man was writhing and moaning continually, making the work difficult.

"Found him in the willows," Bat said curtly. "His soldier-boy friends run off without him."

"You can stop it."

"It ain't my place." He motioned at the watching men. "That there's the uncle of Blackbird's friend, the boy that got hisself killed bringing the horses. He's brother to the feller got shot just after. The women are relatives too. They're all He Dog's folk, Oglalas. They're goin' with us. Reckon to put in with the peace man after what happened today."

"What's Little Hand's stake in this?"

"He's good at it."

The soldier's eyes met Hardeman's and his ghastly lipless mouth made a sound halfway between a sigh and a groan; it rose in pitch to become a wail of agony as Little Hand attempted to peel off a section of skin.

Standing Eagle barked a few words at Little Hand, his voice full of disgust. Little Hand shrugged and moved away from the captive. Standing Eagle spoke again, this time to the women who stood near the fire. Two of the women had their hair cut short and their arms gashed in mourning. They were the first to move, pulling short butchering knives as they ran toward the soldier.

He saw them coming and he screamed. The women reached him and for a moment he was hidden from view. There was another scream, laden with terror and new pain.

A woman threw something small and red to the dogs, where it quickly disappeared. The women drew back, considering what to do next, taunting the soldier, and Hardeman saw that one of the man's testicles had been cut from its sack, which now dripped blood steadily. New gashes crisscrossed the man's chest.

One of the mourning women swung a length of wood as stout as a man's arm against the soldier's chest and there was a cracking sound. The soldier gasped and coughed, and blood trickled from his mouth. One woman shouted her approval, but the others pushed the woman with the stick away and spoke

469

harshly, gesturing at the soldier, apparently arguing for a slower death.

The men were no longer paying any attention to the white captive. They sat in a small group smoking their pipes, discussing the best way to return to the Sun Band's village, and so they did not notice as Hardeman got unsteadily to his feet and began to walk slowly across the clearing toward the soldier.

Standing Eagle was the first to see the scout's advance and he jumped up to place himself between Hardeman and the trooper. Hardeman met the war leader's gaze and looked at the Indian's hand where it rested on his knife, and then he pushed Standing Eagle aside and walked past him. The Lakota moved to stop the white man, but Bat Putnam said a word and Standing Eagle hesitated.

Hardeman reached the soldier, moving through the women as if they weren't there. They protested but drew back, waiting to see what he would do.

The soldier's head was bowed, and saliva and blood drooled from his disfigured mouth. "Oh God," he moaned. "Oh God, help me!"

"You've got to help yourself," Hardeman said, and the trooper looked up with incomprehension in his eyes. "You'll die quicker at the hands of the women, but it's death without honor. The men torture you to let you die bravely. If you cry out, you're not a worthy enemy. You're a coward and you don't deserve their respect."

He watched closely and saw understanding in the miserable man's eyes. The soldier straightened slightly and the tongue licked what was left of the lips to stop the drooling.

"It's up to you," Hardeman went on. "The women'll do it quick but messy. Stand up to the men and they'll see what you're made of. You'll pass out soon enough." He wanted to say more, to give the man some hope, but Bat and Standing Eagle understood English and so he left it there, hoping the soldier would trust him.

He felt himself waver. A haze obscured his vision for a moment and he was afraid he might faint. He took a deep breath and his vision cleared.

Slowly, the soldier nodded. He drew himself up against his bonds and raised his head. He looked beyond Hardeman, at his captors, and from the small group of Lakota came a few approving *hau*'s.

Hardeman turned away and the women moved forward, but they stopped at a command from Bat. The mountain man spoke in Lakota to Standing Eagle and the other men, and Little Hand nodded and said something, gesturing at the soldier, who now waited quietly, breathing deeply, shuddering once with a chill or a spasm of pain, but his head remained high and his eyes met those of his tormentors.

One of the other men spoke and the women drew back to the fire. Little Hand drew his knife and approached the soldier, his face solemn.

The soldier's breathing grew more rapid. Slowly, Little Hand extended the shallow incision in the man's chest. The soldier looked away and tried to close

470

his lidless eyes. Little Hand stopped his work and looked up. The soldier's eyes returned to meet the Indian's.

Little Hand smiled and with a quick slice he removed the loose flap of skin, leaving a new patch of raw flesh that bled freely. The soldier drew a sharp breath but made no other sound, and he kept his eyes on Little Hand.

Little Hand stepped back, holding up the skin, and now from the onlookers came a chorus of approving sounds, loud and strong, which stopped suddenly at the report of a single shot.

The soldier slumped dead against his bonds. There was a hole in his chest over the heart. Hardeman returned the Colt to his waistband even as the Indians jumped to their feet, knives and war clubs raised. Standing Eagle leveled his carbine at the white man.

Hardeman saw the weapons poised and he saw the anger and hatred in the eyes, and the disappointment at being robbed of the barbaric sport, and he didn't care. If they could do this to another human being they were less than human themselves, and to hell with their notion of honor and giving a captive the chance to die bravely. How did they expect a man to be brave when he didn't know their customs? That was why Hardeman had spoken to the boy, so he would understand, and so he might regain his courage. And he had done well. The Indians had seen that the soldier could be as brave as one of their own youths, once he knew what was expected of him. Hardeman had given them just enough time to see that, and no more, before he had ended the boy's suffering.

The Indians were drawing nearer now, closing in on him, and Bat Putnam was with them, his face set and hard. The mountain man had sat and watched the torture, and he had done nothing. The growing friendship Hardeman had once felt for Bat was gone now, and with it any trace of sympathy for the Sioux. The newspapers and the terrified whites who had never even seen an Indian were right: they were savages. They claimed to want peace, but once the fighting began they were as eager for it as the soldiers and they gloried in the chaos of battle; he had seen it in their faces today. Well, they would get plenty of fighting now. The soldiers would come again and again until both sides had had enough of fighting, and then the Indians would be penned in and watched over like wild animals and that was right too. He would do nothing to stop it even if he could. It was out of his hands now and he was glad.

He was clinging to consciousness by a thread, but he strove to remain upright, looking at each dark pair of eyes in turn so they could see his small victory. But the haze rose before him again like sunlight filtered through the yellow leaves of autumn. He swayed, and felt hands take hold of him.

Book Three

LISA PUTNAM'S JOURNAL

Tuesday, March 21st. 5:50 a.m.

With the two heifer calves born yesterday we now have twenty-eight all told; there are thirteen bulls and fifteen heifers. Except for two that are weakly, all are fine specimens. We have lost five. Scours persist among the newborn but my father's remedy of beef broth, pectin and honey has served at least as well as the patent medicine, which is now exhausted.

This is the sixth day of Sun Horse's fast. Since Johnny rode over to the village two days ago and returned with news of this quest for spiritual guidance, worry about Sun Horse has been added to my increasing concern for the safety of Uncle Bat and Mr. Hardeman. It seems they have been gone forever.

Yesterday evening Mr. Tatum informed me that he believes it may be possible to clear a way through the avalanche in another week. The halfway mark was only passed yesterday, but progress is much faster now, aided by the warmer weather, the greater care the men are using with the blasting powder, and most of all the participation of Rama. Mr. Tatum berates himself for not thinking of Rama sooner. The old barnyard scoop, fitted with iron rings for the harness Harry made to fit the elephant, enables Rama to move a great deal of snow and debris in much less time than men with shovels. They now apply all their energies to loading the wagons, and the remaining portion of blocked roadway diminishes daily at a heartening rate.

There is much I would like to say to Mr. Tatum but I have held my tongue. It is best not to let enmity and recriminations out into the open when people are confined together as we are, and he will be gone soon enough. Good riddance, I would say. I have come to share his impatience for the road to be clear and the circus to be on its way. Certainly their early departure will be the best thing for Johnny, and perhaps Amanda herself has realized this. Less than a week ago she was almost throwing herself at him, but for the past several days she has been much more reserved. He still spends what time he can with her, but he is so shy that I doubt there will be any open expression of his feelings, which is just as well. What would he do if he learned the truth about her? I believe it would break his heart. When he is not with her or off working with Hutch, he spends his time with the Waldheims. He has not given them a definite reply to their offer of employment. When the circus leaves he will remain here to await Mr. Hardeman, and I hope that when he is at last ready to set off on his own, Johnny will have given up the romantic notion of chasing after the circus, and Amanda.

It is her I worry about the most. What is to become of her. Things cannot go on forever as they are.

She will be in the kitchen by now and I must go.

After the noon meal Lisa saddled her horse and led him from the barn, preparing to ride down through the meadows for her daily look at the calves, but she hesitated when she saw Alfred Chalmers approaching alone.

It was a blustery day, typical of early spring in the mountains. The snow was soft underfoot. Sunlight and clouds swept across the valley with the wind. Julius had turned three new mothers and their calves out of the heifer lot and he was hazing them down to join the herd. The clowns and acrobats were already at work in the barn and just now the yard was deserted except for Lisa and the Englishman.

"Mr. Chalmers, may I have a moment of your time?"

Chalmers raised a hand and changed course to join her.

For five days Lisa had said nothing of what she had seen that morning in the second-floor hallway, not to Hachaliah Tatum, not to Amanda, not to anyone else.

Amanda had turned, her hand still resting on the latch of Tatum's bedroom door, and she had discovered Lisa watching her. For a moment neither of them had spoken, and then Lisa had invited Amanda to come to the kitchen for a cup of coffee. Together they had made the fire and the coffee, and when Harry Wo brought word that Ling had decided to remain in bed a while longer, Amanda had helped Lisa and Joe Kitchen make breakfast. She had little experience at domestic tasks, but she was a willing pupil and Joe had assigned her to making the breakfast biscuits. They had been widely praised as the best ever, much to Amanda's delight. Since then she had joined Lisa in the kitchen each morning before dawn and they had an hour or more together before Joe and Monty arrived. They had exchanged confidences and become close friends; they had talked of their lives, but never of Hachaliah Tatum.

"Miss Putnam. Another splendid luncheon. Ah, dinner, I should say. I can't get used to calling it dinner in midday. I do try. When in Rome, you know."

"Mr. Chalmers, you must be aware that Mr. Tatum and Amanda are, that is— I don't know just how to put it. They are not simply . . ." She was at a loss.

Chalmers grew serious. The wind whipped his straw-colored mane about his head. "I am aware, Miss Putnam, if I, ah, take your meaning correctly. We are all aware, of course."

"Has this situation existed for long?"

"For several years."

Lisa was shocked. "But then why, I mean how can you..."

"Permit it?"

"Yes. Thank you for making this easier for me."

The wind gusted so hard that Lisa held on to her hat to keep it from blowing away. Chalmers shifted position and raised one arm, extending his cape like a protecting wing to shelter her. "Miss Putnam, we in the circus live in a small world that is closed to society at large, both because of its disregard for us and our consequent disregard for it. Ordinary people will allow us to entertain them but they will not have us sit at the same table, if you see what I mean. Within our own small world we live in intimate contiguity with one another. We have no home except the circus itself. It's rather as if many families lived beneath a single roof; there is little privacy except that granted by common consent. Because of this we have developed our own customs, and the most strictly observed of these is that one does not interfere in the affairs of another unless there is a call for help."

"And there has been no such call?"

"There has not."

"But you can't take her compliance at face value, certainly not in the beginning? She was so young!"

Chalmers looked at his huge feet. "The, ah, situation had existed for some time before we were aware of it. Amanda was in no danger; no harm was being done to her. She made no objection."

"Sometimes the harm is not easy to see."

Chalmers said nothing.

"No one has talked to her, then? None of the women?"

"Perhaps. But I am not aware of it."

Lisa touched his arm. "Mightn't you encourage her to—"

"To what, Miss Putnam?"

Lisa shook her head and dropped her hand. "I don't know. At the very least she should know that her friends care for her. She should know that you would support her if she ever decided to change the situation. To end it."

Again Chalmers made no reply. Lisa gathered up her reins and mounted her horse. "I'm sorry. I have no right to meddle."

"You are not meddling, Miss Putnam. You have made us feel at home here. That means more to us than I can say. We are all very grateful. Amanda respects you and she has accepted you as her friend. You are only expressing your concerns, and believe me, I will think about what you have said."

"Thank you." She gave him a brief smile and rode away.

Her worries for Amanda unsettled Chalmers, coming as they did on top of his own. Ever since Lydia's warning he had watched the girl closely and he had seen the change, too sudden to be genuine. Overnight Amanda had ceased to flaunt her affection for Johnny Smoker. She ate her meals with Tatum and exchanged only pleasantries with the boy in the presence of the circus master, but she was playing a role.

I see it more clearly than the others, Chalmers thought, because I know the theater and they do not. When Hachaliah is about, Amanda is on stage. She plays the young innocent for all the world to see; she is Hachaliah's faithful companion now, with not another thought on her mind, but she overplays the part. Underneath it all, what is she thinking? What does she intend? Can she imagine that she has pulled the wool over Hachaliah's eyes?

The final act of the drama would be played out soon, once the river road was open, and Chalmers' conversation with Lisa Putnam had left him with the feeling that he too would have to take part in the action before it was done.

He spent the rest of the afternoon helping Harry Wo replace a cracked skid on the hay sled. He and Harry had become frequent companions since the arm-wrestling match. Harry usually delighted in teasing the strongman about the opponents he would have to face for years to come in Putnam's Park, but today Harry was quiet, full of concern for his pregnant wife, who kept to her bed for half of each day now, and the two men worked together in silence save for the few words needed to coordinate their labors.

Chalmers found the hard work far more satisfying than practicing with his bell weights and iron bars. Like the rest of the performers he had felt the strain of growing boredom. He was anxious to resume the accustomed routine of daily performances, breaking the tent down and setting it up, moving on to the next town and the next show. Practice served a purpose, but it took performing before an audience to keep the acts honed to a fine edge.

He missed the hunting that had been such a welcome diversion for a time. No one had gone out for several days. The warmer weather made getting around difficult in the mountains; horses and men on foot broke through the surface of the snow and the going was slow, but it was more than this that kept the hunters home. "You cain't whistle up game where there ain't none," Julius had said when Chalmers suggested the two of them go off on snowshoes. "Perhaps it's true that evil spirits have taken the game away," Chalmers had replied in jest, but Julius had answered him perfectly seriously. "Cain't say. I'll leave that to Sun Horse."

Chalmers perceived that the Indians' refusal to hunt had had a greater effect on Julius than the Negro admitted. It seemed that Lisa as well, indeed each of those that lived in Putnam's Park, had grown quieter in recent days, ever since the old chief had undertaken his fast. Only Hutch was unaffected. His infatuation for Maria Abbruzzi kept him intoxicated throughout his waking hours; he remained untouched by the moods of the others and seemed to take great delight in even the foulest day, and Chalmers suspected that in company with the young ranch worker Maria had found ways to relieve her own boredom. If Carmelo Abbruzzi came to share Chalmers' suspicions, there could be trouble.

Hutch was out of harm's way today. He and Johnny Smoker had gone with Chatur to help with the work at the avalanche, and they would not return until suppertime.

When the new skid was fitted to its iron runner and bolted to the sled, Harry thanked Chalmers and went off to the house to assure himself that all was well with Ling. The sun had fallen behind the western ridge and the wind had died away, and already there was a new crust on the snow as the temperature dropped below freezing. Chalmers perched himself on the corral fence to wait for Lydia and the others to emerge from the barn, and he marveled at how soon he had become accustomed to the wintry climate. Wrapped in his cape, he enjoyed the view of the peaceful valley much as he might have enjoyed a pleasant Dorset afternoon. Overhead, the swift low clouds of midday had given way to wispy brushstrokes tinged with pink and red. "Mares'-tails" the circus teamsters called these delicate forms, and claimed they were portents of stormy weather. There had been a ring around the sun that morning and this too was said to presage an end to the warmth that had lasted for four days now. "Never trust a chinook," the wagon drivers said. "It'll snow by Sunday." But Lisa Putnam had scoffed at their predictions. "Oh, it may snow," she had said when Chalmers asked her opinion, "but we have another saying in the mountains: only fools and newcomers predict the weather." And so Chalmers' new interest in mares'-tails and rings around the sun was tempered with caution. To know what the weather would do, one waited until it did it. Perhaps it would be as well to adopt a similar attitude about all things, instead of worrying about what Amanda or Hachaliah Tatum or Carmelo Abbruzzi might do to interrupt the tranquillity of this place.

"I could knit a sweater with the wool you're gathering."

He looked down to find Lydia standing beside him, her black eyes probing his face.

"Just thinking, my dear." He got down from the fence.

"Yes, and I know what troubles you. It's that girl. You know Hachaliah has his eye on her."

"We'll be gone soon enough and it will be over," Chalmers said, hoping it was so.

Others were coming out of the barn now. Lydia took his arm and guided him toward the house, away from ears that might overhear. "Perhaps," she said. "But I think Hachaliah smells a mouse."

"A rat, dear. He smells a rat."

"That too. Can't you see? She is different. Where is all that flirting she likes so much? She is a regular trollop when she knows she'll be gone the next day and some young fellow's heart broken behind her. But look at her here. Quiet and polite, and her eyes everywhere but on that boy when Hachaliah is nearby. I have not seen her this way before, and it worries me. You always said someday she will break away from him, as a child breaks away from the parents."

"Yes. I didn't think it would come so soon. You think that's what it is, then?"

Lydia shrugged. "If it is, what do we do?"

"Perhaps I should have a word with her."

"I will speak to her if you like. The woman's touch might be best."

"No, my dear, this is something I must do. It may be something I have put off for too long."

With his mind made up, he took the first opportunity that presented itself. The supper gong rang before Tatum and the teamsters had returned from the avalanche and Chalmers intercepted Amanda as she entered the saloon.

"May I have a word with you?" He took her by the arm and led her to a table by the windows, far from the line forming at the serving tables. "I have seen no more of that new routine we all liked so well," he said as he seated her. "I hope you won't abandon it."

"No, it's just that, well, Hachaliah wants us to make some changes and we can't agree on them." She looked out the window. The wagons full of men were approaching on the road; as usual Tatum rode in the lead on his white stallion.

"And Sam and Carlos? Do they side with Hachaliah or you?"

"Oh, we all know how we want it to be. It's Hachaliah who wants to change it."

"Often an instructor does not see when his pupil's abilities outstrip his own, my dear. You have come to that point and you mustn't let him stifle you. I think perhaps because I have known you all my life I have taken your abilities somewhat for granted myself. You really have an exceptional talent, you know. Old Sam was saying much the same thing the other day."

"Was he really?" Amanda was both pleased and flustered by this praise.

"Indeed he was. You know, it's possible that a time may come when you will wish to rise beyond the confines of this show. Not that we take second place to anyone, you understand. It's just that sometimes a change is necessary for further growth, if you, ah, see what I mean. Others would be glad to have you, I'm sure. Perhaps even Barnum. And if the day should come when you decide to leave us, your friends will understand." He took her hand in his own. She was looking at him solemnly and in her eyes he saw a maturity beyond her years. It was not the first time he had noticed this quality in her, the ability to be a child one moment and a woman the next, and it encouraged him to discover it again. "We believe in you and we wish you only the best, always. If there is anything we can ever do for you, you have only to let us know. That is really all I wanted to say."

"Thank you, Alfred." It seemed that she might say something more, but then she spied Julius coming through the kitchen door and she jumped to her feet. "There's Julius. I want to ask him if we can play music after supper." She kissed Chalmers quickly on the cheek and skipped away, a child once more.

As Chalmers watched her go he wondered if he should have been more direct. He had planted the seed; when it might grow or whether it would grow at all remained to be seen. He had tried to tell her that when and if she decided to make a break with Tatum her friends would stand by her, but he had done it in his own roundabout way. Directness in personal matters was not in his temperament.

Lydia rejoined him then and together they went to the serving line. The teamsters arrived, hurrying as if the food might be all gone before they reached the tables. Chalmers noted that Henry Kinnean had discarded his sling altogether. Since he had resumed his position as overseer of the unruly teamsters, Kinnean ate and drank by himself and he no longer gambled with the other men.

480

"I think it would be nice if we sat with Amanda tonight, don't you, dear?" Lydia said as they received their plates. When Hachaliah Tatum arrived at last he found an empty seat kept for him between Lydia and Amanda. Gunther and Greta Waldheim were at the same table and Lisa and Joe Kitchen arrived soon after, leaving the last few diners to serve themselves. Throughout the meal the talk was pleasant and inconsequential, but as Amanda rose to go, Tatum put a hand on her arm.

"You look a little tired. This might be a good night for you to go to bed early."

Amanda slipped from his grasp and stood behind Lisa's chair. From a nearby table Johnny Smoker was watching her. "I feel fine. Anyway, Julius and I are going to play music tonight."

"Mr. Ingram will understand if you ask him to put it off until another time."

"He might, but I won't ask him. He's very busy and I will play with him when it suits him. Besides, you said we'll be gone in a few days and there are more tunes I want to learn from him."

Tatum ceased his resistance but he could not conceal his annoyance. "Very well, but don't be too late."

As the meal was cleared away the two fiddlers sat by the potbellied stove. They played reels and waltzes and traded tunes back and forth. Johnny came to sit with them and soon there was a circle of listeners. Hutch brought his banjo and Papa Waldheim his accordion, and the cheerful quartet repeatedly won applause from the small audience.

It seemed to those present that Amanda's music shone with a special brilliance. She played tirelessly, choosing fast tunes and happy ones, and when she followed Julius's lead she appeared to know instinctively where he was going, even when the tunes were new to her. For the most part the onlookers were content to sit and tap their feet, sometimes singing the words to a song they all knew, but a few dancers rose to move among the tables from time to time. Alfred Chalmers took Lydia in his arms and guided her to the darkened corners of the room and twice Johnny offered his hand to Lisa.

In a pause between tunes Hachaliah Tatum cleared his throat; he drew his watch from his waistcoat pocket and looked at it meaningfully. Oblivious to this reminder, Amanda began a new song. Tatum opened his mouth as if to speak, then closed it and stalked from the room.

Others were leaving too, for the hour was late. The weary teamsters had gone long ago, some to their rooms in the house, the rest to the tents. The fiddlers turned to gentle tunes now, ballads and slow waltzes and Negro gospel songs. Maria Abbruzzi whispered in Hutch's ear and soon the two of them went off together. Papa Waldheim squeezed a final chord from his accordion and latched it shut, leaving the fiddles to play for just a handful of listeners, sending their notes across the saloon like birds paired in flight, swooping and dipping and rising together. At last Julius found himself nodding.

"I best get myself to bed," he said, getting to his feet.

Amanda relieved the tension in her bow. "Thank you," she said.

"I should be thankin' you. You put new life in this old fiddle. We'll see you tomorrow."

With Julius gone only Alfred and Lydia and Johnny remained. Lydia's head rested on Alfred's shoulder and her eyes were closed. He patted her gently on the arm.

"Hmm?" She looked up. "Oh, my goodness. Come along, Alfred." With a smile at Johnny and Amanda, they were gone.

"We're all alone," she said.

"I guess we should go to bed too." He didn't move.

How could he even think of sleep? she wondered. Couldn't he feel her excitement? Didn't he sense that she had planned for the two of them to be alone tonight?

"Oh, let's stay a little longer. I haven't even had one dance with you."

"There's no one to play for us."

"I'll play." She stood up and retightened her bow. "Here. You just have to stand a little farther away from me." She raised the fiddle and Johnny put his hands at her waist as she started to play the slow waltz she had played on the night of the circus's arrival, and again on the tightrope. "I've given my waltz a name. It's called Johnny's Waltz now."

"For me?"

"Of course for you. Who else would I name it for?" She could see that he was pleased and she quickened the tempo a bit as they twirled among the tables. She felt that she was gliding on air.

It was all going to come about, now that she had found the way to free herself! She and Johnny would be free together! How could she have been such an idiot? For days she had been close to despair. As soon as she had determined to break free of Hachaliah, he had tightened his grip on her. She had been too brazen in encouraging Johnny, and Hachaliah had demanded repayment in kind. She had been with him every night since then and he kept a closer watch on her during the day, whenever he was in the settlement. He spent an hour or more each day watching the clowns rehearse, and it had taken Amanda only a short while to realize that so long as she remained within his reach he would never relinquish his dominion over her.

Leaving the circus was unthinkable. It was her home and her life. She had imagined herself alone, cut off from her friends, unable to perform, and she had recoiled from the prospect. For a time her determination had waned and she had all but given up hope, and then Alfred, gentle Alfred, in his own bumbling way, had provided the answer.

You have an exceptional talent, he had said, and the very earnestness of his expression had made her see this praise in a new light. The other performers had always complimented her and she knew they genuinely enjoyed her performances, but she had never considered the meaning of those compliments beyond the boundaries of Tatum's Combined Shows, until now. *Sometimes a change is necessary for further growth*, Alfred had said, and the answer to her problems had exploded in her mind. She could have both her clowning and her freedom! Other circus owners would appreciate her talent, and she need not be on her own! Johnny Smoker would be her guide and protector, but unlike Hachaliah he would not control her. Instead she would control him, but he would never dream that her velvet reins rested on his shoulders. He could find work anywhere and he was not afraid to set out for places he had never seen. To him that was the heart of living, making your way in the world and seeing as much of it as you could. It would not be difficult to persuade him to visit the eastern states, and while they were there she could approach another show. Where there was a circus, there were horses, and Johnny had magic with horses. The Waldheims had seen it and others would see it too. She and Johnny would find work together, and who was to say that some of her old friends could not join her later on? When she rose to a position of prominence in the new show she would send for Sam and Carlos, and perhaps Alfred and Lydia would come as well!

Suddenly there was no limit to what she could do. She felt that she scarcely knew the person she had been before she arrived in this snowbound wilderness, for here she had seen how to free herself of her fetters. Not just in her art but in all other things as well she would decide her own destiny. It was Johnny who had awakened this resolve in her and with Johnny's help she had a chance to loose Hachaliah's grip on her until she might slip away and be free of him forever.

She would set her sights high. The Bailey and Cooper circus was going to California this summer and Aaron Cooper might be glad to have her back. There was even talk that Cooper and Bailey planned a European tour. And beyond Cooper and Bailey there was Barnum. Wouldn't Hachaliah turn green if she got a job with Barnum!

Hachaliah was waiting for her now. He expected her to creep to his bedroom when the house was asleep, as she had done so often in recent days. But tonight he would be disappointed. She needed time to gather her strength for the final step. Somehow she must keep away from him for a few days, away from his attempts to hold her by every means at his command. And she needed time with Johnny.

The first step was to make Johnny declare himself. He was so shy! Sometimes Amanda wanted to shake him out of the almost reverential attitude he displayed toward her, as if she were a sainted virgin to be placed in a shrine. But she must be careful. She must not disturb the pure image he had of her. She must kindle a fire in him. He must make the first move. Men needed that. They had to believe that they created a woman's desire and compelled her to submit to them by the force of their will. Allowing them to believe this was a gift women made to men, and the means by which a woman could control any man she chose.

Of one thing she was certain: she would pacify Hachaliah Tatum no more. She must proceed cautiously with Johnny, but time was short and she was ready to dare anything to effect the break now. When the circus left, it would go without her. She would stay behind with Johnny here in Lisa Putnam's comforting home, and when Chris Hardeman was back and Johnny knew his friend was safe, she and Johnny would start out together.

She brought the waltz to an end and curtsied to Johnny. "Thank you, sir. You dance beautifully, as always."

Johnny shifted from one foot to the other, and even in that simple movement she could discern the unevenness caused by his old wound, the trace of a limp that disappeared so miraculously when he danced.

"It is late," she said. "I suppose we should go to bed." She looked him in the eye to see if he suspected her veiled meaning, but she saw no hint of it. "Will you be a gentleman and see me to my room?"

"I don't guess it'd be proper for me to go upstairs with you."

"See me to the stairs then. Is that proper?" She was teasing him now. She took his arm in hers and together they left the saloon and made their way along the darkened hallway to the foot of the stairs. A coal-oil lamp hung at the upstairs landing, its wick turned low. Amanda stood close to Johnny, still holding his arm. "You're worried about Chris, aren't you?"

"He'll be all right. I'd feel better if I was with him, though. It's good to have someone watch your back."

"Shouldn't you go to the Indian village soon to see if there's any news?"

"I thought I might go up tomorrow."

"Take me with you?"

"Sure. You want to go? We won't see Sun Horse, not if he's still shut away by himself."

"That's all right. Hears Twice will be glad to see us and maybe I'll get to see the *heyokas* perform. We could stay overnight, the way we did before."

"What about Tatum? He said you couldn't go off without his say-so."

"He'll be down at the avalanche. Besides, I can go where I like. We can stay with Penelope! She'd be glad to have visitors."

Johnny smiled. "I'd like that."

She pressed herself against him. "It will be fun, just the two of us. Thanks for saying you'll take me."

"That's not much." Johnny seemed embarrassed. "I'd do more for you than that. A lot more."

"Would you really?" Her chin tilted up ever so slightly and she shifted her body toward him. His arm found its way around her, so tentatively it barely touched her. Her free hand slipped up to his shoulder. She wasn't sure if the slight pressure she applied there pulled him to her or if he bent of his own will, but she felt his breath on her face as she closed her eyes.

Their lips met. Seldom was a kiss more chaste, and yet Amanda became aware of nothing beyond that place where their flesh touched, and she felt a warmth that remained when they parted and she climbed the stairs alone.

She had thought she might lure him upstairs after all, leading him on with

484

one kiss and then another, but that could wait until tomorrow in the Indian village, far from Hachaliah's sight and hearing.

She took the lamp from the landing, and once in her room with the door carefully bolted behind her, she sat at the delicate veneered dressing table and set the lamp so it shone on her face. She peered at herself and placed a finger on her parted lips. They felt unnaturally warm to the touch. In the moments when they had touched Johnny's, she had discovered something new about him, something that excited her and fueled her hopes. There was a strength behind his tenderness, one she wasn't sure Johnny himself even suspected.

He was different from the others, the young men whose attentions she encouraged in every place where Tatum's Combined Shows made an appearance. He was so different that she was pressing her attentions on him, although they were concealed in the guise of a young lady's modesty. She stared at herself, eyes wide in the warm yellow light of the lamp. It was true. She was pursuing him. She had never done anything like it before. Always she had simply let herself be seen and the young men flocked around her. She led them on and sometimes let them find the pleasure they sought, and she felt renewed by their adoration. But she didn't want them.

She wanted Johnny.

Her eyes and mouth opened wide in mock astonishment and she covered her mouth with the fingers of one hand, the picture of shocked modesty. She dropped her hand and smiled at herself. Could she control him as easily as the others? It would take more than whims to move him. She would have to know what she wanted, and to know that she would have to be unafraid. In the Indian village she would take him. He would think it was he that had taken her and he would be hers forever. Or for as long as she wanted him.

The doorknob turned. She started and looked fearfully over her shoulder. Damn the lamp! The light beneath the door had betrayed her presence.

"Amanda?"

The voice was soft but she knew it at once and it confirmed her fears.

"Amanda." Again the knob turned and the door creaked as it strained against the bolt.

She arose and crossed the room, her bearing erect and her face calm. She paused to unbutton her bodice halfway down.

"You took your time," Tatum muttered as she stood aside to admit him. She closed the door quickly and silently behind him. He wore a satin dressing gown and soft calfskin slippers.

"I'm tired, Hachaliah. We worked hard today. I'm getting ready for bed."

"Ah yes. Somehow I imagined you would be tired now after playing music until all hours." The edge of sarcasm was cloaked less carefully than usual. His face was placid but the voice was hard. His eyes dropped to her bosom where the petticoat showed through the open dress. She wished she had left the buttons fastened.

He reached for her but she stepped back. "Not tonight."

"Oh yes, tonight. And any night I wish."

"What about my wishes?" Amanda felt the anger growing within her. "Do you think about what I wish?"

"Of course I do. That is why I'm here." He slipped out of his dressing gown and set it aside. His flannel pajamas were dark blue, with white piping. He sat on the bed and began to unbutton the shirt. The hair on his chest was turning gray. On his head he used a pomade that kept the hair there shiny black.

His muscles flexed as he took off the pajama top. His abdomen was firm and flat. He sat back against the headboard wearing only the blue pajama trousers. He was proud of his body and the sight of it caused a familiar quickening of breath in Amanda's breast. She clenched her hands and dug her thumbnail into the flesh of her forefinger, smiling as she felt the pain. "You're so sure about what I want, aren't you?"

"Reasonably so." He smiled too, pleased with himself.

"My teacher."

"Yes. And you have learned well. There's little more I can show you, except my appreciation."

"You're right. I have nothing more to learn from you." She felt a sudden bravado. It was true she needed him no more. The realization made her almost giddy. "Whatever else I have to learn, I'll learn somewhere else."

"From someone else, is that what you mean?"

"Yes!"

In an instant he was off the bed and moving to her side. He seized her arm so tightly that she gasped. "You dare talk to me that way? After all I have done for you? Do you know where you would be without me? In a workhouse with snot dribbling from your nose! Or someplace worse!"

"In a whorehouse?" she suggested defiantly.

"Yes! But I suppose you would take it in stride!"

"Lower your voice!" she hissed.

"Ah!" Tatum's eyes gleamed. "So you would rather the whole world didn't know? Perhaps young Johnny Smoker would no longer follow you about like a lovesick puppy if he knew the truth about us?"

"You wouldn't tell him!" Amanda's tone was brave but she felt a sharp fear deep within her. How would Johnny's feelings change if he knew? Worse yet, what would he do if he should learn that she, and not Hachaliah Tatum, had been the one to initiate their physical relations?

It was true.

For eight years following her parents' death, Hachaliah had cared for her unselfishly, with a genuinely parental affection that never overstepped the normal bounds. And then in a moment of crisis Amanda had changed everything. She was sixteen, feeling the first strength of her womanhood, when she fell in love for the first time. He was a youth of fair appearance and some wealth, four years her senior. He seduced her expertly and she did not resist,

486

for he held up before her a promised life beyond the circus, a life filled with gleaming carriages and liveried servants and gala balls beneath crystal chandeliers. For two weeks while the circus remained in Baltimore he showered her with gifts and promised that the secret romance would be proclaimed to the world on the day before Tatum and the rest departed for the nation's capital. But when the day came, Amanda's swain was conspicuous by his absence. He sent a single rose and a note of farewell. Alas, his parents had made another match for him, he said, and he would be disinherited if he defied them. In a fit of grief, jealousy and rage, Amanda had fled to the comfort of Hachaliah's arms. Through the night she had clung to him, and as the dawn broke and he kissed away fresh tears, she had returned his kisses. At first he had resisted, but she had learned much from her faithless suitor in a short time, and already she knew how to release a man's primal urges. In joining her flesh with Hachaliah's she had sought to guarantee that he would never leave her as the callous youth had done, that she would always find comfort and protection—and pleasure—by his side. It had never once occurred to her that she might one day wish to leave him and that the new bonds she had created might hold her back.

Hachaliah still had hold of her arm. "Wouldn't I? Do you really want to know?" His expression was almost pleading. He relaxed his grasp and stroked her arm lightly. "But there's really no need for us to quarrel, is there? You'll never leave me. I know you too well. I know your needs. And your desires." His voice was low and earnest and his eyes had softened as the anger left him. They were dark and liquid and they held her in his grip even when he released her arm.

"I won't respond," she said, unable to look away. "I won't move."

"You'll move." It was barely a whisper. One by one he unfastened the remaining buttons on her dress until it was open to the waist. He pushed it off her shoulder and slipped the sleeves off her arms, and the dress fell to the floor. She stood absolutely still. He pushed the straps of her petticoat from her shoulders and soon it too lay in a soft heap about her feet. He placed a hand on her midriff and moved it slowly upward. She felt a surge of blood beneath his palm. Her nipples hardened.

"Ah. You see?" His eyes were still locked on hers.

"It's the cold." She pressed her nails into her palms with all her might.

He knelt before her and hooked his fingers into the waistband of her woolen tights. He pulled slowly downward, taking her only other undergarment, that one of silk, with the tights, leaving her naked before him. She stood like a statue; the clothes about her feet were the drapings of the sculptor's pedestal. Her eyes were closed.

Tatum lifted her easily and deposited her on the bed. His arms left her and she heard a movement, then felt his weight descend onto the bed beside her. When he moved against her she felt his nakedness and his desire. She lay rigid. His lips touched hers and moved down to her breasts, touching each one briefly. His hands roamed her skin, stroking and caressing. One moved to her thighs. "Tell me to go," he said softly.

Her mouth opened and she made a small sound that was not a word.

He leaned over her and his breath warmed her face. Somewhere far below he was touching her. "Tell me to go," he said again, and his lips grazed hers.

She fought to keep from responding. This was not the way she wanted it to be. She had planned her escape. He could not hold her any longer. Tomorrow she and Johnny would be off to the Indian village and there they would stay until the gulf between her and Hachaliah Tatum grew so wide he could no longer reach across it.

His lips were at her ear, catching the lobe and teasing it. But he couldn't reach her even now, not unless she let him. And yet so long as he was near her she must give him no cause for alarm, for he could be dangerous if his suspicions were aroused. He must suspect nothing until he saw that the door of her cage stood open and she had flown to safety. She must fool him completely.

As his mouth returned to hers she caught his lower lip between her teeth and held him captive as her arms went around him to pull him down against her. Below, she let herself go, rising to meet his hand, ending the contest of refusal and persuasion they had played out so often before.

When he slept, Amanda lay beside him for a time, matching the rhythm of her breathing to his own, but her eyes were open. At last she lifted the covers and arose, making no sudden motion. The fire in the stove had burned low and the room was cool. She wrapped herself in her gown and sat at the dressing table, where the lamp still glowed. She reached for the jars that contained her clown makeup. First she applied the white, covering every inch of skin, even the insides of her ears. Her movements were careful and controlled, as if she were preparing for a performance of special importance. Next she drew black lines that radiated from her eyes like the rays of the sun. Close to the corners of her eyes the work was made more difficult by the salty drops that ran down her cheeks, but she dabbed them away with a kerchief of Egyptian cotton and applied the last pointed lines to her satisfaction. She inspected her work and smiled. Slowly the smile faded and her countenance fell into the very picture of grief. Then a hand came up, passing before the sorrowful visage, and in its wake the smile shone brightly once more.

She arose and began to dress.

THIRTY-FOUR

For seven days and nights the sticks had remained crossed before the entrance to Sun Horse's lodge, proclaiming that the one within would be left undisturbed. Sings His Daughter had gone to live with relatives in the camp. Elk Calf Woman came and went with wood and water but she took her meals with Mist and Hears Twice and there was no cooking fire in Sun Horse's lodge.

The people glimpsed the headman when he went to relieve himself, but that was rarely now: he ate nothing and had no need to move his bowels. He made *inipi* daily, accompanied always by Sees Beyond. The people paused as Sun Horse passed by. Sometimes he smiled but more often he scarcely seemed to see them.

"He has decided to die," some said, but others disagreed.

"He seeks power for the people," said one.

"He is praying for the *pte* to come help the two-leggeds," said another.

"When the grass is up I will go to the soldier town," said Elk Leggings, pondering what event from the winter moons he would choose to paint on the winter-count robe. How to show that the band had lost its power and fallen away from the Lakota spirit? Unless Sun Horse offered guidance soon, the band would scatter in the spring. Elk Leggings had heard the talk around the lodge fires at night, the men speaking their thoughts softly, none trying to dissuade those who would go to the northern bands, or the others who would turn their ponies toward the place where the sun rose and go to the Dakota reservation. Perhaps this is what he would paint—the tipis of the Sun Band scattering, the camp circle broken and its sacred power lost.

In Sun Horse's lodge, Sees Beyond remained a while after the *inipi* this day. Outside, the sun was shining and the people moved about, smelling spring in the air. Sees Beyond felt Sun Horse slipping away to a place he could not follow. He tried not to show his concern; the old man was wise and knew the dangers of the spirit world. It was for each man to seek power as he knew how. *Wakán Tanka* touched each one in a different way and each must follow his own path.

But he must speak. "Do not leave this world, *Tunkáshila*," he said, and wondered if the old man even heard his words. "Your power is here. Use it for the people."

Sees Beyond was afraid. As Sun Horse became more remote, he felt his own power waning. We are tied together, he thought. Our hands touch. He stands in the world of men, one hand reaching into the spirit world; I stand there, but I see also the world of men, and my hand touches his, keeping me in this life. If he dies, I will die as well.

"My power?" Sun Horse's voice croaked. He took the drinking bladder from the place where it hung behind him and let a little water trickle into his mouth. He swallowed and seemed to grow stronger. "My power is no more than a promise, and I have failed."

Sees Beyond's hand found the stick he used to guide himself when he walked alone, and he rose. "You have led the people for twenty snows and more," he said. "You can guide them still." He tried to sound confident and reassuring.

"Perhaps," was all that Sun Horse said. Sees Beyond found his way around the fire to the entrance, but as he bent to step through the opening, Sun Horse spoke again.

"I would speak to Hears Twice. Find him for me and send him here."

When Sees Beyond was gone, Sun Horse sat in silence for a time. Suddenly he raised his eyes toward the peak of the lodge and cried out, "Oh, Grandfathers! If I may still use my power for the people, give me a sign!"

He heard a wind coming, far off in the tops of the trees beyond the camp circle. He liked to go among the trees and listen to the different voices of the wind. The sound it made in the tops of the trees was his favorite song. He could hear it moving there although it did not touch him on the ground below.

The wind drew nearer and flapped the lodgeskins as it passed. It came from the north, *Waziya's* breath. The weather was changing. All life was changing. Did this wind bring the power to cleanse and heal, or did it come to fight against the life-giving force? It was true that the cold and snow seemed to hold life in abeyance for a time, but even in winter there was life everywhere. There were few creatures about, but those were the ones in which the life-force was strongest, the hardy ones that neither burrowed deep in the earth nor went south to stay warm. There were ravens and woodpeckers and chickadees and eagles, squirrels in the trees and deer and elk and *pte* in the wooded draws, beavers that came out when warm winds let the ice melt, ermine and foxes and wolves, and the snowshoe hare, who grew his own white coat to blend with the snow. The day before, Sun Horse had walked on the mountainside, and he had followed the tracks of a hare, finding where it had stopped to nibble at the seeds from a pine cone and the place where it had rested beneath a snow-laden bough. All this he saw from the tracks. And then the tracks had stopped. In the middle of an open place the tracks simply disappeared. Sun Horse had been puzzled for a moment, until he saw the other signs, the sweeping marks of the wings on the snow as they flapped to rise into the air again with their burden of struggling hare clutched in the claws that even then were crushing the life away. One life had ended that another might continue. Always there was life and death, but winter was truly when life began. Each creature to be born in the spring was in its mother now, biding its time, as if it knew that all too soon it would be flung into chaos to care for itself.

Sun Horse knew that he too should bide his time, but he was impatient. He sensed that this spring would bring chaos to the Sun Band as well, disrupting the pattern of years, and whether or not it would survive the disruption was up to him. But he was no closer to knowing what to do than when he began his fast. For seven days he had cleansed himself in the *ini ti* and for seven days he had eaten nothing, to cleanse his flesh as well as his spirit. Yet he seemed to draw farther away from understanding what he had done wrong, why he had failed to realize the power that *wambli* had promised when the young Snowblind Moon still had horns.

Over and over again he came back to the *washichun*, and each time confusion was the result of his ponderings. His power was to understand the whites, but he could find no way around the central puzzle: *washichun*, a people not at peace with themselves. How then to make peace with them? How to accommodate their power-without-limit to the power of the Lakota so both peoples might live within the same circle of life? How to assure that the Lakota might still walk the good red road that led to an understanding of the spirit? Sometimes it seemed to Sun Horse that the whites were *wakán*, a mystery, and yet they were not like the other mysteries he had studied all his life. They moved beyond the patterns he knew. It was as if they stood apart from the circle of life. There was a proper place for everything in the wholeness that enveloped both the physical and spirit worlds of the Lakota, but where was the place for the whites?

He did not lack for questions, only answers.

There was a soft cough outside the lodge and Sun Horse bid Hears Twice enter. He invited him to sit and together they smoked a solemn pipe, each offering it to the directions, before Sun Horse told the old seer why he had asked him to come.

"I do not know which way to lead my people," he said when the pipe was done. "Perhaps if you listen and hear the sounds of things to come, that will help me decide."

Hears Twice nodded, agreeing to the headman's request, and he left without having spoken a word.

Sun Horse felt powerless. His strength as a leader had been his power to decide, and it had flowed from the power of his vision—the power of the sun, the power to grow—giving him an ability that had rarely faltered, the power to guide his people toward a path of growth both as a band and as part of the Lakota nation. Yet now he felt no direction beckoning him. The power to grow was the power to change, even to make fundamental changes in the way a people lived; in the time of the Ancient Ones the Lakota had lived among forests and lakes in the Land of the Pines, but then some had moved out onto the plains; they hunted the buffalo and made houses of skin, and in time they tamed the horse. They were called *Titonwan*—the ones who camp on the plains—and they were now the last remaining strength of the Lakota nation. All the other bands had been subdued by the whites.

From the first, Sun Horse had seen that the coming of the whiteman would bring great changes and he had dedicated his life to preparing his people for those changes. Now a turning point had been reached and change was demanded, but

491

which way to turn, and how to change without losing touch with the center? Everything depended on making peace with the whites, a peace that would leave the spiritual strength of the Lakota intact.

But the whites did not make war as the Lakota and their neighbors did, and so they could not make peace in the same way. A new way would have to be found.

The Lakota fought to test the bravery of the young men. War was a young man's task, and his teacher. The greatest honor was not in killing but in the degree of risk to which a warrior exposed himself. The trials of the warpath, the risk of going deep into the enemy's land to raid him and steal his horses, to stand before dangerous odds, these taught the young Lakota fortitude as well. Raid the enemy, steal his horses and women, learn bravery and fortitude; treat the women well and give the horses to those in need, and learn the honor that comes with generosity. Bravery, fortitude and generosity; these were the qualitites a young man learned, and above all he learned to use them for the people. He found honor not by thinking of himself but by showing great courage for the people.

But in time even the bravest warrior might give up war and gain still more honor, for to experience war was to learn the value of peace, and none were honored more than the peacemakers. A man laid down the shield and lance if he wished, and from these men came the most trusted councillors, the old-man chiefs who thought constantly of the good of the people.

Among the whites too, such things were known. Sun Horse had heard that the Great Father in *Washing-ton* had been a war leader once, but now no longer wore the warrior's clothes. But there were few other similarities, and many differences, in the way the whites made war. When the plains people fought one another, some died, but never as many as when they fought the *washíchun*, or when the whites fought among themselves. Sun Horse had been astounded to learn that during the whiteman's war between brothers sometimes more men had died in a single day than were numbered among all the bands of Lakota. And the whites preferred to kill at a distance, with little risk. What honor was there in that? None. Worse, they did not go home after a day's fighting and wait until another day, once the honors had been sung and the scalps danced. They fought every day and they fought for the complete conquest of their enemy. Did they not see that war could bring honor to both sides, that neither side need be crushed? It was even said that some whites had traveled far across great waters to fight people of other lands; they fought until they destroyed the camp circles of the enemy, it was said; they kept the enemy in chains for many years, never making them members of the white tribe. Fought on such a scale, how could war teach the young? How could people learn of individual honors and bravery? Surely such a war could teach nothing but shame and sorrow to the loser, and what arrogance might come from winning such a victory? To win over an entire people would make the winner think he was a better man, his people a better people. Only more trouble could come of that.

It seemed that the whites fought to change the life of the enemy forever. . . .

Sun Horse drank again from the water bladder, frightened by what he saw now.

492

It was not only in war that the whites behaved this way. . . . They sought to change beliefs as well.

From his first contact with the black-robe priests Sun Horse had seen the similarities between the beliefs of the whites and those of the Lakota, but the whites saw only the differences. Wherever they went they wanted the plains people to put away their old beliefs forever. They saw the Mystery and called it *God*, but they did not see that the Lakota prayed to the same force because his prayers took unfamiliar forms. They said the Lakota worshiped heathen gods and prayed to animals, and they dismissed his beliefs as "superstition," revealing in their use of the word their own fear of the unknown. They hid away in wooden buildings to pray, cut off from the touch of sun and wind, and they worshiped a cross made of wood; they said *God* lived in these places, but they did not see God, the Great Mystery, in all things and so could not understand how the buffalo or coyote or softly running rabbit could be worthy of prayer. The black-robes came only to "teach," never to listen; they talked of their *God* and denied the spirit power in a thunderhead or the winter wind.

Sun Horse's head ached and he felt dizzy. Not since the early days of his fast had he felt this debilitated. His power seemed far away, beyond his grasp. Perhaps he had been wrong to wait. Perhaps he should have sent Hardeman to tell Three Stars that the people would accept his spotted-*pte* meat and his blankets, and go with him to the soldier town. Perhaps that would have been best.

Outside the lodge the sun emerged from behind a cloud and the dark interior of the tipi brightened somewhat. Sun Horse heard a child scream in play and a mother's voice scolding. Do not disturb Sun Horse, she said, and Sun Horse shook his head. It was good that the little children should play. Even at the time of the Sun Dance, the most sacred ritual of the Lakota, the little children were encouraged to play and shout all they wished, and when someone made *inipi*, a child could put his head in the door and ask questions, for everyone knew that little children were very pure and were favored by *Wakán Tanka*.

How would the child eat today? How could Sun Horse protect the child to-morrow? These were the questions he should be pondering, not the mysteries of the *washíchun*, which made his head spin.

There was a commotion on the far side of the camp circle and several voices were raised, and for a moment Sun Horse felt a chill of alarm, but there was no alarm in the voices, nor the cries of joy that would have sounded if the pipe carriers were seen returning.

Strangers approached the camp. He knew the sounds of his village as well as he knew the sounds of his own lodge. There was a quickening when strangers approached, like the quickened flow of blood in a man when he felt excitement or danger.

Who could it be? Sun Horse found it difficult to return his thoughts to the world outside his lodge. He felt removed, distant, as if it didn't really matter who the strangers might be.

It seemed that his son and grandson and the other pipe carriers had been gone forever. Where were they now? And where were the soldiers? Several days before, a signal had been seen, far off. *Soldiers have attacked a village.* . . . That and no more, as the wind and clouds returned.

Had Three Stars refused the pipe? The pipe carriers might be captives in the hands of the soldiers. Or they might be dead.

Perhaps there could be no accommodation but surrender.

The entrance flap was opened and Sings His Daughter put her head through the opening. "Lisaputnam and the black whiteman are here. There are some of the Strange-Animal People with them."

Sun Horse nodded but made no move. She withdrew. The councillors could meet the whites and hear what they had to say. Sun Horse could do nothing for them now.

There was movement around the camp as men and women went to see the visitors, and then, before these movements had died away, he heard the voice of Dust, the crier, moving around the camp to announce the news. Dust's voice was high and shrill, a tone he used only for important tidings. "The white *heyoka* girl is lost! She left the settlement in the night! The whites ask our help to find her!"

Amanda watched the buildings impatiently as the first rays of sun touched the valley. She saw the first people moving about, walking among the wagons, flowing like chips of wood in a stream toward the Big House for breakfast. She smiled when the tiny figures began running out of the house, to the barn and the wagons, darting here and there. She had been missed.

She wore the buffalo coat Lisa had given her, but beneath the coat she had on only her clown costume, and she had taken a chill in the predawn cold. She moved higher on the ridge to a sheltered spot among a bunch of rocks from which she could catch the warmth of the sun and still watch the settlement. She saw the figures converge on the barn and then larger figures emerging, some going off in various directions up and down the valley and a group riding together up the trail to the Indian village.

"Here I am!" she shouted, but the ants scurrying hither and yon below her couldn't hear.

Her flight had been impulsive, unthinking. It was her own inability to refuse Hachaliah from which she had run. She realized now that she had put herself in real danger by wandering off alone into the hills to the west of the park. Dawn had been hours away when she left the settlement, but the waning crescent moon had helped her to find her way. Higher and higher she had climbed, driven at first by a kind of strange elation. She was making the break at last. She had been badly frightened by an owl that had leaped into the air from a branch above her head, showering her with snow as she shrieked in terror. *Hooo! Hooo-hooo-hooo-hoo,* he had called back to her, each *hoo* softer than the one before. He had flapped away on silent wings and she had seen the tufted horns against the moon.

She had been relieved when the eastern sky began to brighten, and the appearance of the sun had banished the last of her nighttime fears.

She knew that if she started downhill now one of the searchers would find her soon, but it occurred to her that there was some advantage to be gained by putting off her discovery a while longer.

Let them worry about me, she thought. Let them all worry, Hachaliah most of all. He'll think twice before he forces himself on me again.

But Johnny would worry too and she did not want to hurt him. Maybe he would be the one to find her! She could hide from the others! If Johnny came along she would let herself be seen, and seducing him would be easy in the aftermath of a dramatic rescue.

Satisfied that the search was begun in earnest, she left her watching place and climbed higher still, until she stood atop the ridge that separated Putnam's Park from the rising peaks to the west. Of course if she did not see Johnny she must still allow herself to be found before nightfall. She knew where the trail was that led to the Indian village. She would move in that direction and as the day wore on she would find the trail and follow it toward Putnam's Park until the searchers found her. But there was no hurry just yet. She walked along the ridge until she found a place where the sun and wind had cleared a rocky ledge of snow and there she stopped to rest as the sun rose higher. The ledge was sheltered and warm and soon the warmth lulled her to sleep.

When she awoke the sun was at the zenith. She sat up, searching the glistening slopes around her for moving figures.

Whatever could have made her run away? they would wonder. They must be frantic with worry by now.

She gasped aloud as the idea struck her. If ever again Hachaliah threatened to tell Johnny the truth about the two of them, Amanda could silence him with a threat of her own! She would threaten to tell everyone that Hachaliah took advantage of her all those years ago and she kept silent out of fear! She would tell them that at last she had tried to break it off but Hachaliah flew into a rage and took her by force! He raped her cruelly and so she had run away! And they would believe her no matter what Hachaliah said! Why else would she have run away into the wild mountains unless something truly terrible had happened to her? It was a desperate resort; if Hachaliah called her bluff and she had to use the story, Johnny would be shocked. But he would pity her, as the rest of them would, all her friends in the circus and the settlement, for no one but she and Hachaliah knew the truth. When Hachaliah had been dealt with, Johnny's desire to heal and protect her would overcome his shock and she would play the injured innocent to perfection.

Made light-headed by the power of her idea, she clambered down from the ledge and set off over the snow. The crust was soft now and the going was difficult as she broke through every few steps. She found a drifted crest of hard-packed snow at the edge of a steep slope and she walked along the peak, imagining it was a tightrope stretched from one rocky promontory to the next. In the natural amphitheater below her, an imaginary audience watched. She played an invisible violin, slowing her steps to the time of the silent waltz. It was Johnny's Waltz; she would play it for him when they were together again.

She reached the end of the snowy ridge. Her eyes stung and they were beginning to water. She closed them as she bowed elaborately to her admirers. She lost her balance and fell forward.

She cried out as she hit the snow, but fortunately the slope was not long. She tumbled and rolled and came to a stop at the bottom. Above her the slope began to move, breaking into sections that slid at different speeds before slowing and stopping. Amanda scrambled out of the way of the small avalanche. She saw now that streaks and folds in the snow showed where other slides had occurred, all running down into the little amphitheater. She remembered the frightening force of the avalanche that had almost destroyed the circus on the river trail, and as she climbed back up the slope she followed a scattering of rocks that provided a natural ladder out of the bowl. She would have to be more careful of slopes from now on.

She set off for a stand of dark green pines, squinting hard against the glare, which seemed to have grown stronger. Her eyes were watering steadily now and she blinked to clear them. The tears brimmed over and ran down her cheeks. She dabbed at them with her hand, and her glove came away smeared with white paint and a touch of gray where she had smudged one of the thin black star-points around her eyes. She wished she had brought her silver compact with its powder and small mirror. She wanted her makeup to be perfect. No harm could come to her as Joey. Joey always emerged unhurt in the end. Joey was the one who stood in the center of the ring at the end of the performance and accepted the applause alone, before beckoning the rest of the performers to join her.

But the compact had been given to her by Hachaliah and so she had left it behind.

She staggered and nearly lost her balance. She stopped for a moment to shield her eyes with a hand. Not even closing them offered any relief. The light was softer but her eyelids smarted as if her eyes were full of sand. She pulled her clown hat low on her forehead and stumbled on. When she gained the trees she stopped in the cool shade. She swept the snow off a fallen trunk and sat for a while, until the chill underfoot began to penetrate her fur-lined boots and she was forced to set off again to warm herself.

She moved north and a little east, keeping track of Putnam's Park and the position of the sun behind her, making for the trail connecting the park with the Indian village. It helped a little to be moving away from the sun.

But by mid-afternoon she could barely see. Her eyes were swollen and painful and they watered constantly, blurring her vision. When she tried to follow her own tracks to retrace her steps, the sunlight on the snow blinded her completely, and she found herself wandering aimlessly, crossing her own trail. She broke through the crust with almost every step now and the struggle was exhausting her.

496

She stopped to think, fighting off panic. She knew there must be fifty riders out looking for her. If she just went in the right direction she would find help, but her vision was failing. She could still make out the general form of objects close at hand and the shape of the land around her, but no detail. The sun was an awesome glare that filled half the sky; it was lower now, moving toward the west. Putting it behind her she started off downhill, but cliffs fell away before her and she was forced farther to the north. Beyond the cliffs were steep slopes covered with snow and she skirted these too, fearing an avalanche. Finally she found a wooded hillside that seemed to offer a safe descent. She moved through the trees with her hands in front of her to ward off the branches, falling often and sometimes bumping into the tree trunks when she fell, emerging at last in a small meadow.

By peering through her fingers from the shadows at the edge of the trees she saw that the meadow was the bottom of a small valley. Around her, the land rose on all sides. Overhead, clouds covered the sky and she could no longer locate the sun.

She was lost, and night was coming on. A sob escaped her and then another, and she gave in to them, sinking to her knees in the snow. Her head ached and the pain seemed to be spreading to the rest of her body. Her stomach churned and she tasted the bile rising to her throat. Quite without warning she doubled over and vomited violently.

When the spasm passed she wiped her chin and spat to expel the bitter taste from her mouth, and then she became aware of a sound close at hand. It was the sound of a large animal breathing, a whuffling, snorting sound that caused her to go rigid with fear. The hunters had spoken of bears and wolves in the mountains. Why had she forgotten this until now? What had she been thinking of to go off by herself? She managed to turn her head and she let out a stifled cry of terror as she made out a dark shape looming close at hand. She scrambled away on all fours, seeking the shelter of the tree trunks, and when she turned again she saw that the huge shape was moving past her, unconcerned. Curving horns crowned a massive head that hung from great humped shoulders. She knew the beast now. She had seen a buffalo once before, in another circus. Beyond the first there were others. A dozen, two dozen or more of the blurred shapes with the high humps and small hindquarters, all moving in the same direction across the snowy meadow.

A shot startled Whitcomb out of a sound sleep. His legs jerked spastically as he awoke; his horse shied at the sudden movement and Whitcomb fell. He hit the muddy ground as other shots rang out.

"Get him, for Christ's sake!"

The men were shooting at a deer, but the animal leaped a small gully and vanished into a patch of pine trees a hundred yards away as a final fusillade failed to bring him down.

Whitcomb got to his feet and moved his shoulder painfully, but he judged that no permanent damage had been done by the fall. He brushed some wet snow and mud from his buffalo coat.

The day was fair. A gentle breeze from the south was warm on his face. The sun shone brightly and small clouds dotted the sky.

First Sergeant Dupré returned Whitcomb's horse, handing him the reins. "It was Rogers who saw the deer first, sair. He fired without permission."

"It doesn't matter, Sergeant. If he had killed it he'd be a hero. We can't punish him for missing." They had seen no Indians for three days and the men were becoming careless, but no more careless than he for allowing himself to sleep in the saddle. The men were looking around anxiously now, but nothing moved anywhere in sight. They were alone, eighteen men and thirteen horses. Lieutenant Corwin lay on a travois, unconscious. Close to the west, foothills and mountains rose above them. To the east, the plains lay somnolent and deserted.

It was the fifth day since the battle, the third since they had seen another living soul. Two hours ago they had left Clear Fork, the upper portion of Lodgepole Creek, and now they were making their way south along the Big Horn foothills, west of the old wagon road, keeping to cover as best they could. The jerky McCaslin had gathered in the village was almost gone and the deer was the first game they had seen; fresh meat would have cheered the men more than anything except the sight of Crook's column, but Crook was far away, somewhere on the Powder.

"Mr. Reb! Where the hell are you?" Whitcomb turned to see that Corwin had raised himself up on one elbow. He moved to the troop commander's travois, followed by Dupré. "Why have we stopped?" Corwin asked. His face was ashen and the skin was stretched tightly over his cheekbones. There were dark hollows beneath his eyes.

"Private Rogers saw a deer, sir, but we didn't bring him down."

Corwin shook his head as if he had trouble understanding the words.

"There's a grove of trees ahead, sir. There might be some water there. It looks like a good place to rest for a while."

Corwin frowned. "Follow my orders, Mr. Reb."

"Excuse me, sir, but which orders are those?"

"We'll stop as usual when we find a suitable place." Corwin slumped back on the travois. He heaved a long sigh and closed his eyes.

Whitcomb turned to Dupré. "You heard him, Sergeant. That place is good enough. We'll tether the horses in the grove and let the men get some rest."

With Whitcomb and Dupré in the lead the little band got under way again. Although they dared build fires at night now, the men slept better in a patch of sunshine with pickets keeping watch. Hostiles could spring from anywhere and at night the men slept fitfully if at all.

They had had no rest on the night following the battle and the next few days had been little better.

It was only through Corwin's foresight that the abandoned remnant of E Troop had escaped annihilation at the hands of the Indians as the battle ended. Whitcomb had brought his flanking party back to the troop's defensive line in the brush to find that Corwin had sent Sergeant Dupré for the horses and was moving his remaining men to the thickest stand of trees near the river. There was no sign of Polachek and his platoon; Corwin guessed they were pinned down by the renewed barrage of fire from the Indians on the bluffs.

Dupré and his two men had come along the ice moments later, but they brought only thirteen mounts. They had reached the horses to find the animals tethered, E Troop's horse handlers gone, and fighting taking place on the south side of the village as a group of Indians tried to intercept Captain Mills's horses, which were being brought down from the mountain. Fire was coming from the full length of the bluff face above the battlefield, and Indians were once more infiltrating the village, moving out from the base of the hillside. The soldiers still in the village were giving ground and it seemed to Dupré that the situation was precarious. He and his men grabbed fifteen horses, intending to return at once with more men to get the rest, but two of those they took had broken away and bolted when a burning tipi exploded close to the riverbank.

Corwin had ordered Dupré to remain on the line then, sending Sergeant Duggan and Corporal Stiegler with four men to get the rest of the horses. He sent Sergeant Rossi to contact Polachek if he could, but when Rossi had been gone only a few minutes, a group of mounted troopers galloped through the village to where Polachek and Lieutenant Paul had taken position, apparently to save them from being cut off. At the same moment, three Indian boys had brought a dozen or more horses to the warriors in the redoubt. One of the boys was shot, and this had provoked an abortive charge, which was driven back. Corwin could not see the action well from where he lay in the brush, but he could see the mounted troopers withdrawing hastily once the Indians were repulsed, and he saw that they had Polachek, Paul and Rossi with them, together with all the men from that end of the line, the riders screening the men on foot from the continuing fire that came from the bluffs. "It looks like retreat is the better part of valor, boys," Corwin had said, and he prepared the men to mount. But the first bugle call had come then, ordering a withdrawal, and when the Indians saw the troopers in retreat they had burst from cover and poured into the village, cutting off E Troop's escape in that direction and making it impossible for Duggan and Stiegler to return with more horses. With the Indians' attention on Reynolds' column, which was forming up and moving off to the south, Corwin had led his men across the river and they had taken cover in the thick brush there, where Whitcomb had been with his flankers just a short time before.

By a miracle they were not discovered. They had huddled together in their hiding place, weapons at the ready, hands on the horses' nostrils to keep them quiet, and Sergeant Dupré had whispered a prayer in French. The Indians had combed the village to see what could be salvaged and evidently found very little, judging by how soon they had begun to trudge off downstream along the trail on the western bank, the one the women and children had taken earlier. By dusk they were all gone except for a few that plainly intended to remain the night, and the handful of soldiers had dared to move a little farther downstream.

But they couldn't go far. There was no telling how near the main body of hostiles might have camped and they couldn't risk stumbling on the angry warriors in the night. They had found a new hiding place in a larger copse of trees and there they remained, kept warm only by the horses and the foresight of Sergeant Dupré, who had brought several extra greatcoats when he fetched the horses. Each man in the little band had a coat, and the coats had kept them alive through the fireless night.

That night had been a torment. At the first screams from the village the men had wanted to come out of hiding to rescue the poor wretch that had fallen into the hands of the savages, but Corwin had held them back, knowing that the platoon's only chance of survival lay in escaping detection. Some of the men had been near rebellion, but then a single shot had stopped the screams and in the morning the Indians were gone.

The reduced command consisted of Lieutenant Corwin, Whitcomb, Sergeant Dupré, Corporals McCaslin and Atherton, and thirteen private soldiers. Four of the men had serious frostbite; two were unable to walk. Apart from Corwin, none was wounded.

They had crept past the still smoking village and started off upstream, hoping against hope that they would be able to overtake Reynolds and the rest of the attack force at the juncture of the Powder and Lodgepole Creek, where they were to await Crook, but they had been forced to take cover several times during that first day to avoid small bands of Indians moving up and down the river valley, and by nightfall they had made only eleven or twelve miles. The next morning they had been elated to discover the tracks of Crook's four companies entering the valley from the west. The clouds had descended and it had begun to snow in earnest, and the little band had pressed on under cover of the weather, with

McCaslin and Private Gray a hundred yards to the front to watch for Indians. The valley had broadened steadily and the growth of cottonwoods along the stream grew denser, and the soldiers had kept to the trees.

They had halted when Gray appeared suddenly before them, motioning them frantically to take cover. McCaslin had returned a short while later with the disheartening news—they had reached the mouth of Lodgepole Creek but Crook and the reunited command had already gone off up the Powder and the rendezvous site was swarming with hostiles. From the number of mounted Indians it was apparent that the refugees from the burned village had found help somewhere near at hand. Most of the Indians were moving upriver after the soldiers while another group was heading downstream with a herd of horses that included a few cavalry mounts, apparently stolen from the command during the night.

Corwin and his men had kept hidden until the snow thinned and they saw that the wide valley was deserted, and it was then that Corwin had announced his decision: they would make no further attempts to rejoin Crook. The Indians posed too great a risk, he said. There was little chance that such a small force could get safely through the savages. They would do best to stay away from both Crook and the hostiles and make their way alone. They would go up Lodgepole and turn south along the Big Horn foothills. When they neared Fort Reno they would send a patrol to see if the supply train or any part of Crook's force was still there. If not, they would have to continue to Fetterman on their own.

And so they had pushed on with Corwin in the lead, reeling in his saddle. Since leaving the Powder they had seen no one, red or white. On reaching the Bozeman road they found no tracks more recent than their own, made on the march up country, and Corwin, confined to a travois by then, had decided that they would stay away from the old wagon road, keeping closer to the foothills where the terrain offered better cover.

Whitcomb watched the men as the tiny column reached the grove of pines and halted once more. Without being told what to do some of the troopers gathered the horses and took them into the grove to be tethered while others began to gather firewood, but their movements were slow and listless. Two of the men had bandaged hands that were all but useless. One trooper's eyes were completely covered against the glare of the sun and everyone was affected to some degree with snowblindness. Whitcomb still wore his green goggles but few of the others had them.

We're the walking wounded, he thought. Scarcely better than refugees.

"Excuse me, sir, 'e's asking for you." It was Corporal Atherton. He had taken on himself the chore of caring for Lieutenant Corwin. For two days after receiving his wound, Corwin had complained of no pain, although his face was gray and drawn and the effort it took for him to remain on his horse could be seen by all. On the third day he had been unable to keep in his saddle. After he had fallen twice they had built the travois and covered him with a buffalo robe.

"What time do you make it, Corporal?" Whitcomb's gold watch had been smashed in the battle. He didn't know when. Probably when he threw himself on the ground to defend the line against the charge from the Indians' breastwork.

Atherton glanced at the sun.

"Oh, about midday, I should think, sir. It's a nice enough day, isn't it?"

Whitcomb followed Atherton to Corwin's litter. Corwin was singing softly to himself.

> *"Heave away you ruling kings,*
> *Heave away, haul away,*
> *Heave away my bully boys,*
> *We're bound for South Australia.*
>
> *Oh, a sailor's life is a hell of a life,*
> *Heave away, haul away,*
> *Without any money, without any wife—"*

"'ere's Mr. Reb, sir. Excuse me, Leftenant, but that's 'ow 'e asked for you."

"It's all right."

"Ahoy, Mr. Reb! Stand fast, bo'sun! We'll run up the colors when she comes about!" Corwin grinned grotesquely. The troopers were keeping an eye on their commander, watching but not watching. It was plain that his raving made them uneasy.

"'e's like that off and on, sir," Atherton informed Whitcomb in a low voice. "'e'll be like that for a time and then 'e's quite 'imself again."

So far, Corwin had been fit to make each important decision when it came along, but his condition was worsening steadily. What would happen when a decision was demanded and Corwin could not make it? Whitcomb wondered.

"Ask Sergeant Dupré to come over here, will you?"

Whitcomb knelt to untie the bandanna that held Corwin's trouser in place over the wound. He pulled the trouser aside and drew back at the stench.

"You didn't know I was a sailor, did you, Ham me boy?" Corwin was looking at him with steady eyes.

"How are you feeling, sir?"

"Like shit, Mr. Reb. Like the bottom of the post latrine. Damn you, be careful!"

Whitcomb was untying the bandage. "Sorry."

"What sort of progress have we made?"

"Quite good today, sir. I think we've come about ten miles this morning."

"That's good. That's good. Jesus, that hurts! Yes, by God, I was a sailor once. Not the fancy kind, just a working seaman. Christ, I was seasick the whole voyage. No more of that, I said. But I'll tell you something, Ham. The seafaring life has got the songs. The cavalry should have songs half as good as those. Listen to this:

> *"Farewell and adieu to you Spanish ladies,*
> *Farewell and adieu to you ladies of Spain,*

For we've received orders to sail for old England,
And we hope in a short time to see you again."

He sang in a pleasing baritone but with none of the gusto of a sailor leaning to his work on a pitching deck. Instead he raised his head and sang the air softly, like a lullaby or a courting song.

"Well, I didn't have the stomach for it, anyway. The war was just getting started and I joined the Volunteers. Made lieutenant in three months. Hard up for officer material, I'll tell you. General Crook started out as a captain, regular army. By the fall of '62 he was brevetted lieutenant colonel and appointed brigadier general of Volunteers. All he had to do was wait for his permanent rank to catch up with him. But he deserves it, no question about that. He's a hardworking son of a bitch. I'm still waiting. Look here." He tapped Whitcomb on the shoulder. "I may lose track from time to time, but I'm not as far out of it as I seem. The singing and all that—it's just to help me forget the pain."

"You need your rest when you can get it, sir. That's the best thing for you." Whitcomb removed the last wrappings of bandage and tried to hide his reaction at the sight of the wound.

Dupré joined them then and he inspected the wound as Corwin began to sing again.

> *"Me boots and clothes are all in pawn,*
> *Go down, ye blood red roses, go down!*
> *The whalefish swims around Cape*
>   *Horn,*
> *Go down, ye blood red roses, go down!*
> *Oh, ye pinks and poseys—Good Christ!"*

Dupré had gingerly touched the livid flesh beyond the edges of the wound. The skin was dark and mottled. Corwin pushed his hand away and lay back on his litter, breathing hard.

Dupré turned to Whitcomb. "A word, sair, if you will."

They withdrew a short way. Around them the men lay scattered within the shelter of the trees, each in a patch of the warm sunlight. Small fires were burning and a few of the men were making a weak broth by boiling strips of jerky in cups of water. The horses were tethered in good grass, well back in the trees. From a distance any inquiring eyes would see the trees but not those sheltered there. Whitcomb was pleased to see that the faint white smoke from the fires dispersed quickly and was not visible above the treetops. They had all learned a good deal about making smokeless fires in the past few days. Dry willow wood was best and the dead branches of cedar and pine were safe too.

"We did not loosen the tourniquet in time, sair."

"Hmm?" He returned his attention to Dupré.

503

"We did not loosen the tourniquet in time."

During the second frigid night after the battle, Corwin's leg had swollen, which had the effect of tightening the tourniquet and shutting off the slight flow of blood Dupré had permitted to continue. When the limb was next inspected, the foot had shown signs of frostbite, but a more serious affliction had taken hold in the wound.

"Is it gangrene?" Whitcomb felt obliged to ask the question, but even to his inexperienced eyes the putrid state of the wound was apparent.

"I am afraid so. Without medicines, we can do nothing."

Whitcomb noticed for the first time that the ends of Dupré's mustache were no longer waxed and curled. Instead they drooped on either side of his mouth, giving him an almost Oriental appearance. He realized that Dupré was waiting for him to speak, and he pulled himself together. I mustn't let my attention wander, he thought.

"And if we leave it alone, the gangrene will continue to spread."

"Yes, sair."

Whitcomb felt helpless. What would happen if Corwin lapsed into unconsciousness? Who would make the decisions then? "I have heard that sunshine sometimes has a good effect on morbid conditions. We'll leave the wound uncovered today while we rest. It may do no good, but it can't make things worse, can it?"

"No, sair, it cannot make it worse. I have posted pickets, sair. Gwynn and Gray to begin with. I will have them relieved in two hours if you wish to stay longer."

"You should make your report to Major Corwin, Sergeant. He's in command, not me."

"Forgive me, sair, but you should be."

Whitcomb was taken aback. "You're not serious."

"Your superior officer is wounded, sair. Most of the time he is not himself. On campaign an officer must use his judgment in a case like this one."

"You should think twice before you counsel mutiny, Sergeant."

Dupré gave a Gallic shrug that could have meant anything. "You must prepare yourself for the eventuality, sair. What will you do when he gives orders that make no sense?"

"I'll cross that bridge when I come to it. Right now let's see if we can't make him eat something."

With Atherton's help they made Corwin drink some of the jerky broth and eat a few pieces of the dried meat. Afterward, Whitcomb sat with his back to a tree trunk and watched over the little encampment as the men slept.

We're not much of a fighting force, he thought. Not even a full platoon. One first lieutenant, badly wounded; one very junior second lieutenant with less than a month of field duty; a handful of soldiers in varying stages of disrepair—we're the lost platoon of Company E. Thank God for Dupré and Atherton and McCaslin. They're the ones who should be in command if Corwin's unable, not me.

504

A hand shook his shoulder and he realized that he had fallen asleep. He was surprised to see that the sun had moved around to the west. Sergeant Dupré stood over him.

"I imagined that you might wish to be getting along, sair."

"How is Major Corwin?"

"Resting comfortably."

A few hours of exposure to sunshine and fresh air had dried Corwin's wound but the flesh surrounding the mottled area was still livid and tender. As Atherton replaced the bandage, Corwin awoke and groaned.

"We'll be getting along now, sir. With your permission," Whitcomb said.

"Weigh anchor, Mr. Reb." Corwin's voice was weak and his eyes seemed dead.

The little group moved slowly, despite the efforts of Whitcomb and the non-commissioned officers to keep up a better pace. After a time, Whitcomb relaxed his efforts and permitted himself to doze in the saddle, jerking awake every few minutes. Each time he raised his head it seemed they hadn't moved since the last time he looked, but the horses and men plodded on. They moved, but nothing changed; the same looming mountains stood on their right and the same desolate vastness to the left. Even the sunlight couldn't warm the empty landscape.

Where would Crook be by now? he wondered. Once he had resupplied himself from the wagons at Fort Reno he could turn on his pursuers, if they followed him that far. The cavalry would become the hounds once again and the Indians would revert to their natural role as foxes. Crook might bring the wagons up-country this time, along the Powder. Sooner or later he was bound to join forces with Terry and Gibbon and together they would round up the hostiles, but Ham Whitcomb would miss it. His career would get no leg up from this campaign.

There was no help for it. Just now the remnants of E Troop were confronting the soldier's eternal task—survival—in a new and more fundamental form.

He had no more illusions left to be shattered. At West Point he had imagined himself going into battle as part of an army bent on a common goal, with objectives to be taken and lines to be held. Never in his most fearful dreams had he imagined anything like this, being cut off and alone in a land so huge it seemed to be without limit.

We keep moving but we never arrive at our destination. There is no front and no rear; the enemy is everywhere and nowhere. This is what Purgatory must be like for soldiers. We're the Lost Platoon of the Foreign Legion, condemned to wander through Purgatory, forever alert, forever afraid. Is this what all the Indian wars are like?

He found the notion so discouraging that he drew his horse aside and dismounted. He would walk for a while and think of other things. As the rear of the column passed him he fell in beside Corporal McCaslin, who marched there as file closer. The wiry corporal walked a good deal of the time, often giving up his turn on horseback to one of the other men. He seemed to feel the lack of adequate food less than the rest of them.

"How's the snowblindness today, Corporal?"

McCaslin's eyes were red-rimmed and bloodshot.

"Oh, not so bad, sorr. There's some of the boys have it much worse."

Whitcomb removed his green Arizona goggles. "Someone else can use these for a while. Give them to whoever's in the worst shape."

"Thank you, sorr." McCaslin accepted the offering. "Corporal Atherton has a pair as well, and the major won't be needin' his, not while he's restin'. We'll trade them off and make do." He lowered his voice. "Beggin' yer pahrdon, sorr. Did Sahrgint Dupree have a word wid yez about takin' command?"

"Not you too. I thought you told me the men would follow Major Corwin to hell and back."

"That they would, sorr, when himself is himself. But he's not been himself for some days now, and he'll not be gettin' better until we get him to a doctor."

They walked for a time in silence. McCaslin sensed Whitcomb's troubled thoughts and when he spoke again his voice was cheerful.

"If we had some grease, sorr, we could mix it wid a bit of charcoal from a fire and smudge it on our cheeks. Cuts the glare, y' see. We'd look like a lot of haythen Indians, but it'd be a blessin' for the eyes."

Whitcomb considered this. They had no grease and no prospects of getting any unless they brought down some game. McCaslin was watching him expectantly but he could think of nothing else to suggest. He found it difficult to concentrate on anything but his hunger and fatigue.

"I was thinkin' of the horses, sorr," McCaslin said at last. "There's one or two won't go much farther. We could have fresh meat for the boys and a bit o' grease too."

Whitcomb shook his head. "Is that what we've come to? Eating horsemeat? My God, Mac, I never thought it would be like this."

"We're not so bad off, sorr. Except for poor Peter Dowdy, rest his soul. And the major, of course. But we've come through it wid no one else wounded. Just a bit of frostbite here and there. We'll do all right."

McCaslin's good spirits cheered Whitcomb and he felt a little better. He picked up his pace and moved up the column, looking at the horses with new interest. Gwynn's mount walked with an unsteady gait and its eyes were listless. It wouldn't make it to Fetterman, perhaps not even to Reno. Whitcomb was surprised to find the juices running in his mouth at the thought of fresh meat, no matter what the source. Maybe McCaslin's suggestion wasn't such a bad one. He would speak to Corwin about it when they stopped for the night.

Shadows were reaching out from the mountains now, and when they covered the travelers, Whitcomb allowed himself to relax a little. Even if hostile eyes were watching from somewhere out on the plains they would never see the small group of horses and men moving against the dark mass of the Big Horns. Cloud Peak, toward which they had steered until today, lay on the right now. Tomorrow or the next day they would cross Crazy Woman's Fork and from there it was only another day or two to Reno. If they kept up the pace.

He resolved that one way or another he would keep them going. If they had to eat horseflesh, so be it, but they would march every day. At the end of the trail there was rest and proper food, and care for the injured. He prayed Crook had left the wagons at Reno.

The darkness gathered slowly and he realized that the equinox was at hand. What was the date? The twenty-first? No, the twenty-second. The battle had been on the seventeenth; St. Patrick's Day, as John Bourke had reminded him. It was spring, but there was scant evidence of the changing season hereabouts, save for the longer days.

As the dusk thickened he looked about for a place to spend the night. The platoon crested a rounded toe of the foothills and he spied a depression ahead. There was a trickle of water and some brush off to the left where the depression became a gully. He mounted his horse and overtook Sergeant Dupré in the lead. "We better make camp here while there's still some light to find wood," he said.

They moved into the gully where the brush was thickest. A small fire here wouldn't be seen.

Atherton reported that Corwin had mumbled and dozed through the evening march. He had not known Atherton when the corporal gave him water. Together, Whitcomb and Atherton inspected the wound and found that the mottled area had spread. Neither commented on the obvious, but Whitcomb showed the leg to Dupré when he returned with the wood detail, and the Frenchman nodded.

"It must come off, sair. If the bad blood goes above the knee, he will lose the whole leg."

Field amputation was not a specialty taught at West Point but Whitcomb had heard of it often enough. It was the preferred treatment for any serious wound in a limb. A serious wound elsewhere on the body usually resulted in death. Further fatalities were caused by amputations, but if the patient survived he received a pension and a discharge. Some preferred death.

Corwin opened his eyes and looked at them. "Where is the wind, mister?" The voice was not his own.

"The wind, sir?"

"We'll take in a reef if it blows up." Corwin's eyes closed and his breathing became deeper.

"You must take command, sair." Dupré spoke softly. Whitcomb looked at him briefly and then looked away. It was easy enough for him to say; the top sergeant proposed and the officer disposed. What would Dupré do if Whitcomb weren't there? Would he take command or take in a reef?

Whitcomb chuckled and Dupré looked at him strangely. "I'm all right, Sergeant. The leg... Should it be done soon?"

"The sooner the better, sair."

Whitcomb shook his head. Throughout the afternoon he had shut the possibility of an amputation from his mind as resolutely as he might have rejected the thought of his own death. "Leave me alone with him for a while," he said, and he sat cross-legged on the ground beside the travois.

Corwin looked up and smiled. "Well, Ham, we gave them the slip, eh?"

"Sir?"

"The Indians, boy. We gave them the slip."

"Yes, sir."

"You know, I never thought I would want to be back in Arizona, but I could stand it a bit warmer right now. I can't seem to get warm enough. Did I ever tell you about Arizona, Ham?"

"I'll get you another robe, sir. Then you can tell me." When he returned with the robe Corwin was looking up at the heavens, where the stars were winking on one by one. Whitcomb spread the robe over the supine form and tucked it in at the edges.

"There's heaven and hell in Arizona, Ham. All tucked away hundreds of miles from nowhere. Heaven was called Jennifer. God she was beautiful! She was my wife. Did you know I was married?" He looked at Whitcomb and Whitcomb saw that his eyes were brimming with tears.

"No, sir."

"Of course you didn't. I forget that I don't speak of it anymore. But she was beautiful, Ham. We were stationed at Camp McDowell. Then I was transferred and I let her go alone in the ambulance, her and the baby. Things had been quiet and they had just one squad as escort..." He wiped his eyes with an unsteady hand and coughed to clear his throat. "They didn't give 'em the slip that day. Apaches, Ham. God I hate them!"

Whitcomb was shocked. "You lost them, sir? Your wife and baby were killed?"

Corwin waved his hand to brush the memory away. "It was a long time ago."

"I'm sorry, sir. I had no idea." The words were trivial and inadequate, but he could find no way to express the heartfelt sympathy that Corwin's revelation had aroused in him.

Corwin grinned oddly. "I drank a good deal, but it doesn't make you forget, not really. You remember that when you've got something to forget." He lay back and closed his eyes. "There was another girl once. Just as beautiful. If I'd married her everything would have been different." His eyes opened again. "It's all a matter of choices, Ham. You pick your direction and you go, otherwise you stand at the crossroads forever." The eyes closed and it occurred to Whitcomb that he might as well be looking at a cadaver, for all the life that was left in the face. Corwin began to hum a tune and then he whispered the words.

> *"Farewell and adieu to you Spanish ladies,*
> *Farewell and adieu to you ladies of Spain,*
> *For we've received orders to sail for old England,*
> *And we hope in a short time to see you again.*

508

We'll rant and we'll roar like true British sailors,
We'll rant and we'll roar, all on the high seas..."

His voice trailed off and he slept.

Whitcomb got stiffly to his feet and he saw that the men were gathered in a circle around a fire nearby. Overhead the sky was dark. He hadn't been aware of the fire being built or the passing of the last light in the west. Time seemed to be proceeding in jumps, flitting past him when he wasn't watching.

"There's coffee, sir." Atherton held a steaming cup out to him. Sergeant Dupré had found a sack containing three pounds of coffee during the battle, in one of the lodges he had inspected. He had appropriated the coffee without hesitation and it was this precious reserve, as much as the jerky, that kept the men going.

Whitcomb took the cup. He held it tightly in his gloved hands and stood with his back to the fire. Someone handed him some jerky. He chewed each bite of the dried buffalo meat thoroughly and washed it down with coffee, and when he had consumed his share he felt as contented as if he had eaten a full meal. He dropped down on his hocks and let his head droop forward, enjoying the warmth and crackle of the fire.

"That's the last of the jerky, sir."

"Hmm?" He looked up and blinked. He could fall asleep in an instant now. That was what he needed. A good night's sleep. Maybe Corwin's wound would show some improvement in the morning. Wake up early and perhaps find some game at dawn. What had Dupré said about Corwin's leg? It had to come off? Surely that could wait. There was time to decide about that later on.

"It can wait," he said aloud, and realized that they were all looking at him. Sixteen pairs of eyes focused on him.

I'm the youngest here, for God's sake! Why does it have to be me? He searched the faces and he didn't like what he saw. Hope fading, confidence waning. Uncertainty. And questions too, directed at him. What are you made of, Mr. Reb? Now's the time to show us all.

What made it possible for an army to win was the belief that it would win. So simple, until that belief failed. At some indefinable moment the will faltered, first in one man, then in the others, and then defeat followed as certainly as night followed day. "You can see it in their eyes," Cleland Whitcomb had told his son. He had taken Ham to see Lee's surrender because he wanted the boy to glimpse the great man at least once, even in defeat. When the short ceremony was over and Lee emerged from the farmhouse, Cleland Whitcomb held Ham by the shoulders and thrust him forward, and Robert Edward Lee, United States Military Academy Class of 1829, had looked Ham Whitcomb straight in the eye for a moment before passing on.

He saw Lee's eyes before him now, sixteen pairs of them.

"What are your orders, sir?" It was Private Gray who spoke. Whitcomb saw that the gray-haired soldier was regarding him kindly. When Whitcomb had taken his dozen men to flank the Indians behind their breastwork during the battle, it had been Private Gray who showed Whitcomb how to withdraw from his position across the river, making it look as if the line was still held. Gray had been the last man on the line and he had retreated in quick darts, firing from each place he stopped. What would you do now, Private Gray? You helped me then and I could use your help again. What would Captain John Wesley of the Army of Northern Virginia do in my place? You fought your war and you came out of it alive, even though you lost.

But he couldn't ask for help, not of Gray or Dupré or anyone else. The gold band on his hand was his badge of office, and the West Point seal conferred on him a great burden.

"How is your horse, Gwynn?"

"Poorly, sorr. He won't go beyond a walk."

"Very well. We'll slaughter him tonight and pack as much of the meat as we can. Sergeant, how much coffee is left?"

"Enough for four days, sair, maybe five."

"All right. Meat and coffee will keep us going. We should be at Fort Reno in three or four days, but we'll have to march all day from now on. There will be a nooning stop but no time for sleeping." He paused. The burden seemed bearable so far. "We have to protect our eyes. You're no good to anyone if you can't see. The men with goggles will take turns sharing them with the others."

"Excuse me, sir." It was Gray again. "I've heard somewhere that a bit of cloth tied across the eyes is a makeshift sort of goggle. You cut small holes in it. I don't know why I didn't think of it sooner."

Whitcomb was shocked by the simplicity of the suggestion. Why hadn't he himself thought of it sooner? Or why hadn't Dupré or McCaslin or Atherton thought of it, with all their experience on the frontier? Because the first few days after the battle were stormy, and when the sun appeared, he and everyone else had welcomed it. They had squinted and marched on, and now most of the men were affected in some degree by snowblindness. It was the commanding officer's responsibility to foresee such dangers and prevent them.

"We're none of us thinking too clearly, I guess," he said. "All right then, the flankers and pickets will use the goggles and the rest of us will make do with cloth."

"Are you taking command, sir?"

The voice came from somewhere in the circle, but Whitcomb was not sure just where. It didn't matter. The voice asked for all of them. Why did he have to ask? Must there be a formal declaration? Wasn't it enough that Whitcomb was deciding the things that needed deciding now? He took a deep breath. "In view of Major Corwin's condition, I am taking command temporarily until he recovers."

"He won't be recoverin', sorr, not with that leg."

"I agree, Corporal. I'm afraid the leg will have to come off." He set his

510

cup aside and stood up. "There's no sense in further delay. I'll need a sharp knife. Who has one?"

"Use mine, sir." Donnelly offered a long blade, handle first. Whitcomb accepted it and thumbed the edge. It was razor-sharp. He realized that it was the knife Donnelly had used to unman the wounded Indian during the battle, but that didn't seem to matter. Perhaps there was even some poetic justice in using it now; the Indian would have a small measure of revenge on the cavalry from beyond the grave.

"Some of you men bring the major close to the fire," he said. "If anyone has any spirits, I want to know it now."

It was Dupré who reached into his coat and brought out a nickel-plated flask encased in tooled leather. "Cognac, sair. Not the best, but he will not know the difference."

Gentle hands carried Corwin from his resting place and set him before the fire. The movement caused him to grimace and open his eyes suddenly.

"My God damn leg's on fire. Do something, for God's sake!"

"We're going to do what we can for you, Major. I hope you're feeling a little better." Whitcomb felt ridiculous for mouthing such pleasantries. He knelt beside Corwin and placed a blanket under the injured leg. He peeled back the uniform trouser and sliced off the woolen underwear above the knee. Corwin grunted each time the leg was moved. Dupré passed the flask to Corwin, who sniffed it and managed a smile.

"You're a souse, Dupré, you French son of a bitch. Here's to the French." He raised the flask and drank deeply, and then he saw the knife that McCaslin was passing through the flames of the fire. "Oh, I see it now! You bastards want to take my leg! I'm damned if you will!"

He drew back fearfully but Atherton restrained him. "Easy, sir. It's for your own good. That leg is killin' you as sure as an Indian would if 'e got the chance."

Corwin's eyes were wide with alarm and they found Whitcomb now. "It's you, you Rebel son of a bitch! Don't think I don't know what you're up to! You want my command! Well you won't get it! Each of you men is my witness. I'm still in command here! If this Rebel tries to take over, I'll file charges of mutiny. The same goes for any man who helps him."

"Don't be hard on Mr. Whitcomb, sair," said Dupré soothingly. "He is doing what he must do."

"He's a God damn Johnny Reb!" Corwin was agitated and fearful.

"That he is, sorr," said McCaslin. "And so is Private Gray, but he serves you well, just like Mr. Whitcomb here."

Corwin looked at Whitcomb again. "You might as well cut my throat as chop off my leg! I'll go home with two legs or not at all!"

"Lie still, sir, if you please. Private Gray, I'll need you and four others to hold him. Arms, legs and shoulders."

"All right, you bastards," Corwin said as their hands took hold of him.

Rather than have them proceed against his will he gave in. "Have at it. I'll get a peg leg and I'll still kick your sorry asses 'round the parade ground. Give me a minute, boys. Let the brandy take hold." He drank again, and paused to come up for air.

> *"Oh they call me Hanging Johnny,*
> *Away, boys, away,*
> *But I only hang for money,*
> *So hang, boys, hang.*
> *Me father was a sailor,*
> *Away, boys, away.*
> *He should ha' been a tailor,*
> *So hang, boys, hang!"*

He drained the flask and threw it from him. "Lay on, Macduff, and shoot the son of a whore that first cries 'Hold, enough!'" He laughed feverishly.

It seemed to Whitcomb that the amputation took forever. Dupré offered to perform the surgery but something compelled Whitcomb to take the ugly task on himself, and so with occasional advice from Dupré and McCaslin and Private Gray, who held Corwin's shoulders, he proceeded. The leg was cut at the knee; without a bone saw it was impossible to sever it elsewhere. Dupré placed a stick of willow in Corwin's mouth for him to bite on but he bit through it and screamed as the knife severed the first tendon. After that Whitcomb closed his ears to the screams and he breathed a prayer of thanks when Corwin slumped back unconscious.

When the leg was severed he cauterized the stump by heating the knife red-hot in the fire and applying it to the open flesh until the bleeding stopped, choking on the smell. At last he turned away and let the knife fall from his fingers, forcing himself to breathe deeply. He was soaked with sweat. Several times during the operation he had thought he might be sick; he was grateful that he had come through it without that humiliation.

Gwynn and another man, Private Heiss, had slaughtered Gwynn's exhausted horse and there was meat already cooking on the fire. Bile rose in Whitcomb's throat at the thought of eating, but he choked it back. He turned away from the fire and saw the lower part of Corwin's leg lying where he had set it, lifeless and abandoned, and he vomited violently then, falling to his knees and heaving again and again until there was nothing to come up. A canteen was offered and he heard Private Gray's voice. "Have a little water, sir."

He rinsed his mouth and spat and got shakily to his feet, wiping his mouth with the back of his glove. "Someone will have to bury that." He gestured at the leg without looking at it. "I want two pickets posted now. One-hour shifts. Each man to be sure the other stays awake. I'll take the first watch."

"No, sair."

Whitcomb looked sharply at Dupré. Damn it, were they going to turn on

512

him now? Why were they all staring at him? Their faces were different; the look of defeat had gone and it was replaced by something new. What was it? A new sense of purpose, it seemed. Probably all scared to death of Corwin's threats, and they would stand against him now, just when he had his mind made up to take charge. Corwin was right. He had been too familiar with the men, too lenient. He had allowed the Mr. Reb nickname to gain currency. He hadn't reprimanded Rogers for firing at the deer and risking all their lives. He hadn't pushed any of them hard enough and now they thought they could oppose him freely.

He turned on Dupré and his voice was harsh. "I'm in command now, Sergeant, and I said I will take the first watch."

"And with respect, I say no, sair. You must rest."

"Sahrgint Dupree is right, sorr," McCaslin offered. "Ye'll be needin' yer rest. The boys'll post a guard."

"I'll take the first watch, sir," said Private Gray.

"Me too, sir" came from Donnelly, who was rubbing clean the blade of his knife with a handful of sandy soil. Already the others were pairing up, sharing blankets and robes, bedding down near the fire.

Whitcomb nodded dumbly. "Very well. Sergeant Dupré, I'll leave the picket duty in your hands."

He saw that Corwin had been covered with several robes. What else must be done before he went to sleep? There didn't seem to be anything. He spread his own robe by the fire and wrapped it around him like a cocoon.

He felt foolish for ever doubting the men. They hadn't turned on him after all. So he and Corwin were both wrong; Corwin for thinking a commander must be distant and stern, he himself for believing that truly caring about the welfare of the men was all that mattered, when there was something far more important at stake in earning the troopers' loyalty. If they were to believe in you they had to be certain of just one thing—your willingness to lead them. Most men didn't want that responsibility and they looked up to those who were willing to take it on, no matter if they were kindhearted souls or hard-assed bastards.

The last thing he heard before his exhaustion claimed him was a voice that called out softly from the darkness, "Good night, Mr. Reb."

Johnny Smoker sat on a rock and watched the shadows lengthen. The sun moved without moving. The space between the fiery ball and the mountain peaks narrowed and vanished and the jagged summits pierced the disk. The snow glowed with reddish fire and the shadows of the lodgepole pines were dark blue. The mountain slopes were vast, still and trackless.

Johnny had been atop the large boulder for more than an hour, watching all around him. Sometimes the tracker found his quarry best by remaining in one place and letting his eyes do the searching, but Johnny had seen nothing. His horse was tethered twenty yards away in a stand of trees.

Was it possible that she had already been found? He was within sight of Putnam's Park and he had heard no shots, seen no riders reconverging on the settlement. Today even he carried a gun, a Remington Army .44 that had belonged to Jed Putnam. The weight was strange and unfamiliar at his waist. The first of the searchers to find Amanda would fire three shots, repeating them at intervals as he brought her in, until the signal was picked up by the others and everyone had heard it.

It had been Lisa Putnam who discovered that Amanda was missing. When Amanda failed to appear as usual in the kitchen while Lisa was making breakfast, she had thought that Amanda must be sleeping late because of the long evening of music, but when the circus people came to eat and there was still no sign of the girl, Lisa had gone upstairs to wake her and found her gone. Tatum professed to know nothing and no one else had seen her.

Johnny had left the park on his own, not waiting for the others to organize the search. He had moved quickly on horseback while the morning was still cold, but luck had not been with him and he had found no tracks. Amanda had left the settlement on a frozen crust that bore her weight easily. In winter the faint marks she made might have remained for a time, if the day was calm, but today the sun had warmed the surface of the snow and wiped out the nighttime tracks of rodents and other small animals as cleanly as if they were swept away with a broom. Johnny had moved in ever-widening arcs, searching to the west for reasons he couldn't name, but he had learned long ago to follow his instincts when hunting in the wild.

He could remain still no longer. He climbed down and made his way to the horse and his feet crackled on the new crust that was already forming on the surface of the snow. The night would be cold. If Amanda did not find shelter before darkness fell, she would die.

Why had she run away? Was it something he had done? He remembered the kiss of the night before, a magic moment when he had wanted only to hold her and never let go. But he had hesitated. She had offered herself, not merely her flesh but her spirit. She had offered him a chance to say something, do something, to reveal his feelings. But he had let the chance slip by.

He must find her. It was up to him. He had let her get away. Whether or not she had run because of him didn't matter. All that mattered was finding her and never letting go of her again. She belonged with him and he would tell her so.

The horse was nervous. As Johnny untied the reins the animal looked this way and that, its ears shifting about, the nostrils flaring. It heard or smelled something, but its actions lacked the element of stark fear that would have been plain if it sensed a predator near at hand. Johnny had seen no large animals all day, nor any tracks, only squirrels and woodpeckers and a few smaller birds, and three ravens that had dived and swooped as if performing for him alone while he sat on the rock.

As he mounted the horse it tossed its head and whickered. It perceived a distant movement and shied away, and Johnny saw the buffalo.

It was an old bull, standing atop a gentle slope a hundred yards distant, silhouetted against the amber light of the western sky. *Hunh!* it snorted, and the sound reached Johnny clearly in the silence. The head moved, the snout was raised, and again came the *hunh!* The bull turned and walked off, disappearing behind the ridge.

Johnny started up the slope at once. Something had brought the animal to this high place, away from the sheltered valleys where the buffalo preferred to browse for forage. A person on foot or horseback could disrupt the habits of wild animals. . . .

Watch the animals and learn from them, the Cheyenne instructed their children. Johnny sought the bull now as a helper and a guide. It was grasping at straws, a white man might say, but Johnny made his decision with no conscious thought and he accepted the rightness of it without question.

From the top of the slope the tracks of the bull led across a broad meadow into the trees. Johnny followed, wondering that the lone animal should move so fast. A grazing buffalo did not walk as if it had a destination; it wandered, the search for food never far from its thoughts. Only in herds did the buffalo go far and fast, for reasons known only to them.

Johnny followed the bull's trail easily, keeping an eye out for other tracks as well. When he emerged from the trees onto another open hillside, the bull was waiting. It set off again, as if satisfied that he would follow. The animal's behavior was unnatural, and Johnny felt a sudden chill, almost a premonition. It was a feeling he had not known in many years. He had experienced it first in a dream, when a white buffalo cow had spoken to him without words and had predicted the course his life would follow.

515

He kicked his horse into a trot to overtake the bull and he circled the animal as a hunter or a wolf might circle a herd of buffalo, but the bull did not take alarm. Instead it stopped in its tracks and only the great head moved to keep horse and rider in sight as they rode around him. Johnny felt the chill again, stronger now, and a heightening of all his senses. This was a bull, not a cow; it was the same dusty browns of ordinary buffalo, not white, and yet the animal was anything but ordinary. It allowed him to satisfy his curiosity, and when it started off again, Johnny was content to follow at a distance, almost fearful of approaching too close to this beast that behaved so strangely. He could hear the bull's breathing and the sound of its hooves in the snow, both abnormally loud. The crunching of his own horse's hooves seemed deafening. He felt as if he had crossed some invisible line and moved beyond the normal world, leaving behind him everything he had learned in seven years.

Do not be afraid of the power that comes to you, Sun Horse had said to a young boy very afraid of a vivid dream he had had during the night. The dream had filled him with an overpowering awe and he had struggled to wake up, seeking the familiar world of his parents' lodge. He had told his mother of the dream and she had called for his father to listen, and White Smoke had grown solemn as the boy repeated his words. "Go and tell this to your grandfather, just as you have told it to me," his father said, and he took the young boy out of the lodge and pointed to the horns of the camp where the tipis of the Sun Band stood in a place of honor. The boy had wanted his father to lead him, but White Smoke laid a hand on the boy's shoulder. "There is nothing to fear," he said, and the boy went on his own, sure that all eyes followed him. Through the great encampment he walked, paying no attention to the children playing all around. "*Hunhé!*" one man exclaimed. "The White Boy of the Shahíyela has his heart on the ground. Has a young woman sent back your ponies?" But the boy ignored the teasing and kept on. At last he had reached the tipi with the yellow sun painted near the entrance and very timidly he had scratched on the lodgeskins and coughed politely. Sun Horse had listened to the tale of his dream and told him not to be afraid. Little Warrior was a child of the *Tsistsístas* and not a cowardly boy, and after he had talked with his Lakota grandfather for a time he felt proud of the dream and awed by its power, but he was no longer afraid.

So long ago, and even then a vision that came in his sleep, not on the vision quest as part of reaching for manhood. "Do not be afraid of the power," his grandfather had said, and he had accepted it then. But he was no longer that boy; he was a young man who had chosen the white world, in which there were no dreams of power, no visions of buffalo that became young women. A world in which *Ptésanwin* did not exist.

And yet he followed the bull as if it led him by a rope. He followed it higher into the hills, along the top of a steep escarpment and then down again, moving to the north. The sun, which earlier had only dropped behind the mountain peaks in the west, was falling behind the true horizon now, and the light was failing. The bull descended a wooded slope, meandering among the trees as if searching

516

for something, and Johnny's heart leaped as he saw other tracks mingled with the bull's, the small tracks of a human being.

At the bottom of the hillside the bull stepped out of the trees into a small meadow. There were still more tracks spread across the flat expanse of snow but Johnny paid them no attention. He had eyes only for the human footprints, and he followed them quickly, urging the horse forward. At the foot of the valley the tracks ended where a small brown shape lay curled in the snow. It could have been a buffalo calf asleep, or a small deer, but Johnny saw the red clown's hat and the light brown hair, and he was already off the horse and running the last few steps, calling Amanda's name.

Her face was warm to the touch and she moaned as he rolled her over and took her into his arms. "Amanda?"

She seemed to come out of a deep sleep. "Johnny?" She reached up and touched his face. Her own face was streaked with tears, the clown makeup blotched and smeared. The lids of her eyes were almost swollen shut. "Johnny? Is that you?"

"It's me."

"Johnny, I can't see!" A sob escaped her and her body shook.

"It's all right. Everything's all right now," he said holding her tightly.

Night was falling quickly and there was a little breeze. He could hear the wind in the trees, the sound of his own breathing and Amanda's, the creaking of the snow beneath him as he rocked her in his arms. But something had changed. . . . The sights and sounds around him were normal once more; the heightened awareness that had come over him when he first saw the buffalo bull was missing now. He looked around and saw that the bull was gone.

The inside of Sun Horse's lodge was silent save for the sounds of the fire. Hears Twice bent over Amanda's still form, which lay on a pallet near the fire. He had one ear against her chest, listening. At last he straightened up and made a few signs—*I hear no death.*

Sun Horse nodded. Johnny Smoker sat beside him, watching everything that passed between the two men. The Lakota village was much closer than Putnam's Park to where he had found Amanda and so he had brought her here, firing shots occasionally as he rode. He had been within half a mile of the village before the Lakota scouts found him in the dark. Amanda had lapsed into unconsciousness on the journey to the Indian camp and she had not wakened since.

Elk Calf Woman handed Sun Horse a twist of dried grass. He touched it to the fire and blew out the flame at once. He passed the smoking twist along Amanda's body and the pleasant scent of sweetgrass filled the lodge. With his free hand he scooped the smoke from the air and stroked the small form, passing the purifying scent everywhere, finishing with the face and head.

Amanda was still dressed in her clown costume, but her buffalo coat had been removed. Sun Horse spread the coat over her now and pulled a robe atop it, covering her from toes to chin.

From outside came the sound of hoofbeats. Lakota messengers had been sent to the settlement to tell the whites that the girl was found; they were returning now, and by the number of horses he heard, Sun Horse guessed that some of the whites had come to see for themselves that the girl was well.

He spoke to Sings His Daughter and she stepped through the entrance. There was a moment's conversation outside the lodge and then Lisa Putnam entered.

"Is she all right?" she asked in Lakota.

"She is snowblind. If she wakes again, she will live." He had instructed Sings His Daughter to allow only Lisaputnam into the lodge. The others would have to wait.

Lisa bent over Amanda and touched the unconscious girl's cheek and forehead with her hand. She smiled at Johnny. "I'm glad it was you that found her." She stepped back out of the lodge and there was more talk, then the sound of horses leaving. After a few moments, Lisa returned. She sat by the fire near Amanda.

"Mr. Tatum wanted to come in but I said that was against the doctor's orders," she said to Johnny. "You should have seen his face,." She smiled. "I told him that Sun Horse had cured more snowblindness than any white doctor. Alfred and Joe were with him. They'll see he doesn't try to come back until she's ready to see him."

Johnny nodded, not sure why he found this news so welcome, except that Amanda was never quite herself when the circus master was near.

Sings His Daughter entered the lodge and set a bowl of snow beside Sun Horse before taking her seat next to Elk Calf. Sun Horse began to sing a curing chant. He took snow from the bowl and sprinkled it on Amanda's eyes. The paint on her face had not been touched, except to wipe clean the eyelids. The paint was her power and Sun Horse had ordered that it be left as it was.

Again and again he reached to the bowl, sprinkling the snow in small piles that gradually covered Amanda's eyes and grew slowly as the flakes continued to fall from Sun Horse's hands. The snow had taken her sight and now it would restore it to her. So gently did he handle the snow, so carefully had Sings His Daughter gathered the powdery flakes, they seemed to fall on Amanda's face as from a cloud, settling in their own way as they might have settled in a quiet patch of woods.

When the bowl was empty he lit the sweetgrass again and passed the smoking twist along Amanda's body, spreading the smoke with his hand, and he followed the sweetgrass with sage smoke this time, to drive away all but the friendly spirits. When the herbs were extinguished and set aside, he took his ceremonial bag from around his neck and opened it. He held the bag over his palm and shook it gently, and a little dust fell into his hand. He set the bag down and rubbed his palms together quickly, then blew the dust away. The small cloud puffed into the air over Amanda and settled slowly.

It was the last trace of earth from his vision-hill. The symbols of his vision were gone now. He was looking beyond the symbols.

He began to chant the curing song again and now his voice was joined by a second, softer and higher. Elk Calf Woman beat lightly on a small drum in her

518

lap as she sang, and Sings His Daughter shook a rattle made from the dried scrotum of a buffalo bull. It was rare for women to take part in a healing ceremony, but as holy man and healer, Sun Horse had the power to change the ceremonies if he wished, and he sometimes called on his wives to assist him. The healing power of woman was great, and he wanted to summon all that power today. As always, he prayed to the directions and to all living things, each one a separate manifestation of *Wakán Tanka*, and he prayed not just for the clown girl but for himself as well.

Here in his lodge were the two people who had met when the Snowblind Moon was young, when *wamblí gleshka* had spoken to him and he had felt the movement of power all around him. The *heyoka* girl lay before him, her spirit far away. If she died, the promise of power would be broken and his hopes would be gone like the symbols of his vision. When he had heard Dust's voice announcing that the clown girl was lost, Sun Horse had come out of his lodge and he had directed every able-bodied man in the village to join the search. He had sensed then, as he did now, that the solution to his dilemma was still within his reach, but only if the girl lived. If she recovered, he would continue his search for peace.

The warmth of Amanda's face began to melt the mounds of snow that covered her eyes and the water ran down her white cheeks like tears. Sun Horse ended the chant. His wives set the drum and rattle aside and began to prepare sleeping robes on an extra pallet. Elk Calf said a few words to Lisa, inviting her to sleep there, and Lisa readily agreed. She was dull with fatigue after a long day in the saddle.

Sun Horse raised the robe covering Amanda and motioned Johnny to lie beside the girl. "Sleep here with her," the old man said in Cheyenne. "Keep her warm."

Fully clothed, Johnny lay down beside Amanda. Sun Horse covered them both and resumed his seat by the fire. As the others dropped to sleep one by one he remained awake, keeping watch over his grandson and the clown girl. The night was calm and the village quiet. Sun Horse let his mind drift, touching here and there on the separate aspects of his dilemma, and he prayed he would have one more chance to fulfil the promise he had been given so many years ago, atop the small hill overlooking Fort Laramie.

It was dawn when Amanda stirred. She opened her eyes and raised her head, and the slight movement awakened Johnny.

"Johnny?" she said, looking at him as if in a dream. "Good, you're here." She lay back and closed her eyes again.

Johnny slipped from under the covers and knelt beside her. "How do you feel?" She opened her eyes and looked around her. "Where am I?"

"We're in Sun Horse's lodge."

"Oh." She let her head fall back.

"Can you see?" Sun Horse asked in English, rising from his robes.

"Of course I can see." Her eyes suddenly opened wide. "I was lost! Oh, Johnny! You found me and I couldn't see!"

Lisa was awake now and she came to kneel beside Johnny. "You were snow-blind," she told the girl. "Do your eyes still hurt?"

Amanda nodded. "They're sore. But I can see! I thought I was blind."

Lisa smiled. "You won't stand much bright light for a day or two, but your eyes will be as good as new."

On the other side of the lodge Elk Calf left her pallet and moved to the cooking fire, where an iron pot had sat on the coals throughout the night. She spoke in Lakota to Lisa.

Lisa nodded and turned to Amanda. "Can you drink a little soup? You should eat something if you can."

"I guess I am hungry."

Elk Calf passed a wooden bowl and a horn spoon to Lisa, who helped Amanda raise herself to a half-sitting position.

"Oh, that's good," Amanda said as she tasted the broth. Lisa fed it to her a spoonful at a time until it was all gone. The girl lay back gratefully on the soft robes, tired by the small effort of eating and soothed by the warm soup inside her. "I remember now," she said, frowning as she tried to make the memory complete. "I was trying to find the trail between the Indian village and Putnam's Park. I went downhill, but my eyes got worse and worse and I fell down in the trees. And then I was in a field with some buffalo. That's the last thing I remember until Johnny found me. It's all like a bad dream. Except the ending." She smiled at Johnny.

Sun Horse leaned forward and spoke again in English. "It is a spirit animal you see. It led my grandson to you." It had not been *Ptésanwin*, of that he was sure; one such vision in a lifetime was more than all but a handful of men had ever experienced. But he was just as sure that the bull was the spirit of *pte* sent to guide his grandson.

"But it was long before Johnny found me," Amanda protested. "The sun was still up and there were lots of them, all walking past me. They stopped to look at me. I know I saw them."

"There were other tracks," Johnny said slowly, remembering. He closed his eyes to bring back the scene. Even when he was not paying full attention, the number and direction of tracks he saw did not escape his notice. With his eyes still closed he spoke again, moving his hands to show his own movements and where the tracks had been. "I came out of the trees and the bull stopped here. Amanda's tracks went off to the right. The others were in the middle of the meadow, going up the valley." He opened his eyes and looked at Sun Horse, speaking now in Cheyenne. "They were there, Grandfather. They could have been the tracks of buffalo."

Before the day had fully brightened, the scouts and hunters were gathered hastily and Sun Horse addressed them with his white grandson by his side. *Akíchita* were named to control the hunt; no one would be permitted to jeopardize its success; the survival of the people might be at stake.

520

"My grandson will take you to a small valley surrounded by trees," said the headman, "and there you will find the tracks of *pte*."

"There are no tracks," a young scout said arrogantly. "We have looked every day and we would have seen the tracks if any *pte* were near."

Sun Horse did a strange thing then. He lowered his head and made the *hunh!* snort of *tatanka*. He shuffled around the scout, sniffing the air. "If I see you first, will I leave my tracks for you to follow? Do not forget that *pte* is the most holy of the four-leggeds, and wise in ways that men are not. Shall there not perhaps be a small band of *pte* like the Sun Band? Might they not choose to stay low in the mountains in some sheltered place where the grass grows tall and thick in the summer moons? Where they can forage in the winter while others go hungry? Follow my grandson and you will find them as I have told you."

"If they are there, we will find them," said Walks Bent Over, the hunch-backed young man who was head scout of the band. He was given heart by Sun Horse's words and he felt a burden lifting from him. Until the news of the clown girl's disappearance had been brought to the village yesterday, Walks Bent Over had been the only leader to guide the actions of the young men for many days. With Standing Eagle away and Sun Horse retreating into what some said would be his death fast, Walks Bent Over had seen eyes turned toward him for guidance, and he had sent the scouts out to watch the trails, far enough away to give the people time to break camp and move if bluecoats were seen, but not too far. He had placed the eyes of the Sun Band in a ring to guard the people, as the *pte* formed a ring around the helpless ones when danger threatened the herd, with horns and eyes outward. The horns of the Sun Band were few, and those not sharp enough to ward off the far-shooting guns of the bluecoats, and so the eyes must be all the sharper, Walks Bent Over had told his scouts. He had rejoiced when Sun Horse emerged from his lodge to direct the search for the white *heyoka* girl, and he rejoiced now at the renewed strength of the headman. Sun Horse's tone was confident and his eyes were bright with hope.

With women along to do the butchering and pack horses to bring back the meat, the hunters set out. Sun Horse's grandson guided the band unerringly, although he had come down from the hills in the dark the night before. When the band entered the little valley surrounded by trees, the tracks were there. They followed the trail up a draw and over the next ridge and there beyond a small stand of trees they saw the breath cloud of the herd.

The hunters waited as Walks Bent Over advanced cautiously, keeping down-wind, to scout the best route for the attack.

"A big herd!" whispered one young man.

"Any herd appears big to eyes so young," said an older man who remembered herds so vast that *Ina*, the Mother Earth, shook all day and night under the passing feet of her children, as a woman trembled with pleasure in the arms of her man.

"There are five times ten *pte*," Walks Bent Over announced when he returned, and he made signs to Johnny Smoker. *They say that the buffalo-dreamer shall be a great hunter, and the words are true.* He placed a hand on Johnny's shoulder, expressing his gratitude for a job of scouting well done. Then he smiled and made more signs: *They also say the buffalo-dreamer shall get the woman he wants. Good hunting, my friend!* The other men laughed softly and several stopped to place a hand of approval on Johnny's shoulder before moving off toward the herd.

The surround was made on foot, the hunters and scouts spreading out to take position, the *akíchita* watching the hunters to be sure that none fired too soon. Clad in the skins of wolf and coyote, the scouts crept forward. The herd drew in on itself with the bulls on the outer edges, snorting and pawing the snow, but the buffalo did not take fright. They were used to four-legged predators circling the herd to watch for those too young to move quickly or the old and sick that might be easy prey. A healthy bison had little to fear from wolves and coyotes.

But these predators carried guns. When they were in position, the scouts shot the old bulls first, the leaders. Then one man wounded a cow so she moved in circles and started the herd milling in confusion, and then the rest of the hunters started to shoot carefully, taking their time. Whenever one animal took the initiative and tried to lead the remaining ones away, the new leader was shot and once again the *pte* milled about until all were dead in the snow and the hillside echoed with the trilling of joy from the watching women.

When the first of the meat reached the village, the fires were built high and the kettles were filled and great cuts of ribs were placed over the flames to roast slowly. Some women cooked in the old way as well, making a soup in the buffalo paunch by dropping hot rocks in with the meat and water. Children and dogs darted here and there, trying to steal a bite of meat from under the watchful eyes of the women.

It was mid-afternoon when Johnny Smoker returned, riding triumphantly at the head of a long string of horses all packed with meat. He was surprised to see Amanda walking with Elk Calf Woman, coming from the creek, where they had made *inipi* together. Amanda's clown makeup was gone and in place of her costume she wore a simple deerskin dress beneath her buffalo coat. With Amanda delivered back to the lodge and tucked once more in her robes, Elk Calf went off to help Sings His Daughter in cutting up the meat. Sun Horse rose from his seat by the fire and took Lisa Putnam by the hand. "Come," he said in Lakota. "Walk with me. We will walk through the camp and see the people happy." They went out of the lodge and the two young people were left by themselves.

"I asked them to leave us alone when you got back," Amanda said a little shyly. "I have something I want to say to you."

It seemed to Johnny that the girl before him was someone he had never

522

seen before. It was Amanda, but she had changed in some indefinable way. The eyes that met his so calmly revealed a new contentment, as if a persistent worry had finally been put to rest.

He remembered his thoughts on the mountainside, and what he had to tell her. Walks Bent Over's words about the buffalo-dreamer came back to him then and they gave him confidence.

She took one of his hands in her own. "First, I want to thank you for saving my life. I guess that should be the most important thing of all, saving my life, but there's something else I want to say and it's even more important to me." She paused, and then said, "I'm leaving the circus."

Johnny was nonplused; he had no idea of how to react to this news, but Amanda smiled. "It's because of you, really. Without you I never would have had the courage to do it. Hachaliah has taken care of me all my life just the way Mr. Hardeman has taken care of you. But it's time I was on my own. You understand, don't you?"

Johnny nodded. He understood very little except his feelings for Amanda, which were suddenly even stronger than before.

"I don't mean I'm giving up my clowning. I'll look for work with another show. I'm just leaving this circus, and Hachaliah. It's something I have to do."

"Then you won't be going with them when they leave."

Amanda shook her head. "I asked Lisa if I could stay with her until I know where I want to go."

Johnny smiled. "I guess I'll be staying too. I was about set to take that job with the Waldheims, but not anymore. Not now. That was just so I could be near you until I got up my nerve to speak my mind."

She dropped her gaze and her voice was soft. "What were you going to say when you got up your nerve?"

Johnny took a deep breath and plunged on. "I almost lost you yesterday. I don't want that to happen again. I don't know why you took out like that. I don't know that it matters much now. You don't have to say if you don't want to."

"I ran because I didn't know what I wanted. I do now." She raised her eyes to meet his and held his hand even more tightly.

"Does that mean yes?" Hope was plain on Johnny's face.

"Did you ask a question?" She was teasing him, but he was very serious.

"I got nothing to offer you really, just me and a few things you could pack on one horse. But I'll try to make whatever kind of life you want, wherever you want it. I figured I better speak my piece and let you make up your mind before you went off somewhere else." He paused, hoping she might say something, but she kept silent, regarding him solemnly. "I know I'm not making a very good job of this, but I ain't had a whole lot of practice. Come to think of it, I don't guess anyone gets much practice at this sort of thing. It's something you only do one time if you do it right. That's how I'd like it to be."

He asked her to marry him then, and she said yes, and she was surprised to find tears of joy coming to her eyes.

Until today Amanda had had no intention of revealing that she was leaving Hachaliah and the circus, not until she had drawn Johnny out first, making him declare his need for her, his wish for them to be together. That had always been her way, letting her young men think that every action of hers was their doing. But today when she had awakened for the second time, in mid-morning, she had found Lisa and Sun Horse watching over her. She had realized in that moment that she was utterly safe from Hachaliah Tatum, and the feeling had changed her. She was in a world where Hachaliah could not control her; he could not reach her here and if necessary she could remain here until he was far away. For the first time in her life she knew what it was to be free.

And then to her astonishment she had discovered something else. When she learned that Johnny had gone off with the hunters she found that his absence made an emptiness in her. She felt incomplete without him and she was impatient for him to return. It was a feeling she had never known before, and she realized that she did not want Johnny merely as a guide to help her make the break with Hachaliah nor as a paramour to use for a time and then discard. She wanted him as a companion. She wanted to share her life with him.

The discovery had left her dumbfounded and strangely pleased with herself, as if she had wrought this change by her own hand. Her immediate goals had not changed—finding work for the two of them in another circus, adding to her reputation and fame—but this was something she wanted now for Johnny as well as herself. As he had shown her how to stand on her own so she would show him the way to a new life, an exciting life that would take them together wherever they wanted to go.

She had grown impatient for Johnny to come back. At any sound from outside the lodge she had inquired if it might signal his return from the hunt. When Sun Horse had suggested she take a sweat bath to speed her recovery she had agreed readily enough, hoping it would help to pass the time. She had become restless in her confinement and was glad of a chance to move about. She found the fragrant stream invigorating and even her eyes felt almost normal, although they were still a little sore. And when she stepped out of the sweat lodge she saw the world anew. It was as if the sage-scented steam had washed away her past; she felt reborn.

When Johnny returned at last, her heart had jumped at the sight of him and her acceptance of his proposal was heartfelt and genuine.

He rewarded her with a kiss as chaste and moving as their first. She clung to his hands as if she would never let go, profoundly grateful now that she had not given in to her first impulse and pressed a seduction back in Putnam's Park after that kiss at the foot of the stairs. She should have known that the way to make Johnny hers forever was not to give herself but to withhold herself! He saw her as a tender virgin and she would be as pure as he imagined her. They would stay in the park when the circus was gone, spending their days together and their nights apart, until Chris Hardeman returned. Then the three of them would make their way to some town where there was a minister and she and Johnny would be married, and only then would she give herself to him, proudly, as a virgin might, with nothing to hide. It was the way he assumed it would be and she wanted it that way too, to please him, and because the intervening time would allow the memory of Hachaliah's touch to fade until it could be forgotten.

When Lisa returned to the lodge with Sun Horse, she saw the joy on the faces of the two young people. It was a joy she had known once herself, when the cavalry lieutenant had first touched her heart. But when she tried to remember the lieutenant's face she could see only Chris Hardeman. She had very nearly said something to reveal her feelings to him on the day he left, something to say that she was concerned for his safety and would feel his absence until he returned. But she had hesitated, and he had gone.

She had long been aware that in the sparsely populated western territories the paths of separate lives often crossed briefly, never to cross again. At the moment when two paths met, sometimes a chance flared and burned brightly for a short time. But caution was best thrown to the winds at those times, and only boldness reaped the possible rewards. Lisa had honed her awareness of such moments, but with Hardeman she had let the moment pass without speaking. She felt a sudden anger at her timidity. Johnny and Amanda had nearly lost each other because they had not spoken their feelings sooner. If Johny had not found the girl she might well have died. Lisa resolved not to hesitate again when Hardeman and her uncle Bat returned. If they returned. Hardeman might leave anyway, but he would go knowing how she felt.

She stood with the fire at her back and she did not remove her goatskin coat. "It's time for me to be getting home," she said after they had told her their news. "I've got to see to my calves. And I'll announce your engagement." She looked at Amanda. "Mr. Tatum expects to have the road clear in a few more days and there's a lot of talk about the farewell performance. They'll want to know if you'll be part of it."

Amanda brightened. "I forgot! Oh, Johnny, you'll get to see the show!" She turned to Lisa. "Of course I'll perform. Please tell them I'll come down as soon as I can."

"I think it would be just as well if you don't come down right away. It will give everyone a little time to get used to the idea of your leaving them. Anyway, you need another day or two of rest. I'll be back up tomorrow with pack horses for some of this meat. Sun Horse says he's got to repay me for the grain and gunpowder I gave him, even though the Indians made the hunt by themselves. We'll see how you're doing then." She was thinking of Hachaliah Tatum, whose first reaction to the news of Amanda's engagement she couldn't

525

imagine. She hoped that with a few days to consider it, he would see that nothing he could do would change how matters stood.

With scarcely an hour left before sunset, Lisa did not delay her departure. She kissed Amanda, and Johnny too, to his embarrassment, and with a promise to bring Hutch and Chatur back with her on the morrow, she was gone.

That night the Sun Band feasted. Men and women visited from lodge to lodge and invited the needy ones to eat with them, and wood was brought for a bonfire in the middle of the camp circle. Even while many were still eating, the drumming began and the dancers gathered. When the sound of drums and chanting voices grew loud, Amanda and Johnny came out of the lodge and sat with Sun Horse, wrapped in their robes, the young man looking at Amanda as often as he looked at the dancers circling the fire.

Between the dances the *heyoka* performed for the people, often doing their tricks and antics close in front of the white girl so she could see them well. Both drums and voices fell silent and the sounds of wonder came from many throats as the two *heyoka* presented Amanda with sacred presents. She had brought the news of the *pte* herd, which she had seen clearly even with her snowblind eyes. She had brought the life-giving power to the band and the special gifts were made in appreciation. Talks Fast, the elder *heyoka*, painted a jagged bolt of lightning on each of Amanda's cheeks, and then he gave her a wooden cup and *heyoka* bow, the cup representing the water that came from the west, the power to make things live, and the bow the Thunder Beings' power to destroy.

When the first light of dawn appeared in the east, the wind began to gust and clouds moved in to cover the sky. Some of the people turned to their robes for a little sleep, but many remained awake, extending new invitations for others to come and share the meat from their fires. There was a new spirit in the village, one that had not been felt since the autumn moons. The people were strong again and the camp circle was reunited in hope. Yet still Sun Horse had not eaten. He had moved among the people, smiling to see them happy and strong once again, exchanging a few words here and there, but no morsel of *pte* meat had passed his lips. He seeks the path that leads to a lasting peace between Lakota and *washichun*, the oldest of the councillors said; he seeks to unite the power of the two worlds. He takes too much on himself, others said; the band is strong again and we have nothing to fear. Perhaps Standing Eagle is right and we should fight the bluecoats if they come. Sun Horse should eat now, so he will be strong to lead us whatever may happen.

Before the dawn, Sun Horse had gone back to his lodge and the clown girl and his white grandson went with him.

As the morning brightened, the camp grew quiet. Few moved about now; most who were still awake contented themselves with resting in the comfort of a warm lodge and a full belly. A few women resumed the butchering of the meat, which would take days, and some others began to work at a few of the hides. One man who still moved among the tipis was old Dust, the crier.

526

When a family wished to invite another to eat, they might give him a piece of rib roast to pay for his services in announcing the invitation. Already he had eaten more than enough, but until the last vestiges of the celebration died away he would perform his duty and carry any message he might be asked to carry from one lodge to another, or throughout the entire village. He paused in his wanderings to look up and down the valley and he was surprised to see a small group of men and horses moving slowly toward the village from the northern trail.

Surely none of the scouts were still out? All had taken part in the hunt and none had been sent off again. Then who...?

Two of the horses pulled pony drags bearing burdens that looked like men and he saw now that there were some women with the little band. And then he recognized the man who rode in the lead. It was something in his movements, his bearing in the saddle or the way he raised a hand in greeting, for Dust's eyes were no longer sharp enough to discern a face at such a distance. But he was sure now, and he placed a hand over his mouth in wonder.

Could such an honor be his? Usually someone called his name and he went where he was summoned, there to learn what he must announce. This time he was the first to know the news! And it was news all the village had long awaited.

He took a deep breath and faced the camp, his head held high. As he began to announce the glad tidings he walked with stately steps around the circle, moving as the sun moved through the sky and as a man moved when he entered a lodge, calling out in the high penetrating tones he reserved for the most important events. "The pipe carriers return! They are coming now! The pipe carriers return!"

CHAPTER

THIRTY-SEVEN

Within moments the camp circle was alive again. Those who had so recently gone to their robes were awakened by the crier's news and they poured from the lodges. The women working the hides dropped their scrapers to join the gathering crowd. Coming so close on the heels of the successful hunt, the long-awaited return of the pipe carriers seemed providential, and the news of their coming banished fatigue and raised the spirits of the people to new heights. Joyfully the children ran forth, trailed by barking dogs, but as they drew near the riders their cries of greeting died away. They saw the pony drags, one bearing a long bundle, one carrying Blackbird. They saw the strangers, and some smiles from the women and children, but the expressions of relief at finally reaching a place of shelter were overshadowed with weariness and sorrow. They saw the faces of the men daubed black with paint, and even ones so young knew that the black face-paint signified great intensity of emotion about some serious matter. In war, it could indicate either victory or defeat, and often it was a sign of mourning. The children looked from face to face, seeing the tired eyes and bitter expressions, and they saw that one face was missing. Like a flock of birds they turned as one and ran back to the village, silently now. They found their parents in the crowd, clutching the grown-ups' arms and hands as they whispered the sad news, and from some of the women came cries of apprehension.

Sees Beyond went quickly to Sun Horse's lodge, guiding himself with his stick, and he coughed at the entrance. When Elk Calf opened the flap he spoke loudly enough to be heard within. "The pipe carriers return, and their faces are painted black."

Sun Horse had heard Dust's announcement and he had already donned his robe. He stepped out now, followed by Johnny and Amanda and his wives. Penelope came running from her own lodge. She joined her father and clutched his hand.

The travelers entered the village through the horns of the circle and turned left, moving in the ceremonial fashion. The people watched silently and gathered behind them as they advanced. Standing Eagle and Little Hand rode at the head of the band, their blackened faces set and solemn. Behind them rode Lodgepole, who always had a smile for the children and a cheerful word for the women, but he was unsmiling now. His wife ran to his side and touched his leg to assure herself that he was well. He took her hand in his and she walked along beside him. Next to Lodgepole was the *washíchun* Hardeman, and he was wounded. Beneath his coat of waterproof cloth, which hung open, a ragged bandage was visible, binding his left arm against his body. He slumped in the saddle and looked as though he might fall, but now he gripped the saddle horn and drew himself up, raising his head. His face was painted too, and the people wondered at this, for they knew it was not the *washíchun* custom. Next in line were the strangers, the Oglalas. The villagers saw the short hair of the women, the arms gashed in mourning, and the weak condition of the children, but they did not dwell on these things, for their eyes passed quickly to the two pony drags that came last of all, led by the Oglala men. On one was a long bundle, well wrapped and securely lashed down; on the other lay Blackbird, covered with two buffalo robes. His face was no longer that of a young boy ignorant of all manly concerns.

Something very bad had happened, that much was plain. Has there been a fight? If so, with whom? And where was Hawk Chaser? Was it his body in the covered bundle on the pony drag? No one voiced the questions. The answers, and everything that had happened to the messengers since they had left the village, were things of great importance to the people, to be told formally to Sun Horse and the councillors after a pipe had reunited the travelers in the spirit of the band.

The wife of Hawk Chaser stood by Elk Calf, clutching the older woman's hand.

Her eyes searched in vain among the horesemen, and when she saw the pony drags she let out a low moan and closed her eyes. Her daughter Yellow Leaf cried out, a long wail of anguish, and as the riders stopped before the headman's lodge the girl ran forward, dodging among the horses and startling them, stopping abruptly as she reached the rear of the little procession. She looked from Blackbird to the long bundle so like the shape of a man, and back at Blackbird again. She saw the tears brimming in his eyes, and she threw herself on the ground beside him, bursting into a torrent of sobs.

The pipe carriers dismounted and stood before Sun Horse. Johnny made a small sign to Hardeman, wanting to know if he was all right. In return he got an almost imperceptible nod that did little to calm his fears.

Sun Horse looked in the faces of the men and he knew they had failed. He turned to those gathered around him. "Help these relatives," he said, gesturing toward the Oglala families. The women were so exhausted they could barely stand. Women of the Sun Band moved forward at once to take the refugees to their lodges, where they could eat and rest. "Those who have robes or clothing to spare, give it to them," Sun Horse said, and others went to fetch what they had. The Oglala men remained behind as the women and children were led away.

Sun Horse motioned the travelers toward his own lodge. "Come and eat," he said. "Then we will talk." But Standing Eagle made a sign of negation.

"We have traveled for six days," the war leader said, "and we have been hungry all the while. We shared our *wasná* with the Oglala until it was gone. My brother Lodgepole killed an antelope with his far-shooting gun and we ate that, but for the last three days we have eaten nothing, and slept very little. Food will make us tired. We will talk now, while our hunger is sharp to remind us of our difficulties. It will help us to tell them clearly, so the people will hear. Later we will eat and sleep. First we must talk."

"The people must hear what we have to say, Father," Bat added.

Sun Horse looked from one man to the other and than he moved forward to the pony drags, helping himself along with a twisted stick of oakwood that he used as a cane. Bat had never seen his father-in-law use a cane before. Sun Horse appeared much older now than he had when the pipe carriers left the village, just eighteen days and nights before. The old man was very thin and his strength seemed to be failing.

Sun Horse stopped beside Blackbird. The boy had one hand on Yellow Leaf's shoulder and the girl had stopped crying.

"You are tired, Grandfather," Blackbird said.

Sun Horse nodded. "I have not eaten. I have been searching for . . . something. I do not know what it is." With the successful hunt he had thought that the answer to his quest was close at hand; now it seemed more distant than ever. If the peace were broken already, what hope could remain? Was it broken?

"I'm tired too," said Blackbird. "Let the people hear us now and then I will sleep until the grass is green."

Sun Horse felt a stab of fear for his grandson's life. He turned to Standing Eagle. "The wound...?"

"There are two, Father. One in the leg and the other in the side. They will heal. The boy was treated by Ice, the Shahíyela healer, and by Iron Necklace." Here he indicated one of the Oglala men. "He is a bear medicine man."

Sun Horse nodded, greatly relieved. "We will hear what the pipe carriers have to say."

During the time it had taken to receive the travelers into the village, the sky had darkened above the mountains. The wind was gathering strength, gusting among the lodges, and a little snow was beginning to fall. Even as the fire was built in the council lodge the men began to take their seats, and Johnny Smoker found a place beside Hardeman. The youth came alone; Amanda had gone back into Sun Horse's lodge to await him there. He saw his friend's hollow cheeks and sallow complexion and he didn't know what to say. He had never seen Hardeman so tired. His fatigue seemed to be rooted somewhere deep inside him. The scout put a hand on Johnny's arm in greeting and there was no strength in the grip.

"You all right?" the bearded man asked.

Johnny nodded. "Amanda got lost. She was snowblind. I found her and brought her here. She's still getting her strength back, but she'll be all right."

It was just like Johnny to tell a big story in so few words. Hardeman was glad to see his companion again after having been apart from him for what seemed a lifetime. He had noticed the way Amanda stood close beside Johnny, holding his arm, as if that was the only place she felt safe. What he had seen between them before he went away had grown, that was plain, and the knowledge gave him comfort. Whatever ties might help to keep the boy in the white world were all to the better.

"It seems like you've been on a hard trail," Johnny said. It was a term the two of them used to mean a difficult journey or bad trouble, or both.

"Didn't have much luck," Hardeman admitted. "We made pretty good time on the way back, everything considered." His eyes were on Blackbird, who was being carried into the council lodge on a litter. The lodge was filling rapidly now, the councillors talking softly among themselves as they took their places. The scene reminded Hardeman of the council in Two Moons' village and the hopes that were raised there.

"These folks made meat," he observed. He had seen the hides and carcasses.

"When Amanda was lost she saw some buffalo," Johnny explained. "The scouts found them. The hunt was yesterday."

"You and the girl getting on?"

Johnny blushed. "Amanda and I— She's leaving the circus. We're—" He hesitated, not sure he should bring this up just now. The pipe carriers' news was far more important.

"Making plans?" Hardeman offered.

"Just one so far. We're getting married."

There was life in Hardeman's smile and renewed strength in his grip as he put

530

his hand on Johnny's arm once more. "That's good news," he said.

"We ain't got much else worked out just yet. We've got some talking to do."

"Well, you're a pretty good talker when you set your mind to it. You'll get it worked out."

Johnny smiled, feeling uncertain and grateful at the same time. Chris always knew how to lift his spirits, but he had meant it to be the other way around. If anything, Chris was the one who needed to have his spirits raised, but there was no more time for talk now. The lodge was full, the entrance flap secured, and the flames leaped high as buffalo fat was added to the fire to make a bright light. Sun Horse was loading a pipe.

The pipe was lit, and as it was passed around the inner circle the sounds of horses entering the village were heard in the silent council lodge. A moment later Dust put his head into the entrance to say that Lisaputnam was here, and Sun Horse motioned that she might enter. Scarcely had Dust withdrawn when Lisa stepped into the lodge, her eyes darting this way and that until they found first Bat and then Hardeman seated there, and it was difficult to tell which man she was the most glad to see. Her mountain goatskin coat was covered with a dusting of new snow. She accepted a place that was made for her at the bottom of the inner circle.

Lisa and Hutch had come with pack horses as she had promised, and they had brought Chatur to see Amanda. Hutch and Chatur were with the girl in Sun Horse's lodge now. As the three riders approached the village they had seen the clouds that were gathering in the north and felt the strength of the storm that was imminent. They had intended to stay only a short time, but when Lisa was told that the pipe carriers had returned, she had dropped her reins and made straight for the council lodge, and she would stay until the council was done. She might be stranded by the storm but nothing would move her from this spot.

She looked at Bat and was grateful for the smile he gave her. Her eyes moved on to Hardeman, who met her gaze once and then looked away. The brief contact chilled her. She saw a man who was at the end of his resources, both in body and mind, a man who was defeated.

When the pipe had returned to Sun Horse, Standing Eagle was the first to speak. He told of the journey north, of finding the cavalry tracks and seeing the army wagons, and the encounter with the Crow war party at Prairie Dog Creek. He recounted the night attack, and here he invited Blackbird to tell what had happened when he went off alone to try to recover the stolen horses. As always in council, each man told only what he knew from his own personal experience.

Blackbird spoke from his litter. He related how he had overtaken the Crow warrior and been wounded, and how Hardeman had saved his life with the far-shooting buffalo gun. The councillors raised their voices in praise when they heard this, and all eyes turned to the white scout, who sat stone-faced and un-moved, as if he neither heard nor saw what took place around him. But as always Bat was translating the proceedings for Hardeman, and when Blackbird said he had no more to tell, Hardeman spoke up, adding a few words of his own, saying that Blackbird had counted coup on the dead Crow, as was his right. Again the voices of praise swelled loud and Blackbird blushed with pride.

The listeners fell silent as Standing Eagle told of leaving the cavalry's trail and finally coming on the Cheyenne village on the Powder. The smoking pipes grew cool as he spoke of the council held there, and the arrival first of Sitting Bull and then Crazy Horse. There were murmurs of wonder from the councillors then, to hear of these great men gathered to hear the message from Sun Horse. Standing Eagle told of the peace terms that grew from the council, what was to be offered to the whites and what demanded in return. Crazy Horse had agreed to these terms, he said, and in the end even Sitting Bull had given his approval and he had smoked the pipe of peace. There was an outburst of joy in the lodge at this news, but it died away quickly as the men gathered there remembered that the pipe carriers had a man dead and they did not yet know how that came to be, or why the messengers' expressions and bearing told unmistakably of failure.

Standing Eagle moved along now to the night following the council and Bat watched his brother-in-law closely, but the war leader said only that the pipe carriers had left the Cheyenne village before dawn to find Crook, Hardeman going ahead of the others, and when Standing Eagle turned to introduce the Oglalas, who would tell how the battle began, Bat knew the war leader would keep the bargain the two of them had made in private on the journey home. Bat had wrested from his brother-in-law the promise to tell the story this way in exchange for Bat's silence about Standing Eagle's outburst in the council with Sitting Bull and Crazy Horse. "'Tain't like you'd be lyin'," Bat had said, pressing the point in English although the two of them had been riding beyond the hearing of the others. "You jest hold back on a piece o' the truth. What's important is, Christopher saved your boy's life; twice, mebbe. And when the lead got to flyin', he sided with us and fought agin' the bluecoats. Mebbe he was figurin' t' bring the soldiers to the village when he lit out, mebbe not. Mebbe he jest figgered he could do better talkin' t' Three Stars on his own first. I dunno and you don't neither. So you tell it like I say or there's gonna be a heap o' folks hear how you made a fool o' yerself up there in front o' them big fellers."

Taking turns, the Oglalas related how the soldiers had been among the lodges before the alarm was sounded and how the people had fled to the bluffs and fought hard to repel the attackers. One of the men had seen Hardeman enter the battle. He described how the white man had tried to stop the fighting, only to be shot by the soldiers and rescued by two Shahíyela.

Now Bat took over the tale and there was no one to translate for Hardeman, but Bat added enough signs to his narration so that Hardeman was able to follow the gist of it. Bat told how the three youths had brought horses to the stranded Indians, how Blackbird had been wounded while charging the soldiers, and of Hardeman's attempt to save the boy. Bat described how the scout had shot at the troopers, unhorsing one man, and once again Hardeman heard voices raised in praise of his actions, followed by the *ahhh-h*'s of sorrow as the listeners learned at last how Hawk Chaser had died. They understood now why the white scout's face was painted in the Lakota way, and he saw the acceptance in their expressions. Lisa favored him with a kind look and Johnny's face shone with pride for his friend.

They thought they knew it all.

As Bat continued, telling briefly of the return journey, Hardeman readied himself for the moment when he would have an opportunity to speak. He was bone-weary, although his wounds were healing well enough; the persistent exhaustion depleted his spirit as much as it weakened his flesh, but he knew he must gather himself for one last effort before he could give in to the fatigue and let go completely. It was in preparation for this moment that he had risen from his pony drag to enter the Sun Band's village on horseback, and he had thought long and hard about what he wished to say.

On the morning after the battle he had awakened on a jouncing travois. For a time he had not known where he was or how he had been wounded, but the pain in his shoulder had convinced him that he was alive and awake, not dreaming or already beyond the cares of the flesh and its place in the earthly realm. Before long a Sioux squaw had come into sight, looking down on him from horseback, and he had recognized the woman who had cut the soldier's private parts. It had come back to him then, the screams and the scene of torture and his shot that had ended it. Oddly enough, the woman had smiled at him. She urged her horse forward and rode out of sight, and a short while later Bat Putnam came into view, wheeling his horse to ride close behind Hardeman's pony drag. "Reckoned we might lose you, pilgrim," Bat said, and he too smiled. Hardeman had been too weak to make any response and Bat rode near the pony drag in silence for a time. "Well," he said at last, "I reckon you'll be needin' yer rest." And then he had added, "By the by, we give that young feller a proper restin' place; the soldier feller. Built him a scaffold on the benchland. Wrapped him in a cavalry horse blanket. Laid a pistol and a carbine by his side. Wasn't much, but we done what we could fer him." And then he had ridden off to leave Hardeman alone.

Hardeman had been unable to fathom Bat's good will and the absence of recriminations, but he had lacked the strength to unravel those mysteries just then. Soon afterward, he had dozed off again. For much of that first day he had slept, and when he was not sleeping he had lain on the pony drag, letting it take him where it might, while he allowed his mind to drift freely, empty of thoughts and plans. All his thoughts and plans of recent weeks had failed him and brought him nothing, and he was content to do no more than simply exist, leaving his fate in the hands of others.

But as the journey lengthened and his strength began to return under the care of the Oglala healer, Iron Necklace, one by one the men came to see him, almost as if these visits were some kind of ritual, and each man in his own way had made it understood that he had Hardeman's welfare at heart and wished the white man a full recovery. Little Hand had surprised him by delivering his saddlebags, which he had thought lost for good, into his hands. The warrior had made signs to say that he had found them in the village, in the wreckage of Kills Fox's tipi. One of the bags was scorched on the outside but the contents were unharmed.

Standing Eagle was the last to pay his respects, but he too came, and he too brought a gift, which he held up for Hardeman to see before laying it on the pony drag beside the saddlebags. It was the remains of the scout's Sharps rifle. Kills Fox's lodge must have contained gunpowder, for the buffalo gun had been near the source of a powerful explosion. The stock was blown completely away and the barrel was bent. "Ain't much use in it now," Standing Eagle said, "but I reckoned you might want it. This gun saved my boy's life, and I'm beholden for that. Didn't say so before." The war leader's countenance had not been entirely free of suspicion and distrust of the white man. The expression of gratitude seemed to discomfort him and as soon as he had delivered it he took his leave.

The attitude of the Indians had perplexed Hardeman all the more. Why did they no longer blame him for shooting the wounded trooper? And beyond that, surely they suspected why he had left the Cheyenne village in the dark of night, before the battle. Bat himself had said as much. Was it possible that his attempt to save Blackbird from death at the hands of the soldiers had wiped out any blame for what had gone before, and even for his robbing them of their torture victim later? He was sure that could not be the full explanation for their generous treatment of him now, but he had no inkling of their true reasons until one evening when the little band was making camp on the south fork of Crazy Woman's Creek after a long day's march. They had traveled for five days since leaving the battle site, making fair time despite the pony drags, and there was talk that they might reach the Sun Band's village the next evening, or the morning after that. While the men and women went about making fires and small shelters for the night camp, Hardeman's pony drag was placed close to Blackbird's. The travois bearing Hawk Chaser's body was left some distance away. The first two days after the battle had been bitterly cold and transporting the body had presented no problems, but as the weather warmed, the warrior's corpse thawed in the daytime and at night it was unwrapped to refreeze quickly and slow its decay. Removing their dead and wounded from the field of battle was a point of honor among the Sioux and they were taking special pains in Hawk Chaser's case.

Hardeman and Blackbird had seen each other several times during the journey, at one resting place or another, but Blackbird had been as much weakened by his wounds as Hardeman and they had spoken little, other than to inquire about each other's progress.

"You are well today?" Blackbird asked on this occasion, as he had done before, practicing his English on the white scout.

"I'm some better," Hardeman acknowledged. "Iron Necklace has a way with wounds. Dunno why he makes such a fuss over me."

Blackbird was surprised at the white man's tone. "You are one of us," he said. "Iron Necklace is *wapíye,* a healer. He would care for any of us the same."

"I'm not one of you, boy," Hardeman said, more harshly than he had intended. "You best understand that. Everything I did, I had my own reasons, and they're not the same as yours."

Blackbird nodded. "My uncle Lodgepole explained this to us on the night of the fight—the battle, you call it? Your shot made me awake and I looked out of the little hut, the healing lodge. I saw the dead *washíchun* soldier and the men around you like wolves. Then you fell, and my uncle Lodgepole caught you. He brought you—carried you—to the healing lodge. He asked Iron Necklace to care for you. Little Hand said that when you are well he will torture you because you shot the soldier, and my father..." Blackbird hesitated and dropped his gaze. "My father said the same. My uncle Lodgepole stood before the healing lodge and he spoke to them. 'My friends,' he said, 'the *washíchun* do not think as we do. Their soldiers are not taught to die bravely in the way we understand. Some die well in battle, but they do not understand the chance a warrior is given when he is taken by the enemy. The white scout has told our way to the bluecoat and you have seen that the bluecoat was brave then.' 'The white scout shot the bluecoat,' said Little Hand. He is very angry still. 'Yes,' said Lodgepole. 'He knew what we did to the bluecoat, but our way is not his. When the *washíchun* take an enemy alive they put him away in the iron house. Spotted Tail, the uncle of Crazy Horse, was in the whiteman's iron house for many years and you know how he changed. The *washíchun* think it is good to change a man like that, breaking his spirit. They do not understand our way, giving a man a chance to die bravely, with a strong spirit.'

"Then my father said..." Again the young man hesitated, but he forced himself to look Hardeman in the eye as he continued. "My father said, 'Let him die. He is *washíchun,* and no longer a pipe carrier.' 'That is true,' Lodgepole said, 'but he saved your son's life. A warrior died to save him, and he is a guest in our camp.' And then my uncle told them a story of Sitting Bull when he was a young man. He killed a *Kanghí* woman with an arrow, they say. She was a captive of the Lakota, but she was a woman who gave herself to many men, not clean enough to be taken into the band. 'Adopted' is the word? The women wanted to burn her, and they started a fire, but Sitting Bull did not wish to see the torture, so he shot the *Kanghí* woman with an arrow and the people accepted this. Lodgepole told the story and he said to my father and the other men, 'A man does what he must. It is for other men to understand and accept, the Ancient Ones have said so.'"

Hardeman saw how the simple tale had made it impossible for Standing Eagle and the other men to judge him any differently than they would have judged one of their own kind who had killed a captive in similar circumstances, and beyond that, how it compelled a broader acceptance of the white man's different ways and customs. He was well aware of Bat's crucial role in guiding this response. Without the mountain man's thoughtful words to calm their passions, the warriors would have acted on instinct, and Hardeman's body would have been rotting on a scaffold beside the dead soldier, or it might simply have been left on the battlefield for the wolves and coyotes. His life had been saved by Bat's friendship, which he had cast away like an old boot on the night after the battle, and he saw that his willingness to discard that friendship, and any further concern for the Indians along with it, had been born of despair—a despair that arose from his own failure.

On the journey back he had been raised from despair by men who had every reason to regard him as a mortal enemy.

A man does what he must. It is for other men to understand and accept. Was it possible that any people could embrace that simple principle as completely as the Lakotas appeared to do? Hardeman had gone off to find Crook, intending to lead the soldiers to Sitting Bull and force a surrender; he had hoped it could be done without bloodshed, but if the attempt had gone awry he might easily have been the instrument of more deaths than were caused by Crook's troopers in the Cheyenne village. His traveling companions did not know the details of his intentions, but they suspected, and yet they had continued to accept his presence among them and they had sustained him in his time of need. If they had known the whole truth, would they have been so understanding? Would Bat still have spoken in his defense? He had no way of knowing. But they had treated him more than fairly, and as the little band's journey neared its end he had resolved to repay their generosity as best he could. There was little enough he could do now. With Crook no doubt pursuing the campaign against the hostiles, there was scant hope that any of the terms reached at the council in Two Moons' village could be salvaged. The simple question now was, could the Sun Band be kept out of the fighting?

Bat brought his narrative to an end and there was a thoughtful silence in the lodge as the men considered all they had heard. Hardeman saw how some of the councillors glanced at him, to all appearances kindly disposed toward this stranger in their midst. Sun Horse kept his gaze on the white scout for several long moments, nodding thoughtfully. Hardeman looked at Blackbird, resting on his litter, and the boy smiled at him. As much as by the tale the youth had told him, Hardeman had been impressed by the boy's ability to tell it in English. Clearly, Bat Putnam had been taking pains for some time to instruct Blackbird in the white man's tongue. Was it because the mountain man knew that the boy would grow to manhood in a world dominated by the whites? Did Sun Horse realize this as well? Hardeman hoped so. The sooner the Sun Band came to accept that fact, however unpleasant it seemed to them, the sooner they would accept the only course left to them now.

Standing Eagle reached into his robes and drew forth a beaded pipe bag similar to the one in which Little Hand had carried the pipe for Sitting Bull.

Without opening the bag he handed it to Sun Horse, and then he spoke.

"My friends, this was the pipe for Three Stars. I have returned it to my father and I am a pipe carrier no longer. I speak now as war leader of Sun Horse's camp." He drew himself up and looked around the gathering, and it seemed he was glad to be rid of the burden he had carried for so long. "When the bluecoats had destroyed the Shahíyela village, there were none who spoke of peace. 'Now it is war,' He Dog said. He has gone to join his *hunká*-brother Crazy Horse, and all the Oglala went with him, save these men and their families, who have relatives here." He gestured at Iron Necklace and the two other Oglala men. "Two Moons also spoke of war. 'The Shahíyela were at peace with the whites,' he said. 'Now we will fight beside our brothers the Lakota. It is better to leave our bones on the prairie than to surrender to men who make war on the helpless ones.' He sent his young men on the bluecoats' trail to try to recapture the horses the bluecoats stole, and I wished to go with them! I wanted to chase the bluecoats and fight them again to punish them for what they did!" He looked around him, seeking approval, and he saw some men nodding in agreement, their faces dark with anger. But others turned away. They had heard the pipe carriers' tale and they knew Standing Eagle had fought in the battle. Even while he carried a pipe of peace the war leader had taken up arms, and so the power of the pipe was broken. It would seem that Standing Eagle had never believed in his mission, and perhaps that was why it had failed.

Standing Eagle continued, his voice calmer, but still proud. "On the day after the fight we started upstream along the Powder and we met the Shahíyela warriors returning. They had taken back many of the horses and the bluecoats did not come after them!" The men who sided with Standing Eagle voiced their delight on hearing this news, and Standing Eagle smiled. "It seems that Three Stars does not like to fight when the warriors come against him and there are no helpless ones to hinder them. Perhaps he has already gone from our country. I do not know where he is now, but I know this: if we stand strong against him, we can whip him!" His manner grew more serious now. "My friends, before you sent us with the pipes, you said that if we failed, you would take the people to Dakota to make peace with the whites. Well, my friends, the Shahíyela were at peace with the *washíchun* and you have heard what the bluecoats did to them! The Shahíyela lodges are burned and the helpless ones are homeless. They go to Crazy Horse, asking for food and clothing and shelter. Will you still make peace with the men who have done this? Will you have us become beggars who must go from place to place with our hands out?" He looked at his listeners, demanding an answer with his eyes, and then he gave his own reply. "No, my friends, there can be no talk of peace with the *washíchun* now. We are Lakota! Let us live as the Lakota have always lived! Let us prepare to fight! Let us show the bluecoats we are men!"

There were some *hau*'s of approval now, but many men remained silent, and the division in the lodge became more plain to see when Elk Leggings spoke next.

"I am a councillor of Sun Horse's camp," he began formally stating his right to speak. "I am father of the *wichasha wakán* Sees Beyond, who prepared the pipes of peace with Sun Horse. I have the right to advise our people, but I do not speak now to tell others what to do. Each must decide for himself. I will go to Dakota when the snows melt. If the *washichun* want war, there will be war. If we fight the whites, our power as a band is broken. Our power is to understand the *washichun*, not fight them, and by understanding them, to find the way to peace."

There were murmurs of agreement, and before they had died away the scout Walks Bent Over straightened his head on his misshapen shoulders and began to speak.

"My friends," he said, "Standing Eagle has reminded us that before we sent the pipe carriers we agreed to surrender if they failed. Well, my friends, they have failed and war has begun. Have you changed your minds? Do you see some way to avoid surrender and still keep our power as a band? If so, tell me what it is! I wish to know! For myself, I see only two ways: we must surrender or we must fight."

From the back of the lodge came a voice. "To fight the *washichun* is to fight the whirlwind! Sun Horse has said so himself!"

The sounds of agreement were loud now and all eyes turned toward the headman to see if he would confirm his own words, but Sun Horse made no reply and it was Hardeman who finally spoke. He cleared his throat and got slowly to his feet so all could see him, even those in the back. He glanced at Bat Putnam and then he began to talk, and Bat put his words into Lakota.

"You asked me to go with Standing Eagle and Lodgepole and the others, and I went with them because I wanted peace between our peoples, just as you did. In Two Moons' village I saw great men meet to decide on peace or war, and they chose peace. They were willing to give up much, and I believe Three Stars would have accepted the terms. On both sides there are good men who want peace, men like Sun Horse and Three Stars, and Listen Wolf and Two Moons. Even Crazy Horse and Sitting Bull, who have fought hard to defend their people, agreed to the council's terms because they saw a chance for peace with honor, without surrender." Hardeman struggled to keep hold of the thoughts he had marshaled so carefully, which threatened to desert him now as his tired mind tried to place one after the next for greatest effect. He was painfully aware of the need to speak well if he hoped to make an impression on these men. "I hoped that the good men could sit down together and talk quietly, and I hoped they could prevent this war. But General Crook found us before we found him. His soldiers attacked the village and now the fighting has started."

Some of the listeners made soft sounds of agreement. They shared the

538

whiteman's disappointment. They too had hoped for peace and had seen their hopes dashed. But the white scout had done his best, as had all of the pipe carriers; it was not his fault the fighting had begun.

Hardeman heard the sympathy in their voices and he knew they were not prepared for what he would say next.

"Even if the soldiers hadn't come, even if we had found Three Stars in time and he had gone from the country now, there would still have been war."

This surprised the councillors. What did the whiteman mean? He himself had supported the terms in Two Moons' council and had said they might keep the peace. What was this new talk of war?

Hardeman looked at Sun Horse, and he directed his next words to the old man. "You know that the whites fear any gathering of the bands, but still you called for all the Lakotas to come together in the summertime. I know you did this because you believe that peace as well as war can come from strength, but the white man fear your strength. They wouldn't wait to see if you spoke of peace or war. They would look at a gathering like that and they would be afraid; when a white man is afraid, he fights." He raised his eyes and looked around at the other councillors. "Elk Leggings has said that when the white men want war, there will be war, and he's right. But it's not only the whites who love war." His eyes stopped on Standing Eagle and then moved on. "There are many Lakotas who talk of fighting instead of peace."

There were a few soft *hau*'s from those who opposed the war leader's fiery talk.

Hardeman was glad that some, at least, could admit the truth of what he said, and he moved along quickly to press his advantage. "In a great summer gathering the warriors would see the lodges filling the valley bottoms and the pony herds covering the hillsides"—he was caught up in his speechmaking now and he made broad gestures with his one good hand to indicate the extent of the huge encampment—"and they would think that nothing could break the strength of the Lakota nation. Some men would still speak for peace, but would the others listen? Would the warriors accept the terms from Two Moons' council?"

From Sun Horse's expression, he saw that the old man had had these same doubts himself. He waited a moment to let the headman ponder them again, and then he continued.

"One way or another, the summer gathering would have meant war. I knew this the same way a man knows that the sun will rise in the east, and so I tried to prevent it. I left the village alone and no one knew where I had gone. I went to find Three Stars. If I had found him, I would have led him to Chalk Buttes, to the camp of Sitting Bull."

The councillors reacted to this news with surprise and anger, and Hardeman raised his voice to make himself heard above the hubbub. "Not to fight him! To surround him and make him surrender, so there would be no summer gathering! It was the only way to save the peace terms!"

Bat too had raised his voice to make the translation heard, and when the councillors understood Hardeman's last words, they quieted their protests, willing to listen again, but there was no kindness now in the faces that watched him, except, strangely, in the expression of Sun Horse. His look was so benevolent and vague that Hardeman was not sure the old man had all his wits about him.

"With Sitting Bull taken captive, and no gathering of the bands, the whites would think they had won a great victory," he told the councillors. "They would no longer fear you. They might have let you keep this country here, or a part of it. They might even have given you the agency you've always wanted. To keep that hope alive, I would have betrayed Sitting Bull to Three Stars. But I never got a chance. I found the soldiers' tracks and I followed them, but it was too late. The fighting had started and I couldn't stop it."

The hostility that had greeted his confession of what he had planned to do when he went off alone had dwindled. The men who sided with Standing Eagle still looked at Hardeman with dark faces, but the others now revealed something akin to despair, as if they understood what he had done and why, and saw his failure as yet one more chance for peace snatched away by an unkind fate. These men were in the majority, and it was to them that Hardeman spoke now.

"There is no more chance for peace without surrender. You know we met Three Stars' wagons when we were on his trail. There were eighty wagons, all carrying the things he needs to make war. He sent them back to wait for him somewhere." He looked at Standing Eagle again. "That's why Three Stars went upstream. He wasn't running away. He went to his wagons. With new supplies he'll turn back to fight again. He'll keep after the war leaders until he catches them. If he doesn't find them now, he'll keep on through the summer and the fall and winter, if that's what it takes. The war may be long and the men on both sides will fight hard, but in the end it won't matter how many warriors you send against Three Stars, because he will win. Even if you kill a hundred or a thousand soldiers, there will be another hundred or another thousand to take their places, and Three Stars won't give up. That's not his way of making war and it's not the white man's way. When the white man starts fighting, he keeps on fighting until his enemy surrenders."

Hardeman felt his strength failing, but he had little more to say. He turned to Sun Horse. "You wanted to make peace not only for your own people but for all the Lakotas. Now it's too late to save the Sioux nation. You can only save yourselves, and there's just one way to do that. You'll have to surrender."

He sat down, glad it was over. He had done what he could. He had told them the whole truth as he knew it; it was all he had left to give, to repay the Sun Band for trusting him. They knew everything now, and they could judge him however they wished. Like Sun Horse, he too had hoped to make a far-reaching peace, one that would embrace not only the Sioux but the Cheyenne and Arapaho and all the whites as well, and bring an end to war in the northern territories. But he had failed. If the Sun Band would heed his advice and remove themselves to a place of safety, that would be a small achievement, hardly noticeable in the bloodshed that was sure to come, but it would be something.

No one spoke at once to contradict his words, and his hopes rose. Maybe they would see that he had spoken the truth and there was no other way left to the Sun Band. Bat was looking at him, and Lisa and Johnny too. Later he would talk to them and make them understand, if they didn't already. First he would have to sleep. Right now, he could barely remain upright.

The only sounds in the lodge were the crackling of the fire, where the strips of buffalo fat had melted into pools that occasionally spat and hissed beneath the flames, and the noise of men blowing softly through their empty smoking pipes as they waited to see who would speak. Gradually their attention came to rest on Sun Horse. His was the one voice they all wished to hear, the one voice that could change whatever decisions the councillors had reached in their own minds, if his words were persuasive.

Sun Horse was aware of the attention and he knew he must speak now, but still he did not know what to advise. It was as if nothing had changed since the Snowblind Moon was young, when the white scout and the One Who Stands Between the Worlds had first come to the Sun Band's village. The choice remained the same: surrender or fight. Could there be any other path left open now? Walks Bent Over had said not, and Hardeman believed there was only one choice—surrender. The pipe carriers had failed, the war had begun, and by the council's previous decision the Sun Band should go to Dakota and surrender. But the whole band would not go; those who favored fighting would go north with Standing Eagle and Little Hand and the band would be broken. Sun Horse knew his son would never surrender now; he would rather die, and there were others like him.

Yet the pipe carriers had not failed entirely. Unless Three Stars found each of the Powder River bands and defeated them all in turn, there would still be a great council in the Moon of Fat Calves; even now Sitting Bull's news riders might be spreading the word. Many would heed the call, hoping that in the strength of the Lakota nation they would be safe. In his heart, Sun Horse wished to go too, for he knew it might be the last time the nation's hoop was raised. And still he wished to address the council. *Will the warriors accept the peace terms from Two Moons' council?* Hardeman had asked. Sun Horse did not know the answer, but he did know that no man or group of men could deny the people the right to come together to talk and listen. It was for the people to decide such great issues, each man deciding for himself. That was the Lakota way. But Sun Horse knew that if he counseled the Sun Band to stay out now, hoping to avoid the soldiers and reach the great gathering unharmed, some like Elk Leggings would go to Dakota soon, unwilling to take their families where there might be further fighting, and still the band would be broken.

Sun Horse clung to a stubborn hope that there must be another way, some way to keep the band together and the chance for peace alive. It was more than a hope, it was a suspicion that gnawed at him, causing a pain almost as troubling as a wound in the body. It seemed to him that the answer to his dilemma was closer than ever before, as if it lay in something he had heard here today. Yet it hid from him still, as a young man hid in his robe and waited along the river trail until a young woman came for water. The solution was simple, Sun Horse felt certain. Perhaps so simple that he had overlooked it all this time. What could it be? Somewhere lay the path to his power, but he could not find it.

Another pain troubled him too—the constant knot of hunger that had twisted his belly all day. He had not felt it in many days, not since the first period of fasting. The body grew accustomed to the lack of food and the spirit grew light, rising to the place Sun Horse sought, a place free from the limits of the flesh where he might see clearly, but the hunt and the meat it had brought to the village offered him too many reminders of food, the smells of *pte*, both raw and cooked, and the sounds of happy people who for a time at least were well fed. His stomach growled at him now, reminding him of his flesh and its frailty, making it even harder for him to bring some order to the conflicting thoughts that troubled him. The meat posed another puzzle: all was not as it had been when the Snowblind Moon was young; *pte* had returned, a good sign; the village was strong again, but how was that strength to be used? Could it provide a solution to the most immediate challenge—how to assure that the band would remain united? Throughout his fast Sun Horse had felt his people slipping away from him, and he had despaired. That was what he must prevent above all.

He placed a hand on Standing Eagle's shoulder to brace himself and he struggled to his feet. He moved his free hand in an arc that took in Standing Eagle and Little Hand, Blackbird where he lay on his litter, Hardeman and Lodgepole and the Oglalas. "These travelers are tired," he said. "They must eat and rest now. We have heard their words and we have much to think on. We too must rest before we decide what to do. My grandson will come with me to my lodge and I will care for his wounds. Sometimes the young see more clearly than older men and I would hear him tell everything he has seen." Sun Horse did not know whence came the sudden desire to hear Blackbird's version of the journey, but he knew that he wanted to speak with the boy beyond Standing Eagle's hearing, particularly to know what he had to say about Hardeman and the council at the Shahíyela village.

"Let those who have much meat take some to the lodges of these men, who were not here for the hunt. The *pte* have returned to the Sun Band, and *pte* is the source of life. We will eat, warm in our lodges and tonight we will

542

sleep well. Tomorrow we will meet again." The thought of food sent an insistent rumble through his stomach. He would have to eat soon. He had passed the point at which fasting helped to clear his mind.

He remained standing, and now others rose. Those near the entrance began to file out of the lodge. The men would return to their own tipis where they would eat again, and then they would visit among themselves to talk. Some would come to see Sun Horse, if the crossed sticks were removed from the entrance to his lodge. Tonight the councillors would enjoy their wives and sleep the contented sleep of a full belly, and tomorrow they would return to the council lodge. They would be strong in their opinions but they would not agree on what to do. As never before the band needed a leader to guide it. Once again, Sun Horse had managed to delay committing himself to one course or another, but he knew he could not delay much longer, not if he wished to guide the destiny of his band and keep it whole.

As Standing Eagle rose he handed Sun Horse his oakwood cane. The old man gripped it firmly and turned his back to the fire to store up some warmth before going out into the wind and snow. Standing Eagle pulled Blackbird's buffalo robe up about the boy's chin in preparation for carrying him across the camp to Sun Horse's lodge, where the pipe carriers would eat soon.

Bat got stiffly to his feet. For once, he hoped the welcoming meal would not take long. He and Standing Eagle and Little Hand all had families waiting, but custom decreed that the travelers should accept the hospitality of the headman's lodge after a long journey made on the band's behalf. Bat was glad to be home and he wanted nothing more than to retire to his own lodge and be alone with Penelope. But she understood and she would wait for him. She had always waited for him, from the beginning.

Lisa moved to Bat's side and she took one of his hands, squeezing it with both of her own. "I'm glad you're back. I've missed you."

He put a long arm around her. "You heard how it went. Could of been better, but we're safe and sound. All but one." She hugged him close and they were quiet for a moment. "We heard about the avalanche afore we put out. Looks like you're stuck with them circus folks."

"They're digging out the river road. It will be clear in a few more days."

Bat's eyebrows went up. "That so? That's a piece o' work." He looked at the councillors filing out of the lodge, then back at Lisa. "You'll stay fer sump'n to eat?"

"I think we better not. Hutch and I came to pack some meat from the hunt. We should be getting on before the storm breaks."

"We'll send word what the council decides. Might be I'll bring it over myself in a day or two." He didn't say that he might bring Penelope as well, and their lodge, and that he might be leaving the Sun Band for good if they decided to go to Dakota.

"I'd take it kindly if you'd wait long enough for me to grab a bite or two, Miss Putnam." Hardeman had managed to get to his feet unaided. "My fire's just about gone out and I better stoke it up before I head on. That is, if I can impose on your hospitality again."

"Of course," she replied uncertainly.

"Well, time's a-wastin'," Bat said, and he moved to help Standing Eagle with Blackbird's litter. Each man took hold of one end and they rose in unison, holding the litter between them. Bat was in the lead and he was about to step out of the lodge when Hutch and Chatur entered, looking around for Johnny Smoker.

Bat smiled at Hutch. "You gettin' any work done, or you spendin' all yer time with them circus girls?"

Hutch blushed at the accuracy of Bat's guess. "Oh, Julius keeps a person busy, what with calving and feeding and all. We're looking after the circus stock too."

Bat grinned. "I reckon them fillies need lookin' after."

"What spare time I got, Johnny's been learnin' me to rope."

"He's a good learner, too," Johnny put in, slipping into his blanket coat, which he had removed when the council lodge grew warm. "He already knows most everything I do."

"He's gonna learn me about horses next," Hutch added.

"Hmmp. Take you some time to learn all he knows 'bout them," said Bat. With that he bent over and stepped through the entrance, being careful to keep the litter level.

By now all the councillors were gone from the lodge. Sun Horse moved close to Lisa and took her arm. He spoke briefly and she heard him out before translating for Hardeman.

"Sun Horse says there is no need for you to ride any farther today. He invites you to stay here, in his lodge. He says you have traveled far enough and you need to rest." Hardeman's painted face unnerved her. She felt that she was talking to a stranger.

Hardeman looked at the old man and shook his head. "You thank him for me, if you would. Tell him I've got a mind to sleep in a real bed for a change."

He did not give his true reason for refusing. Tired as he was, he felt compelled to go on until he had left behind Sun Horse and the Indians and all the reminders of his failure. He had started his fruitless journey in Putnam's Park and he wished to end it there, where he could disappear into a back room and sleep until the events of recent weeks seemed no more than a troubling dream. "Tell him one more thing," he said. "Tell him he can't stay here forever. He's running out of time."

Lisa and Sun Horse spoke back and forth and Lisa turned back to Hardeman. "He says when the day comes for the Sun Band to leave this place, they will leave."

Hardeman addressed Sun Horse directly now. "If the army finds you they won't sit down to talk, not now that the fighting's started." He turned to Lisa,

544

losing patience. "Can't you make him see that? He's got to understand that there's no more time!"

She kept silent, unable to add her voice to Hardeman's plea but no longer able to oppose him. There seemed to be little enough hope for the Sun Band and yet now at least they had meat. The Snowblind Moon was gone and soon they could safely move. What did Sun Horse intend to do? She knew that he had purposely delayed a council decision today, but why? If he hoped to avoid surrender, why didn't he tell his people what he had in mind?

Sun Horse looked up at the peak of the council lodge where the wind buffeted the smoke flaps. Flakes of snow swirled into the smoke hole and evaporated in the warm air. He smiled benignly at Hardeman and spoke to him.

"He says the winter spirit is not ready to go back to his lodge," Lisa explained. "He saw the new moon last night for the first time. They call it the Moon When the Ducks Come Back. He says the ducks will be late this year. As long as the cold winds blow, the Sun Band will stay here. He invites you to return here when you're rested. He says Blackbird will be glad to see you. He says the true man of peace is always welcome in his lodge."

To Hardeman it seemed that Lisa was not certain he deserved this title or the invitation that accompanied it.

Sun Horse moved toward the entrance, motioning them to follow, saying a few words over his shoulder.

"We must come and eat now," said Lisa. "He says we all need the strength of the buffalo. I gather they attach some spiritual significance to this hunt. They credit Johnny and Amanda with bringing the buffalo back to the Sun Band."

Hardeman nodded, too tired to protest further. There it was again, the talk of spirit power coming from Johnny. No doubt Sun Horse was praying daily to the buffalo or the north wind or the snow gods, or whatever spirits he still hoped might offer some help to the band. But in the end all the prayers and dreams and spirits and imagined manifestations of heavenly intervention would only serve to assure the band's eventual destruction if false hopes delayed their surrender. Hardeman had expended the last measure of his reason in an effort to make Sun Horse see that he must admit defeat, and still the old man was stalling for time. Hardeman could do no more. If the Sun Band sought an early entry at the gates of Perdition, they would have to find their way alone.

Sun Horse stepped out of the lodge and waited for the others beside the entrance. They gathered around him and moved along in a group, Sun Horse leaning on Lisa's arm. Snow was falling thickly. The sky was as dark as dusk although it was midday. The wind was gentle but the occasional strong gusts hinted that the storm was still gathering force on the mountain slopes and would descend in its fury before long.

"You want me to ride over to the park with you?" Johnny asked Hardeman.

He pulled his hat down low to keep the snow out of his eyes.

"There's no need. You stay here and take care of that girl. Get that talking done."

Johnny seemed relieved. "You'll be there for a few days? Amanda and I will come over when the storm's done. The circus is going to give a performance before they go. I know she'd like you to see it."

"I'll be there."

"They'll still want a guide when they head out. You think you might go with them?"

"Me? No idea, Johnny, none at all." It was the simple truth. Until this moment, Hardeman had never given a particle of thought to what he might do once the pipe carriers' journey ended. Just now, putting one foot in front of the other was about the extent of his abilities. He needed no further puzzles to solve. Anything beyond the day at hand was untouchably remote.

He stumbled and caught himself and Johnny took his arm.

"Are you sure you're all right?"

"We'll look after him," Lisa said.

"Between the three of us, we'll get him back home" said Hutch.

Chatur smiled at Johnny. "He will be in good care."

"Oh, I'll be all right," Hardeman grumbled, shaking off Johnny's hand. It annoyed him to be discussed as if he were an invalid, although privately he knew he was not far removed from that condition.

"You're a stubborn man, Mr. Hardeman," Lisa said, and he merely nodded. Her tone managed to convey both a solicitous care for his well-being and a repressed anger. She was probably riled about his plan to betray Sitting Bull to the soldiers, but it couldn't be helped. She had been in the council and she had heard it all.

He realized that he had secretly hoped to return to her with a promise of peace for the Sioux, or at least a future free of warfare for the Sun Band. He had imagined her joy and gratitude and had allowed himself to think that such a deed might win him a place in her affections. But he had failed and she knew the details of his defeat.

The meal in Sun Horse's lodge was quiet. Amanda had fallen asleep again and Sun Horse sat near her in the back of the lodge while his guests ate. He himself took nothing. Elk Calf and Sings His Daughter kept the bowls and platters full, but the food and warmth made Hardeman so drowsy that he could barely hold his head up, and long before he had eaten his fill he rose, preparing to go before he fell sound asleep over his food.

Lisa was quick to follow his example. She cast a meaningful glance at Hutch, who hid his disappointment at having his first meal in an Indian lodge cut short. He was less obvious in his fascination with the Indians and their ways than Chatur, who was still looking about goggle-eyed, but Hutch took it all in with a boyish wonder.

"Well, hoss, you keep yer powder dry," Bat said as Hardeman buttoned his St. Paul coat.

"I'll be seeing you" was all the reply Hardeman could muster.

"More'n likely."

It was a simple exchange, but as Hardeman stepped out of the lodge after a nod to Blackbird and a farewell smile to Johnny, he felt a pleasant satisfaction, as if by those few words he and the mountain man had reaffirmed their friendship. Bat was much like his late brother, and in the understanding that had grown between himself and Bat, Hardeman saw a chance to redeem that other friendship, which he had neglected until it was lost to him. It didn't do to cast friends carelessly aside. Hardeman had wished to do just that after the battle, but Bat had refused to let go and Hardeman was grateful to him.

He followed Lisa to the horses and he saw that a mount had been brought there for him, a pinto from the Sun Band's herd, provided with a saddle. He wondered what had become of his roan after the battle. Probably some Indian had him now, unless the soldiers had taken the roan away with the Cheyenne ponies. The pinto looked small beside the large American horses. While the guests ate, the pack horses had been laden with cuts of buffalo.

Lisa started off in the lead, setting a brisk pace, and Hardeman kept close behind her while Hutch and Chatur brought up the rear with the pack horses. The wind had found its stride now, and the snow flew across the ground. As the riders crossed the divide that separated the Indian valley from Putnam's Park they had to cling to their hats, but as they descended the far slope the wind grew less severe. The snow thickened, obscuring all but the closest patches of trees and revealing nothing at all of the hills and mountains above. Hardeman had thought that he remembered the trail well, but he realized that in his present state he could easily have become lost without Lisa Putnam to guide him. It discomforted him to feel so helpless, but he gave up trying to determine where he was and allowed his head to nod while the pinto plodded along after Lisa's horse.

He felt a hand on his arm and he jerked awake to find Hutch riding beside him, supporting him by his elbow. He had gone to sleep and had very nearly fallen.

After that one of the others rode next to him, talking to him occasionally to be sure he was awake. He forced himself to breathe deeply and sit straight in the saddle. He was determined to make it under his own steam to the Big House and whatever bed he first set eyes on. He rolled his left shoulder and felt the pain start again. He had almost forgotten the wound. He willed the pain to keep him awake, but even that trick threatened to fail him now. Like a horse that had run for too long, his will was growing winded and had begun to slow down. With no hands at the reins it would soon come to a halt of its own accord.

Just a little while longer, he told himself, but his body seemed to belong

547

to someone else. Even the snowflakes that stung his face could not hold his attention.

This time he did fall, landing on the wounded shoulder. Lisa was off her horse and beside him in an instant, helping him to his feet. "He'll have to ride with you," she told Hutch. "You hold on to him. I'll lead his horse."

"I'm all right," Hardeman insisted. He commanded his body to mount the pinto and it obeyed. The pain in his shoulder was sharp now. He started off at once, trusting the horse to find a path through the trees. He heard the others coming along behind him, but he did not look back.

The snow thinned a little and the surroundings seemed more familiar. He came out of the trees suddenly and saw the settlement before him and he reined the pinto to a halt to take in the sight. The storm clouds covered the valley solidly, supported by the ridges. The circus wagons and tents were arranged in rows near the barn, their peaked roofs covered with snow. There were footpaths among the wagons, more paths leading to the house and barn. There was a sense of permanence about it all; the circus was part of the settlement now. Lights shone in many windows, where lamps had been lit against the gloom of the day. Smoke came from a dozen chimneys, large and small. The scene was peaceful and welcoming, and Hardeman smiled. The feeling that arose in him was one he had almost forgotten, one he had not experienced since he was a boy back in Pennsylvania, before he got the urge to wander. Here in this small valley where Jed Putnam had planted his dream and made it grow, Hardeman felt at home.

He knew he was slipping from the saddle again but he didn't care. Here at last he could rest.

CHAPTER

THIRTY-EIGHT

While those in his lodge slept, Sun Horse stepped out into the storm and walked around the camp circle, aided by his oakwood cane. Night had fallen and the wind was strong. It tugged at his robe. He pulled the old buffalo hide over his head and held it close beneath his chin to shelter his face from the driving snow. He moved around the circle as the sun moved around the sky, pausing at the cardinal points. His own lodge stood in the west, opposite the entrance to the camp; the power of the west was to make live and destroy, and resolving this paradox lay at the heart of his search. Would the band be destroyed or would it live? The north was the region of cold and death, but it was also the power of

548

the north to cleanse and heal, and it was for this power that he prayed tonight. At the horns of the camp he stopped to chant a short prayer to the east, praying for the power of true understanding, the understanding that led to peace. The south offered the power to grow and he needed that power too, so his people could grow and change and remain strong through whatever was to come.

When he reached his lodge again he passed it by, stabbing the ground with his cane and hastening himself along impatiently, careless of the cold and wind. He had no more time to retreat into reflections and prayers, no more time to ponder his life and the elusive nature of the *washíchun*. He must decide what to do! Tomorrow the council would meet again and they would demand to know his decision. There could be no more delays.

Your power is in this world. Use it for the people. You can guide them still. Sees Beyond had said this not long ago, just before the whites had arrived in the village with the news that the clown girl was lost.

But how to guide them? Surrender or fight? Nothing had changed.

Everything had changed. Soldiers had attacked a village. The fighting he had hoped to prevent had begun. The pipe carriers had returned. Hawk Chaser was dead.

Just before learning that the clown girl was lost, Sun Horse had cried out to the Great Mystery, asking for a sign that he still had the power to help the people. He had heard a mother quiet a child and he had wondered how that child would eat.

Now there was meat. Were the *pte* the sign he had prayed for? The band was strong again, but how was that strength to be used without leadership to guide it? Which way to turn? To Dakota or to the summer council? And above all, how to keep the band intact?!

Sun Horse continued around the circle until he came once again to the horns of the camp. There he turned and walked straight across the circle to his lodge. The camp circle represented the hoop of the world, and from east to west stretched the good red road, the pathway of spiritual understanding that every man must walk if he is to know peace. As Sun Horse walked this path he prayed, *Wakán Tanka*, help me to understand.

If the *pte* were the sign he had asked for, why then was he still at a loss? Why could he not see the meaning of the sign?

Pte, the most sacred of the four-leggeds. The greatest gift to man, for *pte* provided the essentials of life.

In the lodge they all slept on, his white grandson and the clown girl, Blackbird, and his wives. The fire was built up high. The wind buffeted the lodgeskins; it hummed among the lodgepoles where their naked ends rose above the peak into the breath of the storm. Occasionally a few flakes of snow gusted into the smoke hole, only to vanish before they reached the ground.

The lodge shuddered from a strong gust and it seemed to Sun Horse that even the storm was impatient with him. It blew to urge him onward. It brought the air and the village alive. The world was alive around him, howling its impatience.

549

He imagined the men and women of the village awake and gathered in a ring around his lodge, all blowing with the storm, impatient to hear what he would do.

As he sat down by the fire Blackbird raised his head.

"*Hau, Tunkáshila.*" The boy had fallen asleep after Hardeman and Lisaputnam had gone, while the other pipe carriers were still eating. "I didn't mean to sleep," he said. "I wanted to speak with you."

"But you were very tired and so you slept. Now you have rested and we can talk." Sun Horse moved to the boy's side and unwrapped the dressings on his leg. The Shahíyela healer Ice had used his powers as well. Soon Blackbird would have the full use of his leg. The newer wound on his side was still angry and swollen but it too would heal well. The soldier's bullet had glanced off a rib, breaking it, but Iron Necklace had bound the youth's midsection tightly and the rib would mend. Either wound could have been fatal without proper care.

"Will I limp, Grandfather?" the boy asked.

Sun Horse smiled. "Perhaps, but you will not be crippled. You will still grow up to be a strong man."

Blackbird looked at the pallet where Johnny Smoker lay asleep. "Your other grandson limps, but he is strong. Before I went away with my father you said something about the strength of the warrior who does not fight."

Sun Horse nodded. "You wished to hear nothing of such strength then."

"Tell me about it now."

"Such a warrior does not conquer by fighting but by the strength he keeps inside himself."

Blackbird knitted his brow and pondered this for a time, and then he said, "I would tell you of our journey, Grandfather. There is something I have learned, but I don't yet know what it is."

Sun Horse felt a small surge of excitement. The boy's words described his own feeling as well. Stronger and stronger within him grew the certainty that he had already learned what he needed to know to make his choice. It lurked somewhere inside him, hiding. Perhaps if he listened to the boy... He settled himself and prepared to hear his grandson's tale.

Blackbird began by telling of finding the cavalry's trail and following it, and how the *washíchun* scout Hardeman had wanted to move along quickly while Standing Eagle had seemed to hold back. He told the other events of the trip, each in turn, always being careful to say what he knew from his own experience and what he had learned from others. He passed along quickly to the arrival in Two Moons' village; he spoke of the strength of the Shahíyela camp, the people happy there, and the honor he had felt to be included in the council. And then for the first time Sun Horse heard of Standing Eagle's shocking interruption in the council, speaking loudly for war with the bluecoats even as he carried the pipe of peace. Blackbird left nothing out, telling of He Dog's rebuke and the way Crazy Horse had smoothed away the trouble and made the hearts of the council good again. Blackbird was plainly troubled by what had taken place. He sensed

550

that his father's actions were not those of a man who thought first of the good of the people.

It saddened Sun Horse to hear of these things, but he was not surprised. From the start it seemed that the war leader had not believed in the mission of peace. Why else would he hold back? Could it be that he had actually wished for the bluecoats to find a village and start the war before the pipe carriers could reach them? And once in Two Moons' village, in council with two great Lakota leaders, he had tried to rally them for war, not peace.

Standing Eagle was angry at the whites for all the wrongs they had done to the Lakota, but his anger hurt his own people. It filled his lodge; it filled the councils, no matter if he sat silent or if he spoke. A man should not bring such anger to his people. He should go far away to some place where he could release his anger, and not come among his people again until it was gone. But it was not Standing Eagle's nature to set aside his own passions and think only of the people. Sun Horse had hoped that his only remaining son would change with age, but he saw now that Standing Eagle would not be one of those who chose to set aside the shield and lance and take up the greater burden of leadership. Where then would come the wisdom to guide the Sun Band when he, Sun Horse, was gone?

He took his smoking pipe from the pouch that hung at the back of the lodge and stoked it slowly as he listened to Blackbird tell of waking in the dawn to find his father and uncle gone, catching his horse and seeing the soldiers come riding all in a line, the warning of the blackbirds, and of his part in the battle that followed.

"I was foolish, Grandfather," the boy said, averting his eyes. "When the soldiers passed me without shooting, I thought I would survive the day no matter what I did. But the blackbirds had warned me. 'Fly away!' they said. 'Fly away from the whites!' I didn't listen to them. I forgot that wisdom is more important than strength, and so I charged the soldiers." He looked at Sun Horse, pleading for understanding. "I was the moccasin carrier! My friends and I had some good horses. I wanted to bring them to my father so he would see I was not afraid. Did I do wrong?"

"You did not do wrong."

"A man died because of me," Blackbird said, unwilling to speak Hawk Chaser's name. "Perhaps it was not wrong of me to bring the horses to where the men were fighting. I wanted to help the women get away. But I charged the bluecoats because they killed my friend and I thought they could not hurt me. And because of me the white scout was wounded and a great man died, a man of the people. He rode into the guns of the bluecoats with only a lance! He was strong and wise, and he spoke always of the good of the people. He died for me, but he could have done so much more for them than I can."

"He died that you might live."

"But I am not one of the helpless ones, to be protected by the warriors!"

"You are the future of the people," Sun Horse said, and he felt a sudden chill. It was as if the words had been spoken by another. He heard the truth in the

551

words and he felt the chill of his power moving around him. The feeling reminded him of the day when the Strange-Animal People had arrived in Putnam's Park, the day *wamblí* spoke to him. . . .

"I will miss him, the one who died," Blackbird said. "He used to tell me tales of the people, and I learned from him."

Sun Horse nodded. Hawk Chaser was a storyteller. As an old man he would have entranced the children. But he would never be an old man.

"Who will tell the stories now that he is gone?" the boy asked.

"Others tell the tales."

"But they are the old people."

"In each generation there are those among the young who learn the tales better than the others, those who have the ear to tell them and a way of telling that will make others listen."

"I would like to learn them."

"You know the tales."

Blackbird nodded. "I know them, and I have even told the little children a story sometimes, but I want to be good at it, as he was. I want to be like him, Grandfather."

"Perhaps you shall be."

Blackbird was silent for a time, but then he looked at Sun Horse again. "Another man helped to save me. A *washíchun* came to help me. I do not understand the whitemen, Grandfather. Among the whites there are men as different from one another as the Lakota and the *Kanghí*. I do not understand them!"

"They are very difficult to understand," Sun Horse agreed. "All my life I have tried to understand them and still I know only a little."

"I want to understand them," said Blackbird. "Is it true that they are without number? And that they will never go away?"

Sun Horse nodded. He had told the boy these things too many times to deny them now.

"In the council at Two Moons' village, Sitting Buffalo Bull and Crazy Horse said that the Lakota and the *washíchun* cannot walk the same path. Their feet cannot touch the same earth, they said. If this is so, how can we survive? If they are so many, surely they will win over us some day?"

"We must survive by making peace," said Sun Horse. He felt the chill again, and new hope, born of the change in his grandson.

"If I understood my power better, a man would not have died," Blackbird said glumly. "I thought nothing could hurt me, and I was wrong."

"You heard the warning of the blackbirds and you flew away as they told you. You did survive the day, and you did nothing wrong. Go to sleep now." Sun Horse needed to be alone to put his thoughts in order, but Blackbird was still troubled.

"I have been foolish in another way, Grandfather. One that is even worse. I didn't see it until now." The youth was very solemn. "I thought I had only to be a little older, a little taller, and I would be a man. I wanted to be a warrior like

552

my father so the people would raise their voices when I came back from a fight, and I was angry with the *washíchun* because it seemed they would change the world before I could become a man."

"And now?" Sun Horse felt his skin tighten and tingle all over.

"I see that I wanted to be a man and still play as a child plays, thinking only of myself. I am still a child, Grandfather. I have much more to learn." He sighed and closed his eyes. "There is so much to learn about being a man." Before long the furrows of worry left his brow and he slept while Sun Horse watched over him.

The old man's stomach rumbled loudly and he became aware of the smells of the welcoming feast, which still lingered in the lodge. There was meat in the pot over the cooking fire. He felt the juices flow in his mouth and he struggled to turn his thoughts away from his hunger. Why had it returned to him now to distract him from his quest for power? His search was no closer to its goal than when he started. . . . Or was it? When he was curing the clown girl he had thrown away the last specks of dust from his vision-hill in an effort to look beyond the symbols of his power, trying to grasp its essence . . . and the clown girl had recovered. His curing power was still strong. What of his power to lead? Perhaps it too was as strong as ever, lacking only the understanding of how to use it. . . .

Even his grandson spoke of power and understanding. It seemed that a power had truly come to Blackbird on the morning of the battle. The helper from his becoming-a-man vision had returned to give him a warning. *Fly away from the whites!* the birds said, *and you will survive the day*. The boy had charged the bluecoats' guns, but his first thoughts had been of the people. Only after he had called a warning to the sleeping village, only after he had taken the horses to a place where they were needed most, did he fling himself into the fight to avenge a fallen comrade. And despite being wounded again, he had survived.

Twice on his journey the boy had been badly wounded. He had been close to death, and he was changed by the experience. He wished to learn the true meaning of manhood now; he wished to learn responsibility for the people. . . .

Sun Horse felt his hopes rise.

Two men had ridden to save the boy from the soldiers. One Lakota and one white, united in a common purpose. . . . Why?

Hawk Chaser had died because he was the boy's *hunká*-father, and one *hunká* would do anything to save another.

And what of the other who rode to save him? Hardeman had risked his life twice in a single day. He had tried to stop the fighting and he had failed, but he had been successful in saving Blackbird. And he had saved another boy, long ago. It was in his nature to save a boy in trouble just as it was in his nature to try to make peace. He knew war and he understood the need for peace. He had been willing to do anything to achieve it, even betray the trust that Sun Horse had put in him when he sent him with the pipe carriers. . . .

But it was not only Sun Horse he would have betrayed if he had led the soldiers to Sitting Bull! That was plain from his words here in the council today. He was ashamed of what he had thought to do. *He would have betrayed himself!* The action went against his nature. It was not his nature to betray a trust.

He would have betrayed himself, and of course he had failed, for a man could not go against his own nature.

It was not in Standing Eagle's nature to make peace with the whites, and so he had failed when he carried a pipe of peace. . . .

Sun Horse trembled with the force of the chill that took him now. Outside, the wind gained force; around him the lodge trembled; beneath him the earth trembled; the universe was pregnant with power.

A man cannot go against his nature, neither Lakota nor *washíchun*. . . .

Three Stars won't give up, Hardeman had told the council. *That's not his way of making war and it's not the whiteman's way. When the whiteman starts fighting, he keeps on until his enemy surrenders.*

Could it be that Hardeman was right after all and the only possible end was surrender? In the end the whites would be true to their nature; if only conquest would satisfy them, then they would destroy the hoop of the Lakota nation forever and there would be no accommodation, no joining, no living together protected by the sacred tree that stood at the center of the world, where the red and black roads came together.

If this were true, then Sun Horse's quest, his days and nights of searching for the path to peace, had been in vain. If this were true, then *wambli*'s promise was false, Hears Twice's prophecy was false, his own vision from the butte overlooking the Laramie fort was false, and that could not be! Had not his vision led the people here? Had they not lived in peace for twenty-five snows? Had not Hears Twice's prophecy come true, with the life-giving power of *pte* returned to the band?

The visions and the signs could not be false! They must be true, and they must have a purpose! Had not Blackbird been saved by his vision, his spirit helpers coming to guide him safely through the battle? A boy had nearly died and yet he lived. He had grown a great deal in a short time and his thoughts turned to the good of the people. Why?!

Sun Horse looked at the sleeping youth beside him and he recalled his own words—*You are the future of the people.* . . .

He gasped, and his eyes opened wide in astonishment. For a long moment he remained motionless and then he covered his eyes with his hands and bowed forward where he sat.

He had been blind. As surely as the clown girl, he had been snowblind, made sightless from casting about on all sides, even when the *pte* were found, even when the answer to his search came into his very lodge.

He straightened and opened his eyes, and it seemed to him that he saw for the first time. The sleeping forms around him, the furnishings of the lodge, the fire, even the most familiar objects, appeared newly created and full of hope.

He inhaled deeply, tasting the odor of cooked meat that filled the lodge, the flesh of *pte*, the most sacred of the four-leggeds, and then he began to laugh silently. He shook until he had to hold his sides and he laughed until the tears ran down his cheeks. Except for his broad smile, he might have been crying. His stomach growled and he laughed harder.

Finally the quiet shaking stopped and Sun Horse wiped the tears from his leathery cheeks. He sat looking at Blackbird, smiling still, wishing he could wake the boy to share his good spirits, but his grandson needed to rest and grow strong. When Blackbird awoke in the morning, he would be hungry. Sun Horse would see that he ate well. He would need all his strength for what lay ahead of him.

Blackbird shifted position slightly and began to snore softly, as Standing Eagle had snored when he was a boy, and Sun Horse finally stirred himself. He moved around the fire on his hands and knees, pausing when he reached the sleeping forms of Johnny Smoker and Amanda. He dropped his head low and pawed the ground with one hand, and a new fit of silent laughing overtook him, but he quelled his laughter and grew serious. "Oh, *Tatanka*, thank you for leading my grandson to the clown girl," he whispered. "Truly they have brought a power to help the Sun Band!"

He moved on to where Elk Calf slept and he sat back on his thin shanks when he reached her side. With one wrinkled hand he stroked her face until she opened her eyes. "I will have some broth," he said, smiling, and she looked at him in surprise, coming fully awake in an instant. Tomorrow he would have some roasted meat, but for now just the broth, the life force of *pte*. "And a little liver," he added as Elk Calf sat up. "With gall."

Filled with wonder at the sudden change in her husband, Elk Calf moved the kettle to the center fire and soon the broth was hot. Sun Horse drank one bowl slowly, until his rumbling stomach subsided, and then another, more quickly. With his skinning knife he cut small bites off the liver and dipped them in gall. The yellow gall dripped on his chin and he wiped it away and licked the finger clean. All the time he smiled and said nothing to Elk Calf, but she asked for no explanations. She watched him eat as if she had never seen such a thing before, and when his bowl was placed to show that he wanted nothing more, she returned to her robes. Just as she fell asleep again, she was aware that Sun Horse had left the fire and was slipping beneath Sings His Daughter's robes. Elk Calf smiled. Truly, he was himself once more. When he was ready, he would tell her what he had learned when he was beyond his body and its demands.

Sun Horse fitted himself closely to Sings His Daughter's sleeping form and he felt the smoothness of her skin. His manhood stirred and grew strong and it was this movement that awakened her. She made a sigh of pleasure and moved her buttocks against him, making a place for him between her legs, but he did not take her right away. For a long time he lay close to her, his hands moving very slowly over her body, showing her the peace he felt within him. Finally, when she had nearly gone back to sleep, he enjoyed her gently from the rear and dropped asleep himself, still inside her.

LISA PUTNAM'S JOURNAL

Saturday, March 25th. 12:40 p.m.

Hutch and Julius and I have just returned from feeding. It is blowing a proper blizzard today, although the temperatures remain fairly mild, and the sled got stuck twice in soft drifts. The cattle have taken shelter in the willows. They have survived worse, but I worry about them nevertheless.

The pipe carriers have returned and the war is begun. I am overwhelmed by all that has changed, or I should say by all I have learned, since I sat here to write early yesterday morning. General Crook's soldiers attacked a Cheyenne village on the Powder a week ago and the pipe carriers were there. Mr. Hardeman was wounded in the battle and we have brought him here to recover. (We put him in my bedroom because it is the quietest and most comfortable.) I shall save for another time a detailed account of yesterday's events, the council at Sun Horse's village in which the pipe carriers told their tale, and all I heard there. Today I am full of concern for Sun Horse once more, wondering what he and his advisers will decide. They may be meeting even as I write. I fear that with General Crook still in the country they may not be safe even if they decide to surrender. Will he still offer them safe passage if he encounters them now? Sun Horse suggested that whatever course they choose they will be in no hurry to leave so long as the wintry weather continues, and now I must admit that I have come to share Mr. Hardeman's impatience. Indians do not experience time in the same manner as a white man. They do not mark its passing as we do, with clocks and calendars, nor are they much given to contemplating what tomorrow may bring until tomorrow itself is here. They pack up and move on not according to any long-standing plan but because the day seems right for it. "When the day comes for the Sun Band to leave this place, we will leave," Sun Horse said. Our way is very different and I am not certain it leads to a better understanding of the world and its doings, but I fear that in the present instance Sun Horse's attitude may endanger his people.

So much uncertainty. I try to go about my work and occupy my mind with the tasks at hand. In that regard the storm is some help, as it makes the world beyond the park seem very remote.

Mr. Tatum is pacing about the saloon, fretting. He fears that his long days of work will be erased by drifting snow. I told him that the river canyon is sheltered and there is not much drifting there, but still he worries and is impatient for the storm to end so his men can get back to work. The prospect of imminent departure has created a new excitement among the circus folk, heightened all the more by the preparations for the farewell performance. They all want the show to be top-notch for Amanda's sake. As for Mr. Tatum, he has *not said a word about her to me or anyone else, so far as I can determine. Mr. Chalmers took him aside yesterday and told him of Amanda's intentions, and he got no visible reaction. What can Mr. Tatum be thinking? If it was simply a matter of losing his star performer, I should say he was accepting this turn of events with an admirable stoicism, but because I know the truth about his relationship with Amanda, I find myself awaiting her return with some apprehension. After almost a month of living in close quarters with Mr. Tatum I see a certain unpredictability beneath his polished exterior.*

As for Amanda and Johnny's future, I see no reason why they cannot make a successful life together. Johnny has been under Mr. Hardeman's protection and guidance ever since he left the Cheyenne, but he has self-confidence and an independence of mind, and he had already determined to make his own way in the world from now on. With Hutch he has shown an ability to teach, and since finding Amanda in the mountains, he demonstrates a natural tendency to take responsibility for her and to protect her. Perhaps I am prejudiced in his favor because he knows the western territories and understands what is needed for survival here, and I believe those qualities will stand him in good stead wherever he and Amanda may go. They will find no surroundings more demanding than these.

Julius just came to tell me that he looked in on Mr. Hardeman and found him still asleep. He redressed Mr. Hardeman's wound yesterday evening once we had him settled. If the bullet had struck the bone, I believe he would have lost the arm. He has not regained consciousness since he fell from his horse.

CHAPTER
THIRTY-NINE

Hardeman dreamed. He was in the battle again and the soldiers were shooting at him. Bullets were ripping the air, missing him by inches, and he couldn't seem to run. He was carrying a young boy in his arms. He thought it was Johnny Smoker, but when he looked down he saw it was Blackbird. He had to get the boy to safety.

A bullet slammed into his shoulder and he left the dream behind, struggling toward wakefulness. He realized that he was lying down. He was warm and comfortable. He must be on the pony drag, but why had it stopped? He had to reach Sun Horse and tell him to surrender.

He heard the gunfire again and he opened his eyes. He was in a bed. The gunfire was the rattling of a shutter, latched closed against the storm outside.

Through the slats of the shutters he could see daylight. A lamp turned low burned on the small bedside table.

He remembered now. He had reached the council and he had told them to surrender. It seemed like another dream. How had he come to be here? And where was he?

He tried to raise himself on his elbows and then he remembered his wound. His left arm was bound against his body. He was wearing a man's flannel nightshirt and nothing else. He explored his wounded shoulder with his free hand and found a clean linen bandage there. There was a small bandage on his head as well, but that wound was no longer tender to the touch.

He propped himself up with his good arm and looked around the room. The bed was a mahogany four-poster with a simple gingham canopy. The curtains at the room's two windows had a small fringe of lace. On the dressing table there was a framed tintype of Jed Putnam and another of a woman Hardeman didn't know. A spray of dried flowers and leaves stood in a vase on the chest of drawers against the far wall. A cedar blanket chest at the foot of the bed lent the room a subtle sylvan fragrance. The dressing table had a skirt of blue chintz, and a few ribbons hung from the corner of the mirror. He looked at the tintypes again and saw that the woman had Lisa's hair and the same fullness in the lips. She must be Lisa's mother. This was Lisa's room. It was like her, neat and sensible, yet attractively feminine, delicately scented, and so different from the rooms of the most "respectable" whores in Ellsworth, all frills and satins and perfumes that clung to a man for days.

His buckskins were folded and laid across a chair but he saw no sign of the rest of his clothes, although his saddlebags were hung over the back of the chair.

Beyond the bedside table was a rocking chair with a crocheted shawl laid across one arm and an open book on the seat. She had sat there to read and watch over him. How long ago had she left, and how long had he slept?

He needed to urinate. He swung his legs over the edge of the bed and sat up, then hung his head and held it in his right hand until his vision stopped swimming. He got out of bed and looked beneath it. There was a chamber pot there. He emptied his bladder and climbed gratefully back beneath the covers, tired by the small effort. He leaned back against the feather pillows and gave in to the clean sheets and the warmth of the down comforter, allowing his eyes to close. He drifted for a time, half awake and half asleep. The wind shook the shutters again and he remembered the ride down to the park then, and the storm gaining strength. He remembered too the sense of belonging here that had swept away the last of his reserves once he found himself back in the settlement, and he wished for a moment that Putnam's Park might be his. Ever since Jed had set him to thinking about the day when he would want to find some land of his own, he had imagined a place just like this one, a home in the mountains.

Outside, the wind howled, but it couldn't reach him here. He pulled the comforter up close around his chin. It was almost April and still winter wouldn't give up. Spring was fickle in the mountains, not a season to rely on, as any man who had guided wagons on the Oregon road knew all too well. Set out too early and lose half your stock in a blizzard. Set out too late and find the grass brown and worthless along the trail. Today the snow was falling but in six or seven weeks the grass would be green. What would they be doing here in Putnam's Park then? The feeding sled would be put away and the draft horses turned out for summer, unless there was ditching or plowing to do, and Julius and Hutch would turn to new chores. With the branding done and the cattle gone from the park, irrigating would occupy much of their time. They would spill water from the two long ditches that flanked the eastern and western sides of the meadows, damming and diverting in the smaller channels, spreading the water until it covered every patch of ground, smelling the grass and water, walking in fields that were bright with flowers.

Down in Texas many of the cowhands disdained any work they couldn't do from the back of a horse, but Hardeman had irrigated there one spring. The rancher had wanted hay to feed the dairy cows he was raising along with his beeves. With Johnny's help, Hardeman had seen the irrigation started and the hay crop beginning to grow before they set off for the roundup and the long drive to Kansas. He had enjoyed walking in the hayfields where everything was so quiet and peaceful, the water sparkling in the sun as it rippled among the tender green stalks of grass. What would it be like to see that same grass cut in the fall and fed in the winter, and watch the calves you helped into the world grow to size and be shipped off to market?

He tried to imagine himself on his own land, looking at his own cattle, but the picture in his mind's eye became Putnam's Park in summer. He felt the warmth of the sun on his back and saw the valley all green, with perhaps just a trace of snow still in sight on the western ridge. He saw the lesser ridges that curved around the park like arms, meeting at the bottom of the valley where the river slipped between the fingers. A woman stood at his side, and somewhere down in the fields Julius and Hutch were walking with shovels on their shoulders. And then in the conjured vision other figures appeared; Johnny was there too, and Sun Horse and Blackbird, and the Putnam brothers, Bat and Jed. Hardeman imagined he could hear Jed laugh at him for taking so long to settle down.

He opened his eyes and the image vanished. It was a pleasant dream but he wouldn't be here when summer came. He had tried to lead them all, red and white, to a peaceful settlement, but they would not be led. They would have their war, with each side clamoring for honor and vengeance and the triumph of right, despite the best efforts of good men on both sides. But he would have no part of it. He no longer led men to war.

Perhaps it had been useless from the start. Perhaps the races were simply too different to live together in peace. The whites kept pushing the Indians until they fought back or gave in, and as for the Indians, was it so surprising that they should resist now and again? After all, they only wanted a piece of land to call their own. Now, pushed from all sides, they clung to the last of their domain. They would fight to keep it, but in the end the land they were allowed to keep would be to

559

the east, in Dakota Territory, in country less attractive to the white man.

When the end came for the Sioux, Hardeman would be gone from the northern plains. There was nothing to keep him here now. He had tried to make a peace and he had failed. Johnny Smoker was on his own, and as for Lisa Putnam, she had heard his confession in the Sun Band council. She knew he had planned to betray the Sioux to the soldiers. She had hoped they could remain free and she knew now that he had worked against her hopes every step of the way. All that remained was to be gone as soon as he could sit a horse.

The thought of moving on again wearied him. For seven years he and Johnny had moved on whenever there was no reason to stay in one place any longer, and they had always found something new to try, another territory to see. But this time Johnny would not be riding with him.

The door opened softly and Lisa Putnam entered the room on tiptoes.

"Well," she said when she saw that he was awake. "How do you feel?"

"What time is it?"

"It's afternoon. You have slept for almost a full day. We have had dinner already. Do you think you could eat something?"

"About half a horse, I imagine." He raised himself on his good elbow and once again his head swam, but he tried to hide the weakness from her. "If you'll give me some clothes, I'll get dressed."

"You will do nothing of the kind. I promised Johnny I would look after you and that is exactly what I intend to do. You will have your meal in bed and you will stay here until we see how you feel tomorrow." She moved to his side and touched his brow with a hand that was cool and dry.

"There seems to be no fever."

"At least let me go to my own room."

"If you intend to resist me every step of the way, I shall be forced to take stern measures, Mr. Hardeman. I put you here because this is where I prefer to care for you. I am quite comfortable in your room. It was my bedroom when I was a little girl." As she spoke, she was adjusting the pillows and supporting his upper body with one arm while she propped them beneath him so he could sit up comfortably. He was surprised by the hidden strength in her slender form until he remembered that she was accustomed to doing every chore on the ranch, out of doors as well as in, and only wore a dress in the house. Today she wore the simple gray one. Her skin smelled of soap and cooking, but her hair, incongruously, smelled of sunshine.

"You'll have to settle for buffalo stew," she said when she had him arranged to her satisfaction. "I'm not going to kill a perfectly good horse just to suit the whims of an invalid." She smiled. "I'm glad you have an appetite. My mother always said that was a good sign."

"So did mine."

"Is she alive?"

"Not for twenty years. It was typhoid. She and my father both."

"I was young when my mother died. Here, let me give you some light." She

560

turned up the lamp by the bed and then knelt by the small potbellied stove to add a pair of short logs. "It's not very cold outside, but it's blowing a gale. The room stays warmer with the shutters closed when the wind's like this. There." She shut the stove and rose. "Well, I won't be long."

When she had gone, he looked about the room from his new elevated perspective and found it much the same. His eyes fell on the book on the seat of the rocker and he saw that the leather cover was bare of any printing. He leaned out of bed, supporting himself on the small table. He nearly fell, but he managed to grasp the book. When he opened it he was surprised to find that the pages were filled with handwriting. He leafed to the front and saw that he held in his hand a journal written by Jedediah Putnam for the year 1853. He allowed it to fall open to the page marked by the thin strip of silk cloth that was bound into the binding, the page Lisa had been reading. The entry was dated April eighteenth, written at eight-twenty in the evening:

Today the men and I set the roof beam, and the dream of building my own home is becoming a reality. I am fifty years old this month, and about to have my first real home. A trifle late in the day, I imagine. The place in Lexington was never mine, *not the way this place will be. I will count myself lucky if I have a few years to enjoy it with Eleanor and little Elizabeth. That dream too is within reach. In another month I will go to St. Louis to fetch them here, and if they do not recoil in horror from this wild place, by the first snow in autumn we should be snug enough.*

Sun Horse was down today to see how things are coming along. Just a few more weeks and he'll be taking his people off on the summer hunt. I shall miss them, and Bat too. "Big tipi" was Sun Horse's remark when he saw the house. He thinks white man's houses are a pretty good joke. Bat got in a few digs about this one. Too hard to move, he said, and Sun Horse agreed. The two of them are like peas in a pod, happiest out under the sky and ready to move on whenever the wind blows from a new direction. I know the feeling, but from the minute my axe bit into the first tree we felled, I knew I was ready to plant my roots here. They will live out their days in the nomadic life and think me a fool for abandoning it; meanwhile, I, who have wandered with the best of them (and that's truth!), will get the feel of a different life. If I find I have made a mistake, I can always set fire to the house and pull up stakes again, but I don't think it will come to that. A man's got to make his choices, even if they're wrong, but I've seldom been more certain of one of mine. The day I sold my share in Putnam & Sons to Jacob was like the day I started upriver with Ashley and the Major. (Henry, for you poor souls who live in a time when these men are unknown. Lord, I'm glad I won't live to see that.) If the damn boat had sunk right there I would have swum to another one. There was no going back, not until I had seen what lay ahead. And it's the same now. I imagine each generation must make the same decision (those who have the wits to wonder at

561

all about their destiny and so take a hand in guiding it)—whether to build
something new, to maintain what has been built before, or to allow even that to
crumble and decay. My relatives in Boston maintain the family's business and
its homes; I am cursed or blessed, I'm not dead sure which, with the need to
start from scratch.

Hardeman raised his eyes from the journal and cast his mind back across the years. April of '53. Who was he scouting for that year? Lem Finch again. And by the eighteenth they might have pulled out of Independence already,but he couldn't remember for certain. By autumn in the Big Horns, when Jed had hoped to have his wife and child all snugly settled in with him in Putnam's Park, Hardeman had reached Sacramento and delivered his emigrants and turned his horse back toward the rising sun, hoping to get over the Sierra Nevadas before the first snows. What would have happened if he had come up here then, to make his promised visit? Jed might have offered him work and he might have stayed to help the mountain man build Putnam's Park.

Hardeman smiled. Jed would have offered, all right, but he would not have stayed. The wanderfoot was strong in him still, back then, and as the years passed by, it had continued to hold off the dream of finding a place of his own. That had seemed a notion for a later time, one he could not easily imagine—a time when he would be as old as Jed Putnam, and ready to settle down. During the years when he and Johnny were in Texas he had seen that beef was the coming thing, and he had seen how the men with eastern and British capital set the pattern for the boom, grazing huge herds on public lands, gathering them once a year to be branded and driven to the railheads, and he knew that his own capital reserve, which had sat for so long in the St. Louis bank, biding its time, could never even buy a share in such an enterprise, and so the thought of finding his own place had been left to gather dust in the attic of his imagination. Meantime, here in the Big Horns, Jed had conducted regular spring cleanings on his own imaginings, and without any help from Britishers he might just have hit on the right way to do the thing—a small piece of land and a small herd, just enough that a man could hold it all in his hands and care for it. Beyond that, what else did a man need?

He closed the journal and rested his hand on top of it, scarcely aware of the action, for the realization was dawning within him that the time had come to find his home. There was nothing to hold him back any longer. There was no scouting left, except for the army, and he would not go back to the towns to become like Hickok, all tired and old before his time, convinced that the great adventures were gone forever. A man made his own adventures.

So Jed was right after all. *Wanderfoot's a young man's disease,* he had said. *When it comes your time to stop, you'll know.* At last the time had come. And like Jed he was one of those who needed to start from scratch, building from the ground up with his own hands.

Hardeman smiled. It comforted him to have a new goal. And strangely, knowing what he would do when he left Putnam's Park diminished his urgency to be gone. He needed time to recover from the journey, the battle, and his wound. Time to regain his strength.

His eyes closed. Given the chance, he might sleep the clock around again. How long had it been since he spent a full day in bed? Not since childhood. He felt as weak as a child now. There was time enough for journeying on when he felt stronger. Lisa Putnam seemed to bear him no malice. He would rest here for a while if she would let him remain.

The door opened and Lisa entered, smiling, with a tray in her hands. Hardeman realized then that he was still holding Jed's journal.

"I didn't mean to pry." He set the leather volume on the bedside table.

"It's quite all right. The Putnam family journals are meant to be read by others. Usually only relatives are sufficiently interested." The tray had legs and she set it astride his lap. He remembered his hunger as the aroma from the steaming bowl of stew reached him. In addition to the stew there were fresh rolls and butter and a glass of milk, and canned pears and hot gingerbread, and a small china pitcher of thick yellow cream.

She shook out the linen napkin and tucked it beneath his chin as if he were a child down with mumps. "I'll leave you to eat. I never could stand being watched while I ate in bed. I'll come back a little later."

Hardeman ate quickly, wolfing the stew as soon as it was cool enough. It was much the same as stews he had eaten in the Indian camps, with potatoes and carrots instead of prairie turnips, but there had been no butter among the Indians and no raised bread. It was odd how such small things could do so much to make a man feel at home. He found it difficult to butter the rolls with only one hand, so he slapped on great chunks of butter and ate the bread in large bites, and he was glad Lisa had not stayed to watch.

The food acted as a soporific. Even as he finished the last bite of gingerbread and washed it down with the last of the cream and the juice from the dish of pears, he was nodding. With much care, he lifted the tray off his lap with his one good hand and set it on the floor beside the bed. He lay back against the pillows and closed his eyes and thought he had never been quite so comfortable before.

When he awoke again, the tray was gone and the light outside the windows was fading. The cat Rufus was sleeping on the foot of the bed, apparently not caring that someone other than his mistress lay there. Hardeman was sorry he hadn't heard Lisa return for the tray. The supper gong rang then, the sound of one stroke loud and the next whipped away by the wind, and he knew that she would be busy feeding the circus crowd. He slept again, and when he next awoke the cat was gone and Lisa was sitting in the rocking chair beside his bed, reading her father's journal. The creaking of the rockers had wakened him.

"I'm sorry," she said, "I didn't mean to disturb you. No, that's not true." She smiled at her own embarrassment. "I hoped you weren't sleeping very soundly, because I brought you some soup. Would you like it? It's still warm."

"I haven't done a thing to work off that dinner you gave me, but it seems to have gone away just the same."

She gave him the soup, and buttered bread to go with it, and while he ate she read, not watching him. When he was done she removed the tray and set it aside.

He gestured at Jed's journal. "He writes well."

She seemed pleased. "Yes, he does, doesn't he? And yet other than his journals and letters to members of the family, he wrote not at all. I have sometimes wondered if he might not have become a man of letters if he had been born in different circumstances. What might he have been if he had found no great frontier to explore?"

"He would have been the poorer for it."

She smiled. "You're right, of course. He led a rich life, and he would not have traded it for any other. He was glad to have lived when he did, and perhaps glad that he wouldn't see the changes he knew were coming." She closed the journal and set it aside. "He said that when he first came to the mountains the Indians were the lords of creation. Those were his words. They accepted the white man—the trappers—among them. They taught them what they knew, and they accepted that the whites were different in many ways."

"And they killed one or two," Hardeman added.

"Yes, more than a few. Believe me, I don't harbor many romantic notions about Indians. They are neither the noble children of nature portrayed by the poet nor the bloodthirsty beasts described in popular fiction. As usual, the truth lies somewhere between the extremes. They live a life very different from our own. They have different notions of death, and the meaning of life, and if I live to be a hundred I will never think as they do. But it was those very differences my father cherished. He called theirs a more 'fundamental' life. Part of its fundamental nature was the immediacy of death. It could come at any moment."

She paused, as if unsure whether or not to speak the thought that had come to her. "There is a story he used to tell. He would listen to some passing emigrant or drummer or soldier tell tall tales of the mountains and the Indians and all the fights he had seen and the scalps he had taken. When a man brags like that it's mostly hogwash, as you know. My father couldn't abide such men. So when the fellow ran out of wind for a moment, my father would say, 'Imagine this, if you will, sir. Just for a moment, to show these other good people what life in the mountains means to us.' You'll have to imagine his voice telling it. I'm not very good at storytelling. It's in the life, not in the blood, I guess. 'You are traveling alone and you make camp for the night,' he would say. 'You've eaten your supper, such as it is, when you hear another horse, or maybe you don't hear anything, because it's an Indian who's coming up on you. You look up and there's a man in your firelight. Tell these folks what happens next.' Well, as you can imagine, most of them couldn't think

564

of a thing to say." She looked at Hardeman. "What would you answer?"

He thought for a moment, and shrugged. "Anything could happen. With luck you might make a friend. By morning one of you might be dead, or both of you."

She straightened in her chair, plainly delighted by this reply. "Exactly! A man could step into your firelight and he might be your murderer. Or the two of you might winter together. But no matter what happened, the world would go on, none the wiser. That was what my father liked best of all. You stood on your own and lived and died by your wits, and if you were foolish and died a fool's death, the world went on without you." She sat back and moved the rocker gently to and fro, gazing at Hardeman thoughtfully. "You understand this because you have lived much of your own life under those same conditions, but it was something my relatives could never grasp. My relations on my mother's side, that is. They thought my father shirked responsibility. They saw him pass up the chance to take over the direction of Putnam and Sons. They could not imagine why he would do such a thing and so they mistrusted him." She leaned forward now and there was passion in her voice as she continued. "They could never understand that he took on a far greater responsibility. He chose to live beyond the fabric of civilized society. Most men wrap themselves in that cloth and feel naked without it, but my father found it stifling. He chose to live where a man lived or died by his own actions, without recourse to law, often without recourse to men of his own race in case of trouble. He relished that responsibility and he believed that no one who had not experienced that kind of life could lay claim to the title of free man."

Hardeman nodded thoughtfully. "When you first met him, you wouldn't in a month of Sundays think to find such notions in his head. He'd give you his hooraw and do his best to scare you out of your wits with his stories, but all the time he was taking the measure of you."

"And after you knew him for a time he did talk to you. About the other things, I mean."

Again Hardeman nodded. "He was the damndest talker. If he liked you, he'd talk your ear off. Your uncle Bat's a lot the same."

She smiled. "It hardly seems fair that you knew my father so well and I know nothing at all of yours."

Now it was Hardeman's turn to pause and consider whether to bring forth his memories. When he spoke his voice was softer than before. "My father educated himself while he was apprenticed to a blacksmith. He became a lawyer, like Mr. Lincoln. He admired Mr. Lincoln. While Mr. Lincoln was in Congress, my father sat in the Pennsylvania legislature. He bettered himself and he wished still better for me. I was a disappointment to him."

"I find that hard to credit."

"Oh, it's true enough. He had his own particular ideas about a man's responsibility. He believed that in a free nation each man had a duty to help his fellow man along. 'Bear the common burden,' he put it. He used to say that democracy was not a free ride. He believed in the law and he thought the best way a man could do his duty was to serve in the government, to see that the laws were just, and fairly administered." He remembered what Lisa had said about Jed: *He chose to live where a man lived or died by his own actions, without recourse to law,* and he realized that his own father would have found such a notion frightening.

"He sounds quite a remarkable man," Lisa said. "Surely if he were alive today he would see that you have done your part, although you chose a very different life. During the time of the gold rush, my father knew very well that guiding the emigrants had a part to play in the progress of the nation."

"I know," Hardeman conceded. "He told me all about the sweep of westward progress and those other fancy notions, and I believed it all, back then. Maybe I believed it a little too well. I thought leading the way was a pretty fine thing, and then one day I looked back and saw who I'd been leading. That was seven years ago."

"At the Washita," she said, and he nodded. "And so you left scouting behind you."

"Sometimes leaving off isn't enough. You look for a way to make amends."

She sat gazing at him, rocking slowly, and he became aware that he was stroking the scar on his cheek with his fingers. He dropped the arm to his side.

"You must be tired," she said.

"I haven't done much but sleep all day."

"It's past midnight, I should think." She rose. "I have strict orders to look at your shoulder. Julius will be angry if I forget." She turned her back. "You'll have to get out of that nightshirt so I can undo the bandages. It belonged to my father, by the way. You can keep it if you like."

He wondered what she imagined he would do with a gentleman's flannel nightshirt once he was out on the trail, but he could think of no way to refuse the gift so he said nothing.

"All right," he said shortly, and she turned to see that he had the covers pulled up to his armpits, leaving only the top of his chest and his shoulders exposed. She sat on the bed beside him and began to unwind the bandage.

"I was wondering who did the doctoring," he said.

"Julius's first job as a free man was in a Union Army field hospital. He was just an orderly, but he had plenty of opportunity to watch the surgeons at work. Eventually they let him bandage the simple wounds. There." She lifted the dressing away. "It's doing quite well, I think. There is no inflammation; that's what I was to look for particularly."

To Hardeman, the wound looked ugly enough, but he could see where new flesh was already forming at the edges to cover the damage the bullet had done.

Lisa rose and went to her dressing table where she found a pair of scissors

566

and cut away the soiled portion of the dressing. Returning to his side, she refolded the cloth neatly and applied it once again to the wound and placed his right hand over it to hold it in place while she began to bandage his shoulder.

"I'm going to leave your arm free, but you are to wear a sling when you get out of bed."

"Yes, ma'am," he said obediently.

She smiled, then paused in her work as she noticed a twist of scar tissue on his other shoulder. She touched it lightly.

"How remarkable. It's so similar. Where did you get it?"

"At the Washita."

"And this?" She touched his cheek, the tips of her fingers tracing the small scar there, then brushing his beard as she dropped her hand.

"Same day, same place."

"I see." She returned to her bandaging.

"I suppose I should have learned my lesson the first time."

"Hold still, please. There." She tied the bandage off and looked at him. "But you didn't, did you? Once again you were willing to lead a troop of cavalry to a peaceful village. Was it to make amends?"

"To keep the peace, Miss Putnam."

She met his gaze with steady blue eyes that reminded Hardeman of her father. "I know that's what you hoped to do, but was it really the only way?"

"It was the only way I saw just then. That's what I told Sun Horse, and that's the truth. Anyway, I didn't get the chance."

"I knew Hawk Chaser," she said, taking him by surprise. "When I was a young girl he taught me to ride bareback. He always took an interest in children, telling them stories and making them things. He said the children are the spirit of the Lakota."

"He showed what he was made of, all right." He shook his head. "It was a stupid thing to do."

"Stupid! He saved your life! Yours and Blackbird's."

"We'd have been killed anyway, all three of us, if the soldiers hadn't pulled out just then."

"Perhaps. But that wouldn't have made any difference to Hawk Chaser. He would still have behaved just the same."

"That's why it was stupid. What hope did he have with an iron lance against Springfield carbines?"

"There is always hope! There has to be. I believe in the human spirit. With a strong will, it can find a way. And even if every event in our lives were predetermined by fate, we would still try to change things, wouldn't we?"

"I imagine so. Sometimes we don't get much done for all the trying. I set out to save a people and I ended up saving one boy, and needed help doing that."

"Is it such a small thing to save one boy?"

"I had a chance to make peace and I failed."

"You were not the only one who failed! General Crook failed. Sun Horse failed. Two Moons and Sitting Bull and Crazy Horse failed as well! You cannot place the blame only on yourself!"

"Each of those men did what he could. It's not for me to judge them."

"Nor is it for you to decide for them! You have no right to make a peace by having one band led away in chains in the hope that others will follow! Even if you were successful, what gives you the right to force it on them?"

"That's the way it will end, sooner or later. It's the end of the road for the Sioux."

"Perhaps it is! But they must walk the last few steps as they decide for themselves!"

"And how many dead in the meantime, Miss Putnam?"

"That's not for us to say! Some may choose to die rather than go to the reservation, and they wouldn't be the first people to choose death over the loss of freedom!" She stood suddenly. "Oh, you are a stubborn man!" She turned her back on him and crossed to the window.

"So you said. I didn't argue." He gave her a moment to calm herself and then he said, "Wouldn't you stop the dying if you could?"

She spun to face him and her eyes sparked with anger. "I don't want them to die! But I cannot choose for those people, and neither can you, any more than you could choose for Hawk Chaser or prevent him from doing what he did. You haven't the right!"

He said nothing, and as her anger dwindled she looked away. She moved to the rocking chair and sat down.

"I did not intend that we should quarrel. I would prefer it if we could be friends."

"That was my preference from the start, Miss Putnam."

"Don't you see, if you take too much on yourself, you take away someone else's choice. We must each choose and act for ourselves."

It struck Hardeman that he had heard almost exactly the same words more than once in recent weeks, from the mouths of Indians. *Each man must choose for himself,* Crazy Horse had said in Two Moons' council, and in the Sun Band's village Elk Leggings had repeated the same injunction. The Indians, who were governed by customs rather than laws, accorded certain customs the force of law, and that was one of them.

"I have something to confess," Lisa said now, and her voice was hard, as if she spoke an unpleasant truth. "I had no right to speak to you as I did. You see, I tried to influence them as well. I didn't want Sun Horse to surrender, and so while you were gone I proposed that we should hunt together, Julius and myself and the men from the circus with Sun Horse and his hunters. I thought that if they had enough meat to feed themselves, they would stay free. But the hunt was a failure. Then when Amanda was lost she saw the buffalo and it seemed like a miracle. Now they have more than enough meat.

But you see, now I have changed my mind. I believe they will have to surrender if they hope to survive." She was looking at her hands, folded together in her lap, but now she raised her eyes. "What will they do?"

"They will do what they have to do." *A man does what he must. It is for other men to understand and accept.* In the end the fate of the Sioux nation would be governed by their own customs and the choices each man made for himself, no matter how their friends or enemies tried to sway them. Hardeman recalled the leaders with whom he had sat in Two Moons' council: Crazy Horse and Sitting Bull and Little Wolf and Two Moons and Old Bear, men of the people, sober men who took the welfare of their people to heart; they would defend themselves if attacked, and they would urge the warriors to fight for the people. Now it was certain that they would be attacked wherever they were found.

"It seems that all our efforts have failed," Lisa said. "But at least you saved a life. Surely that must go a long way towards making amends, if there is some fateful ledger in which these things are recorded. Blackbird is alive because of you. And Johnny Smoker."

"That was an accident."

"I don't understand."

He met the blue eyes and saw the trust in them. "I didn't mean to save Johnny's life. That was an accident. I came within a whisker of killing him before I even knew he was white."

She waited for him to continue, and the silence lengthened. Hardeman lay back against the pillows and his gaze came to rest on the dried flowers and leaves in the vase atop the bureau. He began to speak then, and he told her the tale he had told to no one else in seven years, starting with how he had come to be at the Washita with Custer's command. He told her of the meeting with Hickok and the hope of making peace with the aid of Agent Wynkoop and Black Kettle, of finding the Indians' trail and how he had circled around the sleeping Indian camp before dawn and learned that the trail continued on to the villages downstream, of arriving at the battle too late to stop it.

"After Black Kettle was shot, I found Custer in the village," he said, and here for the first time he turned to face her again. "I told him the war party had gone on downriver. I told him these were the wrong Indians and he laughed out loud. He said 'They seem willing enough to fight,' and he rode off and left me there. I was right in the middle of the village with men fighting all around me, and I didn't know what to do. I was sitting there on my horse like a Goddamn statue, and then I saw an Indian boy charge one of the officers—Captain Benteen. The boy couldn't have been more than fourteen or so and he had a pistol that looked about as long as his arm. He could barely lift it. Benteen didn't want to shoot the boy. He waved him off. He made signs that if the boy would surrender to him, he wouldn't hurt him. But the boy kept coming. He was on a little pony. He guided it with his knees and he held that pistol in both hands and he shot at Benteen. The first shot missed,

569

but the second one killed Benteen's horse. I guess Benteen thought two chances was plenty. When he got up off the ground he dropped that boy with one shot. The body fell right at his feet."

He looked again at the flowers in their vase and wondered how they had managed to keep so much color during the long winter months.

"I decided I'd go back upstream and wait with the wagons, maybe. I didn't have much of an idea just where I was going but I knew I wasn't staying there. I started out of the village, but I hadn't gone very far when someone took a shot at me and grazed my cheek." He touched the scar on his face and looked at his fingers. "I saw blood and I looked around to see who was shooting at me, and the next shot hit me in the shoulder. Along about then I understood that someone was trying to kill me. I tried to help them and they wanted to kill me! It made me angry. I don't think I've ever been that angry. The shot knocked me off my horse but I don't even remember falling. The next thing I knew I was on my feet with my pistol in my hand and I had an idea that the shots had come from a lodge nearby. I emptied my pistol into the lodge and then I pulled my knife and went in ready to finish the job. There was Johnny with a hole in his leg."

He turned on her suddenly and his voice was harsh. "You see, I gave him that limp, Miss Putnam, and I damn near killed him. In that first moment, even when I saw I'd wounded him, I wanted to finish him off. If he'd been standing or if he'd tried to run, I would have cut him open without a how-de-do. But he was holding his mother. She was dead and so was the man. They were his parents and he was holding on to his mother to protect her from the soldiers even though she was dead."

"But you didn't kill him. You saved him instead."

"I saw he was a white boy. Maybe it was just because of that, or because his folks were dead. I thought I'd killed the two of them. He told me later they were dead before I came along, but it doesn't matter much."

"It doesn't matter? How can you say that?"

"Because I wanted to kill them! I was ready to kill every mother's son in that village, man, woman or child! That's how angry I was!" He saw the fear in her eyes and he softened his voice. "It's like a madness, Miss Putnam. That's what war does to men. Once you've felt it, you don't forget."

He was suddenly very tired. He lay back and closed his eyes, wishing to remember nothing more, but he had summoned the images of the Washita and they were still strong before him. He saw the burning lodges once more and smelled the carnage.

He heard the rockers creak and felt a weight rest on the bed beside him. A hand, cool and comforting, rested on his cheek, and then Lisa spoke.

"And yet if you hadn't been there, if you hadn't been shot and if you had never entered that lodge, Johnny might have died that same day. Would you change the events if you could?" He made no reply and she answered for him. "I don't think you would. Nor would you change what you did for Blackbird."

"Blackbird will do everything he can to get another chance at the soldiers," he said without opening his eyes. All he wanted now was to sleep. "He'll remember Hawk Chaser and most likely run smack into the guns again to show he's not afraid to die for the people. They put great stock in dying for the people." His voice was bitter. "They're all like Hawk Chaser, the bunch of them. The whole damn Sioux nation would do the same thing if they got the chance, run straight into the guns and die for the people, only there wouldn't be any people left when it was over."

Lisa took his right hand between her own. "Listen to me," she said. "If Blackbird dies fighting the soldiers, it will not be your doing. You have done what you could, and you took on more than any one man should attempt. It is no sin to fail; what's worse is not to try."

She was quiet then, and the room was silent. Outside, the wind had dropped to nothing.

Her weight shifted and he felt her breath on his cheek, and then her lips touched his, dry and quick, as gentle as the touch of a butterfly's wings. He felt her hands withdraw from his own and her weight rise from the bed, and he opened his eyes.

For a long moment she regarded him coolly with an expression he could not fathom, and then she cupped her hand around the frosted chimney of the bedside lamp and with a puff of breath she blew out the flame.

"Why did you do that?" he said into the sudden dark.

"We're running low on coal oil." Her voice came from close beside him.

Even when his eyes grew accustomed to the loss of the lamplight he could see nothing, for the shutters blocked out any faint illumination from the moonless night. There were sounds of wool against silk, silk against skin, and then a hand lifted the bedcovers and Lisa slipped in beside him. She burrowed her face deep in the curve of his neck, and when his good arm went around her, she fitted herself close against him and he felt the smooth warmth of her skin, except for her hands and feet and the tips of her breasts, which were cool at first. She was trembling. He held her still and close and he thought that he comforted her, but it was she who comforted him, she who moved so his lips could find hers, she who guided him without seeming to lead, she who remembered to safeguard his wounded shoulder when he had passed beyond such caution. She gave herself freely and without guile, and when they lay still again, he could feel her heart against him, gradually slowing until its beating was barely perceptible, like the muted ticking of a small clock.

Sunday, March 26th. 6:30 a.m.

I have spent the last hour going through my father's old letters, trying to find one I read sometime during the winter, one that has new meaning for me now, and I have just found it. It was written in April of 1851 and was the last letter he mailed before he and his train of wagons left Independence for Sacramento. He says, "I have taken on a boy this summer, Eleanor. He'll be my assistant scout, or maybe apprentice would be more accurate. He's got a lot to learn but I've a feeling he's one of the ones who'll stick it out. He reminds me of myself, many years ago. His name is Christopher Hardeman and he was born in Pennsylvania. His father's a lawyer and legislator, but young Christopher has got his sights set on the West. He is just about a year younger than I was when I set out up that big river with Ashley and Henry, just as full of spunk and unafraid. When I look at him I think of all I've been through since then; a couple of lifetimes, it seems, and I'm only now fixing to settle down for good. No thought could be farther from young Christopher's mind than that one. What will he go through before he reaches my age? What lands will he see and what people will he come to know? All I know for certain is that he's going to see just about everything there is to see before he slows down enough to plant roots somewhere. He's got wandering feet and a far look in his eye."

Yesterday for a time I allowed myself to hope that Mr. Hardeman might stay on here, but I had forgotten that look, which I noted myself when he first arrived. It is with him still. I imagine I can see it in his face even when he is sleeping. I will not try to hold him against his will.

CHAPTER
FORTY

Hardeman awoke slowly, as he did only when he was enclosed by four walls and a roof, and he became aware that the bed beside him was empty and the sheets there were cool. Her faint scent lingered on the pillow. He opened his eyes. The wind was blowing and the shutters rattled but the light from outside seemed brighter than it had been the day before.

Cautiously he sat up in bed. His vision remained steady and the dullness that had clouded his perceptions ever since the battle was gone. He could feel the cool air on his skin, hear the friendly crackle of the fire in the small stove, see the minutest details of each article in the room despite the limited amount of light admitted by the shutters. His clothing had reappeared, folded neatly atop his buckskins.

He swung his feet to the floor and stood up, and was surprised to discover that he felt quite himself. His first few steps were unsteady, but more on account of stiffness from his long rest than any lingering debility. He used the chamber pot and then turned to the windows to open the shutters. Only when he raised the sash did a sharp pain in his shoulder remind him that he was not to use his left arm.

The shutters swung back to reveal a world bathed in sunlight. Shadows swept across the yard as the wind urged the clouds along. A few flakes of snow were falling still, but the storm had left only four or five inches behind, for all its huffing and puffing.

He saw that the feeding sled was not in its accustomed place in the barnyard. The morning was well advanced and no one had wakened him for breakfast. The thought of food made him aware of his hunger, which was as strong as if he had eaten nothing in days.

A woman passing among the circus wagons saw him and waved, smiling, and he ducked back as he realized that he was stark naked.

In the mirror atop Lisa's dressing table he was greeted by a stranger. He had not seen himself in a glass since setting out with the pipe carriers. His hair and beard were long and unkempt and there seemed to be more gray hairs than he recalled. With his good hand he removed the small bandage from his forehead and he saw that the scab there was well formed. He touched the old scar on his cheek and he remembered then the black paint he had applied to his face with that same hand. Bat Putnam had given him the paint. Bat and each of the Lakota men carried their paints with them, the vegetable colorings and animal fat kept separate until they were mixed together for use. The paint was gone from Hardeman's face now. Someone had washed him as he slept, most likely when they had first put him to bed. Was there supposed to be some ceremony connected with the removal of mourning paint? He had no idea. It all seemed a long time ago, the battle and the journey back, even the council in Sun Horse's village, which he remembered only vaguely. Two days of rest had removed him farther from those events than could be accounted for solely by the number of hours that had passed while he slept. It was as if he had gone to sleep at the moment when he was wounded in the battle and had only now finally awakened from a long period of broken dreams to find himself miraculously healed, or almost so, and transported far from the scene by means he could not imagine.

He was eager to be out and about, wanting to try the feeling of life, as if it were all new to him. He dressed himself in his woolen shirt and pants, which were fresh and clean. All of his clothing had been washed while he lay abed. The bullet hole in the shoulder of his buckskin jacket had been patched with a fresh piece of deerskin and most of the blood had been washed away. The shirt had been similarly repaired. A pair of boots stood on the floor by the chair; they might have belonged to Jed or they might be Julius's, but they fit him well enough.

He rolled up the heavy winter moccasins he had worn on the journey back and set them atop his deerskins.

With a brush and comb from the dressing table he imposed some order on his hair and beard. The cutting of his hair would have to wait until he reached a settlement, and although he often trimmed his own beard he left it now as it was. The wild look he saw in the glass rather pleased him. He resembled a mountain man dressed up to go to town.

When his toilet was complete, he cleaned the brush with the tortoise-shell comb and gathered the loose hairs to throw in the stove, noticing as he did so that a few of Lisa'a fine strands were mixed with his own coarser curls, and he remembered the night before.

Far from blaming him for his intentions toward the Sioux it seemed that she understood what had motivated his efforts and sympathized with his failure. *You have done what you could*, she had said, *and you took on more than one man should attempt*. She had consoled him and she had made it plain that he would be welcome to stay on for a while. But she had sought to be reassured as well, and he recognized now that in his weakened state he had thought only of his own future, the abandoning of one goal and fixing on another, and he had forgotten the threat to Putnam's Park, which was still very real. So long as Crook remained in the field, the war might come here, and when the war was over, the future of the little ranch was far from secure.

Now his weakness of yesterday was miraculously gone. He would need no prolonged period of convalescence. He was strengthened and revitalized and he could sit a horse today, if need be, but there was more he could do here. Perhaps he could even salvage some good from the wreckage of his hopes. The time had come to find his own land, his own home, but there was no rush to be off. He hadn't even decided where he would begin his search. Meantime, the least he could do was try to help Lisa Putnam keep her ranch. He could stay for a time. If the soldiers came near he would intercept them and see that no fighting touched her home. And he would talk to Crook on her behalf. The general's support could be decisive in assuring her title to the park. He would tell Crook that Lisa had fed and sheltered himself and Johnny and had taken them to see Sun Horse, and that she wished for nothing so much as peace between the Sioux and the whites. He would not say that Lisa opposed Sun Horse's surrender. He would tell only the truth, and it might be enough.

And after that? Had her lovemaking been an invitation to stay for longer than a while? To stay forever? Was he foolish to go looking far and wide for his home when it might be right here in front of his eyes? His imaginings of yesterday could come to pass. He could see the park in summer, all aflower, with a woman by his side. But Putnam's Park belonged to Lisa and it would never be his.

Once before in his life Hardeman had thought to stay somewhere because of a woman. It had been in the summer of '68, before the Washita, before he teamed up with a young boy who spoke Cheyenne in his dreams. Fed up with the army and the mulishness of its officers where Indians were concerned, he had turned

574

his back on the frontier posts and made his way east along the Kansas River to the booming town of Abilene, where the talk was of nothing but cattle. He saw the Longhorns for himself and the men who herded them. The "cow-boys," as they were called, for many of the Texas drovers were surprisingly young, had reminded Hardeman of nothing so much as soldiers turned loose at the end of a long campaign. They drank both to celebrate and to forget their hardships and they sought all the luxuries they had been denied for so long. Their fancies were catered to by whores and gamblers and confidence men who had flocked to Abilene as they flocked wherever money flowed freely. Hardeman had lost himself for a time in the section of town south of the tracks, called McCoy's Addition by some and the Beer Garden by others, and it was there that he had encountered the unexpected—an unlikely woman in that unlikely place, the first woman he had ever wished to make his own.

She was a woman in business for herself and her business was operating the best house of prostitution in Abilene. It was called the Bluebird Hotel, and her name was Mary Ellen Tompkins. She was twenty-nine years of age. Her eyes were green, her hair was black, and her skin was like porcelain china. When she was dressed to go north of the tracks on matters of banking or some other business, gentlemen newly arrived in town tipped their hats to this self-possessed beauty and sought to learn where they might call on her. When they learned her true situation they learned as well that she was a solitary woman, unattainable and untouchable; she usually had no trouble diverting their advances and directing them toward one of her girls, who were a cut above the usual run of "soiled doves" and "inhabitants of the *demi-monde*," as the frontier newspapers poetically described the cowtown whores. These young women, whose predecessors had attended the leaves of every army since the world began, now offered themselves to the youthful drovers, giving their masculinity and pride needed recognition after the dusty monotony of the long drives.

Her reputation notwithstanding, Mary Ellen took Hardeman first into her arms and later into her confidence. She let him know at once that she had never lived the life of the girls under her care, and bit by bit, in their private moments together, she had told him her dream until he saw it whole and knew she was offering to share it with him.

Tompkins was not her true surname. She came of good family, a family whose name was known in the society of Boston and New York, and when she came of age she had assessed her prospects and despaired. Her mother had married a man of property, and proposed that as a young lady's highest ambition. She took pains to instill in her only daughter the knowledge that she would need in order to snare the right man. Mary Ellen had been instructed in how to become the guiding force—an invisible force, never to be publicly acknowledged, it was made abundantly clear—behind a powerful man. But Mary Ellen contrived to evade her mother's plans and shake off one wealthy suiter after another, desperately seeking some avenue of escape. It presented itself in the death of an uncle who was regarded as a black sheep in the family. He had gambled and sailed and cared little for the world of financial affairs, and his way with the ladies had caused scandals that never quite managed to tarnish the family name, but there were always raised eyebrows aplenty when he tipped his hat to a married woman. Mary Ellen was his favorite niece and she had returned his affection abundantly. When she was a small girl he called on her when she was sick and read her fairy tales. For Christmas he gave her dresses more suitable for roughhousing and play than for formal dinners with servants in attendance, and she was heartily grateful. When she was older, he gave her presents of jewelry and took her riding in Central Park, and with Mary Ellen at least, his behavior was always impeccable. When they were alone he spoke of the endless opportunities America offered to those with sufficient daring and he debunked the notion that only men should be trusted with the management of money. "Look at you," he said on one occasion. "You've got a head on your shoulders as good as any man's, and a damn sight prettier."

When he died he left Mary Ellen a modest sum of money that was not surprising in itself, for he had been fortunate in investments as well as love and had enjoyed flaunting his money as proof that his wild ways had not led him to the disastrous end his staid relations often predicted. But a close reading of his will failed to reveal any trace of the most common Victorian proviso whenever capital was passed on to a female relative, that she should have access to the interest but not the capital itself. The bequest was without any restrictions whatever. As Mary Ellen was of age, there was nothing her family could do to stop her taking control of her inheritance forthwith. Which she promptly did, and just as promptly disappeared from their lives forever.

She had made her way to the frontier, that land of fabled opportunity, intending in the space of the next five years to make her fortune. She had invested in a business with low overhead and high profits, and in one year she had already deposited in Abilene banks an amount equal to three times her inheritance. At the end of the time she had allotted herself she proposed to sell her business and vanish once again, continuing west under yet another new name. She had her eye set on Colorado, where mining and cattle were creating a new society centered on Denver, or perhaps California, where it was said the weather was always mild. She would let it be known that she was an eastern heiress and when the right man presented himself she would marry. She would seek a man whose dream was as strong as her own, but in their life together she would be his equal; wherever they went, whatever enterprise they undertook together, she intended to be respected and free from want, and she would never surrender her will to a man's whims or weaknesses.

Hardeman had spent seventeen years in the west, half of his life then, and he had not yet tired of leading the way. There was much he had not seen, and although he was not sure where he would stop when the time came, he sensed that his was not to be the settled, respectable life Mary Ellen coveted. Leaving her was like leaving a part of himself behind, but he knew that to remain would mean living her life and not his own, and so he had said goodbye. "I shall be here for four more years," she had said as she kissed him farewell. "Until then I will wait for you."

But he had not gone back for her. Once, years later, he and Johnny had passed through Abilene in wintertime. He had ridden south of the tracks and found the Bluebird Hotel closed and shuttered; Abilene was no longer the railhead, and McCoy's Addition was as quiet as a Sunday-morning churchyard. On making inquiries regarding the former owner, he was told that she had sold out in '72 and gone away, no one seemed to know where, and he had guessed that Mary Ellen had moved on just as she said she would, following her dream. He had realized then that he had cast a life aside when he left her, one of the lives that might have been his if he had taken a different turn.

Since then he had never met another woman who touched him in the same way, until now. Was Lisa holding out the offer of a life together? He was not used to interpreting the unspoken intentions of well-bred women. The women he knew best made their desires plain in a very few words.

If by giving herself she had invited him to stay forever, was that another life he could afford to cast aside? How many similar chances could he let go by before his allotted share was gone? Maybe this was the one he should take.

But all his instincts cautioned him against staying where the land and the dream were Lisa's alone. Dreams were personal things, each taking its own course like the rivulets of spring runoff finding their way down the mountainsides; sometimes two joined and ran together for a time, but with dreams, such joinings were rare.

He became aware that he had been holding the lid off the stove for several minutes and the air in the room was becoming smoky. He dropped the cluster of hairs into the flames and replaced the lid, remembering his hunger and his need to get out into the world, where others had been awake for hours.

With his clothing there was a large square of indigo-dyed linsey-woolsey, obviously intended as a sling for his arm, but he could not tie it in place with only one hand and so he gathered it up with the rest of his things and after a last look around to be sure he had left nothing behind, he went out of the room and descended the stairs.

He went first to the small room in the back of the house where he and Johnny had been quartered on the day they arrived in Putnam's Park. One of the bunks was unmade and a woman's dressing gown lay across the foot of the bed. Lisa obviously thought he would need to stay in her bedroom a while longer. She would be surprised to see him up and feeling fit. He left his belongings on Johnny's bunk and made his way to the kitchen, where he found Ling Wo alone. She smiled as he entered.

"You hungry? I fix breakfast. Lisa say you must sleep all you want, eat all you want."

"Thanks, Ling. I could do with something."

"Coffee there." She pointed at the speckled enamel pot. "You help yourself." She aimed her huge belly at the pantry.

"I could use some help with this." He held up the sling. "If I don't put it on, she'll be angry."

"Don't matter, I think," Ling said cheerfully. "She plenty angry today. Don't know why, anyhow. You come here, I fix it."

He had to bend over nearly double in order for the short woman to tie the sling behind his neck, and while he was in this awkward position there were footsteps in the entryway and Harry Wo entered from the outdoors.

"Morning," said the squat blacksmith as Hardeman straightened.

"Morning." Hardeman poured himself a cup of coffee and sat down as Harry and Ling conducted a short conversation in Chinese.

"Sorry." Harry turned to Hardeman. "We should talk American. I'm trying to improve her. You got to improve all the time or you don't get nowhere."

"It's all right. I'm just getting used to American myself after three weeks with the Sioux."

Harry nodded. "Interesting folks. Hears Twice pays me a visit when he's down. Ain't seen him in some time. You reckon Sun Horse will surrender?"

Hardeman shrugged. "I quit guessing what he'll do."

Harry nodded again. "Well, we got us a stuck sled. I'm off to help dig it out. Snow's soft today. Might be spring after all."

Harry left and Hardeman sat back patiently to await his breakfast, smelling the odors of potatoes and buffalo steak and eggs frying on the stove. The Sun Band would have decided what to do by now. Would they surrender? He was surprised to discover that he was almost indifferent to the outcome. It wasn't his concern any longer.

After he ate, he wandered outside. The mercury in the big thermometer on the kitchen stoop hovered near forty degrees and the day felt even warmer in the sun. He strolled across the yard toward the barn. He would have a look at the packs he and Johnny had brought with them. They would have to split the supplies between the two of them, he supposed, the things that didn't already belong to one or the other. But there was no rush about that, not with both of them staying on after the circus left.

Down in the meadow several figures were working around the hay sled, trying to free it from a drift. Harry Wo had taken along a second pair of work horses and they were being hitched up. Nearer at hand men from the circus were going to and from the red-and-white-striped tent, carrying articles of equipment, and in the barn he found the acrobats and tumblers and clowns hard at work. Everywhere in the settlement, people were going about their tasks, all but Hardeman. Today he would take things easy, and as long as he only had the use of one arm, the amount of work he could do would be limited, but he would find work.

The packs were just as he had left them. He was opening them to look over the contents when a voice spoke his name.

"Mr. Hardeman?"

It was the English strongman. Hardeman didn't know his name.

"Chalmers. Alfred Chalmers," the giant introduced himself. "We did not actually meet on the night of our arrival. Many new faces and whatnot, eh? All seems long ago now. Good to see you up and about. We understand you had quite some adventures. Ah, I believe you have seen Amanda recently?"

"Not for very long."

"But she was well?"

"In better shape than I was, just then. Don't worry, Mr. Chalmers, they're taking good care of her. Snowblindness cures itself soon enough. Sun Horse just helps it along. And Johnny's there to look after her."

"Yes, I know." The Englishman looked around to see if they were being overheard. "Miss Putnam has told us of their, ah, plans. She thought it best that we should have some time to accustom ourselves to losing Amanda. I have told Mr. Tatum myself."

"How did he take it?"

"Quietly enough. He is not an easy man to understand, Mr. Hardeman. You may not be aware that he...he depends on Amanda, you might say. Losing her cannot be easy for him."

"You think he'll make trouble?"

"I believe not. In any event, nothing we can't deal with. Amanda has many friends in the circus and we will stand by her. I just thought you should know."

Hardeman thanked the Englishman for his concern and spent the next half hour going through the saddlebags while the acrobats worked around him. When he stepped outside again he saw that a thin layer of haze had moved in between the small puffy clouds and the sun, diffusing the sunlight. In the meadow Julius and Hutch were feeding hay from a nearly empty sled now, and two riders were coming up the wagon road, Lisa and Harry by the look of them.

When he got a chance he would take Lisa aside and tell her of his willingness to stay and help out. There was more talking to do after that, too. He didn't find it easy to express his feelings but he could make himself plain if he wasn't rushed. Once the circus was gone the place would be quiet and there would be more than enough time for unhurried talk.

A cloud covered the sun and the wind quickened. The air was turning colder. Hardeman thought to get his buckskin coat but as he turned toward the house a movement in the heifer lot caught his eye. One of the heifers was in the throes of giving birth and Hardeman stopped to watch. It seemed to be going well enough; the calf's nose was already in view, and with the next contraction the head appeared with the forefeet neatly tucked beneath the chin. But as the heifer heaved again and more of the calf's body emerged, Hardeman climbed the fence and jumped into the calving lot, feeling in his pocket for his folding knife.

The umbilical cord was wrapped around the calf's neck. He opened the knife as he knelt in the mud by the cow's hindquarters, and severed the cord with a single stroke of the blade. Tossing the knife aside he used his good hand to take hold of the calf by the shoulder and pull gently, trying to help the mother. The thing now was to get the calf out and breathing.

His hand slipped on the birthing fluids and he lost his grip, falling on his side in the mud. He cursed under his breath and slipped his left arm out of the sling. He took hold of the calf with both hands, ignoring the pain deep in his wounded shoulder, and with a final push from the heifer the calf slipped free. It was a bull calf. Hardeman seized a piece of straw from the mud and stroked the calf's nostrils, first one and then the other. Sometimes just tickling a calf's nose would make it sneeze and start breathing on its own, but the calf remained still, its eyes closed. The mother, a heifer no longer, lurched to her feet and sniffed the calf, then began to lick it clean, but Hardeman brushed her away and tried to lift the little bull by the hind feet to drain its breathing passages. There was a sharp pain in his left shoulder and he lost his grip, and as he bent over to try again he was joined by Lisa and Harry Wo, who appeared suddenly at his side.

"The cord was around his neck," he said.

"We better drain him out," said Harry. He seized the calf by the hind feet and hoisted it into the air as easily as a sack of potatoes. Lisa knelt by the calf's head, her elbows in the mud. With two fingers she scooped the calf's mouth and throat clean, then did the same for each nostril.

"Hold his mouth closed," she instructed Hardeman.

He squatted beside her and clamped his hands over the calf's muzzle. She leaned down, covered one nostril with her hand and placed her mouth over the other. She blew hard and released both nostrils, knocking Hardeman's hands aside. The calf coughed, bleated, and opened its eyes.

Harry set the calf down near its mother and spoke soothingly to her in Chinese, encouraging her as she began to sniff her offspring. The calf was breathing regularly now, panting as if to make up for lost time. Hardeman was struck by how different Harry's voice sounded when he spoke English. In Chinese he seemed to be singing some ancient chant.

"These cows all speak Chinese pretty soon," Harry said to Hardeman, and he grinned.

Hardeman leaned against the fence, drained by his exertions on behalf of the calf. It seemed he didn't have all his strength back just yet.

With huffing and stamping from the horses and the creak of wood against wood, the hay sled entered the yard and pulled to a stop beyond the fence.

"You all been rasslin' in the mud?" Julius inquired as he stepped to the ground.

Hardeman looked down at his clothes, which were covered with mud and streamers of birth fluids from the calf. He glanced at Lisa. "I guess I'm in trouble now. This outfit was clean this morning." She didn't meet his gaze. Except for her few words while they worked over the calf, she had neither spoken to him nor looked him in the eye since arriving in the calving lot.

"You in worse trouble with me," Julius said. "I told that woman to make

580

you wear a sling. I didn't mean just hang it 'round your neck."

"It wasn't her fault. She passed on the orders but I needed both hands."

"He got to that cow first," Harry explained. "Without him we might of lost the calf."

Julius scaled the fence with practiced movements and dropped to the ground beside Hardeman. "It's a wonder to me how three folks can get so messed up just saving one calf."

"You can only save one at a time," Hardeman said. Lisa looked at him strangely, and he remembered what she had said about Blackbird. All right, maybe saving one boy wasn't such a little thing. Maybe you could only save one at a time. But at least calves didn't go running headlong into cavalry guns and resist everything you did to guide them to safety.

Julius took Hardeman's left arm in his hands and raised it slightly. Hardeman winced. "Mm hmm." Julius nodded his head. He began to unbutton Hardeman's shirt. "Two bits says you've gone and—yup, you bust it open."

Hardeman looked down and saw fresh blood soaking the bandage on his shoulder.

"You come on with me," the Negro said curtly. "We best get that stopped up. Hutch! You feed those horses and put them out, if you would." The boy already had the harness mostly undone, going ahead with his work without being told.

In the kitchen Julius helped Hardeman out of his shirt and unwrapped the bandage. When the wound was revealed they saw that the fresh bleeding had mostly stopped of its own accord.

"I appreciate all your trouble," Hardeman said. "I didn't mean to ruin your work."

Julius grunted and made no reply. He had no patience for pleasantries just now. Lisa's moods had gone from dark to bright and back again quicker than day and night ever since Hardeman's return, and Julius had no doubt that the scout was at fault. At first Lisa had been all upset about the news of the war starting and Hawk Chaser's death, and although she didn't say so, Julius knew she was worried about Hardeman's wound as well. And then yesterday, she had hummed to herself through the afternoon and evening, staying near the house and spending most of her time upstairs, fixing Hardeman's supper tray herself with everything arranged just so. This morning the cheerful spirits were gone as if they had never existed and Lisa scarcely had a word for anyone. Julius didn't need to know what Hardeman had done to blame him for it.

"You set there and don't move that arm," he said, and went off to fetch a fresh piece of bandage from the medicine cabinet.

As Julius left the kitchen Hutch came in from the entryway. He nodded to Hardeman and accepted the mug of coffee Ling poured for him without a word.

"I reckon Johnny will be along pretty soon, him and Amanda," he said,

581

more as a question than a statement of fact. He sat down opposite Hardeman at the table and couldn't keep his eyes off the wound. He had never seen a bullet hole in a man before.

"Pretty soon," Hardeman agreed.

"I've learned a right smart lot from him while you were gone, about roping and cattle and such. He says everything he knows he learned from you."

"Johnny has a way of picking things up. He didn't take a whole lot of teaching."

"I'm glad he'll be staying on for a bit, him and Amanda both." He fell silent, thinking of Maria Abbruzzi, who had refused his own offer of marriage. She had laughed at his protestations of undying love and she had soothed his wounded pride with her soft lips and warm body, which was so strong beneath the velvet skin. "You are not Catholic," she had said, as if that settled everything. "Besides, you must never marry the first one you make love with, or you will always wonder what the rest are like. If you tell anyone I have said this, I will kill you!" But she kissed him to show she didn't mean it, and she whispered "I will remember you forever. I will name a son for you." Hutch knew of the Waldheims' offer to Johnny and he had given some thought to asking around to see if he too might not get a job with the circus, but he knew now that Maria would never change her mind and he knew just as certainly that the circus life was not for him. They spent their time in the cities and towns, and after their summer in San Francisco they would return to the East. Hutch's life was here in the West, where the land was suited for raising cattle and real men.

He took a sudden breath and spoke again. "Mr. Hardeman, there's something I'd like to ask you."

"Ask away."

"Well, last fall I come by here kind of by accident. Miss Lisa, she said I could stay the winter, and I was grateful for that. She's a fair woman and the pay's all right, but this place means more to me than just a place that give me a job. I feel like I owe kind of a debt and I don't see how to pay it off. I was fixin' to move on come spring, but I'd be willin' to stay on here. You reckon that would help her out?"

"I imagine it would," Hardeman said, considering the sober young man before him. Hutch's seriousness reminded him of Johnny. "It's not an easy time for her. She's worried about keeping the park."

Hutch nodded. "That's it. See, like today she hardly says a word, and a body can feel her worryin' all the while. She makes out like it's just Sun Horse she's worryin' on, and she don't say nothin' about losin' Putnam's Park. The fact is, she don't say nothin' about the outfit at all, and that's not like her. Most mornin's when she's riding down there, lookin' at the cattle, she'll stop by the sled and have a word with Julius and me, about how the cows look and how many calves there are and how much hay's left, things of that nature. Today she didn't hardly say a word even when she came over to help us dig the sled out. I was thinkin' maybe if I said I'd stay on that might cheer her up."

"It might at that," Hardeman said, hoping his own intention to do the same thing would improve her spirits further.

But he found it more difficult than he had imagined to have a word with Lisa alone. It was almost as if she was avoiding him. Julius came back with the bandage and before he was done dressing the wound the dinner gong rang. The circus folk flocked to the saloon and Hardeman joined them, ready to eat again just two hours after his last meal. Lisa kept herself busy at the serving tables and she never did sit down to eat. After the meal Hardeman returned to the kitchen, thinking she would take a moment for him when she was done cleaning up. But almost as soon as he made his appearance she asked if Ling felt well enough to finish up the dishes with Monty's help, pleading some work or other that demanded her attention outside, and she went off so quickly that Hardeman felt he had done something to offend her.

She remained outside all afternoon and as suppertime drew near he resolved to wait no longer. He thought he knew what troubled her, and he could set her fears to rest if only she would give him the chance. As usual she went upstairs to change out of her man's clothing before supper, and when she came down again in her indigo dress with her hair piled atop her head, he was waiting for her in the door of the library.

"Miss Putnam—Lisa. There's something I'd like to say if you have a moment." He took her arm and guided her into the library, where he had built a fire to warm the room.

She turned to face him and there was no welcome in her look, no acknowledgment that they were anything more than strangers.

Her manner took him aback but he went on. "Seeing as Johnny will be staying on here, I thought I might stay on too, just for a while. At least until he and the girl get set to move on. I wouldn't want to miss that wedding." He waited for some sign that his offer pleased her, that her moodiness today had been caused by uncertainty over what he might do and the hope of hearing just such words, but she gave him none. She remained withdrawn, as if shielding herself from an impending hurt. "I wouldn't want to see you get caught up in a war, either. I know the army; it might be I could help, if it comes to that. And I'll do what I can about your deed."

"It may be some time before it's all resolved," she said, offering no encouragement.

"I'm in no hurry to be moving on. I'd like to help."

Lisa sighed. It was time to speak the truth. As she had expected, moving on was the first thought on his mind. He would delay his departure for her but he would not abandon it, and even last night as she fell asleep with his arms around her, she had known somewhere inside her that this was the way it would be. This morning she had awakened and slipped out of bed and looked to the future, and she had felt betrayed by her own impulsiveness.

583

Once again she had permitted herself to care for a man who would soon be gone. Like the cavalry lieutenant he had come to her wounded and she had healed him, restoring to him the strength he needed to leave her. But she would keep to her resolve and do nothing to hold him against his will.

She felt a numbing sorrow and cursed herself for a fool; self-pity was something her father had scorned and she would not give in to it now. But the sorrow was not just for herself. It was for Sun Horse and the Sioux, and for Hardeman too, who was closer to the Indians in habits and ways, if not in social customs, than he was to the people who were already moving west in such numbers to claim the realm that had been secured for them, at what cost they would never know, by mountain men like her father and pathfinders like Hardeman. It had taken the arrival of the circus to make her see just how far things had progressed since her own childhood. A bunch of greenhorns could stumble about the mountains, losing their way, entering the heart of the Sioux hunting grounds without knowing it, and in a few days they would move on without any sense of the dangers they had survived. Twenty years ago such a thing would have been unimaginable. That it was now possible convinced Lisa more than ever that the sun was setting on the roaming ways of the Indians, and all others as well. The time of nomadic freedom was giving way to railroads and farms and fences and traveling entertainments like Tatum's Combined Shows, and it was not only the Indians who would be pushed aside. The trappers were gone and the scouts would soon follow in their footsteps. The West was still a land of many opportunities, but the time was fast approaching when those who did not choose among the opportunities before them would be left behind by the rush of progress, and wonder why only when it was too late. Her father had predicted such a turn of events and she saw it now too, coming sooner than either of them had expected, as if Jed Putnam's passing had somehow hastened the day when he and men of his stature would have to give way to Hachaliah Tatum and his ilk.

She wanted to shout her anger at Hardeman, telling him he was blind not to see how quickly his choices were being narrowed down while he roamed along with the far look her father had noted a quarter century before still in his eyes. Stop looking over the horizon! she wanted to cry out. Look at what's right here! It's good, and I'm holding it out to you! But she could do no more. She had made the offer as plainly as she was able and it remained for Chris Hardeman to accept the gift or reject it. When a man chose to stay with her in Putnam's Park it would be by his own free choice, not because of any persuasions she used to restrain him.

"I do not expect you to leave until you're fit," she said. "I know you'll want to see Johnny again. But if you're going to go, I would prefer that it be as soon as possible."

She turned on her heel and went from the room. If she had remained, Hardeman would not have known how to frame a reply. If she too doubted that there could be a future for the two of them together, then there was nothing left to say. She clearly regretted what she had done last night and she wished him gone.

There was a festive air in the saloon at suppertime. The teamsters were close to breaking through the last of the avalanche and they had high hopes for the morrow. As the meal was cleared away the fat German horse trainer went to fetch his accordion but Hardeman did not stay for the music. His first day out of bed had tired him and he was in no mood for celebration, so he went to the small room at the back of the house where he found Lisa's dressing gown gone and his bed freshly made.

In the morning a gentle snow was falling. Once again he overslept breakfast and by the time he appeared in the saloon it was empty except for Ling Wo and Joe Kitchen, who were wiping off the tables. Hardeman spent the morning sorting through the packs in the barn, dividing the contents as fairly as he could and repacking those items he intended taking with him when he departed. The wound in his shoulder had recovered from being abused the day before and he was confident that he could handle a horse even with his arm in a sling.

After the noon meal he cast about for some way to pass the time and he thought to offer his help to Harry Wo or Julius, but as if in answer to his growing impatience, three riders appeared on the creek trail and once again Joe Kitchen pounded on the meal gong, this time to welcome Amanda and Johnny back to the settlement.

They were accompanied by Bat Putnam, and in no time the three of them were swallowed in a crowd that gathered from all quarters and moved along with them until they reached the barn, where the crowd stopped and would allow them to go no farther until each and every one who had been concerned for Amanda's welfare had welcomed her and congratulated her on her engagement.

"Your eyes, they are well?" Carlos was saying as Hardeman made his way to the center of the throng. "We hear you are blind from the snow."

"They're fine," Amanda said. "Sun Horse cured me. He used a magic chant passed on to him by his grandfather. He told me his grandfather could cure snowblindness better than any man who ever lived." She was wearing her own boots and buffalo coat, and a deerskin dress and rabbit-fur leggings given her by Sings His Daughter. On her head, incongruously, she wore her red clown's cap. Johnny Smoker stood protectively close to her and one of her hands rested on his arm. Lisa Putnam stood at her other side.

"Imagine that old magician working his spells on you," Lydia said, shaking her head. "You must beware of sorcerers, child." She made a sign to ward off evil spirits and addressed herself sternly to Johnny. "You see that you take good care of her, young man. If harm comes to her I will know, even if I am far away, and I will put a mortal curse on your soul."

"When Lydia threatens you, that means she trusts you," Chalmers added quickly, and Johnny looked somewhat relieved as those around him laughed, but Lydia's expression remained serious.

"You mark my words," she said softly, and she drew closer to Chalmers and took his arm.

"So I lose my new assistant before he even comes to work!" Papa Waldheim exclaimed, clapping Johnny on the back.

"I'm sorry. I would have liked working for you."

"Ach! No sorrys, please. You chust take good care of our Amanda. Someone else vill be fortunate to haff you vork for him."

"You won't give up your clowning?" Sam Higgins asked Amanda, concerned. "Miss Putnam tells us you will go to another show."

Amanda dropped her gaze and nodded, suddenly forlorn. "I don't want to leave any of you."

"Come now, my young lady," Lydia admonished her. "We will have no sadness here today. We all understand."

"Indeed," Chalmers added his support, with a meaningful glance at those around him. "There is no need to discuss it and no need to feel sad. Who is to say that we shall not work together again sometime in the years to come?"

Amanda brightened at once, for this was her secret desire. "Oh, I hope so!"

"We've been workin' hard, Carlos and me," Sam said, all good spirits and encouragement. "We've got that new routine down pat, the fisherman and the swell. We'll go over it with you tomorrow and we'll put it in the performance. Goin' t' be quite a show, this one."

There was a distant shout and heads turned to seek the source. Coming up the wagon road at a run, riders were visible in the thin snowfall. There were more shouts now, and raised arms, and behind the horsemen came two wagons, drawn by mules, with men riding in the boxes. Far to the rear came the rest of the wagons, pulled by slow but powerful oxen.

"Looks like you better get that practicing done this afternoon," said Joe Kitchen. "Something tells me we'll be having our show tomorrow."

A few shots came from pistols in the riders' hands and a moment later they swept into the yard, riding in a circle around the circus wagons and finally coming to a stop in front of the crowd by the barn. When their shouting died down and it was possible to make sense of their words, Joe's guess was confirmed. The last of the avalanche had been removed and the roadway was clear, and Hachaliah Tatum had decreed that the performance would be held on the following day.

The wagons clattered into the yard and a new round of cheers was raised by those men. The teamsters on horseback turned toward the barn now, eager to unsaddle their mounts and make for the saloon, for Tatum had promised to buy drinks all around. Some of the performers moved off to join the celebration but Amanda's friends remained clustered around her, the Waldheims and Abbruzzis, Sam and Carlos, Chalmers and Lydia, Julius, Hutch and

586

Chatur, Lisa and Hardeman and Johnny Smoker and Bat Putnam, and all eyes in this group were on Hachaliah Tatum, who entered the settlement last of all, riding in tandem with the one-armed Kinnean. Kinnean saw Hardeman among those around Amanda and he turned aside, taking a more circuitous route to the barn door, while Tatum slowed his white stallion and approached the little gathering at a walk. Amanda drew back but Johnny held her tightly. Lisa moved a step forward as if to prevent Tatum from approaching too near to the fur-coated girl.

Hardeman noted Amanda's fear and the defiance in Johnny's expression, and he remembered Alfred Chalmers' veiled warning.

"Well, I must say you seem fit enough," Tatum greeted Amanda. His voice was full of care. "I am glad to see you looking so well." His eyes moved to Johnny. "No words of mine are adequate to thank you for saving her life. You have my profound gratitude."

Johnny gave a short nod and said nothing.

"If there is anything I can do for the two of you..." Tatum's voice trailed off and his eyes were on Amanda. Then he seemed to collect himself. "Well, we have a show to prepare. If there is any particular arrangement you wish me to make, any alteration in the order of events, perhaps a special farewell, you have only to ask."

He tipped his hat, backed the stallion three paces, then turned and trotted off toward the circus tent.

"It would seem there is no trouble from that quarter," Chalmers mused after a short silence.

"So it would seem," Lisa agreed, although her tone was cautious. She turned to Amanda. "You mustn't stand about in the cold. Come let me make you a cup of tea while Johnny and Bat see to the horses." She took Amanda by the arm and led her off.

"If ve are to perform tomorrow and leave on the day after, ve must feed the horses double," Papa Waldheim said to his sons. "More hay now and grain in the morning."

"We'll help you," Julius said, including Hutch in the offer of aid. The others remembered that they had set work aside to greet the young couple and they dispersed now to return to their tasks, leaving Hardeman and Johnny and Bat Putnam alone with the three horses.

"Come on," Hardeman said to Johnny. "I'll help you unsaddle these animals."

"Now hold on there." But put out a restraining hand. "I ain't come all this way just to take the air. I reckoned you'd like to know that Sun Horse ain't goin' in."

Hardeman stopped and turned. Bat nodded. "Two mornin's ago, the day after you left, he woke up bright as a new penny and he calls a council. 'I will not go to Dakota,' he says. 'We will live in the Lakota way, my grandson and I. Any who wish to stay with us are welcome.' Had Blackbird right there beside him like he couldn't stand to have the boy out of his sight. He says we'll go north when the snow melts and we'll join the hoop of the nation, if there's gonna be a summer gatherin'. He's got a plan to make peace. Didn't say what it was, just that he knew what to do when the time come. Right now we're gonna stick to the Lakota way, he says. Won't surrender, won't fight, just gonna keep clear o' the trouble. And I'm tellin' you, Christopher, it's the doggondest thing. I never seen such a change in a man in all my born days. He's like a young buck again. Eatin' like a grizzly and struttin' about like he was forty again. Threw that cane o' his plumb away. There was sump'n about him, you jest had to believe what he said. Even old Elk Leggin's, him that said he'd be goin' to Dakota come spring, well he ain't goin' now. He's stayin' with the band and so's the rest. We're all puttin' out together when the grass is up. Till then we got the scouts watchin' all the trails. If'n Three Stars comes this way, we'll know in time to stay a jump ahead of him."

It plainly delighted Bat to convey this news and Johnny too was pleased. "You remember how we felt when we left Cheyenne?" the young man asked, and Hardeman nodded. "You had General Crook's go-ahead and we thought we couldn't lose. With a peace man to persuade the hostiles to go in, there wouldn't be any war. You were so sure of it, I believed you."

"It didn't work out."

"No, it didn't," Johnny agreed. "But there's the same kind of look about Sun Horse now. Like he's got something in mind and it's bound to work."

"That ain't certain," Bat said. "A man gets an idea how to lead his people, folks got to believe in him and help out. Everybody's got to do his share. One man alone can't do it all."

Johnny nodded, still looking at Hardeman. "That's right. He'll need help, and I was thinkin' there might still be something you could do for him."

"I did all I could," Hardeman said. "I can't do any more than that."

"Well, I believed that too, but now I ain't so sure. What I mean is, we came to help him right enough, but it was our idea, not his. Maybe that's why it didn't work. What I'm getting at is, the one thing we never done for him was ask what he wanted."

Hardeman was silent for a long time. Johnny had changed. It was no single thing but an impression of many small differences, in the way he spoke and the way he held himself, as if in the time Hardeman had been gone Johnny had grown, not in height or size but inside, where it was harder to see. He stood on his own now and he spoke his mind.

Hardeman remembered the gratitude he had felt toward Sun Horse when the pipe carriers were on the trail north, for giving Johnny the freedom to choose between the worlds. The boy had chosen and the choice had strengthened him. He had taken the last steps into manhood now, and Sun Horse was to thank for that.

"'Tain't like what you done was a perfect bust," Bat said. "There's one thing come out'n this whole deal I thought I'd never see. That's the Lakotas ready to settle down and change their ways. That's what it amounts to, don't y' see? Up there in Two Moons' council them fellers seddown and said they'd take the country from Fort Reno to the Yellowstone and give up the rest. That's like you or me livin' on some dogpatch piece o' ground in St. Louie or Denver so small you could pitch a rock clear acrost it. It's a big change for the Sioux, but they'll make it if'n they get the chance. They see which way the wind blows. Right now it blows from the east and sings the white man's tune. They know it ain't gonna change soon. They're lookin' for a way to keep from bein' blowed plumb flat. Even ol' Sittin' Bull sees which way his stick floats. He's an ornery son of a bitch and he'll walk 'round a mountain to fight the *washichun*, but he ain't stupid. Give him a way to live with his pride and he'll come to water and drink too."

But would the white man drink with him? Hardeman wondered. He remembered how his hopes had been raised in the council in Two Moons' village. It was there that the plan for peace had become something more than his own idea, and there that he had first seen a chance for peace on terms the Indians worked out for themselves. Did Sun Horse see a way to salvage those terms despite the fighting? Hawk Chaser was dead, Blackbird wounded, the Cheyenne and their Oglala friends attacked and homeless, and Crook's column doubtless still on the trail, strengthened now with fresh provisions from the supply train. And Sun Horse was of good cheer.

"Bat says with his brother Jed gone, Sun Horse needs a friend from the white world," Johnny said, looking from Hardeman to the mountain man and back again. "I don't know anybody else who knows the Indians like you do. I'm askin' you to stay on for a while. Call it a wedding present. I don't want nothin' else if you'll do this for me."

"Fact is," Bat added, "Sun Horse said he'd be pleased if you'd come by and stay a spell while we're waitin' for this to quit." He made a gesture at the falling snow and the surrounding mountains, meaning the winter itself, which seemed determined to linger on. "Might be he ain't got nothin' special to ask of you. But his power's to understand the *washichun* and he likes to set 'n' jaw with a feller he can trust. Me, I lived with them folks so long I reckon I think most like them now. But you're fresh from civilized diggin's and you're Johnny's teacher to boot. That's the way he sees it, leastways. Might be he figgers he could learn sump'n from you too."

Even as Bat was speaking, Hardeman knew he would heed the old chief's call. Even without Johnny's plea he would have gone. He had thought to speak with Tatum and offer to guide the circus to Rawlins, but now he was glad he had put off talking to the circus master. Sun Horse was still in danger and he was Johnny's only living relative, and Hardeman's desire to make peace had not been snuffed out by the failure of his efforts, merely pushed aside. And now Johnny had shown him a way to try again. *We never asked him what he wanted*, the boy had said, and he was right. Maybe what Sun Horse had needed all along wasn't someone coming along with his own notions of how to save the Sioux but just a friend willing to listen and do what was asked of him, as one friend helping another. And in Sun Horse's village Hardeman would be close enough to Putnam's Park to watch over Lisa without being in her way. He could see that she was kept safe and with or without her consent he would do what he could about her deed. He would see Johnny and Amanda properly married when the time came. He would do what he could to help Sun Horse. And then he would be free of past obligations and ready to look for his home. He would find a piece of land where he could live or die by his own efforts, as Jed Putnam had done. It was a worthy task, one that could keep a man busy. Maybe even busy enough to forget Jed's daughter, in time.

Bat and Johnny were watching him. "I'll be ridin' back after this here circus show tomorrow," Bat said. "You'd be welcome to bed down in my lodge."

Hardeman repressed a smile. "Oh, I don't know. They're treating me pretty good around here. Three meals a day and a soft bed." Johnny was grinning. The boy knew him too well to be fooled. He knew Hardeman had made up his mind to accept.

Bat snorted indignantly. "We got enough buffler over the hill to keep Rendezvous fed. You ain't lived till you get a bellyful of Penelope's *boudins*, and there ain't no bed in the world softer'n a pallet made o' buffler robes."

Hardeman smiled. "Well, now that's settled, you reckon we could get rid of these horses and go have a drink?" He could think of a dozen reasons to pour himself about half full of good corn whiskey, and his juices ran at the very thought.

A gunshot broke the stillness of the yard. Hardeman's hand found the grip of his Colt as he turned, but he relaxed when he saw Tatum beyond the wagons, standing in a stiff pose with one arm outstretched. Four more times the circus master fired and each time a small block of wood jumped off the railing of the pasture fence a hundred feet away.

From the shelter of the barn door Alfred Chalmers and Lydia were also watching Tatum. They stepped aside as Hardeman and Johnny and Bat led the horses through the door, and they remained standing against the outside wall, two motionless figures on the fringes of a barnyard that was full of comings and goings.

"Hold me, Alfred," Lydia said, and she pressed herself against him.

"With pleasure, my dear." He took her in his arms. "Are you cold?"

"I am frightened."

"Frightened? Whatever for?"

"I don't know," she said, and would say no more. She felt a chill that came from inside, not from without, and it was not the first time she had wondered if her second sight were more a curse than a blessing. In her booth on the circus midway she enjoyed herself, taking the hands of the people who came to have their fortunes told. They were timid or afraid or hopeful, or blustering to show that they did not believe in such things, but they believed, most of them. And Lydia invented fanciful tales, stories that would give a hopeless person hope or make a failure believe he could begin again. But on rare occasions she would take a stranger's hand and feel the frightening chill that overcame her when she saw beyond the present moment and could sense what was to come. On those occasions she closed the curtains to shut away the curious; she concentrated with all her being and she told the stranger what she saw. But even then she told only things that would give hope, for a hopeful person could accomplish much and might even alter fate, while a person told of impending misfortune might bring it upon himself. When she sensed death or calamitious events she kept these things to herself and left the future in the hands of God.

What she felt now was a vague foreboding, as yet unformed.

"Take me to the wagon," she said. "I must rest. But I do not wish to be alone. Stay with me, dear. Stay with me a while."

More gunshots came from beyond the wagons. Tatum was taking glass balls from his pocket and throwing them into the air. One by one he blew them to smithereens.

The saloon was full before the twilight faded, and Hardeman and Bat were among the first at the bar. When the first glass was downed they called for more, and more again when that was gone. Hardeman slowed his drinking then and sipped the whiskey to savor the pleasure the strong drink gave him after such a long abstinence.

From the moment they entered the saloon Johnny and Amanda were the center of attention. Amanda had changed from her Indian clothes into her fawn-colored silk dress and Johnny too was in his Sunday best. When the supper gong rang, several tables were pushed end to end to make a long banquet board, with Johnny and Amanda seated in the center and their friends arrayed around them. The gathering was boisterous and jovial and glasses were repeatedly raised to the young couple. At the foot of the table Bat conveyed Sun Horse's news to Lisa while the conversation dinned around them. She brightened somewhat but he could see that something else was troubling her and then he noticed that she kept a wary eye on Hardeman. The scout too was aware of Lisa, although he never seemed to watch, and Bat divined that some new difficulty had arisen between them. He noted the stubborn tilt of Lisa's chin and wondered if her prideful Putnam nature was at the root of the trouble.

Even before the meal was done the calls for music began. It was to be the full circus band again, complete with tuba, and they wanted Amanda to lead them. "Come on, now," said the circus's second fiddler. "It's the last time we'll all be together. I put your fiddle in the barn, in the clown trunk."

"Tonight ve say goodbye mit music," Papa Waldheim announced. "Happy tunes I vant to hear, so ve can dance the night avay."

Amanda turned to Julius but he shook his head. "We've got time, you and me. Tonight you play for your friends."

591

But Amanda would have none of it. "We'll play together or I won't play at all." She pouted, and Julius relented.

"All right. You go fetch your fiddle and I'll see if I cain't find mine."

As the others began clearing the dance floor and preparing the bandstand, Amanda kissed Johnny quickly on the cheek. "I'll be a little while," she said. "I want to get my things from the barn now, while no one is there. I couldn't stand to do it after the performance tomorrow, when everyone is packing up to leave."

Outside, a few flakes of snow were still falling to earth but stars glittered among the clouds and Amanda caught a glimpse of the slender crescent moon setting in the west. In the barn she found the matches that were kept on a beam near the door and lit the lamp that hung there. Her tightrope and the aerialists' equipment had been moved to the tent. Tomorrow the performers would dress here in the place where they had rehearsed for so long; after the show they would pack up and then even the trunks and costumes would be gone.

Amanda fought off a sense of loss that threatened to overwhelm her. She would not be left alone. Johnny would be with her and she felt that they belonged together. In the spring they would go east and she would show him so many places he had never seen, and once they were there the new jobs with another circus and her own triumphant return to the ring would follow inevitably. Together they could do anything! And hadn't Alfred said that some day she would work with her old friends again? If only she were brave enough now, all her dreams would come true.

She found her violin inside the clowns' trunk in the dressing-room stall. It seemed like something she had last seen in another lifetime. She opened the case and tightened the bow, then set the instrument beneath her chin and plucked the strings one by one, adjusting the pegs. When it was tuned to her satisfaction she began to play Johnny's Waltz to the empty barn, taking stately steps across the floor as if she were walking a tightrope. A barn cat stepped out onto the floor and sat down, watching her curiously.

"You don't have to give it up, you know."

The voice from the dark startled her so badly that the bow flew out of her hand and clattered to the floor. The cat vanished in the blink of an eye. Hachaliah Tatum emerged from the shadows by the door and advanced into the lamplight.

"You don't have to give it up," he repeated. She backed away from him as he approached. He bent to retrieve her bow.

"I didn't hear you come in," she managed to say.

He made a gesture that sought to reassure her and stopped his advance, holding the bow out to her. She came forward cautiously to take it and then stepped quickly back. She returned the violin and bow to the case and picked it up, preparing to leave. She could come back later for the rest of her things.

"Please stay, just for a moment." His voice was soft and confidential. It was a tone he reserved for their times alone together, when he was at his most reassuring. With this voice he had comforted a hysterical child after her parents died in a fire.

She waited.

"I realize it took a great deal of courage for you to take this step. The fact is, I always knew someday you would need to go off on your own and I tried to prepare myself for this moment." He paused and brushed awkwardly at a smudge of dust on the sleeve of his coat. "I'm afraid I haven't done a very good job of it. Perhaps it's not possible. At any rate, I want you to know that I understand what you're doing and I won't try to stop you. You're free to go, of course. But there is something I must ask of you. It's a proposal I have to make for the sake of my business, and perhaps for your career as well. I want to ask that you remain with us just temporarily"—he held up a hand to still the protest that rose to her lips—"on whatever terms you choose. This may seem like asking you to go back on your decision, but believe me, that is not what I mean by it."

"What sort of terms?"

He heard the interest in her voice and he moved a step or two closer as if to take her into his confidence. "Stay until I can find a replacement for you. I would consider it a personal kindness. Not that you owe me any favors. But still, I ask it."

"You have Sam and Carlos."

"They are good clowns but they are supporting characters and neither one is your equal. It will take time to reshape the clown acts and there will have to be another person added. If you will stay, I will take on young Johnny— your fiancé. He could be a great help with the horses. You remember the equestrian parade I've been planning for the grand entrance? The Waldheims will need help with it. He is quite remarkable with horses, they assure me." He paused to give her time to absorb what he had said. "Naturally, the two of you would have your own wagon once you are married."

He moved beneath the lamp and sat on a trunk. "If you would stay through the summer, I could manage after that. Think of it: San Francisco and the nation's centennial. That's what I'm worried about, to tell the truth. You know my hopes for this summer. We simply won't make the impact I want, not without you."

"We could have our own wagon?" Amanda was calculating the risks and the possible rewards. Fresh from a celebrated stand in San Francisco, it would be easy to get employment with another show.

"Of course."

"I'll have to talk it over with Johnny."

"Naturally, I'll abide by your decision. But please tell him how much this means to me. Just until the end of August, that's all I ask. You will have five months' wages in your pockets, both of you. I'll pay him what I pay you." It was extravagant, but it would be a small price to pay if it gave him time to change her mind.

"You would do that for me?"

"Of course. All I have ever wanted was your happiness."

Amanda searched his face and she saw no deceit, only hope. "Thank you," she said, and her gratitude was genuine. Hachaliah had done much for her over the years; he had never refused her anything, and his generosity now touched her deeply. "I'll talk to Johnny. I'm not saying we'll accept, but thank you for the offer." Her voice caught in her throat and she was surprised to find tears filling her eyes. "I thought you would hate me," she whispered.

"How could I hate you? Here now." He offered her a silk handkerchief. She dabbed at her eyes as he put a comforting arm around her.

"Thank you," she said again. She stood on tiptoes and touched her lips to his cheek. His other arm went around her and he drew her close against him, lowering his head to seek her lips with his own. She drew back.

"No, Hachaliah."

"You still want me, don't you."

"Let me go."

"I couldn't stand to lose you. And you couldn't stand to go."

Amanda's happiness vanished. "Please, Hachaliah." His grip tightened ever so slightly. Encumbered by the violin case she could not break free. He tried once more to kiss her but she twisted her head and avoided him and he did not insist. Instead, he smiled.

"Did you think I could simply let you walk away?"

"It was all to get me back, wasn't it?"

"My offer? Yes, to get you back for the show. For the summer. Everything I said is the truth. But I knew there was more that you didn't want to leave behind." His hands moved on her back, one dropping down to hold her hips against his. "Come along for the summer. Bring your young man. Marry him if you like, but of course there's really no need for that. Have your *affaire de coeur*. And when you tire of him—"

"No!" Without thinking, Amanda swung the violin case with all her might. It caught Tatum full on the side of the face, breaking the skin and raising a bloody welt on his cheek. He lifted a hand to ward off another blow and she broke free, running without looking, and found herself stopped by the confines of the stall.

Tatum touched his cheek and saw blood on his fingers. "You shouldn't have done that."

The tone of his voice chilled Amanda. "I didn't mean to hurt you. I just wanted you to let me go."

"Yes. When you wanted me to hold you, I held you, and now you want me to let you go as easily as that. You never once thought about what I want. A young man comes along and catches your fancy and you think you can

594

leave me behind without a second thought. Tell me, is he a better lover than I?"

"It's not like that with him!" She was genuinely shocked by his question. Her time in the Indian village had changed her. She felt purified of all her past mistakes, but now Hachaliah had brought them to life once more.

He smiled knowingly. "Ah. I see. You're playing the virgin for him. How clever. But what would he think if he knew that you have warmed my bed all these years? Would he marry you then?"

"You won't tell him because if you do I'll say you forced me into it from the beginning." There was a dangerous glint in Tatum's eye but she felt a sudden reckless bravado. He couldn't control her anymore. And if she provoked him to hurt her, so much the better. Her friends would take revenge on him and they would quit his employ, and then she wouldn't have to leave them at all. Instead it would be Hachaliah who was left with nothing! "That's not all I'll say," she taunted him. "I'll tell everyone that the reason I ran away the other day is because I told you I was breaking it off and you raped me! And they'll believe me because they're my friends!" As she spoke the final words she swung the fiddle case again, hoping to take him by surprise, but he was on his guard. One hand seized her arm in mid-air and he tore the case from her grasp with the other. He flung it aside carelessly. It struck the post at the corner of the stall and popped open, sending the instrument flying. There was a discord of protest from the strings as the fragile neck hit the floor and snapped.

"I hate you! I hate you!" Amanda clawed at Tatum's face and drew blood before he could capture her hands and imprison them in one of his own. Quite calmly he drew back his free hand and struck her aside the head with a closed fist. She reeled and fell, but he jerked her upright and struck her again, then flung her against the back of the stall where she fell in a heap on a mound of straw. Her skirt and petticoats were crumpled around her stockinged thighs. He could see the garters that supported the silk hose.

He knelt beside her. As she raised her head and looked up uncomprehendingly he hit her full in the face and smiled at the terror that flared in her eyes. He resisted the urge to hit her again. He would take his revenge in a more satisfying way. She was groggy from the blows and stilled by fear, and she did not resist as he raised her skirts up about her waist.

When he arose a short time later, he was no longer smiling. Amanda made no move to get up. Her eyes were open but they did not follow his movements as he rearranged her clothing and covered her with her coat. They merely stared.

Tatum glanced around nervously, suddenly aware of what would happen if someone should come into the barn now, and what would certainly happen when what he had done was known. He had imagined that she would yield at the last moment, that some of her resistance was feigned, as she had feigned it to please him so many times before. But she had yielded only because he

595

had brutually overpowered her, and the savagery her refusal had brought out in him frightened him now. He dusted himself off and straightened his clothing, his mind searching in near panic for a way to avoid retribution for his sins.

He paced back and forth within the light, glancing occasionally at the girl, and then suddenly he paused, for he had hit upon a desperate plan by which he might escape punishment and still keep what he wanted most of all.

"Stay here," he told her with more authority than he felt, and he took the lamp with him to the barn door, where he extinguished it before stepping outside. As he crossed the yard to the house he forced a mask of calm on his expression and his bearing.

In the saloon the music was in full swing and the floor was crowded with dancers. Tatum moved among the people purposefully, pausing only for a moment here and there to exchange a word. He gave the impression that he was on some small errand, nothing of great importance, just a nuisance to be gotten out of the way before he could enjoy this last night of celebration. He noted Johnny Smoker dancing with Lisa Putnam, enjoying himself thoroughly, and then he spied Kinnean across the room. The one-armed man had a glass in his hand and his eyes were fixed on Hardeman, who was leaning against the bar watching the dancers. As Tatum approached, Kinnean tossed down the last of his drink and got to his feet, his face set and hard. He checked the holstered pistol at his hip and started for Hardeman but Tatum blocked his way, taking him by the arm and turning him aside, speaking low and urgently in his ear.

CHAPTER

FORTY-ONE

"I can't see a thing movin' out there, sir." Corporal Atherton squatted beside Whitcomb in the shelter of a small pine tree. They were alone on a low ridge overlooking the plains, awaiting the return of the three men sent out the afternoon before to scout old Fort Reno. The sky was covered with clouds that dropped occasional flurries of snow, and dusk was falling rapidly. In front of them the land was rolling and barren; behind them, beyond the shallow valley where the rest of the men were camped, the foothills rose. Whitcomb could see the campsite because he knew where to look for it, but it was in good shelter and the smoke from the fire could not be seen at all.

As the Lost Platoon drew near the Powder and old Fort Reno, Whitcomb had first thought to make straight for the abandoned post, but it was fifteen miles or more beyond the protection of the foothills and some instinct had cautioned him against such a direct course. He had remembered then the story Crook had told him about being lost in the Oregon country. *We have not been given instincts merely to confuse us,* the general had said. *We should never ignore them entirely.* And so Whitcomb had obeyed his instincts. When he judged that he was as close to Reno as he could get without exposing his men on the open plains, he had given the three strongest horses to Corporal McCaslin and Privates Gray and Heiss, and had sent them to scout the fort. They had more than thirty miles to cover and they had been gone for just over a day. If they didn't return soon they might not find the small campsite in the dark.

Whitcomb prayed they would bring help. If any part of Crook's command remained at the fort, McCaslin would bring some men and horses back with him to assist the lost remnant of E Troop to the army encampment, and by midnight Corwin could be in a doctor's hands. Surgeon Munn's assistant, Dr. Ridgely, had returned to Reno with the supply train, taking with him the wounded beef herder. Ridgely was to set up tents and prepare to treat further wounded when Crook returned to the wagons. But ten days had passed since the battle and there was no telling where Crook and the supply train might be by now.

"How are the men?" Whitcomb asked out of habit. Little had changed. The men survived. Atherton had just come from the camp to relieve him on watch, but Whitcomb had chosen to remain until the scouts returned.

"Private Rogers cut off 'is bad toe, sir."

This gave Whitcomb a jolt. "He did it himself?"

"Luttner and Donnelly 'elped 'im. Rogers said 'e didn't feel a thing. 'e done a good enough job of it, sir. 'e says the walkin' will be easier now."

"How was Major Corwin when you left him?"

"Not good, sir. That leg is killin' 'im. We could cut away some more of the dead flesh but we can't make a proper job of it, not without a saw. 'e needs a doctor's care and bed rest and hot food, and with all that 'e may die anyway."

The report was no worse than Whitcomb expected. On the day following the amputation, Corwin's pulse had been so faint, his breathing so shallow, that Whitcomb had not dared to move him at all. The next morning Corwin had seemed somewhat stronger and was briefly conscious. "Why aren't we under way?" he had asked. Whitcomb had explained that he was afraid the strain of travel would prove too much for Corwin, but Corwin brushed the notion aside. "Carry on, Mr. Reb," he had said. "Don't delay on my account." And so they had resumed the march, but the going was slow. Corwin groaned at every jounce of his travois and several times they had stopped to let him rest. Whitcomb had left Corwin's tending to Atherton and the others at first, afraid that the sight of the stump would make him sick again. That was what he had told himself, but his deeper fear was that the crude butchery would prove to be in vain, and when he dared to look at Corwin's leg again he saw that his fear was justified. The flesh was cracked and oozing where the stump had been cauterized and the end of the stump was livid. He had not needed to see the sober expressions of the non-commissioned officers to know that Corwin's condition was worsening. The wounded officer's lucid moments were few and far between now and he no longer sang songs of the sea.

Whitcomb found himself nodding and he rose to have another look for the scouting party. His stomach was tight with hunger but he did not look forward to his evening ration of horsemeat. Early the day before, he had shot an antelope, a bit of long-range luck that had earned him a cheer from the men. The beast was winter-poor and they had devoured it at a single sitting. Whitcomb had felt sick after eating so much and had almost vomited, and the lean antelope had seemed to give him very little energy the next day. The beast had no fat, Dupré had said. But it was tasty. It would have been better to hoard it and spread it out among the meals of horsemeat. After antelope, horsemeat was even less palatable than before.

Part of the landscape before him moved. He thought at first that his eyes were playing tricks on him in the failing light, but the moving shadows resolved themselves into three mounted men ascending the gentle slope. He waited long enough to be sure the figures were his own soldiers and then he said "Here they come" to Atherton and he started down to meet the scouts.

"There's no one there, sorr," were the first words McCaslin said. "The wagons are gone." He and his men dismounted wearily.

Whitcomb tried to hide his disappointment. When he saw the scouts returning alone he had guessed what they had found, but having his guess confirmed left him feeling helpless and alone. "Did they go north or south?" he asked.

"I can't say, sorr. We left the horses in a draw and Private Gray and meself walked the last mile or two. We got close enough to see there was nobody there and we was about to go have a look at the tracks when we saw a party of Indians on horseback. Six of them, there was. They come ridin' from the south. They rode around the fort and then went down into the river bottom. Makin' camp for the night, I reckoned, and I thought it best not to risk bein' seen, sorr."

Whitcomb nodded his approval. So his instincts had been right. If he had taken the little column to the fort they might have been caught out in the open. Even half a dozen Indians could pose a serious threat to the weakened force. "Well, we've got to go on to Fetterman," he said. "That's all that really matters. Come on now, let's get you to a fire and a meal."

He ushered the others ahead of him, with Atherton in the lead and himself bringing up the rear. Could we have gotten here sooner? he wondered. If he had pushed the men harder, or if Corwin were hale and still in command. . . . There was no use thinking about it. The Lost Platoon had made the best progress possible, given Corwin's wound and the harsh winter weather, which had returned with a vengeance after a brief mild spell. After the wound cost them a day, the weather had cost them the better part of another. On the first day of marching after the amputation they had come upon a recent camp by the banks of a tiny stream, and by the oval sleeping shelters the campers had made, Dupré had guessed it was a small party of Indians. After that the soldiers had kept a renewed watch in all directions. They had seen no further signs of hostiles but they had nearly succumbed to a far more obvious danger. In mid-afternoon it had begun to snow. The platoon had crossed one small watercourse that offered fair shelter, but they had passed it by, hoping to make a few more miles before dark, and then the squall had hit them. They were on a barren plateau, far from any cover or wood or water, and within the space of a few moments the swirling snow reduced visibility to a handful of yards and the men were forced to hold on to a stirrup or a comrade's shoulder to keep together. By good fortune the squall passed after a quarter of an hour but the experience had frightened Whitcomb badly. When the column came on another creek where the steep banks and clumps of brush offered shelter and firewood, he ordered them to make camp, and there they had stayed for most of the following day as the storm continued. They had butchered a second horse and kept close to the fire, eating and sleeping. When the sky finally began to clear in mid-afternoon, they had set out once more and made just five miles before dusk, camping that night by a stream they took to be the south fork of Crazy Woman.

But they had done well yesterday. By Sergeant Dupré's estimate they had covered more than fifteen miles. The days of enforced rest had made the men impatient, and fortified by the antelope, which Whitcomb had shot just at dawn and which they had cooked and eaten at once, they had marched with a will all day.

Whitcomb noticed that Private Gray had dropped back and fallen into step beside him. "Those Indians you saw, were they a war party?"

"There were too few to be a war party, sir. A scouting party, I should think." The cultured Virginia cadences of Gray's speech were incongruous in the rough-clothed and bearded figure.

"I imagine General Crook resupplied himself and took the wagons with him when he returned up-country."

"Well, he did have some wounded, sir," Gray offered. "He may well have sent some of the wagons back to Fort Fetterman to carry the wounded and bring more supplies to a new rendezvous. That's what I would have done."

"And what would you do if you were in command of this force, Private Gray?"

"It's your command, sir, not mine."

"And my first, as you are well aware."

"There is a first time for everyone, sir. I am not sure it is any easier to be promoted to command by departmental orders than to have it thrust on you like this. You'll manage, sir. You have done well for us."

Whitcomb shook his head. "There are times when I'm scarcely able to think. I feel like a blind man."

"Every commander knows that feeling, sir."

"Just now, for instance, I have no idea at all what to do next. We have to make for Fetterman, but if there are more hostiles about..." He left the sentence unfinished. He wasn't afraid to reveal his uncertainties to Gray. Gray knew what it was to command.

"I shouldn't think there are many, sir. My guess is now that they have been attacked they will gather in strength and keep well to the north. The scouts we saw may have followed the supply train to Fort Fetterman, if that's where it went, and they'll be keeping watch for reinforcements. We can't be certain, but I imagine they'll keep close to the road." Gray walked in silence for a moment and then he said, "Do you remember on our first few days of march, sir, when we first left Fort Fetterman, there was a ridge on our left? It had pine trees along the top."

"I remember it." The ridge ran parallel to the wagon road, five or ten miles to the west, most of the way from Fetterman to the Big Horns.

"Well, sir, if we kept to the west of that ridge it would take us straight to the Platte, very close to Fetterman."

"Thank you, Captain."

"I am no longer a captain, sir, and have no wish to be one." Gray touched the brim of his cap and increased his pace to overtake the others, who were a dozen yards ahead.

At the campsite Corwin was awake and calling for Whitcomb. "Why have we stopped, Mr. Reb?" he demanded as Whitcomb approached the litter.

"It's nighttime, sir. We have good shelter here. Have you had something to eat?"

"We've got to press on! Press on! We've got no time to dawdle."

"The men are in no condition to march at night, sir."

"Laggards and malingerers, that's what they are. By God, back in the war we had *men* in the army." Corwin lay back in his robes. "Why am I so tired? When I catch up on my rest I'll show the lot of you. Twenty miles a day. Thirty." His voice trailed off and his eyes closed, and Whitcomb heaved a silent sigh of relief. It was not the first occasion on which Corwin had given orders that made no sense. Whitcomb wondered for the hundredth time what he would do if a real confrontation developed between him and the wounded officer. Thus far he had maintained a pretense that Corwin was in command whenever he was conscious, but if Corwin gave an order that endangered the men, he would have to oppose him openly and risk a charge of insubordination or worse.

He joined the men at the fire and accepted the plate Donnelly offered him, feeling their eyes follow him as he sat on a small log. They had heard McCaslin's news and they were awaiting his orders, awaiting reassurance that their young leader was still willing to lead.

"We're going on to Fetterman," he said. "We'll follow west of the pine ridge, out of sight of the wagon road in case the hostiles are watching it. Each man walks half an hour and then rides, except you, Rogers. You ride from now on. We'll be there in three days."

"Thirty miles a day, sir?" someone asked.

"The going will be easier out on the plains. We'll make it."

In the morning he woke them at first light. An inch of new snow had accumulated on their robes and blankets during the night and the sky was still gray with clouds. Whitcomb wanted a cup of coffee but there was no coffee anymore. They had drunk the last of it three days before, during the storm.

600

After a few mouthfuls of roasted horsemeat for breakfast and more put in their pockets for noontime, the men formed in line without complaint and started off to the southeast. They marched in a column of twos, half mounted and half on foot, a man walking beside each horse to steady the rider if he fell asleep.

They had gone scarcely a mile when Corwin began to moan loudly. The column halted while Atherton and Dupré knelt beside the travois. Neither spoke as Whitcomb joined them.

"What can we do for him?" he demanded.

"Nothing, sair."

Corwin's eyes opened. "Report, Mr. Reb." He looked straight at Whitcomb and seemed to know him, but Whitcomb could no longer tell when Corwin was thinking clearly.

"We're going on to Fetterman, sir. There was no one at Fort Reno."

"Are we on the road?"

"We're keeping somewhat to the west, sir. Corporal McCaslin saw Indian scouts on the road yesterday. We'll follow a course parallel to the road until we reach the Platte."

Corwin looked at Dupré and Atherton. "By God, he's not stupid, is he?" He laughed. It was a rasping, ugly sound. "He's got a head on his shoulders all right. Carry on, Mr. Reb. And wake me when we get there. By God, I want to see Teddy Egan's face when he sees us pull in looking like this. They'll bring out the band to pipe us home!" He closed his eyes, still chuckling, and he made no complaint when the travois began to move once more.

Whitcomb took a position behind the travois, to keep an eye on Corwin. Just when he thought Corwin had his wits about him he said something like that, about Teddy Egan and a brass band welcoming them to Fetterman. Egan was still with Crook, wherever that was, and there would be no band for a bunch of stragglers who had been cut off during the battle and had missed the rest of the campaign.

New snow began to fall, small round pellets that lodged against every ridgelet and obstacle. Whitcomb knew by looking at them how they would feel on his face and what sound they would make underfoot. In four weeks he had become an authority on snow in all its variations.

He felt the air turn colder as the wind picked up and he realized that his field of view had shrunk to a quarter mile. The clouds had descended and the snowfall was thickening. Was there no end to winter here? In Virginia the dogwood would be in bloom.

We're like cattle, he thought, drifting before the wind. But he was almost glad for the wind. On the warm days the men wanted to rest in the sun at noontime. Today they would eat on the march and keep putting one foot in front of the other until he called a halt at dusk. Then they would cook more horsemeat and fall into a sleep close to death. Not too close, please God. I don't want to lose them.

• • •

McCaslin swayed in the saddle and jerked his head up at the sound of laughter. He saw Whitcomb walking nearby with an eerie grin cracking the dried skin of his face. His sandy beard had not grown thick enough in a month of campaigning to hide that golden skin.

"Caught you, by God, McCaslin!" Whitcomb laughed again. "I never thought I would catch you dozing off."

"I beg your pahrdon, sorr."

"No need, Mac. No need. I was beginning to think you weren't human."

"Oh, I'm human enough, sorr. I'd be on me toes all right if I could walk. It's this ridin' that sends me off."

"All right, Mac. Dismount. And keep an eye out when there's anything to see." He moved off up the column, leaving McCaslin to bring up the rear.

McCaslin swung stiffly off the horse and handed the reins to Gwynn. "You ride for a while, Gwynn lad. And don't be fallin' off and breakin' yer head."

Freed of the animal, he shrugged the cumbersome carbine sling off his shoulder and reversed it so he could carry the weight on the other side for a while. He swung his arms to warm himself and did a little Irish jig as he walked along. He hummed the tune off-key to himself, allowing the dance to turn him around, as he had seen the men dancing in the comforting little pubs that seemed to have been sprinkled across the Irish countryside by benevolent leprechauns. How often his mother had sent him for a bucket of beer, or to bring his dad home, and he had always lingered as long as he could, watching the men dance and listening to the fiddle. Happy music it was. No other race knew so many tunes that could lift a man's spirits.

The snow stopped and the wind picked up and here and there a little sunshine shone through the clouds. McCaslin danced in circles with his hands on his hips. Ahead of him the men marched with heads hung down. They were approaching a river. What would it be now? The Powder or one of its forks. The Middle Fork, it should be. And a sad puny stream it was. He hopped in a circle, surveying the countryside. Nothing moved, except the horsemen coming from up the river, riding on the far— Here now, what's this? Horsemen? Lord help us if it's Indians.

"Mr. Whitcomb, sorr! There's riders comin'! Look there!"

"If we don't rest 'em soon, these horses will play out." Fisk got no reply from Tatum and he didn't dare repeat himself. Since the fugitives had left Putnam's Park, Tatum's mood had been as dark as the night, and when dawn greeted them in the broad belt of foothills east of the mountains, the blackness had lingered on in the circus master.

They were seven, carried on six horses. Amanda rode with Tatum, seated before him. Her eyes were open but she took little notice of what went on around her. Fisk rode beside Kinnean in the lead while Tanner and Morton and Johansen brought up the rear. The wagon drivers looked back over their shoulders often, but there had been no sign of pursuit. Around them the foothills were rough and broken, like rubble cast aside after the Big Horns were formed. The country was sparsely wooded in patches and here and there a splash of red sandstone enlivened the otherwise drab surroundings. In such a landscape, a small group of horsemen was insignificant; with new snow beginning to fall, their tracks would soon be covered and the riders would disappear into the vastness.

Tatum had chosen his escort with care, selecting men whose self-interest would override any other loyalties. He had spoken to Kinnean and Kinnean had talked with Fisk; Fisk had found Tanner and whispered in his ear; Tanner had passed the word to Johansen, who had brought Morton along. One by one they had slipped out of the saloon, and when they were all in the barn Tatum had promised them double wages to help him spirit the girl away in the night. He had offered no reasons and permitted no questions. When Tanner asked what he had done, to leave all he had worked for behind, Tatum had silenced him with a curt "Take it or leave it," and he had made it clear that those staying behind could expect no pay at all.

They had saddled the horses and left the settlement under cover of darkness with the gay music from the saloon following them on the still air. Amanda had come willingly enough, or at least she had made no move to resist. There was an ugly bruise on her cheek, but no one had dared to question Tatum about that. If the men knew the full truth of what had caused his flight, they might abandon him even now.

"Are you warm enough, my dear?" He spoke low in Amanda's ear, wanting to comfort her, as if with his concern he might undo what he had done. He had decided against giving her a mount of her own, lest she try to run. The white stallion could easily bear the extra weight. "We'll both be safe and warm before long," he told her. In two days they would reach the old Oregon Trail; in another two, Rawlins; and there he and Amanda would entrain for the east.

He had left a great deal behind him. The hoped-for triumph in San Francisco had been abandoned along with the rest of his plans and the circus that had taken him years to build, but in the end he had run rather than face the Old Testament vengeance that was typical of frontier justice. A rope over a tree limb would be his reward, and for what? For losing his temper with a girl who had given herself willingly to him at the age of sixteen? He cursed his own failure of control.

Once the deed was done he had seen immediately that his choices were few. To flee alone and vanish back in the States? Amanda would tell what he had done and retribution might find him even there. Violated womanhood stirred almost as much outrage in the settled regions of the land as it did here in the territories, where white women were still scarce and hence valued all the more highly. But it was not fear of the long arm of the law that had decided Tatum against that course.

He could not give up Amanda.

When his wife died he had been certain that he would never love another woman as much, but he had been wrong. Amanda had needed his love and he had given it, innocently at first and then more urgently, as his own need grew, until now he was willing to part with everything else he owned before letting her go.

Helena Tatum had hoped for children of her own, but not until her best performing years were behind her, and so she had become like a second mother to the Spencers' only child. She had encouraged Amanda's instruction in clowning and the other circus arts that struck her childish fancy. After the horrible fire, Hachaliah had taken the orphaned girl under his wing in large part because she had been Helena's favorite, and he had sought through her to recapture some of his wife's affection, which she had given to Amanda so freely and which was now lost to both of them forever. Amanda's dependence on him helped to fill that void, and when his time of mourning was past he did not seek to remarry. He and Amanda were a little family by then, content to be by themselves within the larger family of the circus.

Then Amanda had changed everything, and in the new state of things, he had found his love for her growing beyond all bounds. From the first time he was faithful, but she was true to him only for a time. She had learned how to tease him with her suitors and her occasional *affaires*, and he knew he must suffer in silence or lose her. Losing her was what he feared above all. He knew the pain of loss and would not bear it again. And so he put up with her teasing, secure in the belief that she would always return to him. But in Putnam's Park she had sought to betray him completely and his temper had snapped at last, at great cost to both of them.

Even so, he would rise from the ashes of his former hopes, carrying her with him. With new backing he would form a smaller show around exquisite equestrian demonstrations and an act of pantomime and clowning that would match any

604

other in the world. He would add other acts as they came to his attention, but each would be outstanding, and in time the name of Hachaliah Tatum would stand above them all, just as he had always planned. All this was possible still, if Amanda came to her senses and refused to accuse her benefactor. Back at Putnam's Park they would know nothing, only that the girl had vanished and Tatum with her. They would suspect the worst, but without her words to damn him they could never prove their fears. Amanda would recover in time and she would find herself far from the boy she had thought to marry, far from the protection of old and new friends. Once again Tatum would be her only shield against a frightening world and she would turn to the comfort he offered. Together they would start anew.

There might be a brief scandal over the manner in which he had abandoned his former employees, but it would be a scandal of rumor, not of proven deeds, and it would not persist for long.

"We'll walk the horses for a bit," Kinnean said, dismounting. He started off again at once, leading his horse, his derby hat pulled low to protect his eyes from the snow, his long buffalo coat brushing the ground as he walked. The others dismounted and followed him. Tatum helped Amanda down and took her arm to guide her along.

"Gonta storm before long," said Fisk, casting a glance over his shoulder at the back trail and the sky. "We might better find a place to wait it out." His head preceded him as he walked, moving from side to side like a badger's, as if he was looking for a hole.

"We keep going," Kinnean stated flatly. "The snow will cover our trail." It was he who guided the way, not Fisk. During the weeks in Putnam's Park he had talked with Julius Ingram and Harry Wo to learn the lay of the land, and he was sure of his course. Since leaving the park the band of riders had followed the river trail of the Putnam Cutoff, retracing the path the circus wagons had taken into the mountains a month before. A few miles below the park the creek had joined the Middle Fork of the Powder, which would lead them to the plains. There they would turn south, making straight for the Oregon Trail and the railroad beyond.

Kinnean's one regret was that he had been denied the chance to stand up to Hardeman and learn once and for all if the shot that had broken his Winchester had been intended for the gun all along. But Tatum had paid him well to forgo his revenge. Kinnean hadn't settled for the double wages that had bought the other men. To conduct Tatum and Amanda to safety he had demanded and received two hundred dollars in gold. It was enough to buy the new start he had been promising himself since the war, when the loss of his arm had destroyed his army career in mid-stride and sent him westward to seek new opportunities. His loss was no handicap when it came to handling firearms and he had even been a peace officer once or twice, but for the most part the larger settlements wanted a man with two arms for the job, and so he had taught himself to handle a deck of cards and he had made his way by gambling. He had moved from one boomtown to the next, most recently following the rush of prospectors to the Black Hills, but by the time Hachaliah Tatum and his circus came along he had been ready to move on. Gambling was a way to get by but it wasn't the life he wanted. Some day he would find an enterprise at which a one-armed man could excel and until then he would keep looking. Just now Tatum had provided the means. When they reached the Union Pacific, Kinnean would sell his horse and replace the stock on his Winchester, and then he would take the train to California. Maybe there he would find what he was looking for.

For half an hour the six men led the horses and then at Kinnean's command they remounted. The snow thickened and flew at them from all directions for a time before thinning again to reveal the bottoms of the clouds, lower than before, here and there trailing long skirts of grayish white, the patches of falling snow as clearly defined as summer rainstorms.

Where the river ran through a narrow cut, the trail left the course of the stream and rose atop a small ridge. From this vantage point Kinnean stopped to look back the way they had come. He remained motionless for so long that the others turned to discover what kept him and then they too saw what he was watching. A mile or two back up the trail, dark spots moved against the only slightly less dark background of the mountains.

"You said they couldn't trail us at night!" Tanner protested. His deep voice came from somewhere within the curls of his beard as the huge head turned to face Kinnean.

"I said they'd have a hard time of it," Kinnean corrected him. "That boy lived with the Cheyenne and Hardeman's got twenty years of reading sign."

"Let's get moving!" Tom Johansen urged, reining his horse around. He was the youngest of the men and suddenly he wished he had never come.

"You stay put!" Kinnean's voice was full of menace. "A man sitting still might as well be a rock or a tree at this range. They'll drop out of sight soon enough. Then we'll move quick. It might be we'll give them the slip."

"They've stopped," said Fisk.

"Looking for sign."

The moving dots were motionless now. One horseman dismounted, followed by a second. Soon they were off again, the two figures on foot leading the way. Before long they passed out of sight behind an intervening hill.

"All right now. Keep in single file behind me." Kinnean started off without waiting for a reply, with Tatum close behind him. He led away from the trail, keeping to the low ridges that were blown almost bare by the wind, where the riders left scarcely any tracks on the hard ground. When he had gone a few hundred yards from the river he turned to follow its course, keeping always to the windswept areas and the rocks, and when he reached flat ground he increased the pace to a lope.

The snow returned, protecting the fugitive band from distant eyes. Kinnean looked back and then ahead. They were nearing the edge of the foothills, but even out on the plains the country was ridged and rolling and cut with gullies, and a man could rarely see more than a mile or two. Between that and the cover afforded by the snow, they might shake off the pursuers or at least keep ahead of them until dark, when it would be easy work to vanish into the night. But if the pursuers overtook them...Kinnean shrugged inwardly. What happened to Hachaliah Tatum was of little consequence to him. He would get Tatum and the girl safely away if he could, but if not, he would have the satisfaction of an overdue reckoning with Chris Hardeman.

The band rode in silence, each of them looking back often. As they passed over the last hill before entering on the rough grasslands that stretched away to the east, they paused beyond the crest. Behind them the land was arrayed in a series of ascending steps and any movement would be easy to see.

"There they are," said Tatum when only a few minutes had passed.

Kinnean nodded. "Still on our trail. We'll have to move faster."

"Runnin' ain't the way," said Fisk. "We got to make a stand."

Kinnean looked about, considering the possibility. An ambush might kill or wound enough of the pursuers to eliminate any further obstacle to the fugitives' escape. The cover here was sparse, but if the horses and the girl were kept well out of sight it could work. Maybe in the river bottom—

"Jesus God in Heaven!" Johansen was not looking at the pursuing riders. He pointed off to the northwest, where horsemen were emerging from a draw— fifteen, twenty, twenty-five or more.

Kinnean felt a chill as he saw what they were.

"Well?" Tatum demanded, but it was Fisk that answered him.

"Indians!" He gathered his horse's reins to flee, but Kinnean held out a hand.

"Keep still!" he barked. "They'll see the others before they see us. Maybe they'll go after them."

It was true; the Indians were on a course that would bring them on top of the riders from Putnam's Park.

"They've seen them!" Tanner shouted needlessly. The Indians were kicking their mounts into a run, swerving to head straight for the pursuers. But now the whites saw the Indians and they too changed direction, not running from the Indians but moving toward them, arms raised in greeting.

"Damn the luck!" Kinnean swore. "It must be that bunch the Putnam woman knows."

"Lord God, they come to help 'em chase us!" said Johanson, his face white with cold and fear.

"Let's get going." Kinnean reined around and led the way, urging his horse into a run. The thought of an ambush here was hopeless now, with the strength of the pursuing party increased fourfold. Flight was the only chance. If the snow would just keep up they still might get away.

But the snow thinned and then it stopped entirely, and a shaft of sunlight bathed the plains to the southeast. The wind gusted strongly now, pushing the low clouds along. The fugitives rode hard, careless of their tired horses, looking back often, expecting at any moment to see the force of whites and Indians reach the last ridge and spy their quarry in the distance.

"There's more of 'em!" Fisk shouted, jerking his horse up short. He pointed to the front, where a small group of riders was moving slowly toward the river.

"They're not Indians," Kinnean said, struggling to still his nervous horse.

"More from the settlement?" Tatum wondered aloud.

Kinnean tried to count the new party but they were over half a mile away and he could make out only that nine or ten were mounted and the rest afoot. They moved like men on a long journey, plodding slowly, as if they lacked the strength to keep up a faster pace. They were armed, each man carrying a rifle in his hands or over his shoulder, some of those pointing muzzle down, the way a cavalryman carried—

"They're soldiers!" Kinnean exclaimed.

As Lisa approached the Indians she saw that it was Sun Horse himself who led the band. The headman sat straight in the saddle with the bearing of a younger man and he held a flintlock rifle in his hands. He was flanked by Standing Eagle and Little Hand; Walks Bent Over rode beside the war leader. By the looks of it, they had brought every warrior in the Sun Band.

Hardeman and Johnny had stayed back on the fugitives' trail, but Bat and Julius and the four circus men followed Lisa to greet the reinforcements. She spurred her horse out in front of the others, needing the sudden gallop to free herself from the strained tedium of long hours spent tracking in the cold and dark. She raised her Winchester over her head in greeting and reined to a halt as the Indians reached her. Her horse panted and snorted, prancing about. She was very glad to see these feathered men, all clothed in their hides and furs, but as they slowed and swirled around her she recognized a white face in their midst. It was Hutch, watching her warily, sitting astride his mule, Old Joe, and she understood now how the Indians had come to be here. She frowned and tried to adopt a stern expression but she could not find it in her heart to be angry with the youth. She had told him to remain behind when the pursuers set out on Tatum's trail, despite the young man's pleading that he be allowed to come along. With herself and Julius gone from Putnam's Park, there were only Harry and Hutch left to care for the settlement and the cattle; Lisa had feared the pursuit might keep her away for days and so she had ordered Hutch to stay. But he had disobeyed her and she was glad.

"It seems you have a mind of your own." She favored him with a welcoming smile.

"Yes, ma'am!" He grinned from ear to ear, certain now that she did not intend to scold him. It had taken all his nerve to ride over to the Indian village alone in the dark, but he had suspected that Sun Horse would want to know of Amanda's plight. He had been scared half to death by the sudden appearance of the Sioux sentry on the trail, but once the scout had recognized the white youth he had taken him at once to Sun Horse and the old man had lost no time in rousing the village and mounting a war party.

The others from the settlement posse had reached the Indians now, Chalmers

608

towering over the rest as he and the three Waldheims shook hands all around while Bat conveyed in words and signs what little there was to tell of the night's pursuit. Hutch thought of the settlement whites as a posse even though there were no lawmen among them. These men had the same intensity of purpose he had seen as a small child back in "Bloody Kansas" during the late years of the Rebellion, when honest citizens had banded together to protect themselves from Indians, guerrillas and Confederate raiders, who robbed and burned and sometimes carried off young women against their will, or so Hutch had heard. In the posse from Putnam's Park there was no doubt that Amanda had been taken against her will, not after the sight of Johnny Smoker holding up her busted fiddle in front of the hushed saloon.

Johnny had been on the dance floor as soon as the music began, dancing first with Miss Lisa and then with the other women one by one, seeming bound and determined to dance with all of them before the night was done. He had even danced with Maria, bringing her close to the bandstand so she could give Hutch a wink and a smile. She had promised to meet Hutch later for a private farewell. Hutch wasn't sure just how long it was after that when the musicians grew impatient with waiting for Amanda to join them and asked Johnny to go find her. Johnny had returned in what seemed like no time at all, bursting through the kitchen door holding Amanda's fiddle up by the neck, the broken remains of the body dangling by the gut strings. A shocked silence had spread through the room, bringing the music to a ragged halt, and into the sudden quiet Johnny had said, "She's gone. Tatum's gone too."

Things had moved swiftly then. Hardeman and Johnny had gone off to the barn with Bat and Julius right behind them. Miss Lisa had run upstairs to change into her riding clothes, leaving Chalmers and Joe Kitchen to control the circus performers, who were all clamoring to go along, and to choose the few that might be of some use. Hutch had caught up with Miss Lisa in the barn but she had told him to stay behind, trying to make him feel better by saying that someone had to take care of the ranch while she was away.

Bat rode up to Hutch and looked him up and down. "Your ma know you run to fetch redskins when you need help?"

Hutch feared for a moment that he might be scolded after all, but then he saw the mischief in Bat's eyes and he got the joke. He laughed aloud, and it seemed like more than enough reward for passing half the night with his heart in his mouth.

A quarter mile to the south, Hardeman and Johnny were still searching for sign. Once he saw that the warriors were from the Sun Band, Hardeman didn't give the riders a second glance. He was glad of their presence, but there was no time to waste. A new storm was brewing. When it hit, the snow and wind would fill in the tracks left by Tatum and his men. The pursuers would have to close on their quarry soon or lose them.

Johnny dismounted and moved forward on foot, leading his horse across an expanse of windswept ground that was strewn with pieces of shale. From the moment the little band started out on Tatum's trail, Johnny had placed himself in front of the others and no one had questioned his right to lead the chase. Through the dark hours before dawn he had pushed ahead as fast as he dared, close-mouthed and grim all the while. Sometimes he had dismounted to feel the trail with his bare hands, but he had made good time, especially at the start, knowing Tatum and his men would have to keep to the river trail at least until it reached the foothills. At first light Johnny had lost the tracks where the wind had wiped them away, and only then had he turned to Hardeman for help. Together they had cast about as the light brightened, but it was Johnny who found the trail again and since then he had not lost it. Hardeman judged that he himself could not have made better progress if he had followed the tracks alone.

"There." Johnny pointed, finding the scrape made by a shod hoof on frozen ground almost as soon as Hardeman's eyes had settled on the faint mark. The youth remounted and rode forward, bending low in the saddle. His pace quickened as he looked to the front and saw where recent tracks crossed a small drift of snow. Beyond, the ground was covered in white once more and the trail was plainly visible.

Johnny urged his horse into a trot and Hardeman kept pace with him, wondering at the boy's control. Despite his anguished concern for Amanda, Johnny had never once panicked, nor had he forgotten that a man who kept his horse to a steady pace all day would soon overtake another who had gotten off to a faster start.

Hoofbeats came from behind them and Hardeman turned to see the rest of the pursuers, Indians and whites, strung out in a long line behind Sun Horse and Walks Bent Over. As the old chief drew abreast of him, Hardeman made a sign of greeting.

"*Hau*, Christopher," said Sun Horse, and he reined in beside the white man.

Walks Bent Over moved ahead of them but he saw the intensity with which Johnny followed the trail and he kept behind the young man. Like Hardeman, he watched for any signs Johnny might miss and allowed the youth to keep the lead. Ahead, the land fell away toward the Middle Fork.

Lisa and Bat Putnam made their way to the front of the pack, followed closely by Julius. Behind them came the quartet of circus men. Chalmers rode a dapple-gray Shire gelding of enormous proportions and Papa Waldheim was mounted on a sturdy bay stallion. By now even the impulsive Waldheims knew that they must adjust their pace to that of the tracker.

Chalmers was heartened by the new strength of the band. Until now the pursuers had numbered only nine, the number kept small so they would not be hindered by men unfamiliar with the demands of what could be a long and arduous ride, but through the night and into the chill grayness of the stormy morning, Chalmers had grown increasingly concerned about what might happen when the fugitives were overtaken. The outcome of a gun battle between the two groups, so evenly matched, was far from certain, and Amanda would be put in danger if it came to an armed confrontation. Now, with the Indians along, Tatum might see that his situation was hopeless and surrender without a fight.

Chalmers felt personally to blame for Amanda's predicament. When she had run away from Putnam's Park, and after Lisa had brought word that the girl was safe in the Indian village, he and Joe Kitchen and Papa Waldheim had met in his wagon and they had talked over their suspicions that some action of Tatum's must have caused her to flee. "Maybe now's the time for her to get out from under his wing, but she might need some help," Joe had said. "Yes, but how far are ve villing to go?" Papa Waldheim had responded, and Joe had been the first to declare himself. "You fellers make up your own minds, but I'll tell you what. As sure as folks've got to eat, they'll pay me to cook. And they'll pay to see the Waldheim boys do their tricks and to see Alfred here wrap an iron bar around his neck like it was a silk ribbon. It don't matter who runs the show. Oh, Tatum's a great one for getting the show on the road, but he ain't the only one. If I get the boot for standing by Amanda, I won't go hungry for long, and neither will you." Chalmers and Papa Waldheim had immediately declared themselves in accord with these sentiments, and so they had spoken with the other performers by ones and twos, and Lydia had talked with the women, and by the time Amanda and Johnny returned, the performing artists were prepared to form a protective phalanx around the young clown at the first sign of trouble. Chalmers had helped Harry Wo move an extra bed into Lisa's bedroom so Amanda could sleep safely with her there, and he and the others had resolved always to keep Amanda within view until she had gone to bed each night, but Tatum's contrite welcome to the girl and his expression of good wishes had lulled their fears; the high-spirited celebration had made them careless and in the end all their resolutions and good intentions had been worthless.

The riders plunged down a slope to the riverbank. Even unpracticed eyes could follow the trail here.

"If he keeps to the Middle Fork he'll come out of the foothills soon," Lisa said. "He could make good time on the old wagon road."

"So could we," said Julius. "We'd catch him in a couple of hours out there. Even a dude like Tatum won't make that kind of mistake."

"They turn south, they'll come on the South Fork," said Bat. "She twists like a snake but she'll lead 'em stright to the Oregon road. It's a fair little valley too. Give 'em some cover for quite a ways."

Ahead of them, where the river passed through a narrow cut and the trail climbed a rise, Johnny halted by a cluster of tracks and motioned those behind him to stay back. He rode in a broad arc until he found where the fugitives had turned off the main trail. His eyes met Hardeman's. "They've seen us." He set off again, following the tracks with new urgency now. Hardeman had to kick his horse into a fast trot to keep up. Within moments Lisa Putnam overtook him and fell in beside him, where she had been throughout most of the night.

Back in the settlement she had reached the barn before Hardeman had finished saddling the horse he had picked at random from the horse pasture, a chestnut gelding. He had taken one look at her riding garb and the Winchester in her hand, and he had tried to dissuade her from coming along. "Lisa, you can't—" was all he got out before she had cut him off. "Can you ride all day and night if you have to?" she demanded. "Can you shoot a rifle with that bad arm? I can do both, Mr. Hardeman!" A quarter of an hour later the nine riders were on the trail and making for the river canyon. Hardeman and Lisa had spoken only rarely since then. Once or twice he had addressed her as Lisa, but each time she had called him Mr. Hardeman in reply and he had fallen back on his former habit of using her surname. Her manner toward him was the same as it might have been if their intimacy of three nights before had never happened, but still she kept close to him.

The band of pursuers rode in silence, slowing where Johnny had to search out the tracks on bare, frozen ground, increasing their pace where the trail was preserved in patches of snow. The tracks were fresher now.

The snow thinned and stopped and the clouds parted to admit a few rays of sunshine to the country below. Just beyond the last of the foothills the trail turned suddenly again, crossing the Middle Fork to its south bank. Hereabouts the stream flowed for the most part in a narrow channel with banks eight or ten feet high, but the fugitives had found a crossing where the banks were crumbled and low. As the pursuers gained the far bank they scanned the countryside, but nothing moved.

"They're runnin' lickety-split along here," Julius observed with his eyes on the tracks. "Must of spooked when they seen us comin'. I cain't see why they'd keep on like this. They'd do better back in the foothill country. They ever shook us off the trail back there, they could go to ground and lose us for good."

For more than half a mile the tracks led straight as an arrow along the bank of the stream, the fugitives' horses running in line, and then suddenly the trail doubled back, descended a steep bank to the river, and vanished in the water. Johnny crossed the stream and searched the far side, but he found nothing.

Walks Bent Over made signs to indicate horsemen going downstream, hiding their tracks in the water. Johnny understood at once and started off along the far shore, while the hunchbacked Indian advanced on the southern bank. Sooner or later Tatum and his men would have to leave the water.

Sun Horse glanced at Standing Eagle and Little Hand and he made a few signs, motioning them forward along the banks. They obeyed him at once, Little Hand crossing the stream and gaining the top of the bank there, while Standing Eagle galloped off on the near side. Together they would move out

612

in advance of the trackers to see if swift riders might find an obvious trail leaving the river.

The main body of pursuers advanced more slowly behind Johnny Smoker and Walks Bent Over, who watched for signs a man traveling fast on horseback might miss, but before they had gone another half mile Standing Eagle came back in sight, riding like the wind. He made broad signs as he approached and then he swung off toward the southeast, beckoning the others to follow him. In an instant the warriors were off, with Walks Bent Over in the lead and the whites close on their heels. To the rear, Johnny Smoker was already across the river and gaining rapidly on the pack.

"I knew it!" Bat exulted. He had guessed right. Somewhere up ahead Tatum's bunch had left the water and made a run for the South Fork and the shelter of the river bottom there, hoping to throw the pursuers off the scent, but they had failed.

Bat reveled in the thrill of the chase and the sight of the riders around him, whites and Indians together, just like the old days. They were all racing hell-for-leather, eager to close the gap. Standing Eagle led them over one rise and then another, and there was Little Hand waiting for them. He had followed the fugitives' trail from the Middle Fork and now he pointed to the south and led the way. When Bat reached the trail he saw that once more the fugitives had ridden in line, one man leading and the rest following. Why did they take such care to keep in single file? It was an Indian trick, not a white man's, and everyone knew how many men had run off with Tatum, so what was the point?

"How far to the South Fork?" Hardeman called to Bat as he and Johnny Smoker drew abreast of the mountain man.

"A few miles, I reckon. I ain't much of a one fer white man's distance. But I'll tell you what. We'll be there in a jiffy." Bat grinned. "'Bout the time that hits us." He jerked a thumb back over his shoulder. A gray wall of clouds was bearing down on the pursuers from behind, pushed along by the wind, which howled past their ears and whipped the horses' tails about their haunches even as they tried to outrun it. To the west, the mountains were completely hidden. The storm was coming on fast. Even so, the trail was fresh and they wouldn't lose it now. Soon Silk-Hat Tatum and his bunch would be brought to bay and all the questions would be answered, and until then the chase was the thing. It brought Bat to mind of other pursuits long past, like the one on the Green when a large party of trappers and friendly Snakes had wakened one morning to find all their horses gone; it had taken four days, but they had got the horses back and taught the thieving Crows a lesson too.

"Shinin' times!" he said to himself, and be began to tell himself the story under his breath.

"Where in hell have they got to?" Julius wondered aloud, riding nearby. "We oughta catch sight of 'em 'long about now."

"Gone to ground, mebbe," Bat offered, and he put his memories aside to concentrate on the fresh tracks before him. He was a woolly-headed old coot, never content to take what the moment had to offer, always mooning about some time gone by, one he remembered as better. They hadn't all been good times, and that was truth. He knew what it meant to be cold and hungry and a whisker away from death. But he had lived each day and gone on to the next, and that was what he would do now, just get through the day and take it as it came. By the look of things there would be some doin's before nightfall.

He reined his horse back to a trot and drew aside from the pack, looking around warily. When your quarry disappeared, you might be the quarry before you knew it.

Ahead, the trail followed a shallow gully down to the bottom of a dry wash. Beyond the wash the land rolled away to the southeast where the tops of a few trees revealed the course of the Powder's southern fork a mile or two distant. It was a bleak landscape, almost devoid of vegetation, and Bat recalled with longing the pleasant, wooded hills and the lush grass of the lower Powder valley where he had been so recently. Even in winter the northern country seemed rich and fertile compared with this. Let the *washíchun* have the country here if he wanted it. It was little enough to give away if there could be a chance for peace.

Fifty yards ahead of Bat, Hardeman and Johnny were in the forefront as the pursuers entered the dry wash. Hardeman kept his eyes on the tracks, still in a narrow file like those of a party of Indians, who rode that way when they wished to conceal their true numbers. In the bottom of the wash there was a bare patch of sand and a hoofprint clean and sharp, one of the horses showing a cleat much like an army winter shoe...

He looked up suddenly. To the right, the wash curved and twisted away into higher ground, and there was movement along its rim.

"Look out!" he cried, too late.

A crashing volley of gunfire came from up the gentle slope, where clouds of gray-white smoke puffed out along the lip of the wash to reveal the ambushers' position. A horse screamed and in that same moment Little Hand flew backward off his mount, arms flung wide and the rifle falling from his hand; he was dead before he hit the ground.

Hardeman had swerved his horse to one side as he shouted out his warning and he heard two rifle balls miss him by inches, bracketing him. He cursed himself for not realizing sooner what the single-file trail meant. The fugitives had been reinforced! But who had joined them, and how many were there?

A second volley chased the pursuers as they wheeled and scattered, running for safety. Hardeman saw Lisa Putnam riding close in front of him and his first concern left him, but the ambush had taken its toll. Hutch's mule lay on the ground, kicking in its death throes, while the youth scampered away on foot, picked up now by Willy Waldheim. Another horse hobbled in circles, whinnying from pain and fear. In the bottom of the wash the crumpled form of Little Hand lay still. Ten yards to Hardeman's left, Johann Waldheim reeled in the saddle, clutching his side, but he still had control of his mount. Nearby, a young Indian held a wounded arm as he rode.

Hardeman realized that there had been no more gunfire from the ambushers since the second volley and he reined in to look back. Up the slope, the landscape was motionless, devoid of life. The ambushers were keeping low.

Sun Horse and Standing Eagle joined Hardeman, followed by Johnny and Lisa, and the others began to regroup around them. Of the wounds, Johann Waldheim's was the most serious, but already his father and brother were tending him. "I will be all right," he said, waving off the looks of concern cast in his direction.

Hutch was winded but not hurt, and Willy's horse could carry the two of them, at least for now. A young Lakota had caught Little Hand's pony after his own mount was hit. No one was left afoot.

Higher on the slope, Bat Putnam was off his horse and kneeling on the ground, and he fired now at the ambushers' position. Some of the Lakota warriors moved off, circling the wash.

"Keep an eye out for the girl!" Hardeman shouted after Standing Eagle, who galloped away to lead the surround. The ambushers would have to move soon or they would be trapped.

"Where did they get so many guns?" Lisa wondered aloud, just as Hardeman heard distant hoofbeats.

"They're pulling out!" he cried, and he led the way back up the slope toward the battleground.

"There!" Julius pointed and Hardeman saw the riders then, streaming out of a far bend in the wash and over the crest of the low ridge, running off toward the distant river. He counted eight horses. Many of the riders were doubled up, but there was no mistaking the way they rode with the Springfields in their hands. They were soldiers. One man calmly flipped up his trapdoor breech and reloaded his piece at a full gallop, but Hardeman saw no sign of Tatum's white horse, nor any glimpse of Amanda.

Were the soldiers alone? If they were Crook's men, where was the rest of the command?

A few shots from the Indians chased the last of the troopers out of sight, and Standing Eagle kicked his pony out in front of the rest, shouting his war cry. Bat Putnam remounted his horse and joined the pursuit.

Lisa swerved her horse close to Hardeman. "Those are soldiers! We can't fight them!"

Hardeman himself had fought the bluecoats not so long ago, perhaps these very men, but he knew she was right. Tatum must have come upon the troopers and told them some tale to enlist them in his defense. He and his men had probably gone on ahead with the girl. The task now was to get within hailing range of the cavalrymen and tell them the true state of affairs.

"Bat!" he called out, and the mountain man reined back a little. Sun Horse was riding by his son-in-law and it was to the aged headman that Hardeman directed himself. "You'll have to hold back your young men once we get in range! I'll try to make the soldiers parley. They won't side with Tatum once they know what he's done."

"'Tain't gonna be easy," Bat said. "Not with Little Hand lyin' cold back there."

Sun Horse spoke briefly in Lakota.

"Sun Horse says he understands. You'll get yer chance to make the soldier boys talk turkey. He'll keep back the warriors."

The pursuers were cresting the ridge now. The land sloped away before them and they could see the clump of soldiers half a mile ahead of them and riding hard for the South Fork of the Powder. Sun Horse moved out in front of the whites, urging his horse after the foremost warriors. He raised a hand and shouted out; some of the Lakota looked back and slowed their mounts, but beyond them, out of earshot, a single horseman rode, and he was gaining on the troopers.

"Just like Eagle," said Bat. "Runnin' fer the glory. I'll fetch him back." And he was off in pursuit.

Bat delighted in the ease with which the little mare increased her pace. In no time at all he overtook Sun Horse and the warriors and passed them by. Far to the front, a shaft of sunlight shone bright on the land beyond the river, serving as a beacon for the fleeing soldiers, but now the golden rays paled and died away as if a giant hand had squeezed the wick of a lamp between two fingers and snuffed the flame. A gust of wind from behind nearly lifted Bat's winter cap of skunk fur from his head. He clamped it down tighter and pulled up the hood of his capote, looking back over his shoulder. The rest of the pursuers were strung out over a quarter mile, blown like tumbleweeds before the gale, the horses' feet scarcely seeming to touch the ground. Behind them the gray wall of the oncoming storm loomed nearer, building higher and darker as it advanced. It was as if the earlier storm that had welcomed the pipe carriers home and all the clouds and winds and snow showers of recent days were no more than forerunners of the tempest that was sweeping down on the riders now, caroming off the buttress of the Big Horns and rolling out over the plains, perfectly indifferent to the puny creatures in its path.

On and on the little mare ran and Bat was glad he had thought to feed her some oats in Putnam's Park the evening before. A few days' rest and a bucketful of oats and she was up to silk hats and bluecoats today. Once again he recalled other full-tilt gallops made in flight and pursuit and during the hunt. How many times in his years with the trappers and the Lakota had he reveled in the simple pleasure of being borne pell-mell across the prairie by a willing horse? This was the life! And by a miracle, it seemed the good times weren't over yet. Just a few days ago he had thought to leave the Sun Band for good, but the change in Sun Horse had put a stop to that! High spirits had filled the village ever since the headman had broken his fast. The camp was alive with talk and laughter again, dogs barking and fighting over bones, children running everywhere, everyone feeling the good strength of *pte*. Women worked with fleshers to scrape the hides and make badly needed robes and winter moccasins, sinew was stripped for thread, hooves boiled for glue, and once again life had meaning and purpose. True, there was still a dark cloud or two hanging around. No one knew what had become of Crook's soldier boys, and Hears Twice was still keeping to himself, listening for God knows what; Sun Horse had told him he could quit, but the prophet had said, "There is something I must hear," and since then not another word had passed his lips. But Bat wouldn't let that kind of thing discourage him now. Who could tell what the old coot might hear? Voices from the spirit world, no doubt, and sounds of things to come, but meantime there was life to be lived! Just when Bat had thought the Lakota life was going belly up the way the fur trade had done, there was old Sun Horse, full of piss and vinegar and presiding over his people as if he saw nothing but an untroubled future for the Lakota, one generation after another free to come along and live in the same way. Bat knew it couldn't be so, but at least it might last a while longer.

Anger rose within him. Why in damnation did it have to end at all? Why should he have to quit such a glorious life just to give way to the greediest race that ever set foot on the earth? The best part of being a free man was deciding how you wanted to live and sticking with it, and now that freedom was to be denied him—and denied to the Lakota and the Shahíyela and all their friends and enemies as well—just because some politicking yahoos half a continent away couldn't let a few thousand Indians alone! *Politicians!* They wanted something so bad they'd push and shove and stab each other in the back to get it, and anyone who got in the way better look out. They had some notion, something so strong it pushed them along and pushed the Sioux and all the other people of the mountains aside without a by-your-leave. What was so wrong with leaving folks in peace?! He should stick with the Lakota just to spite the damn *washichun*. . . .

"By God I will!" he shouted, and looked around to see if anyone were close enough to hear. Behind him, the rest of the pursuers were far away.

Could it be as simple as that? The bursting joy deep within him told him that it could. He felt all his worries leave him and he whooped at the top of his lungs.

Had there ever been a bigger fool on God's green earth than John Batson Putnam? The blockhead idjit oughta be horsewhipped for thinking all that time that he would have to leave the Lakota just because their glory days were ending! Which race deserved his loyalty now most of all? Hadn't these people welcomed him as no whites would ever welcome an Indian in their midst? He would never find peace among the whites! Not for him, that kind of existence! Far better a life, even a reservation life, among the people he loved than living alone with Penelope among the *washichun*, who would accept neither one of them!

617

For thirty years the Lakota had given him everything they had to give, including acceptance as one of their own, and above all they had given him a life that more than made up for the loss of the trapping days. And what had he given back in return for all that? Not a thing. Oh, he had hunted and fought and done all the things expected of a man among the Lakota, but he owed a special debt that remained unpaid. Well by God he had something to give. He was a white man and he could push every bit as hard and be just as stubborn as any white man ever born. He knew how to parley and how to strike a bargain. He could talk to *washíchun* or Injun and speak his mind, and he knew how to make a fool come to bait. Maybe Sun Horse was right after all; maybe there was a way to talk this war to an end, and if there was, Bat Putnam would sit in council and win something for his people. If not the whole Powder River country then a piece of it. Just a piece to hold on to and live proud, and show folks what it meant to be Lakota and by God the freest people on earth!

He looked around and he saw the world all fresh and clean and new, as if he had been delivered to this spot from his mother's womb. Ahead of him was the river, close now, and the storm was fast overtaking him from behind; all around, the plains lay brown and frozen beneath their thin layer of white, and to Bat it was a world as full of life and promise as any he had ever seen.

"*Hókahe!*" he shouted. He gained a little on Standing Eagle as the mare plunged down a bank and onto the flat of the riverbed. Out ahead, the soldiers disappeared around a bend where a low bluff jutted into the stream. Moments later, Standing Eagle cut close under the bluff and vanished after them, only to reappear an instant later, doubling back as gunfire came from somewhere out of sight. Some of the soldiers had held back to lay for him, but once again they had let fly too soon. They should have let Eagle get on by them and waited for the rest of the pursuers to come in sight. As it was, they had done nothing but give away their position. They'd fall back now and find a new place to fight.

"Wait up, Eagle!" Bat shouted. But Standing Eagle had guessed the same thing and he was already racing off around the bluff again.

They had both guessed wrong. Again there was a burst of gunfire and this time Standing Eagle's horse staggered and fell, throwing him to the ground as bullets kicked up dirt around him. Without hesitation he jumped to his feet and sprinted for the channel of the shallow stream, where a two-foot bank would give him some protection. He fell, dropping his rifle, and Bat feared he had been hit, but he was up in an instant and diving for the bank, where he vanished as more shots chased after him.

Bat reined in as he neared the bluff, keeping out of sight of the soldiers while he plotted his next move. He laughed aloud to see his brother-in-law's gun abandoned in the snow. There's a pretty fix, he thought. Unarmed and pinned down and left it to me to save his bacon. And glad to do it when all was said and done. There was much about Standing Eagle that Bat didn't care for—his stubborn pride, and the satisfaction he could take in any enemy's pain, like that soldier back at Two Moons' camp. But among his own people he was a good enough father and husband and an outstanding warrior, and you couldn't ask a man to be perfect. Eagle was a bullheaded son of a bitch but you had to give it to him, he was a man.

The first of the pursuers were almost upon him and the troopers were still throwing lead at the creek bank where Eagle was hiding. Well, he'd leave it to the rest of them to set the soldier boys straight or run 'em off. Just now he had something to do. You didn't leave your brother pinned down under the guns of the enemy, not if you were a man of the Lakota.

"Get set, Eagle!" he shouted, and he jammed his heels into the mare's flanks. He felt the wind in his face and behind him he heard a six-gun booming. That would be Hardeman getting into action, making the troopers keep their heads down. There were answering shots from the cavalry carbines and a bullet struck the ground in front of the galloping mare. Bat grinned. Didn't reckon they'd plumb forget about Eagle and me. He kept his eyes on the riverbank, seeking some movement. There! Eagle was peering over the edge, getting set to rise up.

Bat steadied the Pennsylvania rifle with his right hand, aiming behind him. We'll show them soldier boys they best mind their manners. He saw the troopers aiming at him and then the rifle jumped and the cloud of smoke whipped away, and the soldiers ducked. He was at the riverbank now and he guided the mare straight along the edge, reaching down a hand to grab Eagle and swing him up behind.

Get ready, Eagle, 'cause I ain't stoppin' to chitchat. . . . There. That's more like it. Get that hand ready now. . . .

Bat felt Standing Eagle's hand touch his own, and then the world turned upside down.

A mighty fist slammed into his chest and suddenly he was flat on his back staring up at the sky, feeling a creeping numbness that competed for his attention with a hard knot of pain located nowhere and everywhere within him. He heard an upsurge of firing, and horses running away. The soldier boys pulling out at last, he guessed, but it didn't interest him much. He felt the wind on his cheek and a few flakes of snow, but he wasn't cold. He didn't feel much of anything.

Bat smiled where he lay. Fifty years in the mountains and they finally got me plumb center. Might pull through and then again I might not. Be a shame to go under now, just when I seen which way my stick floats, but a sight worse to go before, thinkin' I'd of lived out my days with the *washichun*. Better to go like this. You live yer life and it's got to end. Only the mountains live forever, they say. Hooraw fer the mountains!

He coughed, and choked on something warm in his throat.

Hell of a fix. Still, I picked the life I wanted, just like my brother Jed. . . . Now there's food fer thought. D'you suppose that's all there was to that confounded dyin' grin? Just knowin' he'd picked his life each step of the way like a free man? What else is there, when you get right down to it? A man takes his pick of the trails in front of him, not tryin' to figure what makes sense and what don't, just pickin' the one that feels right to him. Why Jed, you sneaky son of a bitch, you saw it all along! And here I reckoned you just couldn't make up your mind. Sure, I stuck to the Sioux after the fur trade while you wandered all over creation, but you picked yer life just as sure as I did. You tried one thing and another but it was all the same life, and you died a happy man! You seen a sight more'n I did, I reckon, but I ain't done so bad. I seen the elephant, and that's truth! Even seen a dancin' bear.

He tried to laugh, but although he felt the mirth deep within him he had lost the power to express it.

He made out Standing Eagle bending over him. Howdy, Eagle, where'd you spring from? He wanted to say the words, but his lips wouldn't move and his throat made no sound. Standing Eagle was talking, but Bat couldn't hear him.

He closed his eyes and saw Penelope's face. I'd like to have another dance with her, he thought. He heard music then, double-fiddle music like it was back at the Rendezvous on Horse Creek in— Which year was it now? The time them two fiddles played so good? It seemed he was moving to the music and he opened his eyes to see where it came from, but he saw only the sky, and Standing Eagle looking down on him with a somber expression.

So long, Eagle. Y'r an ornery bastard, but you know how to live, 'n' so do I.

CHAPTER
FORTY-THREE

"There he is, sair!" Dupré had been riding in the lead as the troopers raced up the river, but he swung around now to join Whitcomb, who was bringing up the rear with Corporal McCaslin. Dupré pointed through the falling snow and Whitcomb made out a clump of cottonwoods a few hundred yards ahead, an unusual sight in the otherwise treeless riverbed. The thicket stood on a small island near the eastern bank of the stream; sluggish water flowed on both sides of it. A figure stood at the tip of the island, waving the soldiers onward. It was Corporal Atherton, who had gone on ahead with Corwin and the civilians.

Whitcomb looked over his shoulder but no pursuers were in sight. The return of the snow had been providential, beginning just as the soldiers withdrew from the second ambush. A handful of shrieking warriors had chased them closely for a time, but they had fallen back.

"Into the water!" He motioned the men to the left. The tired horses, most of them carrying double, splashed into the stream and slowed their pace to a trot. There was no need to make things any easier than necessary for the band of Indians and renegades; they would slow even further when they lost the tracks here and that would give Whitcomb a few more moments to prepare for them. He would need every second.

He surveyed the little island as he drew near it. The patch of trees was small, but it could provide adequate cover for a few dozen men. He wished he had a few dozen.

"Sergeant Dupré, post the men within the trees. I want most of them facing downstream, but send one or two to keep an eye on our rear. When the first Indians come in sight I want a lively fire to drive them back. Make them think twice about coming into range again. Understood?"

"Understood, sair."

As Dupré led the men onto the island, already giving orders for their disposition, Whitcomb reined in beside Corporal Atherton.

"Report, Corporal. How's the major?"

"Bearin' up quite well, sir, all things considered."

"And the civilians?"

"All present and accounted for, sir. None the worse for wear. Exceptin' the girl, that is. She 'asn't said a word. We've been 'ere about 'alf an hour, I should say. I might 'ave gone on a bit, but as you see, sir, there ain't much cover. I thought the trees would do well enough. We've built a fire, figurin' the Indians would find us soon enough with or without it."

Whitcomb turned his head to check the direction of the wind. It was blowing from the north. The Indians wouldn't smell the smoke unless they passed the island by, and there was scant hope of that. "Well done, Corporal. We have a great deal to thank you for."

When Hachaliah Tatum and his party had met the soldiers on the Middle Fork and told their fearful tale, Whitcomb had seen at once that some way would have to be found to transport Corwin on horseback. With the wounded officer on a travois there was no hope of outrunning the marauders that were following Tatum. It had been Corporal Atherton who provided the solution to the problem. In record time he had rigged what he called a "pole harness" to carry Corwin and his litter. He had seen such a device used in the British cavalry to transport the wounded when speed was vital. Using carbine slings and other pieces of belting, Atherton suspended the litter between two horses, each with a rider to guide him, for the harness was fragile and makeshift at best. Two stout willow poles, one attached to the throatlatch buckles and the other to the rearmost equipment ring on the McClellan saddles, connected the horses and kept them a set distance apart. The poles served both to keep the horses moving in tandem and to prevent them from coming so close to each other that they might crush the wounded

621

man between their flanks. With Corwin loaded in the precarious conveyance, Whitcomb had sent Atherton and four privates with Tatum and his men to make as fast as they could for the South Fork, while the rest of the Lost Platoon followed more slowly behind them, serving as a rear guard. The two ambushes had been intended as much to delay the pursuers as to reduce their numbers, for Whitcomb had instructed Atherton to find some defensive position where the platoon might hope to hold off the attackers until nightfall. Atherton had chosen the wooded island, and it would have to do.

Whitcomb looked back downstream. He could see half a mile or more through the falling snow, but there was no sign of movement there. The pursuers had become more cautious. Twice burned, they were twice shy. They would not rush into a third ambush, but in a short while they would discover the stronghold. Without the civilians to think of, Whitcomb and his men might have continued to run, fighting delaying actions where possible, but they could not run for long with most of the men riding double. Better to stand and fight on ground of their own choosing, and this way Tatum's group would have a better chance.

Atherton led Whitcomb in among the trees to where the civilians were gathered by a small fire. Corwin lay close to the blaze, swaddled in his robes. He appeared to be resting comfortably.

Whitcomb wasted no time in preliminaries. "You had better go now, Mr. Tatum. Quickly, please. We'll hold them here as long as we can."

"Go?" The circus owner was taken aback. "I don't understand." His men held their horses' reins tightly, looking fearfully around, all but the one-armed man, who watched Whitcomb thoughtfully.

"If you go now and ride hard, there's a good chance you'll get clean away," Whitcomb explained. "But you must start now, under cover of the snow." He looked at the girl, wondering if she would ever recover from the brutality she had suffered. "If they take her again, she won't live through it," he said.

"He's right, Tatum," said the one-armed man. "If you want to get away, do what he says."

"This way if you please, sir." Atherton addressed Tatum. "There's an opening through 'ere. Lead the 'orses in the water as far as you dare before mounting. You'll go quieter that way and leave no trail."

Tatum extended a hand to Whitcomb. "Thank you, sir."

"Good luck." Whitcomb watched them go, the girl walking docilely beside Tatum. It was a shocking story, the small circus attacked and the girl brutally ravaged by the hostiles before Tatum and his handful of survivors had managed to rescue her. All the more shocking was the presence of renegade whites among the attacking party. That Indians should do such a thing was to be expected, but that white men could take part. . . . Whitcomb said a silent prayer that the girl would get safely away.

The four soldiers who had accompanied Atherton on his flight were holding the platoon's horses near the fire. They were the men with the worst frostbite. Two of them, Luttner and a small red-haired man named Oswald, could barely handle a rifle. With frostbite, the worst pain occurred when the flesh first thawed. But even if there had been no permanent damage, the affected part was very sensitive for a long time thereafter, and grew painful again when exposed to the slightest cold.

"How's the foot, Rogers?"

"Oh, not so bad today, sir." Rogers grinned. "I do better on horseback, though."

As Rogers spoke there were shots from the woods at the downstream end of the island, one first and then another, followed by a short fusillade. Whitcomb ran through the trees until he found Dupré and McCaslin.

"They 'ave withdrawn, sair," said Dupré. "We fired as they came in range."

Downstream, Whitcomb could see no movement in the riverbed.

"They didn't fire back atall, sorr," said McCaslin. "Just skedaddled."

"They'll dismount and come along on foot," Whitcomb guessed. The renegades would approach the wooded island cautiously, and when they were sure the soldiers were there they would try to surround it.

"How much ammunition have we left?"

"Twenty or thirty rounds per man, sorr. When we got here."

Whitcomb calculated rapidly. Four-hundred-odd rounds, if Rogers and the others had the same. Not enough for the kind of defense he had planned. He felt like an idiot for not inquiring sooner about the ammunition. He had hoped to keep up a brisk fire to hold the renegades back and with luck prevent them from completely surrounding the troopers' position before dusk. But dusk was still hours away.

He looked around, assessing his position. To the west the river bottom was broad and the banks on that side were low, but close on the eastern side of the island the bank rose sharply to a rocky ridge. From its rim, the attackers could fire down into the trees. But if the soldiers were no longer on the island when the enemy arrived...

Overhead the sky was dark. The storm would get worse before it abated. Snow was falling thickly now. Whitcomb looked downstream; a squall was approaching, whipping the fresh snow up from the ground and reducing visibility there to a handful of yards.

"Sergeant, I want you to take four men and build up the fire as high as you can with deadwood. Corporal, fetch the pickets from the far end of the island and pick up Major Corwin and the horses on your way back. I'll be waiting for you on the east bank. You have two minutes."

"Sair, what do you—"

"Just follow your orders, Sergeant. Now. At once!"

"Yes, sair!"

As Dupré and McCaslin hastened off to obey, Whitcomb gathered the remaining men and brought them to the island's eastern shore. Moments later they were joined by McCaslin. Donnelly and Gray were with him, carrying Corwin's litter, and close behind them came Dupré and his fire detail, followed by the horse handlers. Whitcomb could see a rising blaze through the trees. "Good work," he said. He waited then, and the men waited with him, none daring to ask what he planned, and when the squall hit the island, filling the air with blinding flakes, he led the men and horses across the stream and up the rocky slope, fearful all the while that the protecting curtain would part and expose them to the renegades' fire. But no shots chased them and they were fully concealed in new positions atop the rise when the squall finally passed. He had placed Corwin and the horse handlers in a sheltered position on the lee side of the rim and the rest of the men along its crest, behind rocks and boulders that offered fair cover from enemy eyes but little from the weather. Upstream there was no sign of Tatum's little band and downstream the attackers had not yet come in sight.

Whitcomb ordered the men not to fire except on his command, and he dared to feel a glimmer of hope. It was not a position he wished to hold for long; here too he could be outflanked by the larger force, but here at least he held the high ground and he had regained the element of surprise. If his daring move worked, the troopers could be back in the shelter of the trees within the hour. The enemy would see the fire and approach the island, and when they discovered that it was deserted they would find the tracks leading across the river. They would think the soldiers had run, but when they massed to follow the trail once more, the Lost Platoon would be waiting. This time the ambush would succeed. With luck they might kill half of the attackers with a single volley and drive off the rest. Once it was dark, the soldiers would slip away.

Unless the surviving renegades pressed the attack and forced the troopers to expend their precious ammunition. Unless their new position were discovered too soon. Unless something else happened that he hadn't foreseen.

He chided himself for letting his hopes run away with him. Live through the next hour and then the one after that. If E Troop's Lost Platoon met its fate here, it would become a legend in the frontier cavalry. Separated from the command, the soldiers' remains discovered a hundred miles from the battle, perhaps after years of searching, and whose were the bones scattered around the platoon's last stronghold? What a mystery that would be!

Whitcomb grinned in spite of himself. He hadn't done too badly.

"Leftenant, sir. The major's awake. 'e's askin' for you." Artherton had crawled up the ridge close behind Whitcomb.

Whitcomb nodded and called softly to the nearest trooper. "Private Gray! I'll be down with Major Corwin. Tell Sergeant Dupré to send for me if anything moves out there."

But when he reached Corwin and the horses he found Dupré squatting beside the wounded officer.

"I need you on the line, Sergeant," said Whitcomb.

"I sent for him, Mr. Reb. This won't take long." Corwin's voice was barely a whisper. He was calm and alert, but very pale. It seemed to Whitcomb that the dark circles around the lieutenant's eyes had deepened noticeably within the past few hours. He fervently hoped Corwin wouldn't give any senseless orders. He hadn't the time for a confrontation now.

"I hope you're feeling better, sir."

Corwin brushed the question aside with a wave of his hand. "Report, Ham. What's our situation?"

"We encountered a party of civilians, sir. Six men and a young lady, pursued by hostiles and renegade whites. I've sent them on ahead while we hold the Indians here. We're on the South Fork of the Powder, as best we can tell. There are twenty-five or thirty in the attacking party. We've killed at least two."

"From bad to worse, eh?" Corwin seemed almost to be amused.

"We're in a good defensive position on high ground and the renegades don't know we're here. We're going to hit them hard and drive them off. After dark we'll get away."

Corwin said nothing for a time. He seemed to be lost in thought. Then he looked at Dupré and Whitcomb in turn. "I want the truth now. Have I been raving?"

Dupré glanced at Whitcomb.

"Raving? No, sir. Well, the fact is, yes, sir. You haven't made much sense at times. You were singing sea shanties."

Corwin made a grimace that was supposed to be a smile. "I'm not surprised. Only tunes I could ever carry worth a damn." He reached out and touched Dupré's knee. "You wouldn't have a little brandy left, would you, Armand?"

"I am sorry, sair. It is gone."

Corwin cackled. "God, what a calamity!" He was racked by a sudden spasm of coughing. Atherton helped Whitcomb and Dupré turn him on his side. They muffled the coughs with the robes until he fell silent at last and lay back, gasping.

Corwin tried to speak but he was unable, and so he motioned them to wait. He breathed with difficulty for a time, wondering if he was doing the right thing. Should he try to hold on a little longer? No. He couldn't take the risk. Each time he lapsed into unconsciousness there was no telling how long it would last or what crises might arise while he was out cold, and if he had been raving—well, the moment had come. He had done all he could to prepare Whitcomb for command, but back at Fetterman he had never dreamed the young officer would have to stand on his own so soon. He had assumed it would be a matter of years, not weeks. Even so, he had known from the start that he would have to bring his new second lieutenant along quickly if Whitcomb were to survive his first campaign and come through it without endangering the men. Like most shavetails, he had been too eager to prove himself. His chase after the beef herd had revealed a boyish recklessness that needed to be curbed, and so Corwin had fallen back on a method he had employed to train his subordinates during the war, when young officers had learned their craft in battle and died if they learned too slowly. He had been a cold and demanding superior. He had treated Whitcomb like a schoolboy, holding him back until he was champing at the bit, just praying for

625

some chance to show what he could do if he were turned loose. And then suddenly Corwin had let him go. Just as he had hoped, Whitcomb had taken the new responsibility well, keeping his recklessness in check because he was so determined that Corwin should find no fault with him. After the platoon was cut off in the battle, Corwin had tightened the reins again, accusing Whitcomb of wanting command precisely to plant the idea in his mind. But if Corwin had passed the mantle too soon, Whitcomb would have feared it and his fear might have led him into dangerous mistakes. Now, with his troop commander worse than useless, the young officer was almost ready to risk a charge of insubordination just to have the matter settled and done with.

He was a good lad. He would do his best, but would it be enough?

"Dupré, I want you to witness this order. You too, Atherton."

"The major isn't himself, Sergeant," Whitcomb began, but Corwin cut him off.

"Shut up, Mr. Reb! You're still taking orders here." He fumbled beneath the robes. "My damned sword. I can't find my sword." He wanted to give his saber to Whitcomb.

"It's back at Fetterman, sir. We left them there." Whitcomb glanced meaningfully at Dupré. Surely by now the first sergeant could see that Corwin had lost touch with his surroundings. Maybe it would be best simply to tell him he was no longer in command and hadn't been for some time.

"Good thing too." Corwin ceased his fumblings. "Useless piece of trash." A fevered light flickered in his eyes. "You should have seen us in the war, Ham. A saber charge! God, what a sight! It'd scare the balls off Tamerlane!"

Corwin had risen part-way up on his elbows but Atherton gently pressed him back. "Don't be strainin' yourself, sir."

Whitcomb cleared his throat. "Major, there's something I must say. In view of your condition I think it's best if I—"

"Dammit, Ham, will you let me finish!" Corwin lay back and fixed Dupré with his gaze. "You're a witness, Armand. This is official." The eyes, almost lifeless now, moved to Whitcomb. "Lieutenant Whitcomb, I'm placing you in charge of the troop, what's left of it. In my present state I'm not fit to command." The eyes closed. "That's all. Carry on."

"Sergeant! Lieutenant, sorr!" Private Gwynn came scrambling down the slope. "They're comin'! And they're showin' a white flag."

When Whitcomb reached the rim he found a place between Private Gray and Corporal McCaslin. The snow had thinned and a mist was beginning to rise from the water of the river as the air turned colder. The mixed band of Indians and whites was approaching at a walk in the river bottom. Two men, a bearded white man and a tall Negro, were well out in front of the rest. Tied to the barrel of the Negro's rifle was a piece of white cloth, which he waved back and forth slowly as he rode.

"It may be a trick," Whitcomb said to no one in particular. He moved along the line, ordering the men to pick a target and wait for his command to fire.

626

The two riders halted when they were fifty yards from the island. "Hello in the trees!" the white man called out. "We want to speak to the officer in charge!"

Dupré glanced at Whitcomb, but Whitcomb motioned him to be patient. To reply now would give away their position. He waited until the main party of pursuers came to a stop.

"Bloody hell!" excalimed Corporal Atherton. "Look at the size of that one, sir."

Prominent in the front rank of the pursuers was a giant of a man on an immense dapple-gray horse. Whitcomb had noticed the man back at the ambush in the dry wash. He wore no hat and was cloaked in a purple cape. It was neither the costume nor the mount of a marauding renegade.

"If they want to talk, I'll talk with them," Whitcomb said. "The rest of you hold on your man and keep out of sight. Range to the main party, about one hundred yards, wouldn't you say, Sergeant?"

"Make it eighty, sair."

"Range eighty yards, and remember you're firing downhill." He cupped his hands to his mouth and turned upstream, hoping his voice would seem to come from everywhere and nowhere. "Who are you?" he demanded.

The two riders turned toward the ridge. They had placed his voice. It was the Negro who replied. "Regimental Sergeant Major Julius Ingram! Formerly of the Ninth Cavalry!" Farther downstream the Indians and whites shifted in their saddles and looked about, wondering if there might be other soldiers in hidden positions around them.

Whitcomb was peering at the man beside the Negro. Beneath his brown oilskin, one arm was in a sling. "I know that man! He was in the battle. He tried to get to Colonel Reynolds, but he was shot by Mills's men." He cupped his hands and shouted again. "Identify the man beside you!"

The white man answered for himself. "Christopher Hardeman! Special scout for General Crook! Who the hell are you?"

"He wasn't one of our scouts, sorr," McCaslin said. "I knew 'em all."

"There was talk of a man sent on ahead of the command," said Private Gray. "Some kind of peace emissary, I think."

Whitcomb shook his head. "I don't like it. I won't violate a flag of truce, but if those Indians move any closer—"

"Oh for the love of God, boys! I've gone 'round the bend. I can't be seein' what I'm seein'!" Private Gwynn was pointing downstream. Approaching along the riverbed, following the trail of the soldiers and their tormentors, was a new band of thirty or more horsemen, and in their midst lumbered a huge elephant with a small man perched atop his shoulders.

Whitcomb stared for a long moment, trying to make sense of what he saw. The two parties in the river bottom had spied each other now and there were shouts of greeting from the Indians and whites below the ridge. The elephant broke into a headlong run and raised his trunk. The sound of his trumpeting filled the valley.

"Hold your fire," Whitcomb said with a calm he did not feel. He rose to his feet and started down the slope toward the river.

Joe Kitchen and Lisa were the last to arrive on the scene, and already the peace was made. The circus men were clustered on the near side of the stream with Rama standing placidly in their midst, while on the far bank Julius and Hardeman were talking with three soldiers. Other troopers were still descending from the rocky ridge, leading their horses, gawking and pointing at the elephant.

The Indians had not lingered long near the soldiers. Sun Horse and four of his men were talking nearby, but the rest of the Lakota were moving off upriver, beyond the island, searching both banks for tracks. Seen through the rising river mists they resembled wraiths. Lisa made out the hatted figure of Johnny Smoker among them. Nowhere did she see any sign of Tatum and his men or the missing girl.

Alfred Chalmers rode forth to meet the two riders, and as he approached, his eyes were on Lisa. He seemed to be searching for something to say, some way to console her, but she spoke first. "She isn't here?"

He shook his head. "Apparently Mr. Tatum and his men were sent on ahead while the soldiers stayed back to delay us. He told them the Indians had destroyed the circus and violated Amanda. He said the rest of us were renegades who took part in the attack. They had no reason not to believe him."

Lisa had imagined that there would be some such explanation for the soldiers' actions. As always, Tatum's smooth talk had served him well.

"We had to come, Alfred," said Joe Kitchen. "I tried to hold them back, but they wouldn't stay there doing nothing." The second band of riders had left Putnam's Park scarcely an hour after the first. Unable to dissuade them, Joe had ridden in the lead. Ben Long and one of the wranglers had some experience at following sign and they had managed to keep on the trail, which was freshly tracked by Lisa and Hardeman and the others who had gone after Tatum.

"I understand, Joseph. But you know we can't go on with all these men. Many of them aren't even armed."

"I know. Just coming this far will satisfy most of them. They'll feel like they done some good. Monty and Ben will take them back."

Lisa moved her horse a few paces off. She would leave it to the men to make arrangements for getting on with the chase and sending the rest back to Putnam's Park. Such deliberations were beyond her abilities just now.

She had stayed with her uncle's body for a time, and the reinforcements from the circus had come upon her there, squatting on her haunches like an Indian with her arms wrapped around her knees, rocking slowly back and forth, oblivious to the chill wind. When the men saw who it was that she watched over, Joe Kitchen had waved the rest of them up the river while he stayed behind. He had said nothing, but he took the reins from her hand and led her horse a short distance away where he held it with his own, waiting patiently. The wind had blown Bat Putnam's gray hair in his face and Lisa had reached out to brush it back. She had felt the unnatural stiffness of the flesh and she had realized that what lay before her was no longer the uncle she loved. It was a corpse, a lifeless remnant. It had seemed less important then that the body would remain unattended for a while, and she had left it after covering the face with the hood of the Hudson's Bay capote.

The men with Sun Horse moved off toward the little island now and he came to join her. When he reached her side he took her hands between his own. Walks Bent Over and Johnny Smoker would find the trail again soon, he told her. The Strange-Animal Man's horses were tired, and he would not be too far ahead. Meantime, the four Lakota warriors that stayed behind would make pony drags from the cottonwood brush on the island for the men who had died. The bodies would be taken to the Sun Band's village, and when the warriors returned, the burial scaffolds would be made and the ceremonies performed. Lisa nodded in reply, not trusting herself to speak.

On the far side of the stream the talk was ending. Julius mounted his horse and made his way back across the river. Hutch joined him as he reached the bank and walked beside him as he rode up to Lisa. The black man stopped close on her upwind side, as if he thought the wind were the source of her grief and he might shield her from it. He held out his hand and she took it in one of her own, feeling his strength and the comfort he offered.

"Miss Lisa?" Hutch spoke in a voice so quiet she could barely hear it. "I just wanted to say I'm sorry. He was a fine man. It kinda made me feel like I knowed your pa, knowing him."

She saw the heartfelt sorrow in his look and she turned suddenly away, blinking hard and choking back the lump that rose in her throat. She was prepared to bear her own pain, but the pain of others threatened to tear her spirit asunder. Why was it so? It had been the same when her father died. She hadn't cried for him until she saw the tears in Ling Wo's eyes.

"Miss Putnam?"

She turned to find Hardeman approaching her, leading his horse by the reins. A young soldier was with him.

"This is Lieutenant Whitcomb. He and his men were separated from General Crook's command at the battle on the Powder. They've had a hard time of it since then."

The young man did not seem old enough to be an officer, scarcely old enough to be a soldier at all. Lisa saw that he was exhausted and her first impulse was to ask him if he and his men had eaten today, but she kept silent.

Across the river, the last two troopers were coming down from the ridge, carrying a litter between them.

"Miss Putnam," said Whitcomb, "I am told that the old fellow who died . . . the one who . . ." He was standing stiffly before her, not meeting her eyes. "I'm told he was your uncle, ma'am. You have my sincere apologies and my deepest condolences, although I am sure they count for very little in the face of your loss."

Lisa could feel no anger toward this youth with the sparse sandy beard. Lies and deception had killed her uncle and it didn't matter who had pulled the trigger.

"It wasn't your fault, Lieutenant. It was no one's fault. Except Mr. Tatum's."

"You're very kind to say so, ma'am."

"What about Amanda? How was she?"

"She was somewhat bruised about the face. And she didn't speak at all. Not a word in the entire time she was with us."

Lisa looked at Hardeman.

"There's no sense worrying about what might be," he said. "When we get her back we'll find out what happened. Right now Lieutenant Whitcomb's men need some food and a place to rest. Some of them have frostbite and his troop commander lost a leg. They'll have to go back to Putnam's Park with the circus men."

"Of course." Lisa was glad of a chance to help others in need and put aside her own loss. She turned to Julius. "You could go with them. If there are wounded—"

"I'll do what I can when we've got Amanda back safe." He would not leave Lisa's side. Not now.

Lisa hesitated and then she spoke to Whitcomb. "We'll be home as soon as we can when it's over. Until then my cook and her husband will do everything they can for you."

Another soldier joined Whitcomb now, a stocky man with a drooping moustache and a thick beard.

"This is First Sergeant Dupré." Dupré touched his cap. "I'll send him with the men. One of my corporals and I will ride with you."

"It ain't your fight, Lieutenant." Julius's voice was hard. He had fought off an impulse to come to attention in the young officer's presence, and recognizing Whitcomb as a Southerner had made him wary. But Whitcomb had been the first to rise from cover, the first to walk down to parley, and now he was the first to refuse an offer of food and shelter until the business at hand was completed.

"I have an account to settle with Mr. Tatum, Sergeant Major," Whitcomb said. "It's a matter of honor."

Julius heard the controlled anger in the young man's tone and he understood. Tatum had hidden behind the soldiers' guns and then he had left them to their fate in order to save his own skin. And but for Tatum's lies Bat Putnam would still be alive. Lisa had put it right when she said there was no one to blame but Tatum. "We best be getting along then," he said.

Dupré spoke softly in Whitcomb's ear for a moment and Whitcomb seemed to slump a little, but he drew himself up as he faced Lisa again.

"I have just been told that our commanding officer is dead. With your permission, Miss Putnam, I'll arrange to have him transported to your ranch. I can't leave him in this place. I hope you understand."

"We have a small graveyard in Putnam's Park," Lisa said gently. "You're welcome to bury him there."

Whitcomb touched the brim of his cap and made a slight bow before turning away. The soldiers were crossing the river now, the litter carriers coming last of all. There too the face was covered. Why do we cover the faces of the dead? Lisa wondered. We're afraid of death, most of us. But not all. Not the Putnam men, it seemed. Her uncle had gone willingly somehow, as her father had gone. Like his brother Jed, Bat had been smiling, and remembering that smile lessened Lisa's pain.

As the litter carriers climbed the riverbank, encumbered by their awkward burden, the man in front slipped in the snow and mud and dropped to one knee. The body rolled half off the litter and was kept from falling only by the quick action of the man at the rear, who lowered his end to keep the litter level. The robe slipped off the upper part of the body, revealing the face. The skin was gray and waxen and the eyes were closed. Only the reddish-brown beard was lifelike.

Lisa touched her heels to her horse and rode the few yards to the river's edge, staring at the dead man as if in a trance. The litter bearers gained the top of the bank and set the litter on the ground. Whitcomb knelt beside the body and regarded it somberly for several moments before drawing the robe back into place.

"What was his name?" It seemed to Lisa that someone else had spoken, although the voice was her own.

"Hmm?" Whitcomb looked up. "Oh. Corwin, Miss Putnam. Brevet Major Francis Corwin."

"Lisa?"

She turned at the sound of Julius's voice to see him looking at her strangely. Hutch and Hardeman and Sun Horse were watching her as well; beyond them Joe Kitchen and Chalmers had been joined by the Waldheims and their eyes too were on her. She saw the concern on every face and her vision blurred. She was unable to speak, scarcely able to think, suffocated by a burden of numbing grief that was suddenly unbearable.

She kicked her horse so hard that he snorted in surprise as he leaped ahead on command, dashing among the other riders, nearly colliding with one or two. She guided him upriver, past the cottonwood island, urging him into a headlong run, needing to leave the senseless death behind her, wanting the wind strong in her face and the sensation of being fully alive that only a horse in full flight could give her. The tears ran down her face and dried there, making numb trails until they ceased to flow.

She did not know how long she rode, but it seemed that hardly any time had passed when she saw the Indians ahead of her. She galloped past the surprised warriors and only when she reached Johnny Smoker and Walks Bent Over did she slow to a trot, following close behind them. They had found the trail. The fugitives' tracks were plain to see in the new snow.

Standing Eagle left the main body of Indians and came to ride beside her. He had mounted Bat's bay mare after his own horse was shot from under him by the soldiers. He nodded grimly. "Won't be long now. We'll settle the score for ol' Bat and Little Hand both. He died good, Bat did. Died tryin' to save me. I guess you know that."

It unnerved Lisa to hear the trappers' English so like her uncle's coming from the mouth of the war leader, and she replied in Lakota. "He would be pleased to hear his brother say he died well."

Standing Eagle said nothing more and they rode together in silence until Hardeman and Sun Horse overtook them as the rest of the pursuers caught up and closed ranks with the Indians. Standing Eagle moved forward then, joining Johnny and Walks Bent Over in the lead, and Hardeman took the warrior's place by Lisa's side. He rode close to her, but not crowding, and she was grateful for his company, as she had been throughout the night. An eternity ago, during the music and dancing of the evening before, Bat Putnam had told her of Hardeman's willingness to remain with Sun Horse for a time, and to help if he were asked. Learning this had made Lisa feel that she and the scout were allies once more, at least insofar as the fate of the Sun Band was concerned, and this in turn had made it possible to set her other feelings aside and allow herself the comfort of his presence during the long pursuit.

Lieutenant Whitcomb and his corporal, a slight man with a sharp nose, fell in place beside Lisa and Hardeman, and Hutch was right behind them, mounted on a horse borrowed from one of the circus men who was returning to Putnam's Park. Farther to the rear, there were more than a dozen circus whites among the pursuers now. Sam Higgins and Carlos were there, both armed. The last to overtake the band were Rama and Chatur. The mahout smiled broadly when some of the Lakota looked back in wonder at the behemoth on their trail. The elephant's lumbering pace was more than adequate to keep up with the horses at anything but a full gallop.

Ahead, the river valley deepened. The stream itself twisted and turned, following a winding course in the broad bottom. The hills on either side were dull and barren, dotted with stunted sagebrush and clumps of struggling grass on the flatter places, while the steep slopes were utterly bare save for a thin covering of snow.

As the leaders entered a long straight portion of the valley they increased their pace, glancing only occasionally at the tracks, which ignored the wanderings of the stream and made straight for the small canyon mouth where the valley narrowed abruptly a quarter mile ahead.

To the west the clouds were breaking. The air had become clear and much colder behind the departing storm and the wind had dropped, as if it had spent all its energy during the violent squalls of midday and needed time to catch its breath.

"Be dark in a few hours," Hardeman observed.

632

Julius nodded. "We don't catch 'em by then, they'll be long gone come day-light."

"Johnny'll track 'em all night if he has to," Hutch protested. "I never seen the like of his trackin'." He was grim and serious, suddenly older. He mourned the loss of his mule, but Bat Putnam's death had overwhelmed any such considerations for now. Like the others, Hutch had but a single goal, a single determination: that the pursuit should be brought to a successful conclusion.

Twenty paces ahead, Johnny and Walks Bent Over rode on either side of the fugitives' trail. The hoofprints were more closely spaced than they had been where they first emerged from the river.

"They're slowin', sorr," McCaslin said to Whitcomb. "Havin' a bit o' rest for the horses. P'raps he thinks we're all spillin' our guts out back yonder." He glanced at Lisa. "Beg pahrdon, mum. I've grown unaccustomed to the presence of a lady."

The corporal's thick brogue and pleasant manner cheered Lisa and she was surprised to find herself smiling.

The trackers were entering the canyon now and suddenly Johnny Smoker held up a hand and pointed straight ahead. As those behind him rounded a slight bend in the narrow passage, they saw horsemen barely a hundred yards away, moving at a walk. Prominent among them was a tall white stallion bearing a large man and a smaller figure seated before him in the saddle.

Walks Bent Over made a peremptory motion to silence the pursuers and he and Johnny led the way at a quick trot, following the soft sand and snow close to the river bank, hoping to close the distance still further before they were discovered. But some noise reached the ears of the fugitives, or perhaps one of their horses gave the alarm, for as one they turned, and seeing the pursuing force so close behind them, they sprang forward at a run and raced off around the next curve in the meandering river's course.

At once the pursuers kicked their horses forward. The Indians whooped with glee and their shouts echoed between the low walls of the canyon. The whites rode in grim silence. There could be no doubt about the outcome now. The quarry would be driven to ground and then all that would remain was to see how it would end—sensibly or with more futile dying.

When the pursuers rounded the next bend they saw that they were gaining on the fugitives. Tatum's men looked back often and one threw a wild shot over his shoulder. Closer and closer the pursuers came, spurred on by their certain victory. Suddenly the figure on the white horse flung out an arm, and in a final desperate sprint he led his men to a jumble of rocks and boulders at the bottom of a high, sloping bluff that was heavily eroded and rounded at the top, affording no rim from which the attackers might shoot or even see into the hiding place below. The little band vanished among the rocks and the pursuers were forced to double back and take shelter behind a curve in the canyon wall as a few shots boomed out from the stronghold. There was a scattering of rocks at the base of the wall, fewer and smaller than those that formed the bulwarks of Tatum's hideout, but adequate to provide safe vantage points from which to survey the short stretch of canyon where the fugitives had taken cover. As the others dismounted, Chatur and Rama arrived on the scene. Leaving the elephant well to the rear, the mahout came forward on foot.

"It's a fair position," Whitcomb said, looking out on the rocky redoubt. The river curved close to the base of the bluff in a channel half a dozen feet lower than the general level of the canyon floor. With the stream serving as a moat to protect their front and the rounded slope guaranteeing their rear, the fugitives had only to defend themselves against approach from either side.

. Sun Horse and Standing Eagle had been talking softly, and now the war leader spoke to four of his warriors, motioning up the canyon. At once they remounted their horses and guided them down the bank to the stream. In an instant they were across and running along the far bank, passing in front of Tatum's stronghold and drawing a few harmless shots as they flew by and disappeared around the next bend in the canyon, where they would take position to prevent escape in that direction.

"Nicely done, sir," Whitcomb muttered, meaning the words for Sun Horse but never for a moment suspecting that the old savage understood him.

"Thank you," said Sun Horse.

Whitcomb was beyond being surprised. Finding himself riding with a band of wild Sioux in pursuit of a kidnapped white girl had exhausted his last measure of that emotion. It was yet another undreamed-of event added to a long list of such experiences he had accumulated in the past month. Together they constituted a second lifetime, equal in breadth and depth to the twenty-two years that had preceded it, and he was certain that nothing would ever surprise him again.

"So, perhaps a few of us should go there too," said Papa Waldheim. "Villy? Johann, you stay." Leaving his wounded son behind, the elder Waldheim remounted. He led Willy down the bank where the Indians had gone before and the two men raced along in the warriors' tracks. At a shouted command from Papa Waldheim, they gripped their saddle horns, dropped off the near side, bounded up and over the horses' backs, then bounced up again and regained their seats as they disappeared from sight to the delighted howls of praise from the Indians.

"Gunther is always the showman," said Chalmers with a wry smile.

"Dangerous bit of tomfoolery, if you ask me," said Joe Kitchen.

"Perhaps not. By, ah, thumbing our noses at Mr. Tatum, so to speak, we make it plain that we have the upper hand. It will give him something to think about."

"He'll see we've got the upper hand," Hardeman agreed. "He'll also see that we can't shoot in there as long as he's got the girl."

Joe Kitchen pointed to the riverbank below the fugitives' redoubt. "We could get pretty close to him down there."

Hardeman shook his head. "We don't want to force his move. Give him some time to think. He'll see he's got no way out and he'll try to bargain with us."

As if he had heard Hardeman's words, Tatum shouted from among the rocks and his silk hat was briefly visible. "Hardeman! Miss Putnam! Can you hear me?"

"We can hear you!" Hardeman replied.

"Let us go or we'll kill the girl!"

"Kill the girl and you've got nothing left to bargain with!"

There was a long silence. Alfred Chalmers cleared his throat. "He is a desperate man. I would not trust Amanda's safety to him. He knows he's lost everything."

"Give him a few more minutes," said Julius. "Pretty quick he'll figure out that his only way out of here is to give us the girl."

"The fact is," Joe Kitchen said, "we don't know just what he's done."

"At the very least he has kidnapped Amanda and caused the deaths of two men today." Lisa's voice was cold. "We can't let him go."

"Not with Amanda." Johnny had scarcely spoken since the pursuit began. The others looked at him now.

"That's the choice," said Hardeman. "We want Amanda, we might have to turn Tatum loose."

Chalmers spoke without hesitation. "We must do what's best for Amanda, whatever has the best chance of freeing her." The circus men nodded in agreement.

Hardeman looked at Lisa and after a moment's delay she too nodded her assent. Nothing could bring back her uncle now. Her first thought must be for the living.

"Tatum!" Hardeman called up the canyon. "Let the girl go and you can ride out of here!"

"We're staying put until the Indians clear out!" another voice replied, and a shot in the attackers' general direction emphasized the point.

"That's Tom Johansen," said Joe Kitchen. "He's got a holy terror of Injuns."

"First we ride out of here!" Tatum shouted. "Then we'll let Amanda go when we're safely away!"

"I was afraid it would come to that," said Whitcomb. "They're not the sort of men to trust simple promises. Once we have the girl back there's nothing to prevent us from doing as we like with them."

Hardeman nodded. "And if we let them ride out of here, Tatum's got no reason to keep his word and let Amanda go."

"It's a Mexican standoff," said Julius.

"We've got to break it somehow," said Lisa.

There was a short silence and then Joe Kitchen spoke. "We can hold them here all night if we have to. Come morning they'll be cold and hungry. It could be they'll be more willing to take our word by then."

"I'm not waiting for morning," said Johnny, addressing himself to Hardeman. "I'll go down under the bank past the rocks to where the river's closest to the bluff. A bunch of men working up close won't do any good, but I might alone. You do something to get Tatum's attention and I'll see if I can't get in there."

Hardeman thought it over and finally nodded. He could see no other way to break the stalemate and Johnny already had his mind made up. "It could work. But you be careful. If they see you too soon they might hurt the girl."

Johnny shook his head. "If they hurt her, they've got nothing left. You said so yourself. Besides, they won't see me." He turned to the others. "Somebody give me a gun."

Lisa drew a pistol from beneath her goatskin jacket and Johnny accepted it without a word. It was the same Remington Army .44 he had carried on the day Amanda was lost. He opened his blanket overcoat and stuffed the gun in his belt the way Hardeman carried his Colt, and then he clambered down into the river channel and began working his way forward under cover of the bank, crouching low.

"We better figure a sure way to keep those fellers watching us," Joe Kitchen said.

"I have an idea that might help," said Lieutenant Whitcomb. "We might even get the girl back without any trouble, but they would still have to trust us. Even if they don't agree, we'll certainly get their attention." He began to explain his plan.

Unnoticed by the others, Chatur left them and returned to Rama. He mounted to the elephant's shoulders and started off down the canyon, urging the beast into a rambling run that quickly took him around a bend and out of sight of the whites and Indians. A few moments more brought elephant and mahout to the mouth of the canyon. There Chatur turned Rama away from the river and guided him up the gentle slopes that led to the canyon's rim, where the land was rocky and rolling on either side of the small gorge. Beast and master made their way back along the heights until Chatur judged that he was above the fugitives' rocky stronghold. He could not see the redoubt, but he knew within a few yards where it was located, by the curve of the river below and the configuration of the canyon wall across the way, which he had noted carefully before setting out. He placed the bull where he wanted him and then descended to the ground and proceeded along the canyon's rim on foot for another hundred yards or more until he came to a place where the canyon's lip was sharp and jutted out over the river, affording him a view of Tatum's hiding place. He could see five men crouched together, watching the attackers' position. To their rear, among the largest rocks at the base of the bluff itself, were the horses and two more human figures. Chatur was not sure he would be able to help Amanda, but should the opportunity arise he was prepared to do what he could.

Below, in the scene the mahout could make out only in miniature, a heated argument was taking place.

636

"We've got to bargain!" insisted Jack Fisk. "There's no chance we'll get away with the girl. She's our ticket out."

"Listen to me!" Tatum ordered for what seemed to be the dozenth time. "We're going to get out of here and we're taking the girl with us. As long as we have her, they won't touch us."

"I ain't going out there to be cut up by those damned Indians!" said Johansen. "I seen what they do to a person."

"Tell them to pull the Injuns back," suggested Tanner in his slow, methodical way. "Then we promise to turn the girl loose once we get out'n the canyon. Nothin' says we gotta do it."

"Yah, sure, and nothing says the damned Indians won't be waiting," argued Johansen. "They'll promise to pull them back, and who's to say the Indians won't just keep out of sight all up and down the canyon? I ain't going out there, not me."

They had stated and restated their fears and positions since being trapped among the rocks, and now they fell silent, eyeing one another more like beasts than men. Fisk's overcoat was raccoon, but his sharp badger eyes moved back and forth from Tatum to Kinnean as he wondered which he should obey if a time came to choose. Tom Johansen, for all his fair appearance and lanky height, was a frightened ferret in a blanket coat. Tanner, bearlike, was the largest, but Henry Kinnean was the most forceful figure, stocky and solid in his buffalo coat. He took no part in the dispute. Like a buffalo he listened and watched, certain in his own power, moving very little except to keep potential dangers in sight. When he moved it would be suddenly and with great purpose.

Only the circus master, silk-hatted and wrapped in his blue cloak, was unmistakably a product of civilized regions, yet his temper was as short as any and his condition the most desperate of all, for he lived under a threat that menaced none of the others. If he were forced to give up Amanda in order to buy his release, Kinnean and the rest would gain their freedom at no cost to themselves, while Hachaliah Tatum, who had already sacrificed everything else in order to keep the girl, would lose his last treasure.

He looked around, seeking some hitherto unseen avenue by which he might flee, but while his present position was well suited to defense, it offered few opportunities for escape. Close against the cliff stood a group of boulders taller than a man; among them, out of sight of the others, Morton watched over Amanda and the horses. Around this central hideaway an irregular ring of smaller stones formed a natural fortification behind which Tatum and the rest were crouched. Beyond the ring, rocks of varying sizes were scattered for a dozen yards in every direction. On the upstream side they extended to the very edge of the river where it curved close to the bluff; a man on hands and knees might gain the channel unseen, but upstream there were Indians waiting.

Tatum wondered how soon the others would crack and force him to surrender. They had been up all night and none had eaten since the evening before. Kinnean had appropriated a few cuts of buffalo from the meat shed outside the barn in Putnam's Park, but there had been no time since then to stop for cooking and here there was no firewood. The men were hungry and tired and their desperation would focus on Tatum when they saw that only he had a motive for escaping without giving up Amanda.

"I'll tell you one thing," said Tanner. "I ain't handing over that girl so long as they got us pinned down like ducks in a washtub."

"Don't be an idiot!" Tatum snapped. "No one's suggesting we should do anything that stupid."

Tanner turned to face the circus master. "Who are you calling stupid?"

"Quiet." Kinnean held up a hand. From the pursuers' position came a new voice.

"Mr. Tatum! This is Lieutenant Whitcomb!"

"That explains how they caught up with us so quick," said Kinnean. "They got to those soldiers and told them the truth."

"You mean we're fighting the army now too?" Johansen's fearfulness increased. He gave the impression of one whose final moments were tolling away and only the manner of his dying remained to be determined.

"Tatum!" came Whitcomb's voice again. "If you'll surrender to me and release the girl, I promise you safe-conduct to Fort Fetterman!"

The fugitives looked at one another. "It's a chance," said Fisk.

"By golly, it is!" Tom Johansen brightened at the possibility of a reprieve. "You think we better take it, Mr. Tatum?"

Tatum hesitated and Kinnean answered the youth in his stead, his voice full of scorn. "You want to explain to the post commandant at Fetterman why we got those soldiers into a fight with a bunch of settlers?" Johansen's face fell.

"I hadn't thought of that," Fisk admitted.

"This is Lisa Putnam!" came a woman's voice from down the canyon. "I give you my word that if you surrender to us and release Amanda unharmed, you'll be free to go with Lieutenant Whitcomb."

"Seems there oughta be some way we could use that lieutenant to get clear of the Indians," said Tanner.

Hachaliah Tatum was thinking hard. Even with Lisa Putnam's promise of safe passage, formidable problems remained, considerations that were unknown to his hirelings. In extremity, he would let Amanda go to save his own life, but to release her unharmed—well, there was the rub. She was bruised a bit and shocked into a stupor from which it seemed nothing would arouse her, but as long as her present condition persisted, the real injury would not be known. Could he risk it? Even if it came to giving her up he could not do so on Whitcomb's terms. The soldiers were in no condition to set out directly for Fetterman. Whitcomb would want to see to his injured and afford them some time to recover their strength, and Putnam's Park was the logical place to do those things. If Tatum were there when Amanda was returned to her friends, she might come to herself and reveal what he had done to her, and then all promises would be meaningless.

The perils surrounding him seemed to increase with each passing moment. If there were a way to escape them and still keep Amanda, he would have to hit on it soon.

"Lieutenant Whitcomb!" he called. "Perhaps we can reach a compromise! Surely you see that we can't surrender the girl while we're trapped like this. Let us ride away and you can come with us. Just you, while the others wait here. Ride with us for a mile or two and we'll give you the girl." Even as he proposed it, Tatum knew the offer would be refused. One man alone with the fugitives could easily be overpowered and the bargain broken. Lacking a more promising course, he was stalling for a time.

"It's no good, Tatum!" came the reply, in Hardeman's voice. "The girl stays here! We're coming out to get her. You meet us halfway and we'll escort you out of the canyon. Sun Horse will take his Indians downstream while you get away." As he spoke, the scout rose from cover and stepped into plain view at the base of the canyon wall where the river curved out of sight downstream. Whitcomb, Julius Ingram and Lisa Putnam joined him. There was movement behind them as the Indians withdrew. Hardeman and his companions started forward. Only Lisa Putnam carried a weapon in view, a Winchester carbine held in the crook of her right arm. Behind the quartet came the boy Hutch, leading half a dozen horses.

"You tell them yes or I will, Tatum," Fisk threatened, made bold by his master's indecision. "We're not all of us going to risk our necks to help you keep that girl."

"Whatever you're going to do, make up your mind," said Kinnean quietly. He withdrew his pistol from its holster and checked his load, smiling slightly, as if he was enjoying Tatum's quandary. While he watched Tatum and the others watched the approaching party, a movement on the upstream edge of the redoubt went unobserved. Except by Amanda.

Back among the boulders, Thaddeus Morton was peering through a narrow gap in the rocks, listening to the others talk. He held the horses' reins in his hand and paid no attention to the girl, who sat on a small rock behind him. She hadn't made a move on her own since leaving Putnam's Park, and like Tatum, Morton assumed she was scarcely aware of what went on around her. Like Tatum, he was wrong.

Amanda had acquiesced in her abduction because she was unable to do otherwise. Hachaliah was her protector, but who would protect her from him? No one, it seemed. He had beaten her and no one came to the rescue; he had taken his way with her despite her efforts to resist. He was the strongest of all and so she had gone with him, powerless to resist him further. When she first saw the soldiers she had felt a flicker of hope, but Hachaliah had bent them easily to his will and her hope had vanished. Now she felt it return. A flash of movement at the edge of the stream caught her eye. Morton didn't notice it, nor did the others. She could hear their voices still, arguing about what to do. "Make up your mind," said Kinnean, but Hachaliah didn't answer. Upstream, among the rocks close to the water, everything was still, and then something moved again. A figure passed from one rock to the next, then to the next, coming closer. It stopped and cautiously raised its head.

It was Johnny Smoker.

Amanda's hope grew strong, but she was fearful as well. When Johnny learned what Hachaliah had done to her, would he still want her? She felt soiled and ashamed, as she had felt during the long night and through the day, but the sight of Johnny reawakened her courage. If he could rescue her, if he could somehow vanquish Hachaliah, then he would become her new protector and they could go forward together, leaving the past behind.

Johnny raised his eyebrows in a silent question. Amanda looked at Morton. His back was to her and all his attention was on something happening downstream. She turned back to Johnny and nodded. His head vanished and a moment later he reappeared, slipping from rock to rock, moving more rapidly now, making no sound as he approached. He reached the boulders and for a moment he was gone from Amanda's sight. When he stepped into view he held a pistol in his hand. He gave her a quick smile, then crossed the small space among the boulders as quietly as a cloud and brought the pistol down hard on Morton's head. He caught the man as he fell unconscious and took the horses' reins from his hand.

"All right, Tatum!" Chris Hardeman's voice came from surprisingly near at hand. Johnny looked between the boulders as Morton had done and saw that he would never have a better moment to act. Fifteen feet away, Tatum and his men were hidden behind their rocks, watching Chris, Lisa, Julius and Lieutenant Whitcomb, who stood on the flat land of the canyon bottom midway between the fugitives' retreat and the place where the pursuers had first taken cover. Now, while her kidnappers' attention was occupied, Amanda might be snatched from their grasp; Tatum would be helpless without his hostage and he could be made to answer for what he had done.

"We'll wait here for two minutes!" Chris called out. "Then we'll let you think about it overnight."

"I'm goin' out there!" Jack Fisk told Tatum. "You do what you like."

"Hold on." Kinnean's pistol shifted in Fisk's direction. "We go together or not at all. What's it to be, Tatum?"

Johnny waited no longer. Moving quickly, he looped each horse's reins around the saddle horn of the next animal until all six were tied in a row, with Tatum's white stallion in the lead. He led the stallion to an opening between two boulders on the upstream side of the redoubt and slapped him on the rump. The stallion trotted off, taking the others with him, their hooves clattering on the smaller stones.

"The horses are loose!" came a shout.

Johnny seized Amanda by the hand. He motioned her to keep low and he

640

led her in the opposite direction, downstream, out from among the boulders and through the rocks at the base of the bluff. He caught a glimpse of Chris and the others and he waved, and at that moment the alarm was sounded behind him.

"He's got the girl!" A shot boomed out and the bullet glanced off a rock by Johnny's head, spraying him with chips. One struck his cheek and he felt the blood begin to flow. There were more shots from behind, but there was firing from the bottomland as well; no longer afraid of endangering Amanda, Chris and the others were shooting at the fugitives.

"Come on!" Johnny let go of Amanda's hand. On his hands and knees he led her along for a few more yards until there was no cover ahead. He pushed her to the ground behind the last substantial rock and protected her body with his own. Bullets from Tatum's men flew overhead, striking the rocks and the face of the bluff, but the pursuers' covering fire intensified now as the circus men in the background joined the fray. The firing from Tatum's men dwindled. By raising his head, Johnny could look out on the scene. Hutch was running to the rear with the horses; Chris and Lisa and Julius and Whitcomb had made for the river when the shooting began and they had taken cover beneath the bank. Now and then one or another would appear briefly to fire at the fugitives, but they couldn't expose themselves for long without attracting return fire. It was a new and more dangerous standoff.

Johnny looked back the way he and Amanda had come. Before long Tatum or one of the others would crawl along the same route and then Johnny would be forced to shoot a man for the first time in his life or allow not only Amanda but himself as well to be taken captive.

Help from an unexpected quarter spared him the decision and broke the stalemate with sudden finality. High up on his cliff, Chatur had seen Johnny make his way into the rocky stronghold. He had seen him overcome Morton and turn the horses loose, and lead Amanda off through the rocks. Had the pair gotten clean away, Chatur might have taken no action at all, for what he planned to do would have uncertain results. But when he saw Johnny and Amanda pinned down by the outburst of gunfire, he threw caution to the winds. Putting two fingers to his lips, he let out a shrill whistle that echoed in the canyon. Before leaving the river bottom, he had noted that rocks of all sizes dotted the face of the bluff above Tatum's hideout, some just revealed, some standing out, awaiting only a few more rains before they too would roll to the bottom. As he had hoped, there were more rocks at the crest of the slope, several quite large. He had placed Rama behind a boulder nearly as tall as Chatur himself, and as he heard the signal now, the elephant put his massive forehead and tusks against the boulder and pushed. The rock was still embedded in the ground but it could not stand against the strength of the huge pachyderm, and at Rama's second lunge it broke loose and rolled, quickly gathering speed, striking other rocks and knocking them loose as it bounded down the slope.

Those in the hideout heard Chatur's whistle, then a brief silence, and then a sudden clattering from above. They looked up to see a cascade of rocks and stones rushing down upon them. Among the boulders, Morton was just coming to his senses. The blow to his head had been partially cushioned by his felt hat and he had been unconscious for only a few moments, but he was still groggy and confused. He saw that the girl and the horses were gone. A sound caused him to look up and he saw an enormous rock plummeting down as if it were falling from the sky itself. It was the last thing he ever knew.

Unaware of Morton's fate, the others rose from cover like quail flushed from a thicket. Johansen ran in blind panic, not looking where he was going, glancing back fearfully over his shoulder. Suddenly the ground disappeared from beneath his feet. He plunged headlong into the river and sat up in the shallow water, gasping for breath, only to find himself looking into the muzzle of a Colt .45 revolver in the hand of Hamilton Whitcomb.

His comrades were less foolish. Tanner sprinted off upstream. Kinnean too had the good sense to run not away from the impending menace but at right angles to its path. He might have run upstream or down, but even in choosing his direction he kept his wits about him. It was he who had seen Johnny Smoker leading Amanda away and he who had fired first, shooting not to kill but only to pin the couple down, for he had realized at once that without a hostage he and the others would be at the mercy of the attackers, both whites and Indians. His urge for self-preservation moved him to sudden action when he saw the falling rocks, but he wished to survive the day as well as the moment, and so when he ran he went downstream, keeping as much as possible within the shelter of those rocks already on the ground, making for the place where he had last seen the young man and the girl.

Two others were close on his heels. Hachaliah Tatum, finding himself suddenly robbed of both Amanda and the horses, had realized in that instant that a point had been reached beyond which his plans and calculations were useless, and so he had turned to Kinnean, whose less refined skills might yet assure his survival. Fisk, although he would admit it to no one, had long recognized Kinnean as his superior, and like Tatum, he followed him instinctively now, seeking protection in the one-armed man's shadow. The three ran with all their might, as if speed itself could protect them from any danger, but they were often within the attackers' view and the gunfire redoubled around them. Suddenly Fisk cried out and fell, clutching his leg. Tatum ducked down behind a rock, but Kinnean kept on toward his goal, bending low, leaping smaller rocks and dodging around the larger ones. A bullet tugged at the skirt of his buffalo coat and another nipped at his bowler hat, but he had his quarry in sight.

"Run!" Johnny shouted, pushing Amanda out into the open. He had kept her with him until now, fearful that a stray bullet might find her if she ran, but he would not let her be taken captive again. She took to her heels without further urging and Johnny turned to protect her retreat. Kinnean came into

642

sight a dozen feet away and dropped into a crouch, smiling as he brought his pistol to bear on the youth. Johnny raised his gun, but he saw that the one-armed man had no further interest in Amanda and he found in that moment that he was not prepared to take another man's life simply to save his own. He lowered the gun and Kinnean's smile broadened.

All around them, others were in motion. Those who had held Tatum and his men under siege were taking advantage of the fugitives' sudden confusion, and they converged from all sides now, each intent on his own purpose.

Amanda's appearance was the event Sun Horse had been waiting for. When the other Lakotas withdrew at his command, he had mounted his horse and remained behind, watching from the shadow of the canyon wall. Since the night before, when the white youth from the settlement had come to the Sun Band's village to tell that the clown girl was in danger, Sun Horse had hoped for a chance to save her. His power had returned to him as a result of her coming together with the One Who Stands Between the Worlds and he owed her a great debt, but he felt that there was something unfinished, something still to be done. Even without such a feeling he would have come gladly to Amanda's aid; his grandson had chosen her for his wife and Sun Horse was personally fond of her, but the nagging sense of incompletion had lent a special urgency to the chase. When he saw the two young people move among the rocks he had tightened his knees to prepare his horse for action, and when Amanda ran into the open, he started toward her, his horse reaching a gallop in a few steps, racing past the Strange-Animal Men, who were only then rising from cover to run forward. From upstream came the whoops of the four Lakotas that had guarded the way there, as they rode forth now to take part in the fight. Sun Horse heard shots on every side and he saw one man fall in the river, but he held to his course and at the last moment Amanda saw him coming and held out her arms to him.

Even as Sun Horse made his move, Hardeman and Lisa and Julius were out of the riverbed and running for the stronghold. With Tatum's men routed by the falling rocks, there was no opposing fire, but at any moment the fugitives might regroup. Fisk had disappeared from view after he fell and there was no sign of Tatum. Only Kinnean was in sight, his head and shoulders just visible near the base of the bluff, and it was for him that Hardeman ran, but Julius had a different goal. He had seen Tanner dart off upstream and saw where he took cover again, and he intended to surprise the teamster before he could pose any further threat, but his concern for Amanda was more immediate, and he hesitated at the edge of the rocks, pausing to see that Sun Horse picked her up safely. The old man wheeled the horse in a sharp turn as he came even with the girl, bringing the animal's body between her and Tatum's men. He leaned over to gather her in his arms, and at that moment a movement in the corner of Julius's eye caught the black man's attention. From behind a rock a few yards away Jack Fisk rose on one knee, raising a pistol in Sun Horse's direction. As Julius turned to confront the danger he saw a second figure, farther away. It was Tanner, and the rifle in his hands was coming to bear on Julius.

There was no time for decision. The Starr Army .44 in Julius's hand bucked once and Fisk pitched over, uttering a soft groan. Julius pivoted, thumbing the hammer back, and as he fired a second time, he felt a red-hot poker stab him in the left arm with enough force to spin him around and throw him to the ground. He heard the report of Tanner's rifle as he fell, and saw the puff of smoke from the barrel. He hit the ground rolling and came to rest in a prone position with his gun at the ready, but Tanner had dropped from sight. Hardeman was almost in the rocks and Lisa was running after him, and farther away Sun Horse galloped off with Amanda before him in the saddle, both of them apparently unhurt. Julius was cheered by the sight. But what had happened to Tanner? he wondered.

Tanner was dead. Lisa had seen the danger to Julius and she had fired as he did. Like his shot, hers was true. Both bullets struck the bearded man at the same moment and Lisa knew from the way Tanner fell that he would offer no more trouble. She wanted to stop and help Julius but she saw him roll and take aim again and she kept on after Hardeman. Until Kinnean and Tatum were accounted for and Johnny Smoker safe, the fight would not be over.

Kinnean didn't intend that it should end as Lisa hoped. Only moments had passed since Amanda ran for safety. From his vantage point in the rocks he had watched the ensuing events without taking part. He had seen Tanner die, Julius Ingram wounded, Fisk shot for a second time and maybe dead too, and the girl whisked away by the old Indian, and through it all he had kept his gun steady on Johnny Smoker. The youth offered him his sole chance to escape. When the gunplay ended there would be a stalemate once more if Kinnean still had a hostage. But there was something else he wanted, something he had put off for too long, and if he had to choose between escape and fulfilling that old obligation, he didn't know what he would do.

"Drop it, Kinnean."

Moving very slowly, Kinnean rose to his feet, Hardeman was a few yards to his right, crouched in the same stance he had assumed in the sudden gunplay back in Putnam's Park on the day the circus arrived, but the scout had only one hand today and he preferred to shoot with two. They were evenly matched, two one-armed men. Hardeman's Colt was aimed at Kinnean's midsection. Twenty feet behind Hardeman, Lisa Putnam came to a stop, holding her Winchester at waist level. It too was pointed at Kinnean. The circus men had reached the rocks now and they halted when they saw the motionless figures with guns trained. From down the canyon came a rush of hoofbeats, and the band of Sioux warriors swept into view, recalled by the firing. They drew near, saw the standoff, and reined in their ponies. Suddenly the canyon was quiet.

To the onlookers it seemed that there was stillness and then there was motion, with no transition from one to the other. Kinnean's gun leaped toward Hardeman, the two pistols spurted flame with a thunderous roar, and stillness returned.

Kinnean lay on the ground, his eyes open but unseeing. Smoke curled from the muzzle of Lisa's carbine as well as Hardeman's Colt. Johnny Smoker straightened up, looking down at the body. The gun that Lisa had loaned him was still in his hand, unfired.

"Johnny!" Amanda came running headlong from the background, where Sun Horse had set her down, but she slowed when she saw that Johnny was all right. He moved to meet her and when he reached her he touched the bruise on her cheek with his free hand.

"Are you all right?" he asked, and she nodded, her hurts forgotten. She was moved beyond words to find him returned to her unharmed.

"Chris." Lisa spoke softly but even the Indians across the river heard her, and they saw what she saw. A half-dozen paces to Hardeman's left, Hachaliah Tatum had risen from behind a rock. He was holding his nickel-plated Colt and his desperate eyes swept the gathering as if searching for a target.

Johnny stepped protectively in front of Amanda.

Hardeman's gun moved in a short arc and found Tatum. The hammer came back with an audible click and the muzzle trembled almost imperceptibly.

Tatum blanched. "Don't shoot, Hardeman. Look, here's my gun." He lowered the hammer gently and tossed the gun into the snow.

Hardeman remained as he was and the moment lengthened, and then slowly, like a man in a daze, he lowered the gun and dropped the hammer back to half cock. He felt the anger leave him, the trembling rage that overtook him whenever another man forced him to kill. There had been no need for Kinnean to die, and the senseless death sickened him. Why had the man challenged him? Over an incident that was a month in the past? There had been more to it than that. He had seen Kinnean's expression just before he made his move, and he had recognized the look of a man who didn't care if he lived or died. The look reminded Hardeman of Hickok's, that day in Cheyenne not so long ago. "I've done my scouting," Hickok had said, and he seemed to be saying that the times had passed him by. Was that how Kinnean had felt today—like a man who saw no place for himself in the coming scheme of things? Fifty years before, he might have been a trapper like the Putnams; not so long ago he might have been a scout like Hickok, like Hardeman himself. But he was a younger man; a violent man who hadn't found a way to live as he wanted to live, beyond the edge of civilization, where he would carry the whole weight of his life and death on his own shoulders, sharing it with no one. Lacking sufficient reason to live, he had chosen to die.

Hardeman looked at the crumpled figure in the buffalo coat. Kinnean's bowler hat had rolled a short distance in the snow and come to rest. The snow on the crown was melting, leaving tiny drops of water, perfectly round. Soon they would freeze. The warmth of a man's life was ebbing from the hat as it ebbed from his body.

Hardeman turned away from the corpse, unwilling to look at it any longer. There had been too much dying today. He walked through the onlookers as if they were so many trees and he let the Colt drop from his hand. He was tired and his shoulder hurt. He wanted to sleep until he could forget the dying, but the memory of Kinnean's visage was before him still and he knew he would never forget it, for he saw himself reflected there as if in a looking glass. He was not so different—always searching, never satisfied. He had better find his own reason for living soon, someplace where there were few opportunities to kill or be killed.

Lisa and the others watched him go. Behind them, believing he was unnoticed, Tatum took a step forward and reached for his gun. Here in the wilderness, far from the places where he belonged, he had been stripped of all his possessions. He was powerless even to save himself now that his last pawn had been taken, and like a wounded animal he lashed out in desperation, directing all his anger at the one who had brought him to this end.

But there were two in the crowd who had not forgotten the circus master.

Seven years of traveling with Chris Hardeman had trained Johnny to be wary when Chris turned his back on danger. He was not aware that he had kept watch, but he saw Tatum move and he saw in his eyes the willingness to kill that marked a dangerous man. A moment before, faced by Chris's gun, that willingness had been absent, but now that his enemy's back was turned, Tatum sought revenge for his humiliation.

Johnny raised his gun and the weapon felt strangely familiar in his hand. As a child of the Cheyenne he had handled pistols and been instructed in their use by the men, before his dream. Since then he had seen Chris shoot a pistol countless times, both during long hours of practice in remote places where the shooting would not be heard, and on the rare occasions when Chris had drawn in self-defense. Johnny had always watched the movements carefully, acquiring the feeling of gunmanship without the actual experience, and the position he adopted now was a near-perfect imitation of Hardeman's two-handed shooting stance. His thumb drew back the hammer as the sights came into view and he felt his finger tighten on the trigger, but he hesitated. Tatum was not aiming at Chris. He was turning, his eyes on Johnny, it seemed. Johnny was surprised and the surprise delayed him, but only for an instant. Something moved on his left, someone approaching as if to stop him from shooting. He pulled the trigger.

It was Amanda who moved toward Johnny, but not to prevent him from shooting. She had kept her eyes on Tatum ever since the moment he appeared; she had seen the malice in his gaze when he looked at her and she feared what he still might do. He had nothing more to lose, except his life. She knew he would try to hurt her, and when he moved to pick up his gun, she was certain he hoped to inflict the greatest hurt of all. He was going to shoot Johnny!

She had to stop him! Johnny had saved her life once already, and today he had risked his own to save her again. He was the source of her strength. Near him, her courage had returned. He was her example and her hope, and she would do anything to protect him!

Hardeman's gun lay at her feet where he had dropped it as he passed by. She bent and scooped it up, fumbling to grasp it with her heavy gloves. Already Hachaliah's gun was in his hand and he was bringing it to bear. Amanda struggled to draw back the hammer of Hardeman's Colt, but the mainspring was strong and her small thumb was too weak to bend it. She tried to use both thumbs, but as she shifted her grip the gun slipped from her fingers and fell, and there was no more time.

Moving with all the grace she displayed on the tightrope, Amanda stepped forward to place herself in front of Johnny. She felt light on her feet. Her eyes met Hachaliah's and she saw his triumph, but it was a mean emotion and no match for her own. Johnny would live and the greater triumph would be hers, for in the act of saving him she knew, if only for a moment, the joy of an unselfish love.

Two shots blended into one, and as Johnny's bullet struck Tatum in the chest, Amanda met the other, which Tatum had intended for her all along.

Book Four

LISA PUTNAM'S JOURNAL

Sunday, April 2nd. 6:40 a.m.

Today the circus and the cavalry are off, and with their departure I will feel that we are done with healing the wounded and burying the dead. The account of the pursuit that I wrote in these pages two days ago has helped me to move beyond the dreadful events of that day, but I am still living from moment to moment.

Lt. Whitcomb and his men will conduct the circus to Fort Fetterman, and with the present uncertain state of things he believes the army will provide them an escort to the railroad at Rawlins.

Yesterday Sun Horse came to the park with Blackbird. The boy is able to sit a horse but I believe his leg still pains him considerably. They brought eight horses which they presented as a gift to Lt. Whitcomb, much to his astonishment. Thus all his men will be mounted when they leave here today, and Lt. Whitcomb has seen at least one instance (two, counting the Indians' aid in our ill-fated attempt to rescue Amanda) in which the "hostiles" have acted to promote brotherhood between the races. It was Sun Horse's visit that gave me the idea for the letter to General Crook. I have written it this morning and I will give it to Lt. Whitcomb before he leaves. In it I have told the general of our friendship with Sun Horse and much more, and I dare to hope this may help protect Sun Horse and his people through whatever is to come.

Almost to a man the soldiers have found opportunities to take me aside and express their personal sorrow for Uncle Bat's death. They have been solicitous and kind, and I cannot regard them as my enemies. Their health is much improved. The sight of a potato is a miracle to them, and the somewhat monotonous meals we have been able to offer them have been proclaimed unqualified culinary delights. They have all gained weight and recovered good color in their four days here, and they have helped with calving, those that have experience in such matters, while the rest of the able-bodied have assisted in many small ways with the ranch work and done what they could to prepare the circus for its journey. From their ranks the burial detail was drawn. They interred their fallen commander with such military honors as they could muster, after which we read a few words over Mr. Tatum, Kinnean, Tanner and Morton. For all our bitter feelings towards these men we felt compelled to give them a Christian burial, and we brought them home to spare ourselves the delay of burying them where they fell. Mr. Fisk and Tom Johansen will be taken to Fort Fetterman, where, I imagine, Mr. Fisk's wounds will require further tending. Neither Fisk nor young Tom could shed any light on what transpired between Mr. Tatum and Amanda before he abducted her, and I believe they are ignorant of those events. Whatever crimes Hachaliah Tatum may have

651

committed, they died with him, and no charges will be brought against his henchmen.

Amanda is on the knoll with my parents. Johnny allowed Julius and Mr. Chalmers and Hutch and Chatur to assist him in preparing the grave. After the service there, which was attended by everyone in the settlement, Johnny and Mr. Hardeman gathered their few belongings and went to join the Sun Band. How long they will remain there, and whether we shall see them again, I do not know.

Do you who read these pages live in a gentler time? Is violent death a stranger to your experience? I hope so. But whatever manner of life you lead, you will eventually know the necessity for grief. On the way home, the moments I found most difficult were when I looked into Johnny's face. Somehow I was more deeply wounded by his sorrow than my own. It seems only natural to me that Uncle Bat should risk his life to save a friend, but over and over again in my mind's eye I see the step Amanda took to place herself in front of Johnny. I saw her face at that moment and it stays with me as clearly as a portrait. She was as calm as if she were performing before a rapt audience. She was serene.

CHAPTER

FORTY-FIVE

The sun shone brightly over the eastern ridge and the morning was springlike as the circus prepared to leave. The yard had been churned into a sea of mud by wheels and hooves and booted feet as the wagons were put in line.

"We're gonta miss you folks," Julius said as he shook Joe Kitchen's hand. The Negro's left arm was bound in a sling.

"What will you do now?" Lisa asked Chalmers. Lydia stood with the Englishman, hugging his arm. Her eyes were red-rimmed, and wet with tears. Already the others had said their goodbyes to Lisa and Julius and taken their places in the wagons. Not for away, Hutch stood at Rama's side, talking with Chatur, who was atop the elephant's shoulders. Maria Abbruzzi approached Hutch and took his hand. The small band of cavalry was formed in a column of twos at the head of the caravan.

"We hope to keep our engagements in Salt Like City and San Francisco," Chalmers replied. "After that, I am not certain."

"Soon as we get to a telegraph, we'll wire Colonel Hyde," Joe Kitchen explained. "He's the money man in 'Frisco. We still got a circus here, and a good one. If he'll put up the place, we'll put up the show."

"There is some talk that we might try to keep the show together and manage it ourselves," Chalmers added, and Lydia nodded hopefully.

"Amanda would like that," Lisa said.

Chalmers was quiet for a moment. "She would, wouldn't she. Then we will have to do our best to make it so."

Lieutenant Whitcomb trotted back from the head of his troop. "Mr. Chalmers? We're ready if you are."

"At your pleasure, Leftenant." Chalmers turned to Harry Wo, who had stood by silently throughout the farewells. "I relinquish my arm-wrestling crown to you, my friend. You are champion once more."

Harry made a slight bow and shook the giant's hand. "You and me, we know who the real champ is." He gave Chalmers a wink.

Chalmers retrieved Lydia from Lisa's arms, where the Gypsy woman had sought comfort for a last time as she allowed her tears to flow freely once more. He helped her to the seat of the lead wagon before climbing up beside her and taking the reins.

Whitcomb cantered to the front of the column and raised a hand over his head, dropping it forward as he took his place beside First Sergeant Dupré. "Forward!" he called, and it struck him that it was the first time he had used the gesture and the command, which he had practiced over and over in front of the looking glass in his room at West Point. He had always imagined that there would be a full-strength troop behind him, the men smart in their field uniforms, with weapons at matching angles over their shoulders, the column of fours starting off in precise step across a landscape of cactus and dust under a bright sun, with the guidons fluttering in the breeze and perhaps even the regimental band along to provide marching music. He had thrilled to the image then, but now he felt no particular emotion.

He could not imagine their return to Fetterman. Fetterman was something that existed only in a dream, a hazy memory from a previous life. This was all that was real—Dupré and McCaslin and his handful of men, and this valley where the Lost Platoon had found escape from Purgatory. Here they had been forgiven their sins; neither whites nor Indians had held them to blame for the deaths they had caused, perhaps because they too had lost one of their own. They were healed now, and their spirits restored. When they left this place behind, everything would be discovered anew.

Whitcomb wondered if he would ever absorb everything he had learned on his first campaign. Just when he was certain he could never be surprised again, Sun Horse had come with his gift of horses, and Whitcomb had been struck speechless once more. Had the old chief done it merely to speed the soldiers from his land or had he been motivated by nobler feelings? In acting to save the girl, it seemed he had been moved by simple human compassion; could it be that he felt a similar compassion for his enemies when he found them in distress? If so, what other feelings might he harbor that neither white soldiers nor politicians dreamed could exist in a savage heart? "Tell Three Stars the horses are for him," Sun Horse had said. "Tell him the Sun Band wants peace."

653

Perhaps everything Whitcomb had learned could be reduced to a single lesson—that the common wisdom about the conflict on the frontier was woefully inadequate preparation for experiencing it firsthand. The realities were far more complex. He felt that he might try for the rest of his life to learn about the western regions and their aboriginal inhabitants and still know only a fragment of the truth. Even so, he would try. What had General Crook said? *Over the years our instincts become tempered by experience.* Whitcomb had followed his instincts and he had survived thus far, and given the opportunity and the time, he would hone those instincts and temper them with the wisdom of experience. He would learn what he could of the Indians and their land, and with luck he might have a hand in bringing the conflict to an end.

The caravan was nearing the bend in the road where the stand of pines sheltered the settlement's little graveyard. Whitcomb's eyes found Corwin's marker, set apart from the rest. He could not read the lettering but he knew what it said, for he had chosen the words himself.

> *Bvt. Major Francis Corwin*
> *Co. E, 3rd U.S. Cavalry*
> *Died 28 March, 1876*
>
> *Laid to rest by his men,*
> *who owe him their lives.*

Julius Ingram had promised to whittle the edges of the lettering in his spare moments, so it would still be legible when the paint faded.

"Eyes right!" Whitcomb ordered, and he held a salute while the troop rode past the grave.

Lisa and Julius watched the caravan pull away from the settlement and then they turned and strolled together to the corral fence, where Harry and Hutch were harnessing the work horses to the hay sled. Feeding the cattle had been delayed past its usual hour so everyone could be on hand for the farewells.

Lisa wore her riding clothes. Soon she would ride through the meadow to look over the calves but just now she felt no urgency to be on her way. For the first time in a long time there was no urgency about anything.

Ling Wo stepped out of the kitchen entryway and came toward the corral, and Lisa realized that the five of them were the only ones left in the settlement. We're six now, she corrected herself. Ling carried little Jed in her arms. Jedediah Batson Wo had been born on the night after Amanda and Bat Putnam died. The birth had been long but not difficult, and was attended by Greta Waldheim and Lydia. When Lisa and the others returned on the following day, having spent the night beside the trail when darkness overtook them on the way home, they found Ling in the kitchen proudly nursing her son while Harry and Ben Long prepared dinner. The soldiers and circus men had arrived late the evening before, bringing word of Bat's death, but the news that Amanda too had died occasioned a new round of grieving, and and in the midst of their woe, circus and settlement folk alike had found themselves visiting the newborn infant in a stream; they wished to touch and hold him, and he was a comfort to them all.

The proud father had waited until the next morning to take Lisa aside and impart to her his thoughts about his son's birth. "My son is American," he had announced. "I wish to become a citizen some day, but my son is born American and I am proud for him. My people have a long history. Many thousand years. The Chinese people are a great people, but that life was not good for me. I am not a man to bow to others. I am a proud man. The Christian God says it is a bad thing to be proud. If my son follows the Christian God he may come to believe that. But I am a proud man. I have done something that is not possible for most Chinese men: I have begun a new life. You made that possible, you and your father. I will teach my son to honor you, not by bowing, but in the American way, as one friend honors another. The life you have given to me, I will give to my son. He is American, and today I am proud for him."

Suspecting that Harry must have rehearsed his speech carefully did not lessen its effect on Lisa, and in sharing his joy she began the process of healing her sorrow.

"Don't know how I can cook just for us," Ling said now, rocking the infant gently in her arms. He was sound asleep, wrapped in a woolen baby blanket that had been Lisa's.

"I reckon to get hungry three times a day, just like before," Julius said. He peered at the sleeping infant. "Don't let that child take a chill." He walked off toward the barn to find some work a one-armed man could do. Tanner's bullet had shattered one of the bones in Julius's forearm. Sun Horse had treated the wound at the scene and Corporal Atherton and Sergeant Dupré had inspected it later. Atherton had told Lisa privately that he doubted the colored man would regain full use of the arm.

Harry and Hutch were done harnessing the team. Ling joined her husband and they talked softly. In the meadow the cows were bawling, but they would be fed soon enough. Harry reached within the folds of little Jed's blanket and stroked his son's face.

"It's so quiet," Lisa said to no one. In the pigpen the pigs were snorting happily, reveling in the mud. The geese waddled into the yard in a group, making small sounds to themselves, the first time this year that they had ventured so far from the springpond. In the willows, blackbirds chattered. The pigs, the geese, the birds, all were normal sounds of the valley in springtime, but Lisa noticed them now for the first time. There had been other sounds here recently, other voices filling the silence; she had grown accustomed to them, and suddenly they were gone.

In a few days the strange caravan would be at Fort Fetterman. In another week the circus could be on the Pacific shore.

She wondered how soon her letter would reach General Crook. Lieutenant

Whitcomb's parting words before he mounted his horse had made it easy for her to ask the favor of him.

"My men and I are in your debt, Miss Putnam," he had said. "I wish there were some way we could repay you."

"There is something," she had said, taking the letter from the pocket of her coat. "You can give this letter to General Crook. Before you attacked that village, Sitting Bull and Crazy Horse had agreed to a peace plan; if they may keep some of this country and have an agency here, there need be no more fighting. I have told the general what I know of the plan and begged him to consider it. I have also told him about Sun Horse. He has influence with the other chiefs. He could be a great help in making peace."

Whitcomb had shown no surprise. "I'll see that the general gets the letter, ma'am. And I will tell him what happened here, including Sun Horse's part in it. My report will include the gift of the horses, and your own generous assistance. Mr. Hardeman also told me of the peace plan in some detail. He asked me to set it before the general myself. Your letter will help me do that. Mr. Hardeman offered to act as an intermediary with the hostiles, if the general should want to use him in that capacity."

It was the first Lisa had heard of Hardeman's message to Crook and the offer to serve as go-between. She wondered if it meant he intended to stay with the Sun Band even after they left their winter valley, but Whitcomb had said nothing more and she had not dared to ask.

Still he wanted peace and he would work for it if he could. And after that, what?

The caravan had reached the stand of pines by the graveyard. As the soldiers rounded the bend in the road, their faces were turned toward the graves.

Lisa had asked Lieutenant Whitcomb to tell her about Major Corwin and he had poured out the story, all unsuspecting. He told her how Corwin had saved them in the battle, getting them away safely and starting them on the trail south, and he told her what he knew of Corwin's career before the present campaign. When he was done, she had asked a question.

"Was he married?"

"Yes, ma'am. He had a wife and daughter. The girl's name was Elizabeth, I believe. They died in Arizona."

And so Lisa had learned what her own fate might have been, but for the grace of God and her own stubbornness. Whitcomb hadn't told her how Corwin's wife had died, nor had she told him that Boots Corwin was the young lieutenant with tired eyes who had ridden into Putnam's Park and into her life in the summer of her twenty-fifth year. It was his eyes that had first caught her interest, and the way he concealed his wound that won her heart. It was a wound of the spirit, not the body, inflicted in no single moment but over the course of two years in a Confederate prison, his career held in limbo while his more fortunate comrades were promoted beyond him and went on to win victories and make names for themselves. Lisa had healed his wound and she had rejoiced to see the change

656

in him, but she had refused his offer of marriage and stayed behind in Putnam's Park, tied to the land.

She felt once more the shock and grief that had nearly overcome her down on the Powder's south fork, when she had first recognized Corwin's body. She turned suddenly away from the sight of the graveyard and the pines and the caravan growing smaller in the distance, thinking to go to her parents' graves to seek the comfort she often took in that place, but she had forgotten the new marker there. A broken violin leaned against the fresh wooden cross. Julius had put Amanda's fiddle on the grave before breakfast, when he thought no one was watching.

Lisa felt a sudden rage. Everywhere around her there were reminders of death! She had had too much of death! It was life she wanted! She wanted to seize it with both hands and wring from it every drop of pleasure and work and satisfaction, all the sheer *living* it contained! And above all she wanted to share it. Eight years after Boots Corwin rode out of her life she had found another man. Like the first, she had healed him in a time of need, and like the first he had risen from her arms and left her. Even before he left she had felt betrayed, remembering Corwin, but she knew she had only herself to blame. By restoring his strength she had made it all the more likely that he would leave, and she refused to use tricks to hold him. In a way it was easier for her this time; she gave no thought to leaving the land. It might be taken from her by events beyond her control, but she would stay as long as she could. If a war forced her to abandon her home, she would go. But only when that ragged piece of deerskin marked with Indian pictographs and Jedediah Putnam's name became worthless. Only when her sole remaining patrimony was what she carried in her breast, the rest gone to become part of the public domain, to be homesteaded and cut up and fenced and squabbled over. Until then she would cling to her home and her life the way the Indians clung to theirs.

She stomped through the mud to the barn and saddled her horse, and as she led him back out into the sunshine she saw the valley anew, and remembered the lines of poetry her father had given her on her twenty-first birthday. *Of thee, O earth, are my bone and sinew made; to thee, O sun, I am brother. Here I have my habitat. I am of thee.*

Perhaps Boots Corwin might still be alive if he had left the army and stayed in this place. It was a life-giving place. Here a man could prove himself and find his true rewards, as her father had done. And Jed Putnam had returned as much to the little valley as he took from it. It had more to give! Would no man ever have the sense to stay?!

She mounted the horse, her jaw set and her expression hard. Some day a man would come, and if none did she would still take her satisfaction from this life, together with Julius and Harry and Ling and any others that chose to accept what Putnam's Park offered.

"Miss Lisa?"

Hutch was approaching her. Behind him, Harry was waiting on the sled.

"There's somethin' I been wantin' to say," the boy began, coming to a stop beside her and looking at his feet. "Everything kept gettin' in the way of it, and now's as good a time as any, I guess. When I first come here, you and me just talked about me workin' through the winter, but I'll be stayin' on a while, if you'll have me." He looked up hopefully, awaiting a reply.

Lisa's anger left her and she blinked to clear a film of water that came suddenly to her eyes, despite the lack of wind. She managed a smile. "I'd like that."

Hutch smiled too, and then he said, "Well, those cows are pretty hungry. I guess we better get 'em fed." His proprietary concern both amused Lisa and touched her. She had wished for a man with the sense to stay in Putnam's Park and one had come to her. He was young, and he was not the man who would share her life, but he was willing to stay, and by his simple expression of that willingness he made it possible for Lisa to believe that winter would finally end and spring would come, and after that there would be summer and fall and another winter, and then another spring and more new calves being born, all waiting in store for her.

Her horse snorted and shied as Rufus the house cat came racing out of the barn with a barn cat in hot pursuit. Rufus had been gone from the Big House all night, hunting in the dark. His emergence from hibernation was a sure sign of spring.

Lisa touched her heels to the horse's flanks and trotted out of the yard ahead of the hay sled. When she reached the wagon road she urged the horse into a canter. She felt the wind in her face and smelled the scent of the pines and the sunshine in the air. She wanted to get back to the house in time to make something special for the midday meal. Buffalo and potatoes were wearing a bit thin. She wanted something festive, so her crew wouldn't feel the letdown of being left so alone. The peaches, that was it! She had saved a tin of peaches. She would make a cobbler. And this afternoon she and Hutch would move the new calves out of the heifer lot. He would enjoy that.

The caravan had reached the foot of the valley. One by one the wagons entered the gap and then they were gone.

LISA PUTNAM'S JOURNAL

Friday, April 28th. 6:15 a.m.

I have been irregular of late about my writing. After the fateful events of last month, it has been comforting that recent weeks have been so ordinary, offering so little of note to write about.

The weather continues cool and the grass is greening slowly. I would think that in another week the cattle could fend for themselves, although at this rate it will be a while longer before we put them out of the park, unless the sun shines more than has been his habit of late. All in all we have not done badly this year

658

once the early bouts of scours were over. The calves are doing well and the absence of any runts strengthens my belief in our breeding program. Julius and I have decided to buy a few new bulls this year and begin increasing the proportion of Shorthorn blood in the herd. It occurs to me that a time may come when we will want to eliminate the Longhorn strain altogether. We are going to have a look at Hereford stock when next one or the other of us has a chance to get to Cheyenne.

We fed the cattle double yesterday and this morning Julius and Hutch and I are going to say goodbye to the Sun Band. Day before yesterday I got up my courage and rode over the hill, which is how I learned that they would be departing for the north country today. Mr. Hardeman took me to see Uncle Bat's resting place. He seemed to know the way very well. It is on a high place overlooking the valley, within sight of the village. Little Hand's scaffold stands nearby. Bat's mare was killed and placed beneath him and his old rifle lies beside him, together with all the things he might need in his final journey. By now I imagine he has made his way to the spirit trail "beyond the pines." Surely after so many years with the Lakotas, his spirit will be admitted to their afterlife. It is a happy place, they say, where the grass is always green and the game plenty, and one sees all the relatives and friends who have gone before. I have come to believe in it almost literally, and although I am aware that it makes no sense at all, whenever I imagine Uncle Bat arriving there, I see my father waiting to greet him.

What with my visit to the camp and our ride together, Mr. Hardeman and I spent several hours in company with each other, but we spoke little. He and Sun Horse were very much at ease together. Johnny Smoker was quiet and reserved with me once more, but he appears to have found a new tranquillity. Twice orphaned by violence and denied his first love by that same agency, he seems to accept death as part of the natural order of things, against which it is futile to protest.

There has been no further sign of General Crook, nor has Sun Horse heard any word from the northern bands. It is as if the earth had opened and swallowed them all, soldiers and Sioux, save for the Sun Band. Sun Horse and his people continue in high spirits. The great change in them gives me as many new worries as it relieves, but I have no cause for complaint. I got what I hoped for. They will remain at liberty, at least for now, and so long as they are free there is hope.

CHAPTER

FORTY-SIX

The Sun Band was already starting off down the valley as the three riders drew near the Lakota campsite. Most of the people were walking beside the pony drags that bore all their possessions. They went at a leisurely pace, the horses pausing here and there to crop the tender shoots of new grass. Children and dogs raced up and down the caravan.

The day was cool and gray, the air still. In the woods the snowbanks lingered, but they were smaller than those in Putnam's Park and the grass here was greener.

Hard-packed circles of bare ground marked the ring where the tipis had stood all winter. Beyond the ring a small group of people and horses awaited the riders. Lisa made out Hardeman among them, and Johnny Smoker. Two days before, Hardeman's left arm had still been supported in a sling but today it hung free. Sun Horse was there with Standing Eagle and Penelope beside him. Blackbird held the horses, all but two. Lisa had given Hardeman the chestnut gelding he had ridden during the chase after Tatum and his men. Together with Hardeman's pack horse it was picketed nearby, saddled and packed for traveling.

A single lodge remained standing in the old camp circle. As the riders passed near, a figure rose from the buffalo robe in front of the entrance. "*Hau*, Julius!" Hears Twice called out cheerfully. "Come and smoke!" Behind him, Mist stepped out of the lodge to see the riders.

"Looks like he ain't goin' with the rest," Julius observed, and he spoke to Hears Twice in Lakota, saying he would return in a short while, once he had bid farewell to those who waited beyond the camp.

Sun Horse greeted the black man as he dismounted and inquired at once about the condition of his shattered forearm, reaching within the sling to feel it. Julius replied that the bone needed more time to heal but the wound no longer bothered him. The old Indian gently probed the arm with his fingers and only when he was satisfied that Julius felt no pain did he nod and turn to Lisa, smiling broadly.

"*Ho, chunkshí*," he said, taking both her hands in his own as always. Lisa smiled wanly, unable to speak. Hello, daughter, he had said, and she realized that having Sun Horse leave her now, if only for the summer, was like losing her last relative in the world. But it cheered her today, as it had two days earlier, to see how well he looked. He seemed to have grown younger in the past two months. In that time the circus had come and gone, a war had begun and many had died, both far to the north in Two Moons' village and on the plains below Putnam's

660

Park, and yet somewhere in these events, or despite them, Sun Horse had found an irrepressible joy.

"We do not come to this place again," he said, surprising Lisa both by his pronouncement and the fact that he spoke it in English. "Too close to the wagon road; too close to the soldier forts. Too easy for bluecoats to find us here. We go north to hunt. In the great council I will speak for peace. Next winter we stay there." He made a gesture to the north, the movement of his hand suggesting a country far away.

"I tried to make him see this is a good place for him," Hardeman said. "The army knows he gave horses to the soldiers and I told that lieutenant he'll speak for peace to the other headmen. No matter what happens to the other bands, he'd be safer here, out of the way." He looked at Sun Horse. He had made the same argument often in recent days, but he knew Sun Horse would not change his mind. "He's a stubborn old man and I told him so. He won't budge."

"We are Lakota," Sun Horse said. "Now we will live in the hoop of the nation. The hoop must be strong in bad times. It will need the strength of the Sun Band."

He spoke the simple words patiently to Hardeman, and Lisa realized that these two men understood each other perfectly. A bond of friendship had grown between them in a few short weeks, and they both seemed to take comfort from it despite their disagreements.

Penelope had stood silently by during this exchange and Lisa turned to her now, holding out her arms to her uncle's widow. Penelope ran into the offered embrace and the two women held each other for a long time, Lisa taking as much comfort as she gave. Sun Horse's news had numbed her. The sorrow would come later, and regret for all that was ending here today. When the embrace ended at last, Penelope kissed Lisa quickly on the cheek, observing the white custom, then turned and ran to her horse.

"I'll be saying goodbye too," said Johnny, offering Lisa his hand. "I'm grateful for all your kindness."

"You're going with them," she said, not as a question. From the disposition of the horses she had guessed that Johnny would go with the Indians while Hardeman went off alone. Somehow she wasn't surprised. She held Johnny's hand for a moment, then took him in her arms and hugged him tightly.

"I reckoned you'd be goin' off one way or another," Hutch said to Johnny when Lisa released him. "I'm glad I had the chance to know you."

"You keep up with the roping. You'll be a top hand in no time." They shook hands, and a general round of hand shaking commenced, in which Lisa and Julius and Hutch each shook hands with Standing Eagle and Blackbird and then with Johnny and Sun Horse again, and it seemed as if the leave-taking might go on for some considerable time. No one was willing to break it off until Standing Eagle took his horse from Blackbird and said a few words in Lakota to his father, gesturing toward the retreating village, which was nearing the lake at the lower end of the valley.

Hardeman stood apart, having already made his goodbyes. Always before he had been the one to ride away, never one of those who stayed behind, but for the first time in his life he was in no hurry to be gone. It seemed to him that he was surrounded by people, both living and dead, who could make up their minds with confident certainty about matters that would surely affect the rest of their lives, while he himself had no notion which way he would ride when he left this place, nor where he might spend the night. He felt like a stranger in such company. Hawk Chaser and Kinnean had chosen death; so had Bat Putnam, or even if he didn't choose it, he had accepted it. Sun Horse had turned his back on what was likely his last chance to go peacefully to Dakota and he looked happy about it. And when Hardeman and Johnny had been in the Lakota village for only a few days, Johnny had announced that he was staying with the Sun Band. He hadn't said that Amanda's death had turned his life upside down in the blink of an eye, nor had he put in words the simple fact that with the Sun Band he would be among people who knew of his loss and understood it. Sun Horse himself had helped Johnny build the pony drag that had carried Amanda's body back to Putnam's Park, and the wound her death had made upon the old man was plain to see. He and many others in the band had set great store by the clown girl, for reasons known only to themselves, and they shared Johnny's grief. In the white world, even with Hardeman, he would bear that grief alone. Maybe that was a good enough reason by itself for staying with the Indians, but Johnny had other reasons too, ones he had been more willing to talk about. His earlier conviction that he belonged in the white world seemed to him like no more than a passing fancy now, he had said, the selfish choice of a young man who wanted to remain footloose forever. And there was no chance he would change his mind again, for Sun Horse had told him at last the full import of his dream. "With the Sioux I have the power to help the people," he had told Hardeman. "That's what Sun Horse says anyway. That's what the dream said. Maybe it's true and maybe not. I'd like it to be so."

And so the dream had recaptured the boy in the end, and Hardeman knew better than to fight it, although he had plenty of misgivings about Johnny's choice. Some time ago he had resolved to be as good a teacher for Johnny as Jed Putnam had been for him, turning him loose to try his luck in the world when he was ready to go. The resolve had been easy to keep when he thought Johnny would be safe with Amanda in the white man's world, but he couldn't go back on it now just because the boy might face danger with the Sioux. He reminded himself once again that Johnny was a boy no longer, but a man.

A man does what he must. It is for other men to understand and accept. Bat Putnam had taught him that.

Johnny and the Lakotas were mounted. Johnny met Hardeman's eyes but he said nothing. They had come to terms with this parting in their own fashion. Not being men much given to speaking their feelings, they had spent the last month recalling the years they had been together, sometimes talking far into the night over Sun Horse's lodge fire, acknowledging the value of their companionship with each memory brought alive in the retelling.

Lisa stood close to Sun Horse, looking up at him. "If you ever come back, the valley will be here."

Sun Horse smiled at Lisa and shook his head. "A power brought me here. Now it takes me away." He looked around the valley, savoring the comfort of it for a last time, remembering the way it had looked in his vision. He would not see it again with the grasses tall and the flowers blooming. From this place he had watched the steady approach of the whites, had seen the impending collision of the two worlds. He had been given the power to understand the *washíchun*, and at last he had fulfilled the promise. In the time that remained to him he must act on what he knew, and so he must leave the watching place behind.

He spoke a few words of Lakota to Standing Eagle. The war leader drew a rolled piece of deerskin from his robe and passed it to Sun Horse. The headman glanced at Hardeman and gestured around the valley with the scroll. "This is a good place. I do not want the *washíchun* to cut the earth or make fences here. I want someone to take care of this place." He held out the scroll.

Hardeman hesitated, but the brown arm remained outstretched, insistent. Hardeman took the scroll and unrolled it. He held it at arm's length and looked it up and down. The top half was covered with Indian pictographs. The first drawing showed a man—a Sioux, by the feather in his hair and the choker around his neck. Above the man's head was a sun and a horse galloping. These things were connected to the man by a thin line. They represented his name: Sun Horse. The man handed something to another figure with a hat. A white man. There were some trees and a circle of tipis, and a stream flowing to a lake. More drawings followed. Below, in carefully lettered English, the scroll proclaimed: *Sun Horse gives the valley of the Sun Band to the whiteman scout, Christopher Hardeman.*

Numb with surprise, Hardeman handed the hide to Lisa.

"The one that died writ it fer y'," Standing Eagle explained.

"He means Bat," Johnny added, smiling.

"That's truth," said the war leader. "He reckoned you knew poor bull from fat cow. Said you knew good pasture when you seen it and savvied some about cattle. This child don't know such. Don't aim to." He looked Hardeman up and down. "Dunno if'n he had you pegged right. Hope so." He turned and rode away, followed by Penelope and Blackbird.

With a last smile at Lisa, Sun Horse reined around and rode off after his son and daughter and grandson.

"Now hold on there," said Hardeman.

"I'll be seeing you," Johnny said, and he too rode away.

"I reckon I'll go and set a spell with Hears Twice," Julius announced. He turned to Hutch. "You want to seddown and smoke a pipe with a wild Sioux Indian, boy?"

"Sure thing!"

As the two of them led their horses away, Lisa looked from Sun Horse's departing figure back to the deerhide document. Sun Horse had planned the gift over a month ago! Bat had known of it, but he had not had time to tell her. He had written the deed before his death, just as he had written a similar deed long ago.

She passed the hide back to Hardeman. He inspected it again, holding it gingerly, as if it were alive and might do him harm. Slowly he rolled it up, looking down the valley.

Lisa followed his gaze. The five riders had broken into a lope to overtake the rest of the band. At the foot of the valley, beyond the lake, the main body of Indians was entering the trees. The horsemen reached the end of the column and two of them stopped. One raised a hand in a last farewell before riding out of sight.

Lisa and Hardeman stood for a long time, regarding the empty valley. Finally Lisa spoke.

"We both have worthless deeds now, Mr. Hardeman. Do you think we will keep our land?" She looked at him and he turned to face her, but he made no reply. Instead he gazed upon her as if seeing her for the first time. She met his gaze and she saw that there was a change in him. Like Sun Horse, he too seemed suddenly younger. And then she realized with a shock what had wrought the change. The searching look had left him. In its place was an expression of calm and contentment.

Back at the abandoned village site, Hutch puffed slowly on the pipe Hears Twice handed him, managing by a great effort not to choke. He was a little in awe of his own temerity. Wouldn't his ma split a gut if she could see him now, sitting on the ground smoking a pipe with a colored man and a wild Sioux Indian? She wouldn't understand at first, but he'd make her see it was all right.

The thought made him remember the letter he should have written months ago just to let her know he was still alive. He would write it soon. She'd be glad to hear he had found the work he was looking for. Oh, it was a small outfit, all right, but he'd tell her there was more than enough for a person to learn here. He'd tell her he had made good friends and was learning to rope and handle cattle, and all about the circus, except Maria Abbruzzi. He wouldn't tell his ma about that. He would tell her one of his friends had died and another was gone away. He had lost Old Joe, his mule, too. It hadn't been all high times, not by a long shot, but he would take it as it came, the good with the bad. He would tell his ma that, and she would understand.

Nearby, Mist was stirring up the fire beneath an iron pot hung on a tripod. They would all eat when the white scout and Lisa Putnam joined them, Hears Twice had said. He and his daughter were going to the reservation in Dakota when the weather warmed a bit more, he had explained, speaking his broken English for Hutch's benefit. He hadn't said why. Just now he and Julius were having a regular gabfest in Indian talk, the old man smiling and jabbering a blue streak, as if he'd forgot every reason he ever had for keeping quiet.

Hutch passed the pipe back and Hears Twice nodded as he took it. "It is good to smoke with friends," he said.

Across the camp, Hardeman and Miss Lisa were standing close together and Hutch could see that they were talking. He wondered what Hardeman would do about Sun Horse's gift of the valley. The piece of deerhide seemed a worthless sort of thing. Miss Lisa had said more than once of her own deed that any land office in the country would laugh out loud to see it.

The two figures turned to walk back toward Hears Twice's lodge and Hutch was surprised to see Hardeman put his arm around Miss Lisa. Her arm found its way around him, and as they drew near, Hutch saw that they were both smiling a small, private kind of smile, as if they had some secret reason to be happy.

Hears Twice gestured at the couple and said something that made Julius laugh. The old man grinned his gap-toothed grin and Mist smiled as she began to dish out the buffalo stew. Hutch wasn't sure just why everyone felt so good, but he smiled too.

CHAPTER
FORTY-SEVEN

Ham Whitcomb emerged from the post trader's store and started off toward the parade ground, keeping to the grassy areas and avoiding the muddy paths. He already wore the high moccasins he would wear during the campaign and he had just purchased a pair of buckskin pants to complete his outfit. Immediately on arriving at Fetterman he had sought out the scouts and inquired about the most practical garb for a summer campaign. "We jest follows the example o' the deer, General," Hank Hewitt had told him. "They wear their skin, 'n' so do we." After six weeks of garrison life at Fort D. A. Russell, Whitcomb was glad to be back at Fetterman and free to adopt whatever clothing he chose as Crook's enlarged command prepared to take to the field once more.

It was mid-morning on the twenty-eighth of May. The day was bright but cool, and a stiff wind held the flag out straight from the flagpole. Whitcomb enjoyed the sunshine, which had been in short supply throughout the long, cold spring.

On every side there was purposeful activity as the command prepared to set out on the morrow. It was a far cry from the dejected post Whitcomb and the Lost Platoon had found on their return from Putnam's Park. They had been astonished to learn that the rest of Crook's column had arrived back at Fetterman two weeks before them and was already dispersed to the various posts of the department, having fought no more engagements after the battle on the Powder. The arrival of Whitcomb and his men had caused quite a stir and set the telegraph lines humming, for they had been given up for dead. The presence with them of the traveling circus had also occasioned great interest, and Mr. Chalmers and his colleagues had given an impromptu performance for the post by way of thanks for the escort that Colonel Chambers, the post commandant, had insisted on providing for their journey to the railroad.

"Ham!"

Whitcomb turned to see John Bourke hurrying toward him. Bourke's thigh-length field blouse was unbuttoned and his boots were caked with mud. He held a packet of papers in one hand.

"Hello, John! You look as if you've been on campaign already."

Bourke grinned. "I've been traveling with General Crook, which is much the same thing. How have you been?" He pumped Whitcomb's hand with enthusiasm.

The two men had seen each other once since the March campaign, when Crook and his aide had stopped at Fort Russell. Bourke had obtained an audience with Crook for his friend, who had delivered to the general the messages from Hardeman and Lisa Putnam. Since then Whitcomb had remained at his post and he had little new to tell as he and Bourke exchanged recent news now. Bourke, in the meanwhile, had accompanied Crook on a journey to the Sioux reservation agencies in an attempt to recruit Sioux and Cheyenne scouts for the summer campaign. The attempt had failed due to a strong reluctance on the part of the agency Indians to take the field against their wild brethren, and Crook had been discouraged to find conditions on the reservation bad and getting worse.

"There's damn little food, Ham," Bourke said. "It's no wonder they'll risk sneaking off. At least in the Powder River country they may find some game. The hostiles have been reinforced, there's no doubt of that. We may have a lively time of it." He lowered his voice as a squad of men passed near. "How are you getting along with Sutorius?"

Whitcomb shrugged. "He's not much like Boots Corwin." Captain Alexander Sutorius had been released from his sobering confinement at Fort D. A. Russell and returned to command of Company E. In the absence of a new first lieutenant, Whitcomb was second-in-command.

"He has almost as much experience," Bourke said. "He's a good man if he stays clear of John Barleycorn. You should get along with him well enough in the field."

Whitcomb nodded. "I intend to."

"By the way, you might like to know that Anson Mills's report says that Corwin transferred command to you before he died, nothing more. You did a fine job, Ham. I mean that with all my heart. We're all proud of you. Oh, and a copy of Grant's letter has been put in your record. Crook saw to that."

Whitcomb was startled by the news. He had stated clearly in his report that he had assumed command on his own responsibility, well before Corwin had seen fit to pass the torch. The report was part of the permanent record, but the fact that Mills, Whitcomb's battalion commander, had chosen to overlook the insubordinate action meant it would almost certainly be forgotten. The deliberate omission would not have been possible without the good will of Dupré, McCaslin and Atherton, all of whom had made verbal reports to Mills on the Lost Platoon's adventures. The faith in him displayed by such worthy men made Whitcomb feel that he had been handed an additional burden of responsibility. As for the letter Bourke had mentioned, President Grant had written to General Crook after the campaign, referring to Whitcomb's feat in admiring terms. The retreat of the Lost Platoon had come to the President's attention in the newspapers, where it had been briefly celebrated. Whitcomb was well aware that such notice might accrue to his benefit, but he was embarrassed by all the praise, and especially that from Bourke, eight years his senior and a recipient of the Medal of Honor.

"I'll be glad to be on campaign again," Whitcomb said. "At least it will mean an end to all this fuss."

"Don't be bashful, old man!" Bourke exclaimed. "Opportunity knocked and you answered. You pulled a miracle out of your hat and saved half of E Troop."

"At the time, all I wanted to do was save my skin, believe me."

"And you did such a good job of it that you brought the men back with you and a train of circus wagons to boot. You should have seen the eyes pop in Omaha when we heard that story!" Bourke laughed, and Whitcomb laughed with him. "Between you and me," Bourke went on, "the general would have liked to promote you first lieutenant, but there was no way to do it. Length of service and all that. You understand. Still, you've made quite a name for yourself in a short time." He glanced at the packet in his hand. "Well, I've got to go. Morning dispatches for the general. Oh, I almost forgot." He dug in the pocket of his blouse. "There was a mail pouch late yesterday. I was looking through it and I found this." He handed Whitcomb a folded letter. "I'll see you tomorrow. We'll have more chance to talk once we're on the trail."

Bourke set off at a trot for the headquarters building where Crook had his temporary office, leaving Whitcomb staring at the letter. It was addressed in his father's handwriting. He opened it and read:

> My dear son,
>
>   I have received a letter from the Yankee general who calls himself the president. As you may well imagine, the opinions of Yankee generals count for very little with me, but from what he tells me, you have aquitted yourself with honor. In war there is no higher duty, next to following orders and gaining the victory, than caring for your men and bringing them safely out of danger. It seems that fortune has tested you and you have met the challenge.
>
>   I am proud of you, my boy.

It was signed, "Affectionately, your father."

"Lieutenant Whitcomb!"

Sergeant Dupré was waving to him from the post gates. The first sergeant's mustache was waxed once again, the points curling jauntily upward. "The troop is ready for inspection, sair! Captain Sutorius requests your presence."

Whitcomb placed the letter in his breast pocket and buttoned it carefully. "Coming, Sergeant."

"Ah, Mr. Bourke." Crook looked up as Bourke entered. The general's black-and-white border collie lay on the floor in front of his desk. The dog opened one eye and his tail thumped the floor at the sight of Bourke.

"Morning dispatches, sir."

"Anything significant?"

Bourke opened the packet and selected a telegram from the top of the pile. "The Gros Ventres told their agent that they were robbed of all their guns and powder when they went south of the Yellowstone to visit the Sioux."

"That means they traded the guns away."

Bourke turned to the next dispatch. "There are reports that another one hundred and fifty Sioux are not to be found at their usual camping place near the Red Cloud Agency. The agent claims they have gone hunting on the Missouri."

Crook snorted and scowled. "Where there is no game whatsoever. We know that and he knows it. I would like to pack all those agents in a wagon and bring them along with us. If there is to be more fighting, I would like them to see what their greed and incompetence have caused! It need not have come to this, you know." He accepted the sheaf of papers from Bourke's hand and began to leaf through them, his face clouded by a lingering frown.

Bourke remained discreetly silent. Ever since returning from the Dakota reservation, Crook's mood had been darker than usual, and he had ample cause for his anger. Rations at the agencies remained woefully inadequate, despite the general's frequent protests both to the agents and Washington City. There were persistent rumors of large bands moving west to join the hostiles, and while the command was off on its late-winter campaign, new scandals in the nation's capital had thwarted the army's hope of regaining control of Indian affairs. Secretary of War William Belknap had been accused of accepting a bribe of twenty-four thousand dollars to appoint a man named C. P. March to the position of post trader at Fort Sill, Indian Territory. Belknap had resigned in the face of certain impeachment, and "Belknapism" had been coined by the newspapers as a synonym for taking bribes. Congress had decided that the War Department was no more fit than Interior to manage the aborigines, and it had struck down the attempt to return the Indian Bureau to the army. On the frontier, Indian activities had increased as the spring advanced. Throughout April and May there had been nearly continuous raiding all along the far-flung borders of the Powder River country, until no one but large forces of armed troops could travel safely in these regions.

Crook held up a sheet of yellow foolscap. "Did you see this? It's the latest figures on the desertions."

Bourke nodded, withholding comment. Crook leaned back in his chair, regarding his aide thoughtfully. "I would be grateful to have your impression of the troops' morale, as compared with the start of our last campaign."

Bourke shook his head. "Not so good, sir. But it's better now that we're here and ready to go. The men will settle down. That's the impression I get."

Crook considered this for a moment, nodded, and returned to his reading.

Bourke hoped he had not been optimistic about the future behavior of the men. They had lost a great deal of faith in their leaders. Following the announcement of the new campaign there had been desertions from posts throughout the department. At the battle on the Powder, not only had part of E Troop been cut off as Reynolds' force withdrew, but the bodies of the dead had been left behind. Persistent rumors that a man had fallen alive into the hands of the enemy had not helped matters. The soldiers were reluctant to serve under officers that abandoned their men, living or dead, to the savage mercies of the Indians. Ironically, only one man, Private Donnelly, had deserted from E Troop itself, a fact that Bourke attributed to Whitcomb's standing with the men and his presence as second-in-command. Ham Whitcomb had emerged from his first campaign with a shining reputation, while heads far more exalted than his rolled about him. Colonel Reynolds and Captain Moore had been formally charged with misbehavior before the enemy, Moore for his failure to prevent the Indians from leaving the village and taking the high ground, and Reynolds because as the expedition's commander he shared responsibility for that failure and others as well, including the disordered withdrawal. The two men were absent from the reorganized command and would be tried by court-martial later in the year. Whatever the outcome, their careers would surely suffer. Captain Henry Noyes had also been charged; he had been tried at Fort D. A. Russell in April and found guilty of conduct to the prejudice of good order and discipline, a lesser offense. It seemed that he had unsaddled his troop during the battle and permitted the men to eat lunch. He was sentenced to be reprimanded by the department commander, but Crook had been lenient. Noting Noyes's excellent Civil War record, he had declined to make a formal reprimand and had placed him in command of five troops of Second Cavalry for the summer campaign, an action of which Bourke heartily approved. Detailed by Reynolds to capture the Indians' horse herd, Noyes had perhaps shown an error in judgment by remaining in the rear while the battle raged, but his testimony and that of others had made it clear that he had not intended to shirk his duty. Fortunately for him, General Crook was a fair man. He would hold any officer or enlisted man to account for a serious offense, but he reserved the harshest condemnation for failures at the level of overall command, where he believed the greatest responsibility lay.

Crook was nearing the bottom of the pile of dispatches. Bourke took a paper from his pocket and held it in his hands. Crook noticed the movement and looked up. "What's that you've got there?" he inquired.

"I was saving the best news for last, sir. Teddy Egan's done it again. He drove off six hundred warriors on the Black Hills road. He got there just as the Indians were attacking a party of miners and sent them running with just his own troop!"

"And of course those miners should never be allowed into the hills in the first place," Crook said with a trace of bitterness. "If there could be a worse example to the Sioux not to trust us, it is our conduct there. Within what is properly their land we are robbing them daily. No wonder their mood is ugly." He was incensed that troops he could have put to better use elsewhere were compelled to protect the miners on the Black Hills road, men whose presence and every action worsened the chance for peace.

Bourke leaned across the desk and leafed through the papers, plucking one from the pile. "You saw this one, sir? The raids have lessened in Nebraska and along the Platte. Surely that's good news."

"Possibly." Crook hoped it meant that the raiders were moving north, along with the six hundred Egan had encountered. He pulled his beard, one tail of the fork and then the other, as he reread another telegram. "Terry and Gibbon confirm their departures. That's something, anyway. Terry left Fort Lincoln on the seventeenth, and Gibbon is en route from Fort Shaw to Fort Ellis." He looked up at his aide. "Mr. Bourke, will you be so good as to find Colonel Royall and the chief of scouts and inform them that I will see them here at five o'clock this afternoon?"

"Sir."

Bourke saluted and left him. Crook leaned back in his chair and put his feet on the desk. It was a minor errand and not the sort he usually gave to Bourke. It could have waited until later, but he wished to be alone to think. Tomorrow he would be in the field, where action was everything, and this time he would succeed come hell or high water.

Three months ago he had hoped to end the war before the advent of spring. Now, under conditions far more favorable to the Indians, he faced a stronger enemy, thanks to the bungling of distant bureaucrats. "The Indian agents will never induce the hostiles to come in and surrender while the people at the agencies are starving!" Crook had informed Sheridan when the division commander had visited Omaha in April. "They can't even keep the Indians they have!" Sheridan had suggested that the reports of agency Indians making off to join the hostiles were exaggerated. "They have no horses," Sheridan had said. The policy of denying horses to the reservation Sioux was his, supporting his oft-expressed opinion that a Sioux on foot was a Sioux no longer. "The hostiles have plenty of horses," Crook had replied bitterly, "including twenty-three of mine."

The loss of the cavalry horses still rankled him. They had been stolen away from Reynolds' force on the night after the battle, along with the Indian ponies recovered by the hostiles. Reynolds had failed to post an adequate guard despite the obvious presence of the angry Indians, who had pursued him all the way to Lodgepole Creek. It was another failing for which Reynolds would be called to account, but at bottom Crook knew that he himself was responsible for the failure of the campaign. There was no doubt that it had been a failure, despite the trumpetings of success in the newspapers. "Crazy Horse's Village Attacked!" they had proclaimed. "One Hundred Lodges Destroyed! Hostiles Routed!" The papers had not said that the spirit of the hostiles remained strong and that the identification of the village was in doubt. Grouard admitted he had identified it as Crazy Horse's because of the presence of the Oglala lodges and some horses in the pony herd that he recognized as belonging to He Dog, Crazy Horse's good friend. He claimed to have seen one of Crazy Horse's favorite ponies too, but Little Bat Garnier had hunted with Crazy Horse and knew him well. He said if the Oglala had been there he would surely have been in the forefront of the fighting, but Little Bat had seen him nowhere. He said too that many of the hostiles were Cheyenne, not Sioux. Hardeman and the Putnam woman had told Lieutenant Whitcomb that the village was that of Two Moons, a peaceful Cheyenne. If that was true, and the Cheyenne now considered themselves at war, then Crook's fears of a renewed Indian alliance were realized.

If only he himself had commanded the attack force. . . . But he had given the opportunity to J. J. Reynolds, and Reynolds had failed him. If Moore had managed to hold the bluffs, Reynolds might have seen the wisdom of holding the village. By all accounts the Indian camp could have fed and sheltered the entire command until the arrival of summer and beyond! Reynolds' orders had been to strike the hostiles and destroy their shelter and supplies, but it was the job of a commander in the field to think for himself and to seize whatever opportunities came his way. Choosing to hold the village would have been within Reynolds' authority. Instead he had burned the village, and by that and his other actions he had guaranteed that the entire expedition would be forced to withdraw ignominiously from the country, leaving the field to the Indians.

Crook and the pack train had reached the rendezvous at Lodgepole Creek at noon of the eighteenth to find half the Indian horse herd already recovered by the hostiles and the spirit of Reynolds' men at low ebb. Their hunger and fatigue were to be expected, but many were without topcoats and gloves, these articles having been laid aside when the battle began and never recovered in the retreat, and sixty of the men were suffering from frostbite. Sixty cases of frostbite, after sixteen days of arduous marching without a single occurrence! Dr. Munn and Steward Bryan had done their best to alleviate the suffering, but with limited success.

With supplies short and so many men unfit for battle, Crook had had no choice but to continue south along the Powder to Fort Reno, pursued by bands of hostiles who fired into the night camps, once again convinced they were lords of the intermountain west. To prevent them from recovering the remaining horses, Crook had ordered the Indian ponies shot. At Reno he had given brief consideration to resupplying his able-bodied men and turning back, but reports from Lieutenant Bourke and Surgeon Munn had persuaded him of the futility of such an attempt. The injured would need a strong escort to assure their safe arrival at Fetterman, and the loss of part of Company E had been a blow to morale. There was a deep unease among the men, Bourke had reported. They no longer trusted their officers. Crook could not restructure his command in the field and so he had bowed to the inevitable and returned to Fetterman.

Court-martialing Reynolds was a necessary evil, but it could not erase the greater evil that had already been done. With the retreat of the soldiers and the recovery of their horses, the hostiles no doubt felt that they had won the

671

day. Now, armed with the new weapons for which by all accounts they had been eagerly trading all spring, and strengthened by new arrivals from the agencies, they would be hot to prove their mettle against any soldiers that dared to enter their domain. The end result of the March campaign, then, had been to increase not only the Indians' will to fight, but their capacity to do so as well.

Crook had planned his strategy accordingly, but it was based on his own reading of the savage mind and so was fraught with dangers. This was the time of year when the Indians customarily grouped together to hunt and dance their savage dances, and he assumed that this year would be no different. With the coming of the warm months the hostiles would move north to gather in the lower reaches of their Powder River stronghold. There they would council to discuss the events of the spring and plan what to do. Emboldened by their "victory" over Colonel Reynolds, would they be confident enough to go about their summer hunt as usual? Crook sincerely hoped so, for based on his guesswork and assumptions, he had taken a tremendous risk in order to bring the strongest possible force into the field. He had stripped bare the posts throughout his command, and left them garrisoned with skeleton guards of infantry. Every able-bodied cavalryman in the Department of the Platte was here at Fetterman, nine hundred of them, and two hundred and fifty infantry. There were twelve hundred horses and three hundred thousand rounds of ammunition. Without the need to carry forage for the animals, without the cumbersome clothing and extra bedding demanded by a winter campaign, his men were at long last on a truly equal footing with their foe. How Terry's and Gibbon's forces were outfitted, he did not know, but his own men were prepared to live off the land. Oh, he had supplies in profusion now. Two hundred teamsters and packers; a thousand mules; a small beef herd at Sheridan's insistence; six hundred thousand pounds of varied provisions. But unlike the March campaign, he could leave it all behind if the occasion demanded. Not just for two weeks but indefinitely, and he was prepared to do just that.

If his assumptions were wrong, what then? If the hostiles had not regrouped in the north, if they remained scattered in small bands and if the raiders that had appeared everywhere in droves during the past two months were merely lurking in the hills and planning their next attack, they would find easy pickings along the Platte and George Crook would bear the blame. But if his calculations were right, the Indians would be surprised in the heart of their buffalo country by the three columns that would soon converge from Dakota and Montana and Fort Fetterman. If Terry and Gibbon did their share, the effect of the combined forces could be overpowering.

Crook picked up the report of Terry's and Gibbon's departures from their respective forts and read it again to reassure himself that both commanders were truly in the field. He had sent a request for this confirmation two days before and it had arrived in time. Neither man had set foot on the trail in

March, although Colonel Brisbin, of Gibbon's command, had ventured as far as Fort Pease to evacuate the garrison there, which had been under constant attack by the hostiles. The weather had been too severe for an extended campaign, Terry had said later. Crook snorted. The weather had not been too severe for his troops of the Second and Third Cavalry. At least the others were on the move now. And Custer was riding with Terry after all, although as his subordinate. As Crook had expected, Custer's testimony before the House committee investigating corruption in Indian affairs had aroused President Grant's fury, and until the eleventh hour it had appeared that Grant would keep the Boy General from joining the campaign. In the end, Custer had written to the President personally, begging that he be spared the disgrace of seeing his regiment march without him. Terry, Sheridan and Sherman himself had endorsed the request, and Grant, ever the old soldier, had relented. Custer would be hot for the smell of powder now and anxious to redeem himself.

At first Crook had thought the split command was lunacy. Once he and Terry and Gibbon were all in the field, communication among them would be next to impossible until—if and when—they joined forces. But at least the orders left him free, answerable only to himself, and now he saw that they suited him perfectly. The others might weary of the campaign if it failed to produce spectacular victories, but he would keep at it. He had learned long ago that when there was a dificult task to be done, he had better prepare to do it himself without depending overmuch on others, and it was with this in mind that he had taken the risk and assembled here the largest force he could muster. This time he would not leave the field without obtaining a resolution. He would continue through the summer and into autumn and winter if need be, and in time the Indians would submit.

That was how the war must end. Before there could be any hope of a lasting peace, the white man must feel he had won the victory. Nothing less would satisfy him. There could be no parleys, no negotiated settlement that seemed to condone or justify the intransigence of the hostiles. All the recent events— the constant raiding, the fevered newspaper reports of every incident, every rumor, the uproar over the Black Hills gold and the demands that something "be done" about the Indians—had created a climate in which there could be only one outcome: there must be a surrender. There might be a single big battle or a series of small ones, but sooner or later the hostiles must yield to the military force and then the public attention would turn elsewhere. The Indians, now pacified, would be forgotten, as they were always forgotten once the alarums of war died away. And that was when Crook might achieve what he had sought all along, a just peace for the Sioux, with fair terms and promises kept, resulting in benefits to both peoples. "It is absurd to speak of keeping faith with Indians," Phil Sheridan had proclaimed more than once, but Crook knew that Sheridan was fatally wrong. Only by keeping faith could the peace endure, and even without that practical consideration, honor would permit no other course.

The campaign would be long and hard. If there were no swift victory the nation would soon tire of reports from the battleground, and when the final surrender came, the public would embrace any terms that brought a secure peace. Crook no longer believed there was any chance for the Sioux to retain their "sacred" Black Hills; the gold was too important. But with that plum secured for the white man, Sitting Bull and Crazy Horse might be able to keep some of the land they cherished almost as much, along the Powder River.

Outside, a bugle sounded recall-from-drill and Crook got to his feet. He would take his midday meal in the officers' mess today. He needed to feel the tension and high spirits that always attended the start of a campaign.

Seeing his master moving about, the dog arose, his tail wagging in anticipation of a walk through the post. Crook bent to stroke the collie's silken ears, daring to enjoy the hope that his plan might succeed. For what seemed the hundredth time he reviewed in his mind the peace terms that Whitcomb had brought him. There were no flaws, no impossibilities. In Hardeman's message and Elizabeth Putnam's there were the seeds of a fruitful peace. The Congress would never approve such terms now, but if a Powder River reservation could be hidden in the terms of surrender so none could call it a concession to the unreconstructed hostiles, it was a possibility. In the general relief at obtaining a final peace with the Sioux, the Congress might be magnanimous in victory and the certain objections of the Indian Bureau overcome.

Crook would do all he could to obtain such a result. But first there must be a surrender.

CHAPTER
FORTY-EIGHT

The water shimmered in the stream and the air shimmered in the rising heat of the day. The great encampment crowded the banks of the Greasy Grass. Gathered in the thousands, the Lakota rejoiced in their power.

Sun Horse sat atop a low hill overlooking the river and the camp. He had come there before sunrise, to pray to the morning star as it ushered in the light. The morning was well along now and the buffalo robe that had warmed him in the chilly dawn was spread on the ground. He sat upon it cross-legged, wearing only a loin cover, giving himself to the heat of the sun. The feeling pleased him so much that he lay back and closed his eyes, letting the sun bathe him from the front and feeling its warmth rise from the earth and the *pte* hide beneath him.

After so much cold and gray and wet, the weather had turned warm at last. The Moon of Fat Calves was waning now, but still rounded. When it was young the snows had come again for a last time before *Okaga*, the power of the south, had finally triumphed, driving *Waziya* back to the north and bringing an outpouring of new life from the soft earth that had been cleansed by the healing snows. Already the grass stood nearly to a man's knees and the hills were covered with flowers.

Sun Horse felt the growing power flow through his body, warming him, and he heard the sounds of the great camp below him in the river bottom—the horses stamping and whickering, children and dogs playing joyfully, many voices making a humming along the banks where the grass grew thick and sweet. The sounds were full of life and he sat up again to look upon what he heard. Clusters of lodges dotted the banks as far as he could see. He spread his arms to embrace the encampment but he could not contain it all. It was too huge. Around the bends upstream and down, there were more lodges, and still more people arrived each day and their horses joined the almost numberless herds that raised great clouds of dust when they went to water.

All during the warming moons the Lakota and their allies had been on the move, drawing together in numbers even the oldest ones had never seen before. From the reservations they came, moving north and west to the streams that fed the Yellowstone, to join the ones already there. The Sun Dance had been held on the Rosebud, and Sun Horse had danced with the others. For two days he had danced beneath the open framework of the Sun Dance lodge, pulling a buffalo skull by thongs tied through slits in his chest muscles, and all the while he had prayed his thanks to *pte* and to *Wakán Tanka*, who gave the greatest of the four-leggeds as a gift to man. It had been good for the people to see the Sun Dance conducted in the old way, with great ceremony. It had made them strong. For a time the wounds in Sun Horse's chest had pained him, but they were already healing. Now, with the sun full on his chest, the wounds were only two spots that felt warmer than the rest, with no pain. Now as then, he gave himself to the sun and the sun healed him.

When the Sun Dance had ended, the grass on the Rosebud was already exhausted by the pony herds, and so the people had moved here to the Greasy Grass, where the council would be held.

All seven council fires of the *Títonwan*, the western Lakota, were here. There were Two Kettles and Blackfeet-Lakota and Burnt Thighs, No Bows led by Spotted Eagle and Minneconjou under Touch the Clouds and Fast Bull and young Hump. The Sun Band was camped with the Hunkpapa, close by the people of Sitting Bull and Gall and Black Moon and Crow King. The names of the famous men were spoken throughout the camp as the people watched the building of the immense council lodge where the leaders would soon gather, but the name mentioned most of all was spoken quietly, for Crazy Horse shunned praise. He led all the Oglala now, and others looked to him as well. In the Moon of Shedding Ponies, the month the whites called May, the Oglala had made their Strange Man a new kind of chief, a headman for leading in peace as well as war, and they gave the position for life. The new honor was not something to be taken away as the Big Bellies had taken his shirt. The people had rejoiced at this choice, and the news carriers had spread the word far and wide, even to the people at the agencies. Crazy Horse leads us all! they said, and from all sides the bands had come.

Far away in the wooded lands where the sun rose, the eastern Lakota had heard of the council and they too had come, the *Ihánktonwan* and even some of the *Isányati*, those who said Dakota instead of Lakota, the ones who survived the war in the year 1862. They were poor people now, called No Clothes by some, but they were led by the legendary Inkpaduta, a great man whose people had been brought to nothing by the whites. He still walked tall and proud and would take a seat high in the council.

Here and there among the Lakota camps were a few lodges of Arapaho, and many Shahíyela, those of Little Wolf and Old Bear and Two Moons joined now by Dull Knife's people and other smaller bands.

Truly the power to grow shone brightly on the Lakota and their friends. They grew in many ways, but they grew strongest of all for war. Throughout the spring they had traded with neighboring tribes for guns, even with their enemies, the Crows and the hated Blackfeet. Relatives from the agencies had brought the guns a friendly agent let them have for hunting, and the halfbreed traders' sons had managed to bring some more. There were many of the back-loading kind and a few of the many-shooting kind too, and powder and lead, enough for every man who needed them. Throughout the encampment the men cleaned the guns and sharpened their knives, and around the lodge fires it was the young men of the Shahíyela who spoke strongest of all for fighting the whites. Until the soldiers struck Two Moons and his people, the Shahíyela had been at peace with the whites, and they were still angry at the whiteman's treachery. We whipped Three Stars and drove him away! the young men said. If he comes back, we will whip him again!

Long Hair will come, some of those from the agencies said.

We know Long Hair! said the Lakotas who had fought him on the Yellowstone two snows past when he came there to make an iron road. There was no iron road yet!

We know him too, said the Shahíyela, remembering the Washita and those who had died there, and they looked at the one they had called Little Warrior in his childhood, before his dream took him back to the white world for a time. The white youth accompanied Sun Horse everywhere now, as did the old man's other grandson, Blackbird. These three were silent when others talked of war, but their silence was lost in a storm of angry words.

Long Hair will not find us sleeping again! the Shahíyela said, and around them the howls of approval grew deafening.

Sun Horse sighed as he looked at the encampment, so peaceful in the morning sunshine. Hardeman had warned that the people would feel invincible gathered together like this, and he had been right.

Off to the southwest, the Snowy Mountains, the range called Big Horns by the

676

whites, stood snow-capped and beautiful against the clear blue sky. Far away in the southern foothills lay Sun Horse's vision-valley, his winter home for so long, but he would not see it again. It belonged to Hardeman now. It was not so much the land itself that had been Sun Horse's parting gift to the scout; by giving the land he had assured that Hardeman would have companionship. It was not good that a man should live alone. Or a woman. Men and women needed one another, and among the whites, who had no tribe to sustain them, they needed one another all the more. Hardeman and Lisaputnam would care for the land and they would remember the friendship that had grown there between Lakota and *washichun*.

Sun Horse missed Hears Twice as well. The old prophet had been a good friend for many years. Once Sun Horse had found the answers to his dilemma and ceased his fast, he had spoken with Hears Twice. Having asked the prophet to use his power to help the people, Sun Horse could not simply tell his friend that there was no further need to listen for the voices of the spirit world, but he had told Hears Twice that he had decided what the band should do, and the seer had seemed happy. "I am glad you have found your power again," Hears Twice had said. "I was afraid for you when you would not eat." Then the old man had touched his ear. "There is something I must hear," he said, and he had continued his silent vigil, keeping to himself, listening still. On the day before the Sun Band left the winter valley he had come to Sun Horse and told him what he heard. "There is big trouble coming. A big fight. The people win, but I hear no victory, no peace. I hear only the sound of tears falling. I hear buffalo gone away, Lakota gone away, everything gone." Here he had passed one palm across the other in the sign that meant *rubbed out.* "I will go to the agency at Red Cloud," he had added, brightening somewhat. "I will live with old friends and smoke the pipe. We will talk about times long ago before the whiteman came. It is good to smoke with old friends."

The spirits had told Hears Twice what was to come, but Sun Horse already knew.

By now Hears Twice and Mist would be on the Dakota reservation, learning what life would be like for all the Lakota in times to come, but before that day arrived for Sun Horse, he had much to do.

His long years of watching from the small valley had not been in vain. He had perceived the true nature of the whites, but he feared the knowledge he had gained, and so he had looked away, pretending it was incomplete. What was worse, he had misunderstood his own power! For so many years he had sought a pathway to peace with the whites, all in vain! That was not his power at all. To understand the *washicun*, yes. To lead his people, yes; and in time he would lead his people to live beside the whites; but it was not his power to force the *washichun* into a peace that was contrary to their own nature! Once the whites began fighting, they kept on until the enemy surrendered. That was their nature, and Sun Horse knew that a man could not betray his true nature, neither *washichun* nor Lakota. In the end, the Lakota would have to yield to the numberless foe.

677

From the start, Hardeman had spoken the truth. Even before he went off with the pipe carriers he had said that the Sun Band would have to submit to the will of the whites, and when he came back he had said the same thing. That evening, when the pipe carriers had eaten and the whites were gone and everyone else was asleep, Sun Horse had finally admitted to himself the truth of the white scout's words, for in his heart he had always known it was so.

Washíchun, a people not at peace with themselves. Uncertain of their own great power, they must conquer others to feel strong.

Confronting this immutable fact, Sun Horse had been led to a dreadful conclusion. He had despaired, and from his despair had come the answer to his prayers.

The conclusion was one not even Hardeman saw: not only would the whites demand that the Lakota lay down their arms and live in confinement, *they would demand a surrender of the spirit as well!*

The whites looked at the Lakota and they did not see men like themselves; they saw the feathers and the paint, the symbols on the tipis, the songs and dancing, the way of life so different from their own. They feared what was different, and so they would try to change it until they feared it no longer. When the Lakota surrendered, the whites would destroy the old way of life. They would take away the weapons and the horses, they would end the hunting; they would destroy all the symbols, seeking in this way to destroy the spirit.

Could the spirit survive without the symbols? If not, then the hoop of the world would be broken; the people would lose touch with the good red road of spiritual understanding and the tree of life would wither. And yet on that fateful night, sitting in his lodge with the storm howling outside, despairing at the thought of the old life ending, Sun Horse had felt a sudden hope.

Look beyond the symbol! Sees Beyond had commanded him when the Snowblind Moon was round and bright, yet until the night of the pipe carriers' return he had not seen just how far beyond he would have to look.

Was not the Lakota way of life itself one all-embracing symbol? The graceful lodges of buffalo hide, the rituals of childhood and manhood, the vision quests, the songs, the dances, the offerings to the spirits, the ceremonies, the prayers— all were part of a great symbol that contained the Lakota spirit. Yet the spirit did not live in the symbol! It was in the hearts of the people, and there it might be preserved!

The people would need a new kind of leader, one who could nurture the spirit and keep it well even when the old way of life was gone. The trail ahead would be long and difficult and Sun Horse knew he would not see its end. He was too old. He could start the people on the new path, but who . . . ?

In that same moment, even as he asked the question, he had seen the answer there before his eyes, in the sleeping form of his grandson Blackbird.

"I want to understand the *washíchun*," the boy had said earlier that evening, and, "There is so much to learn about being a man." "You are the future of the people," Sun Horse had said, little dreaming as he spoke just how true those words might be! The boy was greatly changed by his first brush with war and death. He had fought the whites and survived. Now he wished to understand them, and to shoulder the burdens of manhood. He was prepared to become a man of the people! But with the innate wisdom of youth he had recognized the greatest threat to his learning. In the onrushing flood of *washichun* he saw the one power that could deny him the time he needed. "I was angry with the whites," he had said, "because it seemed they would change the world before I could become a man."

He must have the time! But how to give it to him? Sun Horse had wondered. In two moons, no more than three, the bluecoats would return, yet it would take years for the boy to learn all he would need to know! He must learn every aspect of the old life; he must experience the strength of the Lakota way and know the meaning of all the symbols; only then could he look beyond these things and comprehend the essence of the Lakota spirit, which was all he could hope to save when the day of surrender came.

How could that day be put off for long enough? Sun Horse's despair had threatened to return, but then he had smelled the meat in the lodge and felt his hunger strong within him. And once again the answer to his question had come to him, so simple, so obvious.

Pte, the gift of life for the Lakota. The greatest of the four-leggeds, the greatest gift of *Wakán Tanka*. *Pte*, the strength to live in the Lakota way.

The clown girl had run away and Sun Horse's white grandson had found her. The young man had been led by a spirit animal and the girl had seen *pte*. With the coming together of these two, a power had come to help the Sun Band: the power of *pte*. Had the buffalo returned just so the people could go to Dakota and surrender? No! They had returned so the people could continue living in the Lakota way! In an instant, Sun Horse's confidence had been restored to him and he saw his pathway open before him: Blackbird, the future of the people; to give him time to learn, live in the Lakota way for as long as possible, so it would become ingrained in him, so the spirit would persist when the old ways had been destroyed by the whites!

Flee the whites! the blackbirds had told his grandson before the fight at Two Moons' village. They had spoken wisely and Sun Horse would obey.

Thus it was that he had left his vision-valley behind forever. It was too close to the soldier forts and the wagon road, this was true, but he had left it for another reason as well. The Lakota life was not tied to a place; it was something the people carried with them wherever they might go. From now on the band would live on the move, wintering wherever winter found them, and this too would be a lesson for Blackbird to learn. Sun Horse had brought the people here to the Greasy Grass in order that they should grow strong in the hoop of the nation. In the council he would still speak for peace, but he would not advise surrender. The old life is good for us, he would say; we must keep to it for as long as we can. When the council was done, the Sun Band would go on the summer hunt with Sun Horse's cousin Sitting Bull. After the hunt they might stay with the Hunkpapa war man or go off on their own. Sun Horse would decide when the time came. Above all they would stay away from the whites, away from the fighting, if it came. For as long as possible they would live at peace, without surrender, in the Lakota way. And all the time Blackbird would be learning.

Already the youth had taken more steps on the path to manhood. In the Moon of Shedding Ponies he had gone with his father on a raid against the *Kanghí*. He had stolen horses and left them at the lodge of Yellow Leaf's uncle, Hawk Chaser's brother, with whom the girl and her mother now lived. The horses had been accepted and gifts exchanged. After the great council a new lodge would be built in the Sun Band's camp circle for the two young people.

Sun Horse had encouraged Standing Eagle to instruct Blackbird in the skills of a warrior, but against a traditional enemy, not against the whites. It was good that the boy should spend some time with his father, but not too much. Standing Eagle was a great warrior, a strong man, but he would cling to the old ways so long as he drew breath. He would fight the *washíchun* before the end. He would die rather than surrender. All to preserve a symbol. He could not see beyond the symbol, but perhaps his son could, given time. The boy should respect his father and learn from him, but Blackbird would learn from others as well, men who would teach him what it meant to be a man of the people. Here too his instruction was moving ahead. Before the Sun Dance Blackbird had been taken into the Raven Owners warrior society of the Oglala; there were both Oglala and Hunkpapa in the Sun Band and the society had a lodge there. Crazy Horse himself had spoken for the boy in the ceremony. Blackbird had returned to his grandfather's lodge swollen with pride, but also humbled and awed that the light-haired man of the Oglala should do such a thing for him.

Sun Horse had encouraged this step too, asking the favor of Crazy Horse privately. It was true that Blackbird was still young for marriage and the rigors of a warrior's training, but there was little time. The *washíchun* were an impatient people.

Sun Horse stretched his legs out straight before him and leaned back against his hands. Today his joints and muscles were those of a younger man. The sun had soothed away his aches and pains. Overhead, the blinding orb was nearing the zenith. The day was hot, but it was not uncomfortable. Sun Horse preferred the warm weather. The winter had been long and cold and full of worry. Even his worries were banished by the sun. He was strong again as a leader should be strong, confident in the direction he led his people. In the time that remained, he and Sees Beyond and the others they chose would teach Blackbird everything they knew, moving the boy along fast, hastening his way to manhood, training him to lead, guiding him to see beyond the symbols to the very heart of the Lakota spirit. Blackbird would learn without knowing he was taught, for he was eager to know everything, and in time he would lead without seeming to lead, perhaps even without knowing he was a leader. The *washíchun* would always single out a leader and break his power, but Blackbird would be a new kind of leader, a guardian of the Lakota spirit.

680

As the old-man chiefs kept the coals of the village fire on the journey from one camping place to the next, so it would be Blackbird's task to keep the glow of the Lakota spirit alive during the journey through the troubled times ahead, so that one day the fire might be rekindled for all men to see.

The camp had grown quiet in the heat of the day. A figure moved among the Sun Band lodges and Sun Horse recognized his white grandson by his hat and coat. Like Lodgepole, the youth would keep some habits of the white race, but he was Lakota now, Lakota-by-choice. The moving figure stopped and raised a hand toward the hill where Sun Horse sat. Sun Horse waved in reply and got to his feet with fluid ease. He made broad signs, telling the young man to wait for him, and then he gathered up his buffalo robe and started down the hill, enjoying the feeling of the warm earth beneath his feet. He liked to walk barefoot on the Mother Earth in the spring when she was soft like the flesh of a woman.

The thought caused a stirring in his loins. Last night he had enjoyed both his wives, going from Elk Calf's robes to Sings His Daughter in the middle of the night. From the old to the young.

Sun Horse chuckled as he walked. Even in his lovemaking he saw symbols for the path he had chosen. From the old to the young. From Sun Horse to Blackbird the power would pass, the power to lead the people from the old way to a new one among the whites. As a man planted his seed in woman, so Sun Horse would plant knowledge in Blackbird, seeds that would grow slowly. Only long after Sun Horse was placed on his scaffold and offered to the winds and the sky would the seeds bring forth new life.

Below, in the camp, his other grandson awaited him in the shade of a cottonwood. He would have to choose a name for the young man now that he was Lakota. And before long he should have a wife.

A pain returned, and the smile faded from Sun Horse's face. Had it been necessary for the clown girl to die? He did not know. The answers to such questions were *wakán*, a mystery. He had grieved for her, but even then he had seen that her dying was the final gift, the act that led his white grandson to step between the worlds once more, joining the Lakota as Sitting Bull had foreseen long ago, and so assuring that Sun Horse and his people would remain connected to the white world, as they had been ever since Lodgepole joined the band more than thirty snows ago. As Lodgepole and his brother had shared their knowledge of the *washíchun* with Sun Horse, so Sun Horse's white grandson would share his knowledge with Blackbird. And he would share something even more valuable—the strength of the warrior who declines to fight. That was the lesson Blackbird must learn above all, how to keep his strength within him. For to fight the whites was to fight the whirlwind.

Sun Horse was nearing the bottom of the slope. As he walked he felt the warmth of the day and the softness of the earth underfoot, and the great power of the encampment that was spread along the winding banks of the Greasy Grass, the stream the whites called Little Big Horn. Embraced by the hoop of the nation, he felt his own power strong within him. Would he succeed? Would there be enough time for Blackbird to learn it all? Would the spirit survive? Sun Horse shook his head. He was not one of those who saw the future. His power was to lead his people in this world. He had chosen his course and he would lead his people as best he could. For now he was content.

As the moon of fat calves grew slender, Three Stars returned, seeking the hostiles. They met him on the Rosebud and they fought him, and left him there to lick his wounds. And on the Greasy Grass the soldier chief Long Hair found the great encampment, the hoop of the Lakota nation raised for the last time. Long Hair struck the camp, and he died.

But the triumph of these victories vanished like the wind in the buffalo grass. Again and again the soldiers came and one by one the bands surrendered. When the leaves had fallen once and turned yellow to fall again, Crazy Horse, the strange man who had brought such hope to all the Lakota, was dead, and Sitting Buffalo Bull took his tipis, those of the Sun Band among them, and moved across the invisible line into Grandmother Land, and stayed there for many years. In the end even these came to the agencies and surrendered, to live there among old friends, to talk and smoke and remember the days when buffalo covered the prairie.

Historical Note

It has been my intention to place my fictional characters against a background that is as historically accurate as research and one man's fallible understanding can make it. The fragments of history of the American West presented in *The Snowblind Moon*—the fur trade, the westward migration, the incidents in the Indian wars—are all factually accurate, as informed readers will recognize. Historical personages are not portrayed in times and places where they were not actually present.

Secretary Chandler's letter to Indian Commissioner Smith, reproduced at the start of the narrative, is in fact the document that initiated the process of confining the last free-roaming Sioux on the Dakota reservation.

Chris Hardeman and Johnny Smoker, Jed, Bat and Lisa Putnam and the other inhabitants of Putnam's Park, as well as the park itself and the Putnam Cutoff, are all products of my imagination.

Hachaliah Tatum and his circus and all its personnel are fictional as well, but the appearance of such a troupe in the intermountain West at this time is well within the scope of historical events, as are the individual acts and animals that make up Tatum's Combined Shows. By 1876 the circus was a familiar American entertainment, and many small circuses had toured the frontier states and territories, both by rail and wagon. Several shows, some including elephants, had visited remote regions before this date.

The Sun Band and all its people are fictional. The names of other Indians and bands, and their locations in the tale, are accurate. The council at Two Moons' village at which Crazy Horse and Sitting Bull are present is an invention, but the proximity of the bands at that time is factual, and it is not impossible that these men might have met within the time period of the novel.

General Crook's campaign of March 1876 occurred as related and has not been altered in any significant respect save one: with the exception of Captain Alexander Sutorius, who did in fact miss the campaign because he was confined at Fort D. A. Russell for chronic drunkenness, and Private Peter Dowdy, who was killed in the battle of March 17, the officers and men of Company E, Third Cavalry, are fictional, as is the separation of the "Lost Platoon" from the troop at the end of the battle and its separate retreat to Fort Fetterman. Company E, Third Cavalry, was indeed one of the companies on the campaign, along with the others named in the story, and the fictional characters are not intended to represent any of the real men who served in that troop. Apart from this liberty, the names of officers and men in the command, including scouts and packers, are factual. Robert Strahorn, who wrote for the *Rocky Mountain News* under the pen name Alter

Ego, was with Crook once again for the summer campaign, which left Fort Fetterman on May 29.

The reader may have noticed inconsistencies of rank in references to certain officers. This is in keeping with the confusion that was caused by the existence of brevet ranks. In theory, an officer was entitled always to be addressed by his highest brevet rank, but contemporary accounts make it clear that this practice was not consistently observed. Both Crook himself, in his autobiography, and John Bourke in his invaluable memoir, *On the Border with Crook*, refer to officers variously by their brevet and permanent ranks.

The narrative of the battle of March 17 is based on the accounts of men who fought on both sides. Each of the six companies under Reynolds' command moved independently before and during the battle and I have simplified their movements somewhat in the interest of clarity, but the broad movements related in the story are generally accurate, especially as they would have been perceived by the characters with whom the reader enters and participates in the battle. Captain Moore did fail to prevent the Indians from leaving the village and gaining the high ground, in part through no fault of his own due to the rugged and unfamiliar terrain. Although the withdrawal from the field was ordered well in advance and took nearly two hours to execute, it seemed quite sudden to those on the line of battle; the cavalry dead were in fact left behind, and Bourke says it "was rumored among the men, one of our poor soldiers fell alive into the enemy's hands and was cut limb from limb."

The soldier found alive and unharmed in the village and subsequently tortured by Little Hand is an invention.

Warriors from the village pursued Reynolds and recaptured a majority of their horses. With the soldiers on the run, the Indians regarded the action as a victory, and the news of this event played its part in encouraging agency bands to return to the Powder River country for the summer gathering. The Cheyenne, hitherto at peace with the whites (Secretary Chandler's order applied only to the hostile Sioux), regarded the attack as utterly unprovoked, and they now joined the Sioux in preparing for war. Throughout the spring the allied tribes made extraordinary efforts to obtain new weapons by purchase and trade. Thus the Reynolds attack was in large part responsible both for the number of Indians at the great encampment on the Little Big Horn and their high degree of preparedness.

Crook fought an inconclusive engagement with a large force from the allied tribes on the Rosebud on June 17, eight days before the Custer battle. He remained in the field throughout the summer and autumn, and obtained a considerable victory at Slim Buttes in September. The forces that defeated the Cheyenne under Dull Knife in November were under Crook's command. He left the field for the winter, sending those of his scouts who knew the hostile headmen to try once more to persuade them to come in peacefully. As an inducement, Crook promised that if they would surrender, he would do everything in his power to obtain for them a permanent home in the Powder River country and an agency there. On May 6, 1877, Crazy Horse, the last hope of the hostiles, surrendered with nearly nine hundred people and seventeen hundred horses. He was in the custody of authorities at Fort Robinson, Nebraska, when he was killed on September 5 of the same year.

With the peace secured at last, Crook kept his promise to the Indians. He argued forcefully for an agency on the Yellowstone, at the mouth of the Tongue, and a reservation in that portion of the Powder River country, but his efforts were in vain, as were many similar efforts made by other military men before and after Crook on behalf of the plains Indians. In the end, with all the Sioux confined on the Dakota reservation and certain to remain there, Crook wrote to the headmen at Pine Ridge expressing regret for his failure.

(The Pine Ridge Agency was established after the last battles of the Sioux wars and thus does not appear on the endpaper map. It was just above the Nebraska-Dakota border, north of the Red Cloud and Spotted Tail Agencies. It replaced those agencies, eliminating the last sanctioned camping grounds for the Sioux beyond the borders of the Dakota reservation.)

ACKNOWLEDGMENTS

I am indebted to the following people, who generously contributed their time and expertise and thereby did much to assure the historical accuracy of *The Snowblind Moon*: Marie T. Capps, Map and Manuscript Librarian at the United States Military Academy Library, West Point, New York; Catherine T. Engel, Reference Librarian, Colorado Historical Society, Denver, Colorado; Neil Mangum, Historian, Custer Battlefield National Monument, Montana. Special thanks are due to B. Byron Price, Director of the Panhandle-Plains Historical Museum, Canyon, Texas, who read the sections concerning the frontier army and made many valuable suggestions, and to my friends John and Elaine Barlow and Melody Harding of the Bar Cross Ranch, Cora, Wyoming, and Pete and Holly Cameron of Game Hill Ranch, Bondurant, Wyoming, without whose kindness and hospitality I would know even less about the care and raising of beef cattle.

I am particularly grateful to Dr. Bernard A. Hoehner of San Francisco State University, San Francisco, California, for his invaluable advice in matters pertaining to Lakota language and culture as they appear in the novel. (A *Sihásapa*-Lakota, Dr. Hoehner was given the named Jerked With Arrow in his youth, and is now also known as Grass among his people.)

In including some Lakota words and phrases in a work intended for a general readership I have chosen to disregard certain conventions commonly employed in writing Lakota; I have used no linguistic symbols other than the acute accent and have adopted spellings intended to make something close to proper pronunciation as easy as possible for those with no previous knowledge of the language. These decisions were mine alone. I hope persons familiar with Lakota will forgive these simplifications.

Naturally, any remaining historical errors in *The Snowblind Moon*, whether of fact or interpretation, are my sole responsibility.

John Byrne Cooke
Jackson Hole, Wyoming

About the Author

John Byrne Cooke was born in New York City in 1940. He was graduated from Harvard College and has worked as a musician, filmmaker, rock and roll road-manager, screenwriter and amateur cowboy. He has lived on both the East and West coasts and now resides in Jackson Hole, Wyoming. *The Snowblind Moon* is his first novel.